TRUTH

Book #2 of Bestselling Consequences Series

BY:
ALEATHA ROMIG

TRUTH

TRUTH

REVIEWS

What an exhilarating ride! The players in this game of *Truth* were intense and charismatic, although new people were introduced our old favorites we love to hate got plenty of face-time, namely Tony. If you like a twisty plot with loads of mysteries around every corner, then *Truth* is a must-read! It's a thrilling and thought-provoking psychological thriller at its best! The wait for the final installment is going to be agonizing...2014 cannot come soon enough... Bookie Nookie - *Bookie Nookie Reviews* and *The Romance Reviews*

As I read *Truth* I was amazed by the storytelling ability of Ms. Romig. This is a complex and involved tale, full of tension and drama that will keep you turning the pages. I am not giving any plot details as I don't want to spoil it for everyone. What I will say is that if you enjoyed Consequences. This one is even better IMO. And I believe that there is to be a further addition to this series next year. I can hardly wait! Linda Sims – *Top 1000 Amazon UK Reviewers*

COPYRIGHT AND LICENSE INFORMATION

Acknowledgements

Continued appreciation to my patient family! Thank you for allowing me to pursue my dream and spend hour after hour living in a world created upon my well-worn, slightly damp laptop! (a few tears and some wine!)

A million thank yous to my prized group of readers! Val, Heather, Sherry, Kelli, and Angie... TRUTH would not have materialized as it did without your help. Your honest comments and opinions along with your time and energy helped me in ways I can never express!

Thank you to the many readers of CONSEQUENCES. It may be because I'm new at this, or because I care, but I have read every review and have seen every rating. It thrills me to learn readers feel as passionate about my characters as I do. Hopefully, the twists and turns of TRUTH will be as enthralling and unexpected as those in CONSEQUENCES.

My very last acknowledgement is to Claire Nichols and Anthony Rawlings... never in my wildest dreams did I expect your story to find its way into the hearts of so many!

Be prepared, their saga will continue with CONVICTED, due out the end of 2013!

TRUTH

*It has been said that something as small as the flutter
of a butterfly's wing can ultimately cause a typhoon halfway
around the world.*
- Chaos Theory

Prologue

-July 2011-

The tires of their Chevy Equinox bounced along the worn pavement and dilapidated surface of Bristol Road. Peering through the windshield at the signs of a dying city, Rich Bosley wondered if this was how the *old west* felt when the gold rush ended. Acres and acres of fenced concrete occupied each side of the decrepit street. At one time during Flint, Michigan's prime, cars filled these parking lots twenty-four hours a day. Three shifts of workers came and went from these factories. Today it represented *urban decay* at its utmost.

In 1908 General Motors opened their newly founded headquarters in Flint. Generations of workers walked through the doors; each generation believed theirs would do better than the one before. The tides turned with the oil crisis of the seventies and the nationwide plant closings of the eighties.

But, like rain to the parched ground, *optimism* returned to Flint at the turn of the century. GM invested 60 million dollars to upgrade the plant. Over 2,000 hourly workers and 180 salaried workers frequented the building they passed. Honest work for honest pay. This blue collar haven once again bustled with activity.

Then during the latter part of the first decade, the auto industry suffered collapse. Some plants scheduled for closing were *saved* by private investors. Businessmen and women gave hope where hope was lost. These saviors required assistance. Workers agreed to lesser wages. The dream for *better* became a need for *anything*. Michigan's government granted tax breaks in the supreme effort to keep the factories open and give people purpose.

The tax breaks expired. Workers were asked to accept even lower wages. It was inconsequential; the economy couldn't support the product. Only the bottom line mattered. With no incentive to keep the doors open, men and women in insulated executive offices, miles away, made lofty decisions. The result filled Rich's view: building upon empty building, decaying skeletons of what once was.

Rich thought about his father's recent proposal. The prospect of moving back to Iowa felt like defeat. After all, was the banking business better in Iowa than in Michigan? The economy *was* a national issue. Rich and his wife, Sarah, had faith in this city. They were willing to work to make it better for their son and children to come.

Rich peered to his right and smiled at his lovely wife engrossed in her magazine. "How can you read with all of these bumps?" Her normally styled hair hung from the opening in her baseball cap, and her business attire replaced with jeans and a Tiger's t-shirt. It was their son's first year of baseball, rookie league. It was more about learning team work than learning baseball. However, if you ask the players, it was more about snacks. Sarah provided homemade cupcakes -- a homerun!

"I'm just so amazed by this article."

"What are you reading?"

"Vanity Fair. It's the cover story from a couple months ago. I forgot I'd left the magazine   in here. I just found it." Rich nodded; he wasn't interested. "It's about Anthony Rawlings and his wife. Didn't your dad go to their wedding?"

"Yes, I think so. It's one of the perks of being Richard Bosley, the great governor of Iowa. You get to schmooze with big donors."

"I remember him mentioning it. It sounds amazing."   Sarah rambled, "The wedding was at their estate. So that means your dad went to their estate?"

"I guess. I'm honestly not impressed."

"Why not? It sounds like they're both involved in charity work. Did you know his wife was a bartender when he met her?"

"The man makes his money harming other people."

"It doesn't sound like that. It sounds like an amazing love story. Can you imagine, being an out of work meteorologist, working as a bartender, and falling in love with one of the countries billionaires?"

"Again, where did those billions come from?"

"It says something about the internet."

"Yes. According to my father that's where it started. Anthony Rawlings has managed to take that start and feed off of the unfortunate circumstances of others. He's personally unemployed enough people to fill these factories."

"He also employs enough people to fill these factories." Sarah peered at the barren landscape. "I think people are just jealous. I mean, I could be. What woman wouldn't love to suddenly have Claire Rawlings' life?"

The sound of their son's voice refocused the couple's thoughts. Instead of dwelling on urban decay and the nation's economy, Rich saw the blond hair of hope in the backseat. "Dad, I need to pee." Ryan pleaded wide eyed at his dad in the rearview mirror.

"Ryan, we'll be home in a few minutes. You can wait."

"No, Dad, I can't. I gots to pee now!"

Rich's eyes met his wife's. Her expression said everything he already knew; this wasn't the neighborhood to stop. If they could just drive a little further. However, Ryan's voice whined and his little legs fidgeted with need. "I see a gas station. Stop, pl-ea-se." The last word elongated into three extended syllables.

Against his better judgment Richard Bosley II, turned the Equinox into a parking space outside of a Speedway. He turned to his wife, "I'll go in with him. Besides, it's the middle of the day, and it doesn't look busy."

Sarah smiled and unbuckled her seatbelt. "Okay guys, let's get this over with and back on the road. We have a baseball game to watch. I recorded the whole thing. Ryan, wait until you see yourself get that great hit!"

A film of smudge and finger prints plastered the heavy glass doors. Rich scanned the interior looking for the sign indicating a restroom. The odor of hot dogs cooked to the firmness of rubber permeated their senses. Merchandise sat sparsely upon shelves that packed the room, leaving no discernible path. The dirt and scuffs upon the cracked linoleum were the true indicators of foot traffic. Looking to the cashier, Rich noticed the small unsecured cubical. He scanned the glass square for help, but saw only empty chairs. Then he noticed the open drawer of the cash register.

"Dad, I see the sign." Ryan's voice cut the thick silent air.

Suddenly, a commotion of racket resonated from the hallway containing the bathrooms. Some moments hang suspended in time as if the electrons slow, protons release their pull, and atoms no longer cement into matter; for example, the second a newborn baby releases its first cry. Some instants occur in a flash; like lightening refusing capture upon film. Others are an amalgamation.

A thick man moved toward them, his face concealed behind a black ski mask. Rich's first thought, *it's July, why would you wear a ski mask?* was only a blimp before the realization of their situation, "Run! Back to the car!" The words cascaded from his lips with alarm and authority.

Preoccupied with the search of her purse, Sarah's husband's tone propelled her to flight. She seized her son's small hand and spun toward the smudged glass door. The echoing pop of gunfire erupted so abruptly she never saw her husband fall and thankfully neither did Ryan. The last thing either of them saw was the shower of red as their blood added another dimension to the filth on the floor and windows.

*****

Months earlier and miles away a business executive chose to close a stamping plant no longer showing profits. That one decision resulted in thousands of unemployed workers. One of which was a father with a sick child and no wife. In a moment of desperation the out of work father decided his only option to pay the mounting medical bills and save his son, was crime. A few robberies later, with money too attractive and too easy, he had a new profession...

There is no limit to what a man can do, or where he can go,
if he does not mind who gets the credit.
- Charles Edward Montague

Chapter 1

L ooking around his office, Richard Bosley I contemplated his place in history. The stately office reeked of prestige. Impressive bookshelves covered the walls, and his mahogany desk created a platform of regality. The flags of both the United States and Iowa hung conspicuously behind his leather chair. Only fifteen months into his second term as governor, he had so many goals to accomplish. The voters rallied around him after the tragic death of his only son and his family. They put their trust in him, in his ideas, and in his values. Staring at the *family* photo of him with his son, daughter-in-law, and grandson, he questioned his own values. Perhaps they'd been too lofty. Perhaps if he had stayed out of public office... things would have been different.

The cold March Iowa wind blew outside the window and created a low howl through the insulated panes. Seeing his reflection against the black night sky, Richard Bosley I knew the truth: "perhapses" meant *nothing*! His family was gone and his third round of chemo would start tomorrow. The second round took his hair and energy. The third may very well take his life. If it didn't, the cancer surely would. Seeing his gaunt reflection and viewing his hands, he saw the gray pallor. His skin was merely an oversized casing, loosely hanging over his bones. It reminded him how life wasn't fair. He prayed death would be.

Richard Bosley I would officially resign as governor of Iowa at a press conference scheduled for tomorrow at noon. The lieutenant governor, Sheldon Preston, would immediately be sworn in office for the remaining term. Tonight, alone in the executive office, Governor Bosley chose to make decisions. He had nothing left to lose. To hell with the executive board; tonight the only opinion that mattered was his.

Who can truly say if good done for the wrong reason was still good? Right now, his soul told him to take another look. *Do not leave this place of power without knowing you've done all that you can do.* Easing himself into the splendid leather chair, he decided to do just that. History would write itself.

The stack of petitions for pardon were discussed, debated, and decreased. The news of his impending resignation spurred many requests. The executive board reviewed the multiple *petitions for pardon* and decided upon ten. Ten applicants now serving *time* in one of Iowa's penitentiaries who would soon be free. Ten people, who tomorrow would be informed their verdict was overturned and their sentence was over. Governor Bosley eyed the stack of pages to his left. Within that stack were eleven *other* people. According to the board of review, these inmates would remain in prison. They would serve out their sentences as handed down by the mighty and lofty judges of this great state.

With trembling hands, more from the chemicals within his veins than emotion, Governor Bosley reviewed the stack of prisoners destined to remain behind bars for the eternity of their sentence.

The lists of offenses varied: rapists, burglars, prostitutes. Somehow through the diseased cells infiltrating his brain, Richard remembered his quest. One more time he leafed through the stack. Finally, he found the name he sought. Yes, she'd been married to Anthony Rawlings. Hell, he attended their wedding. Suddenly, Richard Bosley's mouth formed a grin. There had been so few reasons to smile lately. The facial muscles would soon tire, but he enjoyed the brief euphoria.

He reread the file: Claire Nichols - *no contest plea* to the charge of attempted murder, thus not officially found guilty. Good behavior since incarceration. No marks of disobedience. No prior offenses. Sentenced to seven years. Served fourteen months. With the multitude of sins represented by the prisoners already scheduled for pardon, Governor Bosley could question why the executive board allowed this woman to remain in prison. However, he knew. The *board* consisted of five individuals of political power or at least *promise* in Iowa, and each served a four year term. Everyone knew, success in Iowa wasn't found by crossing Anthony Rawlings.

Richard Bosley I found himself with the rare opportunity to avenge his son's death. Dealing with politicians and individuals like Anthony Rawlings taught him many things. Closing his eyes, he saw the esteemed businessman smiling, shaking hands, and making promises. However, Governor Bosley knew Rawlings' decision to close that plant in Flint, Michigan, cost dearly. It may not be Christian to seek revenge, but looking at the page before him, he pondered how anyone but God could present him this opportunity.

Without a second thought, Governor Richard Bosley signed his name to the bottom of the petition. He took the official Iowa stamp and made the document legal. Yes, the original ten names of prisoners receiving pardons were already released to the press. It would be all right. The newspapers would momentarily miss this great human interest story: "State Official Rights a Wrong and Releases Ex-wife of Top Executive from Prison." The newspaper wouldn't miss the aftermath. Richard

Bosley I was confident Mr. Rawlings's publicist would somehow spin this in his direction. However, just maybe, by avoiding the first list of pardons, Ms. Nichols would have the opportunity to write her own story.

The following day, in front of local and national press, Governor Bosley signed ten petitions. Under the Iowa State Constitution, a *pardoned person* was entitled to an expunction of all arrest records relating to the conviction. A full pardon restored all citizenship rights forfeited by law as the result of a criminal conviction and officially nullifies the punishment or other legal consequences of the crime. The person will forever be regarded as innocent and regain the status as if she never committed the offense for which she was convicted.

Most importantly, a pardon granted by a state executive was *final and irrevocable*. Governor Bosley placed the ten documents into the manila folder already containing one. Smiling weakly at the cameras he stood and walked to the podium. "Ladies and gentleman, you witnessed my final act as governor of this great state. It's with a solemn heart today that I resign from this prestigious office..."

The clerk took the manila folder and placed each document inside its appropriate envelope. Counsel representing each individual would be contacted, prisoners would be informed, and if accepted by each prisoner, the pardon could not be overturned. Finally, the courts would be notified of each pardon. With so much activity and emotion, even the clerk didn't realize she had filed eleven pardons instead of ten.

*****

Down the street from the State House, in another office building Jane Allyson, Attorney, paced nervously around her small office willing her telephone to ring. This was her first petition for pardon. She'd waited anxiously for verdicts from juries, verdicts that determined the freedom and future of her clients. Somehow this seemed different -- surreal. Her client had already lost her freedom and future by willingly pleading *no contest* to the charge of *attempted murder*.

Jane remembered standing next to Ms. Nichols with an overwhelming sense of helplessness -- complete impotence -- as they listened to the judge discuss the consequences of Claire's plea. Early in law school, Jane learned to remain emotionally detached from her clients. She usually succeeded. It was a matter of survival. She wouldn't be able to help the next client if her thoughts lingered on the one she failed. However, that day, a year ago, Jane wanted to sit and cry with Claire Nichols. It was all so wrong.

Time passes and seasons change. New clients come and go. Opportunities arise. Esquire Allyson now practiced with a firm in the heart of Iowa's capital. Life was busy. Jane moved on -- until three days earlier, when a courier delivered a certified letter labeled: *Confidential: Esquire Jane Allyson*. Within the envelope she found the completed *Petition for Pardon* for Claire Nichols. No work on Jane's part was required, except to sign as representing counsel. The attached typed note was short:

> *Ms. Allyson, Perhaps you remember a client from about a year ago, Claire Nichols. Enclosed please find a petition for pardon to Governor Bosley. As you are probably aware, his time in office is short. This MUST reach his office today. All that is required of you is your signature. Enclosed please find a certified check to reimburse you for your undertaking. Thank you.*

Perhaps it was the check -- $100,000, made payable to *Cash* or the unsigned note, but accepting this assignment screamed wrong. What attorney in her right mind would accept a task and payment from an unknown source? Her future as well and law license may hinge on this decision. Jane knew she should consult the partners of her firm. That was her intent, until the small digital readout at the bottom of her computer screen caught her attention: 4:32 PM. The governor's office was a ten minute walk.

Jane delivered the signed petition.

Now, she nervously awaited the future. The governor's decision was made. Jane had watched his press conference on the web. Pacing her office, she continued to question the ethics and legality of her decision. If her telephone never rang, if the pardon wasn't granted, no one would ever know she filed the petition. The check would remain in her file cabinet. No matter the governor's decision, cashing the check seemed immoral and unethical.

On the wall in an impressive oak frame, matted against distinguished slate backing was her diploma from the University of Iowa, College of Law. The official seal reflected light even through the glass. Could her decision to help this woman and accept this assignment void those years of education?

She continued to pace the carpeted floor. She had plenty of work she could be doing. But, with the press conference an hour ago, she couldn't concentrate on anything except willing her phone to ring. If the call didn't come soon, it never would.

The memories of Claire Nichols' case flooded Jane's thoughts. The idea to request a pardon had never occurred to her, but it *was* a good idea. The part that scared her – hell, it must have scared the person who sent her the application -- was Anthony Rawlings. The man was extremely influential. There would be repercussions if the pardon was actually granted. Jane pushed those thoughts away. She couldn't think about that now. She could only wait.

Lost in her own thoughts, the ringing of her telephone made her heart race and body flinch. Momentarily, she stared at the devise. Was it her imagination? Were the sounds truly resonating from the small plastic telephone? Reaching for the receiver, with a trembling hand, she utilized her courtroom skills and steadied her voice. "Hello, yes, this is Jane Allyson..."

Jane's grip upon the steering wheel blanched her knuckles. The drive from Des Moines to Mitchellville took less than thirty minutes, and at two fifteen in the afternoon traffic wasn't an issue. The issue which lingered in Jane's mind was her continual work under the radar. No one on planet Earth knew what she was doing. It added to the mystery.

The dichotomous March sky stretched before her, gray upon gray. The shades weren't the same, yet they weren't different. Just clouds upon clouds. Turning east onto highway I 80 Jane thought about the prisoner only a few miles ahead. In her briefcase, on the seat next to her, was the one page document that would change Claire Nichols' life forever.

Three days ago, this document didn't exist. Jane Allyson wondered about the petition and the check. Right or wrong, she decided to keep the assignment to herself. In the world of money and influence, anyone could be tempted to inform Anthony Rawlings of her impending quest.

She wasn't accusing anyone, at any level, of wrong doing. It was only that Claire made claims, real valiant assertions and accusations. Like mist from a lake into the cool evening sky, her testimony evaporated. Over a year later, no one -- not even nosey reporters -- had the slightest inclination of the possible alternate personality of Iowa's golden boy. Some small voice within Jane's soul warned her not to share her current activities. Once complete, she would request a meeting with the partners of the firm. Hopefully, they would understand. At this moment, Jane chose to worry about Claire, instead of possible personal consequences.

Unbelievably, the list of pardoned individuals released to the media following the press conference didn't include Claire Nichols. Yet, the document was in Jane's possession. Pulling into the visitor's parking area, Jane Allyson tingled with anticipation. Fourteen months ago she wasn't able to help her client. Today she would.

The elation vaporized with an unexpected realization. Jane stood statuesque, her hand upon the door, immobilized by a thought, *who has $100,000 available to free Claire from prison?* She'd been so attached to the premise that it was *someone* who feared Anthony Rawlings. What if instead of someone who *feared* him, what if it *was* him? *Could it be? But why?*

By submitting the petition, instead of being a rebel, could Jane be a pawn? What if the freedom she was about to grant Claire was nothing more than an enticement to a web? Her hand held the door handle, and her stomach lurched. Jane couldn't let these thoughts stop her forward progress. Claire Nichols deserved freedom. Jane needed to intercede and assure Claire's freedom wasn't only from the state of Iowa, but *out* of Iowa.

An eerie florescent glow illuminated the small dingy visitor's room. The artificial light added to the coolness of the metal table and chairs.

15

Jane continued to check her watch. *How long does it take to bring a prisoner to this room?*

The answer was thirteen minutes. Nearly thirteen minutes after Jane's arrival to the small colorless room the door opened. Accompanied by a guard, Claire Nichols entered and sat in the opposing chair. She looked much as Jane remembered, with her brown hair pulled back into a ponytail. Although her complexion was pale, even without makeup, her eyes were still the vivid green. Though similar in stature to herself, the prisoner appeared more petite inside her Iowa issued jumpsuit.

"Jane, I'm surprised to see you. Why are you here?" Claire's inquiry sounded amazingly strong.

"Have you heard of a pardon?'

"Yes, it's something the president does before he leaves office. Why?"

"Because it's also something the governor does before leaving office."

Claire's green eyes narrowed as she searched for words. "I don't understand."

"Governor Bosley has cancer. He resigned from office today."

"I'm sorry to hear that. I believe he attended my wedding." She paused momentarily contemplating the information, "What did you just say about a pardon?"

"Claire, he signed a number of pardons before his resignation. The one I came to talk to you about is yours."

Claire heard Jane's words. She tried diligently to process the information, but it wasn't making sense. Words weren't forming. Tears were.

Jane watched as her former client struggled with her new reality. "First, you must accept the pardon." Jane pulled the paper from her brief case and placed it on the smooth surface in front of Claire. "Once you do, *you* are free."

The prisoner stared at the document before her. She read her name and the charges. Governor Bosley's signature was present with the official state stamp of Iowa. Only one line remained blank, the line for her signature. When her eyes left the paper and returned to the woman who'd been her defense counsel thirteen months ago, they sparkled with moisture which now coated her cheeks.

Claire needed reassurance. Too many times in her life she'd been deceived. "Why do *I* have a pardon... and *free*... what does that mean? Free as in free, or free as in I must be watched and monitored..." her voice faded into unsuppressed emotions.

Jane reached across the table and held Claire's trembling hands. "If you sign this petition, you are free. A pardon means all charges are gone. They are expunged from your record. You are forgiven. You may leave this prison today and never look back." As the words tumbled from Jane's lips, Claire's resolve melted. Her shoulders slumped and head bowed. Sounds didn't indicate her sobs; it was the shuttering of her shoulders. Jane squeezed her hands. "You may go anywhere *YOU* want, whenever *YOU* want. Claire, where do you want to go?"

Her green eyes glistened as her gaze returned to her counsel. "Where do *I* want to go?" Claire's mind spun, it had been so terribly long since she'd control of her future. "I don't know."

"I guess the first question you need to answer is: Do you accept the pardon?" Jane watched as Claire's chest heaved. In desperation, the woman in orange attire nodded, words continued to fail her. "Then you need to sign the petition." Claire nodded again.

It took some time for Jane to calm her client. Once done, they secured her signature. There was processing to do, but before this day was done, Claire would leave the penitentiary alongside Jane.

"When will I be released?" Claire found her voice, although more tentative than before.

"I'm not leaving today without you."

Claire's eyes beamed admiration toward her counsel. "What do I need to do?"

"Do you have anything in your cell you want to take with you?"

Claire debated her personal belongings. *Yes, there were pictures, letters, research, and some tokens.* She nodded.

"Then you go back to your cell with a guard. I'll take this pardon to the main office. They'll bring you to me in a short time." Claire continued to nod in agreement. "I have some clothes in case the ones you wore during your arrest don't fit. They'll return all your belongings from that day."

"Thank you." Claire looked down at the table. "I don't have any money to pay you for your work."

Jane thought of the cashier's check. "Let's get you out of here, and then we'll talk reimbursement." Jane's smile proved contagious. Claire returned the smile and squeezed Jane's hands. "Before you go back to your cell, who can I call? Is there someone who can meet you? Someone to take you somewhere? Or do you want to stay in Iowa?" Jane silently prayed her client wanted to leave, and she had somewhere to go.

"Where can I go?"

"Anywhere you want. Who can I call?"

Claire contemplated the question. She wanted to leave Iowa and all its memories as soon as possible. But who could help her? She had no money. Her sister would come, but it would take her time. Besides, Emily didn't have money either. Then she thought of someone, an albeit unlikely friend.

Many months ago, after receiving Anthony's box of secrets, Claire decided to contact Amber McCoy, Simon Johnson's fiancée. She felt a connection, two women done wrong by the actions of Anthony Rawlings. Today, Claire knew Amber was the one person who could help. "Amber McCoy, CEO of SiJo Gaming, Palo Alto, California. I don't know her number."

Writing everything down, Jane answered, "Don't worry, I'll get in contact with her before you reach me in the main office."

"Thank you." Claire stood and walked toward the door. With her hand in mid knock, she repeated, "Really Jane, thank you, I never expected this, ever."

"We'll talk more in the car. Now get your things, there is a big wonderful world waiting for you." Jane watched as Claire lifted her head and squared her shoulders. Next, she knocked upon the door and was led to her cell. For a few more minutes Claire endured the indignation of her prisoner status. The guard didn't know she was now a free woman. Unlike the last time, as Jane watched Claire escorted away, this time, she took comfort in knowing it was only temporary.

Jane wondered why it wasn't more difficult. Removing a prisoner from a medium security penitentiary should be harder. Yet, with the governor's signature and a piece of paper, Claire Nichols was now riding in the passenger seat of her Toyota Corolla, wearing jeans and hiking boots from fourteen months earlier.

Claire chose to wear the blouse Jane brought for her. It was slightly large, but nonetheless, as Jane viewed Claire in her peripheral vision, Claire didn't seem concerned. Instead, she appeared mesmerized by the landscape, occasionally sighing or dabbing her eyes. Jane tried to imagine Claire's state of mind. Of course, her client was emotional; her entire life had just abruptly changed – again. It would be a difficult transition for anyone.

Sporadically, Jane checked her rearview mirror. There were no signs they were being followed. However, if the benefactor of the $100,000 knew about Claire's release, Jane worried he or she might be waiting for their departure.

Breaking the silence, Jane said, "I didn't speak with Ms. McCoy, but her assistant said there'll be a ticket waiting for you at the American Airlines counter."

"I don't have identification." The sudden realization frightened Claire. Could this oversight land her back in prison?

"Yes, you do. Iowa issued you an identification card identifying your personal belongings. You have all of that don't you?"

Claire hugged the small bag. All of her possessions in the entire world were contained within the small nylon bag. Along with the items from her cell, Claire's bag held the blue cashmere sweater and the jewelry she'd been wearing upon her arrest. At twenty-nine, it seemed like such a small accumulation. "I do. I didn't realize the identification card would work outside of prison."

As Jane turned the Toyota south onto highway 235, she inhaled deeply and breached the uncomfortable subject. "Claire, I need to tell you something. The petition for your pardon wasn't my idea."

The trance holding Claire Nichols' thoughts captive released its hold; she zeroed in upon her savior, the person who'd freed her from a life of solitude. However, after so much time alone, conversation was difficult.

Claire tried desperately to fill the silences. If one person spoke, then it was time for the next. Very easy, she could do it. "What do you mean?"

Jane told Claire about the anonymous letter, the almost complete petition for pardon, and the certified cashier's check. She didn't mention her fear as she entered the penitentiary. She waited to see if it was shared.

Claire asked, "Who would spend $100,000 for my release?"

"I don't know."

Claire observed the expression, body language, and tone of the woman next to her. It had been a while, but she believed Jane spoke truthfully. Her attorney didn't know who planted the seed for her emancipation.

Jane continued, "I can tell you, initially, I believed whoever this was, they wanted you released without associating their name. I believed they were protecting themselves from your ex-husband."

Claire ingested her words, it made sense. She reasoned, if Tony knew someone helped in her release, who knows what he might do. Then she registered every word, "Initially? Jane, what do you mean initially?"

As Jane answered, her Toyota headed south toward the Des Moines International Airport. "I have to admit, I've had another thought." Claire didn't speak, but listened and watched. Jane continued, "What if the petition, letter, and money came from an unlikely source, someone to whom $100,000 was nothing?"

Claire's emerald eyes opened wider. The elation which had filled her lungs evaporated. No longer involuntary, breathing required thought. She stammered, "You think it was Tony?" Claire fought an onset of nausea, "Why would he do that?"

"I really don't know. I just know the best thing is to get you out of Iowa especially before the press frenzy begins."

Claire hugged her belongings close to her thumping chest. As she remembered the unrelenting press and more importantly her ex-husband, old fears made her heart to race. Looking again at Jane, Claire noticed Jane's eyes darting between the landscape ahead and the one behind in the rearview mirror. What if Tony or someone else were following her? Claire replied, "Yes, please, let's do that."

The American Airlines' agent at the counter didn't question Claire's Iowa state issued identification. Within minutes she handed Claire her boarding pass -- a nonstop first class ticket to San Francisco, departing in ninety minutes.

Each step toward the concourse removed a little of Claire's heaviness. Although the anxiety and apprehension she'd experienced under Tony's rule knocked at the door of Claire's heart and soul, she tried desperately to suppress those fears. Her counsel's attention and kindness helped to alleviate the burden. Claire truly didn't have time to process her sudden freedom. Turning toward Jane, she inquired, "Tell me again about the pardon. Do I need to check in with anyone?"

Jane explained, "Everything associated with the charge of attempted murder is now gone. The arrest, plea, incarceration... it's all gone. Your record will appear as though it never occurred." She emphasized, "Claire, the last fourteen months never happened."

"Thirty-six." Claire corrected.

Jane looked into her client's eyes. She saw the victim's eyes of over a year ago, not the eyes of an attempted murderer. The sadness combined with confusion told Jane, release wouldn't be that simple. Removing Claire from the walls of Iowa's Correctional Institution for Women was easier than removing the past thirty-six months from her memories. There was nothing Jane could say. Getting Claire safely out of Iowa was her only goal. "Please take care of yourself." Jane said as she pulled an envelope and a card out of her purse. "Here is my card with my cell and office number as well as email. If I can be of any assistance, please don't hesitate to contact me. And in this envelope are a few things I believe should belong to you."

Claire took the items from her attorney and slowly opened the envelope. Staring back at her was fifty dollars in ten dollar bills and a cashier's check made out to *cash* for $100,000. "No, Jane. I can't accept this. This is for you. It's your payment for helping me."

"The cash will help with incidentals until you reach your friend. And, as for the check, it's a ridiculous amount of money for a few hours' work. You get settled. When you can, send me an appropriate payment for my services. Consider it seed money to start your new life."

"But we don't know who it's from."

"No, we don't. If perhaps it's from whom we suspect, wouldn't he be happy to learn it went to you?"

Slowly Claire's lips turned upward; she shook her head. "No. No, he wouldn't." Claire scanned the mingling crowd for a familiar face. Exhaling with relief at the sea of strangers, Claire continued, "And for that reason, I accept." The two women embraced. "Thank you, Jane, for everything."

Claire straightened her shoulders, and turned toward the gate. It'd been sometime since she'd flown commercial, but she knew Jane wasn't allowed past security without a boarding pass. Thankfully, no one else would be either.

Jane watched as Claire passed the TSA agents and disappeared into the crowd of bodies. With an audible sigh, Jane thanked God no one recognized her client, and the reporters hadn't been notified. She had no idea how long it would take interested parties to learn of Claire's release and flight. However long, Jane hoped it was long enough.

Claire Nichols sat in a row of connected black vinyl chairs, holding all of her worldly possessions and soaking in the scene around her. There were people talking, reading, and even sleeping. Periodically the dim background noise shattered with announcements over the PA system.

They told of flights boarding and others delayed. No one noticed her. No one cared that only four hours earlier she'd been a prisoner of the state of Iowa. The buzzing in Claire's brain began to dull, and her pulse steadied. In another thirty-five minutes she'd be boarding a plane. Claire hoped she wouldn't hear an announcement saying her flight was delayed. She may not remember her initial arrival to Iowa, but she was savoring her final exit. Returning was not on her agenda.

Her inner monologue was interrupted by the sound of her name, "Ms. Nichols?" A large security officer bent down to speak quietly near Claire's ear.

Startled by the man's closeness and words, she managed a response, "Yes? I'm Claire Nichols."

"I need you to come with me, please."

Oh God, no! She thought. *Please let me get on this plane.* Involuntarily, moisture returned to Claire's eyes as the shrill sound of alarms reverberated within her head. Trying to speak steadily over the deafening panic, only she could hear, she uttered, "I'm sorry. I don't believe I can do that. I can't miss my flight."

"Ms. Nichols, if you will please come to my office, I'll explain everything."

Claire gripped her bag and contemplated her next move. She shouldn't have left Jane, not yet. She had Jane's card; she could call her. Her voice and tone exposed her apprehension, "I really don't want to go with you." People began to stare.

Speaking in a hushed whisper, "Ms. Nichols, your ticket has been cancelled." She shook her head in protest. "It's all right." Moving his lips near her ear, as to not be overheard, "Please settle down, your ticket was cancelled, because there's a private plane coming for you."

The security officer's voice came through a long dark tunnel. The tunnel closed. Only blackness...

Although the world is full of suffering,
it is full also of the overcoming of it.
– Helen Keller

Chapter 2

Claire woke with a start, her eyes opened wide. The view was no different than from behind her closed lids -- darkness. Utilizing her senses she felt the softness of the sheets and luxurious pillows, smelled the faint aroma of lilacs, and heard only quiet. Her mind tried to replay the past twenty-four hours. There was too much to sort. Nevertheless, she knew without a doubt, this wasn't her cell.

Trying desperately for visual confirmation she searched the penetrating darkness for light. Only a few feet in the distance, she located the illuminated display of a digital clock: 3:57 AM. For the past nine months she awakened every morning at 6 AM. Slowly her mind churned, she wasn't on the twin mattress, not in her cell, and most importantly, no longer in Iowa. She was in California. The two hour time difference explained her early waking. It was almost six in Iowa.

Claire tried to close her eyes and enjoy the new comfortable surroundings, yet her mind swirled uncontrollably with a whirlwind of thoughts. Finally, she gave up and got out of bed. Although she wanted to go to the kitchen, she didn't want to wake Amber, not after everything she'd done. Thinking about her new friend, a smile spread across Claire's face. Truly, until yesterday, she and Amber had only met once face-to-face.

Wearing her new roommate's t-shirt and shorts; Claire made her way to the adjoining bath. Pausing at the door frame, she pushed the light switch and viewed the room where she'd slept. Compared to her prison cell, the room was palatial, containing all the natural furnishings of a bedroom. The queen sized bed had a beautiful headboard covered in ivory fabric. Matching material graced taught boxed valances covering the top of each window. Long vertical wooden blinds kept the room dark, while sleek, modern bedside stands, dressers, and a desk lined the walls. The light golden hue of the blinds contrasted beautifully with the darker wood slats covering the floor. Strategically placed beige shag rugs added warmth and undoubtedly muffling sound.

Turning to the tile covered bathroom Claire smiled at the sink. It looked like a green glass bowl sitting upon a stand. Above the sink was a large framed mirror flanked on each side by lighted sconces. Claire paused, staring at her reflection. It looked different. Her eyes glistened with the realization -- it was the smile! It had been so long since she truly felt like smiling.

Claire assessed herself, she didn't look as old as she felt. Although, the past three years had psychologically aged her beyond the chronological timetable, the more recent lack of sunshine undoubtedly benefited her skin. She remembered a time when she radiated with a bronze sun-kissed glow. She also remembered her hair lighter, both from the sun and highlights. Today her pale china complexion was surrounded by chestnut waves as her hair hung upon her back. It hadn't been trimmed or cut in over a year.

Tip-toeing in stocking feet, Claire silently made her way into the hall. Near the entrance to her room were doors to other rooms. Last night she learned one was Amber's office containing a desk, computers, and everything she needed to stay connected to her responsibilities at SiJo. Additional doors led to a den and an extra bedroom. Amber's bedroom was on the other end of the condo.

Claire continued down the hall, into the living room, and through the archway to the cool kitchen. Everything looked perfect. Although she could, Amber didn't employ a full time household staff. She reasoned, she enjoyed cooking, and often ate out. A cook would be underutilized. There was a woman who came twice a week to clean and do laundry.

Though early, Claire longed for real, non-prison coffee. She eyed the coffee maker upon the granite countertop. It was different than any she'd seen before, some kind of individual cup thing. *Had making coffee changed that much in fourteen months?* She tried desperately to decipher its operation. The metal stand by its side held multiple types of coffee and flavors in small sealed cups. After further investigation and exploration she surrendered and sat at the kitchen table. The quietness of the apartment combined with the freedom to move about as she wished allowed Claire's mind to replay the past twenty-four hours. Staring through the windows into the dark predawn sky she remembered....

*****

When Claire regained consciousness at Des Moines International Airport, the security officer tried frantically to calm her nerves. Once in his office he handed Claire the telephone. On the other end Amber McCoy responded to Claire's obvious distress, explaining, "I'm sorry, I didn't mean to frighten you. It's just after Liz, my assistant, told me she booked you a flight, I started thinking. Maybe I didn't need to take this precaution, but after all you've told me, well, I just thought it would be better if there weren't any record of your travel."

Listening to Amber's steady tone helped Claire regain her composure. "Oh, I think that makes sense. It was just when the security officer said *private plane*, I immediately thought someone else sent it."

"No wonder you freaked. I'm glad I was able to reach you. A SiJo Gaming jet will be there soon. Why don't you stay with security until it arrives? In no time, you'll be out here."

When Claire handed the telephone back to airport security, the nice man offered to get her something to eat or drink. Sipping coffee and fighting feverishly to mend her frayed nerves, she thought about Amber's reasoning. It was the same reason Jane concealed her activities from everyone. Presumably, the reason Governor Bosley chose to withhold her name from the press.

The security guard at the Iowa airport walked Claire to the tarmac where small commercial and private planes boarded and unboarded. She'd never been there before. Tony kept his plane and other Rawlings Industries planes at a small private airport outside of Iowa City. The plane Amber sent had large blue and green letters advertising *SiJo Gaming*, the company started by Simon Johnson. Seeing the insignia reminded Claire of Simon's large blue eyes. A twinge of sadness seeped into her frazzled emotions as she pictured the man she saw only once since the end of their freshman year of college.

While flying across country, Claire tried to fathom her recent change of events. She was truly stunned by so many benefactors. It seemed as though not only were these individuals willing to help her, but it appeared these people saw through the façade of Anthony Rawlings. For so long, Claire truly believed his veneer was impenetrable.

Claire had contacted Amber McCoy after she received Tony's box of information. It didn't seem right for Claire to hide the possible cause of Amber's fiancé's death. She wasn't sure how Amber would react. If Claire's theory were correct, Claire was in essence responsible for Simon's death – if he hadn't tried to contact *her*, he might still be alive.

Claire realized her assumptions were astounding, and she had no proof. Nonetheless, as the two conversed, Claire spun an amazing tale of deceit and vengeance. Apparently she'd been convincing enough to gain Amber's trust. In the months that followed, through multiple emails (Claire had limited computer access while incarcerated) they shared information and research regarding the materials Tony offered in his *box*. Together, they were in the process of recreating much of the information.

The need to recreate was due to Claire's impulsivity. In a moment of weakness she decided to throw most of the information in the prison's incinerator. Sometimes she reasoned it wasn't weakness, but strength -- the strength to rid her of her past, a sort of cleansing. Fortuitously, she'd chosen to save a few non-duplicable items, pictures and the *Top Secret* report.

Claire wasn't sure what she planned to accomplish when she recreated the box of information. She'd planned to have more time. However, she wasn't complaining. Being released from prison almost four years early was worth the uncertainty regarding her intentions. She and Amber would continue to recreate the timeline, understand Tony's past in order to influence his future. Perhaps others would join their quest. Claire didn't know if Emily was up for the challenge.

Thinking about her sister, Claire knew she loved her. However, understandably Claire's arrest and confessions strained their relationship. The accusations and concerns Emily professed and Claire vehemently denied during her marriage were now realized. Claire's deceit cost them both dearly. Truthfully, Tony made the final call, ultimately responsible for Claire's incarceration, John's charges (embezzlement and fraudulent client billing), and every bad thing that happened on planet Earth in the last forty-eight years. Emily tried to support Claire while she was in the Iowa prison. Their interaction was superficial at best. Now that Claire was pardoned, reconnecting with Emily was high on her priority list.

As the small jet cleared the Santa Cruz Mountains, twilight descended upon Silicon Valley. The lights of Palo Alto greeted her, and the airport bustled with commuter planes. It was one of the busiest private airports in the country.

Wishing for invisibility from her ex-husband, Claire prayed one woman on one jet would go completely unnoticed.

As the door opened and the tepid air filled the cabin Claire allowed herself to experience the relief associated with freedom. The change of scenery helped facilitate her emotional shift. Placing one foot in front of the other she disembarked the plane. After three years of constant surveillance, the uncertainty of California's possibilities thrilled and terrified her.

Her future was in *her* hands --such a simple statement of independence. Nonetheless, it could not have been made twenty-four hours earlier. Claire thought about that; it could not have been made thirty-six months ago. Straightening her shoulders and lifting her head high, Claire scanned the concourse.

As if knowing Claire's need for immediate confirmation and reaffirmation, Amber walked silently from an unmarked hanger. She looked much different than she did eighteen months ago at Simon's funeral. Not physically, as Claire recognized the slender brunette instantly. The difference was her presence, no longer grief stricken; Amber radiated a casual confidence and a self-assured aura. Their eyes met and Amber moved toward her.

On the concrete concourse the two friends and strangers, embraced. The day had already been extremely long. Emotionally overloaded, Claire was thankful for her new friend and ready for quiet time. Amber understood and drove them to her condo, with minimal stops on the way for essentials.

Nestled near downtown Palo Alto, Amber's condominium blended perfectly into its surroundings with its stucco walls and orange tiled roof. They parked in an underground garage after waving to the security officer guarding the entrance. When the elevator opened to the fourth floor, Claire recognized the true grandeur of the building, with wide hallways giving access to multiple dwellings. Amber explained, she'd lived there for years, loved the neighborhood, people, and city. As a bonus, SiJo Gaming was near. She didn't need to fight the daily San Francisco traffic.

Hardwood floors, taupe walls, and recessed lighting combined to make her condo warm and inviting. The two ladies settled onto comfortable stools at Amber's high kitchen table and became better acquainted. Claire gazed around the room and took in the simplistic chic style. The understated panache and flair appealed to Claire. It wasn't the grandeur of the mansion she shared with her ex-husband, yet nonetheless, lavish and elegant. The granite counters and table top felt cool and smooth. The high stools in which they sat allowed her feet to pivot upon the cast iron bar.

Their conversation proceeded benignly. Perhaps Amber could sense Claire's dazed realization; during the hours that followed, the two women connected. They shared sushi, wine, and discussed their common bond. As the hours slipped away and the outside darkness intensified, their interaction within became increasingly real.

Nineteen hours earlier, Claire woke in a prison cell. It was the day that wouldn't end. She was physically and emotionally spent. However, Amber must have realized there was a conversation they needed to undergo. Claire wasn't ready for Amber's question, "Did you love Simon?"

Recently conversation hadn't been Claire's norm. So sitting with Amber and being asked something so personal, something that could impact their relationship, frightened her. Claire believed her answer could cost her the one person willing to help her plight. She hesitated, "I hadn't seen Simon since our freshman year of college, until he came to see me in Chicago."

"I know that. But, what I want to know is if you loved him."

Claire bowed her head. The day was too much -- too many changes. She couldn't summon a mask to disguise her true emotions. Her shoulders slumped. Her eyes saddened, though too tired for tears. "I thought I did. When we were at Valparaiso, I believed in fairy tales. I believed in forever. When he left for his internship, I expected him to return. When he didn't, I expected an invitation to join him. It broke my heart I never got one." Claire began to stand, believing Amber would no longer want her to stay. "When I saw him in Chicago, I remembered those feelings. Simon's love was unconditional. You don't know what I went through with Tony, but *unconditional* is not a word I'd use to describe it." Claire hesitated, looked out the large window and saw the quiet tree lined street, four stories below, illuminated by old fashioned light poles. Although Amber remained silent, Claire no longer held eye contact, "Seeing him that day made me sad. I didn't know about you. Honestly, I

26

didn't ask if he were married or engaged. I just knew the love of someone like Simon was something I'd never experience again. I knew I'd missed out on something real, and I'd never know it." Claire pushed the stool under the counter. "Thank you for getting me out of Iowa. Once I cash the check, I'll reimburse you. I'll try to find somewhere to stay tonight."

"Why are you leaving?" Amber's surprised expression echoed her words.

"After what I just said, don't you want me to go?"

Amber walked around the table and faced Claire. The two women were so different and yet so alike: both brunettes, Amber a little taller with brown eyes and Claire more petite with green eyes. Although both were under thirty, life had dealt them more sadness than they deserved. "No, I don't." Claire staggered backwards in surprise. She couldn't take more emotion in one day. "Simon loved you. If his love was unrequited I could easily hate you. But, if his love was reciprocated, if you truly loved him in return, even ten years ago, then all I can do is all I can do."

Claire stared at the woman before her. "I'm sorry." She shook her head. "I don't understand what you're saying."

"I'm saying," she reached for Claire's hand, "I want you to stay here or at least in Palo Alto, and I want to help you find a life." Amber widened her smile. "I want to understand more about your ex-husband, but not tonight. I want to help you do whatever you feel is necessary to repay him for his actions, whether that is revenge or just showing him you can exist without him. I want to honor Simon by having the two women who loved him unite in a common bond."

"Thank you. I'm sorry the two of you didn't get the chance to marry. If I had anything to do with that, I'm truly sorry." Claire held the chair for support.

"Simon had to do with that. Not you. It was just the man he was. Don't feel too guilty. We were friends and colleagues for years; our romance was blossoming. I've been blessed to have Simon in my life. Even without marriage he provided for me forever. Please let me share some of that with you."

"Thank you, but I never want to be dependent upon anyone again. I need to be my own person."

"That's great. If I can help you do that, I'd be honored. Will you let me help you get on your feet?"

Claire thought about her life. Everyone she knew before her marriage was gone. Even her sister was alienated. The friends she acquired during her time with Tony were frightened or truly believed she tried to kill Tony. She and Courtney had clandestine contact. Tony's influence knew few bounds. *Had there been anyone who wanted to help her, just her?* "Are you a patient person?" Claire asked.

Amber's lips and eyes revealed a smile fighting for exposure. "I've been told I have problems in that area."

Claire returned her smile, "I'm glad to hear you don't have a halo. I was beginning to wonder."

"Oh hell, just stick around. You'll learn more about the horns that expose themselves occasionally."

"I'm willing to accept your help to get me back on my feet. I hate that I need it, but I know I do... thank you."

As Claire fell asleep that night she marveled at her new situation. Life had dealt her many changes – this one left her exhausted, eager, and filled with warmth.

*****

Those pleasant feelings continued as she once again sat at the kitchen table, trying to make sense of her life. A little after five in the morning, Amber sleepily found her way into the kitchen. "Good morning, I'm not used to having a roommate. The light startled me."

"I'm sorry. The time difference made me wake early."

"Don't you want coffee?" Amber asked as she selected a small cup and placed it in the top of the machine. Next she pushed a few buttons and the machine came to life. Slowly, Claire walked over to the counter.

"I'm afraid you may have bitten off more than anyone can chew. Apparently, I don't even know how to make coffee."

Amber laughed, "These are kind of new. The hardest part is deciding your flavor."

Claire explained she should call her sister before news of her release hit the media. Amber brought Claire her laptop, "This is to look up your sister's number. You're also welcome to use the telephone and call whomever you want." Claire considered the possibility of unlimited access. Undoubtedly, she would require help with more than just coffee.

Emily's number was unpublished, but Claire remembered it was listed on the information from the prison. Of course, Emily was her emergency contact. Listening to the telephone ring she prayed she'd catch her sister before Emily left for work. It was after eight in Indiana. As the answering machine began to speak, Claire hung-up. She didn't want to leave a message. *What if Emily's line was monitored?* Claire knew she sounded paranoid. But, how does the saying go? Just because you're paranoid doesn't mean someone's *not* out to get you.

While Amber readied for work, Claire continued to browse the laptop. There was so much information literally at her fingers tips. Amber's internet was much faster than the one at the prison. Claire was lost in cyberspace when sounds came from the living room. Someone had entered the front door of the condo.

Walking casually into the kitchen, in worn jeans, a white t-shirt, and bare feet was a handsome man. His blonde hair fell in messy waves, and his face held the telltale shadow of someone who'd yet to shave. Not knowing what to do, Claire sat quietly and watched as he walked in a sleepy haze toward the mysterious coffee maker. After engineering the machine like a pro, he turned toward the table and saw Claire. His smile extended to his cheeks creating small lines around his light blue eyes.

"Oh, hello, you must be Claire." He casually leaned against the counter and took her in.

Suddenly she felt underdressed. Not like she needed to be formal, just more clothes than a t-shirt and shorts. Claire couldn't help notice his firm lean body, long legs, and obvious level of comfort. "Yes, I am. I'm also at a disadvantage. You know my name, but I don't know yours." Other than guards, she hadn't spoken to a man in a longtime. She suddenly realized this man must be Amber's new romance. She couldn't help but think Amber moved on rather quickly. It wasn't a judgmental thought, more an observation. Especially after last night's conversation regarding their *common bond* with Simon. Claire also realized she should stop staring in his direction. He may be handsome, but the last thing Claire wanted to do was cause problems between Amber and her beau.

Offering his hand, he walked forward, "So sorry, my name is Harry. It's nice to finally meet you."

"Finally?" She responded as she shook his hand and recovered her own quickly.

"Well, I've heard all about you since you contacted Amber months ago."

As Harry spoke, Amber returned to the kitchen. She no longer looked like the stylish casual woman of last night or the sleepy robe wearing woman of earlier. Instead, she personified Ms. McCoy, CEO of SiJo Gaming. Everything from her attire to her long hair twisted into a knot at the back of her neck said *professional*. Truthfully Claire wondered if she'd been met by *this* Amber at the airport, would she have felt intimidated. That thought faded faster than the smoke from an extinguished candle when Amber spoke. Her voice brimmed with unabashed joy and enthusiasm. "Claire, I see you've met my brother. Harry lives down the hall and thinks mooching off of me is easier than buying his own groceries." She smiled as she gave her brother a flittering kiss on the cheek.

He smiled in return, "I just really like your coffee maker."

"And my cereal, and my toast, and my..." Laughter interlaced Amber's words. Claire tried to soak in their joviality. She honestly couldn't remember the last time she'd experienced such a refreshing atmosphere.

Sipping her own coffee, Claire asked, "What do you do, Harry? You don't seem as ready for work as Amber."

Amber laughed again, "What do you mean? That is about as dressed up as he gets."

"Hey, that's not true. I wear shoes -- sometimes." He winked at Claire. She felt herself blush. She didn't know why, and neither of the others seemed to notice.

"Well, for the next few days my job is *you*." He said as he took his coffee to the table. Sitting in the chair opposite Claire, he gazed into her stare.

This time she blushed, "Me? What do you mean?"

Amber answered, "I hope you don't mind. I'd like to be the one to help you get things started here in California, but I've got a lot happening at work. There's a new launch about to take place. Harry on the other hand has more flexibility with his job. I asked him to help you do whatever you need."

Claire thought for a moment. "Thank you, Harry. I guess I need to decide what that is."

Sipping his coffee, he offered, "I'm in no rush. But, I was thinking you'll need more identification; so you should request a copy of your birth certificate. Once that arrives you can do things like open a bank account. After that, the possibilities are limitless."

"A telephone." Claire said dreamily, "I'd like to get a telephone."

Harry and Amber smiled at one another. He replied, "That can be our first mission." Neither understood how monumental the common piece of technology would be to Claire.

Lost in her new thoughts Claire continued, "And some clothes. But that can wait until after the bank account."

Amber offered Claire a loan to help her get started. Claire hesitated, but knowing she had the cashier's check, she relented, "After I get the birth certificate, can I get a California driver's license?"

"Can you drive?" Harry asked jokingly.

Claire nodded.

"Then, I don't see why not." Harry answered.

Claire's emerald eyes glowed with anticipation. Who would have thought, she'd have a new home, in California. "So how do I get the birth certificate?"

"How about we eat some of Amber's breakfast foods first?"

Walking toward her bedroom Amber called back to the kitchen, "See what I mean?"

*The secret to getting away with lying
is believing it with all your heart, that goes for lying to yourself
even more so than lying to another.*
- Elizabeth Bear

Chapter 3

J ane Allyson watched the snow and rain pelt the window of her small yet distinguished office. The mixture melted the scene of downtown Des Moines into a sad impressionistic painting. She wanted to concentrate on cases at hand. She had more than enough work to keep her busy, but her mind continually went back to Claire Nichols.

Late the other evening, Jane's private cell rang. Only a week and a half since she'd watched Ms. Nichols fade into a sea of unknown faces, on the other side of security at the Des Moines International Airport, she heard Claire's positive tone. They didn't talk long, but Claire's unspoken message was louder than her words.

She was settled, making a life, and doing well. She also told Jane she mailed her a check for her services. What she didn't say, but Jane heard loud and clear, was a regained resolve. Wherever Claire was, she was emerging from the depths of the past three years – a butterfly finally emerging from the encased cocoon.

It was like Jane could hear the determination her client held during her interviews at the courthouse in Iowa City in 2011. Although Jane moved on to other clients, she could close her eyes and see Claire Rawlings at the steel table, recounting her tortured life with Anthony Rawlings. At the time, Jane felt overwhelmed with compassion and respect for the petite woman. Many victims were unable to share details like the ones Claire described, especially against such a respected assailant. Yet, with each sentence, Mrs. Rawlings grew in stature.

None of it mattered. After the prosecutor, Marcus Evergreen, wove his web around Claire's testimony, she wisely chose incarceration over courtroom drama and further public scrutiny. Despite her circumstances, when the judge proclaimed the final sentence, Claire Nichols accepted the words with dignity and strength.

During the recent telephone call, Jane didn't *just* sense renewed determination. She heard hope and optimism, qualities Ms. Nichols lost.

31

They never discussed Claire's final destination. Jane believed it was better not to know – *plausible deniability*.

As she stared at the frigid Iowa morning, Jane didn't regret filing Claire's pardon petition. Jane believed, no matter the consequences, freeing Claire Nichols was the right motion. Thankfully, after some debate, the partners of her firm agreed.

Earlier this morning, while readying for work, Jane saw Claire's face on the local news. Two weeks after the fact -- the news of her release was out. Jane couldn't contain her smile. She didn't know how Governor Bosley kept it quiet so long, but Jane was thankful.

Word was, Richard Bosley was fading fast -- stage four B pancreatic cancer, metastized to his bones.

Settling into her leather chair, Jane sipped warm coffee and contemplated her impending meeting. Her earlier joy diminished as she entered her office greeted with multiple urgent messages from Anthony Rawlings' secretary. Apparently, Mr. Rawlings learned of Claire's release last night, prior to the news release.

His secretary asked Jane to travel immediately to Iowa City for a meeting with Mr. Rawlings. Jane smiled, wondering how many people drop everything at such a summons. Jane respectfully informed the woman she was involved in very important cases and would need to check her schedule. After a prolonged silence, during which Jane stared aimlessly out her large window contemplating the grey skies and chances of rain, Jane informed the secretary she would be available to make a trip to Iowa City -- a week from Thursday. The woman was obviously dismayed by Jane's refusal to fall prostrate to the great Anthony Rawlings.

A few minutes later Jane's phone rang. This time it wasn't a request. Mr. Rawlings' secretary informed Jane Mr. Rawlings would be at her office by ten *this* morning. Jane thought about stalling the meeting, saying she was busy. But, she decided she wanted to see her client's ex-husband for another reason. She believed Mr. Rawlings' demeanor would reveal if *he* were the anonymous benefactor.

If Jane sensed Mr. Rawlings wasn't Claire's savior, she wouldn't mention the origins of the petition. The benefactor would remain a mystery.

Tearing Jane from her thoughts, her assistant's voice broke through the speaker, "Ms. Allyson, Mr. Rawlings is here, accompanied by his attorney Mr. Simmons."

Jane took a deep breath and exhaled. "Please send them in."

Seeing the strained expression on the entrepreneur's face, Jane knew immediately; Mr. Rawlings did *not* send her the letter. He obviously came expecting answers. She had to wonder, *if it wasn't him, then who?*

"Hello, Mr. Rawlings, Mr. Simmons," she nodded at the men as they entered her office. "Please have a seat." She motioned to the two chairs sitting opposite her desk. Although probably not as grand as theirs, this was her office and Jane would take the seat of honor. Closing the door she returned to her leather chair. "Now gentleman, to what do I owe this honor?"

Mr. Simmons spoke first, "It has just recently come to my client's attention, on March 8th you filed a petition with then Governor Bosley requesting a pardon for Claire Nichols."

"Yes, that's correct."

"My client would like to know why this was filed, on what grounds, and who approached you to make this request."

"Gentleman, Ms. Nichols was never convicted of a crime. She pled *no contest*. That was *not* an admission of guilt. She's had an impeccable record during incarceration. Truthfully, she's the poster child for pardons. And, as for who hired me, I'm sure you're familiar with the term *confidential*."

"Why was I not notified?" Apparently, Mr. Rawlings couldn't restrain himself any longer.

"Why would you be?"

"For my safety. She tried to kill me."

"Have you been threatened," Jane leaned forward, "since her release?"

"No. I just learned of her release last night."

"It *appears* as though you needn't be concerned. She's had two weeks to finish what *you* claim she started," Jane grinned, "and it seems you're still with us."

Mr. Rawlings fought to keep his expression indifferent.

Mr. Simmons continued the enquiry. "Do you know where Ms. Nichols relocated? For my client's safety he should be informed."

"I do not. As I'm sure you're aware, with a pardon, the criminal record is expunged. Ms. Nichols does not owe the court a thing. She is free to go wherever she chooses. And furthermore, she is not required to keep the court or the state of Iowa informed of her whereabouts. I took her to the airport and left her at the gate. There is nothing more I can tell you."

Mr. Rawlings counsel continued, "She had a ticket for San Francisco, but prior to boarding the plane, her reservation was cancelled. Do you know where she went instead?"

Jane truly didn't know about the cancelled flight. She was very glad she'd heard from Claire. If she hadn't, that information would have been upsetting. But, she could appear genuinely surprised. "I don't know anything about her reservations being cancelled. And as I said, I don't know where she is now."

"Ms. Allyson, she had a first class ticket. Do you know how Ms. Nichols could afford such a ticket?" Mr. Simmons continued.

"As I mentioned, some things are confidential." Standing, Jane said, "Now gentleman, if that is all? I have work..."

Anthony's voice resonated low and menacing, "Ms. Allyson, I am not happy with the recent turn of events. I plan to learn of *all* individuals involved in this miscarriage of justice. And it's obvious, you played a role."

Still standing, Jane met Mr. Rawlings' stare. This was her forte -- why she became an attorney. "Mr. Rawlings, I was your ex-wife's co-counsel during her trial. I represented her then and would gladly do so again. If you have complaints about her pardon, I recommend you take them up with Richard Bosley. His signature alone opened the door of her cell." Jane's words slowed, "And I'm certain, a man of your stature did not intend his concern regarding self-preservation to be interpreted as a threat. That would not coincide with your benevolent image and – I'll add -- is illegal."

Standing, Mr. Simmons eloquently interceded, "You are correct, Ms. Allyson. My client is obviously distraught over the recent turn of events. You can understand his concern. After all, Ms. Nichols tried to harm him once. It's only natural for him to be concerned she may try to do it again."

"Yes, Mr. Simmons. I see how *your client* would be concerned that *my client* would cause him harm."

Tony did not appreciate Ms. Allyson's veiled implication. He didn't want Brent informed of Claire's accusations. Standing, Tony summoned his most affable voice, "Thank you, Ms. Allyson. I'm glad you understand my concern and hope you didn't misinterpret my alarm. If you remember anything else regarding Ms. Nichols' departure or learn her location, I would appreciate being informed." Tony extended his hand.

Jane took his hand and firmly shook it. "Mr. Rawlings, you will be among the first I call. Are we done?"

"Yes, I believe we are."

After the two men exited her office, Jane collapsed into her leather chair and exhaled audibly. *Well that was fun.* She smiled to herself. Funny how one petition could continue to bring her pleasure.

*****

The exercise room in the lower level of the condominium sported the newest machines and guaranteed fitness in just minutes per day. Claire usually waited until after seven-thirty for her morning workout. Most of the residents were professionals who utilized the equipment before heading to their respective careers. The small gym burst with fitness enthusiasts every day from five until seven. Since she didn't have a job, waiting until the crowd thinned made more sense.

Flat screen televisions glowed with closed caption from every direction throughout the fitness center. She watched and read. Never again was Claire Nichols going to be uninformed about the world around her. The display on the elliptical machine read nine more minutes. She willed her legs to continue, yearning for her pre-prison tone.

Contemplating the day's activities, she made a mental *to do* list. At eleven o'clock she had an appointment in San Francisco with a jewelry broker. Since obtaining her birth certificate she'd fulfilled many of her needs: driver's license, bank account, clothes, telephone, computer, cosmetics, a used car, and insurance. Truthfully, Claire was proud of her *new to her* Honda. It was the same make she owned in Atlanta, just a few years newer. Of course, she sent Jane Allyson a Money Order for her services.

Claire wasn't advertising her location. However, short of assuming an alternate identity, she knew she couldn't stay completely hidden. In an effort to avoid a trail of credit card receipts or loans, she utilized cash as much as possible. The recent expenditures took their toll on her $100,000. Although she currently had no living expenses that would inevitably change. A one bedroom condo on the third floor would become available soon. Claire weighed the pros of living close to Amber and Harry, her only two friends against the cons of her unknown future employment.

Obtaining work was high on her priority list. However, it wasn't easy. She wanted to work in meteorology. Her lack of recent experience and desire to avoid any station or weather organization connected to Rawlings Industries severely limited her options. *Six minutes left on the elliptical.*

Without a job, she needed more money. One evening while talking to Emily on the phone, the subject of her jewelry came up. When arrested, Claire was wearing diamond earrings, a diamond journey necklace, a diamond watch, and of course her engagement and wedding rings. If it had been up to her, she would've only been wearing the rings. Now as she struggled to complete the final five minutes on the machine, Claire smiled. If only her ex-husband knew how his insistence for her to wear the jewelry would probably net her a fine profit. Today's meeting was to determine the value of her bounty.

Harry recommended Mr. Pulvara. He only deals in high quality jewelry, not a common pawn broker. It didn't take an expert to know Claire's jewelry was very high quality. However, Mr. Pulvara only sees clients through recommendations and by appointment. Thanks to Amber she had both.

Claire valued Harry's recommendation. His connections in the Bay Area went beyond his real job as President of Security for SiJo Gaming. Amber joked about being her brother's boss. Nevertheless, with a degree in Criminology and five years' experience with the Bureau of Investigation and Intelligence, under the California Department of Justice as an investigator, Harry was more than qualified. *Two minutes remained on the elliptical display*; thankfully the resistance lessened.

Claire returned her attention to the TV. Suddenly, her lungs deflated, not from exercise, but from the picture on the screen. She stared helplessly at her wedding picture, the one released to the media. Although closed caption flowed across the bottom, she couldn't concentrate. Finally her mind focused, and she read, *"...Bosley, diagnosed with stage four pancreatic cancer. It is unclear why Ms. Nichols's name was not released to the public. Governor Preston has promised a full investigation. Mr. Anthony Rawlings' publicist stated Mr. Rawlings is shocked by this turn of events. He has no comment at this time. MSNBC has not been able to reach Ms. Nichols for comment."*

Her legs no longer moved; the machine moved her. She gawked at the television as the newscaster progressed with other stories. When her feet hit the solid floor, her muscles tightened. Claire knew she should cool-down properly, and although her legs yelled in protest, the voices inside her head conquered.

Claire looked to the mirrors completely covering one wall of the gym. Normally she didn't like seeing herself hot and sweaty. However, today she couldn't look away. She wondered; *do the other people watching the same program recognize me?* The bride in the picture beamed photogenic. Her porcelain complexion, blonde hair, and designer dress looked so different from the woman in the mirror. Other than her eyes, which Claire immediately diverted to the floor, the differences outnumbered the similarities.

Her thoughts swirled as she rode the elevator to the fourth floor. Entering the condominium, she called to Amber -- no answer. *She's probably already left for work.* Claire sat at the kitchen table. Ignoring the perspiration dripping down her back and between her breasts, she booted up her new laptop. While the PC came to life, she searched for her telephones. She actually had two! It was probably silly, but she had her real iPhone with a blocked number and a *pay as you go* phone. The latter was used to communicate with Emily and Courtney. Claire was trying to stay under the radar. Her iPhone was on her bedside stand, but she couldn't find the other, which was strange. That phone rarely left her side, being her primary source of communication with her sister. The two siblings were working on their relationship. They'd talked more during the past two weeks than in years.

Back in the kitchen, she drank a glass of water, made a cup of coffee, and began to read the homepage. She saw two photos: her wedding picture and the cover of Vanity Fair. Her stomach twisted as she read the article. It divulged her public life during the last two and a half years: her marriage, lack of prenuptial agreement, lavish trips, high-end shopping, charge of *attempted murder*, plea of *no contest*, and sentencing. As she began the part about the pardon, she heard the front door. Turning to the source, Claire watched as Harry came toward her. His liquid blue eyes flooded with compassion. *Obviously he's seen the news.* He held her other telephone in his outstretched hand.

Trying to sound strong she took the phone, "Thank you, I guess I left that at your place last night." Amber may have better food, but Harry had the better television. Last night the three of them watched a Lakers game at Harry's. Claire wasn't really a basketball fan, which goes against her Indiana roots. It's just that the Hoosier glory days were before her time. She'd heard stories, but they never ignited a passion for the sport.

Her expression, the moisture in her eyes, and her obvious interruption from a work-out, told Harry Claire saw the news. Handing her the telephone he said, "This keeps chirping, I think your battery is about to die." He looked into her green eyes, "Claire, are you all right?"

She sat straighter. "Yes, I'm fine. Thank you for asking."

36

His compassion changed to surprise, "Oh, I just worried that ... well, when I saw the news... all right." He turned back to the coffee machine.

Claire checked the telephone – two text messages and one voice mail. She checked the texts. The first was from Courtney, sent at 10:45 PM last night – *TONY JUST LEARNED YOU'RE OUT OF PRISON. YELLING AT BRENT. NOT HAPPY. WANTS ANSWERS. LOVE YOU. WILL TELL MORE WHEN I CAN. STAY SAFE.*

Claire stared at the screen. *Why didn't I see this last night?* She didn't hear it beep with the game. Fear swept through her in a wave as her heart beat wildly in her ears.

"Claire, what does it say?"

She looked from the screen to Harry and shook her head. She tried to hide her fear, but she couldn't hide the tears slipping from her eyes. She hit another button and continued to read.

Sniffing, she wiped her eyes, tried to appear composed, and read through blurred vision. The time read 6 AM - only two hours ago, also from Courtney, *PRIVATE DETEC TRYING TO FIND YOU. KNOWS ABOUT CANCELLED TIX TO SAN FRAN. CHECKING OUT INDIANA. CHECKING EMILYS PHONE RECORDS. HEARD TONY'S VOICE W/ BRENT. NOT HAPPY!!!! BE CAREFUL.*

Silently, Harry stood motionless, intently watching Claire's every move.

"I'm sorry," she offered, "I need to check this voice mail." She didn't want to answer his *what* question, and hoped he'd leave her alone to listen. He didn't, although he went back to his coffee on the counter and gave her some space. Claire activated her voice mail and listened to Emily's voice:

"Claire, it's a little after four in the morning here. That's what? Two there, I think. I know you're asleep but you need to know, I just got a call *at this hour*, from some man named Roach. He said he's a private investigator working for a *mutual friend*. He said you may be in danger and needs to know your location, *for your protection*, he said. I didn't believe him. Please call and tell me you're safe." Claire's tears multiplied as she listened to her sister's scared voice. "He said he knows I've been talking to a disposable phone in California and asked if it's you. I just kept saying, *I don't know where she is and I have no other comment.* Finally, I hung-up on him. Can they really look into my phone records? I'll get one of those phones too. I'll call you later with the number... so even though you don't recognize it, please answer. I love you, and I really do believe all you've told me. Let me know you're safe. Bye."

Warnings and alarms rushed through Claire's mind as time stood still. Her body involuntarily sought to run -- the flight instinct. However, *that* monologue had been talked to death -- run where? She'd started a life. Therefore, flight wasn't an option. Therefore, biology told her to fight. Not physically, Claire *knew* that wasn't possible. This scenario was what she'd hoped to avoid. The text messages and voicemail confirmed her fear.

TRUTH

Naïvely she'd hoped -- no prayed -- since she hadn't heard anything for two weeks, maybe Tony would just let her go. It may've been fantasy, but the two week reprieve was heavenly.

Claire stood to go to her room. She would finish the article on her laptop, later.

Harry tried again, "Claire, please tell me what's happening."

"Nothing, I'm fine." She made to the hallway before Harry touched her shoulder.

The contact initiated an immediate flinch. Straightening her spine, she spun to face him. A look of terror and panic filled her beautiful eyes. The expression shocked him. Harry expected sad or maybe mad, but what he saw was unbridled fear. It took his breath away. While an investigator for the Bureau he'd seen that look. Without thinking, he asked, "What did he do to you?"

Her eyes muted, a haze covered the brief glimpse into her true feelings. Claire's countenance turned stoic. "Harry, I need to take a shower. Thank you for checking on me. I'm fine, and I know you need to get to SiJo." Mustering a forced grin she continued, "I hear your boss is getting upset about all your recent time off."

He wanted to question her. Inquisition procedures were his specialty. However, she wasn't a suspect. She was his sister's friend – no, his friend. During the past two weeks they'd spent countless hours working as a team to put pieces of her life back together. He knew about the box of memories Anthony Rawlings sent her. He knew she looked like a child at Christmas when she purchased a telephone. He knew she did *not* attempt to murder her ex-husband. Of course, that was just Claire's word, but Harry believed her.

He didn't know about her life with Mr. Rawlings. Somehow, whenever the subject came up, she eloquently changed it. Now the churning in his gut told him why. This petite, funny, friendly, pretty, delicate, kind woman in front of him was hurt. Maybe, just maybe, it was only a broken heart.

It has been said, people drawn to law enforcement have a sixth sense, an ability to see what others do not. He prayed he was wrong. His sixth sense said there was much more than a broken heart in Claire's past.

Harry pushed his questions away, "Your right, I do need to get into the office. Are you still going to Mr. Pulvara's?"

"Yes, my appointment is at eleven. I really need to get ready."

"I'm sorry if I overstepped some bounds. I won't push you; it's none of my business." The haze covering her eyes evaporated; the emerald green began to shine. Harry added, "If you need anything, you know my cell."

She smiled up at him and sighed, "Thanks, Harry, see you later." She turned toward the hall, speaking over her shoulder. "Please lock the door on your way out."

Claire closed the bedroom door with the weight of her shoulders. The glossy wood felt smooth behind her head. She strained to hear the sound of the front door close and lock. The still coolness of her room filled her lungs. After enough time passed, Claire allowed more warm tears to flow. Her trembling hand pushed the small button on her door knob. She produced a mental checklist: security guard, locked front door, and locked bedroom door – was it enough? Suddenly chilled, Claire wrapped her arms around her torso and felt the shuddering of her chest as sobs resonated uncontrollably. After a few minutes she blinked away the moisture, tried desperately to calm her unsteady hands, and sent Emily and Courtney a text: *GOT YOUR MESSAGE. THANKS. IM GOOD. CALL WHEN YOU CAN. I LOVE YOU TOO.*

Hot water pelted her upturned face as she stepped into the shower. The sensation of warmth flowed over her. Slowly, the heaviness washed away from her soul. By the time her feet hit the tile floor her thoughts centered on the future. The past was gone. She had survived. She wasn't the same woman Anthony Rawlings took three years ago.

As Claire exited the elevator with *her* telephones in tow she inhaled the unique scents of the parking garage. Easing herself into the leather driver's seat of *her* car, she relished her new found independence. Yes, life threw her some obstacles; she was stronger for them.

The GPS instructed her to turn right from the garage. The morning fog had begun to dissipate revealing patches of pale blue sky. She turned her Honda into traffic and thought about the jewelry inside her purse. Her lips turned upward as she pondered the value and remembered Anthony's perpetuity for appearance. This time, she hoped it would work in her favor.

Light thinks it travels faster than anything, but it is wrong.
No matter how fast light travels, it finds the darkness has always got
there first, and is waiting for it.
- Terry Pratchett.

Chapter 4

Sophia watched her husband pack his suitcase. "Derek, I just got back from Florence. Can't you stay home?"

"I told you, they want to meet me face-to-face."

Sophia sighed and smoothed the t-shirts he'd so precisely placed into the bag. It was so different from the way she packed. But then again, they were different. Some of their friends called them *Darma and Greg.* Looking at Derek's suits, pressed shirts, and cuff links, they definitely had different styles. However, those differences brought them together and kept them united.

Her bare feet allowed her head to fit perfectly under her husband's chin. Standing to wrap her arms around Derek's neck she smiled lovingly, "I know, just please hurry home."

His light brown eyes mellowed as he stared into her tender expression. "I'll come back as soon as the interview process is done."

"Tell me again, who are these people, and why do they want you?"

Derek tipped his head to Sophia's and grinned, "I've told you. You just don't listen."

Her hands wandered down the buttons of his white silk shirt. "Maybe it's because I get distracted. I keep thinking about wanting you for myself."

"I think you're trying to distract me so I'll miss my flight."

"Oh, well, so you leave tomorrow, instead of tonight." She nibbled his neck, "Would that be so bad?"

Punctuality was Derek's thing, not Sophia's. She was a free soul -- an artist. Perfect for her personality, she could work, sketching and painting, whenever the impulse hit. Sometimes that was three in the morning. Often Derek would wake to find her covered in chalk dust, still wearing the night gown she'd worn to bed.

40

Despite their differences, their love was intense, passionate, and real.

*****

Just south of thirty, Sophia had given up on happily-ever-after. She'd had her share of romances, but something always seemed to intervene. Most of the time, it was her art. There were few men willing to take a backseat to a sketch pad.

If she chose to reminisce, there was one man that met her requirements. He did a great job schmoozing with investors, but honestly preferred spending time alone with her. He understood her art and said everything right. However, as time passed, their goals grew incompatible. It was as if he could see her dream, but it didn't matter. He wanted things she didn't understand. One day he received an unbelievable job offer, requiring travel. They promised to stay in touch. The final act proved lonely.

Then unexpectedly in December of 2010, her life changed -- she met Derek at a mutual friend's Christmas party. It happened so fast. In January of 2011 they married-- a whirlwind elopement to Paris. Sophia shared her affection for Europe and memories of Paris while working on her Master's degree. Derek surprised her with a prearranged wedding. They exchanged vows in the park at the foot of the Eiffel Tower. Afterwards, they dined in a small French cafe with their witnesses. Derek secretly flew both of their sets of parents to Paris. It was the dream wedding she'd given up ever having.

Occasionally, her love of art and a desire for self-promotion required her to travel for art exhibitions. Personally, her art was gaining notoriety. Recently, she'd accepted an invitation to exhibit her work at the Florence Academy of Art during a three week exhibition. Although she didn't like leaving Derek, they both knew this was a remarkable offer.

And now that she was home again, in Provincetown, Massachusetts, it was Derek's turn to follow a remarkable offer. Shedis-tics, a software Fortune 500 company in Santa Clara, California, recently contacted him. The parent company, Rawlings Industries, wanted this branch of its empire to be again in the top 100. They believed Derek could help them achieve that goal.

It wasn't that he didn't already have a great job and career. He did, in Boston for a major electronics company. Everything was going so well. He was satisfied with his career, and Sophia was happy in the community she loved. That all changed when he received the phone call from a Shedis-tics' representative. The contact person told Derek he came *highly recommended*. Now -- he wanted more.

Truly, the offer seemed too good to be true. Unsolicited propositions rarely happen in today's economy. He was rightly cautious; however, after days of research Derek found everything with Shedis-tics legitimate. He also reasoned the new job would allow him the ability to greater support his wife's passions. Even with notoriety, art didn't pay well. Derek loved her passion and wanted to make her every dream come true.

*****

His warm breath bathed her cheeks, "You know, I don't like leaving." He kissed her nose, "I'm doing this for you, for us."

Sophia's gauze skirt brushed the tops of her bare feet as she purposely pressed her scooped necked t-shirt against his chest. "I love you for it. But I don't want you working yourself to death to support my art. I want it to support itself."

He encircled her trim waist. "It will, Baby. You're so talented, one day it will." His lips lingered on her pouting lips. "Someday you can support me. Let me do it now, and get you that bigger studio."

She exhaled, melting against his chest. "Please call me before you accept anything."

Derek nodded, as his lips found her slender neck, brushing her dark blond waves away, and sending chills down her extremities.

"You know I won't make a decision without talking it over. We're a team, Baby."

Sophia looked into his eyes, marveling at his long lashes. "I just wish our team could play on the same court more often."

Derek pulled away and glanced at his watch. "Are you driving me to the airport? Or do you want me to leave the car there?"

Sophia slipped her feet into her flat canvas shoes, "Oh, no, if you're leaving for an undetermined amount of time, you're not getting rid of me until the gate."

"Sorry, Sweetie. I've got a commuter from Provincetown to Boston, so no two hour drive in your future."

Sophia pouted again, "So, I have to give you up sooner rather than later. Well, you aren't parking there either. I'll see you all the way to the tarmac."

Provincetown had its distinct advantages: first and foremost -- its reputation in the world of art, also, its small population, close to 3,000 -- until tourist season. During prime summer months it's estimated there were as many as 60,000 people in their small town -- each one a potential art buyer. The free spirited world of the Cape fit Sophia perfectly.

The greatest disadvantage was its proximity to the rest of the world. Out on the tip of Massachusetts, transportation took time. Being late March, the cold wind and ocean spray off the Atlantic, could make Highway 6 potentially dangerous.

Derek flew the private commuters daily to his office in Boston. To him the thirty minute flight was as common as riding the T in Boston. He counted it a small price to be with Sophia in the community she loved.

Settling back into the living room of their cottage, Sophia debated a fire in their fireplace. Spring weather on the Cape changed without warning. Yesterday was in the sixties; today with overcast skies and strong ocean winds, it would be fortunate to reach fifty. Sophia settled onto the soft sofa, curled her long legs under her body, as her skirt swept the wood floor.

Sighing, she thought lovingly about their home, a quaint cottage built in 1870. Many amenities had been added since the original structure: a modern eat-in kitchen and two full baths. Sophia loved the clawed tub in the first floor bath. The wood floors, trim, and built-in bookshelves were original. The second floor held two bedrooms perfect for Derek's home office and Sophia's home art studio.

Sipping warm Jasmine tea, she contemplated Derek's job offer. *How often does a company like Shedis-tics seek out a potential employee?* It was truly a great opportunity, and he always supported her opportunities.

Along with notoriety, her art provided some financial profits. Occasionally pieces sold, and she enjoyed a cult following of buyers, people who required sporadic pacification with fancy dresses, champagne, and exhibits. She'd even been commissioned for a few specific pieces. A large portrait of a woman in her wedding gown had the greatest payoff. The anonymous buyer required her to sign a letter of confidentiality. She couldn't even sign the painting. Sophia recognized the woman from magazines -- the wife of a businessman.

Her work had become bolder since she'd married Derek. His love and support strengthened her to try what she'd previously felt too risky. That same love provided her with stability. Over the years, her parents worked desperately to help and support her. But, they were getting older, and she'd been a financial burden too long. Nonetheless, Sophia knew she wouldn't have her small studio on Commercial Street, if it weren't for them. She longed to prove she could make it on *her own* with her art, even if *on her own* meant *with* her husband.

Finishing her tea, Sophia reached a decision. If Derek needed to move to California, she'd move too. Their cottage and her studio would sell. Being together was more important than living her dream.

From her upstairs studio, Sophia looked south, out to the bay. The waves blended into the overcast sky. She pulled out her stool near her drawing table and found the note:

I love you, if you found this, you're doing what I love seeing you do... Create me something special, I miss you already and will be home soon!

Sophia smiled as the East coast chill evaporated, and she filled with the aura of warmth. Turning on her laptop Sophia reasoned she couldn't slip a note into his suitcase, but she could send a quick email. He would receive it on his phone when he landed.

As her fingers hit the last exclamation mark, she remembered the publicity photos of her Florence exhibition. Clicking through the different shots, she saw the pictures in their entirety. She didn't scan the crowds, didn't enlarge the masses. If she had, she would have notice a reoccurring face. In most shots only the gentleman's dark hair was visible. However, his dark eyes were visible in a few. A profiler might notice those black-eyes watched Sophia, not her art.

Securing her sketch paper to her table, Sophia closed her eyes and envisioned her subject. The charcoal darkened her fingertips as it brushed the surface of the thick cotton paper. In time the heel of her hand blackened, rubbing and shading the image. It wasn't a drawing for future exhibits. Never would it glean the walls of a studio. This self-portrait was meant for one man. The shades of charcoal gray transformed the blank page into a dreamlike scene creating Derek's *something special*.

The hair Sophia drew blew gently in the ocean breeze. Though the windows were shut, she felt the wind on her cheeks and smelled the salty air. The body she drew was presumably better than the one she concealed under her t-shirt and skirt, but not by much. She was slender, yet shapely. Her long legs often spent hours walking the beach or nature walks around Provincetown. Drawing her own breasts, Sophia's thoughts filled with her husband and her nipples rose under the cotton shirt. Smirking, she drew the same reaction. Sophia reasoned -- *if I were to walk naked on the beach, it would be cold.*

Dinner forgotten, the sound of her cellphone pulled her from her artistic trance. Beaming as her darkened hand reached for the small devise, she read Derek's number and name. "Hello, Honey."

"Hi, Baby, did I wake you?"

Sophia laughed, "What do you think? I'm working on your *something special.*"

Their call lasted only minutes. Shedis-tics had a car waiting to drive him to the hotel.

"They're pulling out all the stops. I really think they want you," Sophia said.

"We'll see what they say."

"Derek?"

"Yes?"

"I know we haven't talked about it. But, I know this may mean moving. I don't care, as long as I'm with you." Sophia heard her husband exhale.

"You don't know how much that means. I won't do anything without calling, I promise. I need to go. I love you, and I can't wait to see my *something special.*"

"I love you too." They hung-up.

Things do not change. We change.
- Henry David Thoreau

Chapter 5

Phillip Roach, Private Investigator, contemplated his information; by triangulating cellphone towers near a Palo Alto, California, street he narrowed the origination of calls from a disposable cellphone making multiple calls to Emily Vandersol, Claire Nichols' sister. The area contained restaurants, cafés, and residences; Phil didn't know for sure it was Claire Nichols or if she called from one of the businesses or a residence. Nonetheless, his intuition told him, he was close.

Phillip had useful associates possessing resources he didn't. Undoubtedly, he'd be asked to fulfill favors in the future -- *Quid pro quo.* It was the way of his profession. With a client like Anthony Rawlings, there was no deal Phil wasn't willing to make. Hell, he'd shake hands with the devil to continue this alliance.

Forwarding the telephone number of the track phone and narrowing Ms. Nichols location to Palo Alto would momentarily pacify Mr. Rawlings. Phil composed his findings into a text message and promised more information in the future. He hit *SEND.*

*****

Claire's GPS directed her to the heart of San Francisco's financial district. Although the tall buildings and steep streets created a maze, the computerized voice navigated her to the two hundred block of California Street. "You have reached your destination."

Goosebumps, incited by the late March wind, rubbed against her smooth silk blouse as Claire walked from the parking garage toward her goal. Just south of Chinatown, the streets bustled with patrons. Yet, it wasn't the people which momentarily held her attention but the picturesque scene. Down from the hills, a thick white blanket of fog covered the bay, penetrated only by the pillars of the Golden Gate Bridge.

Since her release from prison, every view, every scene held wonder and awe. Claire vowed never again to take freedom for granted.

Over the last two weeks she'd contemplated her presence. Although seemingly unimportant, one question she'd pondered was her clothing style. Her attire before her life with Tony --and during -- were worlds apart. Shopping for herself, her desires, wants, needs, and choices proved more difficult than she'd anticipated. Eventually, she concluded her taste fell somewhere in between. Shopping alone and with her money brought back the elation of finding great deals. Now, she enjoyed *Mrs. Rawlings* quality clothing at reasonable prices – she even perused sales racks. There was no question; intimate apparel was her favorite purchase. Claire now owned more pretty panty and bra combinations than one woman should have. She justified it as overdue, well-deserved, and three years' worth.

Today, personifying the professional, Claire donned wool slacks, a silk blouse, a complementary jacket, and heels (with white lace panties and bra no one would see – but made her happy).

Although, the suite number was the only outward sign, Mr. Pulvara's office was easy to find. Claire double checked Harry's note; *yes this was the right one*. Once inside, she entered a small waiting area with a receptionist behind a glassed partition. It reminded her of a doctor's office. She confidently approached the gray haired woman behind the window.

"Hello, my name is Claire Nichols. I have an eleven o'clock appointment with Mr. Pulvara."

"Yes, Ms. Nichols. May I see your identification?" Claire retrieved her new driver's license and handed it to the woman.

The receptionist took the small card, made a copy of both sides, and returned it to Claire. "Mr. Pulvara will be with you in just a moment. Please have a seat."

The soft leather chairs were neatly arranged in an L shape in the corner of the room. The incandescent lighting created a soft appearance. To pass the time, Claire removed her iPhone and pulled up the article from earlier that morning. She scanned the article:

...The pardon was legally granted on behalf of Ms. Nichols...Unable to overturn once accepted... Question remains; why was her name concealed by the governor? ... Governor Preston intends to avoid the perception of impropriety... cannot be overturned... complete history of arrest through incarceration expunged... could not reach Ms. Nichols for comment...

"Ms. Nichols," the voice returned Claire to the present. She hadn't considered the pardon being *overturned*. She sighed, relieved that wasn't a possibility. "Ms. Nichols?"

"Yes." Claire said, as she followed the woman through a solid door. Once behind the partition, she was amazed at the room before her. There were lights, magnifying glasses, scales, and other instruments designed to inspect small delicate items. A gentleman on the other side of the counter stood her height with skin the color of lightly creamed coffee. Special glasses with extended magnifiers hung from his neck. His voice contained a Middle Eastern accent and exemplified aptitude. His smile as he extended his hand in greeting, reassured her. Claire accepted his hand and introduced herself.

Mr. Pulvara wasn't one for small talk. Time was money and Claire currently had his time. She pulled a small blue velvet bag from her purse and removed the watch, diamond stud earrings, and journey necklace. Placing his glasses upon his nose, Mr. Pulvara remained expressionless as he inspected her jewelry. His skilled hands rolled each piece between his fingers as he studied the gems and gold. After a few minutes with each piece, he set it upon a black cloth.

"Ms. Nichols, these are fine pieces. Do you have anything else in that bag of yours?"

"I do." Claire emptied the bag into the palm of her hand. She extended her open hand with her engagement and wedding ring glistening under the lights.

He glanced from her palm to her eyes. First, he picked up the platinum wedding band embedded with diamonds. After a few minutes he set it down and took the platinum engagement ring. Without speaking he turned the diamond ring every which way. He then used a few gauges to measure the face of the gem. Finally, he broke the silence, "Ms. Nichols, do you know from what merchant these rings were purchased?"

"I was told Tiffany's in New York. I wasn't there. So, I'm not sure."

"I am assuming you have a receipt or insurance policy something indicating you are the owner of these pieces."

"I do not. They were gifts."

"Perhaps you could contact the giver of these gifts? You understand I must be sure these items truly belong to you."

"Mr. Pulvara, these items were given to me by my ex-husband. I have no plans to contact him. If you are not interested in purchasing them, I will gladly look elsewhere. Thank you for your time." Claire began to reach for her jewelry.

The broker gently touched the top of Claire's hand, stopping her movement. She looked up to his face. He said, "I am *very* interested. It is just -- I believe this wedding set is of the highest quality and quite valuable. The cut alone is extremely rare. I must be sure..."

She cut him off, "I have no proof of my ownership. I will take them ..."

"Ms. Nichols, may I ask Mr. Nichols's first name?"

Claire hesitated. "Mr. Pulvara, am I certain of your confidentiality?"

"Of course, I would not have the customers and reputation I currently enjoy without complete confidentiality."

"Forgive me, but I would like that in writing. I don't want to see on tomorrow's news that I sold my wedding rings." She recognized such information could make headlines.

"That can certainly be arranged. Now Mr. Nichols?"

"Nichols is my maiden name. My married name was Rawlings, as in Mrs. Anthony Rawlings."

The broker stood silently for a few seconds taking in her words and looking at her anew. Claire watched as the light of recognition filled his eyes. "Ms. Nichols, you've changed your hair since your wedding. I saw a picture today..."

"Yes, Mr. Pulvara, many things have changed since my wedding, including my desire to wear these rings. Are you interested in assessing their value and sharing that amount with me?"

"Please, Ms. Nichols, have a seat and allow me some time. May I remove the stones from the settings?"

"If I do not like your price, will you put them back?"

"Of course."

Claire saw chairs against the wall. She nodded to the broker, sat, and watched as he weighed, measured, and performed other tests. Then he consulted his computer and made notes. Claire remembered *Vanity Fair* estimated the value of her engagement ring around $400,000. She honestly had no idea if that was accurate or sensationalism. If it were accurate, it would make *one* bit of information in that article factual.

Almost forty minutes later, Mr. Pulvara finally spoke, "Ms. Nichols, if you would please join me, I'll explain my appraisal."

Claire stepped from the bank onto the sunshine warmed afternoon sidewalk. The multitude of people filled her with exhilaration. She'd just met with the bank's investment specialist and diversified her new found riches. Employment was still desired. However, the need was no longer dire. Tony's desire for quality and appearance now allowed Claire time. It was the time she would use to complete her research.

Before entering the parking garage Claire removed her iPhone, checked the time, 4:32 PM and typed a text: *IS ANYONE AVAILABLE TO CELEBRATE? DINNER IS ON ME!* She entered Amber and Harry as recipients and hit: *SEND*.

A few hours later the three sat chatting at an authentic Brazilian steakhouse in the heart of downtown Palo Alto. Neither Amber nor Harry argued with Claire's declaration to purchase dinner. They ordered wine, read the menu, and debated appetizers and entrees. Although they were surrounded by other patrons, the three talked and laughed about their day's activities. Their goblets touched in a toast to Claire's transaction.

Amber entertained them with multiple stories of SiJo focus groups. Apparently a recent group had extreme varied opinions on one of their newest games. It amused Claire how Amber could laugh about negative reviews and joke about comments. That wasn't to say the creators didn't consider the opinions of the focus groups. They did.

As their celebration concluded and Claire added cream to her coffee, her disposable cellphone buzzed. Pulling it from her purse, she apologized, "I'm so sorry, but this is probably Emily. She said she's getting a new phone. I need to answer it." Her chair scooted back as she hit the *CALL* button. She hadn't noticed the number on the screen as she said, "Hi."

Claire intended to move to a hall or outside to speak, but the voice in her ear caused her knees to buckle and her face to blanch. She recognized it immediately, "Good Evening, Claire."

She collapsed into her chair. Both Amber and Harry watched in horror. "Are you all right?" They asked in unison.

Claire managed to shake her head. *No*, she wasn't all right. She still hadn't spoken.

The husky, deep, baritone voice coming through the ear piece did. "Now Claire, we've been through this before. It is customary for one person to respond to the greeting of another. I said, *good evening*."

"Hello," she managed, finding her voice. It was difficult to allow her voice to exit while keeping her food down.

"Very good. I thought perhaps we would need to review common pleasantries." Tony's voice was smooth, strong, and domineering. She closed her eyes and saw him, looming near the fireplace in her suite. It wasn't the Tony Rawlings she married. Her vision was of Anthony Rawlings, her captor. The time and place continuum shattered. She was no longer with her friends in a bustling restaurant; she was three years in the past. Visions played like Tony's surveillance videos behind her closed lids as her body trembled.

Forcing her eyes to open, she searched for her friends. She fought to inhale as she sought desperately through a dense fog. Faceless people spoke. Their voices were a background din to the deep voice in her ear. Her head shook in response to her ex-husband's comment. The movement was so slight that without the movement of her hair, it would have been unperceivable. Conversely, inside she shook vehemently. *No, I can talk, review isn't necessary.*

Swallowing the overwhelming mixture of emotions and food fighting the natural peristalsis, she summoned a stronger voice. "Good bye, Tony."

"Claire, you should know, I learned of your release less than twenty-four hours ago. As you can hear, I already have your telephone number. How long do you think it will take for me to learn your location?"

Sitting straight and squaring her shoulders she found strength. It was a strength she'd always possessed, but in the past it was used to keep Tony pacified. Today she used it to declare her thoughts. With each word, her voice gained resilience. "It seems *you* have lost the ability to perceive meaning. *Good bye* means this conversation is over. For the record, that includes future conversations. I'm sure you remember, once a discussion is closed, reopening it is not an option."

The response came in the form of a laugh, a deep, resonating laugh, and then words. "I have always admired your strength. Such a brave speech from someone hiding across the country..." Claire didn't hear any more. She removed the phone from her ear and hit *END*. The fog of isolation lifted; she saw the saucer sized eyes of her concerned friends.

"If you'll excuse me, I'll be in the restroom." Claire stood, "If you see the waiter, I believe I'm ready to leave." She walked away from the table before her friends could voice questions. Halfway to the bathroom the trembling resumed and tears escaped her eyes. Nevertheless, not until she was inside the stall did she allow herself to take a ragged breath. Unintentionally, an audible sob seeped from her chest.

Again her purse vibrated. She needed to look; it could be Emily. The screen read *Blocked Call*. It stood to reason, if Emily were getting her own *disposable* phone, a blocked number wouldn't be necessary. Claire hit *ignore*. Thirty seconds later the symbol indicating a text message appeared. Hesitantly she opened it. *ONLY I CLOSE DISCUSSIONS. THIS ONE IS STILL OPEN. I LOOK FORWARD TO RESUMING IT IN PERSON...*

I guess we are who we are for a lot of reasons. And maybe we'll never know most of them. But even if we don't have the power to choose where we come from, we can still choose where we go from there.
— Stephen Chbosky, The Perks of Being a Wallflower

Chapter 6

-1980-

Anton made his way to the lower level of his family's estate. The scene he just witnessed between his grandfather and father ran in a continual loop through his mind. With each step toward the entertainment center of the mansion, he tried desperately to forget his family and think about life back at Blair Academy. More than anything he wanted to be back on the campus of his boarding school, away from the charade he called *family*.

It wasn't like he had many good friends at Blair. It would be easier if he were part of a group, if he participated in extracurricular activities. Heaven knows his stature benefitted him in the area of sports. He continued to grow taller and broader each year. Anton enjoyed intermural lacrosse and basketball. The coaches watched his obvious talent and asked him repeatedly to join one of the Blair teams. And, although his refusal met animosity from fellow students, little did they realize, it wasn't his choice. The other boys thought he was too *stuck-up* to participate. The truth was, grandfather forbid participation. Of course, Anton didn't admit that to anyone. If he did, it would show others he wasn't allowed to make his own decisions. That wasn't something Anton was willing to reveal. Go ahead -- think Anton Rawls was a jerk; he didn't care. He would make the only man whose opinion mattered proud. Besides, he would show those other boys one day.

Nathaniel never experienced the benefits of a private education. He wasn't able to offer that luxury to his own son. Now, he expected his only grandson to reap the benefits only money could buy. Nathaniel expected Anton to succeed. To Nathaniel, academics should be Anton's only focus. Therefore, it was.

Well, except for Anton's past-time of following his family's company. Anton may only be fifteen, but he could read financial reports, follow the NASDAQ and Dow Jones. He understood investments and could dissect quarterly reports. He never discussed this with anyone. His father treated him like a child and would never take Anton's thoughts seriously. His grandfather was too busy to discuss business with a fifteen year old. Anton yearned for the day when he was the one on the other side of the desk, discussing profits and losses with his grandfather. Someday, Anton knew -- Nathaniel would see him as his greatest asset.

Enduring his fellow students' snide comments was better than listening to his father and grandfather's argument. When Anton was Nathaniel's top advisor, he fantasized they wouldn't argue; they would work together, conspire and collaborate to make Rawls Corporation the greatest industry America ever saw. Exxon, General Motors, and Mobil wouldn't hold a candle to the possibilities of Rawls with Nathaniel and Anton at the helm.

Just before reaching the entertainment center of the house, Anton turned the corner to meet his grandmother. "Anton, where are you headed in such a hurry?"

"Grandmother, I didn't mean to be going so fast. I guess I'm just thinking about other things."

"Of course you are. You're a growing young man. You probably have a lot of things on your mind, perhaps a young woman?" Anton didn't reply. Sharron continued, "Are you planning on watching television downstairs?"

"Yes, it's the final season of *Hawaii Five-O*. I didn't want to miss the show."

"Oh, I've heard of that show. May I watch it with you?"

Anton feigned a smile, of course he wouldn't tell her *no*. Nevertheless, he didn't want her there. Not because he didn't love his grandmother, but because she'd talk throughout the entire program. He much preferred quiet. Nonetheless, he responded, "Sure, come on down."

Sharron followed her grandson toward the seldom used television room. Once they reached their destination, Anton turned on the large television, and Sharron settled onto the soft sofa. It was then she asked, "Nathaniel, what is it we're watching?"

Anton exhaled and turned to his grandmother, "We are watching *Hawaii Five O* and I'm Anton."

She smiled lovingly at her grandson, her expression a combination of love and confusion. Slowly the clouds passed from her gaze, and she stared directly at his deep brown eyes. "Yes, *Hawaii Five O* and of course Anton, why would you tell me your name? You are the light of our lives."

He smiled. It wasn't a smile of happiness, more a pacifying act to quiet her reasoning. He'd heard it before. She could talk her way out of any misstep. Actually, as long as he could remember she'd been doing that: saying something totally off base, or doing something weird, and justifying it, like it was the most natural thing in the world.

Half way through the episode, Anton gave up on hearing the actors speak. "Grandmother, I just remembered my mother wants me upstairs. I think I should go up there."

She smiled, "Yes, of course. Please give Margarete my love."

He walked to the television and turned off the set. It wasn't worth the correction or explanation. Margarete was his great-grandmother, Nathaniel's mother. Dying before Anton's birth, she was someone he'd never met. "I will Grandmother. I'm sure she feels the same."

His grandmother snickered, "We both know that isn't true. But, please tell her anyway."

"I will."

Anton wondered if his grandmother was talking about her relationship with her mother-in-law or her daughter-in-law. He didn't wonder enough to question. The answer would take longer than he was willing to commit. Besides, Anton knew from experience, at the end of the conversation, his question could easily remain unanswered.

You gain strength, courage and confidence
by every experience in which you really stop to look fear in the face.
You must do the thing you think you cannot do.
– Eleanor Roosevelt

Chapter 7

"I don't think it's a good idea." Courtney's apprehension came through Claire's newest disposable cellphone. It was her second *pay as you go* phone. Only Emily and Courtney had this number, and Emily had a new similar phone she used to communicate. Of course, Courtney would also only call with a *pay as you go* phone, and yes, she had a new one. None of these numbers could be traced back to the number Tony knew.

"If you won't give it to me, I'll get it some other way." Claire's voice rang strong and resolute.

After Claire collected herself from her meltdown in the bathroom stall the night before, she decided to meet her problem head on. Her problem: her ex-husband Anthony Rawlings.

"Seriously Courtney, don't you understand? I'm not going to live my life running. I won't let *him* have that control. If I flee every time he's near, he wins. I'm making a life out here. I want to live it."

Courtney sat in her kitchen and stared into her backyard. The Iowa spring was struggling to break through the gray veil of winter. Patches of ice and snow speckled the pale remnants of lawn. In another month the grass would begin to green and life would renew. Courtney contemplated her friend; she deserved renewal too. "Claire, how will having his private number help that?"

"Because he thinks he can call and disrupt my life. The only way to stop him is to turn the tables. I need to have equal opportunity to initiate contact."

"I guess I understand. But, don't you think he'll wonder how you got it? I mean – it's blocked. I know you know that."

"I do. I've seen his contact list, it has lots of people. He isn't as isolated as he thinks. It just takes one of those many people."

Courtney continued to watch the scene outside of her window. Near her elbows on her table sat a list of Saturday afternoon activities. Julia, her future daughter-in-law, would be over soon they had many things to accomplish before the quickly approaching wedding. Next to her half full mug of coffee was her list of proposed guests. She glanced at the list of rehearsal dinner locations and caterers. They had appointments with three of them this afternoon.

Their son, Caleb, recently started his own investment company in a Chicago suburb. It was the only plausible reason he would leave Tony's employment. Luckily, Caleb was convincing when explaining to Tony his desire to - *make it on his own*. Being an entrepreneur himself, Tony actually encouraged Caleb's independent spirit. This scenario also gave credence to the removal of some of Brent and Courtney's Rawlings stock options. They wanted their capital to help finance their son's endeavors. Courtney's thoughts kept her from responding.

Claire misinterpreted the silence, "I understand. I really do. If you can't help me, I'll find someone else..." her disappointment audible.

"No, I will. Let me get my other phone, it's programed in there."

Claire quickly replied, "Thank you. I really appreciate it."

Before Courtney could respond to Claire's gratitude, the sound of multiple voices came through Claire's receiver. She sat cross legged on her bed fifteen hundred miles away listening to the conversation.

Courtney was so caught up in her conversation and thoughts she didn't hear the doorbell or her husband's voice, until he and Tony reached the kitchen.

Brent spoke first, "Look who stopped by."

"Hello Courtney, I'm sorry for the intrusion. I was on my way home and wanted to talk to your husband for a few minutes." His deep voice contained its usual friendly tone he used with Courtney.

She covered the phone with her hand and smiled her brightest smile, "Oh Tony, so nice to see you." Courtney stood to give him a customary *hello* hug and hoped he wouldn't notice her accelerated heart rate. "I'm just trying to finalize some wedding plans, if you two will excuse me. It'll just take another minute." The two men nodded and looked at the papers on the table. Brent opened the refrigerator, handed Tony a bottle of water, and noticed Courtney's small black phone, not her usual Blackberry.

"Come on Tony, let's go to my office. Believe me; you don't want to be in her way when there're wedding plans to finalize."

Tony laughed. "That's fine. This will only take a few minutes." Turning back to Courtney, "It's nice to see you."

She nodded toward the men as they left the kitchen. Courtney grabbed her Blackberry and stepped through an archway to the sunporch, increasing the distance from her husband's office. "Shit." She whispered into the small telephone.

"Oh god, Courtney, I'm sorry."

"No, don't be sorry. Let me get you the number. Just please wait until he leaves before you call."

"I will. Honestly, I'm not sure when I'll call. I just want to know I can."

Momentarily, Courtney smiled as she scrolled her contacts. Looking toward the archway and back toward the kitchen, she quietly gave Claire the ten requested digits. Then she added, "I hope you know -- I truly hate him for what he did to you."

Claire nodded. "Thank you, but you've been his friend for a long time. I appreciate your help, but I understand..."

"No, you don't."

Courtney's tone surprised Claire. Anger -- fervor, she wasn't sure she'd heard such vehemence in Courtney's voice ever before. "Perhaps I don't." Maybe she'd pushed Courtney's allegiance too far by requesting Tony's number. "I'd better go. Thank you again."

"Claire," Courtney's voice was more of a whisper, "I'd like to see you. I need to be honest with you about what I know and how I feel. It'd be better in person."

Emotions swirled. Claire wanted to see her friend, yet part of her wondered, *is she truly my friend*? Hearing Tony's voice, so casual in her kitchen, could this request be a trap? And *know* -- what could Courtney possibly *know*? Claire lied to her, just like she'd lied to everyone else. Was the tone Claire heard directed at her or about Tony?

Claire reminded herself Courtney was the only person to go out of her way to communicate with Claire in prison. She was one of the few people to offer support. Claire replied, "I'd like that too. First, why don't you concentrate on your company? We'll work out details later."

Courtney nodded. "You're right about time. We've known him a long time. However, sometimes you know someone and still don't *truly* know them. Other times you learn the truth right away." She paused, but Claire didn't respond, so Courtney continued, "I hope we can work it out -- to get-together. We'll talk later."

Claire replied, and the line went dead. Courtney placed the small black slender phone in the pocket of her jeans and took the Blackberry back to the kitchen. Julia would be over soon; they had a busy afternoon ahead.

Claire stared at the number on the note pad. There it was. Now, he wouldn't be the only one able to initiate contact. She added the number to the telephone Tony called the night before. Claire shook her head. There were three telephones before her. All she wanted was *one*; now she had three!

Courtney wasn't the only person opposed to the idea of Claire calling Tony. Harry also thought it was a bad idea. Surprisingly, Amber understood Claire's reasoning. Harry replied with the analogy of poking a bee hive with a stick.

Claire finally smiled and explained, "My dad had a friend who raised bees. We used to go and help him extract honey -- fun but scary. The bees would buzz all around his garage as we worked inside getting the honey out of the combs."

Harry and Amber listened, probably thinking the bee analogy was meant metaphorically. Claire continued, "When I was little, I was afraid to help. After all, the bees were really mad. You can't blame them. We're taking their honey. I remember asking dad's friend how he got the combs out of the bee hives without getting stung. He showed me this funky hat with netting and a thick material suit and gloves, boots – you know the whole bee garb?" The other two nodded. "So don't you get it?"

Claire watched waiting to see some realization in her friends' eyes. When she didn't see it, she answered her own question. "I promise not to poke the stick in the hive until I'm sure my outfit is fool proof. I don't intend to be stung ...again." Claire was sure she saw sparks of admiration in her friends' eyes.

Now that she had his number, Claire needed to work on her beekeeper's outfit. Until last night, she wasn't sure what she'd do. California was turning out better than she ever imagined. Honestly, she'd hoped maybe she could start a new life and forget the last three years. Then the whole paradigm changed; Tony called.

Claire knew in the pit of her stomach – depths of her soul -- it would never be over. He shared in his *box* that he'd been watching her since at least the time of her parent's death. No, actually – if, and she still isn't sure of this -- if he purposely lured Simon away with the job offer – he'd been watching since her freshman year of college.

Yes, Anthony Rawlings was the one who callously threw her away – left her to be incarcerated for a crime she never committed. However, multiple times she thought about his offer. Before she pleaded *no contest* to the charges, he offered her another *out*. He offered her the option to plead *insanity*. He even had an institution ready to take her as a patient. *If* she'd accepted his offer he would still to this day, possibly forever, be in control. Somehow Claire believed Tony expected her to take his option.

She grinned, realizing that without trying, she'd defied his plans. Feeling a small amount of pride, Claire grasped the unusual feeling. If she could defy Anthony Rawlings out of instinct, instead of intention and survive, it seemed the possibilities were limitless, if she put her mind to it.

Tony would never allow her to exist away from him. Somehow she needed to remove his power. Claire realized hiding from the sound of his voice, strengthened it. Conversely, the opposite would weaken it.

Last night, after returning to the table at the restaurant, Claire announced to her friends she was ready to continue the work on their quest. She currently had the time and thanks to Tony, the money. She would accept help, but without a doubt, Tony's phone call cemented her resolve – Mr. Anthony Rawlings had a lesson to learn and Claire claimed the role as teacher.

Amber and Harry saw her red blotched face. Yet, instead of pity or even acknowledgement of her current condition, both friends smiled.

Amber got up and hugged Claire, "I hope you know you have my full support and any help I can provide."

"If you two scorned ladies will allow, I would like to be involved in this quest." With that, Harry encircled both women in his arms. Their group hug lasted only seconds, but the common goal and support energized Claire beyond any depletion from the phone call.

This morning she woke with new purpose. Her phone call with Courtney didn't diminish that purpose, it increased it.

As she dressed for her day, Claire marveled at again hearing her ex-husband's voice. Twice in two days! Hearing him speak to Courtney, sounding casual and friendly, there was a time she worked diligently to keep that tone in his voice. It was refreshing to not concentrate on *his* feelings, but on her own.

Claire smiled at herself in the mirror. She liked her chestnut brown hair, jeans, and tennis shoes. She liked wearing very little make-up. From now on *her* concerns were going to be *her* focus!

She'd spent the last fourteen months grasping at straws of self-worth. It was a difficult process especially while in a federal penitentiary. At one time she wondered if living was worth the trouble. Today, she knew it was.

His voice, through her phone, divulged more to her than merely words. Tony had once said she knew him better than anyone. In the pit of her stomach she knew he would seek to find her. And beyond a shadow of a doubt, he'd succeed. Anthony Rawlings rarely, if ever, failed.

This reality fueled her need to suddenly become visible. Her original plan of anonymity was to avoid him. She failed. Being invisible would make her an easy target, no matter his intention. The more visible Claire Nichols was to the world, the harder it'd be to remove her. This, hopefully not too late realization, made her cheeks rise and a smile radiate beyond her lips to her green eyes.

Honestly, the prospect of seeing him, talking to him, being near him frightened her. The fear didn't just stem from *his* possible actions – but, hers. Claire knew, she couldn't predict her own actions, emotions, or responses when the time came to meet him face-to-face. Despite their history, Tony had the ability to manipulate her thoughts and beliefs. Her personal pep talks were all well and good while he remained at large. Nevertheless, Claire could not honestly predict how *she* would respond, when push came to shove.

She reminded herself, unlike three years ago, she now knew the rules and boundaries to *his* game. Rule number one, there were no boundaries. Anthony Rawlings was capable of anything and would stop at nothing to get what he wanted. Yet, even Superman couldn't overcome kryptonite. Catherine once told Claire, she had the *rare opportunity* to know Anthony Rawlings as few do. Claire knew his intimate beliefs. She knew his kryptonite – appearances!

58

She also knew without a doubt, he'd be in California. It may be days, weeks, or hell, only hours, but he would step foot on the west coast. It would happen. Claire needed to be ready, her beekeeper suit intact.

She sat on the tall stool in the kitchen, her laptop open and began to *ego surf*. Before she could change the perception the world possessed of her, she needed to know what that perception held. The results were nauseating.

Entering CLAIRE NICHOLS RAWLINGS into the Google search engine landed her over fifty thousand hits! She began to click and read. Yes, there was factual information: born October 17, 1985, to Jordon and Shirley Nichols. One sister, Emily Nichols Vandersol, married to John Vandersol. Claire graduated from Hamilton Heights High School in Fishers, Indiana, and obtained a Bachelor's Degree in meteorology from Valparaiso University. She completed a one year internship in Albany, New York, and then worked for WKPZ as a meteorologist assistant in Atlanta, Georgia. After WKPZ was bought, she worked at the Red Wing, a restaurant in Atlanta, until 2010. It's at that point the history of her life becomes mostly conjecture.

One of the few facts: on December 18, 2011, she married Anthony Rawlings. Claire had read the information before about her being a *gold-digger*. However, the ferocity of the newly found articles surprised her. It was as if some of these reporters were truly hell-bent on righting the wrongs done to *Anthony Rawlings*.

Claire scrolled numerous articles which made her every sin public knowledge. She read about her changing hair color and shopping habits. There were accurate and inaccurate reports of travels. Thinking that perhaps this was a journey she shouldn't have taken, she clicked and discovered an unlikely ally – a redeemer of her reputation. The article appeared in *Rolling Stone*, February 2012, following her arrest – prior to her plea. It was entitled, Mrs. Rawlings, No longer a Mystery - But Seriously a Killer? by Meredith Banks. The article discussed Claire Nichols, the real person, student, sorority sister, daughter – grieving the loss of her parents following their tragic deaths, intern, meteorologist assistant in Atlanta, bartender . It went on to discuss the impromptu meeting in Chicago and the unlikelihood of Claire Nichols attempting to murder her husband. Meredith mentioned Claire's hesitation to discuss her future husband. *Hesitation, I didn't discuss him!* Meredith also discussed the obvious -- with as much money as Anthony Rawlings possessed, why would Claire want to kill him? She used the travel, shopping, and pampering spas as evidence. Why would Claire want to kill the handsome generous husband who showered her with luxuries? She had access to all the money she wanted and Anthony was making more. Meredith concluded killing him made no sense.

Claire couldn't help but see the irony – the first, perhaps only, positive and accurate article was written by the same woman who wrote the article eighteen months earlier which almost cost her, her life!

Claire opened another page on her laptop and Googled *Meredith Banks*, independent correspondent based out of Long Beach, California. The website contained her email and phone number. After a quick check of Google Maps, Claire learned Long Beach was a six and a half hour drive from her current location. She pondered that information. With Tony's current state of mind, perhaps a 400 mile drive wasn't a bad plan.

Claire considered her new option. She could contact Meredith. She could promise an exclusive interview. But, what was she willing to reveal? If she couldn't look Amber and Harry in the eye and talk about her life as Mrs. Rawlings, was she ready to do it with Meredith?

Off the dining room were two sets of sliding glass doors leading to a courtyard with a small outdoor sitting area and hot tub. Claire eased her way out into the *yard* and into a chair. Holding her mug of warm French Vanilla latte, she looked up toward the sky. The clouds had parted revealing patches of blue. She knew the entire disclosure process needed to be well thought-out. Claire reminded herself not to act impulsively or without forethought. Perhaps, as stunning as it seemed, Meredith may be the answer she'd been seeking. Yet, before she attempted to make contact, Claire needed to be sure of what she intended to share. Her article years ago with *Vanity Fair* taught her that every question must be thoroughly reviewed and dissected. Each impromptu answer must go through the same scrutiny.

If she planned on informing the world the *truth*, she needed to be sure it came across the way she intended. The question looming in Claire's mind -- could she trust Meredith Banks to write that article? Claire truly didn't know the answer.

White filmy wisps of condensation moved ever so gently across the sky as beams of sunshine continued to win their battle. Tilting her face toward the sun, Claire closed her eyes and inhaled the fresh spring air. The warm rays and warm coffee reminded Claire that no matter her decision, the reality remained, it was *her* decision.

Suddenly an old question resurfaced, *how did he do it?* How did he make her disappear, without anyone questioning her sudden departure? This information seemed incredibly important. She needed to be sure, history would not repeat itself.

Every journey into the past is complicated by delusions,
false memories, false naming of real events.
-Adrienne Rich

Chapter 8

Claire gripped the phone tighter, "What texts and emails are you talking about?"

"It must've been in March, if I remember right. March of the year you left Atlanta."

"That is what I've been saying, Emily. Tony *took me* away in March, March 17, 2010, and I was at his house on the 20th. I never sent emails or texts."

"Yes, you did. You sent out emails telling about a new job possibility. They said how excited you were about it." Although Emily couldn't see, Claire shook her head. "Actually you also sent out emails via Facebook. I remember thinking, you must really be excited."

"I never sent those. Did you respond?"

"I did and you replied. Then about a week later you sent a text saying you'd be getting a new phone number and would call. As you know, you didn't call for months, and your old number no longer worked."

Claire pondered this new information, "I wonder if messages went out to other people?"

"I know John received the same emails and texts – you know, like you did a mass send? And when we didn't hear from you again for a while, I called your apartment complex. They said you'd moved out and paid to break the lease. They also said something about a new job opportunity but couldn't remember any details."

"Why didn't you ever mention this?"

At first Emily remained silent. When she spoke it was with a recent reoccurring sharpness to her tone, "And when do you suppose I should've done that? Maybe while your every word was scrutinized or perhaps while my every word was overheard?" Those details, about their conversations during Claire's marriage, were just recently revealed by Claire. Obviously Emily still found them upsetting.

"No, Emily. I'm sorry. I know you couldn't have said anything then, but now?"

"Well, perhaps I've been busy trying to get to know my sister again and oh yeah – my husband. Details of your disappearance three years ago, when I thought you just didn't want me in your life, well, they haven't been high on my priority list."

Claire inhaled deeply and exhaled. Emily's anger was justified. "I want you to know I did not, and would not, just email or text you or John out of my life. If it happens again, please know it isn't me."

Emily's end of the line went silent. She finally responded, with distress not resentment, "Why? Are you seriously afraid it could happen again?"

Claire didn't hesitate. She no longer wanted to delude her sister. "Yes."

"I promise, if I can't get ahold of you, or I get those kinds of messages – I'll have the police break down Anthony Rawlings' door."

Claire smiled. "Thanks, Sis. Hopefully, that'll never be necessary. Right now I'm learning what I can about how he did it last time."

The two spoke for a while longer. During her time in Iowa, her calls were not only monitored but time restricted. The two sisters relished their new lengthy soul revealing conversations. Emily informed Claire she'd be going to New York the first week of April to bring John home. With his sentence complete, the condition of his probation required regular interaction with a probationary officer. As long as he did that, he could travel, or live, anywhere within the continental United States.

Due to the charges of fraudulent billing, The New York State Bar Association suspended John's admission to the bar, disabling him from practicing law. For any chance at redemption, an appeal must be made to the governing body's disciplinary committee. Emily wasn't sure what he'd do. She was just happy they'd be together.

Claire wanted to ask to join Emily in New York. However, instinctively she believed her presence was currently unwelcome. She hoped it was only momentary, besides Emily and John needed private time.

Amber arrived home to find her dining room table covered in piles of disheveled papers. It was the information Claire saved from Tony's box, along with new information Amber and Harry helped accumulate. Harry's connection to the Bureau of Investigation and Intelligence was definitely advantageous.

From the *box*, Claire saved pictures. Looking through the stack, she placed them in chronological order. The first series was from her parent's funeral. If she hadn't stared at them for hours, in her cell in Iowa, the subject would be upsetting. Instead, the circumstance of their existence dominated her thoughts. The photo in her hand was of the grave site. She saw the vibrant autumn trees surrounding the double plot and a seemingly appropriate gray sky. The faraway shot showed Emily with

John on one side and Claire on the other. There were many people behind them. The next one caused Claire's stomach to churn. It showed a close-up of her, alone -- her name handwritten on the back. She recognized the distinguishable writing. She'd seen that same script on many notes throughout her two years with Tony.

She didn't meet Anthony Rawlings until almost five years *after* these pictures were taken. Yet, the looming question remained; did he personally shoot these photos? It added to the mystery. She wished for pictures of the crowd, some way she could scan for his familiar face. Thinking back, Claire remembered news coverage -- her father was a policeman, and even though his death wasn't in the line of duty, it was considered newsworthy. Suddenly, she wondered if the footage still existed. Working at a television news station, she knew many videos were disposed of after a certain length of time. Nonetheless, if she could watch, even a few seconds of the crowd, Claire would find Tony -- tall, dark and handsome -- if he were present.

The next stack of photos revealed images from Emily and John's wedding, with the same alarming close-ups of Claire with her name written on the back in Tony's handwriting. The sea foam green dress made Claire smile.

She realized if she took these pictures to the police, they didn't prove Tony's presence. Of course, he could pay someone to take the pictures. Yet, Claire was certain a handwriting specialist could verify his handwriting.

The other bit of information, Claire retained, from Tony's box of confessions, was the *Top Secret report*. Over the past four months she'd wondered how he obtained the document. It looked official, containing the Top Secret watermark. Originally, she placed it in the box of information to burn. However, just before leaving her cell, Claire decided to remove it. Looking back, she chastised herself for taking the box to the incinerator at all.

She couldn't really justify her actions, only that at the time she wanted freedom and separation. Watching the contents burn proved temporarily therapeutic. As the flames enveloped the box and its contents, she felt her life with Tony shrivel into parallel nothingness. At the time, it was cathartic.

In the days and weeks that followed, she realized the error of her ways. With time to meditate, muse, and contemplate her life's milestones, it seemed that at many junctures she'd acted impulsively. Whether it was refusing to leave Atlanta after the loss of her job, signing a seemingly benign napkin, getting into a car and fleeing Anthony's estate, or burning a box of confessions, the choices and their consequences continued to return and rear their ugly heads.

The *Top Secret* report told the true identities of two important players in the downfall of Nathaniel Rawls; securities officer, Jonathon Burke and FBI agent, Sherman Nichols. It was the glue that held Claire to Tony's well played plan of revenge.

After contacting Amber, they worked together to regenerate the information Claire could recall. If only she hadn't burnt it. Regrets were useless. Their progress thus far was all that mattered.

Claire was lost in her thoughts of the photos when Amber entered the condominium. Claire looked up at her roommate and said, "Hi, I didn't expect you this early."

"The day is too nice to spend cooped up in my office. What're you doing in here?"

Claire explained her less than conventional pile system. First, she had the stack of Rawls information. She was surprised how easy it was to obtain supporting documentation that Nathanial Rawls not only existed, but was married to a woman named Sharron, had one son named Samuel. Samuel married a woman named Amanda and they had one son, Anton. The information was all available through public records from New Jersey. She'd even been able to access the appropriate websites online while in prison. The birth records confirmed Anton Rawls was born February 12, 1965, not surprisingly, the same day as Anthony Rawlings. His change of name didn't include a change of birthdate. Claire wondered why he didn't change that too. It seemed like a serious piece of evidence to overlook. He must not have deemed it necessary. Claire doubted he ever considered his identity would be discovered. Truthfully, without his box of secrets, it would have remained hidden.

As Claire and Amber discussed some of the information, Claire picked up a police report from Santa Monica Police Department. Claire asked, "How did Harry get these reports about Samuel and Amanda's deaths?"

"Since it occurred in California, I think he called in a few favors from some investigators he used to work with."

Claire scanned the report, "I haven't seen this before. It tells all about the scene and even has statements from neighbors and..." flipping another page, "oh my, here's the statement from their son." Claire pulled out a chair and sat. She imagined a young Tony finding his parents dead in their Santa Monica bungalow. Being only twenty-four, she shuttered at his endured horror. Imagining wasn't difficult; the report gave a very detailed description of the crime scene. Thankfully there weren't pictures.

Claire's parents' death at only twenty-one was tragic, but she wasn't the one to find them. Suddenly thoughts triggered. Could *Tony* be responsible for the death of her parents? Could *he* be responsible for the death of his own parents?

In the information she read about Nathanial Rawls' trial there were actually *three* people responsible for Nathanial's conviction. Besides the security officer and FBI agent, there was Samuel Rawls, Tony's father. He testified for the state. The articles said his testimony played a significant role in the conviction. After all, being the son of the defendant and present during most of the business dealings, he knew details. Samuel testified he was against the avenues his father pursued to increase their income. And although he voiced his objections, his father was very strong willed. Claire recognized that familiar trait.

As she learned more and more about Nathaniel Rawls, Claire felt as though she knew him. She knew someone who took after him in more ways than just dark eyes.

Claire checked the dates... Samuel and Amanda were found by their son in September of 1989. Nathanial died while incarcerated May of 1989. She continued to read the police report:

Anton Rawls recalled entering the home, via an unlocked door at approximately 8:30 PM. He stated the television was on, and he called for his parents. When they didn't answer he walked in and found his mother on the floor of the kitchen. He ran to her. She was unresponsive. He noticed blood and yelled for his father. He found his father lying on the bed in the master bedroom. The suspected weapon, a Weston revolver, was found beside Mr. Rawls' body. After discovering his father, Anton left the house and used the neighbor's phone to call the police.

Patrick Chester, neighbor, stated he heard loud voices at the Rawls' home earlier in the day in question. Mr. Chester saw a small blue Honda but not the license plate. He believed the car belonged to Samuel's sister whom he'd seen once before. He recalled Mrs. Rawls saying the woman was Samuel's sister. He didn't know her name.

Claire quit reading and went back to her computer. The website she accessed months before was entered into the search engine. She used the web address from the bottom of the printed pages holding the information regarding Nathanial and Sharron's records. While she waited for the site to load she went back to the police report.

Mr. Chester stated the sister left during the afternoon. He remembered, because he was outside working in his yard and saw her leave. He heard voices from within the Rawls' bungalow after she left. He was unable to confirm if the voices were of the Rawls or the television. He didn't see Anton Rawls until he knocked on his door to call the police.

While scanning the computer screen, Claire called to Amber, "Did you read this police report?"

Amber came through the archway from the kitchen. "I did. It didn't mean a lot to me. Why? Do you see something interesting?"

"I didn't remember Nathanial having two children. Yet, there's a statement about Samuel's *sister*." Claire typed the necessary information into the New Jersey public record's website. "I'm trying to see if I can find any record of her under Nathanial's information."

Amber stood behind Claire as she typed. The information popped up: *Children: 01. Samuel Rawls*. Claire tried another avenue; she typed in Sharron Rawls and waited. The screen read: *Children: 01. Samuel Rawls*. She looked up at Amber and shook her head.

Amber exhaled, "Is there a name listed?"

"No, not on this report." She scanned the pages. "I wonder if they pursued this angle. The article I read before, said the crime scene *looked* like murder – suicide. Why would they decide that, if someone else was there?" She hoped Tony wasn't truly responsible for his parents' death. Maybe he included the article because he felt their deaths were *a product of* the work of the securities officer and FBI agent who testified at Nathanial's trial.

"I don't know. Maybe they decided that person wasn't connected." Amber offered.

Claire shrugged and went back to the report. It contained the dialogue of the 911 call. She read, thinking of Tony calling about his own parents. No doubt, this kind of trauma would have long lasting effects. His grandfather died and then only months later his parents. She knew she shouldn't, but Claire's heart ached for the young dark-eyed man. No wonder he had issues with relationships and control.

Amber went back to the kitchen as Claire settled into the high backed dining room chair. The dialogue on the printed page incited goose bumps on her arms. She read:

21:02:36: Caller: I'm at 7208 Mongolia Drive. Please send the police. I just found my parents and I think they're dead.

21:02:39: Operator: I will send the authorities immediately. Please tell me your name.

21:03:02: Caller: My name -- my name is Anton Rawls.

21:03:09: Operator: Anton, are you in the house?

21:03:47: Caller: No. I'm next door.

21:04:07: Operator: Good. Don't reenter the residence until the police arrive. Did you see anyone else?

21:05:02: Caller: No. Send someone fast.

21:05:27: Operator: The Santa Monica Police are on their way. They'll be there in three minutes. Please stay on the line with me. (silence) Anton? Are you there?

21:06:18: Caller: Yes -- I'm—I'm -- here.

21:06:49: Operator: Good. Did you see a weapon?

21:07:13: Caller: I don't remember.

21:07:42: Operator: Are you sure they're dead?

21:08:29: Caller: My mother is. I checked her when I found her on the floor. (Gasp)Oh! There's blood on my hands, I didn't even realize...

21:09:42: Operator: Did you say there's blood? (Voices in background) Anton? – Anton?

21:10:52: Caller: This is Patrick Chester. Anton is sitting down. The cord doesn't reach that far. Are the police on their way?

21:11:03: Operator: Yes, Patrick. Who are you?

21:11:28: Caller: I'm the neighbor of the Rawls. Anton called from my phone. Oh, I hear the sirens. Can I hang up now?

21:12:01: Operator: Just another minute. Let me please speak to one of the officers when they arrive.

21:13:12: Caller: All right, let me go answer the door. (Silence – voices) This is Officer Griffiths – ten four. (Line disconnected: 21:14:03).

Claire stared at the report and felt moisture coat her cheeks. Yes, she hated her ex-husband for the things he'd done to her, but no one should have to experience what she just read. She placed the pages on the shiny polished table and pushed back the tall upholstered chair with her feet. Dabbing her eyes, she tried to focus on the melting stacks of pages before her. It was too much. They were acquiring evidence to prove Tony's guilt, but at this moment Claire didn't feel vengeance. She felt pity for the man she'd loved.

Unconsciously, she used her sleeve to wipe her eyes and massaged her throbbing temples. She couldn't stop the awful images of Tony's parents that floated through her mind. Trying desperately to think of something else, she remembered Amber saying it was a nice day. She'd spent most of it inside. Claire needed a break from all this information.

As she put the report on a stack of pages, another title caught her attention: *Santa Monica Coroner's Report.* Her stomach lurched. Claire didn't want to read more; she was on overload. Closing her eyes she contemplated the unread information. Would it tell the estimated time of death? If it did, would it condemn her ex-husband, or absolve him? Did she want to know the evidence? Or could ignorance allow her peace?

Opening her eyes she looked at the clutter. The pounding in her head and twisting of her stomach told her to walk away. She placed the coroner's reports in a manila folder, closed the folder, and allowed her hand to linger on the smooth cardstock. The information wouldn't go away. She could read it another time. In more of a dream state, she continued to fight the visualization of Amanda Rawls lying on her kitchen floor, a dark red puddle of thick liquid surrounding her form.

By the time she and Emily were asked to identify the bodies of her parents, they were cleaned, laid on cold silver tables, and covered with clean white sheets. The coroner reported they both died instantly; their deaths were quick and painless.

Claire often hung to that information. Losing people you love is difficult. It wasn't a conscious thought process, but those who remain often contemplate the final moments of their loved ones lives. Claire imagined her parents driving down the dark country road, talking jovially, laughing about some story her mother was undoubtedly telling about one of her students. Her mother often dominated the conversations. Claire's father didn't mind, actually he seemed to enjoy the sound of his wife's voice. The endless chatting created a melody which sang continually throughout Claire's childhood.

The wet roads combined with wet leaves made the road slippery. As physics would prove, their tires lost their grip. The moisture and wet leaves widened the separation. Within an instant, the car slid and the automobile connected a royal hundred year old oak. Due to force and speed, her parents didn't have time to regret their drive or worry about their children. They just transcended from a loving, happy discussion, directly to a heavenly sleep. Many times in the months and years that followed, this story, this fantasy, gave Claire peace. She never shared this account with anyone, even Emily. Truthfully, she'd compartmentalized the entire momentous event away. Nonetheless, it occasionally decompartmentalized.

Groggily, she got up and walked into the warm kitchen. Amber stood near the counter cutting vegetables. When she looked up from the bright red, yellow, and green peppers, she saw Claire's tears. "What's the matter?"

"I just read the 911 call from Samuel and Amanda's crime scene. I feel bad for Tony."

At first Amber stood silently scanning Claire's face and expression, finally she spoke, "Do you remember saying you thought I might have a halo?"

Claire nodded.

"Well, I think you'd be a better candidate." Amber rinsed the vegetable juices from her hands and dried them on a towel. Empathy no longer evident in her voice, "I find it very difficult to feel compassion for the man who's caused you so much distress and could -- according to your theories -- be responsible for my fiancé's death."

Claire walked to the kitchen table and looked out at the street. Long shadows from the trees covered the ground as the setting sun neared the western horizon. Watching the pedestrians four stories below, she saw people wearing only light jackets. It appeared the temperature had indeed risen. Maybe she needed air.

"I think I'm going to go for a walk."

Amber exhaled, "Claire, I wish you'd talk to me. Tell me why I should feel compassion? I don't get it?"

To be honest, Claire didn't *get it* either. Nonetheless, she was mad. Involuntarily, her neck stiffened and shoulders squared. Intellectually she knew this was ridiculous. Why would she be mad at Amber? Why did she feel the need to suddenly defend Tony? "I think I'll get something to eat at one of the cafés. I'm sorry if you're cooking me dinner." Claire turned to leave the kitchen.

Focused on her light jacket in the hall closet she stepped into the living room. The swirl of emotions combined with her pounding head and queasy stomach stymied her footsteps. She became mesmerized by the tall floor to ceiling windows. Flooding the luxurious room were hues of red and orange; the panoramic expanse radiated colors of the setting sun as it reflected off the purple haze covered mountains. Momentarily she became awestruck by the beautiful view.

Amber switched on the lights, filling the room with sudden brilliance and taking away the outside. Claire turned from the now dark window back to reality, which now included the glare of her roommate, accompanied by an unfamiliar angry tone, "Don't you get mad?"

Claire stared at Amber's expression. She'd met more intimidating expressions before. Slowly she responded, "Yes, I get mad." Nonetheless, her true emotion remained concealed by her calm tone.

"Then show it!" An eternal silence pursued. Eventually, Amber huffed and returned to the kitchen.

The sound of cabinets closing too loudly declared Amber's ability to show her emotion. Claire knew she should talk – she had no idea what to say. So instead, she reached for her jacket, grabbed her purse, and walked out the front door.

Palo Alto had many small cafés on University Boulevard, only a short walk from their condo. Most were open during the early hours, with all kinds of delicious coffee. While many of these establishments closed their doors in the evening, other street fronts brightened with dining choices as the sky darkened and the lights of the city came to life. When she opened the door and walked from the brightly lit foyer of their building, the cool dusk air hit her face. The street lights illuminated the sidewalk, and people hustled along the pathway. Suddenly, Claire realized it was Saturday night.

She didn't want to go to a real restaurant. She didn't want to sit and watch happy patrons chat and eat. No, she wanted time alone, time to sift and consider her thoughts and feelings. Without thinking, she turned toward the northeast, away from the setting sun and toward the water.

During her first week in Palo Alto, Harry showed her a beautiful park along the San Francisco Bay. Perhaps she'd lived too long on private property. Her desire for fresh air and nature overtook concerns for the descending darkness or abandoning side streets. With each step toward her goal, the tension in her head and neck eased.

Could it be possible to hate and love someone too? Claire wondered. The overpowering compassion back at the condo wasn't just for a young man in a tragic situation; it was for the young man who grew up to become the husband she had loved. She blinked her eyes against the breeze and remembered good times. Theirs was a heated passion. She contemplated the man who made her hate her own existence one moment and love it the next.

As her unconsciousness flooded with memories, feelings stirred deep inside. Concurrently, her consciousness screamed for her to remember his atrocities, the cruelties which outnumbered the kindnesses. However, her heart ached and argued -- perhaps, his positives could overtake his negatives. After all, doesn't everyone have a good and a bad side?

This is why I'm not ready to face him. This is why I can't face anyone right now.

Claire knew her thoughts and feelings were wrong. He'd given her every reason to hate him, seek vengeance, and aid in his destruction. *So why was this so hard?* She tried to push Tony back into his assigned compartment.

Her thoughts moved to Amber. Instead of crossing Middlefield Road, Claire should be back at the condo talking to her friend. However, after spending so much time alone and years hiding her true emotion with Tony, Claire wasn't comfortable sharing her feelings.

She couldn't control the way she felt. Apparently her mask wearing skills were rusty.

Hopefully a walk along the shore will help me sort out my feelings and revive my energy. Then maybe I can face Amber. She deserves that.

*****

Parked near a four story stucco condominium on Forest Avenue, Phillip Roach compiled his information for Mr. Rawlings. Although Claire Nichols hadn't used the phone with the number he'd determined was hers since she received the calls from Mr. Rawlings, Phil believed this was her place of residence.

In the past twenty-four hours, Phillip learned a lot about Claire Nichols: She'd applied for her birth certificate and social security card – all matters of public record. She opened a bank account with a deposit of $100,000 from an unknown source – not public record.

He also discovered, just yesterday, her account received a life-giving infusion. Phil wasn't the investing type, but from his scan of the information, Claire Nichols had an impressive investment portfolio. The notable wealth came from a wire transfer. The originator of the transfer was an account in Switzerland. To most people that would be the end of that transaction. Phillips's sources were not that easily deterred. The monies came from a high-end gems and jewelry broker named Pulvara operating in San Francisco. Phil planned to visit his business Monday.

He gave Ms. Nichols credit. She'd tried to remain under the radar, even using a post office box at the Palo Alto Post Office. It would have worked, except the federal government, as well as the Indiana state government, didn't accept P.O. Box numbers as an acceptable address to send official documents. Ironically, Ms. Nichols adherence to domestic laws led Phillip Roach to the corner of Forest and Gilman.

Phil wasn't willing to relay all of this information to Mr. Rawlings. First, he wanted to visit Mr. Pulvara to learn more before he jumped to conclusions on her recent windfall. Second, he wouldn't divulge the exact address without visual conformation. After all, she could have deceivingly listed a friend's address. Or perhaps, she paid someone for the use of their mail box. Phil glanced between the large luxurious building and his laptop, as he worked to compile a detailed report. He planned to say he was getting closer to pin-pointing Ms. Nichols' whereabouts when he saw a petite brown haired woman suddenly visible through a large window on the fourth floor. He strained to see the woman, stories above. Yes, it looked like Claire Nichols.

Reaching for his camera with the telephoto lens, she walked away from the plates of glass, and he lost sight of her. Momentarily questioning his vision, he debated adding her address to the report. Then like a gift from the surveillance gods, Claire Nichols stepped through the front doors of the building.

Wearing a jacket to protect her from the spring wind, the brunette turned toward the northeast. Phil watched her bury her hands deep into the pockets of her coat. The breeze blew back her hair, exposing her face and slender neck. Utilizing the long telephoto lens, he zoomed in on her features. Due to the wonders of technology his camera's illumination element diffused light, creating the illusion of daytime even in dusk.

Despite the brown hair, Phil's intuition told him this was the same woman in the photos he'd studied. Without question, the surveillance gods had offered him Claire Nichols. Depressing the button on his camera, multiple photos snapped in seconds. Phil pulled his car out of the concealed parking space and slowly eased his way along Forest Street. He drove ahead of where she seemed to be going.

In his rearview mirror, he watched Claire progress along the sidewalk, only feet from his newly parked car. He snapped her photo. She clearly appeared absorbed in her thoughts. Forcing her into his automobile would be easy, but that wasn't Mr. Rawlings' request. Mr. Rawlings wanted information.

An investigator's job was not to question. Therefore, he would never do so aloud. Yet, internally, Phillip Roach wondered why, if Mr. Rawlings was concerned about the woman who reportedly tried to kill him, he only wanted facts. As Phil observed the attractive lady his instinct told him he hadn't been hired to keep Mr. Rawlings safe. No, he'd been hired to report the every move of a woman Mr. Rawlings wasn't willing to emancipate.

As Claire passed, Phil pretended to look down. Once she passed, he eased out of his car, onto the sidewalk and fell into rhythm with her steps.

*Things are not always what they seem;
the first appearance deceives many.
The intelligence of a few perceives
what has been carefully hidden.*
-- Phaedrus

Chapter 9

Phillip Roach reread his email:

To: Anthony Rawlings
Date: March 23, 2013
Subject: Claire Nichols
From: Phillip Roach

Mr. Rawlings, due to the late hour in Iowa, I'm emailing the information I've acquired thus far:

I had visual confirmation. Claire Nichols has been located -- her address: 7165 Forest Ave. Unit 4 A, Palo Alto, California. She recently obtained a copy of her birth certificate, social security card, and a driver's license. She isn't employed. Her bank account is healthy, opened with the deposit of a $100,000 Cashier's check. This was traced back to a bank in New York; it was purchased with cash. I have some top notched associates working on this, but it seems to be a dead end. It was purchased the week before her release.

She spent much of the original money on necessary items: a car (2011 Honda Accord LX), clothes, personal items, telephones, computer, etc.

Her bank account recently received another deposit of $50,000, and she created an investment portfolio worth near $750,000. The source of this money is still being investigated. I hope to learn more Monday. I have confidence this information will be obtained.

Attached are photos taken Saturday night.

I will await your directives for continued observance and will remain completely devoted to this case until you instruct otherwise. Phillip Roach

Phil double checked the attachment: Multiple photos of Claire walking along a street, the close-up views were quite detailed. He continued to click. The numerous photos gave the illusion of Claire Nichols literally walking down the street. He slowed his clicks; she now sat on a park bench. Next she held an iPhone. The conversation changed her expression – relieved, happier. A few more views of her on the bench and then there's someone with her.   Click, they're talking -- the other person who wore a jacket and baseball cap was a man. Although the hat concealed his features, Claire's expression suggested familiarity. The next shot showed the two of them walking from the bench to a waiting car. No physical contact, however both of their expressions appeared relaxed and casual. As Phil clicked, Claire opened the passenger door of the blue Mustang while the man opened the driver's. The last photo showed the license plate.

Phil smiled; satisfied with his report and hopeful Mr. Rawlings would feel the same. *SEND.*

*****

The cool clear water refreshed Derek Burke as his plane descended toward Boston. Below the clouds and between the buildings he saw sprouts of green. As April began so did spring on the East coast. He'd been gone two weeks, making five weeks since he and Sophia were in the same city. He knew it wasn't either of their preference, but after accepting Shedis-tics job offer, he worried it'd be their future.

Relishing flying first class with wider seats and increased leg room, Derek closed his eyes and nervously awaited their reunion. The anticipation combined with apprehension obscured the roar of engines. He considered Shedis-tic's final offer... the next time he flew from coast to coast it would be in a private Shedis-tic's plane. They offered him unlimited access and ability to fly from Santa Clara to Provincetown in hours, without the hassle of commercial flights.

The enticement package was incredibly appealing. The salary alone was more than Derek had ever considered requesting, and the signing bonus would alleviate most of their debt. Sophia's larger studio could become a reality sooner, rather than later.

Throughout the negotiations he'd done what he promised and called Sophia discussing each offer. When he explained the financials and necessary living requirements, she was on board. However, her attitude changed when he mentioned the travel component. Not just traveling to and from the west coast, but weeks and months traveling outside the country. It was inferred, most of his travels would take him to the Orient, the location of the world's major software players. After all, Shedis-tics didn't expect to overcome the competition by watching from afar.

Unfortunately, Shedis-tics required a decision prior to his return home. With a heavy heart, Derek accepted. The pros far outweighed the cons. His new position officially began May 1. He prayed his wife would see why he gave them an affirmative answer.

Imagining Sophia's beautiful slate gray eyes, amazing scent, and soft skin -- anticipation conquered his apprehension.

"Sir, you may exit the aircraft."

Lost in his own thoughts, he'd completely missed the landing. Derek nodded. The attendant had his bags ready near the door. Yes, this first class thing was nice. And to think, this would be *slumming* compared to the Shedis-tics private plane.

Derek took his phone out of *airplane mode* and it immediately vibrated. As he approached the luggage carousel, Derek read Sophia's text message: *I HAVE A SURPRISE FOR YOU! TAKE A TAXI TO BOSTON HARBOR HOTEL. THERE'S A PACKAGE FOR YOU AT THE FRONT DESK -- Smiley face.*

It was funny how a colon and half of a parentheses could bring a smile to Derek's face, but it did.

At the front desk of the Boston Harbor Hotel, Derek retrieved his mysterious envelope and tipped the concierge. He surveyed the contents of the envelope: a key to suite 523 and a beautifully scribed note: *Come see your surprise.*

His enthusiasm amplified with each step of this faux clandestine encounter.

Opening the door to suite 523, he beheld his *something special* leaning against the wall, illuminated by candles. Scattered near the sketched self-portrait of his beautiful naked wife and through the suite's sitting room were thousands of rose petals. If the petals didn't indicate his directed path the assortment of lacy under garments at each two step intervals did. Following the erotic GPS, Derek found his beautiful wife, dressed exactly as she was in the sketch, lying upon a large four poster bed. The candles provided a sweet sexy fragrance combined with the perfect flickering glow.

In mere seconds Derek was dressed to match – or rather *undressed*.

Hours later, wearing thick hotel robes, they settled onto the intimate dining table on the balcony of their suite. Boston Harbor's lights glimmered in the cool spring night air. Sophia surveyed the feast before her as she felt her husband's gentle fingers lift her long disheveled hair and his lips kiss her exposed neck. Despite the warm terrycloth, goose bumps appeared on her arms and long slender legs. She closed her eyes, as a purr escaped her lips.

His warm breath bathed her ear as Derek whispered, "I love my surprise."

Sophia's smile radiated her entire face. "Good, I'm glad. I've missed you."

"I've missed you, too."

"Tell me about your job prospect; I promise I'm listening." Her toe wandered up his warm leg.

"Hmmm, I think you're trying to distract me."

Sophia beamed, "No, I think, if I wanted to distract you, I could."

Derek's cheeks rose, as admiration radiated from his gaze. Without a doubt, if there was one thing Sophia was good at doing, it was distracting him. Actually she was good at many things. Beholding her now, hair beautifully tousled and wearing only a white robe, he prayed *being understanding* was among her list of attributes. "The company is one of the biggest players out there. They have potential to be even bigger."

"And you want it?"

Derek looked down. This was easier on the phone, not seeing her beautiful trusting eyes before him. "I do."

"Then tell them *yes.*"

"But, what about us? What about living arrangements? Travel?"

Sophia left her food untouched, fell to her knees, and sat back on her heels before her husband. "I love you. Did you say I could stay in Provincetown and you'd be there every weekend?"

"Yes, unless..."

"Unless you need to be out of the country."

"Yes."

"Where will you live during the week?"

"I guess I'll have an apartment or condo in Santa Clara." He smoothed her blonde hair. This was going so much better than he'd expected.

Sophia continued, "And didn't you say they offered you transportation back and forth?"

"Yes, but that's a lot of time apart."

She lifted herself to encircle his neck. "If you want this, if it's your dream, and if we'll be able to afford both homes, I can travel too. I can spend some of my weeks in Santa Clara and some weekends too. We can both spend time in Provincetown. I can paint, draw, and sketch -- anywhere."

Derek dropped his head to hers, sighing audibly. "I didn't think you'd take it this well." She kissed his cheek. He asked, "You'd be willing to travel?"

"I'm willing to do whatever I need to do, to be with you."

"I anticipate long hours, during the week."

"Have you ever known me to shy away from late nights, or early mornings?" Sophia asked with a sultry smirk.

Derek smiled, "Late nights no, early mornings -- not really your thing."

"So, I'll just consider early mornings to be later nights. It all blends together. Besides, if you're some big wig, you need a wife by your side."

He lifted her body as he stood. "Mrs. Burke, you're right, as always." His hands began to roam under the thick robe as his lips found the place where her neck and shoulders met, the spot that sent tingles throughout her body.

"What about dinner?" She murmured, "I ordered your favorites."

"I think I need some more of my surprise appetizer."

Sophia didn't argue, or agree. Her mind was lost in her husband's touch.

The next morning they awoke to their new reality. They were moving to Santa Clara, and they needed a place to live. Stepping into the spacious glass shower, she thought about their impending adventure. Although Sophia traveled all over Europe, she'd never been to California. Being born and raised in New Jersey, the East Coast was always home.

Her parents lived in the same house where she was raised. They'd lived there for over forty years. Feeling the warm water coat her body and inhaling the fresh clean scent of body wash, Sophia realized home was a feeling, not a place. She liked that feeling. It made her feel safe, loved, and wanted.

Rinsing the floral scented cream rinse from her long hair, she suddenly shivered as cool air penetrated her warm moist haven. Before she could turn or comment, Derek caressed her trim waist and hips. He was her home. He gave her that feeling. It even transcended her art, allowing Sophia to use bolder colors, attempt more abstract drawings, and create beyond previous boundaries. If he could do that for her, moving to the West Coast was a small price to pay.

Wrapped in a thick luxurious towel Sophia combed her wet hair. Droplets of water rolled down her bare back as she contemplated drying it. She didn't like using a hair dryer. It was bad for her hair and used a lot of energy. But the cold April wind didn't support wet hair. Smiling, she thought about her parents and heard her mother's voice, *"Don't go outside with wet hair, you'll catch your death of cold."* At first her parents may not like the idea of her moving west. But, after she explained the two homes and her ability to visit while Derek travels, Sophia anticipated understanding.   After all, that's what they had always provided -- understanding.

Derek pulled her from her thoughts as he entered the glass and tile bathroom. "I just went down to the front desk to pay the bill. It was paid."

"I gave them our credit card."

"No." He shook his head, "Shedis-tics paid it."

Sophia smiled, "That's nice." Then her expression darkened, "But weird, how'd they know we were even here? I mean you didn't know until last night."

"I don't know." Derek smiled, "But man, this company has perks!"

Sophia tried to push the uneasiness away. Obviously Derek saw this as a positive. She wouldn't be the one to bring him down. She smiled, "I guess that means more money for breakfast."

Derek encircled her waist, spooned his wife, smiled into the mirror, and mused, "Mrs. Burke, I don't think you can eat that much."

Sophia removed her phone from her purse as Derek slipped their car into Boston traffic. The icon indicated missed calls. She listened to the messages, two from her mother.

Sophia's expression said it all, something was amiss. Derek waited while she listened. Finally he spoke, "What is it?"

"It's my pop. He's been in a car accident. Mom thinks he'll be okay, but I need to call."

Derek nodded and reached out to squeeze his wife's hand. As he watched her fumble with the screen of her phone, he changed the direction of the car. No longer were they headed to the Cape. He turned onto I-84 West. Before Sophia realized where they were, they were in Connecticut headed toward New York and on to New Jersey.

"Thank you. I'll feel better seeing him in person."

"What happened?"

"Mom isn't sure. She kept saying, *I was supposed to be with him, I should have been with him.* She'd stayed home with a migraine. She's blaming herself. His car went off the road near Sourland Mountain Reserve. He's driven those roads a million times. The police speculate wet roads caused the accident." She turned to her husband's profile. "You know I'm proud of you and your new job? But maybe we shouldn't mention it to them, not yet."

Derek nodded, "Your pop will be fine. He has your mom to look after him."

Sophia fought her emotion, as tears moistened her cheeks. "You know, I didn't think about others. I got so wrapped up in myself and us." Her chest heaved, "I never considered them when thinking about moving to California. If we were in Santa Clara we couldn't just jump in a car and be there."

"No, we'd jump on a plane," he reassured, "which, considering this traffic, might be quicker."

Sophia smiled. "Private planes, right... something to get used to!" Sighing, she leaned her head against the seat, watched the world pass-by, and settled in for the five hour drive.

*****

The gray clouds settled over Princeton, raining down and draining color from the urban landscape. Sophia considered drawing the scene, thinking about chalk, she'd need only black -- devoid of color, the sketch would come to life in shades of gray.

She liked her hometown of Princeton, New Jersey. After all, it was where she experienced childhood, learned to walk, talk, and color outside the lines. And although her parent's home wasn't in the Borough, it was still Princeton, the home of the acclaimed university.

Sometimes growing up she hated the prestigious school. It seemed like the entire world revolved around it. Unlike so many of the locals, she knew in her heart the world offered more. However, now Sophia was eternally grateful for Princeton, especially its medical center.

Rubbing her eyes, Sophia yawned. She'd been in the hospital room, looking out the window, sitting in the plastic chair, and pacing the linoleum floors for hours. The monitors beeped at appropriate intervals without alarm; everything indicated her father's progress. Sophia just wanted him to open his eyes.

Derek finally convinced Sophia's mother, Silvia, to get some food. It was the first time she'd left Pop's room since he returned from surgery. Sophia's promise to stay near, allowed Silvia the reassurance to leave, if only for a little while.

Tears lingered in Sophia's eyes as she watched the man who'd always been her rock. Nearing seventy, with declining stature, he wasn't any taller than Sophia. Of course, he'd never been taller than five eight, but with age even that lessened. Yet, when she closed her eyes, Sophia saw the mountain of a man who'd scoop her into his arms and put her on his shoulders.

Throughout the five hour drive, she tried to convince herself she would arrive to find him sitting up and swearing at the nurses. The image made her smile. Pop was the sweetest man, as long as you played by his rules. And when you didn't, he was more bark than bite. His contagious deep and harmonious laughter shook his too large stomach with joy. She imagined him arguing about the hospital gown, food, or television stations.

Yet, reality didn't match her memories or dreams. The man before her, attached to wires and tubes, didn't seem like her father. Nevertheless, the small bracelet on his wrist read: *Rossi, Carlo*; confirming he was indeed her pop.

The rain drops continued to silently pelt the glass pane. Sophia stared at the view. Instead of trees and buildings blurred by sheets of unrelenting spring rain, she saw memories she'd put away, as the saying goes -- for a rainy day. She saw the hardworking man who came home from work each day. She saw her mother, wearing an apron in the kitchen, fussing to have dinner ready precisely by 6 PM. She saw the couple standing proudly and awkwardly at New York art exhibits and her Paris wedding.

Sophia thought how different she was from them and how much they'd given her. Instead of fighting her artistic side, they embraced it. They never belittled her dreams. Now, standing by her father's bedside, she wanted to do the same. She wanted to support them any way she could. Currently, that meant hours of diligent vigil.

Sophia must have fallen asleep in the hard plastic chair she'd pulled up next to Carlo's bed. She awoke with her head near his feet, her back bent and sore, to the swish of the door across the linoleum floor. She blinked away the sleep from her eyes and watched as a nurse entered the room. The wipe board on the wall read: *Kayla*.

Sophia remained silent as Kayla made her rounds, checking fluids in the hanging bags and making notes, reading monitors and making notes, and lifting Carlo's hand, feeling his pulse and making notes.

When it appeared she was done, Sophia spoke, "Hello, I'm his daughter. Can you please tell me how he's doing?"

Kayla checked her notes. "Can you tell me your name; I need to verify you're on the list." (Her R sounded like a W... a reassuring inflection to someone raised near the Borough)

"Sophia Rossi Burke."

Kayla double checked her notes. "Yes, Sophia. Is your mother near?"

"Yes, she's with my husband in the cafeteria."

"Do you expect her to return soon?"

"I do... what time is it?"

Kayla checked her watch, "It's almost eight thirty. The doctor is doing her final rounds. I'll tell her you're here, and she'll inform you of your father's progress."

His voice sounded groggy, but Sophia would recognize that deep gargle anywhere. "If your talk'n bout me, you might as well talk *to* me."

Sophia's smile filled her face while the pent-up tears slid over her raised cheeks. Both women turned toward the bed. Carlo continued, "And what in Sam Hill are all these damn tubes. I don't need damn tubes. I want them out!"

Sophia hurried to his side and threw her arms around his neck. "Pop, you're awake?!"

"Damn right I'm awake. Where's your mother? And why aren't you with that husband of yours?"

"Mom's with Derek in the cafeteria. She's been by your side the whole time. We finally convinced her to get something to eat."

Carlo nodded approvingly at his baby girl.

Kayla interrupted long enough to lift Carlo's bed so he sat up, asked a few questions, and promised to send the doctor. Once they were alone Sophia held her father's hand and looked him square in the eye. "Pop, what happened? How did you crash your car?"

Carlo returned her gaze, "My car? I don't remember."

She tried to reassure him, "It's fine, just rest."

"It's not fine, Sophie. You're saying I crashed my car? Is Silvia all right?"

"Yes, Pop. She wasn't with you. You were alone... out by Sourland Mountain Reserve."

Sophia watched as Carlo eyes closed. Finally he spoke, "I... I'm... I just don't remember. Sophie... don't tell your momma. I don't want her thinking I can't remember. Baby, I need you to help me with this. Tell me what happened so I can get it straight."

"Pop, I don't know. They just found your car. You ran off the road and hit a tree. Your right leg is broke, but not your hip. The doctor made a big deal out of that. Momma's been real worried. You also punctured a lung. But the doctor said everything should heal just fine."

"What about the other people, in the other car?"

"Pop, what other car?"

"That one that started to pass and pushed me off the road."

Sophia stared at her father. "Pop, do you remember another car?"

Carlo looked at his hand. He followed the IV line up to the dangling bag. "What's this shit they're pumping into me? I can't think straight!"

"I think it's pain medicine."

"Sophie, get your momma."

She kissed his forehead. "If you promise not to go anywhere," she smiled, as big as she could, her eyes twinkling.

"Now tell me how in Sam Hill I'm supposed to do that, with all this bloody crap hooked to me." Beneath the pale complexion and gruff exterior, Sophia saw her father's loving sense of humor.

"Pop, I'll get Momma. But, I think you should know I'm not leaving until you're better!"

As Sophia turned toward the door, she once again heard swoosh against the linoleum. The large barrier opened and the sound of her mother's voice filled the room.

"Caa-ar-lo-oo!" Silva cried, creating a four syllable word where there'd only been two. Within seconds she was kissing his graying hair and fussing over his blankets.

Sophia looked up to see Derek's tired quizzical expression. She took his hand and they walked into the hall. The sound of her mother fretting and her father minimizing elated Sophia. However, Derek's sad eyes grounded her emotion.

"Derek, what is it? Did you speak to the doctor? Is there something I don't know?"

Derek shook his head. "No. It isn't your pop. It's what you just said to him. Are you planning to stay here, in Princeton?"

Sophia collapsed against the wall. "I don't know. I just can't leave them."

"What about finding a place to live in Santa Clara?"

"We have a month. We don't need to fly out tomorrow." She watched her husband's neck and shoulders stiffen. This was a new version of their one main disagreement. He liked plans and details. Sophia lived in the moment. This morning she would have willingly flown across the country. However, things changed. Now she didn't know when she'd be ready. "Can I please not make a decision right now? It's been a very long day."

He reached for her waist, pulled her closer, and rested his chin on her head. "I have some bad news."

She didn't ask. Inhaling his aftershave and listening to the beat of his heart, Sophia braced herself for the bad news.

"I tried to tell your mom we'd get a hotel." Sophia snickered into his shirt; she knew where he was headed. He continued, "But, she wouldn't hear of it."

"Don't tell me..." Her tired gray eyes twinkled up to his sullen expression.

"Yes, we're sleeping in your old room tonight." His lips brushed her forehead and gently kissed her nose. "So Darling, it's *also* going to be a long night."

She molded into his comforting embrace and thought about her cramped bedroom. It was great when she was ten, but now... the standard bed was probably older than both of them put together. "I think staying in my old room is your plan to make me want to leave sooner."

"Is it working?" Derek asked -- his brows elevated.

"If Pop could get up and walk, we'd be home by morning!"

Derek smiled as he held her close. "I can't take more than two nights in that old bed."

"Deal." They reentered the hospital room, hand in hand.

When one door of happiness closes, another opens;
but often we look so long at the closed door
that we do not see the one which has opened for us.
- Helen Keller

Chapter 10

Most mornings Claire sat at the table, perused the web, and waited for the others to arrive. She enjoyed the quiet time, as much as the morning ritual of coffee and pleasantries. Of course, she was usually the first in the kitchen; after all, Amber and Harry needed to get ready for work. Claire only needed to be dressed to workout.

Her options for connectivity continued to expand. Whether she used her laptop, her tablet, or her phones, she could stay in touch with the world, anytime – anywhere. This also allowed her to see her personal life laid out for everyone whenever she chose. Having technology denied in past, she now felt compelled to read *everything*. And apparently since her unusual prison release, Claire Rawlings Nichols was once again deemed newsworthy.

Often her face would appear on the cover of esteemed magazines, the kind which lined the check-out lanes of the grocery stores. Today she saw her picture in a thumbnail on her homepage. Still alone, Claire scanned the link and found the corresponding article: The Rawlings Moving On. It claimed to enlighten the reader on their lives after marriage, complete with pictures. Tony appeared exquisitely dressed with a pretty woman on his arm. According to the article, she was associated with a large hospital in Iowa where her father was CEO and Administrator. The article alluded to the implications of this affluent union, since Mr. Anthony Rawlings was among the top contributors to the hospital. In the opposing frame Claire sat with Harry eating at a café in Palo Alto. According to the article Claire, left penniless, was unemployed and living with Harrison Baldwin, a security guard at SiJo.

The clicks of Amber's heels upon the hardwood combined with the opening and closing of the front door brought life to the quiet kitchen. Looking up from her laptop, Claire apologized, "I'm so sorry for bringing the two of you into this media mess."

Amber snickered, as she finished making her cup of coffee, "I've never seen anything so ridiculous. I can't believe reporters think this is news!"

Leaning against the counter, Harry brushed his tussled blonde hair from his eyes and puffed his chest. Claire chuckled, the pictures and article before her forgotten. She found it amusing, no matter the occasion, his golden curls continually fell softly across his face. She wondered if he owned a comb or brush, anything that could possibly tame his unruly mane.

Musingly she fought a new desire to reach out and brush the curls away, to better see his soft blue eyes. The impulse surprised Claire. She gripped the handle of her mug in an effort to stop her hand. Thankfully, her momentary insanity went completely unnoticed by Harry as he postured in preparation for his speech.

In reality, only a second or two had elapsed. However, the rush of blood to her cheeks made Claire lower her face, in a feigned attempt to inspect the contents of her ceramic mug. Slowly, she raised her eyes as Harry spoke, "Actually, I saw today's article, and I'm honored. I've never been a celebrity before."

Laughing, Amber brushed her brother's shoulder and glanced toward Claire with a sly smile, "Guess what, Harry? You aren't one now!" Amber started to walk back toward her bedroom and turned to Claire, "Don't worry about it. Life's much more exciting with you around."

Avoiding Harry's gaze, Claire looked toward her computer's homepage, until Harry's jovial voice brought her back to reality, "So, what do you think? Just in case I end up in *People* magazine or something, is this shirt all right? Or, do I need something nicer?"

She returned her gaze to the man before her. From behind the soft curls she saw small lines surrounding his sparkling cobalt eyes, and his cheeks raised in a boyish smirk. Claire looked at his collarless black woven shirt with the SiJo Gaming emblem. The shirt wasn't tight but accentuated his muscular abdomen, broad shoulders, and defined arms. Her eyes scrutinized his attire as they descended to the khaki slacks emphasizing his trim firm waist.

Slowly she realized he was teasing her. "Actually, I think you should change." Her smile radiated emerald shimmers.

"You do?"

"Yes, maybe something like the jeans you wore last night. You know the ones with holes – it highlights my penniless status."

With his grin in full gear, he reached out and covered Claire's hand. Never before had this familiarity ignited the tightness she now felt. Claire fought between the desire to turn her hand over and return the contact and the need to pull away and run to her room. Seemingly unaware of her sudden mixture of feelings, Harry said, "If I ever do live with a penniless woman, I can only hope she has a portfolio like yours."

"Oh, is that your only requirement?" Her brows rose in question.

"No..." his gaze captivated her, holding her prisoner. "It's probably the least of my requirements. The first is that she doesn't tell me what to wear."

Pulling her stare away, she nonchalantly replied, "Hey, you asked. But, I guess that leaves me out. Should I alert the press?"

He winked, "No, let me enjoy my fifteen minutes for a while."

Claire shook her head, "Okay, our secret living arrangements are safe with me. Oh, and about fifty other people who live in this building and know the truth."

"They won't tell." With that Harry walked toward the front door, toward his true home.

When the door closed, she exhaled and scolded herself. The easy atmosphere of Amber and Harry's company was a gift. The last thing she wanted to do was complicate it with feelings which surpassed *friendly*. In an attempt to dismiss the unfamiliar tightness, she refocused on the article.

Claire knew she should share the nonchalant attitude of Amber and Harry. It was only she'd been taught an engrained fear of *public failure, appearance,* and *opinion*. Unconsciously, while out -- at a store, a café, or walking on the street -- Claire found herself scanning the crowds for cameras. On some occasions she would think she'd see one from her peripheral vision, and then upon second glance, the perpetrator would disappear. The photographers had to be there. How else could she grace so many magazines? A new *laissez faire* perspective would take time.

Claire knew her *star status* would soon extinguish. After all, California was inhabited by many famous people. That meant if her story was to be newsworthy, she needed to strike while the iron was hot. That was her thought process as she reached for her telephone.

Claire's heart beat rapidly as she considered the repercussions of her intended actions. For once, she wasn't being impetuous. She'd thoroughly debated this decision, knew her guidelines, her limits, and even wrote them down. Her stipulations were sitting on the counter in front of her as she dialed the phone.

Justifiably shocked and surprised, Meredith Banks willingly dropped everything to speak with her old sorority sister. Sounding businesslike, yet friendly, Claire explained her desire to *get her story out with someone she could trust.*

Candidly Claire asked, "Meredith, is that you?"

Without hesitation, Meredith replied, "Claire, I never doubted your innocence; yes, I would be honored to help you with this."

Claire knew Meredith saw dollar signs and the potential for fame. She needed to know if she could trust her. To that end, she presented Meredith with a litmus test. "Before any interviews or work on my story, I want you to publish a *very* overdue retraction regarding our 2010 interview. I want you to tell the truth and explain it wasn't an interview, but an ambush, resulting in an unauthorized article. The retraction must also clarify that during our conversation I never mentioned the name Anthony Rawlings. You made assumptions based solely on conjecture." Before Meredith could respond, Claire added, "If and when I read your published retraction, the exclusive rights to my story are yours."

Verbally Meredith agreed. Claire had heard verbal promises before. She informed Meredith everything would be summarized in a written contract. The breach of said agreement, by either side, would result in a hefty financial penalty.

Claire agreed to one concession. Meredith could promise a *real* interview with Claire Rawlings Nichols in her printed retraction. Without a doubt, *that* piece of journalism would reach Tony's publicist Shelly, and in essence -- Tony. Eventually they would learn of her interview and impending article anyway. This plan put Claire in control of the timing and gave her visibility. She reasoned *visibility* gave the world *cause,* if she suddenly disappeared, making Anthony Rawlings the most likely suspect.

Claire was no longer hiding or being played by Tony; for once, she was in control! The two women agreed to meet for a series of interviews and editorial sessions, after the publication of the retraction. They left the specific details in flux.

Smiling, Claire disconnected the call with a sense of satisfaction. She believed it was the right decision at the right time. The public had too many misconceptions. They needed to know the truth. They needed to know the real Anthony Rawlings before he repeated history with her, or heaven forbid with someone else.

Satisfied with her call, Claire sipped her coffee and noticed the blinking icon on her iPad indicating an email. It was the confirmation of her impending trip. She'd paid for both the airline and hotel reservations with her new Visa. That wasn't done recklessly. Claire knew her plans were now visible. She even felt a twinge of pride showing her ex-husband her new found independence. Of course, it was all a ruse; instead of flying into Corpus Christi where she'd spend her holiday, Claire was flying to San Antonio, where she'd rent a car, check into a very nice hotel, and then slip away and drive three hours to the coast. The deception was for Courtney. The two friends wanted time together, and their relationship needed to remain clandestine.

Although Claire wasn't sure, she believed her movements were being monitored. After all, Courtney said Tony hired a private detective. And in the two weeks since Tony's call, she'd received two lovely floral arrangements. The first came a few days after their short conversation. It contained cherry brandy roses, lilies, dark blue delphinium, hot pink larkspur, silver dollar eucalyptus and no card. Nevertheless, the meaning was clear... *Tony knew exactly where she lived.* The second arrangement came a week later with a card simply stating: *I have business in California soon. Perhaps we could dine?*

Although Amber called it a waste of beautiful flowers, Claire threw both arrangements directly into the trash. After her reaction to his call,

Claire decided she wasn't ready to face him or talk to him, in person or on the telephone. She could eliminate his voice by disabling her voicemail. Unfortunately, she still received his text messages. They mostly consisted of polite greetings to which she never replied. She hated to admit; even his typed word affected her. Sometimes she missed the pleasant Tony.

Contradictorily, the voice on the phone that sent chills down her spine and sent her running to the bathroom. That Tony she didn't miss. Besides, Silicon Valley was beautiful in April with flowers at every turn. They didn't need flowers indoors too.

Claire spent her favorite part of each day walking outside. True, the Palo Alto streets weren't like hiking in the Iowa woods. But, it was outside, and as much as she tried, Claire couldn't shake the memories of her incarceration. Yet, when the breeze blew her hair and the sun warmed her face, the chains of her imprisonment melted away and her wounded spirit began to heal. With each step in any directions she chose, her lungs filled with fresh air, and she felt her strength grow beyond that of pre-prison, to a place -- pre-Tony.

*****

Unbeknownst to Claire, her outings were diligently photographed and submitted to Mr. Rawlings along with her daily activities. Phillip Roach had never been paid so well for so little. Claire's predictable routine, as well as traceable internet usage, made for detailed reports and photos. He would often sit within the same coffee shop or cafe while Ms. Nichols lived in her own world. A few times Phil worried she saw his camera, but with the paparazzi vying for her image, he blended into the crowd.

Mr. Rawlings seemed pleased with his reports, although not always with their content. The disclosure regarding the source of Ms. Nichols' new found fortune (the sale of her jewelry) was met vehemently. Following Mr. Rawlings' directives, Phil returned to Mr. Pulvara's office. And although the price seemed extreme, Phil followed orders and retrieved the rings at *any* cost. Not trusting couriers, Phil personally delivered the rings to Rawlings Industry corporate offices, in Iowa City.

While he'd seen the tycoon's picture and talked with him on the phone, it was their first face-to-face meeting. Admittedly, within seconds of entering the CEO's regal office, Phil sensed Mr. Rawlings' commanding dominance. The expression Phil witnessed as Mr. Rawlings opened the velvet box was contrary to the millions of photos he'd seen. Obviously, the sale of his ex-wife's rings upset him. Thankfully the sparkling diamonds satisfied Mr. Rawlings and verified Phil's willingness to complete directives.

For a split second, Phil worried about the sweet looking woman who'd become his new dedication. He wondered how she could end up with someone like the man before him. Although he'd read every bit of published information, she seemed no match for Mr. Rawlings' power.

Phillip Roach learned years ago, not to include emotions in his line of work. This was emphasized during military training, reinforced in special ops, and ingrained as he covertly monitored person after person. Expectantly, his targets during military and special op usually ceased to exist following their discovery. Phillip even followed orders and aided in their demise. This training and dedication earned him the kind of money he currently demanded. On more than one occasion his work required his own disappearance. With no personal connections, that wasn't a problem. If he relocated or moved for a year or two, it was just part of the game. His alliances could fulfill any necessary relocation -- for a price.

This assignment was different. He'd located his assignment, yet his orders remained reconnaissance. As opposed to setting the sights of a high powered rifle on the enemy of a high rolling gambler or a threatening politician, this was well paid babysitting.

*****

Claire made her way through the crowd and settled at a small round table near the bar of a local Palo Alto restaurant. Although Harry and Amber weren't due for another fifteen minutes, Claire was ready. Tony made it clear early on, he had no patience for tardiness. Now, punctuality was her mantra. She really didn't think about it, it just was.

While waiting for her friends she ordered a martini and thought about her ensemble: a pair of slacks and blouse from Neiman Marcus and a pair of Dior pumps from Saks. Truly, she was allowing the press to get to her. She wanted to look like Mrs. Rawlings... to quiet their attack. Suddenly, she worried she was being photographed from every side.

Last night, when they talked about getting together before Claire left on her trip, Claire suggested eating at home. She even offered to cook. She liked cooking and contributing to the household duties. Her life in Palo Alto was a beautiful meeting of her previous two, not as tedious as her day to day survival in Atlanta, nor as opulent as her life in Iowa. It was real and comfortable – a perfect restart.

However, her friends insisted on going out to celebrate her impending vacation. They knew the *press thing* bothered Claire but argued she needed to be free to live her life, without worrying about other's perception. After a deep sigh, Claire agreed.

Lost in her thoughts, Claire didn't see Harry until he was right before her with his hand on her shoulder. Looking up to acknowledge him, she noticed how nice he looked, wearing a sports coat and button down shirt. His hair was even gelled and combed back in an attempted style. Before she could speak, he bent down and kissed her cheek. She felt warmth flow from her face to her insides as he took a seat across the small table.

"Well, hello. That was an interesting greeting." She mused.

Harry's blue eyes sparkled, illuminated in the low light of the restaurant. "I noticed how nice you look. Is that a new outfit?" Then he leaned a little closer, "And, that you're being watched from a table to your left." He reached for her. "Don't look, it'd be too obvious. I thought I would give them something to write."

"Maybe we should go somewhere else." Claire really wanted to say, *I want to go home.*

"This won't last long. We can leave, if you want, but I think your plan to make yourself visible is working. You shouldn't run from it now." He squeezed her trembling hand.

Claire looked at his serene expression and took comfort in his calmness. She exhaled, "Thank you, for being such a great sport about this."

"Well, like I said, I've never been a celebrity before."

"And, how do you like it?" She couldn't help notice the twinkle in his intensely blue eyes.

"I'm getting used to it. Just this morning, the barista at Starbucks recognized me and gave me free coffee."

Claire giggled, "Are you serious? I'm supposed to be the penny-less person. Why don't I get free coffee?"

"Well, I'm not exactly destitute. But," he mused, "I won't turn down free java."

The waiter came and took Harry's drink order. When he asked if they were ready to order, Harry turned to Claire, "Do you know what you want? Or, do we need some more time?"

Claire turned to the waiter, "I believe I'd like a little more time, please." She slowly picked up her martini and took a long sip, suddenly unable to make eye-contact.

Harry saw her sudden change in mood, "What's wrong?"

"It's really stupid." She said as she sat her drink back on the linen tablecloth. Peering above the flickering candle she saw his concerned expression and gained strength to continue, "I know I don't talk about my life with Tony very much. Maybe I'm not sure how I feel. But, from very early on, actually the first time we ever went out, he ordered my meal. He ordered my drinks, everything."

"Well, some men do that. Did you like it?"

"Not at first. I mean, he never asked me what I wanted. Even on that first date. How could he possibly know what I liked? Then later, I guess I got used to it. Other than the first time, I never questioned it." Claire became transfixed by the flame of the candle, flickering in the center of their private haven, moved by some unperceivable breeze.

Harry didn't know if he should encourage this conversation. It seemed to make Claire sad. However, it was the first time she'd opened up about any personal aspect of her life with Mr. Rawlings. He pushed, "Why?"

Claire looked up from the orange and blue glow. "Why what?"

"Why didn't you question it? I mean if you didn't like it, if you wanted to order for yourself, why didn't you tell him?"

Claire exhaled.

Harry watched as her eyes and face which were deep in thought, slowly took on perfect features. He recognized what she was doing. She was becoming the pretend Claire, the one who kept others at arm's length and said everything perfect.

"It's very complicated. Let's just say, no one tells Anthony Rawlings what to do or how to do it." She picked up her menu, "So what do you think sounds good?"

"I think it all sounds good. You should order whatever you want."

The smile Harry spotted behind the large leather bound menu, made his chest thump with pleasure. It wasn't the pretend one.

As they discussed their cuisine options, both of their phones buzzed: a text message from Amber. *SORRY. SOMETHING HAPPENED AT WORK - NOTHING SERIOUS. CAN'T MAKE DINNER.* Claire felt a twinge of guilt. Truthfully, until that moment, she'd forgotten Amber was absent.

By the end of their meal as they sipped coffee, Claire also forgot about the reporters. She'd been listening to Harry talk about things at SiJo. She didn't know anything about electronics or gaming and even mentioned she hadn't played a video game since college.

Shocked, Harry replied, "Then, it's settled. We're going back to my place and you're getting a lesson on the advances in gaming."

Claire smiled and shook her head. "I don't really think I'd be very good, I mean it's been years. Everything I knew is outdated. Besides, I'm sure you have more important things to do."

"What? More important than playing video games, are you kidding? Besides, just because you haven't done something in a while, doesn't mean you aren't good at it. With a little encouragement I bet you'd be very good."

"Are you that good of a teacher?" she asked. Harry's sly smile suddenly made Claire rethink her question. Perhaps the subject had changed without her realizing.

"I guess that remains to be seen."

Although, she could feel the blood in her cheeks and her increased pulse, she tried diligently to keep the conversation in check. "Well, the most advanced system I ever played was the Nintendo Game Cube, over ten years ago. Has it gotten more complicated? As I recall," she peered over her cup, "I was pretty awesome at Zelda."

When they stood to leave, Harry casually placed his hand in the small of Claire's back. She considered moving away but consciously decided to continue the contact. Harry joked, "That *is* an impressive resume. I'm not sure why SiJo hasn't snatched you up as a gaming specialist before a competitor learns of your secret talents."

Phil's camera caught it all.

"Oh sure, make fun. I bet I can beat you at Zelda, and I might even remember Mario's secret chambers, if I try."

"You're on!" They stepped into the spring air.

The next day Claire surveyed her new luggage and stacks of clothing. One benefit of Claire's time with Tony was Catherine. She possessed the uncanny ability to think of everything Claire needed. Looking at the items before her, Claire wondered if Catherine would think of something she'd forgotten. There were sundresses, shorts, shirts, beach cover-ups, flip flops, and sunscreen... it seemed like all the essentials for sun and fun.

Thoughts of Catherine made Claire sad. She truly loved the woman. Catherine was like a mother to her during a very difficult time in Claire's life. The idea to call and talk occurred more than once. Yet, Claire was afraid. She knew Tony's staff was incredibly devoted. What if Catherine believed Claire tried to kill Tony? The fear of hearing rejection in Catherine's voice stopped Claire from attempting communication. She didn't want anything to change the kind loving Catherine in her memories.

As Claire's trip approached, her excitement at seeing her old friend grew. Courtney's first choice of destination was Cancun. Claire would have liked that; she'd never been. Unfortunately, Claire hadn't applied for a new passport. That was fine. Corpus Christi was a beautiful destination in mid-April -- prime Spring Break time. The hotels and resorts would be bustling with patrons. Two women in a suite, walking the beach, and enjoying the pool would blend in. The last time Claire enjoyed a beach was in Hawaii, eighteen months ago. Allowing her mind to uncompartmentalize the months locked away from sunshine only added to her exhilaration as she contemplated white sand, hot rays, and blue waters.

Her items weren't bulky – the smaller suit case worked well and would be easier to negotiate through the busy airport. Claire glanced at her watch. Her flight left San Francisco International at three-thirty. With security regulations she planned to arrive by two-thirty. Currently a little after eleven, she had time for lunch.

On her way to the kitchen, the doorbell changed her direction. Her thoughts were already basking in the Texas sun; they weren't thinking about unwanted telephone calls or reporters with cameras.

Their condominium building was secure. In order to enter, one had to pass a security guard in the garage or one in the lobby. If you weren't a resident, an ID and signature were required for entrance. This could be perceived as inconvenient, but for inhabitants it was reassuring.

Opening the front door Claire could only see a stack of boxes labeled *Neiman Marcus*. With a sudden overwhelming dread, she realized the boxes obscured the delivery person's face. However, before she could shut the door, she heard a young man's voice and noticed inexpensive scuffed shoes.

"Ms. Nichols?"

She remembered to inhale. "Yes."

The young sandy haired man moved the boxes to the side and peered around the bounty. "These are for you. Could you please sign the delivery confirmation?"

Relief lowered her defenses. "I'm sorry, there's been a mistake. I didn't order any merchandise."

The young man struggled to balance the boxes and his electronic pad. He surveyed the information and confirmed her name and address. Pity overtook her, she finally responded, "All right. Bring them in and place them in the foyer."

Claire signed the electronic clipboard and accepted the unknown merchandise. She shut the door and moved the boxes to the dining room table. An envelope was attached to the top box. Claire debated: open the envelope or the boxes? Choosing the envelope she read:

I'll be in town after you return from Texas. Shall we dine? Perhaps you would enjoy wearing something more appropriate for our reservations? Since you seem unable to answer your phone, I'll send a car to your condominium, Wednesday 7PM. I look forward to our reunion.

Her fingers forgot to grip; the card floated to the floor.

A revolt erupted within Claire's stomach. The contents of the boxes were still undetermined; however, the meaning of his words came through loud and clear. Translation... *I know everything about you. I know about your trip. We're going to dine on Wednesday.* It wasn't a request -- his customary mandate.

She contemplated leaving the boxes sealed and throwing away the merchandise. However, curiosity won. Reluctantly, she opened each one. The small top one contained shoes; beautiful, high-heeled, Sergio Rossi, black sandals. The next box was larger; tentatively, she opened the lid. The black and white, Christian Dior, off-the-shoulder dress took her breath away. The final box contained a Chado Ralph Rucci trim coat, crepe with sheer chiffon at cuffs and hem. As Claire's fingers caressed the chiffon, she fought the desire to try it all on with the need to send it all back. Settling for somewhere in between, she stacked the boxes in her closet, and compartmentalized any thoughts related to them away for another day.

It was a lesson learned from Scarlet O'Hara, *Fiddle de de, I'll think about that tomorrow.* Today she wanted to concentrate on her impending vacation. Her ex-husband's invitation and clothes could wait. She'd deal with those later.

Things do not pass for what they are, but for what they seem.
Most things are judged by their jackets.
-Baltasar Gracian

Chapter 11

-1983-

"Yes, Anton, we'll be at Blair by the time of the ceremony." Amanda's voice came through the telephone receiver.

"It starts at two," he reminded his mother.

"We know that. You know Nathaniel would never be late."

That went without saying; Anton's family was punctual. "Mother," Anton hesitated, "is Grandmother coming?" He debated voicing the question but needed to know. After all, his relatives portrayed the perfect family. That image was becoming increasingly difficult to depict with Sharron Rawls' erratic behavior. Besides, he had enough issues with his classmates. He didn't need a *crazy grandmother* added to the mix.

"She is. It will be fine. I promise." Anton didn't answer. Amanda continued. "Nathaniel hired Sharron a private assistant. She accompanies your grandmother everywhere. With her assistance, Sharron is doing much better. It keeps her organized and focused."

Anton liked the sound of that. "That's good. I'm glad to hear it."

Two days later, dressed in his cap and gown, Anton peered out into the auditorium searching for his family. Bright lights shone directly onto the stage, limiting his ability to see the audience. However, he knew they were there. The Rawls may be many things, but undependable or unreliable, were not among their list of inadequacies. If a commitment were made, it was completed.

Following the ceremony, Anton met his family in the grand hall of the Center for the Arts. It was the perfect location for graduation from this prestigious private academy. Scanning the crowd, he found his parents and grandparents, and an unfamiliar face. Walking toward the group he waited for accolades that would never come. How could Anton ever imagine he'd receive praises for graduating third in his class? Third, what a disgrace! That his GPA was above the perfect 4.0 and he'd been accepted by every university to which he'd applied were not important. He wasn't number one.

Feeling the slap on his shoulder, he turned to see his father's reserved, yet kind eyes. "Congratulations, Son, we'd like to take you out to dinner. This is the end of a very important phase of your life."

Anton nodded in his direction; it was a form of acceptance. He looked toward his grandparents. Nathaniel's expression revealed nothing. If he were proud, if he were disappointed, Anton wouldn't know, until later. Sharron on the other hand appeared quite content. The young woman on her arm whispered in her ear as Sharron smiled and nodded.

The only positive aspect of the day, Anton could salvage, was his grandmother's new sense of calm. His mother gently touched his elbow, "Anton, this is Marie. She's Sharron's personal assistant."

Anton presented his hand, "Hello, Marie, nice to meet you."

The young woman smiled bashfully and presented her hand, "Hello, Mr. Rawls."

He noticed Marie's sweet smile and soft eyes, contrasting the dark in the members of his family. He wondered her age and guessed not much older than himself.

What credentials did one need to be a personal assistant? She must have some education beyond high school, mustn't she?

During dinner Marie impressively kept Sharron in line. Anton's grandmother didn't yell, complain, or argue. This even affected Nathaniel's demeanor. He was more relaxed than Anton had seen in years. Anton even saw his grandfather occasionally smile at his wife, who smiled lovingly in return. The look in her eyes, as she focused on her husband was like one peering upon a Roman god. It wasn't that Nathaniel didn't deserve the reverend gazes. Anton presumed he did. After all, his patience with Sharron was more than Anton or anyone else witnessed in any other facet of Nathaniel's life. Nonetheless, Sharon's praises for her husband were lessened by her ability to remember anyone other than him. Her memory seemed to concentrate on their life, pre-child, before Samuel, before Amanda, and before Anton.

Being Anton's graduation, he thought it would be nice if he were the subject of someone's compliments. But of course, the weather was a more important subject.

On multiple occasions, Marie reminded Sharron of her duties at hand, and the elderly woman immediately refocused. It was obvious, Sharron wanted more than anything to make her husband proud. She could in fact do as she was told, with some assistance. Sharron could follow the rules.

Samuel gripped the edge of the table. His mother was no child. She didn't need a damn nurse, and she sure as hell didn't need to worry about his narcissistic father's concerns. Sharron Rawls should be concerned about herself, not anyone else!

Of course, each time Samuel tried to discuss this with her, she'd smile serenely and ask about Nathaniel; where was he? When would he be back? And oh, yes, what was your name?

Between his father's business deals and his mother's declining mental health, there were days Samuel thought he should be the one to go completely insane. Thank god he had Amanda to keep him stable and Anton.

It went without saying, they were very proud of their son. Anton graduated third in his class from a prestigious private academy and would attend Columbia University in the fall, majoring in business and computer technology. It was no secret his son inherited a prowess for business. Samuel only hoped Nathaniel wouldn't ruin Rawls Corporation before Anton could get his feet wet. There were so many wrong decisions being made.

Seeing his mother's sudden agitation he started to help. However, Marie immediately assisted. It surprised Samuel to witness his mother's sudden composure. Perhaps having a non-emotionally involved assistant wasn't a bad idea. Although young, the girl seemed to possess a sense of calm the Rawls admittedly lacked. In some ways it reminded Samuel of his mother, before this terrible illness took hold.

In the face of the storm, otherwise known as Nathaniel, Sharron calmed the winds, rains, and rough waters. His entire life, Samuel wondered how she did it. Rarely, did he ever witness a disagreement between them. Superficially, she appeared to submit to his every demand. Yet, there were times when they looked at one another and Samuel knew, without confrontation, Sharron had made her feelings and desires known.

Samuel failed miserably in that category. He didn't have the ability to communicate nonverbally with his egotistical father. Their confrontations were predictably loud and boisterous. Perhaps, it was a two way street. Nathaniel needed to want that communication. He accepted the glances and body language from his wife, but not from anyone else, even his only son.

Samuel believed his parent's union had a history of rough patches, yet Sharron never complained. And now, as her mental facilities slowed, hell – derailed -- the reality in which she chose to dwell was not that of a mother, or grandmother, or even a wealthy businessman's wife. She saw the world as it had been when she and Nathaniel were first married. She looked at her handsome, yet aging husband and saw the twenty year old soldier she loved.

Samuel supposed on some level, he resented Anton for looking so much like his father. It wasn't as though Anton could control his genetics. That would be Samuel's doing as well. It was only that when Sharron looked at Anton, she smiled so sweetly and her eyes melted into the liquid calm reserved for her true love. Yes, it was Nathaniel she saw.

Nonetheless, she never asked Anton his name; she only called him Nathaniel.

How in the world Samuel found Amanda, and had forged out some semblance of normalcy was beyond him. Talk about nature verses nurture -- shit, he was screwed either way. Peering at his son, Samuel prayed Amanda's influence would overpower the messed up Rawls blood flowing through Anton's veins.

Yes, although the mother he once knew was rarely visible, Samuel knew Sharron's influence was his saving grace. Therefore, if this young girl helped Sharron transition from her world of make-believe to the present, maybe Samuel could learn to accept her.

A friend is someone who understands your past,
believes in your future, and accepts you
for who you are today.
--Unknown

Chapter 12

The warm gulf water lapped the shore, as the soft, moist sand enveloped their bare feet, and the sun bathed their tanned skin. Clad in swim suits, Claire and Courtney picked up the occasional shell as they walked along the beach. Although the third morning of their secret get-a-way, neither friend had run out of things to share.

Their reunion was everything Claire imagined and more. When Claire arrived late Tuesday night, or early Wednesday morning, to their rendezvous suite, Courtney was anxiously waiting.

Courtney hadn't changed. Her bright blue eyes and brown hair were exactly as Claire remembered. Courtney jokingly said, "Honey, my hair is only the same because my beautician hasn't decided to change colors!"

Claire's commercial flight to San Antonio took almost four hours. Flying first class, she reasoned was a gradual downgrade from private jets. She also knew some reporter could take her picture, and the penniless thing was getting on her nerves. After landing in San Antonio, she secured a rental car, drove to the Hotel Valencia Riverwalk, and checked into her suite. It was truly beautiful, complete with a balcony overlooking the famous San Antonio Riverwalk. While there, she messed up the bed and threw some towels into the whirlpool tub. *It kind of looks lived in.* She thought, as she made her way back to her rental car.

Next, she drove two and a half hours to Corpus Christi. Along the way she stopped for a healthy McDonald's salad, anything fast to get her to Courtney. Thankfully the rental car's built-in GPS directed her around an accident on I-37, south around Mathis. The voice knew about the back-up. And although rerouting added about thirty minutes, it was better than sitting in stand still traffic. By the time Claire reached their hotel, it was almost two in the morning, local time.

Just like her suite in San Antonio, the floor of their suite was only accessible with a key. Claire's key was waiting for her at the front desk, under the name *Julia*. (Courtney's future daughter-in-law)

When Claire opened the door and stepped onto the tiled entry, she heard the familiar scream resonating from one of the two bedrooms. She barely had time to see the lovely white living area and brightly colored furniture before her entire body was encased in Courtney's full embrace. In no time, their joyous reunion became tearful. Perhaps it was sleep deprivation; more than likely, it was their eighteen month separation and the circumstances surrounding it.

Leaving her unpacking until morning, the two sat on the sofa, knee to knee and talked until dawn. Their conversation focused more on the future than the past. There would be plenty of time for that as the week progressed.

Courtney told Claire all about the preparations for Caleb and Julia's upcoming nuptials. She desperately wanted to have Claire attend the event; however, as long as their relationship remained secret, they both knew it wouldn't happen. Courtney also told Claire about Caleb's recent entrepreneur endeavor. "He's doing very well in Chicago. It's an investment firm and he already has some great clients."

Claire couldn't hide her surprise, "I'm shocked he'd want to leave Rawlings. I mean with Brent and Tony's friendship, I'd think Caleb's future would be set. Tony always liked your children."

"Tony was very supportive. Being an entrepreneur himself, I think he admired Caleb's desire to succeed on his own."

Somewhere deep inside, Claire thought: *Yes, I'm glad he can be understanding... I know it's possible, just not usual!* "I'm glad it's working out."

Claire told Courtney all about California, Amber, and Harry. Of course, they'd discussed much of this on the phone, but face-to-face was so much nicer. The subject of Claire's financial backing slipped into the conversation as they talked about some of the recent reports of Claire's life. She assured Courtney she wasn't living with Harry, and she wasn't penniless. She even divulged the information about the mysterious $100,000.

"Where do you think it came from?" Courtney asked as she sipped her wine. It was their second bottle of Cabernet, something which likely added to their honesty and freedom of dialogue.

"I really don't know. It's weird. At first, both Jane and I feared it was from Tony."

"Why'd you think that?"

"Well, who else has that kind of money to throw away?"

"Good point, but maybe the donor didn't feel they were *throwing it away*?"

Claire smiled, "I hope not. Whoever it was, I can never thank them enough. They gave me my life back." She continued thoughtfully, "Prison wasn't as bad as it could have been – I guess. I kept to myself a lot."

Claire fell silent as she gazed out the dark balcony doors to the still black sky.

Courtney put her hand on Claire's knee, "You can talk to me."

Claire fought the tears, "I know. It's just -- I haven't spoken to *anyone* about this. I mean, I like Amber and Harry, I really do. They've been wonderful, especially considering we hardly knew one another when Amber went out on a limb and sent a jet to get me. I want to open up to them, but I'm so confused about so many things. I just don't know."

"Did you have anyone to talk to in prison?"

"There was a counselor, actually a psychiatrist. Her name was Dr. Warner. She took an interest in me. We met three times a week. At first I didn't say much. It's just hard to know who you can trust. But, over time I said a lot."

"But, no other prisoners?"

Claire shook her head, "No. Once people found out who I was married to... well they'd be... not nice." Looking down into her lap, she explained, "I never felt like I acted better than anyone else. I mean, I was a prisoner there just like everyone else. But, apparently they thought I did." Claire inhaled deeply, "It was just easier to stay by myself."

Talking to Courtney was so easy; it had always been.

Courtney scooted closer and squeezed her friend's hand. "I'm sorry I couldn't do more for you while you were there," then in a quieter voice, "or, to keep you out of there."

"I really understand." Claire smiled at Courtney's sad blue eyes, "But you did do something. When your letters started to arrive, I can't tell you how much they meant to me!"

"I'm so glad. And I'm sure our entire correspondence went under the radar. Believe me, if Tony knew, Brent would've heard."

Fighting her emotions, Claire said, "I know it was a big risk. Thank you."

"So, you're convinced it wasn't Tony, the money, I mean?"

"Yes. Well, you helped convince me. You sent me a text saying how upset he was when he learned about my release. I mean, if he'd sent the money and letter to Jane, he'd have already known. I know it wasn't in the papers, which is just another of the amazing miracles, but I know Tony. If he'd spent $100,000, he would've followed up to learn if it paid off."

"I think you're right."

"And... when he called me, he said he'd just learned of my release. No, I don't think it was him."

"Any other ideas?" Courtney asked.

"No, not really, but whoever did it, took quite a risk. Not just with Tony, but also with Governor Bosley. That isn't all; Jane could've refused to file the petition. There were a lot of pieces of a puzzle that needed to fall into place." Claire sipped her wine and settled against the soft sofa cushions, "I don't know who my angel is or how it all worked; I'm just thankful it did."

"I can't believe Jane Allyson gave you the money. Was that *your* angel's* request?"

"I don't think so. I think it was supposed to be her payment for filing the petition. I tried to refuse the check, but she said it was a ridiculous amount of money for such a small amount of work. Apparently, the petition was complete except for her signature. All she did was sign and walk it to the governor's office." Claire took another drink. "I don't mean *all*-- obviously that's a lot. But, she told me to consider it *seed money* to start my new life and pay her an appropriate fee. I could hardly refuse. I really believed I had nothing."

Courtney's eyes glistened. "You did have something, didn't you?"

"I did." Claire answered slyly. "It was actually Emily's idea. I hadn't considered selling my jewelry and had no idea of its value."

"Do you miss it?"

"No! – Oh," Claire played with the rim of her wine glass, "I answered that too quickly. As you know, I haven't worn any of it for over a year. The rings were beautiful and when I received them, I loved them. Wedding rings are supposed to be a symbol of a feeling. Without the feeling, they're just metal and stones." A little more empathically, "I always disliked the journey necklace."

"Really? It was lovely and you wore it often."

"Yes, I did." Claire allowed the rim of her glass to loiter on her lips, less than a subtle hint she'd said all she was saying on the subject.

"And, the earrings?"

"They were beautiful too. Tony gave them to me for my birthday, right after that party we all attended. Remember, at Eli and MaryAnn's?"

Courtney knew, from the copy of the preliminary brief Brent obtained, what happened in California. She knew when Tony and Claire were alone on that trip he'd physically abused her. Claire didn't know she knew. Courtney planned to share that during this visit, however, now didn't feel right. "I remember the party. Afterwards, the two of you went to Yosemite, right?"

"Yes." Claire's expression lightened as her lips turned upward and her eyes began to sparkle. "I've considered buying myself some diamond studs. Everyone needs a nice pair, don't you think?"

Courtney smiled, seeing her friend's pride, discussing *her* ability to do as *she* pleased. "Well, yes! Everyone needs a nice pair of diamond studs!" Courtney agreed.

Courtney also talked about Tim and Sue. Their baby, Sean, just turned one! She showed Claire a picture on her phone from his first birthday party.

"I can't believe their son is actually one. I've missed so much."

"Honey," Courtney's voice reflected her look of concern, "there're some people who truly believe you tried to kill him."

Claire looked down into her glass. "I assumed."

"Just so you know, I'm not one."

"Brent?"

"No. He doesn't believe it either. Let's just say, we have a different perspective than most."

Claire reached out and grabbed Courtney's hand. Her green eyes glistened as tears teetering on the rims. "Thank you, for believing in me. I know I can't prove it. But just knowing there're people who believe me and support me; it means the world."

They cried and laughed. They chatted, laughed some more, and cried some more. When the sun rose they were both exhausted. Sleepily they stood at the railing and watched the dark sky fill with light as a red hue spilled across the Gulf of Mexico. Eventually, the red became orange, brightening the sky until the black became blue. They both agreed; sleep was in order.

So many memories of their friendship filled Claire's mind as she settled into the queen sized bed. Instantaneously, sleep overtook her.

Unbelievably, she didn't stir until after 1 PM. Looking at the clock, she couldn't believe the time. Walking into the empty living room she found a note:

> *Hi Honey – I'm at the pool. There's coffee in the pot. Before you come join me, please look at some papers on the kitchen table. I hoped it would be easier for you to read this without me looking over your shoulder. Brent accidently received this information via Marcus Evergreen. He never should've had it, read it, or shared it with me. There'd probably be stiff legal ramifications if it were discovered. Of course, Tony doesn't know we have it or read it. Those ramifications don't need to be said, we all know they'd be stiff. Please know we love you and believe every word. I hope you'll come down and talk to me when you're finished.*   *Love – Cort*

Although, only about seven yards from the living room to the kitchen, Claire's feet suddenly weighed a ton apiece; with each step, her goal seemed farther away. She could see the binder thick with pages. At one time, before she married Tony, he showed her the article written by Meredith Banks, and another time, he had the news release of Simon's death. Both of those experiences came rushing back. Claire wasn't sure what the binder held. Somehow, she knew, it wasn't good.

Sitting her mug of coffee and muffin on the table, she exhaled and opened the binder. Inside she read: *January 31, 2012, Paul Task, Attorney At Law - Preliminary brief - State of Iowa vs. Rawlings, Claire.* Claire thumbed through the pages, catching a word here and a phrase there. She didn't need to read it word for word, she'd spoken it. Hell -- she'd lived it. The account of her life with Tony, *the truth*, was right there in black and white. It wasn't all inclusive, that was even stated, but it was descriptive. From her abduction, to his abuse, his punishments, his controlling nature, her near death *accident*, his change of behavior, their marriage, his control, his domination... and the reason she drove away from the estate. At two thirty her cup was empty and the muffin was cold, stiff, and still wrapped in a shiny tin.

Claire stared at the open binder and wondered what to do, what to say. Other than outsiders, her attorneys and Dr. Warner, she hadn't discussed any of this with anyone. She felt a twinge of panic, *if Tony finds out that they know... Oh God! It's a direct violation of his rules.*

Leaving the binder open she went to her bedroom to put on her bathing suit. Claire realized *this was the information Courtney wanted to share-- in person. She really did know.* Claire remembered the cathartic feeling she experienced when divulging all of this to her attorneys. However, with Dr. Warner it was different. Claire felt ashamed, like it was somehow her fault; she allowed all these things to happen. Dr. Warner agreed, well -- in so many words. Claire allowed Tony to dominate her.

How could she face Courtney and look in her eyes, knowing she had allowed herself to be abused and had lied?

Claire meant to go to the pool. However, somewhere during the process of getting ready, she collapsed on her bed and released years of suppressed tears. They didn't stop. Unknowingly, she drifted to sleep wearing her new white bikini. Wakefulness came with the sensation of a warm soft hand rubbing her exposed back. She didn't turn around. Instead she kept her face buried in the damp soft pillow and choked out her apology, "I'm so sorry."

Claire expected compassion. Instead Courtney's voice was stern, "*You* are sorry?" Heavy emphasis on *you*, "Claire, please turn around." Slowly she did. Courtney looked at her puffy eyes and tear stained cheeks. "Girl – what in the hell do *you* have to be sorry for? It seems to me, the rest of us are the ones who should be sorry!"

It didn't make sense to Claire. She was the one who allowed Tony to abuse her. She was the one who lied to everyone, especially Courtney. How many times did Courtney ask Claire if everything was all right? And every time, she lied.

The tears resumed, "I lied to you. I lied to you -- many times. I let things happen."

"Honey, *everyone lets* thing happen around Anthony Rawlings. What were you supposed to do? Do you think if you'd stood up to him more, he'd have backed down?" Claire couldn't answer. She didn't want to discuss any of this. It made her head hurt. "Let me tell you something, it may not be physical -- like you endured -- but we're all victims of your ex-husband. Do you think for a minute we would've let you go to jail, much less to prison, if we weren't scared of what Tony might do?"

Claire stared at Courtney in disbelief, wiping her nose with the back of her hand, Claire asked, "What do you mean, scared?"

"I mean scared, like frightened. We're putting all of our cards on the table, right?" Claire nodded; Courtney continued, "We all know Tony has power – a lot of power. Brent isn't ready to retire, and there's no way he can walk away from Tony. Besides, most of our money is tied up in Rawlings Industries' stock, or it was. We never discussed a fear of physical retaliation, but Brent convinced me our lives and possibly those of our children would suffer unseen consequences if we came clean about this information."

"How long have you known?"

"Since before your divorce. The file was on a pen drive from Evergreen's office. Like my note said, it shouldn't have been there, and Brent shouldn't have read it."

Claire turned her head into the soft pillow and exhaled. Slowly, she sat and looked her friend in the eye. She truly was at a loss for words and completely uncomfortable with the mixture of emotions swirling inside her chest.

"Claire, I understand why you didn't tell me. I wish you would've. I had this feeling things were different than they appeared. Truthfully, I had no idea the enormity of the situation. I understand you couldn't say anything."

"If I would've, I wouldn't have been allowed to see you." A sob came from somewhere deep, buried under years of suppression. "I needed you."

The two women hugged like never before. After a time Courtney started to laugh, "Aren't you glad you came all this way, for all this fun?"

Claire looked into her honest blue eyes now reddened like her own and snickered, "At this moment, I'm not too sure."

"I am. I needed you to know what we know. I needed you to know we understand. And, if for some reason you feel responsible, or like you deserved something, anything that happened to you... you're sadly mistaken. I told you once; I loved and hated your husband. That's still probably true. He's capable of wonderful things. We just never knew the extent to which he's capable of terrible things."

Courtney continued, "Claire, you're a saint for loving him despite all of that. Please, *never* think you deserved any of it. No one should endure what that brief says you endured." Courtney shook her head, "The thing I keep thinking is -- I really believed he loved you. I believed you loved him too. As his friends, we worried about a woman wanting him for his money. I never got that feeling from you."

"I wish I could explain it." Claire replied, "Hell -- I wish I could explain it to myself. When I met him, I didn't know who he was. Even after he took me to his house, I didn't know who he was. Believe me, I hated him. I told him how much I hated him, multiple times. Maybe it was the isolation; I didn't have contact with anyone but him. Yet, overtime I did love him, or I thought I loved him. And, he *did* get better, a lot better." Claire smiled a sad smile. "I think it's true. Love and hate are very close emotions, both intense and consuming. Even after he left me in jail, and still today, I find myself struggling with those two emotions." Claire shook her head. "I know it doesn't make sense. It's just that when he was good, he could be *so* good. When he wasn't... It was just... there

102

was always so much stress and pressure." Claire thought about Brent. "I think *you* do understand. I think if anyone would, it would be Brent and you. I've seen that same stress on Brent's face."

Courtney nodded, "I'm glad you believe me. We wanted to help you. We weren't sure it would pay-off. Honey, it wasn't throwing away our money. It was more than worth it!"

Claire sat straight. Her mouth gaped with surprise. Finally words came from her lips, "Oh my god, it was you?" Courtney nodded again. "Of course, the petition was filled out. An attorney would know how to do that. Brent's an attorney." Claire's voice sounded shrill with amazement and gratitude. "Let me pay you back. I can now. I sold the jewelry."

"No. Consider it guilt money. We were so helpless, wanting to do anything to stop what was happening to you -- like you said, it was a risk -- a good risk that paid off."

Claire hugged her again. "So it's true, Brent does believe me."

"I said he did."

"Yes, I know you said... but he *really* does. It's just when he came to the prison..."

Courtney interrupted, "Tony warned him. He said the tapes from those visitors' rooms were available for a price. He told Brent the visit was strictly business."

"Did Tony ever watch the video?"

Courtney smiled, "I don't know. Brent hoped he would."

"Why?"

"Because, when Brent came home he was so impressed by you. He didn't know what to expect and didn't want to face you."

"He didn't have a choice, did he?"

"No, he didn't. Yet, afterwards he was glad he went. He talked about your strength, resilience, and determination. I don't know if you remember, but you told him to tell Tony to bring on the liable case, that you'd be glad to testify to a larger audience." Claire grinned and nodded, she'd said that. "Of course, Tony wouldn't tell Brent what warranted such a case, but Brent knew. He also knew – there was no way Tony would pursue it. It was some stupid mind game. Honestly, we don't know if it was meant to hurt you or Brent, but I can tell you, it inspired Brent."

"Inspired?" Claire asked.

"Yes, we knew before then we wanted to distance ourselves and Caleb from Rawlings Industries. Seeing your strength, being away from him – in prison no less -- has been a constant reminder to us to stay the course."

"I'm glad. I remember feeling bad for Brent when he left." Claire's eyes were drying. She couldn't believe she had this support – from Tony's *closest friends.*

The two ladies went to the pool and ate lunch. They lounged on chairs at the beach and sipped drinks. They walked along the shore and talked about everything. Claire even told Courtney about her mixed feelings regarding Tony. She hated what he did. Nevertheless, sometimes she'd remember good times and miss him too. Claire knew he wanted to see her and the idea terrified her. She wasn't afraid of a physical threat; she was doing everything she could do to avoid a repeat of that history. Honestly, it was *her own resolve* she questioned. If the charming, loving, friendly Tony approached her – she wasn't sure she could resist him.

Claire told Courtney about the dinner invitation. Surprisingly, Courtney didn't try to dissuade her. A few weeks ago a similar subject caused an argument with Amber. Claire reasoned; *Courtney knows Tony and truly understands.*

During the course of the four days Claire told Courtney all about Tony's box, his confession of sorts. She hadn't planned to divulge, but sharing felt too liberating. She explained why Tony came for her in the first place, all stemming from *her* grandfather's help convicting *his* grandfather for multiple white collar crimes. "It's like everyone connected to the scenario thirty years ago and their family has been made to pay, even Tony's parents."

"Do you think he hurt his own parents?"

"I did at first. Maybe it's just wishful thinking, but now I'm not sure. I think he had some influence over my parent's death or maybe it was coincidental?"

"I had no idea Rawlings wasn't his birth name. I wonder if Brent knows."

"I think Tony also had some influence with Simon Johnson's death. It's too coincidental, him dying after I saw him in Chicago."

Courtney shook her head. "I knew he was capable of a lot, but I can't believe how deep this all goes. He really sent you pictures showing he's been watching you for years before you ever met him?" Claire nodded. "What about Emily? If he's getting everyone related to your grandfather, wouldn't he do something to her too?"

"I think he did. I mean not personally. But by hurting me and John, he hurt Emily."

Courtney confirmed, Brent told her Tony was responsible for John's difficulties. "Is it done?" Courtney asked, "Is there anyone else he believes deserves to pay?"

"I don't know. I mean he seems to be after me again." Claire shrugged, "I don't know if he thinks I didn't suffer enough. Or, maybe he thinks I did. Perhaps, he believes his vendetta is over and I'll want to resume our relationship. Thankfully, Emily and I are the only descendants left of our grandfather."

"Well, Honey, only you can decide what to do." Smiling with blue eyes shining, Courtney continued. "Just remember, this time it'll be *your* decision." Then as an afterthought, "I guess be glad you don't have cousins."

"Yeah, I'd hate to think of anyone else enduring what I did."

"Now, tell me more about this Harry guy. He's kind of cute in the pictures I've seen in magazines."

Claire blushed, "He's just a friend. But you're right, he's kind of cute. I'd say his most endearing quality is he's nothing like Tony."

"So?"

"So, nothing, we're friends. He's Amber's brother and has been very helpful with rebuilding my life and researching Tony's past."

"Sure, I believe you."

Watching the waves flatten the sand, Claire confessed, "And... he might be an excellent kisser, but I can honestly say nothing more has happened."

"Does he make you smile?"

Allowing her grin to surface, Claire nodded.

"Do you live in fear of upsetting him?"

Claire shook her head.

"Honey, if you go to that dinner with Tony... will you do me a favor? Remember those two questions and your answers."

The lump in Claire's throat didn't allow her to verbally answer; she nodded. She'd remember.

*****

The rented Chrysler 200 rolled along the hot Texas pavement driving toward San Antonio. While music filled the car, Claire contemplated Courtney's confession. Never in a million years would Claire have suspected Brent and Courtney were her angels. Tony considered them his closest friends, yet Claire was driving north on 37 toward her hotel. If it were up to him, she'd still be locked away.

The days spent by the pool and on the beach gave Claire's skin a much needed dose of Vitamin D with a golden brown bonus. It had been so long since she'd enjoyed intense sunshine. The get-a-way strengthened her in so many ways-- mentally and physically.

Courtney left Corpus Christi earlier in the morning. As Claire looked at the clock, she thought, *she should be back to Iowa by now*. Claire wasn't scheduled to fly to San Francisco until tomorrow.

Around four thirty, Claire pulled into the parking garage adjacent to the Hotel Valencia Riverwalk, the suite was still hers for another twenty four hours. Obviously the housekeeping staff knew she'd been gone for most of the week, but she wasn't trying to fool the housekeepers.

Searching for the key to her suite, which was really a card, she stepped into the shiny golden elevator. The doors closed but the compartment didn't move. She remembered putting the card someplace *safe*, if only she could remember which compartment of her purse that was.

The elevator doors opened again and a tall, middle-aged, white haired gentleman entered. Claire smiled politely as she dug into another zipped compartment within her cavernous Gucci handbag.

He showed a reserved smile and acknowledged Claire with a nod. Then he inserted his card and pushed eleven. She exhaled as she found the key, "Here it is." Her voice was barely a whisper, not intended for anyone but herself.

The man stepped to the side exposing the control panel, "I'm sorry. Am I in your way?"

"No, actually you've already accessed my floor."

He looked at the small suitcase near Claire's feet. "You'll enjoy this hotel, the staff is wonderful."

"Thank you, I've been here for a few days." Realizing the suitcase, "I just had a few things in my car I needed to retrieve."

She didn't know why she was lying. Nevertheless, she'd rehearsed her story and was glad it sounded slightly plausible.

"Well, enjoy the rest of your stay." The elevator stopped, and the doors opened. He politely held the door allowing her to exit.

She smiled, "Thank you, you too."

Claire walked toward the right, while the gentleman walked to the left. Unlocking her door, she quickly entered the sunlit suite. As she turned to bolt the lock she mindlessly peered through the peep hole. Directly across the hall from her room she saw the same gentleman opening a door. *That's odd, why'd he walk the other way if his room was there?* She contemplated. *He looks familiar. Maybe I saw him when I originally checked in? Or, maybe I'm just paranoid!*

Within the bedroom, upon the bedside stand, was the only item she'd left at the hotel, one of her telephones, her *Tony* phone. She left it *on* and plugged in.

Not hearing from him in four days was refreshing. Allowing the signals from *this* phone to be sent from *this* location was priceless. That bit of deception plus a lengthy GPS erasing procedure were Harry's idea. His past police experience made him suspicious. That same experience gave him invaluable knowledge. Claire couldn't have begun to erase the GPS permanently, without his directions. Claire would do anything, no matter how laboring, to protect Courtney.

She opened the French doors to her balcony and inhaled the warm spring air. The beautiful wrought-iron railing added to the French ambiance. Looking down she watched the people stories below on the famous Riverwalk. It was beautiful, filled with flowing water, flowers, people, and giant cypress trees. A faint breeze blew the curtains of the open doors as she relaxed upon her king sized bed and checked the phone. There were seven missed calls and three text messages. Claire closed the phone. The get-a-way was too fresh in her mind, too many good memories. Her mood was too high; she would read the messages later.

Next, she checked in with Emily, her daily *I'M FINE* text. Today she added, *I'M BACK IN SAN ANTONIO. MY FLIGHT IS TOMORROW ABOUT NOON FOR SAN FRAN. CALL IF YOU CAN. LOVE YA!*

With Emily's husband John, back in Indiana, the two sisters no longer spoke every day. However, they made a point to *check in* daily. Claire spoke to John a few times since his prison release. At first it was even more uncomfortable than her first talks with Emily. Thinking about her time with Courtney, Claire decided they needed some face-to-face time. It was much better than phone calls.

She also sent text messages to Amber and Harry informing them of her location. Knowing there were people who cared and worried about her, added to Claire's euphoria. Closing her eyes she debated napping. The distinctive *Emily phone's* ring stopped her descent into the drowsy abyss. Eyes still closed, she reached for the small black cellphone. "Hi."

"Hi, Claire, I hope you don't mind me calling." The voice caught her off guard, her eyes opened wide. Napping disappeared from her radar. She hadn't heard this voice since last July at Iowa's Woman's Penitentiary.

"Brent?"

"Yes." She held her breath, unsure what to say. Brent continued. "Courtney's home safe."

Claire's mind spun. She wanted to trust him; after all, according to Courtney he was also responsible for her freedom and was too a victim of Tony. Claire knew that. She'd witnessed their interaction. "I'm glad." She swallowed and continued, "Brent ... thank you."

"Please don't thank me. I've done much more to hurt you, than help you."

She heard the anguish in his voice. "Just tell me, of all the things you've done, which ones did *you* want to do?"

"I wanted to help you. I never wanted to hurt you, even before I read the preliminary brief. It's just that sometimes I had no..."

Claire stopped him, "I understand." She inhaled and continued, "You know that though -- don't you?"

"I do. And, we understand you."

Her entire body filled with warmth. She'd known this man for less than three years. Her ex-husband claimed him as his best friend, and he'd endured much of the same domination as Claire. She couldn't suppress her smile as tears trickled down her cheeks. "I offered to pay Courtney back. I can now."

"She told me. I agree with her. Please, keep your money. Watching and listening to Tony's response when he learned of your unorthodox release, seeing him unable to control or influence the situation, more than made it worth every penny."

"If there is anything I can do for either of you..."

"Actually, there is..." The two continued their conversation for almost an hour. Brent wanted to know all about Tony's box. The information fascinated him. He also asked about the information she'd learned from their detective work. Brent vowed to do what he could from his end. He also explained the things he'd done to hurt Claire: the divorce with no financial compensation, his attitude when he visited her in prison, hiring a private detective to find her, and supporting Tony along the way.

Claire reassured Brent, she understood. He didn't have a choice and she appreciated his current clandestine support. Fearfully, Claire asked Brent a question she'd contemplated of and on again for a while, "Is Jane

Allyson all right? I mean, has Tony done anything to her?" Claire's heart skipped a beat as her question met silence.

Finally, he answered, "She is, for now."

"Can you please elaborate?"

"When we left her office, Tony voiced his displeasure." Claire nodded, although Brent couldn't possibly see her from Iowa. He went on, "I've tried on numerous occasions to remind him, if something would suddenly happen to her up-and-coming career, immediately following your petition for pardon, it would appear suspicious."

Claire smiled; Brent knew the game. Tony's kryptonite was indeed *appearance*. Claire replied, "I don't want her to pay because she helped me."

"I put her in that position. I promise I've done all I can to protect her." Brent replied, then he chuckled. "She knew what she was doing when she did it. That's why I chose her. She is one tough lady and a great attorney! You should've heard her when we went to her office."

"I bet. She's the only one, in a room full of males, who stood up to Tony, at the jail in Iowa."

"Other than you."

Claire stammered, "I... me... I didn't stand up to him. I never did."

"That isn't true. You never would've survived if he didn't consider you a challenge. He truly thought you'd take the insanity plea."

"Well, the fact I didn't, probably confirms, I am insane."

Brent laughed. "That's why you and Courtney get along so well."

He went on to tell her about Phillip Roach, the private detective who's been watching her for the last month, sending photos and information to Tony. Brent wasn't privy to all the information, but Tony's attitude regarding Claire seemed to be changing. Brent assessed, he's no longer upset; *obsessed* would be a better word.

Brent assured Claire she'd successfully lost the private detective during the last week. "If Tony knew you and Cort were together I would have heard. I even called Mr. Roach once to confirm my theory. He was rather allusive about the past four days and promised more information in the future." Claire heard the smile in Brent's voice, "It's all making Tony a little crazy."

"Have you met this Phillip Roach? What does he look like?" Claire asked.

The clock read 7:23 PM. Originally, Claire planned a quiet evening with room service. Her TV had an attached gaming system, and she'd contemplated practicing her skills in anticipation of another gaming session with Harry. However, finishing her make-up, stepping into the Marc Jacobs white silk sundress, and fastening her Prada sandals, she mentally reviewed her new plan.

'Charm' - which means the power to affect work without employing brute force, is indispensable to women. Charm is a woman's strength just as strength is a man's charm.
- Henry Ellis

Chapter 13

The final slam of the cottage door muffled Sophia's sigh. On the other side of the wooden barrier was their home, life, and private haven. With a turn of the bolt and the closing of heavy shutters on creaky hinges, she'd successfully closed it tight --storing everything away for a season.

Sophia's mind swirled with memories of their first home: late nights slipping out of bed, making her way upstairs to her studio, while Derek slept -- light brown hair disheveled, mouth slightly open. She relished the security of knowing when sleepiness overtook her creativity; she could crawl back into their bed and be enveloped by his warmth. Leaning against the door, she remembered the first time Derek made a fire in their fireplace but forgot to open the flue. Once the smoke cleared, they laughed until they cried. And the way the golden sunshine streamed into her studio in the late morning. It was her favorite time to paint; the colors looked so real. These recollections made her smile despite her heavy heart.

Begrudgingly, she allowed herself a window of self-pity. That being said, as soon as she was once again face-to-face with her husband, she vowed to keep her true feelings hidden. After all, this was Derek's big break. Sophia wanted to be the supportive wife. She kept telling herself, *if the roles were reversed, he'd support me.*

Undoubtedly, the uncertainty added to her unease. They didn't know when they'd be back to Provincetown or who'd be returning. It could be both of them or only Sophia. It all depended on Shedis-tics.

Since graduating high school, Sophia controlled her life. Having the people of Shedis-tics dictate her living arrangements, travel plans, and everything else, made her anxious. Yes, she'd submitted to the occasional investor, agreed to show her work, or attended a private wine-and-dine session; but, all at her discretion. She'd always had the option to say *no.*

Sophia knew marriage meant collaboration, a partnership. She'd watched her parents successfully share a similar arrangement her entire life. When she said *I do*, Sophia willingly accepted her role as half of a whole. However, now she questioned her percentage. Was she in fact half? Or was she less? Was Derek still half? Or was he more? Perhaps Shedis-tics was now part of the equation?

Originally his new job was scheduled to begin May 1st. Nevertheless, they called him out to Santa Clara only two days after her father's accident, over four weeks early.

Little did Sophia realize, when Derek said he couldn't take more than two nights in her childhood bedroom, he'd meant it literally. Truthfully, Derek hadn't known either. As he explained, when the company president calls and invites you to meet with parent company executives, you don't say, *No Thank you*.

Lingering on the stoop of their cottage, she looked toward the Harbor, inhaled the salt air, and listened to the soft din of the sea. The sound of the surf created a continual soundtrack for life in Provincetown. While something she rarely thought about, she knew she'd miss it terribly.

Yesterday, she closed her studio on Commercial Street. The sign in the window read: *Closed for an Undetermined Amount of Time*. The neighboring businesses promised to keep a watchful eye on everything. Sophia knew nothing would physically happen to her personal slice of cramped heaven. It was the emotional toll that concerned her.

On her way to the airport, Sophia took a detour and found herself at the shore enjoying the calm water rippling beneath the crystal clear blue sky. Tears streaked her cheeks as she bid adieu to Provincetown Harbor. Through her blurred vision she saw the Cape across the sea. Sophia absorbed the scene, savoring it -- preserving it. If she kept it safely sealed within the recesses of her mind, it would never completely be gone. In times of need, she'd will it forward, out of the depths of her memories, and into her thoughts.

Recognizing the inevitable, she made her way to the small Provincetown airport. From there she'd fly to Boston. In Boston she had tickets for a first class flight to San Jose, the closest airport to Santa Clara.

Even with a short layover in Denver, she anticipated feeling Derek's strong arms by four o'clock, Pacific Time. When she did, she planned to melt into his embrace and show him why they should never be apart again. Then, she reasoned, the world would once again be right.

*****

When the elevator doors opened Phillip just about lost it! She entered almost sixty seconds earlier and should have been to her floor, not still within the golden mirrored cubical. Practicing his covert skills, Phil Roach assumed a calm passive persona and spoke casually to his number one assignment, Claire Nichols. This hadn't been his plan.

110

Nevertheless, now that they'd conversed and she hadn't recognized him, she might be his lifesaver.

Anthony Rawlings was suspicious and becoming increasingly untrusting. Phil did a good job for a few days giving generic reports and letting Mr. Rawlings assume his ex-wife was vacationing alone in San Antonio. However, the lack of specifics and pictures were beginning to spark too many questions.

The per diem and generous expense account made it difficult for Phillip Roach to confess he'd *lost* his assignment. Claire Nichols flew to San Antonio with Phil on the same flight. He knew of her hotel reservation and followed her to the Hotel Valencia. It was late; he assumed she was sleeping safely within her room until the next day. However, when he returned to the Riverwalk later the same night, Ms. Nichols was AWOL. Her car was gone, she was gone, and her cell phone continued to send signals from her suite. Phil panicked knowing he'd been duped!

He also knew Claire's reservations at the Hotel Valencia extended until Sunday morning. Having no idea where to look, he continued his surveillance of the hotel on the famous Riverwalk. When he saw Ms. Nichols enter the lobby Saturday afternoon, it took all of his self-control to not hug her. Thank God she was alive and safe – if something had happened to her in a place he hadn't reported her being. Phil didn't even want to consider the consequences. It didn't matter; she was all right.

She wasn't just all right. She was relaxed, tan, and happy. He was sure she'd been with a man, but who? He'd confirmed Harrison Baldwin's presence in Palo Alto during the last four days. There was no doubt Mr. Rawlings would want answers. Phil's exuberance at her presence could be blamed for the unplanned meeting in the elevator. However, as he reviewed the encounter, he assured himself *no harm no foul!*

Currently, she was settled into her room, presumably for the night. Phil had watched her for almost three weeks. She wasn't the wild and crazy kind. Room service was a 99.9% assured outcome. Rarely was Phillip Roach wrong.

The electronic sensor startled him back to reality. It was a non-conspicuous devise attached to her suite door. As long as the door remained closed the devise remained silent. When the door opened and separated the connection, an alarm sounded in his room. Immediately, Phil jumped to the peep hole, expecting to see a waiter delivering room service.

Instead, stepping from her suite, dressed to *kill* was Claire Nichols. *No wonder Mr. Rawlings was so interested in this women, she's frig'n hot!* Phil thought as he watched the petite frame in the flowing white sundress and high heels. Although his view was somewhat distorted due to the domed glass peep hole, the woman he saw looked more like the woman in the pictures. She looked like Mrs. Rawlings.

Phil grabbed his sport coat, combed back his hair and splashed his face with water. 57 seconds after Claire left her room, Phil double stepped it down the stairs to the lobby, only eleven floors down.

The firm soles of his shoes hit the marble floor of the main lobby. Phil inhaled and exhaled, regulating his breathing as he walked toward the large glass entry. Being Saturday night, the hotel as well as Riverwalk bustled with people, most paired and appropriately adorned for evening revelries. It was after all, a five star establishment. The magnitude of private conversations created a dim drone as Phil scanned the open foyer. The ceiling towered many stories above, the enormous fireplace blazed, and the tile floor echoed with the clicks of stiletto heels. An occasional whiff of food cooking in the distance reminded Phil that Citrus, the hotel's finer restaurant, was nearby.

His tenacity was rewarded as Phil passed the glistening, metal, beaded, chain curtain separating the ultra-sleek Vbar from the Hotel Valencia. Just beyond the semi translucent drape, he saw the beautiful outline of Claire Nichols. Her white dress shone like a beacon within the dimly lit tavern.

Phil followed the piano music and entered the posh lounge. The low lights, red carpet, and intimate groupings, created a chic romantic atmosphere. He watched from afar as her face, illuminated by a flickering red candle, smiled and spoke to the attentive waiter. Using his phone he casually snapped a few photos. Walking nonchalantly through the busy lounge Phil positioned himself on a leather stool at the shiny black bar. Each time he raised his head Ms. Nichols sat directly in his field of vision. He ordered a Blue Moon and waited.

Fifteen minutes passed; no one joined his assignment. She didn't seem worried, wasn't fidgeting with her phone; yet, her attire screamed *date*. He waited, but no one joined her, perhaps no one was coming. Phil contemplated the woman he'd spent the last three weeks getting to know. Many women sitting alone in a bar would be self-conscious. Ms. Nichols looked completely content, composed, and confident. She sipped a glass of red wine and gazed around the room. Suddenly, their eyes met. Phil fought the urge to look away. He reminded himself, they'd met on the elevator. His mind wheeled as she smiled and tipped her glass his direction. *Could this be an invitation? Perhaps if I talk to her, maybe I can learn where she's been?*

Phil smiled and raised his mug in response. The bartender broke their trance, "Sir, would you like another beer?"

Phil became aware of his near empty mug. Maybe the stress of the last four days had gotten to him. "Yes. And could you please send the lovely lady in the white dress another glass of wine, with my compliments."

"Certainly, sir."

He covertly watched as the waiter gallantly delivered the wine to her table. He couldn't hear their conversation but read her body language: surprised, pleased, and appreciative. When she turned toward him, she lifted the new goblet and mouthed *thank you*. Phil bowed his head. When he looked up, her gaze was no longer his. Had he expected an invitation? Fifteen more minutes, she remained alone. Phil puffed his chest, exhaled, and eased himself from the tall leather stool.

Lost in thoughts she didn't acknowledge him until he was directly in front of her. "Thank you, for the wine." If he'd startled her, there was no reflection in her voice. He assessed, *she is either considerably calm or an ice princess*. Her vitality penetrated the calm veneer. Energy sparkled in her emerald eyes. Phil became consumed by the fire he observed in those amazing eyes. An *ice princess* would never be able to conceal that kind of heat. She'd surely melt.

"You're welcome." He remained standing while she lounged gracefully in the soft high backed chair.

"I suppose I should've been the one to buy you a drink."

He smiled, "And why would that be?"

"Well, you're the gentleman who saved me from remaining within the confines of the elevator, forever."

"I do believe you would've rescued yourself. After all, didn't you find your key as we began to ascend?"

Claire smiled acknowledging his affability. "Thank you, again."

Phil gestured toward the empty chair in Ms. Nichols' grouping. "Would you mind if I sat and joined you for a while?"

Abashed, "Oh, of course, I'm sorry I didn't offer sooner. Please, help yourself."

Phil lowered himself onto the plush cushion and pursued their conversation. "Hello, I'm Phil." He extended his right hand.

Accepting his hand Claire responded, "Hello, my name is Claire."

He couldn't help notice how her green eyes glistened in the candle light. If only he could take her picture now. It would make Mr. Rawlings forget the absence of information during the last four days. "I couldn't help notice your tan. Did you get that here at the pool?"

"Texas sun is quite intense."

"I've been here since Tuesday. I find it hard to believe I've not seen you during the last four days..." He continued to fish for information. Unfortunately, Ms. Nichols stayed true to her story. She'd been here at the Hotel Valencia for the last four days enjoying the local sights including the Alamo and a boat ride on the river. It was a well-deserved retreat which included sleeping late, bedding early, and the completion of two novels. They'd been talking and laughing for about thirty minutes when Claire received a text message.

"I apologize, this is rude. It's just that I'm expecting some very important information."

"Please, go ahead and check your phone." Phil wondered if he called the number he'd given to Mr. Rawlings if the phone in her hand would ring. He doubted it. The glow in her eyes and the obvious smile indicated her satisfaction with the information in the text.

Still holding her phone, Claire took her wine goblet and slowly sipped the red liquid. Setting the glass upon the small table she looked directly into his eyes. "Phil?"

"Yes?"

"I believe given the circumstances, I'd feel more comfortable addressing you as Mr. Roach."

His back straightened. He hadn't told her his last name. "Excuse me?"

"Yes, Mr. Roach," she paused for effect. "I mean, I don't really know you, not as well as you know me -- since you've been following me for the last month." She allowed her lips to linger upon the glass's rim teasing the liquid. Her eyes stayed on his.

He contemplated his options: lie, act ignorant, or come clean. "I'm not sure what you're talking..."

"Let's cut to the chase Mr. Roach. You were hired by my ex-husband to keep tabs on me. You've done your job quite well, that is until you lost me last Monday. Now, the way I figure it, you have two choices: be honest with Mr. Rawlings, tell him you don't know where I was, or lie and give him just enough information to keep him pacified?" She sat the glass down. "How am I doing?"

"I assure you, I don't know..."

"Given your inability to be honest with me – I'd assume you chose deception with your employer as well."

"Ms. Nichols, I'm not sure how you've reached your conclusions."

"For starters, I never offered you my last name." She waited, he remained silent. Claire continued, "I decided to confront you tonight -- or should I say to have you confront me – for this discussion. Mr. Roach, I do not wish my where-a-bouts for the last four days to be known. Let's both say I've been here in San Antonio alone, and you'll confirm that, as the truth."

"Ms. Nichols, tell me why I would possibly agree to this?"

Her broadening smile made her sun kissed cheeks rise. Without saying a word, Phil knew she had a plan. "Let me show you the text I just received. Actually it's a multi-media attachment." Claire extended her hand, with her iPhone angled for his maximum viewing pleasure.

Phil looked down onto the small screen and saw a picture of him standing near her table. She brushed the screen and another photo appeared; him sitting across the small table from her. She brushed the screen again; they were leaning toward one another across the small void.

"I don't understand," he confessed.

"Come now, Mr. Roach. You infringe upon people's privacy for a living. That information is often used in less than scrupulous ways. Surely you recognize the same being done to you." She waited; he remained silent. "You haven't divulged the truth to Mr. Rawlings over the last four days. He's suspicious and asking questions. I'd be glad to forward these pictures to the press. They do seem to enjoy writing about me. Or, perhaps I could send them directly to my ex-husband with information regarding our secret rendezvous."

His mind spun. *Shit! This isn't happening.* "Why would you do that?"

"To get you fired Mr. Roach. I don't appreciate having a shadow everywhere I go."

"I'd deny everything; explain that I was only talking to you for information."

"That sounds plausible. However, I presume you were instructed to keep me in sight, not to make contact."

She was right. That was his instruction. He bowed to her manipulation. "What do you want me to do?"

"I want you to report exactly what I told you. I've spent the last four days relaxing in sunny San Antonio and enjoying the sights."

"Why haven't I sent photos?"

"You were having problems with your computer, or your SD Card, or your camera... I don't care. Tomorrow I'll gladly don different clothes and allow multiple staged photos... adjust the date on your camera, and your story will be complete."

"What's in this for me?"

Claire stood, "Would you like to join me on the terrace?"

Phil stood. They slowly stepped through the open French doors onto the crowded stone terrace illuminated by large lit torches. The spring air blew warm against their faces, and their attention moved to the magnificent view. San Antonio was before them. Below, the Riverwalk and cypress trees faded into shadows. In front of them, the buildings beamed with artificially induced colorful hues accentuating the wondrous architectural structures. Claire continued their conversation. "It's a beautiful city. I think it would be nice to spend four days here."

Her Cheshire grin infuriated Phil, he repeated, "You haven't answered my question. Why would I agree to your plan? What's in it for me?"

She responded ever so coyly, Phil thought he heard the faintest evidence of a southern drawl. He'd read she lived in Atlanta for a few years. "That should be painfully obvious, Mr. Roach." The word *painfully* stretched for four or five syllables. "For starters you get to keep your job."

Phil considered her threat. If she followed through and sent the compromising photos to Mr. Rawlings or the press, he would undoubtedly loose his assignment. "For starters? Are you insinuating there's another benefit... to me?"

"I'll allow you to ponder the possibilities." She lifted the bulbous goblet to her lips intentionally savoring the rich dry liquid. "My ex-husband is a powerful man. I do not believe he would take kindly to you *moving in* on me, your *assignment*. I'm not saying that to imply a mutual affection. Rather your mere presence indicates his sense of proprietorship. Not only will these photos imply a relationship between the two of us, but your recent inability to confess your short comings in the area of *trailing* will support the claim." Claire gazed out over the

Riverwalk. "Mr. Roach, let me be the first to warn you. Lying to Mr. Rawlings is not recommended. That said -- getting caught lying is even worse. My plan will have mutual support and after tomorrow's photo shoot, substantiating evidence."

"What are you trying to hide?"

Claire finished her wine and sat the glass on a nearby tray. "My plane leaves before one tomorrow afternoon. Of course, you know that, don't you?" Phil smiled and she continued, "I'd like your decision regarding my proposal. I need to plan my wardrobe for your photos."

Phil stood at least six inches taller than Ms. Nichols. He glanced at her feet. The golden sandals had tall heels. He wasn't sure of how tall but wondered why women chose to walk in such uncomfortable shoes. As his eyes scanned upward settling on her intense emerald eyes, he fought the new feelings he had for Claire Nichols. Contempt and respect were currently contending for first place. How could this petite polished woman so easily reduce him to her accomplice? He leaned down to lower his voice. "For such a beautiful woman who appears deceivingly meek," She turned toward him, stupid grin still intact. "You really are a bitch."

"Thank you, Mr. Roach." She extended her right hand. After only a moment's hesitation, he accepted. "I've had a marvelous teacher. I believe we have a deal, am I correct?"

"Yes, Ms. Nichols, we have a deal. I certainly hope you've enjoyed your relaxing stay in San Antonio."

"Thank you, I have. Oh, Mr. Roach. If you're considering tampering with the GPS in my rental car, let me save you the trouble. The data's been permanently deleted. Shall we begin tomorrow with breakfast, let's say 7:30?"

Phillip thought how helpful that information would have been earlier this evening, before he spent forty five minutes trying to extract recent destinations from the built-in Global Positioning System within her Chrysler 200. There was no question in his mind – he'd seriously underestimated this woman. He wondered if he were the only person to make that mistake. He truly doubted it. "I'll be lurking in the shadows at 7:30. Forgive me; I don't want to be included in future photos."

"Then we've never met." Claire turned to leave then glanced back, "Until tomorrow."

He nodded and watched her walk away. Her posture exuded confidence, straight spine and slightly raised chin. The backless dress exposed her feminine lean body. A faint white line from a slender bathing suit strap was visible across her tanned back. Below the bare skin, covered with the soft white material was one of the most perfect round behinds he'd ever seen. Watching it sway with just the perfect amount of sultry yet aristocratic movement, he concluded: *she does a fine job walking in those shoes. A clandestine four days with her in this five star hotel wouldn't be a bad tour. Hell, it might even be worth losing his job.*

The body of Mr. Roach's email was short and simple:

Mr. Rawlings, I apologize for the inconvenience and delay. My laptop decided to reject the SD card from my camera. I'm glad to say the kinks have been resolved. As you will see, I have multiple photos of Ms. Nichols from throughout her four day holiday. I honestly expected to see her with someone. However, it seems this was truly a four day get-a-way meant only for her personal rest and revitalization.

I have a return ticket on her plane. We should arrive in San Francisco at approximately 5 PM PST, 7 PM CST. I'll be available by telephone after that, if you need to reach me. Again, I'll remain dedicated to this assignment until I learn otherwise. Thank you, Phillip Roach

Tony clicked the attachment. A parade of pictures: Claire eating breakfast, lounging at the pool, at dinner, in a bar... After a fast pass through all fourteen photos, Tony went through them again, slowly digesting the contents.

He wondered about San Antonio. *Why? Why would she go there? It didn't make sense. But, then again why not? She'd always enjoyed warm weather and sunshine.*

A man growing old becomes a child again.
– Sophocles

Chapter 14

-1984-

Marie combed Ms. Sharron's thinning hair and talked endlessly about nothing. Mrs. Sharron Rawls enjoyed hearing her talk. When Marie would momentarily pause, to collect her thoughts or take a breath, Ms. Sharron would gently tap her arm, indicating for her to continue. Marie wondered if the sweet elderly lady understood the words being said, or if she just liked the sound of her voice. Heaven knows, even with the large staff, the enormous house could be incredibly quiet and lonely. There were times Ms. Sharron would allow the sounds to be the radio or the television, but without a doubt, she preferred voices. When Marie spoke, Ms. Sharron's breathing would regulate and her expression would calm.

It would seem that after a year and a half, Marie would have run out of things to say, but she hadn't. She could ramble at length about nothing. Truthfully, she hadn't planned on staying with the Rawls for this long. She, of course, never saw herself as a nurse maid. Yet, given her circumstances, this job was a god send. And now, barely twenty–three years old, she feared it would end too soon. After all, Ms. Sharron was barely a shell of who she'd been when Marie began.

In the beginning, it was sad to see the way she struggled for words and their meaning. Nevertheless, as Marie spent day and night by her side, she found humor in the most unlikely places. Surprisingly, Ms. Sharron found humor too. This shared bond and most absurd witty view of an unfortunate reality, bound these women despite their drastic differences. The rest of the family was too serious. Especially Mr. Samuel Rawls, Ms. Sharron's son. Marie shuttered to think how he would react if he knew the way they laughed at some of her mishaps.

Marie never had formal caregiving training. Then again, is someone formally trained to *care?* Wasn't it as simple as being observant to needs and fulfilling them? If Ms. Sharron looked toward her cup, she needed a drink. If she fidgeted in her bed or seat, she needed to get up and move. It wasn't rocket science, yet other than Mrs. Amanda Rawls, whose presence for some reason agitated Ms. Sharron, the men in this family were hopelessly incapable. Even when they tried, they were often too self-absorbed to notice the slight clues Ms. Sharron put forth.

Marie's duties transformed as Ms. Sharron's disease progressed. In the beginning, Ms. Sharron tried diligently to maintain certain responsibilities. Being that she always oversaw the household staff, she felt it necessary to maintain that assignment and appear competent to her husband. After all, he ran a million dollar business. With tears in her eyes, she explained – over and over, it was her duty to be sure *his* home ran efficiently. Marie caught-on quickly to the roles of the different employees. She helped Ms. Sharron not only monitor job performance, but payroll. Ms. Sharron didn't write checks, but she compiled the information for Mr. Rawls' accounting staff; Marie made sure Ms. Sharron's figures were correct. Eventually, Mrs. Amanda Rawls took over the responsibility. In actuality, it happened before Ms. Sharron became aware. Ms. Sharron believed she and Marie were still in charge, but they weren't. In time, she forgot about the staff and household responsibilities. After all, in her mind she wasn't the wife of a tycoon, but of a handsome young soldier.

Mr. Nathaniel Rawls spent a lot of time with his wife. It broke Marie's heart, to see the look in his eyes as he attempted to make conversation. For the most part, Ms. Sharron was beyond speech. However, if her eyes saw the real world, which rarely occurred, they lit-up when she saw her husband or grandson. Marie learned early that Anton looked remarkably similar to Nathaniel as a young man.

When she was more lucid, Ms. Sharron enjoyed passing the hours looking through old photo albums. Marie learned a great deal about the Rawls' family history from those albums.

Marie also researched dementia and Alzheimer's disease and learned recalling memories from the ancient past was somehow easier than recent memories. That inability to recall recent events aided Marie's monotonous dialogues. It wasn't like she needed to talk about new things every day or every hour. Ms. Sharron likes the sound; content was unimportant.

There were only so many stories a twenty-three year old could tell. At first she talked about books and movies. For someone so young, her mature interests made good stories. She enjoyed foreign films and biographies. Marie found learning about people and why they did what they did, fascinating. Sometimes instead of telling stories, Marie would read aloud. The mansion had a large library. Marie could find book after book that filled her interests and needs. With time, she also talked about her past. It wasn't like it mattered. Ms. Sharron couldn't remember or repeat her sordid story.

The Rawls home was like nothing she'd ever seen, at least not in real life. When she applied for the position, she had no idea of the opulent

119

lifestyle she would enter. And still, behind the gated drive, inside the stately walls, and amongst the luxurious furnishings, they were still just people. It took her a while to realize; but once she did, it made everything less awkward.

Even the great intimidating Nathaniel Rawls was in reality a man, as they say: who puts his pants on one leg at a time. Perhaps it's the hours they've spent at Ms. Sharron's side, but Marie actually enjoyed his company. And if she wasn't imagining things, he appeared to enjoy hers. To allow Ms. Sharron the gift of their voices, they discussed unlimited subjects. At first it was superficial, he didn't seem open to anything else, and Marie was too hurt by her own family to open up with another one. Then with time, they'd comment on books or movies or news. Marie didn't know the protocol for a job such as hers, and without a doubt, she worked too well with Ms. Sharron for Nathaniel to call her out on her shortcomings.

The end result was a twenty-three-year-old woman who'd argue her points and opinions with a sixty plus year old CEO. She didn't realize this was wrong. After all, he brought up the conversations, why wouldn't she answer honestly.

She spent so much time sequestered with Ms. Sharron she didn't know she was the only one who spoke to Mr. Nathaniel Rawls with such candor. The realization suddenly became apparent at a family dinner. Anton was home from Columbia University, and the mission was to appear as a family united. Conversely, Marie felt tension bubbling from every pore and rippling through the air, resulting in an undercurrent which swallowed everyone's words and happiness.

Marie knew there were issues at Rawls Corporation. Sometime during their long conversations Nathanial spoke about decisions and risk taking. Marie increasingly admired Mr. Nathaniel's business sense.

That dinner was a wake-up call. She hadn't noticed the undercurrent in the beginning of her employment; there was too much to take in. But, this perfect family suffered from serious dysfunction.

Marie understood Alzheimer's as a sad, degenerative disease. She also wondered if on some level Ms. Sharron wasn't better off in her own world. The toxic quality of the one around her could cause anyone the desire to escape.

She also understood why Ms. Sharron saw the world as it had been, not as it was. The man who sat by her side, conversed with Marie, and religiously kissed his wife each morning and evening wasn't the same man who presided over the family meal. What Marie didn't understand, was why he wouldn't share his caring side with the rest of his family.

As Ms. Sharron weakened, she no longer made it to the family dining room. Instead her meals were eaten in her suite. At first they were served on a small dining table within the large suite. With time, her eating became less regular. Many times, physical feeding was required. For some reason, she'd only accept this action from Marie or Nathaniel.

The other members of the family faithfully visited every day. Well, Samuel and Amanda did; Anton would when he was home. Marie didn't blame the young man for staying away. Actually, she understood the need to distance oneself from certain people. And, while Sharron's son and daughter-in-law were kind to her, they both treated Marie with a kind of superior disregard. Perhaps it was because of Ms. Sharron's affinity for her. Marie wasn't sure what she'd done to warrant their acrimony.

Attached to Mrs. Rawls large suite was a smaller one, where Marie resided. The job also included generous pay. However, with no definition of hours, she rarely had time to spend her new found wealth. Besides, she had all her needs met: a place to live and food to eat. With time, Nathaniel offered to purchase clothing. Marie declined. She had plenty of money in her account and didn't want to take advantage.

One evening, following her refusal of his generosity, she entered her closet to a complete new wardrobe. That incident taught Marie the tenacity of Mr. Rawls' resolve. If he wanted to do a kindness, he wouldn't be stopped. Later she would learn the opposite was also true. If he had a score to even... there would be no holds barred.

Anyone can hide. Facing up to things, working through them,
that's what makes you strong.
— Sarah Dessen

Chapter 15

The water wasn't colder or clearer in first class, nonetheless, it was refreshing. Claire thought about Phillip Roach sitting somewhere behind her, in economy. She'd seen him at the airport. The uneasy way he turned away, as she inclined her head in his direction, made her smile. Having Courtney and Brent's support filled Claire with more resolve than she could imagine. The feeling of invincibility wouldn't last forever, but she'd savor it for the time-being.

With her new found strength, Claire forced herself to concentrate on the stack of boxes in her closet. She should have immediately sent them back to Neiman Marcus. She should have called Tony, and said, "Thank you, but I'm busy." Unfortunately, Claire didn't do any of those things. Now, she had three days to prepare for a dinner with Anthony Rawlings.

Peering around the first class cabin, she took in the leather seats and heard the hushed voices, barely audible above the drone of the engines. Laying her head against the seat, she wondered how many of the women around her would consider an invitation from the great Anthony Rawlings an honor. Amused by the thought, she reminisced about a time when she didn't know the name Anthony Rawlings. Unfortunately, she couldn't allow the memory to linger. Claire knew his name, both current and birth. And most importantly, she knew she'd allowed too much time to pass, to cancel their *date*. Now, she needed to contrive a plan to control the evening.

Upon arriving home, Amber asked all about her trip. Claire told her about the reunion with her friend. Although she didn't share the discovery of her saviors, she made no attempt to hide her joy at the way the week progressed.

Claire hesitated telling her friends about her impending reunion. She knew they wouldn't be happy. On the plane, she decided to concentrate on the angle of *learning more about Tony* and *getting clarification on his confessions*. She couldn't hide from him forever. Actually, she was no longer hidden. This reunion would take place. Claire needed their support to tilt the odds in her favor.

When Amber retired, prior to Claire's announcement, Harry smiled and asked, "So are you tired from your trip, or would you like to go next door for another video game lesson?"

Throughout her vacation Claire spent some time thinking about their last gaming lesson. Truthfully, she wasn't looking for a romantic interest. It was even difficult to image herself with anyone but Tony. Yet, as they sat a week ago, side by side, holding the newfangled controllers and laughing at her avatar's jerky movements, she sensed a mutual admiration. It showed in his soft blue eyes and his encouragement and support. There was no domination or instruction. After her recent loneliness, Harry's comfort was refreshing and so different than anything with Tony. The light-heartedness, warmth and mutual appreciation allowed her to lower her guard. When he gently eased his arm around her waist, she was only mildly surprised. Instantly, Claire realized she didn't want to protest. Therefore, when his lips neared hers, she'd intended to submit willingly. But, before she could he stopped.

Claire opened her eyes unsure of what happened. His honest and even timid expression reflected in his words, "Claire, are you sure you're all right with this?"

His unexpected need for permission flooded her with admiration. Claire didn't answer, she wasn't sure if she could trust her voice. Instead she nodded and leaned toward him.

Harry pressed forward and their lips united. She felt his warm chest against her breasts. It had been so long, she unconsciously molded against him.

They didn't take it beyond kissing and caressing. However, multiple times throughout her vacation the memories of that gaming session infiltrated her thoughts. Lying in the sun she'd suddenly remember his strong arms, unruly hair, or the scent of his aftershave, and uncontrollably she'd feel a tightening somewhere deep inside. It was an old feeling. However, having it brought about by a new source was surprisingly refreshing.

Now, he was asking if she wanted to play video games. She knew he didn't mean *video games*. With a twinkle in her eyes she answered, "I don't know, do you think I still need lessons?"

Harry glanced toward his sister's room. Turning back to Claire he whispered, "No, I don't think you need lessons at all. Maybe we could just play?"

"Hmm now that's an offer a girl can't refuse."

He took her hand and led her toward the door.

She'd been in Harry's condominium many times. Though smaller than Amber's, the one bedroom unit was equally lavish in design with quality craftsmanship, wooden floors, handcrafted woodwork, granite counters, and ornamental lighting. Nevertheless, what continued to bring a smile to Claire's face was his amusingly eclectic decor. While obviously equipped by a man, technology was the main focus. Couches, chairs, and tables were secondary to large screens, speakers, and surround sound. All he needed was a pool table in the dining room to have an official bachelor pad. The first time Claire entered his condominium, she half expected to turn the corner and find one, or perhaps foosball, but surprisingly he did indeed have a real dining room table.

"Would you like anything to drink? I have some Cabernet." Harry asked as they passed the threshold, into his abode. Claire noticed the low set, indirect lighting. She smirked, wondering if she were indeed that predicable.

"Sure. Do you want me to get the PS3 out?" Claire asked with a grin to her voice.

"Unless, you want to practice your skills on the Wii? It does requires more hands-on, you know, use of your entire body."

"I've never played that."

He was calling from the kitchen. Claire could hear the pop of the cork. "I bet with a little help, you'll catch on fast."

Harry entered the living room and handed her a goblet. Smiling, he leaned in for a kiss.

She absorbed his warm smile and willingly accepted his puckered lips. "Can we talk before we try the Wii?"

"We can do whatever you want." Harry sat on the sofa.

Claire eased herself a few feet away and turned toward his handsome gaze. She never expected this to be so difficult. "I didn't have a chance to tell you about a delivery that came just before I left on my trip."

Harry sat his glass on the coffee table and asked, "Delivery? Did you receive more flowers?"

"Not flowers..." Claire went on to tell him about the note and the clothes. She watched as tension tightened his neck muscles. For someone who was mostly calm, the subject of Anthony Rawlings, in more than an abstract sense, initiated obvious unease.

"And you plan to go on this outing? You plan to get into this car *he's* sending?"

"Well, I've given that some thought. You see, he still doesn't know I have his private cell number. So, I've decided to call him, but not until Wednesday afternoon. Then I'll inform him of a change of plans."

Harry picked up his glass and listened while Claire explained her ideas. She would tell Tony that since she *knows the area* she made reservations at a nearby restaurant. And, she'd meet him there at seven. She wasn't sure how it would go, but she wanted the ability to leave of her own free will.

"If I ask you, will you tell me something about your relationship with him?"

Claire sipped her wine, "I don't know. It's difficult for me to discuss." She looked at the man only feet away. She entered his condo willing to take their relationship farther. Did she honestly feel better sharing her body, than her memories? He patiently waited, finally she exhaled, "What do you want to know?"

Harry scooted closer, removed the glass of wine from her hand and placed it on the table. She waited for his question. Instead, he leaned down, his lips brushed her neck and he gently kissed that spot between her neck and shoulder. The round scooped neckline of her shirt exposed the sensitive site. Shivering at the light touch of his lips to her skin, tingles descended toward her arms, to her fingers, and down her legs, all the way to her toes.

Claire gasped as she inclined her head, granting him greater access. Before she realized, she was sandwiched between him and his leather sofa. His lips were no longer brushing her skin; they were connecting her lips and skin with a new found urgency. Her body arched as his hands roamed over her tight t-shirt and caressed her lacy bra covered breasts. When her mind caught-up to their actions or more accurately her reactions, she whispered, "I thought you wanted to ask me questions."

He supported his head, near her face and looked down into her beautiful gaze, "I needed to know if I *could* ask." He gently kissed her lips, "Right now, I'd rather do something else."

Claire smiled and purred, "Good, there're better things to do right now." She arched her back, feeling her nipples rub against the weight of his chest and nuzzled his neck. The aroma of his aftershave combined with the stubble on his neck electrified desires she'd compartmentalized away.

There was no question, those desires weren't gone. They spilled out with a vengeance.

*****

As the airliner taxied to the San Jose gate, Sophia summoned her brightest smile. It wasn't too difficult. After nearly two weeks of separation, she was truly excited to see her husband. Without fail, they'd spoken every day. Unquestionably, that wasn't the same as being together. She longed to feel his embrace and taste his lips.

Sophia consulted the screen of her iPhone and retrieved an email she'd received earlier in the day. It wasn't from Derek, but from Danny, Derek's new personal assistant. Sophia wondered if the term *Personal Assistant* was manufactured so men wouldn't feel awkward being identified as secretaries. Danny not only handled Derek's business at work, he'd assisted Derek with apartment hunting and learning the area.

The email said Derek would be waiting for her in Terminal B near baggage claim. She felt her anticipation rise as she stood to exit the plane.

With all of Sophia's experience with international travel, San Jose's small easy to maneuver airport made locating her desired destination simple. She did however, have trouble locating her husband.

A gentleman in a chauffer's uniform stood near the baggage carousel. Subconsciously Sophia read his sign: *Mrs. Derek Burke.*

After three years of marriage she should recognize her name. However, momentarily it confused her. First, she expected Derek. And second, her name was Sophia Burke. Other than on guest books at weddings and funerals, she's never referred to herself as Mrs. Derek Burke. The sensation of the shutters came back. The clamor of voices dissipated as she listened to the rusty hinges creak. *What happened to Sophia Rossi Burke?* She wondered.

Sophia sat in the back seat of a company limousine, while the chauffer drove her to Shedis-tics. In an effort to remain calm, she peered through the tinted windows at the unfamiliar terrain. Occasionally she'd see the mountains Derek promised. Admittedly, she enjoyed their blue hue.

Apparently, Derek had an unexpected web conference he couldn't miss. He was very sorry. The apology came through loud and clear -- on a text message. He promised a better reunion, once they made their way to their new home.

The limousine pulled into a generous semi-circular drive with a large fountain surrounding the Shedis-tics sign. Tall palm trees intermingled with soft pines created a landscaped barrier to the road. The multi-leveled glass building was more spread out than office buildings on the East coast. The building was actually a complex of interconnected glass and mirrored structures.

The car stopped, the driver opened Sophia's door, and she thanked him for the ride. "What about my luggage?" She wasn't sure if she was supposed to take it into Derek's office.

"Mrs. Burke, I believe I am to wait for you. We will leave it in the car until I hear otherwise."

Sophia agreed, all the while questioning her own ability to make decisions. Why would the driver be waiting if she were leaving with Derek? Tentatively she entered the glass building.

The large impressive lobby glowed with natural light. The white walls, huge windows, plants, and fountains made her feel like she was still outside. Sophia made her way to the information desk.

Three women were behind the tall counter. Two wore blue blouses, *Shedis-tics* embroidered on the front. The other wore attire screaming executive; a black pencil skirt, white blouse, and tall black pumps. While the well-fitting clothes accentuated her feminine gender, they also confirmed she meant business.

Sophia approached a woman in blue. "Hello, perhaps you could help me? I'm looking for Derek Burke."

Before the young lady could reply, the executive woman turned to Sophia. "Hello, you must be Mrs. Burke."

It wasn't a conscious decision for one woman to evaluate the other, but it happens all the time. Sophia took in her features. Immediately she noticed the woman's petite frame, probably four or five inches shorter than herself, undoubtedly younger, with blonde hair, fixed into a low bun and a beautiful smile. The assessment took only a millisecond. Sophia extended her hand as she responded, "Yes, please call me Sophia."

The young executive eagerly accepted and shook Sophia's hand. Her strong voice was eager and energetic, "It's nice to finally meet you. I'm Danielle, but please call me Danni. I'll be glad to take you to Derek's office. His web conference should be almost done."

*****

Claire's plan progressed smoother than she'd hoped. She hadn't heard Tony's voice since she answered his call, over three weeks earlier. As she dialed his number, she wondered what big meeting she may be interrupting. While married, after she had a cellphone, she was specifically instructed to only text during business hours. Actual calls were prohibited, except in the case of an emergency. After all, he's a busy man. He didn't want her interrupting some multimillion dollar deal. The memory of that instruction came rushing back as she listened to the rings on her end. Utilizing the telephone that he called, she knew her number and probably name, would appear when he checked the screen.

Surprisingly, he answered on the second ring. She heard a combination of amusement and surprise in his voice. "Hello, Claire. I hope you're not calling to cancel our plans."

Her heart momentarily forgot to beat. Damn, if he wouldn't have used her name – but he did. Feigning strength, she pressed forward. "I wouldn't do that, Tony." She could use his name too. "That would be rude, to cancel something at the last minute."

"I must admit, I'm surprised to receive your call... on my private cell."

"I presume you are. I wanted to contact you about tonight."

"Yes?"

"You see, I've been living in this area for a while. There's a lovely French restaurant I believe you'll enjoy." She didn't wait for him to respond, she continued, "I realize you made reservations, but so have I. I'd be glad to meet you at Bon Vivant on Bryant, at 7."

"Well, there is a car coming to pick you up..."

She interrupted, "I appreciate that. It's very kind of you; however, I have my own car and am more than willing to drive." She heard his soft chuckle.

"If that is what you prefer."

She exhaled, "I do."

"Very well, I must return to this table of directors and web conference. Until tonight."

"Yes, good-bye."

Her next decision involved attire. The outfit he sent was exquisite. She tried it on and expectantly, everything fit perfectly. However, the day before their reunion, she returned it to Neiman Marcus, having the money returned to the purchasing credit card. Claire planned on presenting the receipt to Tony during their meal.

She decided to wear the white dress and Dior sandals she'd worn during her discussion with Phillip Roach, in San Antonio. When considering hairstyle, she purposely styled it in a way she knew her ex-husband liked. She also figured this outing would make at least one or two publications and most likely be plastered all over the internet before she settled down for bed. Claire Rawlings Nichols intended to look the part.

Before she walked to the parking garage, Claire exited the elevator on the ground level. It was 6 PM, and the restaurant was only minutes away. She was ready to go. Her nerves were stretched to an inflexible tautness which didn't allow her to linger in the condo any longer. Besides, Amber was out of town on business, and Claire wasn't ready to face Harry as he returned from SiJo. She'd feel better talking to him after the dinner. Until then, she couldn't stand to see that look in his soft blue eyes. For some reason, the way they looked at her made her feel like she was cheating, which was ridiculous. Especially since she and Harry didn't have anything official on which she could cheat. Their mutual admiration hadn't yet progressed to sex. Although when Claire recalled their encounters, she felt like a school girl, warm and aroused, anticipating the next move.

Exiting the front doors of the condominium, Claire walked boldly to Phillip Roach's inconspicuous grey sedan. She watched him shake his head, as she knocked on his window. Suspiciously, he lowered the pane. "Yes, Ms. Nichols? I see you're wearing your trapping clothes."

Claire smiled, "I'm not sure if your employer informed you, but we're meeting for dinner this evening. We'll be dining at Bon Vivant on Bryant." She handed him an envelope; slowly he accepted. "The restaurant is often crowded, and I didn't want you to miss the fun. There's a small shadowed table reserved in your name, please accept this gift certificate and enjoy your meal on me." With her eyes twinkling, she turned and walked toward her building. Claire felt Phillip's eyes upon her, not an unfamiliar feeling.

*What happened in the past that was painful
has a great deal to do with what we are today.*
--William Glasser

Chapter 16

Arriving thirty-five minutes early, Claire noticed the parking lot wasn't as busy as normal. She'd only eaten at Bon Vivant once, but found the service exceptional and the food delicious. It was a popular and highly acclaimed destination in Silicon Valley. Her last visit was a weekend, and it had been packed with patrons. Claire reassured herself, this was a week night; many people were still at work.

The maître d' politely greeted her as she entered alone, "Good evening Mademoiselle, do you have reservations?"

Claire looked around the nearly empty restaurant. "Oui, deux pour Nichols." (Yes, two for Nichols)

"Oui, Mademoiselle. Your table is not yet ready. Perhaps you would like to wait for your companion in our lounge. I will personally inform you when your table is ready."

"Thank you, I left specific instructions for a conspicuous table, near the center of the main dining room."

"Oui, we will do everything we can to accommodate you and your companion. The lounge is to the right."

"Merci." Thanking the maître d', she followed the piano music and made her way to the posh lounge. Years before, when Claire accompanied Tony to a French restaurant, she was at a complete loss as he spoke to the wait staff. While in France, she began to pick-up a few words. However, it was while in prison, she had time to study both French and Italian. She wouldn't be considered fluent in either; however, she could understand what was said around her. Undoubtedly, her speech held a very American accent.

The lounge was beautifully contemporary, mostly white with colored lights, creating an awe-inspiring ambience. She noticed a few other couples at nearby tables. Claire checked her watch, as the other couples were escorted from the lounge. At two minutes before seven, she found herself sitting alone, in the great expanse of the lounge. Maintaining her mask of calm she watched as the archway filled with the man from her past.

Memories of their last meeting in the Iowa City jail flooded her consciousness. Tony's presence filled the otherwise empty room. The earth no longer rotated on its own axis, but on him. She had compartmentalized away his utter dominance. As much as she tried to appear aloof, the mixture of emotions raging through her, threatened to propel her from the soft luxurious seat. Unconsciously, she gripped the arms of the chair, hoping for stability. Claire feared, if not for the anchor, she might possibly become airborne.

Her breathing labored as his gorgeous form advanced closer. With each step, he narrowed the vast fifteen month divide. He hadn't changed. His perfect appearance was just as she'd remembered, from his dark thick hair masterly styled in place, to his brown eyes sparkling with electricity. His cheeks were raised, revealing a closed lip grin. And of course, his suit was silk, tailored specifically for him, with cuff links shining from the edge of his jacket sleeves. If anyone else had been in the room, they would have disappeared into his all-encompassing aura. But alas, no one else was present, except the piano player. And momentarily, even the music dissipated.

From the archway to Claire's table could be traveled in a few seconds; however, it seemed as though Tony's casual stride fought an unseen tide. The seconds lasted minutes, hours, or perhaps days. During the elapsed expanse of time and space, Claire remembered every moment of their time together. Three years of memories compressed into a fraction of time. Finally, accomplishing his journey -- because Claire knew Anthony Rawlings rarely failed at any endeavor -- he stood before her table. She fought diligently to remain calm and serene, as he politely nodded in her direction.

His voice filled the cavernous room, engulfing the otherwise empty molecules and stirring the cauldron of emotions within her chest. "Good evening, Claire."

She'd fought this fight before. Admittedly, she'd rarely won, but nonetheless, the battle was familiar. Claire pressed on, "Good evening, Tony. Won't you please have a seat?"

"Thank you." He pulled the chair from the table and lowered his tall lean body into cushioned seat. She watched as his dark eyes remained fixed on hers. Perhaps the rest of the world was gone. It was the most plausible answer. Heaven knows she couldn't see or think of anyone else. That must be the answer, they were the only two people left, as the Earth spun into a timeless abyss.

Claire once read time doesn't pass at normal speeds within a black hole. If one were to travel into a black hole for only moments and return again, centuries would have passed. That explained the sensation she felt, once again peering into his dark gaze. She wouldn't look away; she'd trained herself better than that. Then again, she reasoned, it wasn't an option. She couldn't divert her gaze if she wanted. The hold upon her stare was stronger than any ropes or chains made by man. Claire knew from experience, submitting to the hold was her best chance at survival. Fighting was a futile waste of energy.

As she felt herself slipping into her old station, she remembered her cause. Claire remembered her friends and their support. She recalled the advice of a good friend. She needed to ask herself, *am I in fear of upsetting him? Does he make me smile?* She thought about her cellphones in her purse and her car in the parking lot.

No! She could fight and survive. She had! Within the milliseconds that transpired, she clawed her way out of the abyss, time had not elapsed. She continued their dialogue. "It was nice of you to accommodate my change in plans." Taking a sip of her water, she fought the dryness threatening her mouth and gestured toward a bottle of wine. "I took the liberty of ordering us a bottle of wine."

Tony smiled a devilish grin. Claire's insides tightened. His eyes lightened as he lifted the bottle and assessed the label. "Excellent choice."

Before their conversation could continue, the waiter appeared at their side. "Monsieur and Mademoiselle, your table is not yet ready. May I open your wine?"

Claire spoke before Tony could answer, "Oui, grazie." She noticed Tony's smile broaden. In the past she learned amusement wasn't always a good thing. A small voice in the back of her head warned her to proceed with caution.

After the waiter poured the wine, he left them alone, literally. Claire couldn't help notice the absence of others. She tried diligently to keep her increased unease hidden.

"My, Claire, you continue to amaze me. I see you're trying to show me the new independent Claire Nichols." She didn't speak. He continued, "You don't need to work so hard. I've been observing you from a far and am already impressed."

"Tony, my goal is not to impress. My goal is to show that I don't need your observation. I'm doing quite well on my own."

"I believe you have surpassed my expectations, once again."

"And for the record, I was independent before our encounter."

"Yes," pause, "I can see how you would think that." He sipped his wine, "Now tell me, what the point was with the change in venue?"

"No point. I've eaten here and thought you'd enjoy the cuisine."

"I see," he continued to sip the wine. "That's good. I was afraid you were trying to manipulate our visibility..."

Before he could continue the maître d' approached their table. "Excusez-moi, your table, it is ready."

"Gaize," Tony replied as he stood. While Claire gathered her handbag, Tony politely helped her with her chair.

As she stood, she continued to fight the old pull. It was as if she were slipping into Mrs. Anthony Rawlings, perhaps not slipping, pulled – by an irresistible force. She needed to remain diligent to be the independent woman she longed to be.

Walking across the empty lounge, Tony placed his hand in the small of her exposed back. She didn't fight the contact. Actually, she fought the sudden desire to melt toward it. Memories came rushing so fast, she barely had time to blink -- the feel of his caress -- his ability to elicit emotions and desires -- the warmth and security of his embrace. Although her resolve diligently fought, her heartbeat quickened and fantasies interlaced her recollections. Not only did she remember his large strong hands; she also remembered his tender mouth, firm steady chest, and tight abdomen. The slight touch evoked memories of ecstasies they'd shared. Highs, which before him didn't exist, and elations she feared were forever extinct.

When his tall body inclined, allowing his lips to hover near her ear, her body tingled. Then, without warning he whispered, and her fantasy evaporated. Reality struck with a slap that only real life can elicit. "I'm glad visibility was not your goal for this evening. I would hate to disappoint you."

Before Claire could respond, they stepped from the lounge into the dining area. She gasped. Her neck stiffened as she took in the empty restaurant. No longer was her subconscious filled with memories of love and pleasure, but control and manipulation. The harshness deflated her lungs. Claire fought to breathe, battling the sensation of suffocation she'd suffered during the years of his domination.

With new found determination, she turned toward the sly smirk of her ex-husband and asked, "What have you done?"

"I wanted to spend time with you, without the diversion of others."

"Where are the other people?"

"I believe they accepted an unbelievable offer. In essence, I rented the entire restaurant. After all, you said it was delicious, and I wanted to enjoy the food and company."

Claire stared incredulously, "You bought-out the entire place?"

"Yes, Claire. Shall we sit? I believe you requested this central table."

Her blood boiled, looking around she wondered about Phil, where was he? She'd become accustom to seeing him periodically throughout her day. Feeling incredibly vulnerable she sat, allowing Tony to push her chair under the table.

Fighting her instinct to run, Claire straightened her neck and met her ex-husbands smug expression and sparkling darkening eyes head-on. The waiter delivered their wine, including glasses to their new location. After he left, Tony lifted his glass and proposed a toast, "To you, the only person in this world, who can keep me on my toes."

Claire held her glass. Tony moved the goblet to his lips. Slowly, she raised the rim to her mouth. Just before she took a drink, he laughed. Placing the glass back onto the linen tablecloth, Claire said, "I hope you're amused. I believe I'm getting a headache. We'll need to postpone this dinner for another time." She placed her hands on the table to push back her chair.

Tony reached across the table and covered her hand. The touch ignited her skin. She wanted to hate the man with her entire being; yet, his touch, the sound of his voice, smell of his cologne, and sight of his incredibly handsome face turned her insides to jelly. The two contrasting memories of love and domination, played simultaneously within her head. Unwillingly, she looked into his soft chocolate eyes and sighed.

In a much gentler tone he said, "Claire, I would like you to stay. Your plans are to be commended. You probably know, but even without the clothes I sent, you are stunning. Now, if we are done with this ridiculous posturing, I'd like to talk with you for a while."

"This was not meant as posturing! And I assure you, my head does hurt."

"I have missed you terribly."

She stared. What did he just say? It didn't make sense. She was gone from him, from his life, due totally to him.

He continued, "I have missed your voice, your strength, your smile, and mostly your eyes. My god, Claire, you have the most amazing eyes!"

"Stop it."

Abashed, he asked, "Excuse me?"

"I said, stop it!" Her voice was harsh yet hushed. "The last time we spoke, in person, I begged to go with you back to your home, *our* home in Iowa City. As I recall, you offered me a psychiatric institution. So why would I be interested in listening to your drivel today?"

"Well, first, because you accepted my invitation."

"I accepted your invitation for one reason, to convince you to leave me alone. We are done."

"My dear, it is not that simple." His expression revived a suppressed fear.

She fought to steady herself as the room wobbled off center. It was the finality with which he spoke, as if his comment were beyond reproach. "It is." Her voice less convincing than she'd hoped. She inhaled to emphasize her next word, "Anton."

His back straightened, and his eyes intensified, "My name is Anthony. You may still address me as Tony."

"That's very gentlemanly of you. Do you not think as your wife, I deserved to know your true name was Anton Rawls?" Claire watched an internal battle launch and rage within her ex-husband. She knew him and could read his non-verbal clues. Others may not recognize the scene before her, but she did.

Externally Tony remained stoic as he fought for control. Finally he spoke, his voice deceivingly calm, "Where could you possibly come up with such a story?"

"Why, Anton, it was in your box of confessions."

Tony stared in utter shock and disbelief. Claire wasn't sure if she'd ever seen his facade shatter as quickly. Though he remained still, she imagined him scurrying to pick-up the pieces of his usually intact veneer. His voice gained strength with each syllable. "I assure you, I have no idea what you are saying."

"The information you sent me in prison."

Before they could continue, a waiter appeared beside their table with menus. Placing the binders in front of each, he asked if they were interested in hearing about the specials. Concurrently, they answered, "No." The waiter apologized for the interruption and meekly backed away from the table. Tony reached for the leather folder; his fingertips blanched, as he squeezed the helpless menu.

It didn't make sense. The writing on the note was his, as was the writing on the photos. Although Claire was reasonably certain he'd ended this conversation, she decided to go ahead and ask the question screaming in her head, "Are you saying you didn't send me a box of information?"

He didn't need to answer; his expression and body language spoke louder than words. Nonetheless, he managed to articulate, "I can assure you, I did not send you anything while you were in prison." Continuing to regulate his external calm, he added, "And, speaking of prison, congratulations on your early release."

Sarcasm dripped from his final statement; however, Claire was still mulling-over his first declaration. *If he didn't send me that information, then who did?* When his words registered she decided to dial down the conversation. Yes, her old instincts were guiding her through this mine field. Those instincts saved her life in the past. He'd changed the subject, and experience warned her to take heed. Any discussion of his box or his alternate persona would need to wait. "Thank you, I promise, I was as surprised as you must have been."

He *harrumphed* as he took another drink of his wine. The contents disappeared. He poured himself another glass. "That, my dear, is debatable."

Claire smiled; he may have manipulated her plans. Nonetheless, she'd just acquired invaluable information. He didn't send the box; he hadn't known she knew about his past or his vendetta, and she could obviously influence his demeanor. That knowledge seemed more powerful today than it'd ever been. She looked at the menu and discussed the entrees she found appetizing.

Truthfully, neither of them possessed much of an appetite; nevertheless, the dinner progressed. As expected, Tony ordered their meals. However, as he spoke to the waiter, in French, Claire smiled when he ordered the selection she'd suggested.

After the waiter left, Tony turned to Claire and continuing in French and said, "I see you have broadened your language portfolio."

Also in French, she replied, "Yes, I decided to capitalize on my gift of time."

He grinned and shook his head ever so slightly. Now in English, "Claire, how is your headache?"

"I believe the wine is helping."

"That's good. Tell me about San Antonio."

Momentarily, she savored the robust thick liquid that contained a hint of sweet floral flavor, and contemplated her response. If his obvious knowledge of her whereabouts was supposed to threaten or alarm her, she disappointed him again. Meeting his gaze she smiled, "It was lovely. I've always enjoyed sunshine and warmth."

"Yes, I can see your lovely tan."

Maybe, he could make her smile. Yes, there was a twinge of concern about upsetting him. But even empty, they were in a public place. She knew he wouldn't do or say anything harmful while in the sight of others. Truthfully, she felt a new sense of empowerment. If it had been present before, she'd been too close to see it. But now, Claire sensed her ability to affect him. She could upset him and she could calm him. Few people held that power. Perhaps, others did, but were not brave, or stupid, enough to try.

Claire chose to use the word *brave*.

When Claire entered her condo she heard unexpected noises resonating from the den. Making her way down the hall, she found Harry lounging on the small loveseat watching a baseball game. The way his long legs hung off the end of the sofa added to the comedy of the scene. Especially considering the large comfortable couch and five times larger television in his condo. "Is your television broken?"

He turned to speak. Her appearance momentarily muted him. Eventually he managed to answer, "No, it's fine. I just thought you might need some moral support."

"Tell me you aren't here to be sure I came home."

Harry stood and approached one of the most beautiful women he'd ever seen. "Not like you may think. I really wanted to be sure you were all right. I know I haven't asked directly. And I don't need to know anything you don't want to say, but I get the feeling there were times in your past, your ex-husband didn't treat you well." He tried to read her eyes; they were changing into that stoic noncommittal stare. "Claire, stop the pretense."

She backed away from his sudden harsh tone. "Excuse me? I haven't said a word."

"No, you haven't. But you're doing what you always do. You're hiding behind some mask of indifference."

The night was overwhelming. Her head *did* hurt. She'd just left dinner with Tony and was suddenly in another confrontation. Claire honestly wasn't up for more conflict. Plus, his word: *mask*. That's what she used to tell herself to wear with Tony. Did she really wear one with Harry too?

"My head *is* aching. I'm sorry if you find my expression unappealing. I appreciate your concern. I'm home safe and sound. And, I did learn some valuable information. Perhaps, I can share it with you tomorrow."

He stepped closer and placed his hands on her waist. She didn't back away. Yet, she filled with guilt as her thoughts centered on the man at the restaurant, not the one before her.

When Harry touched her waist, his fingertips landed on her warm skin. He hadn't realized the back of her dress was open. He leaned around her shoulder and took in the stunning view. "You look lovely. I'm sure this will be on every magazine in a day or two."

"No, it won't."

Surprised by the finality of her statement, Harry asked, "How can you say that? We go to Starbucks and make the internet. You looking this gorgeous will warrant the cover of every national gossip magazine!" He continued to hold her gently around the waist. Claire shook her head back and forth. Then half-jokingly he whispered, "Apparently, I've not warranted such an amazing dress."

Her neck stiffened, "It's not new. I wore it in Texas. And I can assure you, you won't see my picture in this outfit or any other with Anthony Rawlings, at least not until *he* is ready to have it out there."

"What happened to your plan for visibility?"

"I was trumped. I should have seen it coming, but I didn't."

"What happened?"

"I promise to tell you all about it, tomorrow. Right now, I want out of this dress and these shoes." Harry moved ever so slightly toward her warmth, until her next words changed his plans. "If you'd please lock the door on your way out, I'm going to bed." She pulled away from his embrace and turned toward her room.

Before she passed the door frame she heard Harry's voice. "I would really like the chance to understand you better, the real you."

Softly she said, "Good night, Harry," and proceeded to her room. Truthfully, his comment regarding a *mask* caught her by surprise. She didn't mean to hide her feelings, well not usually. Nevertheless, tonight she couldn't possibly look into his soft blue eyes or feel his gentle touch and not think about the man that challenged her sanity. It wasn't fair to Harry, be with him and think about Tony.

It wasn't fair to Claire to have to make decisions about her true feelings. She needed time; time to sort out the mayhem that continued to be her life. Luckily, the medicine cabinet in her attached bath contained a big bottle of acetaminophen. Finally, she settled into her welcomingly cool and pleasantly lonely, comfortable bed.

*Ideologies separate us. Dreams and anguish
bring us together.*
- Eugene Ionesco

Chapter 17

Claire's body dripped with perspiration; her breasts pushed toward his solid muscular chest. She craved the sensation of his tight muscles and soft chest hair against her sensitive nipples. Inhaling deeply, the fragrance of cologne reached the depth of her lungs, filling her senses and intensifying her irrepressible desire. The tips of her fingers gripped the soft Egyptian threaded sheets; her manicured fingernails threatening to gouge the luxurious linens, potentially returning them to fibers, in the heat of passion. Arching her back, Claire's lips sought to taste the stubbled neck, which with each exaggerated pulse of his carotid artery, provided the amazing scent. It was so close.

Yet, as much as she tried, as much as she pushed toward the warmth, she couldn't reach her target. Claire's body ached to feel him, to have him, to take him or more accurately, to be taken by him. It'd been so long, and she could no longer suppress her desires. No one else's opinion mattered. Willingly and without regret she submitted to the mounting passion. The train she rode couldn't be stopped, even if she wanted. But, she didn't want to stop. Every fiber of her body was in agreement. She wanted what only *he* could give. She wanted...

Her eyes opened to darkness. It wasn't the darkness in her dream – not the dark eyes, which unpardonably consumed her heart and soul. It was the darkness of night, of her room, of her lonely, empty bed.

Claire looked at the clock on the nearby table. Damn, it was only a little after two. Being the third time she'd awoken since leaving Harry down the hall. She decided it was the night that *never ends*. *Lamb Comps* sang in her head, a G rated childhood memory running in loops, kindly drowning out the echoes of XXX rated passion.

Freeing her bound legs from the tangled mess of sheets and blankets, Claire relished in the cool fresh breeze from her open window, detecting the slightest scent of the impeding summer. She inhaled the promise of warmth, chlorine, and freshly cut grass.

The night had been a never ending ride upon a carrousel, up and down, around and around, the same scenes over and over. One minute feeling cold, she'd ensconce her body with a soft cocoon and drift to sleep. What seemed like moments later -- she'd awake, violently thrashing to free herself from the sweltering coverings. Thank god, Amber was out of town. Claire believed a few times, she'd actually cried-out audibly. She wasn't sure if her screams were from the ecstasy of her dreams or the pain of her reality.

These weren't mysterious nightmares which left her wondering their meaning. No, these were vivid, lifelike dreams that caused her to gasp with disappointment each time her eyes opened to the cold reality. Although, the visions were no more real than her memories of an Iowa summer or her lake shore, she still laid panting for breath and clutching the helpless, innocent pillow.

Claire knew her unconscious, carnal yearning had once again forsaken her. It wasn't the first time. Last time, she gave in to its perfidious pleas. Last time, the object of her desire was close, too close to fight. She hadn't had the strength, not to fight him and her rebellious longings.

Allowing her eyes to adjust to her surroundings, she concentrated on the stucco ceiling illuminated only by the light of the clock. The stupid, red numbers refused to change, giving her more time to do nothing but think. Claire focused on her breathing, willing her pulse to slow and her skin to cool. She argued with her traitorous body. Surely with enough reasoning, she could make it cooperate.

Claire reminded herself that her memory banks held a litany of scenes involving Anthony Rawlings. She had plenty to supersede the erotic episodes she was currently viewing -- no, reliving. She knew the other memories existed. It's just she'd worked to compartmentalize them away. So when her eyes closed and she remembered sharing a table with him, only hours before, the lock on the negative part of their past remained secure.

Then again, during that dinner she had plans. And once again, he thwarted her plans, utilizing his unlimited resources and cunning psyche to conquer her desired consequence. Appearing suave and debonair he'd managed to reduce her well laid idea to rubble, while maintaining the perfect smile.

That wasn't completely true. His veneer definitely cracked when she referred to him as *Anton*. That bombshell unquestionably permeated his facade. Claire still couldn't wrap her mind around this new revelation. Of course, she'd assumed the box was from him. She was certain of the writing, although the note wasn't signed. Claire wished she still had the note. But, she had the pictures. The writing on the back of those, she was certain was his.

Again, thankful Amber wasn't home, Claire chose to forgo another all-consuming dream and get-up. She wanted to review and work on their research.

138

With a warm cup of coffee in tow, Claire made her way to one of the spare bedrooms. Turning on the light she marveled at the magnitude of papers. Slowly, she was taking over more and more of Amber's space. Although she mentioned finding a place of her own, she admittedly liked the company. And thus far, Amber had been more than accommodating. It was Claire who suggested moving the mountains of findings to the small bedroom. She felt bad burying the dining room table with her stacks of research.

The queen-sized bed created the perfect palate for Claire's unique filing system. There were piles from one end to the other. In a paperless world, she'd managed to personally decimate a tree or two. The information was also saved on her laptop. Nonetheless, holding the pages in her hands, gave Claire a sense of reality. She knew from experience the internet could contain false truths. However, when she held a story, a blurb from an article, dates from public record, and pictures, in her hand – it gave them validity. The small desk contained her laptop while a dresser held the printer.

Claire moved toward the bed and stacks of information. She wondered, could there be something in their accumulated data she'd missed? She wasn't the only one gathering information. Harry pulled strings to get police information containing invaluable reports unavailable to the general public. Amber willingly spent hours surfing the net, *back-dooring* company websites. She understood the business side of their research much more than Claire.

That being said, the depth of Claire's business knowledge surprised them all. Apparently, the days she'd spent in Tony's office weren't wasted. She remembered sitting hour after hour while Tony worked, required to be at the ready, in case her services were demanded. At the time she saw it as his display of power and control over her time and body. Today, she grinned at the new perspective: those wasted days were actually educational.

How many people receive the opportunity, to watch and listen to one of the country's most successful entrepreneurs at work? Although she usually spent those days reading, she subconsciously listened. Perhaps, he felt she didn't care, or couldn't understand. Claire opted for the answer: he didn't even consider eavesdropping. He was busy displaying his power over her schedule, the rest of the world be damned.

She shuttered at the estimation of hours spent in that office during the nearly two years on his estate. After they were married, most of the time was voluntary. Nevertheless, she'd listened to web-conferences, webinars, and unnumbered telephone conversations. Hell, she listened to those in cars and even on his plane. Her presence never inhibited his words. Actually, she got good at recognizing the subtle changes in body language as his words remained amicable.

When in his office and perturbed, he had a habit of rolling an old key ring in his hand. It was some old trinket he kept in the upper right hand drawer of his large desk. If Claire looked up from her book or magazine and saw the stupid ring running laps on his right hand, she knew he was upset. Yet, the person on the other end of the discussion would never know. His features and voice never wavered. They couldn't see the tarnished silver charm or strangely shaped key being passed from one finger to the next. Claire came to know the speed at which the ring ran a lap in his large hand, was proportional to his state of agitation.

Contemplating those memories, Claire's stomach twisted. His unease was directly proportional to the downturn of her day. Not only did he control her comings and goings, he was the barometer for the tone of her life. If he were happy, the day could be manageable, maybe even good. If he weren't...well, she really hated that stupid key ring.

Her business knowledge was unrealized until she read an article about a company under investigation by the SEC, Securities Exchange Commission. Claire remembered hours of discussion about that same company. Some of the issues that, according to the article were just brought to light had actually been debated ad nauseam years before.

Amber found her information very intriguing. After Amber pulled up more details on the company, Claire was shocked to realize she actually knew, or at least recognized, the names and faces of many prominent players. They were people Claire had been responsible for entertaining at business dinners. She'd met them, talked with them, and dined with them. Her knowledge base was much broader than she'd previously expected.

Settling into a comfortable chair, feet on an ottoman, wrapped in her warm robe, Claire began rereading documents. Anthony was obviously surprised by the use of his name, Anton Rawls. He flat out denied it. Well, he called it *a ridiculous story.* She didn't directly ask if he was once Anton Rawls. She only asked him if he sent her the box. That he categorically denied.

Claire decided to start at the beginning: Nathaniel Rawls, born 1919. Served in U.S. Army, WWII deployment, returned to USA 1943. Married Sharron Parkinson Rawls 1943. Began working for BNG Textiles in 1943. 1944 Samuel Anton Rawls born. 1953 BNG Textiles became Rawls Textiles. The company expanded. 1975 Rawls went public, traded on the NYSE. At this point records are easier to obtain. The biggest problem was lack of technology in 1975.

Today a wealth of information was available on every publicly traded company: assets, liabilities, ownership equity, profit and loss sheets, management analysis and much more. The same information was presumably available in 1975 but not at a click of a button.

Claire debated traveling to New Jersey to access microfiche files. The woman on the telephone told her they *should* have it. However, the state of New Jersey doesn't have the inclination, time, or manpower to track the old information. She invited Claire to come and investigate the bowels of their storage. Although a lovely invitation, Claire hadn't decided if it were necessary.

January 1986 rumors involving Rawls Corp resulted in a drastic drop in stock price. Investors wanted their money returned. 1987 Nathaniel Rawls was convicted and incarcerated at *Camp Gabriels*, a minimum security state prison, located in northern New York. He was sentenced to thirty-six months, one of the heaviest penalties dispersed for a white collar crime. 1989, twenty-two months after conviction, Nathaniel Rawls died of a heart attack.

Harry found a list of civil cases involving Nathaniel during his incarceration. He said it wasn't uncommon for prisoners to be sued. Many wronged investors want *blood from a turnip*, so to speak. Claire hadn't read the various cases. Harry admitted he'd only scanned them, but believed many stemmed from rumors Mr. Rawls hid money prior to his incarceration. Although he may have had the opportunity while remaining outside of prison, on bond awaiting trial, the allegations were unproven. Judging by the lengthy list of plaintiffs, there were many bidders for a piece of his hidden bounty.

Claire read a blurb suggesting his money was hidden outside of the United States. However, those closest to Mr. Rawls, vehemently denied this, stating Nathaniel was known for his American bravado. They speculated he'd never trusted *foreigners* with his money.

After hours of reading, and not finding anything she hadn't read before, Claire decided to move on to Samuel. Reaching for his stack of information, she noticed the faint sunlight leaking from around the blinds. Refocusing on the clock at the corner of her laptop, she saw it was almost seven thirty.

Claire decided to table – or bed -- the Samuel reread and opt for a shower. She wasn't sure, after the way she left Harry last night, but he usually came over for coffee about eight. She moved stiffly from the soft chair and lifted her empty coffee cup. If she were to survive her incredibly long day, Claire needed more caffeine.

Feeling almost human after another cup of coffee and shower, Claire decided to dress causal, wearing yoga pants, a camisole, and an oversized t-shirt. Not wanting to be busy with the hairdryer when Harry arrived, she combed her wet hair back into a low ponytail and managed a little mascara, lip gloss, blush, and perfume. Claire wasn't the stunning model from last night, and although she wanted to tell him she was sorry, if he walked in and saw her dressed to the nines for coffee, he'd rightfully be suspicious. She wasn't sure of her daily plans. However, as her bare feet padded along the wood floor of the cavernous condo, she smiled at the sunshine streaming through the unblocked windows.

Some research, coffee, warm shower, and fog-free blue skies did wonders to put her life in perspective. Claire's dinner with Tony momentarily sent things off-kilter, but all was neutralizing again. She needed to focus on her mission involving Tony. And that mission wasn't sex! It was retaliation. He may not have sent that box, but her research continued to validate its contents.

As Claire set her laptop on the kitchen table she typed in *Newsweek*. Like so many other publications, *Newsweek* required a subscription in order to access previous editions. That was fine, she thought, *Phillip Roach can have fun figuring out why I'm suddenly so interested in news magazines.*

Starting the coffee maker for another high octane injection, she typed 1975, the year Rawls went public. She remembered a magazine article with a picture of Nathaniel and his family in front of a house like Tony's. She wanted to find that picture, to verify – if only to herself -- that Tony was indeed Anton Rawls. If it wasn't in *Newsweek*, she assumed it must be *Time*. She had an online subscription to that publication, too.

Two hours later she found the picture with the house, Nathaniel, Sharron, Samuel, Amanda, and Anton. Claire couldn't wait to show Harry. She'd tell him about Tony's denial, and then show him the picture to validate her suspicions.

Then Claire realized -- two hours. It was almost ten. Surely, Harry's at SiJo by now. He hadn't come over for coffee. Claire staggered at the sudden disappointment flowing through her. She hadn't realized how much she enjoyed their morning chats, until now, when he didn't show.

There was no question; it was her fault. She'd been rude last night. Would she have ever treated Tony that way? The answer was no, not because she didn't want to, but because he'd never have allowed it. Had she really spent half the night fantasizing about someone who dominated her entire life, including emotions and reactions, when there was a kind understanding man in real life?

Claire went to the bedroom to find her phone. She wanted to send Harry a text, tell him she missed him this morning. Hopefully he'd respond, and maybe she could meet him for lunch.

The screen indicated four missed calls. Picking up her *Emily* phone she had texts, one each from Emily and Courtney. They both wanted to be sure she was all right, after her dinner.

Darn, she'd meant to call them last night. The whole evening just messed her up. She sent a text telling them she was fine and would talk to them, when they had time. Walking toward the kitchen, she added, *I HAVE SOME NEW RELEVANT INFO TO SHARE!*

Honestly, she hadn't checked her Tony phone. That could wait. She needed more time in the sunshine, without his voice and the darkness that swallowed her into its abyss. Smiling, she checked the iPhone. Two calls were from Amber; oh yeah, she'd forgotten to check in with her, too. One call was from Harry, no message. At least he called. She didn't recognize the other number, no message.

When almost to the kitchen she heard a knock at the door. *Wow, Harry must be upset, if he is knocking.* Claire didn't care, as long as he was there. Smiling her biggest grin, she opened the door with a light hearted, "Did you forget your key?"

Her heart stopped beating, and the air dissipated from her lungs. She wasn't staring into Harry's soft blue eyes, wavy blonde hair, or his SiJo fitted black shirt. No, it wasn't his chest with the nicely stretched Under Armor across his wide pecs in front of her. This one was covered by an Armani tailored suit. Claire's smile shattered, as dark eyes once again sent her world into a spiral. The axis which had taken her most of the night to correct was once again wobbling uncontrollably.

Straightening her neck, she suddenly wished for shoes, preferably heels. It was a stupid wish. If a Genie had just given her three, it would be a waste. However, as he loomed, at least six and a half feet high in her doorway and she stood barefooted, she felt incredibly small. Claire didn't like the sense of vulnerability rushing through her nervous system, sending off flares of panic at every synapse.

His voice registered deep, "I don't have a key, but I'd be glad to get one. Just tell me where to sign-up." After so much time of evaluating his looks, eyes, movements, and voice, she immediately assessed: he sounds restrained, yet amused.

She wanted to say, "Go to hell, and let me know when it turns cold – because, that's when you can expect to receive a key!" However instead, she squared her shoulders and tried to display a small amount of decorum, "How did you get up here. You can't be on this floor without a key."

He was still standing in the hallway. Claire held the edge of the door, ready to slam it, if necessary. "Perhaps you could invite me in, and we can discuss it?"

"Tony, why are you here?"

He smirked, "If we're playing one hundred questions, I admit defeat. May I come in?"

Momentarily, Claire stared. Her stomach twisted with the realization, he'd asked the same question twice. It was another of his old pet-peeves. As much as she didn't want to allow him entry, she didn't want risk him asking her a third time. She stood back and nodded. He walked in and surveyed his surroundings with an air of approval.

"My, Claire, you are living much better than I expected. When I first learned of your release, I pictured you destitute."

"I'm sure you enjoyed that scenario. I'm sorry to disappoint."

He snickered, "Disappoint? On the contrary, your ingenuity is to be praised."

Still standing on the marbled floored entry, Claire asked her question, again. "Tony, I will repeat myself, at the risk of being redundant." She could sense the increased intensity in his stare. "Why are you here and how did you access my floor."

"I gained access by the security guard on the first floor. He tried to call you, but you didn't answer." Claire thought about that unknown number. She needed to program *Security* into her phone. "I explained, we are old friends, I'm leaving town, and since I had recently talked with you, I knew you were home and expecting me."

As he spoke her iPhone rang. It was the unknown number again. "This is security. I'll tell them I don't want you here, unless you quickly tell me why you're here." The phone rang again.

Rarely, if ever, did Anthony Rawlings receive an ultimatum. Now faced with one, he didn't anger or hesitate, he answered, "I want to know more about your prison delivery."

She eyed him, more assessment: honesty. Apparently the conversation wasn't *closed* the night before, only tabled until today. After the fourth ring, she brushed the screen and answered. "Hello." "Yes, this is Ms. Nichols." "Yes, he did." "Thank you." "Yes. I will. Good-bye." Tony watched intently as she spoke. She had the sensation of a bird, being evaluated by a cat. Should she fly away, had she just thrown away her only chance of ejecting him from her home, or would she be consumed by a power greater than she could manage?

After her conversation with security ended, she turned back to her *guest*, "I have plans today. Please make this quick."

His eyes scanned up and down her petite form. "Yes, I see you are dressed for business. What do they call that, *business casual?*" The vulnerability of her light weight pants and top made her uneasy. Refusing to take his snide bait, Claire remained silent. His tone turned sultry, "I'm not complaining. I always found the *casual Claire* as sexy as the one who rocked designer dresses."

Dreaming or awake, we perceive only events
that have meaning to us.
- Jane Roberts

Chapter 18

Claire looked up into the sparkling velvety brown eyes. Damn, she'd been seeing those same eyes and that Cheshire expression all night long. Crossing her arms over her breasts, she exhaled, "Please, I have lunch plans, and I'd like to change. Question what you want and go."

"Do you only entertain in the entry, or may we sit?"

His gentlemanly tone was difficult to resist. "We may sit." She led him to the living room. As they sat, him on the sofa and her in a chair, she added, "I know you enjoy coffee, I'd offer you some. But, the last time I got you coffee, it didn't work out so well for me."

Tony smirked, "God, Claire you're something else. I can't imagine anyone else joking about that."

"Well, see, you misinterpreted. I wasn't joking. I'm actually still pissed as hell." This wasn't something she could have said while they were married. And definitely not something she would have said in a restaurant, even a restaurant devoid of other patrons. Some details of their life could only be discussed in private. His rules regarding privacy and appearance were as ingrained as punctuality.

"Good for you." He leaned toward her, his eyes devouring her entirely, until she questioned her own presence. "Your ability to admit your displeasure is refreshing. It encourages me to be honest, too."

Claire did her best to glare, "Honesty. That would be a refreshing change."

His expression remained soft and so were his words, "You should know ...I am sorry."

The world as Claire knew it, shifted. Perhaps it was an earthquake, they do happen in California. Why couldn't he be domineering or abrasive? *That* she could resist. But, apologetic, in the depths of her soul, she never expected to hear those three words.

"What?" She tried unsuccessfully to subdue the overpowering trembling. The volume of her voice rose exponentially with each phrase,

"You're sorry?" The years of submission, incarceration, and domination bubbled out. No, not bubbled -- gushed. This was not *his* house. She was not sequestered away from the love and support of others. She'd say whatever she wanted, and then tell him to leave. If he didn't – she'd call security. They were after all, on her call log. "Well, Tony, I believe I need a little clarification. Tell me what *exactly* you're sorry about. I'll gladly give you a few options."

The fury surging through her veins wouldn't allow her to remain seated. She stood and paced, around the coffee table, in front of the large windows, back to the chair and again to the coffee table. She felt his eyes on her, as she made multiple slow and methodical loops. Her mind was a whirlwind, a tornado, of words. Each syllable vehemently rushed to get out. Instead of opening the flood gate, Claire took a few deep breaths. She wanted to proceed slowly, clearing away the debris cluttering her mind, and choose the right words. Finally, she began, "First, you're *sorry* for invading my privacy for years, years before I even knew you existed. Second, you're *sorry* for kidnapping me, isolating, controlling me, and manipulating me. Third, you're *sorry* for lying to me, pretending you cared and oh yeah, marrying me. Fourth, listen carefully Tony, this is a big one... you're *sorry* for framing me for attempted murder, resulting in incarceration in a federal penitentiary." She sat back down, arms once again crossed over her breasts. It was the most direct she'd ever spoken to him, and it felt liberating. Unfortunately, the resentment coursing through her veins wouldn't allow her to relish her new found independence.

She expected her words to incite anger; after all, she'd experienced his anger before. Nevertheless, carelessly and unapologetically Claire forged ahead, "I would prefer the words, but you are welcome to say, one through four, if that's easier for you."

He leaned forward. Cautiously she looked up into his face. Her body trembled. The cause may have been the fury she'd just released, or perhaps fear of his anticipated reaction. Then she took in his expression and without warning the trembling stopped. His eyes were soft, the color of melted chocolate -- even sad, overflowing with regret. He reached for her hand and gently tugged. Slowly, Claire released her appendage, allowing it to sit in his large palm. Tenderly he closed his fingers encasing her petite hand.

"I am deeply sorry for one and four." He rubbed the top of her hand with his thumb. "I did provide you with an alternative destination for number four." Claire exhaled audibly, Tony continued, "I am not proud of two, but three would never have happened without it." His tone deepened and slowed, "I am not, and never will be sorry for three. And, for the record, I never *lied about* or *pretended* to love you. I didn't realize it at first, but I have loved you since before you knew my name." He slowly lifted the hand he held and lowered his lips to the firm soft skin. "And, you forgot our divorce. I am sincerely sorry for that also. Had I known you would be released so soon, we could still be married." He placed her left hand on her knee, and stroked her empty fourth finger. "You could still *officially* be mine."

Was he implying that *unofficially* she still was? He waited.

As Claire contemplated Tony's words, she thought about her rings. Did he know she'd sold them? Then she noticed him eying the two cellphones on the table, in front of her. She quickly reached for her *Emily phone* and slid it into her camisole between her breasts. Yoga pants don't have pockets.

Tony closed his eyes and gently shook his head. "If I didn't want to see that phone before, I sure as hell do now."

"It's my *work* phone." *When had lying become so easy?*

"Oh, I was unaware of your employment."

"Really, I guess I forgot to inform you or your spies." She didn't think it was appropriate to use Phillip's name.

"Claire, I want to show you that I can change. Have as many damn phones as you want. Two seem excessive, but go for it."

"Thank you for your permission. I don't need it. I can have fifty phones, if I want."

Tony nodded, with a stupid grin and a spark in his eyes. Claire continued, "It's documented, when a person is forbidden something, once it's made available, they tend to overindulge."

Tony met her gaze, his tone a sultry melody, "Before it is made available, a person may dream of it, long for it, and fantasize about it. Especially if they once had it and know how amazing it is."

God she hated him, and not! Her insides tightened as the feelings from last night returned. The inappropriate sensations, deep inside, threatened her irrelevant tone. "I don't recall availability being an issue for you."

"Be careful, Claire. That could be interpreted as an invitation."

"Then once again, you would be misinterpreting." She stood.

He stood and stepped toward her. She remained strong and defiant, straightening her spine and standing as tall, as her five–four frame would allow. At the same time, she wanted to crumble. Their bodies stood resolute, untouching, separated by inches. Those inches might as well have been miles. The space created a deep chasm, filled with a magnitude of baggage and memories. Impassable, the gorge served as an insurmountable barrier.

Or, could the gap be closed? His voice held more than a hint of sensuality, "I believe you want, what I want, as much as I do."

Claire feigned strength and ignorance. What had she told Phillip Roach? She said, she didn't recommend lying to her ex-husband. Yet, here she was, giving it her all. "If you're suggesting I want you to leave, you are absolutely correct. If you're suggesting anything else, it couldn't be farther from the truth." His cologne penetrated her subconscious, the same exhilarating scent that infiltrated her dreams.

His head bowed slightly. Claire feared he would kiss her. She wanted to back away and at the same time, she wanted to feel his lips on hers.

She fought the urge to lift her chin toward him, surrendering her hungry mouth.

The only possible conclusion she could ascertain was Tony was a giant magnet. His pull affected everything, from the rotation of the earth, to her mind's ability to reason. Losing her battle, she slowly tilted her face upward.

He gently held her chin, as his voice continued with its seductive undertone, "You, my dear, have never been a good liar."

In a moment of strength, Claire backed away and sat, exasperated. She'd willingly admit defeat in this stupid stare-off. His proximity was more than she could bear. She needed air and space. Her arms once again crossed her heaving bosom, igniting friction on her disloyal nipples. Frustrated, she admitted, "You're right. Your deceitfulness far exceeds my modest attempts at dishonesty. I bow-down to your superior duplicity."

Tony retook his seat on the sofa as his knee touched hers. "I know you have no reason to believe me, but I thought you should know why I came to California."

She looked up into his genuine gaze, "Why?"

"To take you back to Iowa."

Claire stared at her ex-husband. A momentary feeling of panic filled her senses. She sat dumbfounded, unable to respond, afraid to trust her own voice. The appealing idea to slap his smug face and scream at him, danced through her consciousness. She knew she couldn't do it. She'd already pushed her luck with her earlier verbal tirade. Nevertheless, the fleeting thought made her smile. Simultaneously, she fought the desires she'd been experiencing all night. That traitorous part of her wanted to forget all reason and take whatever he offered, and more. Eventually, wisdom prevailed; she responded, "Well, since *this time* I have a choice, I'm going to say *no*."

"Catherine misses you."

She searched his face for insincerity and found none. However, she'd misjudged that in the past. The sound of the woman's name made her heart ache. Claire had no reason to lie, "I miss her, too." Hesitantly she asked, "Does she believe I tried to kill you?"

His half smile and softened eyes disappeared. Breaking the connection he looked down at his own hands. Shaking his head slightly, he answered, "I'm not sure. We've never discussed it. I know at first she was worried about me. Then once I was well, she was upset, but I don't know for sure if it was at you or at me. The subject's never come up."

"Then how do you know she misses me?"

"I just do. When word came of your pardon..."

She interrupted him, "You were angry."

This time he stood and paced. Claire watched his jaw clench and unclench. She'd seen it before; his attempt to maintain control. Part of her wanted him to lose it, not a masochistic desire, more clarification. The frightening domineering man was much easier to resist than the sensual, apologetic one.

148

Tony stopped at the large windows. His back toward her, he seemed to be absorbing the view, taking in the mountains and sunlit sky. Silently she waited and watched. Eventually his shoulders squared, and with his back still toward her, she heard his restrained voice, "I was. I admit I was... stunned. Governor Preston informed me of your release *two weeks* after it occurred." He emphasized the two weeks. "I was angry at everyone, at *you* for being pardoned, at Jane Allyson for presenting the petition, at Governor Bosley for signing it. Hell, I was even mad at the clerk that filed it." He turned toward her. She knew those black eyes. He may have restrained his voice, but his true emotion shone like beacons through his intense gaze. Refusing to look away, Claire met his stare with her own intensity. He went on, "I finally figured out, the person I was the most upset with, was *me*. For the first time in *years*, yes more than three -- you know that now-- I'd lost track of you." His volume increased, "My god, you were gone!"

There were so many things churning in her brain Claire couldn't speak. There were statements, accusations, and questions. None would make themselves known. She just watched, knowing she'd done what she'd subconsciously wanted. She'd pushed him to the brink. Tony lingered on the precipice; a slight breeze could push him into a complete meltdown.

Her heart beat rapidly, as he walked toward her. There was no violence. His tone and eyes mellowed. He resumed his seat. "Damn it, Claire. Nothing has been the same without you. The house is just a big empty hole."

She exhaled and asked, "Tell me why?"

He looked puzzled, "Why is it empty? Because *you* are not there."

"No, Tony. Why did you do it to me? Why'd you set me up, worse -- arrange my entire life to look as though I was after your money, setting you up for the kill? You know I continually told you, I didn't care about the money. But everything from the beginning was manipulated to make me look guilty. Now you say you loved me. You don't do *that* to someone you love. Tell me why you did it."

"It isn't past tense, Claire. I still love you. And I thought you knew why."

"I want to hear it from you."

"What was in the box, you said you received? What information did you think I revealed?"

She didn't have time to filter her answers, the words came tumbling out. "There were pictures, articles, and a letter. It all explained that your birth name was Anton Rawls, you changed it after the death of your grandfather and parents." As the words flowed, she realized the thing she'd been missing. She didn't say grandparents and parents. What happened to Tony's grandmother? Could she still be alive? She would be very old. Maybe, she sent Claire the information? Or maybe, she was behind this vendetta. Would it lessen the sting if Claire learned it wasn't *all* Tony's doing?

"Was it handwritten? Where is it? I'd like to see it."

"Yes, the note was handwritten. I thought it looked like your writing. It wasn't signed, but you never signed anything." It was Claire's turn to look down. "You can't see it," She exhaled, "I burned it."

She heard him laugh, "You what?"

Looking up, squaring her shoulders, she repeated, "I burned it, all of it. I took it to the incinerator at the prison and watched it burn."

He stared for a moment and exclaimed, "You are serious. You have no proof of anything you just said? You burned it." His shoulders relaxed. The tension that glued his muscles together, dissipated before her eyes. He continued, "I don't know who sent it to you. I did confirm, today, that you received a box in October of last year. The prison said the return address was Emily's."

Claire nodded. "Yes, I assumed it was books or something."

He exhaled again, "Burned it. Why?"

"I've asked myself that same question a thousand times. I believe it was a cleansing of sorts, my way of removing you from my life."

Tony smirked, "How is that working for you?"

The tension in the room disintegrated, like the ashes of her information. She couldn't help but grin. "Not as well as I'd hoped." Claire glanced at a clock, 11:16. "I really do need to get ready for my lunch *date*." There was no reason to emphasize the last word, but she did. "If we're done, I'd like you to leave." Her voice no longer held the urgency from before. While the ability to direct *his* movements empowered her, the memory of destroying the evidence subdued her.

"I would like to ask you one more thing?" She nodded; her strength to fight him was waning. "Who was the expected recipient of that dazzling smile?"

Claire's mind spun. *What smile?* "What are you talking about?"

"When you first opened the door, your smile was earth shaking. Who were you expecting?"

"A good friend."

Tony raised his eyebrows, but Claire didn't respond. She didn't have to. She'd answered his question, the first time he asked. She didn't owe him anymore. Truthfully, she no longer owed him that.

Claire stood, "If you'll follow me, I'll show you to the door."

Tony stood, "I will not give-up my quest." Though his tone was friendly, his words were both a promise and a threat; they both knew it.

The living room and hall continued to stretch making the walk to the door endless. Finally they reached her destination.

"Please give Catherine my love." As she reached for the door handle she continued, "*If* you have truly changed, as you claim, you will respect my decisions. *If* that is the case, you are wasting your time."

"I have invested much more." He paused, "One last thing," his words slowed, "do not share your unsupported theories -- with anyone."

Claire straightened her neck, once again facing off with her ex. "I'm sorry. It's too late for that."

150

He reached for her hand. Her thoughts were forming too slowly to react with enough speed, to save it from his clutches. He lowered his lips to soft skin as his fingertips brushed her palm beneath. Waves of warmth radiated throughout her body. Before releasing her captured appendage, he warned, "Be careful. You don't want to disappoint me." He dropped her hand as his dark brown eyes peered into the depths of her soul.

She maintained eye contact, "That – is no longer my concern. Good-bye, Tony."

He nodded, turned and strode toward the elevator. She watched his tall, elegant body disappear down the hallway.

It took her a minute; finally, she shut the door and collapsed with her back against the hard wooden surface. Her *Emily phone* fell from her camisole. The sound of shattering, refocused her thoughts. The small black devise lay helpless on the shiny marble floor. Dropping to her knees, she retrieved the phone. Opening its cover, the screen was black. Not registering the implication, she remembered Tony's eyes. *When he left, were they black, or had he kept them under control? Could he really change? Could she ever forgive him?*

She tried to focus. The phone would not turn on.

Closing her eyes and absorbing the coolness of the marble floor, she fought to think. Each thought was epic and yet minuscule. She needed to get another phone. She also needed to call Harry. It was too late for lunch; she was too drained. Maybe she should nap, and later she'd face life's decisions.

Dragging herself to the living room, she found her iPhone, so heavy. She managed to complete her unfinished text to Harry. Focusing, she read what she'd started an hour before: it talked about missing him at breakfast and being sorry for her behavior the night before. She just hadn't pushed *send* before Tony arrived. She added: *WOULD YOU JOIN ME FOR DINNER?* And hit *send.*

Her bed seemed too far away. Yawning, Claire noticed the soft inviting sofa. Nestling onto the indulgent, cool leather she reached for a throw pillow and inhaled *his* scent. The brief exhilaration morphed to disappointment, questioning her future. Would Tony ever let her go? *What exactly did he mean by his comment not giving up his quest?*

Waking at two in the morning was not a good idea. Sudden exhaustion engulfed her. Claire was so tired. The large glass windows filled the room with sunshine. She glanced toward the mountains in the distance, appreciating their beauty, as their purple haze filled her vision with color. Dreamily, she observed the sky above. The amazing clarity reminded her of a Midwestern sky, crystal blue with light fluffy wisps of clouds. She wondered when the high pressure system had settled in, very unusual for Palo Alto this time of year. She knew that from meteorology, not experience. After all, she'd only lived on the west coast over a month. So much had changed in such a short time.

Normally, on a beautiful day like this, she'd go for a walk. Her daily hikes provided fresh air, exercise, and a wonderful view of the city. They took her to places she might not see by car. Surprisingly, there was something reassuring about Phil's surveillance. His omnipresence gave her confidence, like the cameras back in Iowa. She was being monitored. She could choose to focus on the negative, or she could relish the positive. Claire was confident Tony didn't know she and Phil had spoken. Nonetheless, if anything threatened her, she knew, Phillip Roach would be there. Inhaling Tony's cologne, Claire surmised Phil would intercede with any perpetrator -- except his employer.

That was apparent with Phil's departure from the restaurant last night. Claire made a mental note to question Phil. Thoughts were becoming too elusive, slipping away. Her attention was once again outside. The blue of the sky melted into the purple of the mountains, bleeding into a swirl of color until her eyes could no longer focus. Finally, succumbing to the tremendous weight of her eyelids, Claire closed out the light and color. The darkness absorbed her thoughts. Everything else could wait; she needed a little nap.

Claire tried to wake, but was that possible from within a dream? The one, from the night before, was back. Again, it felt so tangible. Why couldn't her subconscious just let her sleep?

It began with Tony's voice, coming from a fog, "Put your arms around my neck."

The directive was not demanding; yet, she struggled to resist. Undaunted, he controlled her movements. Not with words, that she could resist. No, he manipulated her thoughts and actions with the most devious means of persuasion, a kiss -- his warm full lips engaged hers. Conscious reasoning evaporated into the fog of her dreamlike state. Tony didn't need to repeat his command; her arms encircled his neck. Her obedience was rewarded with more of the kissing, more warmth, more bliss. Then the world moved. Claire had the sensation of Tony lifting her, or maybe she was floating. That can happen in dreams, can't it? There's even a line in a song: *in dreams our feet never touch the ground*. Claire reassured herself, this wasn't real.

She'd watched him walk away and locked the door. Didn't she?

Convincing herself this was only fantasy, Claire nuzzled into his chest and allowed the illusion of his powerful, yet tender arms to transport her through the condominium. Familiar sights passed blurrily before her eyes. Was it from the dream, or the speed with which they traveled? Claire closed her eyes and accepted the journey, anticipating the destination.

Somehow she was on her bed. When she woke at two in the morning, she didn't straighten the bed clothes. The exposed, soft sheets were cool against her skin. Gently, the clip was freed from her hair, allowing her auburn trusses to fall in waves onto her soft pillow. Piece by piece her clothing disappeared. She obeyed the simple commands, "Lift your arms over your head." Her oversized t-shirt was eased over her head, then the camisole. Claire moaned as the cool air caused her nipples to harden. Her physical reaction did not go unnoticed. His now gentle fingers lightly caressed the hard nubs. Closing her eyes, with her arms above her head, she arched her back, surrendering her vulnerable breasts. She ached for more.

Next, her yoga pants were eased past her ankles, exposing her black lacy panties. The barely visible material was but a scant hurdle on the road to their destination. Nevertheless, a streak of panic ran through her, like ice on overheated skin. Goose bumps formed on her arms and legs. The sudden alarm intensified everything, from the sound of their breathing to the touch of his hands. The small lace barrier was another direct violation of *his* rules. She watched his expression as his fingers traced the delicate trim. In the center, inches below her bellybutton was a small, black, satin bow. His strong hands encircled her hips as his thumbs teased the tiny adornment. She was a present – a gift, wrapped only for him. He didn't speak, but his chest rose and fell, as his breathing deepened. She sighed with relief, when the tips of his lips turned upward into his handsome, devilish smile.

The panties were gone.

"This isn't real. This is a dream." She wasn't sure if the words were in her head or if she'd spoken them aloud.

They must have been said aloud, because Tony responded. "Do you want it to be a dream?"

She shook her head, *no.*

No, she didn't want it to be a dream? Or no, she didn't want it to be real? She didn't know. "It isn't real." Claire repeated, a little less confident of her words or her ability to speak.

It felt real. The fragrance of his cologne filled her room, as only she filled his sight. It was that all-encompassing gaze, the one that removed everyone and everything from the world, leaving only them. The heat radiating from his amazing body was overwhelming; she wondered if it could burn her. Yet, she wasn't concerned. This wasn't the man who hurt her. The man in her dream was the one she loved and loved her. Her mind searched for reason. He'd proclaimed that love again, in the living room. Now her subconscious wanted to fulfill its desires. She submitted to the dream. Fighting would take too much energy. Even her unconscious knew her energy would be better utilized in other ways.

His clothes were also gone. When had he taken them off? Time can be so elusive in dreams...

He was talking; asking questions and voicing appreciation of everything before him. Nevertheless, his words didn't register, only the rhythm of his deep sensual tone. That cadence, along with the strong beating of his heart, within his massive, heat-radiating chest, calmed and excited her. Claire listened and nodded, even though she was unsure of what she authorized.

Her senses were on high alert. The amazing sight of him, unclothed, his distinctive scent, the warm commanding touch of his hands, the sound of his sexy breathing, so close to her ear, and the taste of his soft lips, produced gasps and moans. The unrelenting provocation generated overwhelming desire. She heard her own voice, pleading for more. Yet, she wasn't conscious of speaking. Everything was in another dimension. Involuntary actions and reactions overtook her mind, words, and body. When had fantasy ever taken her to this height?

His hands felt so real, as they caressed her skin. Each touch intensified the electric sensations and passionate desires. She'd been fighting these images all night. She couldn't do it anymore. The man of her dreams didn't take, as the real one could. He asked, as Harry had done.

That was it, Claire reasoned. Her subconscious created a combination, an amalgamation of sorts. When the husky voice requested permission, her body screamed with need, "Oh god yes, please!" His smile, too, seemed real. Reaching up, she longed to touch his face. Unlike the night before, her fingertips connected their target. She caressed the smooth, freshly shaven skin of his cheeks and wove her fingers through his thick black hair. Her sensitive nipples pushed toward his chest. Instead of feeling them against his warm skin, Tony bent down and suckled the vulnerable hard tips. Again and again, her back arched. She wanted everything. It had been so long.

What truly wakes one from the depths of sleep? Was it external, like the sound of a ringing phone and noises from the street below? Or was it internal, like the twisting in your stomach from ravenous hunger? Snuggling into the soft, smooth sheets she thought about food. When had she last eaten? Slowly her consciousness took over, and an unreasonable fear filled her being. It was the fear that when she opened her eyes, she'd no longer be in Palo Alto, but in *her* suite -- in Iowa.

Trying unsuccessfully to subdue the rising panic, Claire did the only thing she could. She opened her eyes.

Relief escaped in a deep exhale as she viewed the inside of her room, in Amber's condominium. She rolled toward her clock, 5:17. Was it that early? She closed her eyes. No, it wasn't that early... it was that late. She'd slept the entire day away. Pulling back the covers she revealed her clothed body. The only piece of clothing she no longer wore was the large t-shirt currently lying on the rug near her bed.

Walking toward her bathroom she remembered her dream. She stopped and took a moment to survey her room. Nothing seemed out of place. Yet, hadn't she fallen asleep on the couch?

When she was young, her mother told her she would sometimes sleepwalk. Perhaps, that's what she'd done. Turning on the warm water of the shower she decided to freshen up before dinner. Removing her clothes she inspected herself in the mirror. There were times when she was with Tony, that her body displayed evidence of their intimacy or his domination.

Her skin appeared untouched. Nevertheless, her body felt ... she wasn't sure how to describe it... content? The unrelenting tension she'd been experiencing since Harry's first video game session was gone.

Satisfied -- yes, that's how she felt, content and satisfied. It was as if she'd been thoroughly taken, filled and pleased, by a memory.

Claire stepped under the soft hot spray. When the water struck her nipples she flinched and shielded them from the assault. *That's strange,* she thought. *Why am I so tender?* As she poured the shampoo into her hand, she briefly inhaled the fragrance of Tony's cologne. Her next breath was filled with the scent of flowers.

Claire shook her head as she massaged the floral cream into her hair. Her imagination was working overtime. She needed to compartmentalize Tony away. Hopefully, she had dinner plans with Harry. He could help her leave the world of fantasy and concentrate on reality. She wanted to tell him about Tony and about the bombshell of him not being the sender of the box. There was something else too... stepping from the shower, onto the soft mat, she tried to recall.

As she dried her skin, she remembered. It was Tony's grandmother. She wanted to research Sharron Rawls... Something in the mirror caught Claire's attention. It was her pile of dirty clothes. She picked up the camisole and the yoga pants. Hadn't she been wearing under wear?

The most authentic thing about us is our capacity to create,
to overcome, to endure, to transform, to love,
and to be greater than our suffering.
– Ben Okri.

Chapter 19

-Early 1985-

Marie didn't want to care this much, not about anyone. Then why was she sitting in her nightgown, at three in the morning, watching Ms. Sharron breathe? It wasn't like she was anything to most of this family, other than hired help – and she sure as hell didn't have a family of her own.

The breaths came, inconsistent, with a rattle. *If the doctors could just stop the damn rattle.*

Marie sat in the high-backed Queen Anne chair and wrapped her arms around her knees. The doctor, who'd been to the estate earlier, said the IV medication would fight the infection. Marie just hoped Ms. Sharron was strong enough to be the battle ground. What good was a strong army if the earth crumbled under their siege?

Marie didn't have medical training.

Hadn't that been said, about a hundred times in the past few days? Mr. Samuel and Ms. Amanda made no bones about the fact someone *more qualified* should be at Ms. Sharron's bedside. Not only did they express their dissatisfaction with Marie's medical qualifications, they also didn't want her to be the sole person with Mrs. Sharron when she moved from this life to the next.

As was the case with everything, the decision wasn't theirs to make. Marie would remain as long as Mr. Nathaniel Rawls wanted her there. He didn't argue; he declared, "Sharron is comfortable with Marie. She'll stay." It may not be up for debate, but Samuel and Amanda made no attempt to hide their disproval.

Even without medical training, Marie knew Ms. Sharron was in pain and laboring. Everything Marie had read said Alzheimer's disease was unpredictable. She could pass away today or live another five years. As Marie watched and listened, she felt the need to pray for today. This wasn't a life she wanted Ms. Sharron to endure any longer. Then again, if she passed, what did that mean for Marie? It meant she would leave this estate and go on her way. Although, it would undoubtedly make Samuel and Amanda happy, Marie wondered about Nathaniel? It surprised Marie to realize she'd actually miss her talks with the stubborn old man.

Marie chuckled softly, *old*? He was in fact old, at least a lot older than she. In the past eighteen months he looked even older. Nonetheless, for a man with so many concerns weighing him down he was incredibly attractive. And the power he wielded, outside of this room, was impressive. Yet, the part of Nathaniel Rawls Marie would miss was the part no one else saw. Not the ostentatious, narcissistical, tyrant making deals and barking orders. She would miss the handsome, seasoned gentleman who sat for hours, holding a hand that rarely held back. The man who propped himself on the bed, held his wife's frail body, and watched her sleep upon his chest.

"I thought I told you to go to bed?"

The deep voice startled Marie back to reality. She turned her tear stained cheeks toward the man who'd been in her thoughts. "I tried, but I couldn't sleep."

"So, can you sleep better in that chair?"

Marie smiled, "No, but at least I'm doing something."

Nathaniel pulled another chair beside Marie's, sat and squeezed Marie's hand. "I can hire someone else to sit with her at night, so you can get more rest."

Marie turned away and tried to breathe, her emotions were overwrought. Her question came through with more dejection than she intended, "Do you also think I'm incapable of doing my job?"

"Marie, are you crying?"

"No." She lied.

His strong hand still covered hers. "I think you are more than capable. I just think you need a break. You can't be by her side twenty-four hours a day."

"What about you?"

"What about me?"

"You sit here half the night and work all day. You need sleep, too."

He smirked, "Do I, now?"

"You do. You can't go on burning your candle at both ends. I suggest some time away from work, or more time sleeping." His sly smile made her feel self-conscious; was he making fun of her? "All right, now why are you grinning? Are you laughing at me?" she asked.

He tried to hide the smile showing through his dark sad eyes. The smile was a nice change to the solemn expression he often wore while observing his sleeping wife. "I'm not laughing; I'm amused."

"Fine, be amused. Just get some sleep."

"I don't remember the last time someone told *me* what to do." Nathaniel sat back and watched his wife. Marie didn't go to bed; she sat and allowed him to talk. She couldn't take away his pain. Perhaps, if he felt comfortable enough to express his thoughts, the ache would lessen, in some way. Nathaniel continued, "I do actually."

They were no longer looking at one another or touching. Both sat with their heads resting on the plush winged sides of the Queen Anne chairs, watching Sharron. Marie encouraged, "You do?"

"Sharron, she was the only person who was ever able to tell me what to do," he chuckled, "and how to do it." He went on describing the love of his life, her incredible beauty and tenacious will. "When I came home from the war, it wasn't over, but my tour was. She'd written to me, and I her. We still have those letters in a box somewhere. I couldn't wait to see her again, to hear her voice, and hold her." He reached forward and picked up her frail hand. "I should show you pictures. I know what you see -- isn't what I see. I still see the vibrant strong-willed girl I rushed home to marry."

Marie didn't comment. The tears she'd shed earlier now had companions. Her heart broke for this man telling a beautiful love story, one which she knew had a cruel sad ending.

"Did I ever tell you, her family didn't approve of me?"

That was difficult to believe. After all, Nathaniel Rawls was an esteemed businessman. "No, why not?"

"Well, first her father didn't like me," and with a chuckle, "Believe me, the feeling was mutual. But mostly, it was because they had money. Not a lot, but they were comfortable. I barely had two pennies to rub together. He didn't believe I could provide for his daughter, *in the style to which she was accustomed.*"

Marie grinned, "You proved him wrong!"

"I did." His voice didn't sound triumphant, more melancholy.

"Did he ever admit he was wrong?"

"No. And that's understandable; real men don't apologize. Besides, he died before I made my first million. This," he gestured with his hands, "has all been for her. And now, I have to keep going for her. I refuse to back away from any of it. Even if she isn't with me, I'm still doing it all for her."

"She still loves you." It was surprisingly easy to carry on heartfelt conversations while not looking at one another. "Your voice excites her. Her heart beats stronger when you're near."

"Do you think she still knows?"

"Some days, some times. When I first started, she liked to look through old photo albums. I think it was her way to hold on to memories. She'd tell me stories about the two of you, when you were young, and about Mr. Samuel and Mr. Anton. You two had -- I mean have -- something very few other people are ever blessed to experience."

Nathaniel looked at his watch, "Marie, it's after three thirty. You go get some sleep. I'll stay here until morning. You can relieve me in about three hours."

When she didn't move, he stood and took her hand. She noticed the gleam in his eyes. He was thinking about another time and another place. "I mean it. I want you to get some rest."

She allowed herself to stand, her hand still in his. "Good night, Nathaniel." While in the presence of others, she addressed him formally. However, during their private talks, the *Mr. Rawls* was long gone.

It wasn't planned. It wasn't right. Nevertheless, as he stood there holding Marie's warm soft hand and their chests touched, with only her robe covered nightgown and his robe covered t-shirt separating them, something changed. They both knew it, but neither one uttered a word.

Nathaniel Rawls took what he wanted in life. What he wanted, above all else, was his wife. Life was cruel, and he couldn't reach her, no matter how long or how hard he tried. He'd worked his entire life to give her the best of everything. However, he couldn't give her health.

Standing in front of him was everything Sharron had been and had ceased to be. In his hand was energy, vibrant and strong-willed, embodied in a lovely caring young woman. As he looked down into her soft gray eyes he noticed a sparkle only recently doused with tears.

Although he still held tight to her hand and their hearts beat frantically within their touching chests, Nathaniel watched as Marie turned her twinkling eyes away. He didn't want to lose that vivacity. It was more life than he'd be held in a long time. He gently raised her chin and spoke with a deep throaty voice. In all of their talks, she'd never heard this tone before, "You need to go to your room. May I suggest locking your door?"

His tenor terrified her. Not that Marie feared Nathaniel; she feared the desires stirring within her. After all, she hadn't been with a man for a long time, and never consensually. For the first time in her life, she experienced consensual thoughts and feelings. How could she possibly be thinking like this, with Ms. Sharron only two feet away?

Her voice also came from somewhere deep, almost unrecognizable, even to herself, "Does everyone do exactly as you say?" She liked the way he smiled. It was so much better than his grief.

"Everyone, who is smart."

"I've never claimed intelligence."

Nathaniel stood over six six. Marie was about five eight. When she was younger her height made her feel awkward. At this moment, it felt perfect. Her head fit perfectly under his chin. And with her chin tilted, as it was in his hand, and his face inclined their lips were but millimeters apart. The next minutes lasted hours. His lips moved forward and she made no move to stop them.

It could be argued that she moved toward them, possibly lifting herself onto her toes. Honestly, there was such a small space to cover -- the *who* was inconsequential as at the moment was the *why*. What mattered was the *what. What were they doing?*

His lips were full, warm, firm, and right. They'd both been overwhelmed by the sadness at Sharron's recent decline. Perhaps, within a cold gloomy New Jersey winter where hope seemed lost, a glimmer of joy could exist.

"If you don't tell me to stop – now -- I can't promise I'll be able to stop in the future."

Marie remained silent. When he tugged her hand toward her attached suite, she willingly followed. She wasn't hoping to cure her loneliness as much as his. Could a *wrong* relationship actually be *right*, in the middle of this desolate life?

*Strength does not come from winning. Your struggles
develop your strength. When you go through hardships
and decide not to surrender, that is strength.*
--Mahatma Ghandi

Chapter 20

Claire licked the spoon, followed by a satisfied, "Yum." She lifted the pan of creamy cilantro sauce and set it aside to cool. Her empty stomach twisted in anticipation of the appetizing aromas. Amber's kitchen glowed with warmth and the rich fragrance of baking fish. She pushed the *light* diagram on the screen of the wall-oven and illuminated the small cavern. Inside, she spied fresh tilapia filets sizzling in a warm bath of liquid butter and lemon juice. Claire reread the clock. *Harry should be here any minute,* she thought.

Walking toward the stove top, she checked the water level in her sauce pan. It would soon serve as the perfect basin for asparagus to soften to *al dente*. The mixed green salad, lightly tossed with raspberry vinaigrette dressing, was already on the set table as was an open bottle of cabernet. Claire placed wineglasses next to the tall, filled water goblets.

After her shower, she found her iPhone in the living room and read Harry's response: *DINNER SOUNDS GREAT. WE SHOULD TALK.*

Claire wasn't sure why the word *talk* sounded so ominous, but it did. She immediately responded: *AMBER'S GONE, HOW ABOUT DINNER HERE? MORE PRIVACY FOR TALKING?* She finally exhaled when his, *SURE,* came in reply.

Claire checked the clock again, three more minutes. It seemed as though the world was spinning in slow motion. Claire hit a few buttons on Amber's whole house sound system and listened as Michael Buble's rich voice filtered through hidden speakers.

Unlike most evenings where Harry was home by 6:30, tonight he'd sent a text apologizing for unseen delays. Claire didn't start the tilapia until 7:45; after he messaged he was on his way. With traffic, the short drive could take half an hour. Without traffic it should take less than ten minutes. She looked at the timer, four more minutes.

Clock: 8:17. *Where was he?*

When the timer sounded, forcing Claire to face the reality of her still lonely condominium, she removed the fish from the oven and placed it in the microwave to stay warm. Her instincts told her to call or text Harry.

161

However, she didn't listen. Instead, she poured herself a glass of wine and walked aimlessly around the condominium.

In the living room she peered through the large windows into the night sky. The bottom of the vista twinkled with illuminations from the valley, the glow of the street lights, cars and buildings. The top half reminded her of velvet with the mountains intensifying the black sky; only the top quarter lessened the darkness with faint flickers of light. Unfortunately, the city lights overpowered the potential glow of the distant stars.

Momentarily, Claire thought about the stars in Iowa. From her balcony at Tony's secluded estate she could see millions. Instantaneously, Claire remembered Tony's quest and wrapped her free arm around her torso. Would he succeed? Would she be back on that balcony?

Still wandering, Claire found herself in the spare bedroom containing her unorthodox filing system. She reached for the stack of information she'd put down almost twenty four hours ago, the information they'd accumulated on Samuel Rawls.

Claire knew she needed to research Sharron Rawls, but it could wait until tomorrow.

She leafed through the documents and found herself staring at the *Santa Monica Coroner's Report* for Amanda and Samuel Rawls. It was something she'd put off reading, but as they say: there's no time like the present. She settled herself on the corner of the bed and began to read.

There were a lot of technical terms discussing the injuries, explaining the trajectory of bullets and the damage that ensued. Claire skimmed the information until she came to the section entitled: *Coroner's Assessment.*

She cautiously read the opinion of the elected official: *It is the judgment of this office Amanda Rawls died of multiple gunshot wounds. While she was struck in the leg, spinal cord, and right shoulder, the lethal shot connected her right ventricle. Death occurred due to rapid loss of blood. A bullet struck the C-5 vertebrae severing the spinal cord resulting in immediate paralysis. It is believed the victim was unable to move during the last minutes of life although she would have remained conscious. Time of Death: based on body temperature believed to be approximately 1600 hours. The trajectory indicates a taller assailant standing at least five feet away.*

Claire tried desperately not to internalize the information as she flipped the pages of the report. She found the same section of Samuel's report. *It is the judgment of this office that Samuel Rawls died from multiple gunshot wounds. He exhibited injuries in both legs and his spinal column. The fatal shot occurred with a bullet to the right temple. His right hand tested positive for residue consistent with the placement of the weapon.*

The weapon found near Mr. Samuel Rawls has been confirmed to be the weapon used with both Mr. and Mrs. Rawls. Time of Death estimated at approximately 1600 hours.

162

Claire sighed. She'd put off reading this report, fearing it would implicate Tony instead of Samuel. Although tragic, she found the information comforting. The times of death exonerated Tony, proving he wasn't responsible for his parents' death.

Then again, the reports raised new questions: Why would Samuel have multiple injuries? Most people committing suicide don't shoot themself in the legs or back? What about the neighbor's statement? What about the other woman? Samuel's sister? After minutes of scanning, Claire determined the other woman must have been a dead lead. No sister existed or was mentioned in any other reports surrounding the deaths of Samuel and Amanda Rawls.

Finishing off her glass of wine, Claire read the clock, 9:07. *Where is Harry?* The room wobbled slightly. Her head felt light with wine and lack of food. She left the research on the bed and went toward the kitchen. On the shiny granite countertop, her iPhone sat all alone. Claire reached for the devise and pushed buttons. Immediately the icon for missed calls appeared with the number two. As she changed the screen to see the numbers, she saw a text from Harry:

IM SO SORRY. IM ON HAMILTON AVENUE. ACCIDENT RIGHT IN FRONT OF ME. IM FINE BUT STAYING WITH VICTIM UNTIL POLICE AND PARAMEDICS ARRIVE.

She immediately called his number; it went to voice mail. Claire hung up and called again. She felt an unwelcome tightening in her chest as she ran for the door. Hamilton was just a block or two away. She could be there in minutes if she walked fast, sooner if she ran. The phone rang as she threw open the door to her condominium. If she hadn't looked up, she would have run right into him.

*****

Derek quietly entered their dark condominium. Coming home much later than he'd planned, he placed his keys on the small table in the foyer and gazed down the dark hallway. Seeping from around the door to Sophia's new studio he saw golden beams of light. He slipped off his shoes and walked soundlessly toward the glow. With each step his anticipation mounted, would he finally find his wife drawing or painting? She'd been on the West Coast for almost two weeks and hadn't so much as touched a sketch pad. With each step he realized, more than anything, Derek wanted to see his wife lost in her world of creativity.

Of course, over the past fourteen days she'd given every excuse for avoiding her new studio; adjusting to the time change, getting to know the neighbors, learning her way around Silicon Valley -- all valid, especially his favorite, getting to know people at his work. When Derek worked in Boston and Sophia spent her days and nights on the Cape, she rarely interacted with his fellow workers. He often wondered if it were proximity or personality. It was no secret, they lived in different worlds. Nonetheless, her lack of daily interaction didn't hinder her presence at social functions, where she mingled beautifully, being her gregarious self.

163

Derek often felt a twinge of pride when coworkers noticed his lovely wife. Some of the Boston associates even commented about Derek's *perfect life*, a gorgeous wife patiently waiting miles away, leaving his days free to *explore* what Boston had to offer. Derek didn't agree. He had more woman in Sophia than he'd ever dreamt; exploring wasn't on his radar.

Truthfully, it wasn't just Sophia's looks, although he approved; it was her uncensored zest for life -- her ability to see the world in a way he never would. As Derek anticipated her arrival to their new Santa Clara home, he readied himself for a whirlwind of excitement.

It never happened.

From the moment Sophia stepped into his new office, he noticed the difference. Her beauty never wavered, yet her spark and drive did. The spark which drew him to her, like a moth to a flame, was gone. In the past two weeks, she's unpacked their condo, shopped, made regular appearances at his office, attended a few business dinners, and waited patiently for his return home. Derek wondered if he'd unknowingly married a Stepford wife.

He longed for the woman he'd left on the Cape, the woman who would paint all night, crawl into bed before his alarm, nuzzle close, and pout when he finally pulled away from their early morning encounter. She filled his fantasies. Yet, of all the sudden changes, Sophia's lack of *art* bothered Derek most. She'd made no attempt to organize her new home studio. Even after Derek ordered her a new desk and some of the basics, she'd done nothing to make it hers. Now, as Derek slipped down the bleached wooden planks, toward the light and resonating soft jazz music, his anticipation grew.

He read his watch: 11:27. His meeting turned to dinner, into more discussion and into more drinks. It wasn't the first time since Sophia's arrival he'd disappointed her by not coming home at a decent hour.

Leaning around the slightly ajar door, Derek peered into the light *at the end of the dark tunnel*. His chest filled with love, seeing Sophia's long blonde hair secured by a big clip and the deep swoop of her nightgown. She was turned the other direction, sitting cross legged on the floor, with her sketch pad on top of an unpacked box. Her hand moved urgently as the charcoal brushed the surface of the linen tablet. He saw his wife's slender neck all the way down to the middle of her back. Though the room was still in disarray, he noticed a few new bags of art supplies.

Derek fought the desire to break his wife's trance. He realized the woman before him, on the floor with darkened fingertips and bare feet was the love of his life. And watching her in this state, almost drugged by her own creative muse, was Derek's favorite aphrodisiac. The scent of her perfume mixed with charcoal filled his senses. Gripping the door jamb, Derek stopped his impulse to nuzzle her sexy exposed neck.

They had a beautiful king sized bed, in a large suite with a magnificent view on the other side of the condo. However, as Derek stood watching, he fantasized about taking his wife right there, right now on the wooden floor. Closing his eyes Derek thought about Sophia's gaze, as they made love. He imagined her stunning gray eyes clouded with a blue haze as their passion ignited. Sadly, Derek realized, he hadn't seen those blue clouds since New England.

That realization, combined with the woeful reverberation of saxophone music prompted him to turn silently toward the hallway. He couldn't disturb her, not for his own desires. Seeing her in her state of euphoria was enough. He eased his way to their room and climbed into their large empty bed. Derek's only solace, as he drifted off to sleep, was that Sophia was once again drawing.

The linen page filled with different shades of black and gray. Sophia bought colored chalk at the supply store, but charcoal seemed more appropriate. She wasn't sure what propelled her to the art supplies store in Palo Alto. Perhaps it was her desire to see the numerous art studios in that area boasting wonderful exhibits. After all she'd received a postcard inviting her to one of the exhibits. It wasn't really to her. It was one of those promotional mailings, but it intrigued her. While perusing the displays, she felt the familiar desire to create. It was so overpowering she couldn't resist any longer.

It wasn't that she'd been resisting. It was more like she'd put it away -- somewhere. Since coming to California there were more important things to do. She needed to be *Mrs. Derek Burke*. No, she *wanted* to be. However, with each passing day, Sophia questioned if she wanted to be Mrs. Derek Burke for her or for him. As an executive in a large and upcoming company, didn't he deserve that? The pretense was draining. Sophia constantly argued with herself... if she *wanted* to be what Derek wanted, than why did she feel so unhappy?

While in an art studio on Hamilton Avenue in Palo Alto the curator approached, and they began talking. They discussed the displayed pieces and debated the use of mediums and color. With time Sophia revealed she too was an artist and mentioned her studio in Provincetown and exhibitions in Europe.

The gentleman asked to see her portfolio. It was at that moment Sophia realized it was still in Massachusetts. That realization struck her with unseen force. Her portfolio -- her life in synopsis -- was back on the Cape. She'd left her life to be with Derek.

Some of her better works were accessible through her website. She typed in the address and showed Mr. George her art. He appeared more than impressed.

"Mrs. Burke, I like your work. It has a fresh raw quality."

"Thank you Mr. George. Please call me Sophia."

"I want you to know this is out of character, to offer a position to someone without checking references, but I've recently found myself in need of a trusted employee." Sophia listened, "I have space in the back where you could create, but mostly I need someone to look after the studio a few hours during the day. It would also require the occasional evening and weekend."

Sophia didn't know what to say. She hadn't been looking for a job. Nonetheless, the past two weeks she'd felt like a fish out of water. The idea of being surrounded by art thrilled her. But at the same time, she knew Derek didn't want her to work. He wanted her to be free to create. She wished she could explain how her new found freedom felt stifling.

"Mr. George, I'm honored. I really should discuss this with my husband. And you should know I plan to make some short trips to Provincetown during the summer. I hate having my studio closed throughout the busy time of year."

"I understand. We can meet again to determine if details can be worked out. Would you consider shipping some of your work here, for display?"

She couldn't help beam. It would have been impossible to hide the smile. "I'm truly honored. I'll give it all serious consideration. Could I please contact you tomorrow?"

They made the necessary arrangements and Sophia took his number. The renewed excitement gave her the strength to purchase new supplies. She couldn't wait to tell Derek. However, he called and told her he wouldn't be home for dinner. Then there was the text message explaining his meeting was going longer than expected. She tried to busy herself while she waited.

Sometime during the evening Sophia found herself in the room he'd planned as her studio. Looking around she knew it needed to be organized. However, as she began removing the new items from the bags, she gave in to impulse. Although new, the charcoal felt smooth and amazing under her fingertips. Without thought or provocation she surrendered to the desire, and began to draw.

When the white page was no longer white, she sat back and looked at the whole of what she'd created. It was a beach with rolling clouds and rough seas, no place in particular and yet -- East Coast. Looking around the cluttered room Sophia wondered about the time. Surely Derek should be home by now. Making her way down the hall she found his shoes by the door. Sadness swelled in her chest, a muffled sob escaped her lips when she discovered him sleeping alone in their bed. Why didn't he come down to her?

Softly she shut the door to their bedroom and went back to the other hall. Next to her studio was another room, a spare bedroom, decorated with light colors and natural textures, for visiting friends and family. As she eased herself into the cool sheets and inhaled the fresh newness surrounding her, her thoughts traveled across the country to their cottage on the Cape. No matter how hard she worked to eliminate the scent of age, it lingered below the surface. It probably was a combination of sea, moisture, and mildew. The ingredients sounded foul, yet it wasn't. Lying on the new bed, in the newly painted room, she longed for that fragrance. Allowing quiet tears to escape her eyes and moisten the soft pillow case, she drifted into a restless sleep.

Be who you are and say what you feel
because those who mind don't matter
and those who matter don't mind.
– Dr. Seuss

Chapter 21

When Claire looked into Harry's tired, sad eyes, her anxiety melted into relief. She flung her arms flung around his neck and buried her face into his chest. She'd never expected to be so concerned, but she was. Her muffled words flowed without hesitation, "I just got your text. I was so worried. I was going to find you; to be sure you were okay."

Slowly his arms encircled her frame and his chin settled upon her head. "I am."

She led him into the apartment and offered him something to drink. He asked for water then changed his mind to wine. She attentively tended to his needs, as he explained what transpired.

"I would've been here sooner, but just as I was about to leave SiJo, we had multiple false alarms. I have no idea what was happening. We had sensors indicating people where there were no people. Sensors ignoring people where there were people." He rolled his shoulders in an attempt to release his pent-up stress and continued, "I know it's a computer glitch. I probably could've figured it out, but honestly, I wanted to get here. So, I left Jackson to deal with it and headed home." He emptied his glass of wine. Claire refilled it and returned it to his hand. After a few sips he continued.

"You know, usually Palo Alto is quiet and calm." Claire nodded. She didn't have a clue how Palo Alto was *usually*, but in her short time it fit the description -- calm. He went on, "I was almost home, on Hamilton, when this car pulled out of a parking space. It was like some kind of movie, happening fast, yet in slow motion." He finished the wine, placed the glass on the nearby table, and took Claire's hands. "I don't mean to sound vain, but if it wasn't for my quick reactions, I think I would've been the one placed in that ambulance." He squeezed Claire's hands as she remained silent, "Honestly, I wasn't paying attention. I was thinking about you and our talk. When everything happened, I just reacted."

167

Claire wanted to know about that talk, but he needed to discuss the accident.

"Before I knew it, this car pulled out of a parking space, heading the other direction, and then this taxi came up on my right. There wasn't really a lane. He must have been in a hurry." Harry closed his eyes and watched his private recall. Finally he spoke, "The car in front of me swerved, I hit the brakes, and the taxi moved into my spot. Suddenly, the car from the parking spot went into the oncoming lane and collided head on with the taxi. The driver of the car from the parking space was a young girl, only sixteen. I don't know if she hit the gas instead of the brake." He shook his head solemnly, "We'll never know."

Claire took a drink of her wine, definitely not a *sip*. She thought about Harry's words, *if it wasn't for my quick reaction....* She'd experienced too many questionable situations to believe in coincidence. Finally she asked, "How is the taxi driver?"

"Distraught and injured, but not life threatening. He was on his way to a fare; so he didn't have a passenger." Claire kissed Harry's cheek and asked if he wanted more wine or if perhaps he was ready for some dinner. When he nodded, she led him by the hand into the kitchen.

He looked around at the set table and pans on the stove top. "I'm sorry, I messed up your dinner. It smells wonderful."

She smiled a wary smile, "I don't think my dinner's as important as you. You're okay, that's what matters." She squeezed his hand. "Why don't you pour us some more wine and start your salad. I'll warm up this food. It'll be fine."

He continued to talk about the accident as Claire warmed the fish in the microwave and heated the sauce on the stove. Next, she refilled the sauce pan for the asparagus. As the faucet gushed water she heard Harry's voice, but her mind filled with other words -- Tony asking, "Who was the expected recipient of that dazzling smile?"

Tears came to her eyes as the realization struck. Her presence wasn't making Amber and Harry's life more exciting; she was putting them in danger.

The memories of her parents and Simon's untimely deaths paralyzed her movements. Water overflowed the pan as she stood motionless staring at the tiled backsplash. It wasn't the mosaic design holding her trance; it was her new thoughts about Amber. She's flying home tomorrow from meetings in Houston. Simon died in a plane crash. Claire's heart began to beat erratically.

Harry appeared behind her. So deep in her sudden rational or irrational terror, she didn't hear him approach. She jumped as he grasped her shoulders. As if from a tunnel she heard his voice, echoing against the cavern walls, or maybe he was repeating himself, "Claire are you all right? Claire, Claire are you all right?"

Her grip on the handle of the pan failed. The metal pot fell to the depths of the sink as water droplets splashed violently coating the tile, granite, and porcelain. Her body trembled as she tried to speak, "It's me. I have to leave. We need to call Amber."

"What's you? What are you talking about?" Harry tried to calm her; however, she barely heard his words through the commotion within her head.

Finally in desperation she screamed, "Call Amber, now!"

Still unsure of the reason for Claire's sudden outburst, he turned off the water, reached for his phone and led Claire's unsteady body to the table. Harry dialed his sister. Once the connection was established, he handed Claire the phone.

Her words ran together as she tried to explain everything to Amber. Claire told her about Harry's accident, about Tony's visit, and about her fear. Harry listened to every word. When she spoke about Tony visiting the condominium, Claire saw his neck stiffen and jaw clench. She pushed on.

Amber listened to what some might consider a mad rant. As Claire finished, her voice slowed, reflecting her utter exhaustion. She listened to Amber's steady voice of reason as tears slipped from her downcast eyes. Her fatigue wasn't physical; she'd slept until after five. It was psychological. All of the research was well and good. She could plan and possibly implement a great demise. However, none of that mattered, if her friends were lost in battle.

Only after Amber promised a thorough inspection of the SiJo plane prior to departure, did Claire hand Harry back his phone. Harry spoke to his sister for a few moments, hung up, and reached for Claire.

She wanted his embrace, his comfort and support. Nevertheless, she knew if she took what he offered, she'd in fact be condemning him. Resolving to keep him safe, she stiffly returned his embrace. With her head safely against his chest the trembling ceased. She started to speak, but Harry spoke first.

"I want to hear more about that visit. Why did *he* come here?"

"I was going to tell you about it and other things I learned..." She pulled from his hold and reached for the water goblet. It shook as she tried to make it reach her lips. "I just haven't had a chance." Her voice sounded stronger than she appeared.

Harry watched as Claire regrouped. He saw a mixture of emotions passing like clouds before her emerald eyes. Once again, he put his arm around her shoulders, "How about we eat some of this delicious food and then talk?"

Claire stared momentarily into his pale blue eyes. The intensity she'd witnessed as she told Amber about Tony was gone. Now, she saw concern. Claire replied, "I think I need to find a new place to live."

"Let's eat and sleep and then discuss it."

Claire steadied her stance. "We can eat. We can sleep. But it's my decision and I'm not putting you or Amber is harm's way for my vendetta."

Harry carried the dish of tilapia to the table and walked back to the stove for the sauce. Drizzling the white cream over the rewarmed filets, he said, "It *is* your decision. But I'm the head of security at SiJo Gaming. I'm pretty sure I can take care of myself. And as for Amber, we'll arrange additional security." He smiled a feigned smile. "Now eat. Someone made us a wonderful meal."

Claire obediently picked up her fork. With her hand lingering above the plate he'd dished for her, she considered his words. Finally, she nodded.

Taking his seat across from Claire, Harry added, "And as of tomorrow, you'll also have around the clock security. No more surprise visits."

Her chewing stopped mid-mastication. Swallowing became difficult as her mouth dried. She didn't like his authoritative tone; she'd lived through that once and didn't plan on doing it again, no matter how pure his intentions. After a much needed drink of water, she said, "I don't think that's necessary. Tony won't hurt me. He wants me back in Iowa, besides; I have Phil Roach watching me."

Harry started to speak when Claire interrupted, "What are we going to do, ask Phil and the security detail to share a car? I mean with the occasional paparazzi, a private detective *and* a security guard, I might as well lead a parade."

Ignoring her attempt at humor, Harry asked, "What do you mean he wants you back in Iowa?"

Claire looked back to Harry. The intense stare from earlier glowed. It surprised her, how the normally soft shade could stay the same, yet appear so different. She answered, "When he was here, he told me the reason he came to California was to take me back to Iowa."

"Did you respond?" During the last two months, Harry witnessed Claire's transition from a quiet guarded woman, into one who spoke more freely. Nonetheless, he wasn't sure she possessed that ability while with Mr. Rawlings. That was part of the reason he'd waited for her after their dinner. He wanted to be sure the stronger Claire still existed. Last night, he wasn't sure.

"Of course I responded. I said *no*."

"And he was fine with that, and left?"

"He left. He isn't still here." Claire looked down at her plate as she stabbed another leaf from her salad. "He didn't argue, but..."

"But what?"

"He said he wasn't giving up *his quest*." She ate some more salad and added, "I'll consider the security."

Harry nodded, and Claire began to relax. The food provided the much needed subsistence to her weakened body and mind. Without saying it aloud, they'd agreed to table the Tony, security, and housing discussion until later. Soon they fell into a benign chat about superficial monumental events. Apparently the Giants were tied one to one in a three game series with Boston. The next game was tomorrow; Harry wasn't sure the Giant's pitcher would be ready...

170

They fooled themselves, if they thought their conversation could be avoided the entire evening. After dinner, they moved to the living room. It was hard for Claire to fathom earlier the same day she'd sat in the same room with Tony. Now instead of sitting one on the sofa and the other on the chair, Claire sat nestled into the crook of Harry's arm. Somehow the embrace didn't feel sexual, only protective.

With her head against his shoulder, she pulled from his strength and thought about his patience. In the last hour she'd dropped a few bomb shells, and she had more to drop. Yet, unlike her ex-husband, Harry didn't demand answers. Instead, he provided space and support. She said she would tell him more; he waited, allowing her the luxury of choosing her time and words.

With a deep inhale followed by an audible exhale, Claire began. "What do you want to know?" The warmth of his embrace on her shoulder and side, as they both stared into the Palo Alto night, fueled her courage. Before the night was done, she'd share the secrets of her life with Anthony Rawlings. She didn't know what it would mean for their relationship, or if this was what he'd wanted to *talk* about. However, she couldn't imagine being with a man who didn't know her past, to understand her present.

When her history became difficult to articulate, he'd rub her shoulder and remain silent. There were times as she spoke about her *kidnapping, agreement of duties, glitches, or her accident*, she felt his body tense. Never once did he question her choices. It was if he knew she'd questioned herself too many times to count. She'd asked herself: *Why did you agree to marry him? Did you really fall in love? Did you think he loved you? Why did you keep up appearances?* Asking questions was much easier than answering them.

Harry continued to listen without judgment. Many times he squeezed her shoulder or kissed the top of her head. Each affirmation fortified her resolve.

She didn't spare any aspect of her life with Tony. She also didn't dwell on details. No secrets remained. Nearing dawn, she told him about the dinner. She explained how Tony arranged for an empty restaurant. Then she told Harry about Tony's reaction to her knowledge regarding his birth name.

For the first time, Harry asked for verification, "Are you saying he didn't send that box of information to you in prison?"

"That's what I'm saying." She turned her weary eyes to his face. "He was really stunned. That's why he came here, to find out more about what I know."

"Did you tell him?"

"I told him the package held pictures, articles, and a letter. He wanted to see it."

Again Harry prompted, "And?"

"And I told him I'd burnt it -- he laughed. I could tell he was relieved. But before he left, he told me not to share my information with anyone." Her eyes widened. "Oh my god!" She jumped from Harry's embrace to see his eyes, "I told him it was too late." Her trembling resumed. "That's why you were almost in that accident. He thinks I've shared the information with you and Amber. I need to get a hold of Emily. And..." Claire just remembered, "I dropped the phone I use with her and Courtney. It's broken. I need to reach them." Her words came in short increasingly sharp stiletto sentences. "I can't let anything happen to her or John."

Harry held Claire's hands, restraining the explosive panic that surged through her no longer calm body. His voice was now calm and slow. "Do you possibly think you're giving him too much credit? That accident was caused by a sixteen year old girl, how could that conceivably be traced back to Mr. Rawlings?"

Claire shook her head, "I don't know. What about the sudden computer *glitches* at SiJo?"

"Sometimes shit happens."

"I'll feel better after I talk to Emily. But, I need another phone."

"I understand the need for another untraceable phone to speak with Courtney, but why Emily? He knows where you are. He knows where she is; you're sisters."

Claire stared at him momentarily, "You're right." She reached for her iPhone.

*****

The angry sound of Derek's voice brought Sophia out of her restless sleep. She could hear his tone and see his expression; she couldn't understand the cause. With his hands on her shoulders, he turned her to face him. "Why Sophia? Why in the hell are you sleeping in here?" Disorientation from the sudden wake, muted her ability to speak. "I reached for you and you still weren't in bed. I thought you might still be drawing. But you're sleeping, without me!"

Her mind reeled, "How did you know I was drawing?" Her soft voice didn't mirror his irritation, though it did a poor job of hiding her unhappiness.

"What's the matter? Why are you crying?"

This time a little stronger, "How did you know I was drawing?"

"I watched you." As he spoke and her body convulsed with repressed sobs. "You looked so beautiful with your hair up, that sexy nightgown and charcoaled fingers."

"But, you didn't say anything. I never knew you were there."

"I didn't want to disturb you. It's the first time you've drawn since you moved here."

She tried to turn her face away. His expression was no longer upset, she saw the man she loved. Even with limited light she could see the concern and relief in his soft brown eyes.

"Please don't look away. Talk to me."

172

She couldn't move her arms with his hands on her shoulders, so she lifted her head to reach his lips. His hands left her shoulders and scooped her body into his arms. Between kisses, surrounded by his embrace, she whispered, "I thought you didn't want me because I can't be what you want."

Derek stopped kissing and looked into Sophia's beautiful gray eyes. The sadness made his heart wrench, "What are you talking about. You're everything I want. When did I ever say anything different?"

She pushed herself up to sit. "You didn't. But ever since I got here, I feel like I'm expected to be someone else, you know, *Mrs. Derek Burke.*" She wiped her eyes on the clean sheets, "I've been trying..."

"Stop trying. Stop trying to be someone you're not. I love *you.*" His embrace squeezed the air from her lungs. Her body collapsed against his. "I've missed *my* Sophia. Besides, who the hell is *Mrs. Derek Burke?*"

Sophia smiled from behind her tears as the sparkle returned to her eyes. It was the glimmer Derek hadn't seen in what seemed like ages. It was the most beautiful sight he could behold.

The last two weeks of stress melted into a fury of passion. For the next few weeks, every time Sophia walked by their guest room, she'd blush.

Together they reconnected their bodies and minds. Glorious sensations sent both of them to untold heights. When their exhausted bodies finally fell into tender embraces, their words revealed more of their misconceptions.

"I don't want you to be anyone else. Not, Mrs. Derek Burke. You're Sophia Burke and I love *you!*" His heart swelled with the recent vision of blue clouds floating across his wife's beautiful eyes.

Sophia revealed her insecurity around people like Danielle and how she felt inadequate amongst the professionals in his life.

While allowing his lips to roam over her full breasts and tight midsection he tried to ex-plain and demonstrate his approval. Yes, she's his wife. Nevertheless, he didn't want her identity to be a reflection of him, only of her. "If you want to work at an art studio, and it'll make you happy," his smile shimmered in the darkened room, "go for it. Do what makes you happy." Never once did he want to marry someone like him. Truthfully, he never wanted to marry, until he was awestruck by the most amazing, energetic, caring, and possibly crazy, woman he'd ever met.

They both knew they'd just overcome a difficult time for their marriage, learning a valuable lesson -- the need to communicate. Neither should assume they know the other's thoughts. They don't. That ignorance keeps life exciting.

Inhaling deeply, Sophia nestled into his warm shoulder, listened to the beat of his steady heart, and drifted into a peaceful sleep. When she awoke he was gone, presumably off to work. For the last two weeks she'd tried to get up and make him coffee and breakfast. Smiling into the tear stained pillow, she realized he didn't want or need that. He wanted *her.* Relishing the soft sheets of the guestroom bed, Sophia drifted back to sleep.

Before you embark on a journey of revenge,
dig two graves.
-- Confucius

Chapter 22

Claire reread the email:

To: Claire Nichols
Date: May 8, 2013
Subject: Printed Retraction
From: Meredith Banks

Claire, here is the final copy of the retraction we discussed. It will appear in coming issues *of People, Rolling Stone, Vanity Fair* and various on-line publications. There is always potential, in this mass media world, for it to be picked-up by other sources. I hope you find this final draft acceptable. If I do not hear from you, it will be submitted. Therefore, if you request changes, please contact me immediately. I look forward to furthering this agreement. I appreciate your decision to work with me on this endeavor. I promise to represent your interests to the best of my ability. Meredith

Claire clicked the attachment:

"Journalist Seeks Redemption"
In pursuit of stories, many reporters and journalists close the gap between perceived and truth. We make this jump for the benefit of our readers. In September of 2010, I made such a leap in an article I wrote concerning Claire Nichols and Anthony Rawlings. There were speculations regarding a relationship between this unlikely couple. I used my familiarity with Ms. Nichols to learn more. I spoke to Ms.

Nichols in Chicago; it was not an official interview. I purposely made myself available to an *old friend* and asked to *chat.* Following that discussion, I wrote a story insinuating a connection between Nichols and Rawlings. While that connection proved in time to be accurate, I am publically declaring Ms. Claire Nichols did not reveal the relationship to me during our chat.

She has, however, promised me exclusive rights to her story, promising an enlightening view into the world of her true relationship with one of this country's wealthiest men, as well as the truth about her arrest, plea, incarceration and unconventional release. Please stay tuned, the wait will be worth it!

Meredith Banks, Independent Correspondent

Still dressed in her work-out clothes and sipping coffee, Claire approvingly read the attachment. Savoring the warm liquid, she considered the implications and wondered if she'd hear from her ex-husband. No, Claire wondered *when* she'd hear from him. She hadn't heard his voice since he left Amber's condominium nearly two weeks ago. And although Harry continued to declare her paranoid regarding Anthony's influence, she knew in her heart, Tony's power was limitless.

Thankfully, the inspection of the SiJo Gaming air fleet came up clean. There were no signs of tampering with any of the company's aircraft. Emily and John were well and would soon be in California for a visit. And, Amber and Harry remained accident free.

Claire conceded she may have an active imagination. Smiling, she remembered finding her black lace panties inside her yoga pants after a *very* vivid dream. For a moment she'd actually thought it could have been real. Nonetheless, Claire's great imagination didn't nullify Tony's influence.

To save her friends, Claire offered again to find her own place to live. However, honestly she didn't want to live alone. Isolation reminded her too much of her cell in the Iowa Penitentiary or her suite at Tony's estate. Therefore, as long as Amber consented to Claire's presence, she'd stay. Claire justified: *if I move because of Tony, I'm giving him power.* She refused to relinquish her power; she'd done that before.

Breathing a sigh of relief, Claire realized the attached article wouldn't hit the newsstands for a couple of days. Quickly, she fired back a response, approving the attachment and thanking Meredith for the advanced notice. Claire also sent her cell number and asked Meredith to call to schedule their interviews. The last time they spoke, Meredith suggested the possibility of doing a series of articles. It all depended on the extent of information Claire would reveal.

Claire decided the articles would concentrate on *her* life with Tony, not his hidden past. She didn't believe it was her place to disclose that information. For some reason, someone wanted her to know his secret history. If they didn't, she wouldn't have received the mysterious box. Although, Claire struggled to understand the reasoning, she didn't feel sharing it with the world was her place.

The haunting questions that infiltrated her thoughts continued to be... *who* sent the box? *Why* did they send it? And *what* did they hope to accomplish?

Merely moments after she hit send on her email to Meredith, her iPhone rang. The excitement in Meredith's voice reverberated through the cellphone. Meredith made it clear she was more than willing to travel to Palo Alto as soon as possible to begin their interviews. During their conversation, Claire recognized a desire to travel. Since Harry's near miss of an accident, she'd been stressing about everyone and everything. She needed a break. Meredith lived in Long Beach, and would be in San Diego during the next three days on business.

"Meredith, I think I'd enjoy a get-a-way. Could we meet in San Diego?"

"Really? Sure! That would be great. We can get started right away!"

They agreed to meet in Claire's hotel suite, the next night. Claire promised to text Meredith her accommodation information as soon as she booked a room.

Claire assumed text messages were less traceable than emails. It was only an assumption. Phil Roach would probably know the minute she booked the flight and room. She sighed and started her research, purposely checking multiple destinations and dates of travel.

She found three different flights leaving tomorrow, but purposely decided to wait until first thing in the morning to book one. This gave Phil less time to follow. She also found multiple acceptable places to stay. That too could wait until the morning. She made a list of flights and rooms. Pensively she wondered, would she ever be able to live without constant surveillance?

During dinner, Amber presented Claire with an interesting proposition, "So, there's this big fundraiser gala in a couple weeks. It's a joint endeavor between many of the top gaming companies in Silicon Valley. We all pledge a percentage of certain sales. Individually it's very minimal, like a quarter of a cent per download, but the cumulative amount is surprising. This money all goes to fund the National Center for Learning Disabilities."

"That's nice. I didn't know you did that."

"Well, it's something Simon was passionate about. There are studies showing people with learning disabilities can benefit from some of the electronic games. Hand-eye coordination and sequencing... it's all very interesting."

"I think that's great." Claire said with a smile. She remembered Tony's regard for philanthropic funds and thought how nice it was to have people donate, for the right reason.

"Yes, well here's the thing, I don't enjoy fundraisers. I mean, I'll do it, sometimes. But honestly, I don't do the chatty small-talk thing that well."

Claire sensed a question coming. She smiled and raised her eyebrows.

Amber grinned, "So, I was wondering if you'd be interested in representing SiJo Gaming for me?"

"I'd be happy to do it, but do you really want *me* representing your company?"

"Don't be silly. Why wouldn't I want *you* representing SiJo?"

"Well, I don't know, maybe because I have a dubious past."

"Seriously, you'll be talking to the top two percent. Each plate is $30,000. Everyone there has a dubious past!" Then in a quieter tone, "If you're lucky and someone has too much to drink, you'll get to hear one or two of those stories. Some people like to be very chatty and the information can be quite entertaining!"

Claire smiled looking at Amber's expectant expression. She was thrilled to be able to do something for Amber, after all she'd done for her. "Then yes. I'd be honored to represent SiJo Gaming for you and for Simon. Am I going alone, or will there be someone else with me?"

"SiJo has two tickets. I kind of assumed you'd want Harry to go with you, but if you have someone else in mind."

Claire's eyes flitted to her plate to avoid Amber's direct gaze, "No, I'm relieved to have someone I know. I thought there might be another SiJo representative you wanted there."

Amber giggled, "Harry's been avoiding these things for years. After Simon died I tried numerous times to get him to accompany me to formal events. I like the idea of manipulating him into going." Her smile indicated possible knowledge of Claire and Harry's increasingly familiar relationship. Nonetheless, she didn't verbally acknowledge it, she just said, "I'm sure Harry will be relieved you don't have another companion in mind. And, it's formal so he'll have to wear a tuxedo." Amber's voice flowed with unbridled excitement at the prospect of making her brother dress formally. "Now, if that doesn't deter you, there is one more thing you should know before you totally sign on."

A sudden feeling of foreboding settled over Claire, she hoped it wasn't anything that would make her retract her offer. "And what would that be?"

"One of the companies well represented at this festivity is Sheds-tics, a subsidiary of Rawlings. It was the company where Simon started. He was always fond of his start and stayed close with the local executives. The two companies have shared a table in the past."

Claire's stomach twisted at the prospect of sharing a table with Tony. Her mind went over the numerous formal events she attended with Tony over the years. Her eyes squinted as she processed, "I don't remember this being an event Tony and I attended while we were married."

"I checked. He hasn't attended in three years, since May of 2010. And Shedis-tics hasn't submitted their attendees for this year. They have four tickets."

Claire's mind went to May of 2010, "He went to this in 2010?"

"Yes, that's the information I saw. Why? You weren't married until December right?"

"Right."

"Well, he was there with someone else, early May. I didn't recognize the name of his companion or remember the exact date. But it was in 2010."

Claire thought about being in *his* house while he attended events with other women. Why had she never thought of that before? It wasn't until late May of 2010 that she went to the Symphony with him. All those lonely evenings and nights when he was *busy*. Unconsciously she clenched her teeth. Oh, she didn't want to go there. Claire tried to focus on Amber. "Oh, I guess... I'll still do it. I owe you this and more."

"You don't owe me anything. However, I was thinking if *he* does come, wouldn't this be a great opportunity to be seen near him, in public? You know, since he spoiled your plans for visibility during your dinner."

Claire shrugged. "I suppose it could be." Slowly a smile spread from her lips to her eyes, "And if *I* knew *he* was to be there, but *he* didn't know *I* was... hmm," she pondered, "I think this could be good."

"I won't have Liz send your and Harry's name in until the last minute."

"Thank you." Claire leaned across the tall kitchen table and asked, "Tell me, is this an occasion for a new dress?"

"Oh girl, do you need an occasion? Seriously, you're welcome to borrow one of mine. Check out the closet in the spare bedroom; any one is fine."

By eight fifteen Friday morning, Claire sat comfortably in the wide plush leather seat aboard a non-stop *United* flight to San Diego. If she stayed true to her schedule, she'd pick-up her rental car and be in her hotel suite before noon. Claire felt devious and clever, booking her flight at four thirty in the morning, and not confirming her hotel until she was in the first class lounge awaiting her flight. Undoubtedly, Phil Roach would follow, but the momentary slip fortified her ability to manipulate the people who worked tirelessly monitoring her every move. She relished the brief reprieve from knowing eyes.

Just before take-off, Claire sent a text to Meredith proposing dinner in her suite while they discussed the impending journalistic expose. She hadn't received confirmation and now that the plane was in the air, her iPhone had to be off. With the scrutinizing eyes of the seemingly friendly flight attendant, Claire followed the rules and kept her phone neatly stashed in the pocket of her purse. She'd check for Meredith's response once she landed.

Preoccupied with following signs to the luggage carousel and retrieving her larger suitcase, Claire didn't remember to turn on her iPhone until she was standing in line for her rental car. When she turned the telephone on, she saw multiple emails, text messages, two missed calls, and one voice mail message. She opted for the voice mail. After entering the necessary information she clasped her hand over her ear, trying to shut out the noisy airport clamor and listened to the voice coming from her phone. She needn't worried. The voice was loud and clear.

"I hoped you could answer *this* phone, since you refuse to answer the number you know I know. I will assume you have a good reason for not answering but will call me back immediately. Shelly just called. I expect you remember she's my publicist. We need to *talk*. If I do not hear from you by noon, my time, I am boarding a jet and heading to you. The choice is yours."

Claire didn't realize she'd been holding her breath, until the voicemail ended. Finally she exhaled. Looking to the screen she saw the time, 9:57. She tried to remember the time difference. *Shit, three minutes.* Why did everyone want to *talk*? That word no longer held a positive connotation.

Claire stepped from the line and indicated for the next patron to progress toward the counter. She wasn't surprised Tony called her iPhone. She knew once she and Emily started communicating through it, it'd be easy prey. Honestly, at that moment she was happy he had. If he'd left this message on her other phone, she probably wouldn't have heard it until he was already in California.

Claire dialed Tony's number, while simultaneously sifting her emotions. Fear was among the top contenders; she wasn't stupid. Nonetheless, it held a mild third to determination and revenge. She'd made up her mind. When she thought Harry was the victim of Tony's consequence, Claire knew, he had to be brought down. His power needed to be lessened. She admitted having erotic thoughts about her ex-husband, along with thoughts of lust and perhaps -- love. Nonetheless, if he could table his love to fulfill his agenda of revenge, she could do the same.

Regulating her breathing, Claire listened to the ring of his private line.

On the third ring she heard the same voice, less menacing than the one on the message, yet still irritated, "My, Claire, you do like to cut it close, don't you?"

"I just turned on my telephone. I hope I caught you before you made an unnecessary trip."

"I don't make unnecessary trips."

"Please enlighten me. What did Shelly tell you that has you so worked up?"

She heard his grin, "*Worked up*? My dear, you have no idea."

"I would argue, but I'm on a schedule. Could you please tell me why I called, so I can continue with *my* agenda?"

"Of course, I'm sure your schedule is excessively hectic." He paused, emphasizing his sarcasm. "Meredith Banks? Really Claire, haven't you made that mistake before?" Though his tone was deceptively lighter, his words sent chills down her spine.

She waved the next person to the counter. The retraction wasn't scheduled to be released until tomorrow. Why was Claire even surprised he'd already seen it? "If you'd read the release, it states I actually *didn't* make that mistake before. Which I believe I told you. And yes, I remember the *accident* resulting from your misconception."

"Are you trying to push me?"

"No. I'd be more direct if that were my goal. I'm trying to tell the world the truth. I've read numerous false accounts and believe it's time to set the record straight."

"Know my legal team will stop anything, including this retraction from ever seeing the light of day. You are wasting your time."

"Funny, I remember telling you the same thing -- recently."

"I warned you not to disappoint me. I recommend you reconsider your actions."

"I need to go. I'm in the middle of something. As always, it has been a pleasure."

As Claire moved the phone from her ear to hit *end*, she heard him reply, "Not as much as last time." Touching *end*, she wondered what exactly he meant by that.

As Anthony Rawlings ended the call with his ex-wife, he noticed the small symbol indicating an email. Despite the fact he had an untold number of people paused on a web-conference, he swiped the icon. Within the list of unread emails he saw one from Phillip Roach, dated today, received 10:23:04 this morning. Tony must have overlooked it earlier. He touched the screen and the document came into view.

To: Mr. Anthony Rawlings
Date: May 9, 2013
Subject: Ms. Nichols
From: Phillip Roach

Mr. Rawlings it seems Ms. Nichols booked a flight early this morning for San Diego. She left San Francisco at 08:12:00, PT. Her flight is scheduled to arrive in San Diego 09:43:00. I have confirmation of her hotel booking at the US Grant on Broadway. I could not manage a seat on Ms. Nichols' flight. I am however scheduled to arrive at 11:17:00. As soon as I learn more, I will forward the information to you.

Smiling, Tony realized Claire did return his call as soon as she could. He immediately replied to Phillip Roach.

To: Phillip Roach
Date: May 9, 2013
Subject: Ms. Nichols
From: Anthony Rawlings
Check to see if a reporter named Meredith Banks is staying at the same hotel or even in San Diego. I have reason to believe the two are meeting. I want to know if my suspicion can be confirmed. Contact me immediately upon learning this information, or any other. AR

Tony knew Phil Roach wouldn't receive his email until his plane landed in San Diego. He could wait, looking at his watch, another hour and a half.

Suddenly, realizing he had other things to do, Anthony Rawlings resumed his seat and hit the enter button on his computer. He was once again visible to seventy-two finance officers at various Rawlings' subsidiaries. The web-conference resumed and Mr. Rawlings performed perfectly, despite the fact his mind was elsewhere. While discussing profit strategies, he held his iPhone out of camera range and sent a text to his driver, Eric.

IT SEEMS AS THOUGH I NEED TO TRAVEL TO SAN DIEGO. PREPARE TO PICK ME UP AT 2:30. HAVE THE JET READY FOR FLIGHT.

The next text went to his secretary, Patricia. *CANCEL MY APPOINTMENTS THIS AFTERNOON AND TOMORROW. I MUST MAKE AN EMERGENCY TRIP TO SAN DIEGO. IF THERE IS A PROBLEM HAVE TIM OR BRENT HANDLE IT.*

All the while, he never missed a question or hesitated with a response. The web-conference progressed without a flaw.

Out of suffering have emerged the strongest souls;
the most massive characters are seared with scars.
- Kahlil Gibran

Chapter 23

Tension permeated from every corner of Claire's luxurious hotel suite when she allowed Meredith entry. However, like vapors over warm water, the warmth of an old friendship soon rose above the cool, edgy, businesslike atmosphere. Wisp by wisp the strain evaporated and Claire and Meredith's old relationship prevailed. This first evening was about overcoming their past and becoming reacquainted. Although it was never said, they both knew their future partnership depended upon it.

Boldly, Meredith approached the prime obstacle, "Claire, I know I took advantage of you and of our friendship. I knew it was wrong, and I did it. I wanted the story everyone was trying to get. I'm sorry." She looked sufficiently apologetic. Claire fought the urge to look down at her hands; instead she kept her gaze upon Meredith, as Meredith continued, "After you were arrested, I wrote another article. I meant every word, but I think in retrospect, I wrote it to rectify what I'd written earlier."

Claire inhaled. This wasn't the time for her to inform Meredith of the consequence she suffered for Meredith's coup; it could wait. Looking her old friend in the eye, Claire chose not to see the seasoned reporter. Instead, she saw the young college student, ten years younger -- her friend. Claire said, "After I was out of prison, I did some research and found your second article. You're one of the few people to write anything supportive of me." She smiled her biggest smile, relaxed her shoulders and added, "That's why I called you. I'm glad you agreed to help me."

Meredith exhaled on cue, "Thank you. I didn't know if you'd read it."

"I did. And it means the world to me. But there are a few things you should seriously consider before taking this journey." Meredith nodded, waiting. Claire went on, "Mr. Rawlings has a lot of connections. I know without a doubt, he'll make this difficult. You need to know what you're getting into."

"I was going to talk to you about some strange things with my retraction. It's already met unusual editorial scrutiny. *People* and *Rolling Stone* will only agree to print the retraction, not the information regarding future information. *Vanity Fair* completely passed, even after they'd accepted in concept. I just received a generic refusal from them moments ago."

"His influence is very far reaching. Believe me; I'd understand if you want to pass on doing this article? It's okay. We can call this a reunion and go on with our lives."

Claire watched the twenty year old peek through Meredith's thirty year old eyes. Claire saw the spark she saw ten years ago when they skipped class to watch the Cubs.

"Hell no! If my simple retraction is generating this kind of reaction, can you imagine what our *series of articles* will do? Besides, the world of publishing is changing by the second. I'll blog the stuff about the impending information. My blog reaches hundreds of thousands. Then with that, *Twitter* and other social sites, the audience is global." The excitement in her tone crackled like electricity through the suite. "Sweetie, it takes more than money to stop social media. Once something is viral, it can *not* be stopped!"

Claire pondered the possibilities. When she first was taken by Tony, social media was in its infancy. While with him, she had no access to media. It was only a little better in prison. Slowly, she was beginning to understand its potential. There's a world that can take a spark and create an inferno. Looking at Meredith's large blue eyes, filled with anticipation, Claire believed her old friend knew how to fuel that fire. Nonetheless, Claire owed her one more warning, "There's something else."

"Yes?"

"There's a history of ill fortunes coming to people who cross my ex-husband. I don't want anything to happen to you. If you want to do this, you need to go into it with your eyes open."

Meredith exhaled and sat against the sofa cushions. She kept her eyes on Claire, waiting perhaps for the punch line. When none came she spoke. "I'm a reporter, a journalist. I've always dreamt of infiltrating some enemy camp and learning the deep secrets of some foreign dictator. In my dream I'd tell the world of his atrocities. My life would be threatened, and I may even endure incarceration for my stance. But in this dream, I did it. I believe in the freedom of speech."

Claire smiled sadly, "That sounds very idealistic and romantic, but this is real life. You have a husband and two children. I'm not saying anything will happen; I just want you to know, we're talking about upsetting a colossal force. Are you sure you're willing to do it?"

"I'm willing to help you tell your story. I have no idea what it is, but my instinct's telling me, it's bigger than I ever imagined."

Claire nodded.

Conviction grew with each word. Meredith went on, "I'd be honored to tell the world what *you* want them to know."

Ten years earlier they shared a sorority house at Valparaiso University. With all life dealt Claire, those ten years might as well be a million. Yet, throughout the evening that timespan shortened. They recalled names from their past, people Meredith stayed in contact with. She knew the latest news on so many people. For a few hours they were once again two girls, gossiping about sisters and fraternity brothers.

Claire realized she couldn't totally blame Tony for her lack of connectivity with these people. It started years before she became aware of him in her life. She chose to put her energy into her work and career.

After dinner Claire took their dirty dishes into the hallway. If she'd been more observant, perhaps she would have noticed the small sensors, connected by a thin hair like wire linking her door with the jam. Each time her door opened, that sensor simultaneously sent a message to Phillip Roach and to a camera hidden in a potted plant across the hallway.

The camera's technology was impressive. It filmed continuously; however, only data received three minutes prior and post signal was recorded and stored. That information was streamed simultaneously to Phil's laptop. An alarm sounded in his suite when the sensor activated.

Approximately every ten minutes, Phillip would text his employer the status of Ms. Nichol's door. Mr. Rawlings was in a car outside the hotel, waiting for Ms. Nichols' guest to leave. Phillip confirmed Ms. Nichols' guest was indeed Meredith Banks, Claire's college classmate and journalist. The confirmation of his suspicions didn't please Mr. Rawlings.

Sitting on the sofa and reminiscing, the two women reconnected. This kind of emotional bond wasn't necessary for men, or for many scenarios, but Claire needed it. She needed a safe, intimate environment for her memories. Harry gave her that, an invisible blanket of acceptance, no matter what she revealed. She'd never be able to trust her stories with a stranger. After all, this endeavor was more than disclosing information; she was entrusting it to someone who would then share it with the world. That was why Claire chose Meredith.

Part-way through the evening, Claire presented Meredith with a *Confidentiality Agreement*. If Meredith signed the CA, she agreed not to speak to anyone about the information revealed by Claire Rawlings Nichols. Once the information was approved by Ms. Nichols, it could be reviewed for editorial purposes. During the interview process, no one else could know. All the information would be kept secret, until the appropriate time.

They hadn't talked money or substance, but as Claire opened her door, and alarms sounded in Phillips's suite, Claire confirmed their goal, "I feel good about this, Meredith; you think about it. We can met again tomorrow night and let me know your decision."

Meredith hugged her sorority sister, "I know I'm in. What time tomorrow?"

"Here at seven, some dinner and we'll begin."

Meredith smiled sweetly, "I can't wait. See you then." She watched Claire a moment and asked, "The retraction isn't coming out until tomorrow. Would you mind if I blogged tonight?"

"As long as it stays in our perimeters."

Meredith relaxed, "I'll send you the copy before I post it."

Claire nodded her approval.

"I can't wait to get started on all of this. See you tomorrow." With that, Meredith walked down the hall.

Claire shut the large double door and looked around the luxurious living room. Near the table where they'd eaten dinner was a high boy, complete with various shaped glasses and a bucket of ice. Inhaling the sweet serene quiet of her resolve, Claire moved toward the mini bar. She hadn't ordered wine with dinner; she wanted to be in complete control of her senses. But now that the evening was done, she sighed, *Yes, I deserve a glass of wine.*

Gazing at the small, one serving bottles, she decided a real bottle was in order and called room service. Claire reasoned, she may not finish an entire bottle, but with the stress of her first face-to-face with Meredith, she deserved it and would give it a good start! Considering a snack, Claire decided wine was sufficient. The server, on the other end of the line, promised prompt service with delivery in five minutes. Claire smiled. Hotels were always so willing to accommodate their nicer suites.

Settling on the plush sofa, Claire kicked off her shoes and mentally reviewed her time with Meredith. As she replayed each interaction she felt satisfied. It was exactly what she'd hoped for, maybe more. Meredith seemed competent and eager. And Claire had to admit, it was fun to hear about so many people from her past. Her bright disposition clouded with the thought of their articles, how would people react to the information? Did she truly want the world knowing her private misery? After a moment of self-reflection she reassured herself, *this isn't about me. This is to inform the world about Tony. I was the victim; he's the villain. I need to get that information out!*

Her thoughts turned to Harry. She was eternally grateful for the way he reacted to her private confessions. That, plus the memories of Courtney and Brent continued to fortify her resolve. Unconsciously, she wrapped her arms around her chest and felt a twinge of loneliness. Harry asked to accompany her to this meeting. Claire just believed she'd be more effective with Meredith one-on-one, and now that the first meeting was complete, she knew she'd been right. The entire evening was better than she could have ever anticipated.

Claire reached for her iPhone to call Harry, when a knock came from the door. Instead she reached for her purse and pulled out a ten dollar bill; the bottle of wine would go on her hotel tab, but she wanted to tip the waiter. Leaving her phone and her purse on the table, she went to the door.

*****

Even though Mr. Rawlings released him for the evening, Phillip Roach remained online with his video surveillance. It was like the night at the French restaurant in Palo Alto. Even though Claire gave him the gift certificate, Mr. Rawlings made it clear Phil didn't need to continue his observation within the restaurant. Actually, Mr. Rawlings specifically told Phil to wait outside until Ms. Nichols left the establishment, follow her, and report when she made it home. Sometimes Phillip felt more like a babysitter than a private detective.

Tonight he didn't know which title he should accept. He'd informed Mr. Rawlings of Ms. Nichols' early departure from San Francisco. He decided truth about his minor slip, would help him avoid another devious exchange with Ms. Nichols. Then he followed her to San Diego. Thankfully, she actually stayed at the hotel where she'd made reservations. It was there Phil wired her door and set up the necessary cameras.

Now, watching the video feed, he saw his employer, dressed in casual khaki slacks and a button down shirt, waiting patiently for Ms. Nichols' door to open. He glanced at his watch, almost ten thirty. Although Mr. Rawlings looked calm, Phil knew differently. Throughout the day and their multiple conversations, it was obvious Mr. Rawlings was not happy about whatever Claire was doing with Meredith Banks. Phillip Roach, seasoned private detective, knew he should turn off the video feed and stop watching, but he couldn't. Claire Nichols was now his obsession, admittedly, as much as Anthony Rawlings'. Phil didn't understand his fascination, other than the obvious money he earned watching her. It was just that sometimes he worried about her, with Rawlings. It wasn't his place to make assessments. Not to mention, it's highly out of character. However, Phil reasoned, he was usually in and out of a job in days. He'd been watching Claire for almost two months.

Glancing from the monitor, he noticed the time, 10:28:07. His eyes returned to the screen, seeing Ms. Nichols open the door to her suite. Phillip saw her immediate change in body language. Her normal carefree presence transformed instantaneously. She immediately stiffened. The intensity of her stare caught Phillip's attention. The normal sparkle in her eyes morphed to a glare.

This was his job. Phillip Roach watched... perhaps, his correct title was *voyeur*.

*****

Claire stared in disbelief; words failed her. The expression glowering down at her was not the same one she'd seen a few weeks ago. This was one she'd seen before, one she preferred to keep compartmentalized away. It contained all the signature features of the man she wanted to avoid, eyes black as night, a tightly clenched jaw, and the visibly strained neck muscles. Angst filled her chest sending a rush of alarm through her veins. Without thinking, she went into defense mode, straightened her neck, and returned his glare.

Through clinched teeth, Tony said, "Let me in. We need to talk."

"I don't think we have anything to discuss. You made an unnecessary trip. Please go." Her voice sounded small yet strong.

Tony stepped toward the entry, "We are not having this discussion in the hallway. I'm coming in." With that he pushed past her into the suite. Claire immediately stepped back avoiding contact. He closed the door behind him. Tension filled the suite as they stared at one another. She contemplated her strategy while evaluating his movements. Then the reality hit her, and her momentary intimidation changed to indignation.

"We're not married and I'm not your prisoner. You can't just bully your way in here." His glare would stop most people in their tracks. Claire was sure it had. It'd stopped her before, but not today. "I want you to leave." Each phrase grew stronger.

Ignoring her demands, Tony circled the living room of Claire's suite, like a lion sizing up its prey. His presence dwarfed the once large room. Unknowingly, she held her breath as she watched his still clenched jaw and listened as his words came as a low growl, "What are you doing with *her*?"

"I'm having an overdue reunion with an old college friend." Feeling slightly more confident, she continued, "Besides, it's really none of your business. You shouldn't even be here. " She observed the dark deepen in his gaze. Watching from a new perspective, Claire decided the darkness wasn't just his eyes, but his entire expression, the way his brow furrowed and his jaw tightened. While her eyes saw only him, his ferocity filled her other senses. She waited for the sound of his reply. So much could be interpreted by the tone, tenor, and speed of his words. The room also filled with his scent. The cologne she'd dreamt about was once again penetrating her senses. Yet, her thoughts weren't sensual. Seeing him stalk toward her, she remembered fear, and reconsidered her boldness.

Without warning his hands forcibly seized her shoulders. His words came with hot needy breaths upon her face. Her gaze never wavered, with each syllable she continued to stare into the darkness. "You think I'm stupid? You're talking to her about me, and I won't have it." Claire chose not to reply. Tony exhaled and growled, "Damn it, Claire, you infuriate me!"

Before she could register his words and actions with enough sensibility to form her thoughts, he released her shoulders and stomped toward the windows. The dark San Diego sky turned the multiple glass panes into a mirror. She watched his eyes close in the reflection, and his shoulders sag from behind. The distance gave her needed clarity. The fact, he wasn't wearing a suit suddenly caught her attention. Her heartbeat calmed, and she listened to his words, "I flew across the damn country and have been sitting in a damn car waiting for your little reunion to conclude."

Claire shivered at the idea of him monitoring her movements so thoroughly. "Tony, you need help. I can't believe you're watching me that closely. Get over it!"

He looked at her with disbelief, his voice no longer harsh. What did she hear? "Don't you understand? I can't. You know from your prison delivery, I've been watching you for a very long time."

"And I think it is beyond creepy. Why? Tell me why. You didn't answer my question before."

Visibly calming, Tony's clenching ceased. He ran his hands over the back of a chair as a mischievous grin slowly formed, shattering his angry expression and mellowing his gaze. "Creepy? I've been called many things, but I think that's the first time someone has called me *creepy*."

Claire tried to hide her smile, "To your face."

After a moment, his amusement reached his eyes, bringing light to darkness, "Touché," he nodded, "that may be true."

"I guarantee it. Now if you're going to bust into my hotel room, answer *my* question. I don't owe you answers if you're not going to give them to me."

Tony looked at the sofa and back to Claire. "If you're asking me questions does that mean you aren't throwing me out?"

Claire crossed her arms across her chest and debated. A second ago she wanted him out, but his fight toward calm was a step in the right direction. "I don't recall ever having the ability to *throw you out* of anywhere. Maybe times do change?"

"People change, too."

He sat. Before she could join him in the sitting area another knock came upon the door. Tony looked at her with surprise. "Are you expecting company?"

"I ordered wine from room service," she said, as she walked to the door. This time she looked through the peep hole.

"That must be why you opened the door earlier. You obviously didn't look the last time." He smirked.

"You're right; it's a habit I need to work on." She opened the door. A young man dressed in a burgundy uniform entered, pushing a linen covered cart. Upon the cart was a bottle of Merlot and two glasses. He smiled politely at them.

"Ms. Nichols." He acknowledged. Claire confirmed. She realized the scene looked far different than reality. The young man requested, "Please sign this." He presented her with a small black folder, a smile and a slight bow.

Claire took the binder and opened the small folder. To her surprise the paper within wasn't a receipt, it was a note:

Ms. Nichols, I'm entrusting your silence.
Just making sure you are all right. P.

She looked to the waiter, who watched expectantly. Nervously, her gaze went to Tony who too was watching. She took the pen and wrote:

Yes – Thanks C.

Next, she closed the folder. Finding the ten dollar bill, she handed both to the waiter.

"Thank you."

"Thank you, ma'am. May I open the bottle?"

Claire nodded. After releasing the cork, he bowed again. Claire thanked him, and he left with his small black folder.

Claire returned her gaze to Tony as she thought, *Your creepy stalker, Phil Roach, is concerned. It's almost comical.* She didn't know if this declaration was good or bad. The ludicrousness made her giggle. If she'd been alone, it may have bordered on hysteria, but as it was, Tony's voice returned her to present.

"Did you order two glasses?"

She shook her head and tried to focus, her words came through muffled laughter, "No, but since they're here, would you like some Merlot?"

He approached her warily. "You know, you are the only person who can have me pissed off one minute and completely dazzled the next. Why are you laughing?"

Claire shook her head, "I don't know, shock, absurdity? It seems I never know what's coming. As much as I plan, I'm continually blown away."

Tony poured wine into each glass and handed one to Claire. "Do you remember when we had wine at the Red Wing?"

Claire closed her eyes, recalling the scene from a lifetime ago, and nodded. "I do."

"I'd been watching you for years. I was so nervous that night. I thought I was planning your acquisition." He looked into his red liquid.

Her stance straightened, "If you're using business metaphors, may I suggest *hostile takeover*. It's more appropriate."

He took a sip of wine and exhaled, "Yes, Claire," standing close he looked solemnly down into her emerald eyes, "and I have apologized for that." He paused for a moment, collecting his thoughts. "What I didn't know, despite all my research, as we sat talking was you. I mean, I knew everything about you." He shook his head reflectively, walked back to the sofa and sat down. His long legs stretched out in front of him. Claire noticed for the first time, how tired he looked. It was after all, almost two in the morning in Iowa. "Yet, I didn't know you. Truthfully, at first, I had no desire to."

"Oh, really?" She asked with intended sarcasm. "Because, I recall some pretty up close and personal contact."

Tony smirked, "Yes, I wanted *that*. I didn't want to *know* you, like the real you. I fought it for months. But you were this light that kept sucking me in. It wasn't supposed to be that way. *We* weren't supposed to happen."

"What was supposed to happen?"

"Well, the *takeover*," he emphasized the use of her term, "was supposed to stop you. I never expected anyone to flourish under such circumstances." He looked at Claire with a gaze of admiration as he continued, "You didn't just flourish. You conquered." He took another drink of his wine. "I've continually underestimated you or perhaps I should say, you've continually exceeded my expectations. You still do. You are the only person who has ever derailed me. And more than anyone, you know me, not Anthony Rawlings, me."

Claire knew she'd had the *rare opportunity*, as Catherine so eloquently told her once. She pushed forward, "The real you. Would that be Anton?" His expression morphed. Sadness fell like shadows over his face. The despair reached into her chest, physical ache came at seeing his expression.

He exhaled, "I suppose, yes, but not anymore. I had it legally changed. So, you see, I didn't lie. My legal name is Anthony Rawlings, and it has been for a long time."

Claire stood. She wouldn't allow herself to feel pity. Instead she did what people do when trying to avoid their true emotions; she lashed out, "You share this with me now, but not when we're married. That tells me that you never trusted me, *the only person to really know you*." The last clause emphasized. "Plus, you threw me away and left me to rot in prison." She exhaled in exasperation, "You say you love or loved me, past or present. You don't know what *love* is. You have an obsession and it really needs to stop. Stop watching me. Stop having me watched. Your fun is done. It's over."

He returned his gaze to the red liquid, slowly swirling it within the confines of the crystal globe. His words weren't rushed, instead a slow release, divulging hidden truths that only recently he'd come to know, "I don't know how to explain it. It was a loop hole. Don't you understand?"

Claire stood motionless; she didn't understand.

"I tried to help you." His eyes stared with need. "Anyone else would have jumped at the insanity plea. I had a hospital all set; your commitment time would've been negotiable. But no." He stood once again, "No! You refused! By doing that, you took your sentence away from *me* and gave it to the state of Iowa. I no longer had influence over your release." He turned to face her and his volume increased, "Why did you have to be so damn obstinate?"

"Me? You're accusing *me* of being obstinate? I didn't want you in control of my life any longer. I was willing to let the state of Iowa decide, rather than you."

Tony looked perplexed, "It was the only way to save you."

Claire tried to comprehend his words, "I have no idea what you're saying. Save me, from what?"

Tony looked down, his tired eyes suddenly dark and gloomy and his voice flat with restrained emotion, "Me."

The temperature of the room dropped. Claire felt the goose bumps materialize on her arms and legs as she instinctively wrapped her arms around herself. Slowly she sunk into the chair to Tony's left. The silence stretched between them, little by little filling each available molecule in the suite. The intensity of the quiet, made the air difficult to breathe. Claire tried diligently to fill her lungs with oxygen. She wasn't sure what he meant, but somehow the confession seemed monumental.

The sound of her vibrating telephone shattered the silence. She jumped as the small devise danced ringlessly across the table before them. The screen flashed: *HARRY CELL.* She saw Tony's eyes read the name before he turned away.

His question sounded strangely distant, "Are the news stories accurate?"

"You should know the accuracy of news reports." She replied as the phone continued to vibrate.

"Perhaps I should answer it?" Tony offered. His voice now clipped. The spell that encased the suite and isolated them from the rest of the world was broken. She wouldn't learn anymore about his attempt to *save* her this evening.

"No, thank you. I'll be just a minute." Claire reached for the iPhone, stood, walked into the bedroom, and accepted the call. "Hi." Although she was trying for light and carefree, she feared she failed miserably. Her mind was still reeling from Tony's declaration.

When we were children, we used to think
that when we grew up we would no longer be vulnerable.
But to grow up is to accept vulnerability;
to be alive is to be vulnerable.
- Madeleine L'Engle

Chapter 24

Harry's tone brought light back to Claire's dark suite. "How did your meeting with Meredith go?"

The insinuation of dread no longer lurked in corners and unknown hiding places; radiance flowed with the promise of better things. She absorbed the positive energy, closed the door between the bedroom and living room, and answered. "I think it went well. Mostly, we just reconnected."

"That's probably a good first step." He paused, "I miss you. I still think I should be there."

Claire exhaled, knowing he deserved honesty. Her voice was hushed, "I have a surprise visitor."

She heard the change in his countenance. His voice suddenly tensed as his words came too fast, "Is he still there? Are you all right?"

"Yes and yes."

"I'll get a SiJo jet and be there in an hour and a half."

"That isn't necessary," she continued to keep her voice low, "although, I would love to see you. But seriously, you need to work tomorrow; I'm fine. I'll call when he leaves."

"He isn't the only one who can jump on a plane to see you."

Claire shook her head. "You know, I never wanted to be someone *people jump on planes to see.*"

"I'll be waiting for your call. If you change your mind and want me there sooner call, text, or send smoke signals." His attempt at levity made her smile; he continued, "I'll be there."

The grin traveled through the phone, "Thanks, I will, I promise."

"I like hearing that smile. Just remember... it's for me."

"How can I forget?" she asked. "I'll call soon."

"I hope so. I'll be waiting. Bye."

"Bye, soon I promise." She disconnected the line.

Claire saw her phone, now solely used for Courtney, flashing on the dresser. She checked the screen, one text message, and hit the button: *BRENT JUST CALLED. TONY'S MAKING AN UNSCHEDULED TRIP TO SAN DIEGO. YOU AREN'T THERE, ARE YOU? JUST WONDERING... THOUGHT YOU SHOULD KNOW.* Claire smiled, fortified by the support of others.

Hesitantly, she approached the door to the living room. Her hand seized the handle; the cool metal calmed her nerves. She took a deep breath and pulled it open.

She half-expected to find Tony standing directly on the other side of the closed barrier. Opening the door and stepping through the threshold, she saw him standing again at the windows, holding his wine, and looking at the nocturnal vista. Claire wondered if he'd heard her open the door. If he did, he didn't turn around. Slowly, she approached and joined him at the window.

"I apologize for the interruption." She said, looking at the lights below.

He turned toward her, looking down from above. "Do you now, Ms. Nichols?"

Claire noted the change in his tone, more businesslike. "I do." Perceiving the meaning of her last name, she confirmed, "You're correct, I am Ms. Nichols, not Mrs. Rawlings." She considered adding, "you're doing, not mine." However, she didn't; she'd baited him enough.

Momentarily Tony stood, facing her, close enough to touch, yet, a million miles apart. Making no attempt to lessen the expanse, he replied, "I'm sure you are busy. If I were *him*, I'd be on a jet right now. According to my calculations, that gives us about ninety minutes to discuss what I came to discuss."

Claire considered enlightening Tony on the difference between the two of them, explaining Harry wouldn't be arriving because she asked him not to. She could talk about trust and communication. Instead she walked toward the sitting area, refilled her glass, sat down compliantly, and asked, "What do you want to discuss?"

"You will discontinue your discussions with Meredith Banks and any further plans you've entertained regarding speaking with the media." It was a very poorly worded plea, sounding more like a mandate.

She sat back against the chair and smiled, "Will I now?"

There was no hint of humor in his reply, "Don't push me. I'm tired and suddenly not in the mood."

Inwardly she smirked, knowing Harry's call upset him. With each such instance her sense of empowerment grew. "Well, I'd like to discuss something else."

"I would like to stay on topic."

"Then it seems we're at an impasse. Perhaps you should go. We can continue this, another day, or not."

"You're not changing the subject. The non-disclosure of our relationship is nonnegotiable."

"I don't recall signing anything, well, other than a blank napkin. We didn't even have a prenuptial agreement. So I have no legal restraints on what I can and cannot disclose."

Tony stepped closer, "Legal, no. What about ethical or moral?"

"Did those concerns come into play during your *acquisition* or our *relationship*?"

"I have tried to explain, not at first, but they did."

"Tony, I'm tired, too. I don't have the energy to figure out your puzzles. I don't plan on disclosing anything about your true identity to the media, if that's part of your concern. I have however, learned of many misconceptions regarding *me* during our relationship. I do plan on correcting those errors."

"Why?"

She sat straighter and used the words he'd said to her, "Because I can." His micro-expression revealed his displeasure, "The world wants to know, and I'm willing to disclose."

"It won't happen." He sat his glass on the table and leaned forward. "I came here to emphasize *this* is a waste of your time. Currently my legal team is working diligently to stop any information regarding our marriage or relationship from public media. If anything appears on the internet or anywhere else, a civil suit will immediately follow, against you, Meredith, and the offending sites."

Claire allowed the glass to linger on her lip and watched as Tony laid the gauntlet at her feet. Finally she spoke, "Well, at least this time you have the nerve to deliver the ultimatum in person, instead of sending Brent."

The reference to Claire's prison visit caused Tony to straighten his stance. "I was angry about the plea."

"You've made your point, now it's my turn."

Tony smirked, "Yes, I recall, you did like your turn."

She ignored his implication and went on with her request, "I want a promise -- from you."

"What promise do you want from me?"

"I want a guarantee the people in my life, the associates, and friends I've acquired are not in harm's way."

"My Claire, you give me too much credit. I'm a businessman. I don't have the ability to cause harm to anyone much less those associated with you."

This time Claire straightened, "Simon, John... do these names mean anything to you? How about my parents, your parents? Are there more? I can't seem to process right now."

"I do not take responsibility for that entire list. And explain exactly what you're requesting."

"Actually, I don't believe I'm *requesting* anything. I'm saying, beyond a shadow of a doubt, if anything happens to me, my friends or associates, my story and the truth behind our relationship will be public. I will continue to work on the articles and stop production before everything is public. *However*, if anything happens to me or my friends, everything will be public knowledge. You're welcome to do damage control but only be after the initial public response has been made and broadcast globally. As you know, once a perception is set, it's difficult to change."

Tony's grip on the stem of the wine glass intensified as he changed the subject, "I don't want you with anyone else. You're mine and have been for a very long time."

Although his words sent a shiver down her spine, Claire managed to respond incredulously, "That isn't your choice. You sent me away!"

"No. You left, *you* drove out of our garage." His words were stifled by his clenched jaws.

Claire stood, "Tony, I'm done with this conversation. I'm tired; however, I have a few other demands." She didn't wait for him to acknowledge, but continued, "John is out of jail. I want his law license reinstated. You took it away, don't deny it. Now, bring it back. I will consider that proof of you commitment to this agreement."

"I never liked him."

"I'm pretty sure the feeling is and always has been mutual. Nonetheless, he never deserved what you did to him. By the way, do you know who sent me the box?"

Tony stood, walked toward the door, but stopped and faced her, "Yes," his voice confident, "my dear, the information isn't known by many. My list of candidates was quite limited. It didn't take long to confirm my theory."

She followed him toward the door. Looking up at his face she asked, "Who?"

"Good bye Claire, for now. May I have your hand?"

She spied him suspiciously, "Why?"

He didn't answer; instead he held out his hand and waited. Reluctantly, she placed her right hand in his upturned palm. Tony bowed and touched his lips to her knuckles. While the warmth radiated up her arm, he turned her hand over. "Close your eyes."

Weakened by his strong yet benign command, she obeyed.

"Keep them shut," he whispered. She nodded as he reached into the pocket of his slacks, brought out a white gold chain with a pearl upon a white gold cross and placed it in her upward palm. Next, he closed her fingers around the delicate necklace and squeezed her hand. "My sign of commitment -- end this with Meredith." He kissed her closed fingers and opened the door.

By the time she saw her grandmother's necklace lying innocently in her hand, the scene blurred. Tears overflowed her lids and cascaded down her cheeks. She turned to Tony, but he was gone.

Claire's trembling fingers fumbled with the small clasp. With intense concentration she managed to put the delicate chain around her neck and secure the fastening. Hastily, she ran to the mirror and watched the small

195

white gold cross with the large pearl, move up and down upon her chest, accelerated by her now rapid heartbeat.

With time, her eyes moved from the necklace to her own face. The concentration and determination from before were gone. Her cheeks were now blotchy and smeared with mascara.

The stress of her reunion with Meredith -- the unexpected meeting with Tony -- complete with multiple confrontations -- and now the reality of her grandmother's necklace sucked any remaining strength from her core. Claire collapsed onto the bed, stared up at the ceiling, and fought the urge to cry. She couldn't stop the tears streaming from the corners of her eyes. But the sobs that screamed for release from the confines of her chest -- those she worked to contain.

Cradling the large soft pillow, now damp with tears, Claire curled into the fetal position, and closed her eyes. The combination of stress and emotion brought back her once familiar aching head. In time, slumber surrounded her, isolated her, and comforted her, creating a safe haven from the storms continually confronting her life.

The sound of pounding interrupted her peaceful bliss. She fought the disorientation associated with waking suddenly in an unfamiliar place. Groggily she saw the clock: 3:17 and forged toward the door of the suite, toward the source of the pounding. Nearing the large double doors she heard a key in the lock and *his* panicked voice, "Claire, Claire, are you in there?"

O, shit, I didn't call Harry.

Claire ran toward the doors. She'd used the chain lock; their key couldn't open the door completely. Just before her destination, she glanced at the large mirror near the entry, seeing her clothes from yesterday. The silk blouse, now untucked, hung wrinkled above her rumpled linen slacks. Dark black circles of melted mascara graced the underside of her swollen, red eyes. She mindlessly tried to smooth her messed hair, as if that would help her sad appearance. Quickly she called to the man on the other side of the door and fumbled with the chain. "Please wait, just a minute." Sliding the chain and pulling the freed door inward, Claire gasped at Harry, two men dressed in the hotel's signature burgundy, and a woman in a San Diego police uniform.

She stood in shock at the crowd before her.

Any anger she'd heard in Harry's voice through the door evaporated as he took in her appearance. "Are you all right?"

Before she could respond, he hugged her shoulders, and pulled her into his embrace. She didn't resist, melting against his chest. Unconsciously, she inhaled his masculine scent as her cheek felt the rhythmic beat of his rapidly pumping heart.

"Are you alone?" Claire nodded. "Did he hurt you?" She shook her head.

Harry turned to the others, "You may go." Speaking to the woman in uniform he said, "We'll let you know tomorrow if there're any charges."

Harry's unwavering embrace impeded her view, yet Claire struggled to free herself and turn toward the police officer, "There are no charges." Looking up Harry's soft blue eyes, she continued, "I'm sorry. I just fell asleep." Looking back to the woman in blue, she said, "Thank you for your time. I'm sorry for any misunderstanding, but there are no charges." Harry pulled her back into his embrace. She felt his heart slowing to a steady rhythm. "I'm sorry I worried you." She mumbled as they walked into her suite.

The comforting tone of his voice dwindled and agitation prevailed, "You said you'd call. You promised."

She stepped back from his touch, suddenly defensive. "I'm sorry. I don't know what else to say. I was upset when Tony left. I didn't mean to fall asleep. I just did."

Harry reached out and wiped smeared mascara from her cheek. "You've been crying?" She nodded. "What happened?"

She exhaled and recalled the evening in a synopsis of the finer points. "We argued. He told me not to speak to the media about our relationship. I told him to leave the people I care about alone. Then, when he left, he gave me this." Claire pointed to her necklace.

"He gave you a necklace?"

"It was my grandmother's. It's the only thing he saved from my Atlanta apartment, my only connection to my life before him." She fought the sobs bubbling in her chest and whispered, "It means more to me than anyone will ever know." Claire tried to compartmentalize the realization that lurked in the back of her mind; *Tony knows how much it means to me, he's the only one who knows all about me.*

Harry's voice helped clear her thoughts, "If it's something you want, I'm glad he returned it. But, why now?"

"He said, *as a sign of commitment.* In that box of information, there was a picture of it at an auction of my things. I thought it was gone forever."

Harry took Claire's hand and led her toward the sofa. On the table in the middle of the small grouping sat the almost empty bottle of wine and two glasses.

When Harry's grip tightened, Claire felt the need to explain, "I ordered a bottle of wine before he showed up. It came with two glasses, and I offered some to him."

"Very hospitable of you."

Claire wrenched her hand free at the crispness of his tone and turn toward the bedroom. This time she didn't get the chance to dismiss him. He followed, seized her shoulders, and turned her around. Peering down with the softest blue eyes, Harry spoke, "I don't care about the wine. I only care that you're safe. I called and called. You didn't answer. His jet left the private airstrip about 12:30. I panicked. After what you told me about last time, I was scared to death you were on that jet, involuntarily."

"I really am sorry. I don't know why I didn't hear my phone." She picked it up, from the table near the wine. The screen's message said eight missed calls, as well as text messages and emails. She checked the ringer, it was silenced. "I guess I never turned on the ringer after my meeting with Meredith." She looked up into his caring expression. "Thank you for your concern. What're you going to do about work tomorrow?"

Harry smiled his first smile since arriving, giving Claire the sensation of sunshine breaking through a cloudy day. "I know the boss. I'd better text her and let her know you're all right, but she gave me the day off."

Claire grinned, enjoying the sensation of raised cheeks instead of ones dampened with tears, "I've always heard it helps to have connections."

Harry leaned down and kissed her nose. "I like your smile much better than the sad face."

"Me too." She tipped her face up and allowed her lips to linger on his. "I know I look like hell. I'm gonna go clean-up. Why don't you text Amber?"

"I think you're beautiful, but go do whatever you want. You need some more sleep and so do I. I'll text her."

Wrestling butterflies and insecurities, Claire opened the door from the bedroom to the living room as her hand trembled slightly on the cool door knob. Scanning the suite, she immediately noticed Harry's bed. He had a sheet, blanket, and pillow on the sofa. Continuing to search, she found the man she sought. Irony struck when she realized he stood exactly where Tony stood hours before, at the large window, staring out at the dark San Diego skyline.

Worried that he'd reject what she had to offer, she tried to push the doubts from her mind and press forward -- barefooted across the light carpet. As she neared him, she saw the glass in Harry's hand; it wasn't one of the stemmed wine goblets from the table, but a small tumbler from the bar. He swallowed the last of the wine.

Quietly she moved next to him and touched his elbow. Lost in thought and startled by the contact, he turned his gaze to her. She watched as his blue eyes devoured and his expression morphed. She was only inches away, her face clean of makeup and tears, her hair brushed, and wearing a silk, floor length, light green nightgown.

She remained motionless, nervously awaiting his response. When he didn't speak, she tried for levity, "You're awfully tall to sleep on that sofa."

Keeping his eyes fixed to hers, he replied, "I was thinking the same thing as I put the blanket there." His hand gently went to Claire's shoulder, teasing the delicate spaghetti strap. She closed her eyes and exhaled, causing her breasts to move as her lungs deflated.

In unison, they stepped forward. Her nipples hardened as they brushed the silk nightgown and pushed against his hard chest. They'd been close to this numerous times, always stopping before making the ultimate leap.

Claire knew the consequence of her clothing choice. She had shorts and t-shirts for her morning work-outs. If she'd chosen that for her sleeping attire, she'd have sent an entirely different message. But she didn't. Her decision wasn't made hastily; she'd been debating it for weeks.

Harry's voice resonated deeper than usual, "You've had a long night. Don't you want some sleep?"

Her body shivered with anticipation, and her response came breathily, "Eventually."

He pulled her petite frame to him. Within his embrace, her body became liquid, molding against his. "Are you sure? I didn't come here for this."

She nodded, smiling a shy tight lipped smile and wrapping her arms around his muscular torso. "I know. You came because you were worried about me." It was Harry's turn to nod. She strained her tip toes to kiss his cheek, "And I appreciate your concern."

He lifted his brows, "So this is your way of saying thank you?"

Claire gazed through her lashes, "No. I said thank you, I think. *This* is what I want."

With only a moment's hesitation, he took her hand and led her toward the bedroom. Her insecurities faded with each step. When they reached the threshold, Harry stopped and asked, "Are you letting me in, or pushing him out?"

Claire's smile faded as she contemplated the question she wished he'd never asked. Feeling his warm hand encasing hers, she replied honestly, "At the risk of losing you to the sofa, I don't know."

He reached down and scooped Claire into his arms. She giggled in surprise as her feet left the ground. "At the risk of sounding like a man, at this moment I don't give a damn. I just want to be sure you know what you're doing."

She wrapped her arms around his neck and spoke with purposeful breaths into his ear. "I promise I know exactly what I'm doing. It's you and your actions I'm uncertain about," she nuzzled his neck, "and the anticipation is driving me crazy."

His blue eyes twinkled, "Ms. Nichols, crazy is just the way I like you." He laid Claire upon the king sized bed and watched as her long chestnut hair fanned behind her lovely face, highlighting the intense shimmer of her emerald eyes. After kissing her sweet lips he expressed his true observation, "You are so beautiful!"

Claire felt her cheeks blush as she lifted her head to watch Harry pull his shirt over his head. She'd seen his bare chest before, usually when they'd worked out together. Tonight she stared, thinking it looked wider than she'd remembered. The sight of it heaving with each breath, took her breath away. Happily, she replied, "I must say, I like my view, too." Her smile flowed from her lips, to her cheeks, and settled in her glittering green eyes.

When he started to unbuckle his belt, Claire sat up and asked, "May I?" Harry nodded and watched as Claire reached for the buckle.

She was a divorced twenty-nine year old woman, not a teenager. There was no need to portray false purity. Harry knew her past. As she unzipped his slacks and his boxer shorts tented in expectation, it was obvious he wasn't deterred by her boldness.

Standing in only his boxers, Harry reached for Claire's hands and helped her stand. With their chests once again touching he whispered, "My turn."

First uncertain, she then nodded, understanding his meaning. Slowly he bent down and secured the hem of her silk gown. With painstaking patience he eased the soft fabric over her hips, torso, and breasts. Only the gasp that escaped his lips, as he uncovered her supple firm body, could be heard until he spoke with the raspy tenor of desire, "Lift your arms." She acquiesced, and he eased the gown over her head, dropping it to the floor in a puddle of silk.

Harry's smile made her feel sexy, as she stood before him wearing only a small white pair of lacy panties. His eyes never left hers as he stepped toward her. Though his words directed her movements, his tone spoke with desire, "Lie down."

She stepped back, their eyes locked with need and gratification. Feeling the bed against her legs, she did as he bid. He gracefully followed her onto the soft mattress. His soft blue eyes danced with yearning. The emerald – blue contact ended as Claire's eyes closed, in response to Harry's caresses. Next, his lips contacted her soft exposed skin eliciting moans from deep inside of her. His kisses began at her cheeks, moved to her neck, shoulder, and down to her breasts.

Claire's breathing labored at the feel of his fingers massaging the small white lace triangle and his tongue tantalizing her hard nipples. Her back arched toward his touch and fingers twisted his blonde hair. She pushed his shadowed stubbly chin against her throbbing breasts. The sensation overwhelmed her deprived senses. She craved more.

She kissed his head, tasted his shampoo, and inhaled his after shave. It'd been so long. Claire knew what she wanted and the sexual assault upon her electrified nerves made her patience dissolve. She wanted him - - now.

Harry didn't show the same urgency, patiently caressing, feeling and kneading her most sensitive areas. Though she pleaded for more, he continued his reverent worship. Between kisses he showered her with adoration and compliments, "You're amazing." "Your skin is so soft." "I want you so much." The longer he denied her, the more intense her desire. Never had a first time been so intense. Never had Claire been made to feel so adored.

Her body tensed when Harry asked if she was on the pill. It hadn't occurred to her. The birth control insert that she had implanted long ago had passed its expiration. Thankfully, Harry was prepared. She didn't question why he carried a condom. At the moment her only reaction was relief. When they finally united, they were both hot with carnal longing.

Her dreams seemed real and exciting. But reality was magic. The undercurrent pulled her into Harry's rhythm as her body moved in sync with his. In time the current became a wave. Starting at her toes and moving north until it titillated the hairs of her scalp. She reached for his shoulders, arched her back, and unknowingly uttered a deep primal moan. The tidal wave took them all the way to a deserted exotic shore where he spoke the same primitive language.

Once the aftershocks calmed, she collapsed against Harry's chest. It seemed almost incomprehensible to Claire, that after such a stressful evening she could feel so relaxed and content. Her eyes closed as the sound of his heart lulled her tranquil body toward sleep. Encircling her shoulder he squeezed, momentarily waking her. She buried her face into his soft chest hairs and murmured, "I don't know what this means for the future." Enjoying his embrace, she added, "I really don't know what I want this to mean. I'm not looking for forever, but thank you for tonight."

He wrapped both arms around her, securing her gently to his chest. His voice made his chest vibrate against her cheek. "I don't know about the future either." He kissed her hair. "However, I don't think I can look at you the same way in Amber's kitchen wearing those shorts you wear." Claire lifted her eyes, sighing at his shy smile as he continued, "I mean, now that I know exactly what's under the shorts and t-shirt."

Claire shook her head, "Oh my, I hadn't thought of that." She let her hand trail over his pectoral muscles and down toward his waist. "I might just need to blush myself, knowing what's hidden by those delicious ripped jeans you like to wear."

"Delicious?"

"Hmm – mm," she murmured, hearing his laugh.

Stroking her hair, his voice became more serious. "Honestly, I'm not looking for forever, either. But if we're giving out thank yous, *you* should be on the receiving end."

"I think I was."

He chuckled, and went on, "I confess, I've been thinking about this since you bought your first cell phone."

Claire lifted her head. This new position gave her visual access to his soft blue eyes. "What? My cellphone, why?"

Harry grinned, remembering the scene. "I didn't know your story or even much about you. It just struck me as odd – you were so excited about a phone. I mean everyone has phones. Yet, you were almost giddy. I remember you looked like a kid at Christmas. At that moment, I fell head over heels for your excitement, enthusiasm, and innocence."

Claire lowered her head to his chest, "Harry, don't be deluded. I'm hardly innocent."

He lifted her chin and kissed her lips. "I'm not deluding myself. Innocence refers to lack of guilt and pretense. While often reserved, you fit that description. You're also very honest and naively trusting." He rubbed his thumb over her chin and stared into her clouding eyes. "Those, too, are admirable qualities. Besides, I think you've given me a pretty complete bio. You deserve the same." Claire tried to subdue a yawn, it was almost dawn, "And I'll give it, another time. Right now, let me enjoy the moment."

Claire nodded as she nestled her head once again upon his chest. "I'm rather enjoying it myself." His arm tightened around her soft bare shoulder. For the first time in weeks, she fell into a sound dreamless sleep.

Of all the animals, man is the only one that is cruel.
He is the only one that inflicts pain for the pleasure of doing it.
- Mark Twain

Chapter 25

-Summer 1985-

Despite the rising outdoor temperature and humidity, the mansion remained cool, too cool. Marie longed for a momentary reprieve. Emotions were running too high. Sighing, she settled onto one of the comfortable lounge chairs Nathaniel had ordered to Sharron's balcony and accepted the sun's warmth on her upturned face. A slight breeze tempered the June rays, as Marie inhaled the fresh country air. Sitting barefooted in a pair of shorts, she stretched her long legs out before her, and attempted to read. Despite the lovely afternoon, concentration was difficult. After all, the doctor was completing his most recent examination of Sharron on one of his now daily trips to the estate. Since he usually had one or two nurses for assistance, Marie found it better to allow them their space. When he was done, he'd sit down with Marie and Ms. Amanda and give his daily report. Of course, if Nathaniel or Mr. Samuel were home, they too would be included in the conference. Although, Marie knew Samuel and Amanda didn't approve of her presence, she appreciated they'd momentarily quelled their objections.

Ms. Sharron continually outlived every prediction made by the physician. But, as Marie listened to the monitors and witnessed her expressions, she knew Ms. Sharron was ready to go. The beautiful, elderly, frail woman believed in a higher being, a merciful God and a heavenly paradise. After spending over two years at the woman's side, Marie believed Sharron refused passage due to an unseen binding, bound to this earth by the chains of love. The afterworld, full of beauty and peace, was waiting. She just needed to let herself go.

Some would call it cruel, but after careful consideration, Marie and Nathaniel decided to be honest with her. Although her eyes hadn't registered any recollection in months and her mouth no longer spoke, there were times when holding her hand she'd momentarily squeeze theirs, in return. The physician explained this as mere muscle contractions. He reasoned emotional humans try to read meaning into scientific phenomenons, where in fact, there was none. Marie didn't care about his explanation. She believed there were times, Sharron could hear, understand, and communicate any way possible.

They'd discussed their speech many times. These discussions occurred alone in Marie's suite --usually in her bed. If Sharron wouldn't leave this world because of her bond to Nathaniel, he needed to tell her to go. Not as he would dismiss a servant or an employee, but with love and understanding. He needed to explain, he wanted her suffering to stop, and he would survive. He would live again. And this was the part they debated -- he was living again. Not only living, he was loving.

They both hoped the knowledge of Nathaniel's new life and new love would allow Sharron the peace to cross over. She could go where her body once again worked, where she could smile, sing and most importantly where pain, physical and emotional, ceased to exist.

The opportunity came only two nights ago, sometime after midnight. They'd been sitting in the plush high backed chairs, talking about something from Nathaniel's work when Marie noticed Sharron's eyes flutter and her hands open and close. Silently, Marie approached the far side of Ms. Sharron's bed; Nathaniel did the same on the near side. Without speaking, they created a circle. Marie remembered the warmth and strength coming from Nathaniel. It was such a stark contrast to the cool fragility of Sharron.

It was one of those instances in your life where time ceases to exist. When Marie's gaze went from Sharron's uncharacteristically clear and knowing eyes, to the dark intense stare of Nathaniel, she felt her heart break and swell. Was that how it happened? Similar to a turtle's shell, it shatters before it can grow. The pain that no medicine could treat produced tears which unapologetically streamed from Marie's eyes. However, it wasn't until she saw the same moisture escape from the dark eyes of the man she loved, that she felt the impending sobs within her chest, threatening the loving silence which filled the room.

Marie knew it wasn't her place to speak. Oh, she didn't have a problem directing Nathaniel while alone, but this was his speech. He needed to proceed at his own pace. It may be the only time she ever heard his voice crack, but she did. It was a gift few others receive, a forbidden view into his heart and soul.

"Sharron, it's all right. I want you to let me go." He continually exhaled, at a seemingly disproportionate rate to the breaths he took in. Finally, he continued, "I love you. I will always love you. And I know you love me. But you need to move on, for you, for all of us. Samuel and

Amanda will be all right. Anton will be fine," more exhaling and inhaling, "and we will miss you, but we will survive."

Sharron squeezed both of the hands that held hers. Her eyes appeared to flit from one face to the other. Did she know? Was she giving her blessing? They'd never know for sure, but they could believe. Nathaniel's voice gained strength, "I will never forget you, but I've found solace. Marie came into my life for you, but she's helped me, too." More breathing, "We've found comfort in one another."

When he fell silent, Marie spoke, "Ms. Sharron, I promise to take care of Nathaniel, as much as he will allow. He will not be alone."

Nathaniel's eyes moved from his wife, to his companion, to her midsection. Marie looked away. Did he really want to reveal their secret? She couldn't do it; again, it was his decision. "Sharron, this may shock you." He grinned through the grief; Marie believed she heard a low laugh. "I know it did me. But dear, there'll be another Rawls in the house. Our name will continue. We have a baby due the beginning of next year."

Did she understand? She squeezed both hands again. Her eyes seemed to register every word, and she blinked two times. The next breath she took was one of the deepest she'd taken in a while. One more squeeze of their hands, and she fell asleep. Sharron hasn't awoken since.

The sound of the French door opening behind her brought Marie back to the present. She moved her focus from the vast green landscape to the person now looming beside her chair. Expecting the nurse, Samuel's presence caught her off guard.

Marie spun around, her feet feverishly pushing into her sandals. "Mr. Rawls, I didn't know you were home."

His stare was intense, as he lowered himself onto the adjacent lounge chair. Instead of speaking, he looked out at the blue sky. The growing silence magnified Marie's unease. Only the rustle of the trees in the breeze was audible. Finally she asked, "Did you want something? Or are you waiting for the physician to finish his exam?"

"You like this lifestyle, don't you?"

"Excuse me?"

"I had you investigated. Did you seriously think I would allow someone to live in my house, care for my mother, and seduce my father without knowing her past?"

Marie stood abruptly. She moved toward the rail debating her response. If this were Nathaniel and they were alone, she would meet him head-on. This wasn't Nathaniel. And she'd always addressed Samuel with respect, a kindness obviously not reciprocated.

"Mr. Rawls, your tone is making me uneasy."

He stood, "Really, my tone? My words aren't bothering you? The fact I just accused you of seducing my father – calling you what you are, a whore."

"I believe you're overwrought by your mother's illness. I'm sure you don't mean everything you're saying."

"You're wrong. I mean every damn word. I will admit, the investigation was tricky, seeing as though you don't use your first name."

She turned and glared, her gray eyes speaking the retort she wouldn't allow her lips to say. He continued, "My investigator told me you were disowned by your family – they don't want anything to do with you, after you disgraced them, after you gave birth to a bastard!"

Her blood boiled; she couldn't contain her words. "Your investigator doesn't have the whole story."

"When my father hears this, once my mother is gone, you'll be out on your ass!"

"Good luck with that." Marie's chin rose in defiance. "Your father knows the truth. I've told him everything. The truth is..." Marie straightened her stance and contemplated. After a protracted silence, she continued with more control and less emotion, "The truth is -- you don't deserve to know what happened. It's none of your damn business."

Samuel took a step toward her, infuriated by her insolate words and tone. This conversation could go so many different directions. Fortunately the destination would remain unknown as a petite blonde nurse offered a welcome interruption, politely knocking on the glass paned door, purposely making as much noise as possible, as she entered the stone balcony. "Excuse me, Mr. Rawls, Ms. Marie, the doctor would like to speak with you both."

Samuel's look would stop most people in their tracks. His brown eyes glowed with frightening intensity. Many people would be intimidated by the darkness; Marie was not. She knew beyond a shadow of a doubt she had Nathaniel's support. That knowledge propelled her forward. She'd seen those eyes before, in the man she loved. However, they hadn't been directed at her, but at the man before her. Perhaps that was Samuel's true source of animosity. She possessed the love and support he'd never received. Pity threatened her indignation until fear took over. What would Samuel do if he knew she were pregnant?

The report was the same: Ms. Sharron's vitals continue to diminish. The IV kept her hydrated but without nutrients she'd be gone within hours or days. This time, the doctor did not expect a reprieve. Samuel, Amanda, and Marie listened as the doctor explained the probable sequence of internal events ultimately releasing Sharron from her earthly prison and stopping her respirations altogether.

The three sat in silence as the doctor and his staff gathered their belongings. "Mr. Rawls, I will once again offer my nurses to stay with Mrs. Rawls during these last few days. This is a difficult time for those emotionally bound to her. We can have a rotation here twenty-four hours."

Nathaniel wasn't present, granting Samuel the supreme position as decision maker. Marie sat straight and looked to Mr. Samuel. She wanted compassion, understanding, perhaps even respect for her years of service. She wanted to be the one monitoring the sweet lady. Instead, what Marie saw was contempt. Samuel's sinister expression displayed his sudden ability to thwart her plans. His voice was smug and restrained, "Thank you, Doctor. I believe that would be best. Please have your nurses begin immediately."

Amanda looked from her husband to Marie, back and forth. Finally, with a pompous smirk she spoke, "Then I guess it's settled. Marie, you may pack your things. It seems everything is covered."

"Thank you, Mrs. Rawls." Despite their cruelty, Marie conducted herself with poise and dignity. They were after all in Ms. Sharron's room. It wasn't the place for an argument. "I believe I'll wait for Mr. Rawls' return before I begin that endeavor."

Amanda smirked, "Marie, perhaps you've forgotten, I'm in charge of household staff. Nathaniel has more important issues than dealing with the help. Your services are no longer required."

Ignoring Amanda's directive, Marie walked toward the bed and squeezed Ms. Sharron's hand. With tears in her eyes, Marie nodded respectfully to the nurses, gathered her composure and walked toward the door of the suite. She needed air. The day was beautiful. Her goal was the pool or perhaps gardens, anywhere away from Samuel and Amanda.

Marie's mind spun as she approached the grand staircase taking in the gorgeous entry. The space below shone brightly and full of light, the high ceiling sparkled with reflective gold flakes glistening above the large glowing chandelier. A story below, sunlight seeped through beveled glass, creating prisms of color. Momentarily, Marie paused at the railing mesmerized by the rainbows dancing on the reflective sheen of the marble floor. It was as if the beautiful foyer was unaware that death lurked in the shadows.

After descending a few steps Samuel's gruff voice stalled her movement. Gripping the rail she remained facing forward, refusing to turn toward him. His words reached her loud and clear, "I would appreciate you to remember, staff uses the back stairs." When Marie chose not to respond, Samuel moved closer, descending a few steps. "I am speaking to you."

Her gray eyes shot shards of hate through the moisture she shed for the woman upstairs. "I can assure you, I heard you. Would you like me ascend, so I may descend again?"

"I would like you to ascend so you may fulfill the task my wife instructed."

Marie turned away, exhaled audibly, and continued her descent. This time he stopped her progress with a tight grip to her right arm as he propelled himself in her path. "My father has a lot of important things happening with his work; he doesn't need to be concerned with the employment of *servants*." His heavy emphasis on the last word did not go unnoticed.

Marie's chin rose in defiance. She stared directly into Samuel's eyes. "I am aware of his concerns."

"Oh, really?"

She didn't owe Samuel anything. Nonetheless, she hoped her knowledge would stop his barrage, if only momentarily. "Yes, your father is currently in a meeting with Mr. Clawson and Mr. Mathews. That's why he wasn't able to be here for the doctor's examination. However, he plans to be home as soon as he can. Your son is coming too."

Samuel chuckled, "Well, I guess it's true. If you want to know everything about someone," he paused, "share a pillow."

Marie freed her arm and attempted to step around the detour Samuel created. The prisms of light and color continued to dance across the floor, far below.

"We want you gone by the time he gets home." It wasn't a request.

Marie spun again, "I will not leave this home until your father asks me to do so."

"So you actually think you will stay, after my mother is gone?"

"I think you disrespect your mother by speaking as if she's already in heaven."

His rage was fueled by multiple sources. His mother's illness and impending death was unjust. She deserved so much more than she'd experienced. She deserved love and kind-ness, something Samuel couldn't imagine she'd ever received from his tyrannical father. As he stared at Marie's vain expression, he wanted to remove it forcibly from her smug face. He had never struck a woman, yet he questioned this woman's true status. Believing her to be nothing more than a gold digging whore, Samuel questioned how Nathaniel could be deceived by this slut. Samuel reasoned it was due to his father's increased stress with Rawls Corporation and Sharron's worsening health. Fighting to contain his instincts, he reached once again for her arm, "*I* am dis-respecting her, when you're fucking my..."

The front door opened as the prisms disappeared in a shower of light. Samuel and Marie's loud, angry voices carried throughout the vast foyer and beyond. Nathaniel and Anton's attention immediately went to the two people half way up the grand stairs.

Nathaniel's booming voice superseded the two coming from above. He saw the tear stained face of his love and the menacing expression of his son. "What in the hell? ..." He watched as Marie's expression turned toward him with obvious relief.

The next instant would replay over and over in his mind. Samuel's hand was on Marie's arm. She spun toward Nathaniel. Anton rushed forward, as if sensing the future. Amanda appeared at the rail above, seemingly to witness the commotion. But no, alas she had her own agenda. His daughter-in-law's voice transcended the foyer, "The doctor said we all should be in Sharron's room; it's almost time."

Samuel moved upward toward his wife. Did he push Marie? No, she simultaneously pulled away from his grip. Physics were nonnegotiable. The law of conservation of energy states energy can neither be created nor destroyed. It can only change form or be transferred from one object to another. As the two angry individuals exploded from their point of origin, they each used the contained momentum to propel themselves in their own desired direction.

The stair on which Marie stood was maybe ten or eleven inches wide. In her haste to reach Nathaniel, her sandaled foot misjudged the step. In slow motion, Nathaniel watched helplessly as his new love and the life of his unborn child tumbled downward. Her form rolled vulnerably, hitting each step with increased speed and power as she neared the marble landing.

Anton's agility and quickness allowed him to reach her before she connected with the rock hard floor. Nonetheless, Nathaniel, Amanda, Samuel, and various curious staff, gasped in horror and stared powerlessly as Anton held Marie's limp body.

*The most precious possession that ever comes
to a man in this world is a woman's heart.*
-Josiah G. Holland

Chapter 26

C laire woke slowly, enjoying the soft luxurious hotel sheets against her bare skin. Before her mind registered her location, she snuggled happily into the blankets. Suddenly, her knee contacted a warm leg. Claire gasped and stilled. Only inches away she heard the unfamiliar sound of rhythmic breathing and felt radiating heat. Opening her eyes she saw Harry's tussled blonde hair. Momentarily, her mind replayed scenes from the night before as her knee mindlessly moved against Harry's leg. It'd been so long since she'd awakened with anyone. She smiled and relished the softness of his leg hairs against her smooth skin.

Turning slightly toward the clock, Claire adjusted her eyes and read the numbers: 10:27. At first, she wondered where the morning had gone. Then she remembered dawn breaking through the dark sky, when they finally submitted to exhaustion and yielded to sleep. Dismissing the idea of leaving their secure haven, Claire peacefully closed her eyes, curled her body close to Harry, and savored the closeness.

In the recesses of her mind she recalled Harry's confession; he'd anticipated them together since she purchased her first cellphone. Smiling, she contemplated her first thoughts of a union – when Harry first asked her to play video games. Although, she told Courtney his anti-Tonyisms drew her in; she acknowledged to herself, his unwavering kindness, concern, and support held her captive.

Grinning into her pillow, she recalled Harry's prowess between the sheets. Prior to Tony, she'd been in a sexual slump. Simon was many years earlier, and they were just children. Between the two, there were a few nameless, meaningless men. Unquestionably, Tony's sexual abilities were boundless. Nonetheless, the daunting reminder of his nonconventional introduction into her life and bed darkened every positive memory.

Gratified with Harry's skills, Claire snuggled into the soft sheets, enjoyed his warmth and floated in and out of consciousness. Nearing eleven, Claire stirred as Harry eased his way out of bed. Her damaged self-esteem waited patiently for him to return. When he didn't, she freed herself from the warm cocoon, shyly wrapped herself in her robe and wandered into the sitting area.

Tentatively stepping into the bright room, Claire found Harry standing in the sunshine, peering through the large window. A glistening vista filled with buildings and shimmering sea filled the large pane beyond his silhouette. Despite the beautiful view, Claire's gaze focused on Harry's firm bare torso, trim waist, and perfectly faded jeans. They were the same jeans from last night and hung perfectly around his hips with the top button undone. As she admired the vision, she noted the absence of visible boxer shorts. Suddenly contemplating their location, her insides tightened. *If they are still in the bedroom -- it meant -- under his jeans...*

Smirking, Claire shook her head and listened as Harry spoke on his Blackberry.

"That's fine, send the email to me and I'll review it." "No, that can wait until Monday." "Be sure Lee knows." "Yesterday?" "No, I wasn't aware." "Have Lee call me as soon as he's off the call." "Thank you Rachel. I'll check in later today." He turned around and saw Claire.

Momentarily she feared her eavesdropping would upset him. However, Claire's anxiety dissipated as Harry's eyes lightened and a smile filled his handsome face. Slowly he walked closer keeping his glimmering eyes locked on hers.

Though he spoke into his Blackberry, his expression revived Claire's feelings from last night. "Yes," he said, "forward everything to my personal email. I can get it from my phone." His eyebrows rose as he neared and discontinued his conversation, "Good bye, Rachel. You know how to reach me."

He hit the disconnect button and flung his phone onto the couch.

Harry's change in countenance eased Claire's uncertainties about the night before. Suddenly her facial expression was beyond control. No longer did she wear a mask, her cheeks rose involuntarily, and the tips of her lips moved upward. She remembered Courtney's question: *does he make you smile?* She knew the answer and momentarily considered calling her friend and screaming -- *YES, he does!* However, her desire to remain within Harry's grasp prevailed.

"Hey, Beautiful Lady, I called room service and ordered coffee." His wrapped his arms around her waist. "It should be here soon." He moved so close, Claire needed to look up to see his blue eyes.

"That sounds wonderful. It's way too late for my first cup."

Lowering his lips to her forehead, Harry asked, "Did you sleep well?"

Her arms encircled the torso she'd been admiring, and she murmured, "Hmmm, I did. You?"

"Much better than I would've on that couch."

Claire grinned into his chest, thinking so many questions. What did this mean for their friendship? Truthfully, she wasn't looking for anything long term. And she didn't want to hurt him, but selfishly, the closeness felt wonderful. Every inch of her craved more of what they'd shared.

"Harry," she began shyly, "maybe we should talk about..." His hand gently lifted her chin, slowing her words. When their lips connected, her words ceased.

"How about we talk later?"

Claire didn't reason or think. Instead, she nodded and her body responded carnally without modesty. His hands untied the belt of her robe and slowly eased the fabric from her shoulders. As it fell to her feet, she pushed toward his warmth and security. From within the confines of his jeans, Claire felt his straining erection against her hip.

Moving his gaze down her body and back up to her emerald green eyes, Harry asked, "Do you know how gorgeous you are?"

She fought the urge to look down modestly and replied, "You make me feel that way."

"You should always feel that way." His hands cupped her behind as he pulled her nude body against him. The rough denim fabric burnished her suddenly sensitive skin. Their mouths united as Claire welcomed Harry's tongue through her parted lips.

This time she remembered the condom. "Do you have any more protection?"

Harry released his embrace, grasped her hand, and led her to the bedroom. Going to the bedside stand, he opened his wallet, and with a triumphant look produced a small silver square packet.

Claire's smile and lifted eyebrows begged the question, *did you expect this?*

"What can I say? Once a Boy Scout ... always prepared." His infectious levity made her giggle. Harry crawled on the bed and patted the mattress. She willing followed, unable to restrain the large ridiculous smile overtaking her face.

Gently easing her onto the pillows Harry moved to the foot of the bed. With his own devilish snicker, he allowed his lips to brush the skin of her ankle, calf, knee, thigh, hips, and stomach. By the time he reached her breasts, Claire's expression morphed into a pleasure clouded gaze, and her back arched as he teasingly suckled each nipple.

Weaving her fingers through his unruly hair, she asked the question burning in her mind, "How many of those packets do you have?"

Harry lifted his eyes to hers. "This is my last one." She exhaled. "I suppose we'd better make it count."

The thought alone electrified her skin, taking her beyond words. She gasped as her head foolishly bobbed in response.

She heard him say, "I know a few other ways to utilize our resources," as his kisses moved back toward her stomach and south.

Acquiescing to his suggestion, Claire fell against the soft pillows and allowed her body to enjoy the excursion.

212

******

Phillip Roach reviewed the video: 23:42:34 Mr. Rawlings leaves Claire's suite. Phillip notes she appears unharmed, perhaps slightly stunned, as she closes the door. Phil rubbed his temples and ridiculed himself for sending the note. Thankfully, since he hadn't heard from Mr. Rawlings, he assumed Claire managed to hide its existence from his employer. There was something in Mr. Rawlings' voice as he waited in that car, something which alarmed Phil. Now, shaking his head at the stilled image of Ms. Nichols closing the door while simultaneously looking into her closed hand, Phil acknowledged Claire's talent. This petite woman could influence Mr. Rawlings, in ways few others could.

The video restarted, 03:17:25, Ms. Nichols had a crowd at her door. Listening to the dialogue prior to the door opening, Phil determined Harrison Baldwin to be the one to gather the group. Baldwin looked and sounded tense while he banged on her door. As Claire appeared, she looked recently awakened, having slept in her clothes. Though her face was barely visible through the crowd and Baldwin's embrace, she looked uncharacteristically disheveled.

The others went away while Baldwin entered the suite. Phil rewound the feed and listened again. Though difficult to hear everything, it sounded as though they said something about *charges*. Claire specifically said *no charges* to the police woman.

The camera didn't activate again until 11:13:48, when Mr. Baldwin opened the door to allow room service to enter with a cart, the exchange polite and short. Baldwin wore the same clothes from the night before.

13:37:16, Mr. Baldwin pushed the cart into the hall and left the suite. 14:16:32, Ms. Nichols exits her suite wearing a beach cover-up, hat, sunglasses, and flip-flops and carrying a beach bag.

Phil decided to get a closer look at Claire's suite. He stopped on his way to the pool. When he reached her door, he found it ajar with a housekeeping cart parked before her entrance. Casually Phillip Roach stepped around the cart and waved to the housekeeper, in the bedroom changing the sheets. Noticing the blanket and sheet upon the couch, Phil grinned and clicked a picture. Although, it was none of his business, he suspected Mr. Rawlings would be as happy about this discovery as he.

Phil clicked a picture of the coffee table with an empty bottle of wine and three glasses. Next, he nodded politely to the housekeeper, left the suite, and walked toward the pool.

Easing into a lounge chair shadowed by a large umbrella, Phil's eyes settled upon his new obsession. Despite her eventful night with multitudes of visitors, Claire looked rested and relaxed, casually lounging under a deep burgundy umbrella, her bare legs stretched out before her, wearing a black bikini. On the table to her left, Phil saw her iPhone, a plate with part of a sandwich, and a tall glass with amber liquid. The lemon upon the rim and the small bowl of various colored sweetener packets indicated the glass contained iced tea. Her sunglasses were on top of her head as she read from the iPad.

He leaned back, snapped a photo and began his email to Mr. Rawlings.

******

Claire adjusted her eyes to her iPad. As long as she kept it out of the sunshine and her sunglasses off, she could read the screen. Sighing, she reread Meredith's blog for the third time. The content wouldn't change. She wasn't seeking new information -- only assessing. The procedure felt strangely familiar, evaluating each new situation for possible fallout. She'd lived two years of her life that way, taking-in everything around her, and gauging if, no not *if* -- *how* Tony would react. Claire no longer feared physical retaliation; yet, part of her felt the need to placate Meredith's blog, hoping to mellow his response. Claire reread:

Freedom of Speech

While Freedom of Speech is protected by the First Amendment of the United States Constitution, it is not apparently immune to money and influence. I wrote a retraction scheduled to appear today in *Rolling Stone* and *People Magazine*. It was a retraction to an article I wrote over three years ago. (Hyperlink to 2010 article)

As an independent correspondent, I have experienced the highs and lows of our ever changing world of media. In the past, I've proposed ideas which have been accepted or rejected in principal. Never, until now, have I had a publication refuse to print my finished product, **after** first accepting the concept.

(Hyperlink to Rolling Stone article) and (Hyperlink to People Magazine article); for the record, my retraction was to include additional information which these esteemed publications have since refused to print. A third nationally recognized magazine refused to print any of my retraction.

In an effort to inform the public, as **is** your **right** to know, my blog will serve as the sounding board designed to reach the masses. Here, as **is** my **right**, I will write what no magazine was willing to print:

Ms. Claire (Rawlings) Nichols has agreed to sit down with me and openly discuss her relationship, marriage, and divorce with Anthony Rawlings. Mr. Rawlings is one of this country's leading entrepreneurs and listed as one of the top ten wealthiest people in the United States. His influence in the world of business is without bounds. That same influence has been working overtime to stop Ms. Nichols' right to free speech.

As of yet, I do not know any details of their relationship. It is, however, my opinion that since Mr. Rawlings' legal team is working diligently to contain her voice, the final product will be worth writing... and reading!

Continue to follow this blog to learn more about the TRUTH only Ms. Nichols can share!

Claire looked at her phone and wondered if she should call Tony. After all, she didn't want Tony's *fine legal staff* presenting Meredith with a restraining order. Claire tried earlier to reach her old friend, but she was busy in another interview.

Claire closed her eyes and debated the effectiveness of *her* case, she would tell Tony: *I was upset after you left last night. You should know that. I fell asleep before I could call Meredith. The blog was already up and viral by the time I woke-up.*

There were over 300,000 hits. Her planned words were all true. Claire just wasn't sure if she could talk to Tony, after what happened last night with Harry.

Thinking about last night ... and this morning... caused a smile to sneak onto her face, momentarily forgetting the blog. She lowered her sunglasses over her eyes, placed the iPad face down on the small table, and relaxed against the soft lounge chair.

Absorbing the sunshine, she recalled her night and morning. When she and Harry finally talked about what they'd done, Claire was reassured by their like mindedness. Neither wanted to jeopardize their friendship, and both thought they were comfortable with the additional benefits. After all, they're both consenting adults.

Harry previously accused Claire of being distant regarding her past. If that were true, he was in another state. Until this morning, he'd kept his personal past hidden. Even Amber hadn't mentioned anything.

After their morning's use of Harry's last condom, he wheeled the cart with coffee into the bedroom. Sitting on the bed, sipping coffee, wrapped only in a sheet with Harry once again dressed felt absolutely licentious. Despite all they'd done, the decadence was stimulating. She remembered peering at him over the rim of her coffee mug, secretly wishing he had more silver packets, and knowing their daily coffee chats would never be the same. She listened as Harry offered a small glimpse into his history:

He only had, had two serious relationships. He acknowledged other sexual encounters, but there were only two he considered *girlfriends*. One started in college and lasted three years. Claire listened, thinking that was longer than her time with Tony. The most recent lasted about a year and a half and ended a few months before Claire arrived in Palo Alto.

At first it surprised Claire she didn't know any of this. Then she realized how little she knew about Harry's past. He'd been very forthcoming regarding his work at SiJo and previous police work. But that was all in relation to his investigating skills with Tony.

This morning he told her about regular medical care and his belief that he was healthy and free of all communicable diseases. He even offered to have a routine check if it would ease Claire's mind. He winked and his blue eyes twinkled when he mentioned with a clean bill of health and her on the pill, they could avoid the bothersome condoms. While Claire appreciated his candor, she wondered if this was what dating had become, the exchange of medical records. It wasn't like she ever had a chance to consider that with Tony. And she had seen a doctor in prison, without a doubt, her medical record was clear. The pill -- that was something worth considering.

As he volunteered a larger glimpse of his personal history, Claire wondered why she'd felt the pressing need to share her past despite knowing so little of his. She reasoned it was due to his help researching Tony's past. After all, Harry hadn't asked Claire to investigate his ex-girlfriend.

It was the name of Harry's most recent *girlfriend* which caused Claire to twinge. She wasn't sure what it meant. Could it be jealousy? She didn't think so. However, not only had she met his ex, she'd talked with her. Now the more recent coolness she'd noticed from Amber's personal assistant made sense: only months before, Harry and Liz had cohabitated.

"Do you find it weird working with her every day?" Claire asked.

"No. It's over. We both know it. Besides she's great at what she does." *Wow, that was an open ended statement*, Claire thought. "And Amber doesn't want to lose her, just because we had a thing."

"That's incredibly mature. Does she feel the same?"

"Well, I think so," he shrugged. "We haven't talked about it." Looking closely over the rim of his mug with a look of disgust, he added, "Not everyone hires private detectives to follow their ex's every move."

That reminded Claire of Phil's secret message from the night before. With everything else, she'd actually forgotten. Harry's eyes widened with curiosity when she told him about the wine delivery and the note.

Taking her empty cup, Harry kissed her nose and said, "My, your list of admirers continues to grow. How did I end up being the one to stay the night?"

The idea of Tony or Phil staying made Claire uncomfortable. Mostly because she'd fantasized about one and hardly knew the other. But Harry's tone made the blood rush again to her cheeks. She couldn't believe she was blushing like a school girl. "Lucky, I guess, Mr. Baldwin."

"I would have to agree." His smile warmed her.

They also talked about her last night in San Diego. Despite Mr. Rawlings' *request* (*more of a mandate*, Claire thought), to stop her discussions with Meredith, she had a scheduled meeting and planned to keep it. She planned to do what she'd told Tony -- go on with the interviews but halt production. Recounting the sickening feeling of fear for Harry, Amber, John, and Emily, she believed this might just be the ticket to keep them safe. However, she did worry about Meredith's reaction. Undoubtedly, she would want her article or articles published, preferably sooner than later.

Harry asked, "So would you mind company for the rest of your stay? I'll make myself scarce while you and Meredith are working." Claire smiled and remained silent. She liked his requests. They were so much nicer than decrees. Harry continued, "I think with all of your visitors, I should stay... for your safety."

"Didn't you say Tony's plane went back to Iowa?"

"Yes." He hesitated and then asked, "Does that mean your answer's *no?*"

"It means you need a better reason." Her eyes twinkled.

"How about, I want to?"

"That works for me. But maybe you could..." She raised her eyebrows.

This time his cheeks reddened, "Yes, I was thinking a stop at the drug store was in order." Claire didn't respond verbally, she just nodded.

*****

The vibration of her iPhone, against the glass surface of the small table, pulled Claire from her memories. She read the screen: *TONY CELL.*

*Turn your face to the sun and
the shadows fall behind you.*
-Charlotte Whitton

Chapter 27

*T*ONY CELL, Claire read the words from her iPhone. She wanted to be the one to call him, but her memories faded into dreams as she lay on the sunlit lounge chair. Mindlessly, she realized her plate was gone and her tea was full. The vibration and ringing confirmed her earlier concern; Tony or Shelly must've seen Meredith's blog. Claire knew she needed to meet his confrontation head-on. If she didn't, she risked him flying back to San Diego. And seeing as how her sleeping situation had recently changed, that wouldn't be good. After the fifth ring she squared her shoulders and swiped the screen.

"Hello, Tony."

"Claire."

She couldn't determine his mood by his one-word response. "To what do I owe this honor? First a visit -- now a call." Claire tried in vain to sound nonchalant.

"It seems that your *friend* blogged about your impending disclosure."

"Yes, I read that."

"We discussed this yesterday. I was under the impression we'd reached an agreement."

Claire reached up and touched the pearl dangling daintily from her neck. "As I recall our agreement states the articles won't be printed, unless something happens to me or someone associated with me." She attempted to maintain her businesslike tone. "I said I would go on with the interviews."

Sarcastically he asked, "Tell me Claire, do you expect bodyguards for everyone? I'll need a list of names."

She shook her head, "I expect distance and respect."

"And I expect my directives to be followed." Claire recognized the change in Tony's tone. It was harder with increased volume. "Her blog no longer exists."

"That's unreasonable." She replied, "She didn't know anything about your directive. I haven't had the chance to speak with her."

"That's your undoing, not mine."

"Actually, I beg to differ. I was upset by your visit last night, more accurately by your gift. Instead of calling, I fell asleep. By the time I woke, she wasn't available and the blog was viral." As Claire spoke, she powered-up her iPad and searched for Meredith's blog. The web address she'd used earlier was met with the Error Response: *Server not found.* "Shit, Tony, what have you done?"

"I believe I presented you with a sign of commitment, and now I have presented you with a warning. Following my rules isn't optional. I expect you to remember that, if you want your *requests* to be considered."

Claire's blood boiled. She remembered his rules and his redundant lectures regarding those rules. However, as much as she wanted to argue and fight, she wanted her loved ones safe, and John's law license reinstated. With great effort, Claire's voice strained with projected compliance, "I will speak with Meredith this evening. Nothing more will appear in print or on-line as long as people stay safe and John gets his license."

"Your second request will take some time."

"Tony, it wasn't a request."

"Your bravado is appreciated, but I won't be swindled. I don't make mistakes or unsubstantiated threats. It would do you well to keep that in mind."

"From business metaphors to chess, the thing is, for a swindle to have occurred I would need to be losing. On the contrary, I'm in California and you're in Iowa. I would say I have the initiative."

"Well, I see your weakness, your *hole*, and I'm confident that you'll blunder. The queen will be mine."

"Yes, I know the term. Now, didn't you tell me last night that I continually exceed your expectations?" She didn't wait for a response. "I think you've forgotten -- to win at the game of chess it isn't the queen you seek, but the king."

"You may consider Meredith's blog to be a gambit, but I doubt she shares your point of view. I look forward to the end-game."

Claire sighed, "I will talk with her tonight."

"By the way, I like the black bathing suit, but I'd prefer it here at the estate where it wouldn't be seen by as many people."

Her head darted from side to side. Behind the trunk of a palm tree, under the shade of an umbrella she saw Phillip. "Good-bye, Tony." She disconnected the line, before he could comment. She stood and made her way toward Phil's umbrella; they needed to *talk.*

The late afternoon temperature was perfect. The low humidity combined with a light breeze made the pool oasis a haven for relaxation.

However, as Claire approached Philip Roach, his expression looked anything but relaxed.

She didn't ask permission to sit in the chair next to his, she just did.

His voice was curt, "Ms. Nichols, I thought we weren't to know one another. Can I assume we're being photographed?"

"I was about to ask you the same thing." Holding up her phone Claire continued, "It seems my ex-husband is receiving up to the minute updates. He even knows what I'm wearing."

"What can I say, I have a job. I do it."

"Then tell me what last night's note was all about."

Phil looked away. Eventually the enticement to see Claire sitting next to him, in nothing but her black bikini, was too strong. He returned her gaze. Mindlessly he wished she wasn't wearing the large sunglasses. He so rarely was able to look at her this close. He wanted to see her eyes. Finally he responded to her question, "It was a display of unwise judgment."

"Unwise?" Her voice softened, "I thought it was kind."

"Well, Ms. Nichols, I'm not paid to be kind. I suppose I momentarily forgot my place in this equation."

Her anger regarding Tony's knowledge of her attire faded. She gently touched Phil's outstretched leg and said, "Thank you. He *was* upset when he arrived." She smirked, "He's not too happy right now. But he calmed last night, he'll calm again."

"You seem to have an uncanny ability. My concerns were unfounded."

"No Phillip, your concerns were admirable. Thank you."

He nodded.

Claire went on, trying to give Phillip some sense of understanding. "This is nothing but a game to Mr. Rawlings. Unfortunately for me, he has the ability and resources to keep the game going into untold overtime. And you are a piece of that game."

"Game? That wasn't the impression I've received."

"It's like chess. I make a move, he makes a move. Eventually one of us will declare check-mate."

"From my short experience, I believe you're a worthy opponent."

"You see, that's where I'm confused. Sometimes I think I'm an opponent. Other times I think he believes I'm the prize. Thing is, I'm not interested in being a prize."

"Maybe instead of chess, it is archery. And you, Ms. Nichols, are the target."

She pondered his observation. That scenario would take more consideration. She asked, "By the way, what happened to you at that French restaurant?"

"I had an offer I couldn't refuse."

Claire nodded. "Thank you again for your concern. I'm in hope of you being dismissed soon, but I doubt that will happen. And at this time I don't want to break in another bodyguard. So I'll leave you to your work."

As Phil watched, Claire walked back to her chair. He considered her words and thought to himself, *bodyguard -- that does sound better than paid voyeur.*

After her time by the pool, Claire went back to her suite and made some calls. A lot had happened with Tony since she'd last spoken with Courtney. Claire told her all about Meredith and the agreement she hoped to secure with her tonight. She also told Courtney about Tony's surprise appearance the night before.

Courtney filled Claire in on the progress of Caleb and Julia's wedding. With it less than a month away, Courtney was trying to be as helpful as possible. Claire smiled, listening to her friend go on and on about dresses, rehearsal dinner, and tuxedos. Claire told her how much she'd like to help. They both knew that wouldn't happen. Nevertheless, Courtney promised lots and lots of pictures.

Just before they hung-up, Claire mentioned her other late night visitor. Claire couldn't tell Amber about what they did. It was refreshing to have a friend with whom she could talk to about Harry. Courtney didn't judge; she listened. When Claire said Harry *did* make her smile, Courtney said she couldn't wait to meet him. Her last comment on the subject caught Claire off guard. Courtney remarked, "Can you imagine if Tony realized his visit was the push to advance your relationship with Harry?" Claire hadn't thought of it like that. She remembered Harry's question. If Courtney's observation was right, was she pushing Tony out, instead of letting Harry in?

Harry returned to the suite later in the afternoon looking delicious in new jeans and a new black t-shirt. Since he hadn't planned on staying in San Diego, he was forced to do some shopping. With a boyish smirk, he handed Claire a plastic bag containing a box. She looked into the bag and returned his smile from under her mascaraed lashes. It seemed silly to feel shy about the box of condoms. However, when she noticed the number on the side of the box she exhaled. She didn't know they were sold by the dozen.

Her thoughts went back to Palo Alto. Did his bulk purchase mean he intended this arrangement to continue back at the condominium? She wasn't opposed. It would just be different. This get-a-way was more like a holiday. Another issue requiring more thought.

Just before seven o'clock, Harry asked Claire, "I was thinking, instead of flying back to Palo Alto tomorrow, maybe you'd be interested in driving?"

"Driving? How long of a drive is it?"

"About eight hours."

Claire stared in disbelief. "Eight hours?! Why do you want to do that?"

"Because, Santa Monica is about two and a half hours from here. And a friend of mine, known for his amazing research, tracked down Patrick Chester."

Claire contemplated for a moment, "Chester? The neighbor of the Rawls? The man whose house Tony went to, to make the 911 call?"

"Yes, one and the same. If you want to visit, I'll call him this evening and see if we can arrange a meeting."

Her mind spun. That wasn't something she'd even considered. Claire thought *if Tony was upset about me visiting with Meredith, this would throw him over the edge.* But then again, she did have a reservation to fly back to Palo Alto at nine in the morning. If she didn't cancel, Phillip would once again lose track of her, at least temporarily.

A knock came on the door of Claire's suite interrupting their conversation. Looking through the peep hole, she saw Meredith. Just before opening the door, she turned to Harry and replied, "If he's willing to meet, let's do it."

Harry leaned down and kissed her. His voice sounded huskier than before, "I'll be back after your meeting. Have a nice dinner."

His smile made her pulse increase and her stomach clench. She replied, "You, too. Sorry you're eating alone."

"I'll survive."

With that, Claire opened the door and Meredith entered. Claire made quick introductions, "Meredith this is Harrison Baldwin. Harry this is Meredith Banks." The two shook hands and made quick pleasantries. Harry excused himself and left.

When the door shut, Meredith's eyebrows shot up, "Is he the man I've seen you with in the magazines."

"Are we off the record?"

Meredith smiled, "Yes."

Claire returned her smile, a little more shyly, "Yes."

"My Claire, you certainly know how to attract the good looking men. If I weren't married, I'd ask your secret."

Their easy banter quickly disappeared as Claire explained the loss of Meredith's blog.

Meredith stared in disbelief, "I thought there was a problem with the server due to the excessive number of hits. I never dreamt it could be due to Mr. Rawlings." She sat in silence for a moment and added, "So, is this an example of what he can do?"

Claire nodded. "It is. Are you sure you want to do this. He was here last night, and I can promise he isn't supportive."

"He was here? So you two are still talking, after everything... the prison thing and all?"

Claire nodded, "Honestly, I don't know if I'd call it conversation. I'm speaking, he's speaking... well you get the picture."

Meredith nodded affirmatively.

"He set some boundaries." Claire explained briefly, "At this time I'm inclined to respect them. It's a quid pro quo thing."

Meredith laid her purse on the table, pulled a small laptop from her bag and turned it on. "All right then, lay it on me. What are the rules?"

Claire snickered, "Oh, you have no idea."

She and Meredith discussed the new rules: They would continue to meet, Claire would tell her story, it could be written, but it would only be published *if* Tony failed to keep Claire and her close friends safe. During the conversation, Claire realized Meredith needed compensation for *lack of publication*. Claire could help with some of that, but decided if Tony wanted to keep this quiet, he could help float the bill.

After dinner, Claire gave Meredith a small sample of what she could expect. It began with the story of a twenty-five year old woman working at a local news affiliate in Atlanta, Georgia. After ten, Claire decided she was done talking for the night. Their story ended with that same woman waking in an unknown room. Claire didn't begin to describe the woman's physical condition, just the terror of a lost day and the unknown.

Meredith typed feverishly and conceded, "I want this story. I'm willing to do anything and follow any rules to be the one to write it."

They agreed to meet again in a week. This time Meredith would travel to Palo Alto.

Claire's airline reservation required her to leave the hotel early. Even though she wouldn't board the flight, Harry and Claire chose to stay on schedule. It would help their illusion with Phillip Roach. Their night hadn't been as late as the night before. Nonetheless, Harry's trip to the drug store wasn't for naught.

When Harry and Claire arrived at the airport, they traded Claire's Mazda 3, for a Mustang Convertible. As Harry lowered the roof on the bright blue muscle car, Claire secured her hair in a ponytail. She smiled and chose not to respond to Harry's comments as he put Claire's luggage in the car. He mumbled something under his breath about how happy he was he didn't have luggage. Claire's suitcases seemed to fill most of the trunk. Shaking his head he repeated, "It was only a three day trip."

The ocean breeze helped disperse the clouds and create bright blue patches high above, matching the paint of the Mustang. Harry eased the rental car into the light Sunday traffic of I-5N. Claire laid her head against the seat and enjoyed the sun and wind on her face.

She didn't often allow herself to think about prison. It was easier to keep it compartmentalized away. Nevertheless, sometimes the isolation and incarceration came rushing back. The memories of days, weeks, and months with limited interaction, fresh air or sunshine would infiltrate an otherwise happy day. It happened as she listened to Led Zeplin sing about a stairway to heaven. Closing her eyes behind the Oliver Peoples sunglasses she relished the warmth and tingling on her cheeks. It was all such a contrast to those dark months. Claire didn't even realize she was lingering on her own sad memories until she felt the tears slip from her eyes. Harry reached for her hand and squeezed, offering comfort.

He turned down the music and leaned toward her, "Are you all right? If you don't want to do this, I understand. Amber told me the police reports upset you."

Claire took a tissue from her purse. "It isn't that. I really haven't given this whole meeting a lot of thought."

223

"What is it?"

She exhaled. "I just love the sun and wind."

Harry smiled and squeezed her hand again. "Well, if it makes you cry, maybe we should avoid things you love."

Claire grinned through her tears, "How about I try not to cry, and we enjoy lots of sun and wind."

"You don't need to *try* anything."

A few minutes later, Claire volunteered softly, "Sometimes I remember what it was like to only see the sun for an hour a day."

Harry exhaled. His grip intensified upon the steering wheel, "I forget about your time in prison. You never talk about it." She shook her head. His eyes screamed compassion as his blonde unruly hair blew in the wind. "You can cry, laugh or scream, anything that helps. Go for it."

She squeezed his hand, laid her head against the head rest, closed her eyes, opened her mouth and screamed! It was like nothing she'd ever done before. She didn't look at Harry; her eyes stayed closed tight. They were traveling at approximately seventy miles per hour, with the wind blowing wisps of her tied back hair and the sun bathing her cheeks.

Although her first attempt was weak, Claire didn't quit. She pictured her cell, the cement block walls, and sparse furnishings. She tried again. This time she felt the sound begin in her diaphragm, travel up her throat, and explode through her lips.

Without thinking she felt the smile creep onto her face. Despite the memories, the outlet filled her with hope. When had she last screamed? Really screamed? There were plenty of opportunities, but she'd never done it.

Feeling the release, from her toes to her eyebrows, Claire scrunched her eyes tighter and gave the scream one more try. This one lasted longer, going on and on. Her eventual silence came only due to the deflation of her lungs. Nevertheless, once they inflated again, the sound morphed to a giggle, starting as a lonely chuckle and propagating. By the time she opened her eyes, tears leaked from her lids, not from sadness, but from the rush of release.

Harry tried to maintain his focus on the highway. There were other cars as well as big trucks. The lack of roof made the rush of wind and sound so much louder than it'd be normally. However, the woman beside him filled him with awe. When he'd said to scream, he never expected her to take him up on it. But there she was head back, emerald eyes hidden behind lids and sunglasses, with her mouth open wide.

His peripheral vision refused to release her image, even for one second. The second scream was louder. The third was beyond belief. For a moment he thought about Claire in a prison cell. In that instant his chest filled with angst for her plight. Yet, that thought was but a flash. Claire started to laugh. Yes, Harry couldn't believe his ears. Her chuckle grew becoming infectious. His expression of disbelief changed, as if his lips started at below zero and within seconds became zero and soon forty-five degrees. When she finally opened her eyes, he couldn't contain his own laughter.

Never could he remember feeling the admiration for someone he currently felt for Claire Nichols. How could anyone let her go?

At that second, Harry realized, no one could. Anthony Rawlings would never let her go. If Claire were to be part of his life, so would Anthony Rawlings. He forced a smile and glanced toward her hidden eyes.

Claire's voice transcended the rush of air, "Thank you. I really do like the car and the drive."

"You're very welcome, anytime."

With her cheeks still raised and her lips turned upward, she moved her glance to the right. He thought about the woman who arrived at Amber's apartment; would that woman have screamed at the top of her lungs, on highway 5-N? Would she have joined him in their activities over the last two days? Harry wasn't sure. He knew the petite brunette at his side was a mass of contrary emotions and actions. Beyond anything, he longed to explore every one of them.

Claire glanced back at Harry as he suggested, "I know this great place in Oceanside for Sunday brunch. Are you up for stopping on our way to Santa Monica?"

"Yes, it sounds great."

All secrets are deep. All secrets become dark.
That's in the nature of secrets.
 - Cory Doctorow

Chapter 28

With the wind in her hair, Claire's thoughts disappeared into the ribbon of white sand and rolling waves. She watched as a few lone souls, in wetsuits, walked the shore carrying surfboards in search of the perfect wave. The table she shared with Harry at the Beach Break Cafe was covered by a blue umbrella. Under that same table, Claire's sandaled feet rested upon a carpet of sand. Inhaling the salty surf she relished the perfect atmosphere for Sunday brunch and sipped her coffee.

Harry remained uncharacteristically quiet as Clair enjoyed the glowing vista. The glistening sun reflected off the waves creating silver caps rolling upon the turquoise blue ocean. Wistfully she remembered other sandy beaches. She loved the soft gritty sensation as she wiggled her sand covered toes under her chair.

After the waitress refilled their cups of coffee, Harry's soft voice penetrated the sounds of the sea, "If this is too difficult for you, I can go to Patrick Chester's house alone. I'll just call and reschedule."

Claire looked up. Despite his concerned expression, it was his long unruly blonde hair moving in the ocean breeze that made her smile. Only once had she seen it controlled, the night they'd met at the restaurant and he'd used gel. She remembered he'd also worn a jacket, a sexy look, but not as sexy as his jeans and well-fitting t-shirts.

"No, I can do this. Honestly, I haven't allowed myself to think much about it. I guess I'm torn." Harry lifted his brows, and Claire clarified, "I'm curious, but apprehensive. The police reports were upsetting. I'm not sure I want to hear more gory details."

"That's not why we're going to see him."

Claire listened.

"I asked a friend, who works at SiJo, to help me with research."

Claire interrupted, "Harry, please don't do that. I feel bad enough with all Amber's done for me. She doesn't need to be paying people to research my vendetta."

"Well, Lee's my friend; we went to academy together. After Simon made me head of SiJo security, I called him and offered him a job. There were openings and he was more than qualified. He's got a wife and two kids. The increase in pay was too hard for him to turn down. Most of all, he's been a tremendous asset to SiJo. Amber isn't wasting money on him, no matter what he does.

Anyway, he's always been a master at digging for information. So, I might have mentioned that there were some inconsistencies in the Samuel and Amanda Rawls case."

Claire sat her coffee cup upon its saucer. "Because... you often bring up old homicide or suicide cases during lunch break?"

"I might have also mentioned you... and your ex... but I promise, Lee's professional. I told him about the ballistics and the reported COD. He agreed, it seemed... well, fishy."

"Is that supposed to explain why we're going to Santa Monica?"

Harry remained silent as the waitress interrupted their conversation, delivering food. The smell of sand and salt disappeared into a cloud of decadent aromas. Claire noticed the attentiveness of the cute voluptuous blonde, of course, all directed toward Harry.

She watched as Harry returned the server's adoration with restrained politeness. Momentarily Claire remembered being at restaurants with Tony. There were times when waitresses or hostesses blatantly flirted. However, as *red hot sexy* as *People Magazine* said he was, Anthony Rawlings was also intimidating. More often than not, Claire witnessed shy smiles and platitudes from servers, *"Thank you, sir." "If there is anything else I can do..."*

Harry, on the other hand screamed sexy, with his tight V-neck, relaxed *7 For All Mankind* jeans, and tussled blonde hair. She thought about his *free* coffee, after their article appeared in popular publications. Grinning into her quiche, Claire inadvertently shook her head.

Harry looked up from his eggs Benedict to see Claire's actions, "What?"

She looked up with big bright emerald eyes, trying for her most innocent; *I have no idea what you're talking about* look.

After a bite of his eggs, complete with Hollandaise sauce, Harry continued their conversation, "Well, Lee is thorough. He, on his own, decided to do a better investigation of the neighbor, Patrick Chester."

Claire nodded, interested in Harry's information, almost as much as her fresh fruit.

"It seems Chester was awarded a settlement in November of 1989."

"That's not long after Samuel and Amanda's death. What kind of settlement?" She managed between bites of succulent pineapple.

Harry went on to explain the origin was fuzzy. At first glance it appeared as though Chester was a litigant in a class action suit. However, upon further investigation, the beneficiary seemed to be an independent international company, based in the Cayman Islands. The actual monies were siphoned through a law firm in Los Angles. Of course, this law firm refused to answer questions or divulge any information."

"What kind of settlement are we talking -- how much money?"

"The first installment was only 20K."

Claire had to ask, "The first?"

"Well, his bank account has received infusions every year. I want us to go to him with the pretense of justifying his story."

Claire looked puzzled.

Harry explained, "You're newly involved in the distribution of wealth. You're just checking your beneficiaries, making sure they deserve *your* annual supplement."

"I have no idea what you're saying. So, if I'm supposed to be clueless, I've got this!"

"Follow my lead. I used to be very good at this kind of thing. Patrick Chester still lives in Santa Monica, but not on Mongolia Drive like twenty-five years ago."

While heading east on highway 10 toward Santa Monica, Harry asked Claire if she wanted to drive by the bungalows owned by the Chesters and Rawls. She declined. What benefit would she gain from seeing the home where Samuel and Amanda Rawls died? She wasn't a pathologist and what clues would be available twenty-five years later?

Exiting Highway 10 onto Lincoln Avenue, they wove around side streets on their way to Riviera Estates. It was a posh neighborhood with an amazing view of Riviera Country Club. Claire revisited their plan, "Did you actually speak with Mr. Chester?"

"Yes."

"And he's willing to talk to us?"

Harry turned toward Claire, "Yes. Well, kind of."

"What do you mean, *kind of*?"

"He was hesitant until I told him you're a Rawls. And you needed to talk to him."

"I wasn't a ..."

"Theoretically you were." He interrupted, "Just let me do most of the talking"

Claire looked at him pensively.

"Do you think you can do this?"

Claire exhaled, "I guess."

Harry squeezed her hand again, "It'll be fine, I promise. And, if my gut is right, this could be enlightening."

Claire laid her head back, closed her eyes, and fought the onset of a headache, "All right, are we almost there?"

"A few more minutes."

Claire watched as the houses grew and the yards became expertly landscaped. Slowly Harry pulled the Mustang up to large iron gates and stopped at a guardhouse.

"May I help you, sir?" the uniformed man asked.

Harry removed his Ray-Bans and responded, "Yes, Harrison Baldwin here to see Patrick Chester."

The man in the small building referenced an electronic tablet and nodded, "Yes, sir. 100023 Fairway Drive. You'll just need to continue left, then right at the round-a-bout."

Harry thanked the man and eased the car forward.

Claire leaned toward Harry, "This is a very nice neighborhood. What does Patrick Chester do?"

Harry hadn't replaced his sunglasses. Claire saw the twinkle in his eye, as he answered, "He's retired. But before that, he was in retail."

"Retail? Like he owned some amazing chain or overpriced boutique."

"He didn't own anything. He was middle management at a mid-priced chain."

They pulled onto a wide stone and slate drive. A sprawling, stone and stucco house created an "L", with a four car garage perpendicular to the street. One bay of the garage was open. Harry put the car in park, in front of the open door, behind a sleek silver Audi S5.

Claire continued in a low whisper, "Then how did he end up with *this* house with *that* car?"

"That's what we're here to find out." Harry's light blue eye disappeared momentarily as he winked in Claire's direction. "I'm thinking it has to do with that mysterious settlement. Let's give my theory a run?"

She smiled, "Okay, but if I forget my name is Rawls, elbow me in the side."

"If you say so," Harry teased as they both stepped from the Mustang and moved toward the front door.

Before Harry and Claire could reach the stoop of 100023 Fairway Drive, the wide front door opened. A balding gentleman wearing a black Burberry Brit Zip Hoodie, gray t-shirt, and sweat shorts, stepped outside. If he'd been wearing running shoes instead of flip-flops, he might look as if he was about to jog around the neighborhood. Harry and Claire stopped. The man hastily closed the large front door and rushed toward them.

As the distance narrowed between them, Harry spoke, "Mr. Chester?"

Glancing right and then left, the man answered, "Yes, yes. You must be Mr. Baldwin and Miss Rawls?"

Claire extended her hand, "My name is now Nichols."

Patrick Chester took her hand and assessed the woman before him. "So are you Anton's daughter or his cousin?"

Claire's back straightened. She saw the smile sneak from the corner of Harry's lips. Yes, she could chronologically be Tony's daughter, but no one had ever said that to her before. While she fought with her answer, Harry spoke, "Mr. Patrick, Ms. Nichols has been given the responsibility of overseeing certain funds. She's here today to confirm the need to maintain one of those funds."

Patrick glanced back toward his house. "Let's go around to the pool, my family's in the house. They don't know anything about my settlement. I'd like to keep it that way."

Harry replied, "Of course. We'll follow you."

He briefly reached for Claire's hand and squeezed. She chose not to reciprocate, deciding instead to press her lips together and exhale. If he'd known her better, he would've understood the displeasure screaming from her eyes. Instead he goaded, "How's Daddy?"

She leaned closer, "So far, I'm not enlightened!"

They followed Patrick Chester through a large wooden gate situated within the tall stone wall. Entering the rear yard, Claire's step stuttered at the majesty. A kidney shaped swimming pool surrounded by lavish furniture served as the feature of the lower level. It was a three tiered yard. A few steps up, the next level contained an outdoor living room, complete with fireplace, sofa, chairs, and encased technology center. Currently country music lofted from the speakers. Claire looked even higher and saw an orange grove on the upper level.

"Your yard is beautiful Mr. Chester." Claire said as she sat at an umbrella covered table near the shallow end of the pool.

"Thank you, Ms. Nichols. I don't mean to be impolite, but let's get this over with. This is very unusual and quite frankly, makes me uncomfortable."

Claire went on, "I was in the area and decided today would be as good as any. Thank you for seeing us."

Patrick nodded.

Harry went on, "We're here to confirm you're the true recipient of the ongoing settlement."

"Is this some kind of joke? I've kept my end of this bargain." He turned toward Claire, "Your family better keep theirs."

Without missing a beat, she replied, "Let's not get hasty. We just have a few questions." She looked toward Harry.

Harry asked, "Are you certain your original testimony involving the presence of Samuel's sister has been contained."

Patrick looked skeptically toward them, and finally answered, "I think I need to see some identification. How do I know you're who you say you are?"

Claire reached for her purse and grabbed her wallet. Before she could open it, Harry took it from her hand and spoke, "Mr. Chester, how do we know you deserve to see identification?"

"You contacted me."

"True, but give me something. How do I know you're the Patrick Chester who Ms. Nichols needs to contact?"

"What do you want?"

"Tell us exactly why you deserve your annual settlement."

With sarcasm dripping from his voice, Patrick answered, "I don't remember."

Harry pushed, "What don't you remember?"

"You see, that's the problem. If I remember -- your mom," he looked toward Claire, "or your aunt -- well, there's no statute of limitations on murder in California."

Claire remained silent while Harry opened her wallet and handed Patrick her American Express credit card with *Claire R. Nichols* embossed on the front. Patrick took the card, read it, and handed it back to Harry. Claire watched as each man's eyes glared back and forth.

She reached for her credit card placed it back in her wallet. Breaking the silence Claire said, "Thank you, Mr. Chester, I'll relay your information, but I can't make you any promises regarding future installments."

His glare turned toward Claire. "I think you can, and you will. Tell Anton my memory's not so bad for an old man."

She sat taller, "I will."

Harry interjected, "Do you really want to threaten the man who's provided you with all of this?"

Patrick sat back against the chair. "I agreed to meet with you because I wanted to see you." He tipped his head toward Claire. "I haven't been able to find or contact Anton in twenty-five years. I wanted confirmation he still exists."

Harry replied, "Your yearly payments weren't enough?"

"No trace of their origin. Glad to know he's still kick'n. He was a good kid."

Claire asked, "So what message do you want me to give that *good kid*?"

Patrick stood and the others followed. "Tell him to contact me only through the suits in L.A.. I don't want any more surprise visits."

Claire nodded and Harry extended his hand as he spoke, "Good bye, Mr. Chester. I believe Ms. Nichols has enough information."

Going the direction they came, Claire and Harry silently made their way back to the blue Mustang. It wasn't until they were outside the iron gated community that Claire finally spoke. "Why did you show him a credit card?"

"I didn't want him to know your address."

His words added to the unease she'd been feeling at the end of their interview. "Oh, thanks, I didn't think of that."

Making their way back to I-5 North, they settled in for the almost six hour drive. Claire inclined her seat, listened to the music from the speakers, and absorbed the sun's rays.

Her mind wandered from Patrick Chester to Tony. Claire still didn't know who this mystery woman was, but now they'd confirmed she exists, or existed. Who would Tony be willing to protect with annual payments? He never mentioned another woman. Actually he said he never wanted to be with anyone else. But could she believe anything he ever said? Maybe the woman really was his aunt. However she never heard of any family members. Even the *Vanity Fair* article said he had no other relatives. Could that woman be the one who sent Claire the box? Why would she willingly upset the man who'd financed her freedom from prison for murder? Or did she or someone else have another motive for sending Claire that information? Maybe the person wanted the box to affect Claire differently? It seemed the new information did nothing but create more questions.

Claire closed her eyes under the sunglasses and fought the ache threatening her temples.

As she was about to drift away when she heard Harry say, "I'm sorry. I shouldn't have exposed you to that creep."

She shrugged, "I've met a creep or two before. No harm no foul. I'm just not sure what we gained."

"We now know for sure there was a woman. Someone Patrick believes is Samuel's sister. I'd put money on the fact, she killed Samuel and Amanda."

Claire added, "And Tony is willing to pay yearly to keep that knowledge hidden."

"Who's the woman?"

"That seems to be the million dollar question!" She said as she watched the beautiful scenery.

Compromise - better bend than break.
— Scottish Proverb

Chapter 29

L eaning against the countertop in the kitchen of their new condominium, Sophia traced the edge of the cool granite, as her mind wheeled in disbelief. She tried desperately to make sense of the voicemail she heard for the second time. Mr. George, from the Civic Center Art Studio in Palo Alto, received a call from a buyer, representing an anonymous customer. This mysterious person wanted to purchase *three* of Sophia's pieces, the entire collection Mr. George commissioned from her Provincetown studio. During their earlier discussions, she agreed to three of her older works, after painstakingly debating the pieces on her website. The paintings were still in Massachusetts and had only been on Mr. George's website for twenty-four hours. Now they were sold.

Mr. George wanted Sophia's entire portfolio, yesterday. Apparently the buyer was enthralled. Yes, Sophia couldn't believe it. That was the word Mr. George used – *enthralled* with her art. The mysterious buyer may even be interested in additional works. Mr. George wanted to know how soon Sophia could fly to Provincetown and ship her *entire studio* to Palo Alto. He promised to make it worth the expense.

Although Sophia and Derek had recently reached an understanding, well, more than an understanding -- a coming together of monumental proportions. She wasn't picking up and flying east without discussing it with him. Looking at her calendar she realized the only conflict, if she suddenly flew to P-town, would be some fundraiser dinner they were supposed to attend. Some top executive wanted Derek to attend this dinner as a representative of Shedis-tics. Apparently, this was an annual big deal.

Sophia wondered if she could possibly do both. Considering the probability, she realized she would either need to tell Mr. George to wait, or tell Derek she couldn't do the dinner. The timing was just too unfortunate for both. Packing the art work would take days, possibly a week. The event was in five days. This was one of those compromises they'd discussed. The concept was much easier in the figurative sense.

Like a child, she crossed her fingers, unconsciously bit her lower lip, and dialed the phone.

Danni's voice on Derek's private line no longer surprised Sophia. Sophia even shamefully felt a twinge of superiority with Derek's recent confession. He swore total ignorance regarding Danni's hidden agenda. Perhaps part of Sophia even felt a bit sorry for the pretty young blonde. No, given the circumstances, she didn't.

"Hello, Danni, it's Sophia."

"Yes, Mrs. Burke, Derek is in a meeting right now. May I take a message?"

Sophia noticed, despite many attempts to change Danni's salutation, she was still addressed as *Mrs. Burke* and Mr. Burke was still *Derek.* "Yes, please let him know I need to speak to him as soon as possible. As a matter of fact, I'll be going out later and can come by his office this afternoon."

"Yes, well, his schedule is quite full. Perhaps, I can have him call when he's available."

A week ago that would have stopped Sophia, but not today. As soon as she hung up with Danni, Sophia would text Derek's cellphone. When Sophia explained her insecurities during their reconnection, Derek promised only he would answer his text messages.

Sophia smiled into the phone and replied, "You can let him know I'll be in the area from one to three. Please call me with the best time to stop by."

"Yes, Mrs. Burke."

"Bye, Danni."

She hung-up and sent the text. Seconds later her telephone buzzed. She swiped the screen, *I ALWAYS HAVE TIME FOR YOU! CAN'T WAIT. GOT A WEB CONFERENCE AT 11. BE DONE BY 12:30, ANY TIME AFTER AND I'M ALL YOURS. – NOT TRUE, ALWAYS YOURS! LOVE YA BABY.*

She grinned. Technology was wonderful! She wouldn't let Danni, or anyone else, make her feel insecure about her husband. After swallowing the final drops of Jasmine Tea, she stowed her tea cup in the dishwasher, wiped down the breakfast bar, and began contemplating the extent of art in the Provincetown studio. Her mind spun with displayed and stored artwork. Suddenly the ring of her telephone brought Sophia's thoughts back to Santa Clara. Looking to the illuminated screen she saw: *Derek's office.*

"Hello?"

"Hello, Mrs. Burke. This is Danni."

"Yes?"

"It seems that a meeting has been rescheduled, Derek is available after 12:30 this afternoon."

Sophia's smug expression couldn't be contained. "Thank you, Danni. I look forward to seeing you and Derek then."

"Yes, ma'am." The line disconnected.

Glancing at the clock, Sophia realized she had three hours before she needed to be in Derek's office. She decided to go to Palo Alto and talk to Mr. George in person. Maybe he called the wrong person. After all, who would buy three pieces of art without seeing them in person?

The Civic Center in Palo Alto was in the heart of a cafe haven. Easing her car into an available space, she contemplated stopping at one of the many shops she passed. As in Santa Clara, parts of the city gave Sophia the wonderful *small town* feel.

The fog that so often encased the Silicon Valley was gone, dissipated into the shining blue sky. The buildings, trees, and mountains all glowed with the spring sun. As Sophia walked along the crowded sidewalk, inhaling the fragrant aromas emanating from the coffee shops and cafes and listening to the murmurs of pedestrians, she found herself bemused by the recent turn of events. This new life wasn't as bad as she'd made it out to be. Derek *did* want her here.

The revelation or epiphany came in the knowledge that he wanted *her* -- not some perfect wife. That support strengthened her, rejuvenating her confidence as she approached Mr. George.

Entering the small studio, she noticed the contrast in noise. The sounds from the busy street silenced as the glass doors closed to faint music, impeded only by a soft chime indicating a prospective customer. Sophia took in the white walls, indirect lighting, and lovely pieces of displayed art on canvas as well as three-dimensional pieces on podiums. At the beck and call of the protective bell, Mr. George appeared from the depths of the back rooms.

Since their initial meeting, they'd only spoken on the phone. Sophia wanted more information before she shipped her entire collection to this man.

"Oh, Mrs. Burke!" Mr. George exclaimed with perhaps too much glee.

"Mr. George, please call me Sophia."

"Yes, Sophia. I'm so glad you came in today." His bright smile threatened to rupture his ruddy cheeks as he positively swelled with excitement. "Did you receive my voice mail?"

So it was meant for me, she thought as she answered, "Yes, that's why I'm here. Can we discuss this transition?"

"Most certainly, I agree it's unusual. But I want you to know, I've verified the funds, although I'm unable to confirm the identity of the buyer. It's real. Someone offered 2.3 million for all three works."

Sophia's bravado dissolved. She struggled for air. Her lungs collapsed, and her legs wobbled. "I'm sorry; did you just say 2.3 million?"

"Oh, didn't I mention the amount on the message? Yes, initially the buyer asked me the price. I told him I'd need to discuss it with the artist. He didn't want to haggle, so he offered what he believed would be the top bid." Mr. George's grin enlarged even more, showing his too white, too perfect teeth, and the pink gums above. "I think he succeeded. However, I still told him I'd need to discuss it with you. Of course, the studio collects fifteen percent. The rest is yours."

Before her legs gave out entirely, Sophia found an empty chair. Her mind subconsciously computed the math, while her lips fought diligently to speak, "Mr. George, I'm going to talk to my husband, soon. I'll be getting those works for you as soon as I can." *One million nine hundred and fifty thousand dollars!* "I just don't know about my *entire* collection. I don't want to close my Provincetown studio."

The two of them discussed the possibilities and opportunities. They decided upon a sampling of her works on display in Palo Alto, with the entire collection available online. If this buyer or another wanted one of the works still in Provincetown and were willing to pay appropriately, Sophia would return to Massachusetts.

An hour later, Sophia entered Derek's office. As her long gauze skirt brushed the tops of her feet and her high heeled sandals clicked the marble floor of his private reception area, Sophia chose to ignore Danni's looks and innuendos. Her mood was too high to worry about the immaculately dressed PA or the plush surroundings. She casually walked past the pretty blonde without speaking and stepped into Derek's regal office. Brazenly, she wrapped her arms around her husband's neck and kissed his parted lips. Before she could introduce her tongue teasingly into his willing mouth, Sophia realized Danni followed her into Derek's office.

They both turned to see her standing in the doorway. Before Derek had the chance to recover from his wife's licentious greeting, Sophia took the liberty of dismissing his assistant, "That'll be all, Danni. Please close the door on your way out."

Danni looked questionably at Derek, who smiled uncontrollably, barely able to take his eyes away from the spirit filled woman who'd just fallen into his lap. Finally, he glanced toward his PA and confirmed Sophia's wishes, "Yes, Danni, and please hold my calls."

Danni's incredulous expression as she backed out of the office and closed the door added to Sophia's euphoria.

"My, my, Mrs. Burke," Derek managed between kisses, "To what do I owe this lascivious reception?"

She explained the unbelievable procurement of *three* of her oil paintings. Derek stared, open mouthed, when she disclosed the bid. Eventually, he found his voice, "Wow, Baby! I love your work, but I'm shocked at that amount of money."

Sophia pouted, more in jest than reality, "What? Don't you think they're worth it?"

He immediately pulled her against his chest and spun her around in his large leather chair. Sophia curled her legs into his lap and threw her head back, allowing her long hair to fan out and fall over his shoulder as his office became a blur. Leaning his mouth to her exposed neck he breathily whispered, "I think they're worth ten times that! But, if you're willing to part with them for a measly 2.3 million, I guess that's your prerogative." His lips connected her warm sensitive neck, immediately instigating purrs from the depth of her throat.

When his lips slowed, Sophia pulled away and made eye contact. Looking suddenly serious, she went on, "There is a problem. The buyer wants them yesterday. I need to fly to Provincetown and ship them back here. Mr. George also wants me to ship some other works to put on display and photograph the rest of my collection. It'll take me days to get them all packaged for mailing."

"That dinner for Shedis-tics is Friday. Will you be back by then?"

"I'm sorry. I don't think so." She looked passively into his soft brown eyes, "If you want me to wait, I can ask Mr. George to contact the buyer, have him contact the mystery person, and see if it can wait." Sophia watched through seductive lashes as Derek's expression changed before her eyes. She saw pride, disappointment, indecision, and resolution.

Eventually his light brown eyes glimmered as his cheeks rose in conjunction with the tips of his lips. "You know, when Shedis-tics asked me to come out here early, they promised me some time off. How about, I travel with you? If we work together, we can package your art much faster. We might even make it back for this big dinner thing. I'm not sure why, but *they* really want me there."

Sophia stared at her husband in disbelief, "You'd really be willing to go with me?"

"Sure," he kissed her lips, "we can consider it a romantic get-a-way." Then with a predatory grin he added, "And maybe we can use one of those private jets they promised in my interview?"

"You know, Mr. Burke, I've always wanted to belong to an exclusive club."

"Really, Mrs. Burke, what club would that be?"

"I believe it's called *The Mile High Club*."

Derek closed his eyes and shook his head at the woman who'd swept him off his feet three years ago. Regaining his focus he replied, "I'll be sure to find the criteria regarding entry into that exclusive club. I've heard initiation can be strenuous. Perhaps you're not up to the challenge?"

"Mr. Burke, you check out the specifications, and I'll concentrate on my aptitude."

He tried, unsuccessfully, to keep his grin concealed, "Aptitude isn't an issue, Mrs. Burke. I believe the component in question is altitude."

Sophia buried her lips into the crook of his neck. "You provide the altitude, I'll provide the aptitude."

"We can do a test run at sea level, just to be sure."

Sophia amusingly shook her head. This was a battle of wits she didn't want to win.

"Perhaps, when I get home?" Derek didn't wait for an answer from his wife as he picked up the phone, his voice no longer playful, "Danni, make the necessary arrangements. My wife and I need a Shedis-tics jet to fly to Provincetown, Massachusetts, leaving tomorrow and returning Thursday." Sophia listened to his side of the conversation.

"That can be rescheduled." "That, I can do from anywhere." "Do you have any other concerns?" Sophia heard the agitation in his voice. She wondered if Danni recognized it too. Derek continued, "That is fine. Let me know the final arrangements." "Thanks, Danni." He hung-up. Smirking ear-to-ear he proposed, "The next order of business it to research the requirements for that club."

Sophia squeezed his neck, "Thank you! We can work day and night to get back for that dinner."

Derek caressed her waist as his eyes muted ever so slightly, "I think I know a better way to spend our nights."

Sophia giggled, "Really? We can debate the pros and cons of each proposal."

"No. I think I'm evoking the *helpful husband* card; you'll have to agree to my proposal -- no debating allowed."

She didn't argue. "I see your point. However, I'll need at least an abstract of your ideas presented tonight at home." Her eyes twinkled as she stood and smoothed her skirt.

"You drive a hard bargain." Derek replied, "See you tonight."

They kissed and Sophia opened the door of his private office. Walking past Danni's desk, her mind filled with Derek's affection and playful banter. As she turned toward the impassive gaze of his private assistant, Sophia summoned her sweetest voice and said, "Thanks, Danni. Bye."

From gritted teeth, Danni replied, "You're welcome."

Walking along the still crowded sidewalk, Sophia felt the sensation of floating. Had someone really offered 2.3 million for her art work? It didn't seem possible. And her conversation with Derek went in such an unexpected direction. She'd expected him to be supportive, yet reserved about missing the dinner. After all, how important could attendance at a fundraiser really be for a Fortune 500 company?

Despite his executive pretense, he was just a man. Sophia told herself; she needed to remember that. After all, she was just a woman. That makes the two of them compatible in a remarkable way.

Wanting to speak to Mr. George in person, Sophia drove back to Palo Alto. She wanted to let him know she and her husband would be packaging her work and getting it west as soon as possible. Before facing *Mr. White Teeth*, Sophia decided to stop for a cup of tea and some lunch. Working her way into a bustling cafe on the same street as the Art Studio, Sophia scanned the crowd looking for an empty seat.

The cafe hummed with the drone of conversations at most every table. The aroma of freshly baked bread, rich coffee, and tangy spices made her empty stomach twist with anticipation. She stepped toward the counter to read the menu above, when a woman near the window with an electronic tablet, cup of coffee, and salad caught her attention. She looked vaguely familiar. Sophia didn't want to stare. It just seemed strange that she'd know anyone eating in Palo Alto.

*****

The chatter of the busy cafe surrounded Claire, soothing her aching temples. She mindlessly picked at her half eaten salad while simultaneously skimming the latest news on her iPad. Relishing the temporary reprieve, she enjoyed one of her first free moments in the last week. She realized the irony of solitude in a crowd.

Last Saturday, her sister, Emily, and brother-in-law, John, arrived in San Francisco. Since then, she's hardly had a minute alone. Wistfully she thought about Harry; *they* hadn't had a minute alone either. Actually, since San Diego, a week and a half ago, they'd only had one opportunity to utilize his procurement of resources from that drugstore.

Multitasking, Claire read each headline on her newsfeed. However, her thoughts were of her sister and brother-in-law. They'd asked to borrow her car and take a day trip into San Francisco. She was thankful for them to get some time to themselves.

The face-to-face reunion between the three of them washed away all doubt and hard feelings from their past. When Emily walked through the archway at San Francisco International Airport last Saturday and their matching green eyes met, they melted in a sobbing embrace. It was minutes before John was able to separate the two of them, before he got his own chance to hug Claire.

Being the ever accommodating hostess, Amber offered the Vandersols the use of her third bedroom. It meant re-filing all of Claire's research, but it was worth it. For five days Claire's sister and brother-in-law would be only a door away.

It also thrilled Claire that Emily and John got along so well with Amber and Harry. The ease of conversation and similar interests created a comfortable atmosphere, very dissimilar to the one while she'd been married to Tony.

After a few days, Amber began to talk business with John. The two shared similar philosophies and work ethics. What started as discussion over a few interesting Rawlings Industries dealings soon turned to SiJo Gaming strategies. While the two talked shop, Claire and Emily enjoyed one another's company. The sharing and camaraderie was wonderful.

Nevertheless, Claire couldn't understand why she continued to fight her aching head. She was being more open and honest with her family than she'd been in years, yet she had the strange feeling of teetering on the edge of a looming argument. Her emotions felt stretched. Truthfully, she had no idea what the impending argument entailed or why it was stressing her out.

Looking up from her iPad, Claire scanned the cafe. People moved about in every direction within the cafe and outside on the street. Sitting by the window, she watched people pass the glass. Occasionally she would have the sensation of being watched. It was both annoying and familiar.

In a moment of self-reflection, Claire asked, *when in the past three years haven't I been watched? Or did it date back further than that?*

Later tonight Claire, Emily, John, Harry, and Amber had reservations at a local restaurant. They were going to meet Amber's new *friend*. She met him a few weeks ago, at an out of town conference. He works for Google. Amber claimed it wasn't serious, but the gleam in her eyes as she mentions Keaton made Claire smile.

It also made the idea of telling Amber about her and Harry easier. Claire reasoned if Amber were also involved with someone, she'd take the news much better. Claire assumed Amber and her family had suspicions. But no one asked, and Claire and Harry hadn't volunteered. For the most part, the two of them kept their new familiarity private.

Claire looked up again and saw Phil Roach standing in line behind a pretty blonde woman. Her nervousness quelled. That nagging feeling of being watched was easier to deal with when you know the voyeur, or as Claire liked to refer to Phil, her bodyguard.

She wondered how he handled losing her at the airport back in San Diego. Smiling to herself, Claire realized she sometimes too thought of parts of her life as a game. And unquestionably, she enjoyed controlling the metaphorical chess board.

Refocusing her attention to the electronic tablet, she read a headline on MSNBC about Megatone, a subsidiary of Sony. She read about concerned investors. There was a recent selling frenzy of stock resulting in a plummet of share prices. Just since this morning they'd fallen from $77.12 to $48.13. Claire glanced at her watch. It was almost one-thirty, four-thirty on the East coast. The stock market would close soon. It didn't sound good for Megatone.

The Associated Press article discussed *personal wrong doing* on the part of the CEO. Concerned shareholders questioned ethics in the boardroom. The underlying insinuation was if an individual in a place of power made poor personal choices, investors rightfully or wrongly transferred that to business choices. Megatone and its board of directors maintained the company's position of strong integrity and principal. Currently no evidence of corporate wrong doing was evident. Yet, with up to the second news, the stock continued to dive.

Claire searched her stock market app; Rawlings Industries stock currently sat at $168.78 per share. That was up $2.04 since the same time yesterday. The company had been experiencing an upward spiral, despite the economy, for the last five years.

*****

Sophia searched her mind as she stood in line. Each time she snuck a glance at the brown haired woman, she analyzed her features. Finding a small table, Sophia sat sipping her tea and waiting for her salad. Suddenly, she realized it was the hair that was wrong. The woman that this woman resembled had lighter hair. Nonetheless, as an artist she dissected the woman's features. Sophia knew without a doubt, in every other way, the woman at the window was the same woman Sophia had stared at for days and weeks. Not only had Sophia stared at her, she'd painted her, wearing a beautiful Vera Wang wedding gown.

Suddenly, Sophia wondered if she should approach her. After all, Sophia signed a confidentiality statement regarding that painting. While Sophia debated, the woman seemed lost in her tablet.

With her salad now secured, Sophia resolved to approach the woman at the window. Without warning an attractive blonde haired man sat down opposite the woman. Sophia watched as the concern and concentration the woman had been devoting to the tablet dissolved. The blonde haired man appeared to take all of her attention. Sophia wondered, *could that be the man who hired me to paint the picture?* If it was, she should remain silent. Breach of contract would require payment. Since she didn't have the 1.95 million yet, talking to the woman she'd once painted was no longer an option.

Without a doubt, the possibility of an encounter with this mystery woman seemed odd!

Sophia sat back, enjoyed her lunch, and watched the man and woman converse with a heartwarming sense of familiarity. She hoped they liked her work.

The strength of a family, like the strength of an army,
is in its loyalty to each other.
– Mario Puzo

Chapter 30

His sparkling blue eyes were right in front of Claire before she noticed Harry's presence. His rich voice rose above the clatter, "Your color looks much better. How are you feeling?" Claire beamed toward the handsome face and turned her cheek making it available for his friendly kiss. "I'm feeling much better, thank you. I'm not sure what my problem was this morning."

Harry took the seat opposite Claire.

She continued, "I love having Emily and John here. I don't know why I'm so on edge."

Harry leaned over and covered Claire's hand. "Your sister is thrilled to be here with you. Just enjoy the time. They're leaving Thursday."

Claire looked down toward her half eaten salad. "I know," she looked up and her emerald eyes twinkled, "and on Friday I get to see you in a tuxedo!"

Harry shook his head from side to side, "It's not too late. We can get someone else to go to that gala. It's nothing more than stuffed shirts acting all self-righteous about their donation."

Claire smiled smugly, "I know what to expect, been there done that. But, I haven't seen you in a tux, and I want to do that. Besides, I promised Amber."

Harry picked a strawberry from Claire's uneaten salad and plopped it in his mouth. Immediately, she thought about his lips as they closed around the small red fruit. She tried to compartmentalize the thought smoldering deep within her. To aid in her diversion, Claire chose to speak, "I thought Amber said you hadn't been to any of these things with her. How do you know what to expect?"

"I haven't been, as a guest. I've worked security at events like this, as a cop and for SiJo." He reached for a sleek slice of orange.

Claire giggled, "Do you want the rest of my salad? I'm really not hungry."

Bashfully he replied, "No, you should eat it. I don't think you had much breakfast. Besides," his voice slowed, "I was wondering..."

Looking up, Claire saw his expression change subtly, with a gleam to his eyes and a crease on his forehead. She couldn't pin point the exact difference, but whatever it was, it caused that fire she'd felt moments ago to reignite. Trying to sound more seductive than shy, Claire leaned toward Harry, "Yes?" She allowed the word to be drawn out, asking a question, not answering one. "What were you wondering?"

"Well, you see I was at work -- minding my own business -- when I received this text."

Claire raised her eyebrows, yes, she'd sent a text. It wasn't intended as a request.

He went on, "It said something like: *hope your day's going well. Heading to Clancy's on Hamilton for some lunch. Emily and John took my car for a road trip to San Francisco for the day.*"

"Yes, I believe I know about that text. I sent it. And I received one in return. It said something like: *have a good lunch.* Oh, there may have been a smiley face."

Harry shrugged, "Well, yes. But then I started to think about you... all alone."

"I'm a big girl."

His eyes now held the same smoldering fire she'd been trying to conceal. "Yes, you are." His fingers rubbed the top of her knuckles. "You see, I wasn't sure how you would handle being all alone back at the condo. It seems like with your company, you haven't been alone in a while."

Claire's grin caused her eyes to twinkle; the fire now glowed behind the green. "You're very kind to leave work just to assist me. Maybe, I do need some help."

He seized her hand as she started to push her chair away from the table. "I'm here to assist, anyway I can."

She leaned closer to his ear, "What would your boss say about you playing hooky?"

"My job definition is open to outside security."

"Oh, so you're providing me with security?" She smiled, looking back at Phil sitting with a sandwich and tea. "Should we tell Phil to take the afternoon off?"

Harry shrugged, "I don't think it'd do any good. Now Ms. Nichols, what assistance do you need?"

Claire felt her cheeks flush, "Well, maybe from here to the condo, we can think of something?"

The Brazilian restaurant offered amazing cuisine with impeccable service. Keaton, Amber's friend, held his own in their small crowd. He jumped right in, as the conversation moved from person to person. Claire enjoyed hearing her brother-in-law banter jokingly with the others. Her shoulders relaxed realizing the stress she used to feel whenever John and

Tony were together was now gone. Maybe that old feeling was what had been bothering her.

Harry laughed as Emily questioned Claire's diet. "Why are you so hungry?"

Claire smiled... perhaps her afternoon activity had helped return her appetite. "I guess I really like this restaurant."

Emily couldn't see Harry's hand squeezing Claire's dress covered knee.

After the waiter cleared the dishes from their main course, Claire noticed glances, bemused smiles, and nods between Amber, John, and Emily. Her curiosity got the better of her, "What's going on?"

Amber raised her glass of wine and said, "I'd like to propose a toast."

Claire obediently lifted her Chianti filled goblet and listened, "To Claire," the temperature of the room rose as Claire felt self-conscious at the sudden attention. Amber went on, "The past three months, well almost three, have changed Harry's and my lives. We've not only found a good friend, but learned about life in the spotlight." Everyone giggled. She continued, "You've done more than that. You've brought others to our life. Thank you." Everyone sipped their wine. Amber continued, "Now to John and Emily. When Claire spoke to me about your visit, I was thrilled to have you stay with us, for her. But as the two of you know, it's become more than that. Here is to a long relationship between us and more importantly, between you, John, and SiJo Gaming." Again glasses went to lips.

Claire's glass didn't move. Her stomach lurched; she had to ask, "What does that mean?"

Emily leaned toward her sister; their shoulders touched, "It means we're moving to Palo Alto."

Claire glanced around the table still in disbelief. Amber continued, "John and I spoke about the possibility of him working for SiJo. I called an emergency meeting of the board yesterday and they agreed. SiJo needs someone to spearhead our investment division. Diversifying is essential and we're lacking. Claire, your brother-in-law is very intelligent and I'll be forever grateful that we've met."

Stammering, Claire looked at the wide eyes around her. Turning to Harry, "You're on the board, you knew about this?" He nodded. Looking to Emily she asked, "Did you go to San Francisco today?"

Emily shook her head, "No, we spent the day at SiJo. John had paperwork to complete and people to meet."

Claire placed her glass on the linen covered table and exhaled, "So why'd everyone know about this but me?"

Staying quiet during this personal conversation, Keaton interjected, "I didn't know."

Claire smiled a weary smile, "Wow, I'm shocked." Tears filled her eyes as she turned to Emily. "I never dreamt we'd be together again."

Emily embraced Claire's shoulders. "Honey, we're thrilled. Are you all right with this?"

She nodded into Emily's shoulder. The entire table laughed as Harry patted Claire's back.

Emily whispered, "You're so emotional. Are you sure you're on board with this?"

Claire sat up and wiped her eyes with the napkin from her lap. "Shocked, that's all." Then as she beamed at everyone she added, "It's a very good shock! Thank you, Amber, and welcome, Emily and John. When are you moving?"

John answered, "We have some things to do in Indiana. A few legal hoops to jump through, but we're hoping to be here by the first of July."

Claire leaned back, rested her head against Harry's shoulder, and settled into his comforting embrace. When she refocused on the table, she saw everyone's questioning looks. *Oh, that's right, they don't know about us.* She thought as she glanced up at Harry and grinned. He shrugged and remained quiet. Claire followed his lead and allowed conversations to resume.

Back at the condo Amber, John, Emily, Harry, and Claire relaxed in the kitchen before retiring for the night. Claire was coming to terms with her family living near. "Near, not in the same condominium," John smirked.

"I'll be glad to start the search for your new place, if you'd like," Claire offered.

Changing the subject, Amber announced, "Liz submitted your names to the National Center for Learning Disabilities Gala today."

Claire didn't know if the statement made her bristle due to the mention of Liz's name or the apprehension regarding SiJo's and Shedistics' shared table. "I still don't have a dress."

"Oh, I'll help you with that tomorrow, if you'd like." Emily offered. Claire nodded enthusiastically. Yes, she'd like having her sister near.

Amber continued, "And Liz also gave me the names of everyone at your table."

Both Claire and Harry stiffened.

Amber smiled and said, "I didn't recognize any of them."

Claire and Harry exhaled together.

Emily looked at the two of them, "You two are scaring me. You're breathing in unison."

Claire realized the cause of her recent headaches. She hadn't really talked to Emily about Tony since she'd had dinner with him. That was the argument Claire had been anticipating. Emily knew she and Tony had a few discussions, but even on the phone, the subject caused tension. The only time Emily or John were open to discuss Tony was in the context of revenge.

The only person who knew Claire's mixed emotions: the way she hated Tony and still loved him, the way she pitied him for the tragic loss of his parents at a young age and became exasperated by him every time he foiled her plans, was Courtney.

Harry knew about Claire's *requests*, no *demands* of Tony, regarding her friends and specifically John's law license. Nevertheless, Claire found it difficult to discuss any amicable or enlightening interactions with Tony with the people around her. To them, Anthony Rawlings was a monster. Claire realized she *could* also see him that way. However, she knew it wasn't the entire person, only one side of the multidimensional man.

With Claire lost in thought, Amber responded to Emily's statement, "SiJo shares a table at the gala with a local company, Shedis-tics; it's a subsidiary of Rawlings. In the past Claire's ex has attended this event. We were waiting to submit SiJo's attendees until we knew if he were attending."

Emily obviously stiffened, "So if he *were*," she paused and looked at Claire, "you wouldn't go, would you?"

The familiar throbbing erupted behind Claire's temples. She stood straighter, looked to Harry for reinforcement and responded to her sister, "We promised to attend, no matter what."

Emily's tone hardened, "Claire that's ridiculous. Why would you willingly put yourself near *him*?"

Harry squeezed Claire's shoulder and spoke, "Your sister is a very tough lady. She can handle any confrontation." He added with a sense of pride, "She has many times."

Shit! Claire thought. *Emily doesn't know how many times I've seen him.*

Emily stared directly at her sister, "What does he mean *many* times? I thought you just had dinner that one time."

Claire didn't like Emily's tone. It was the *I'm the older sister you need to listen to me* tone. Maybe their move to California wasn't such a good idea. Claire answered, "Don't worry about it. I'm good. *If* he were at the gala, Harry and I'd still be there. Things change, *I* can handle myself. Besides, I wouldn't be alone. Harry'd be with me."

"When else have you seen him? Besides the dinner, I mean."

Amber and John remained silent, hanging on each word. Emily and Claire's stares intensified as each woman's emerald eyes bore into the other. While Claire contemplated her answer, Harry spoke. The soft tenor of his voice eased Claire's head, "Claire is quite capable..."

Emily interrupted, "I'm sorry, Harry. That's very nice of you to support my sister. But I doubt you know the complete history."

Claire found her voice, "Actually, Emily, he does."

Harry's calm voice released the tension from the room, like the air from a gently deflating balloon. Everyone relaxed as he spoke, "I'm sorry if I mentioned something that has overshadowed our wonderful evening." Refocusing the conversation, he added, "It's great that the two of you are moving here. John, Amber has high hopes for your assistance with SiJo and the rest of us on the board are anxiously waiting to see if her hopes payoff."

John nodded, "It's a new job description for me, but I'm excited to jump in with both feet."

Amber smiled to her brother. She appreciated his ability to defuse the situation. Addressing John, Amber said, "You won't be alone. You'll have a staff to help with your research. And I don't expect miracles overnight." Looking to Harry, Amber added, "Neither does the board. Don't let Harry stress you too much."

As the conversation within the kitchen went to SiJo, Claire mouthed, "Thank you" to Harry.

He embraced her shoulder and whispered, "Sorry, I didn't know she didn't know."

Claire whispered, "It's okay. I'm not used to the protective motherly attitude."

"Really," he whispered with a grin, "I'd think *protective* would be old hat to you by now. After all, you've got me and don't forget your bodyguard."

Stifling a yawn, Claire smiled and nodded into his shoulder.

"I think you'd better call it a night."

The others were talking about something; Claire had lost track of their conversation. She turned to Harry and raised her eyebrows, "Maybe I should have taken a nap today?"

She watched his cheeks rise and his eyes do that half open -- half closed thing, "Perhaps the next time you nap, you'd rather sleep."

Blushing, Claire whispered, "That's not what I said; maybe I should have slept, *too.*"

Harry addressed the group, his voice once again loud enough to be heard by all, "Good night everyone. I'm headed home."

"Good night," came from the crowd.

After the front door closed, Claire turned to a room of questioning eyes. She feigned her most innocent expression and asked, "What?" Without waiting for them to answer she added, "I'm tired too. See you all in the morning." Claire turned to walk to her room before anyone could propose the unspoken questions. Besides, she didn't want to revisit her conversation with Emily.

Courage is not the absence of fear, but rather the judgment
that something else is more important than fear.
  – Ambrose Redmoon

Chapter 31

S ophia settled into the plush, white, leather seat and fastened her seatbelt. The tranquility of the plane's luxurious cabin enveloped them. Just as Sophia's tired eyes began to close, she felt the warm reassuring presence of Derek's hand covering hers. Lifting her heavy lids, she glanced at her husband through her lashes. Despite the haze of sleepiness, Sophia saw his soft brown eyes intently watching her every move. The tender look filled her with affection. Smiling, she whispered, "Thank you so much, for all your help. I'd have never gotten so much done without you."

His chocolate eyes sparkled. His hand squeezed hers and he replied, "It was a fun break from routine."

Jokingly she asked, "Oh, now I'm a break?"

"Mrs. Burke, you're the fun part. Coming back to Provincetown was the break. In such a short time, I've forgotten how quaint and beautiful the East coast is, so different from the West."

"They both have their charm," Sophia confessed, while rotating her hand so their palms united. Instantly their fingers intertwined. "The most important thing is being together."

A gentleman in pressed navy slacks and a starched white shirt appeared through the door of the airplane. "I apologize for the delay, Mr. and Mrs. Burke; we will be taking off in another five minutes."

Derek responded, "That sounds wonderful. Do you have all of Mrs. Burke's art stowed below?"

"Yes, the last crate was just secured."

"Thank you."

Once the gentleman was in the cockpit, Sophia whispered, "This is so cool."

Derek's eyebrows rose, "I think it's pretty neat, too."

"I'm glad you thought of bringing the art back with us. I feel much better having those three pieces on board then handing them over to Fed Ex."

"I don't blame you. They're kind of valuable."

Sophia shook her head and closed her eyes, "I still can't believe it. And the twenty other pieces should be in Palo Alto by next week."

A second gentleman entered the plane; they heard the stairs move away and the outside door close. "Mr. and Mrs. Burke, we should arrive in Palo Alto in six and a half hours. Once we reach altitude, there will be refreshments available."

"Thank you." Sophia and Derek said in unison, as the second man in uniform nodded and joined the other in the cockpit.

Derek leaned toward his wife, "Alone again." His eyes glistened.

"Why Mr. Burke, whatever do you have in mind?"

*****

As Derek and Sophia drove behind the logistics van containing her art toward Palo Alto, Derek asked, "Do you have a dress for tomorrow night?"

Sophia's expression fell. "Oh no, I've been so excited about this sale and everything we had to do, I haven't had a chance." She glanced toward her husband, "I don't expect this is an occasion for a dress I already own."

"Well, apparently not. The other day I learned we're attending with my boss, Jonas Cunningham and his wife. But, the big news is the CEO of our parent company is one of the featured speakers. His name is Rawlings, Anthony Rawlings. I haven't met him, but I've listened to him on web conferences. Since we are one of his companies and he'll be there, everyone is supposed to do it up right."

"All right," she said apprehensively, "what does that mean?"

"It means I'm glad you didn't get a dress yet."

"You're glad?" She asked surprised.

"Yes, if you'd gotten one before, it would have been on my meager salary. Now you'll have your money from the sales and can get whatever your heart desires."

Sophia pressed her lips together, "Your salary is hardly meager, and I have no idea how to shop with that kind of money. My heart's desire is cotton gauze."

"Would you like some help?"

She giggled, "Now you're a professional shopper?"

Laughing, "No, but I do know what I like to see you wear," he glanced toward his beautiful wife, "and what I enjoy you not wearing."

"Well, although easier to shop for, it sounds hardly appropriate for this gala. I do have a hair appointment tomorrow afternoon. Do you have your tuxedo?"

"I do. And I was serious about that help. I'm sure Danni..."

"No, thank you." Sophia interrupted.

"I was going to say, I'm sure Danni knows where you could go."

"And she'd be glad to tell me."

"I think you read too much into things. Do you want me to ask?"

"Well, since I'm in a pinch, fine. But don't call her now, it can wait until tomorrow."

Their car pulled into a parking space near the paneled van. Mr. George eagerly emerged from the front of his studio. Before they could enter, he spoke rapidly on the street, "Ms. Sophia, I'm so surprised you were able to get all your art work settled so quickly. Of course, it is wonderful. I heard from the buyer today. The mystery investor will be in town tomorrow night and wants the paintings delivered to his hotel."

Sophia nodded, "Well, can that be done?"

"Oh, yes!"

Listening to Mr. George's words, Sophia looked to Derek and her heart filled with pride as she saw his delighted expression. Finally her manners returned, "Mr. George, this is my husband, Derek Burke."

The next day, sitting in the stylist's chair, Sophia mentally went through her wardrobe for the evening. The day had started early with her visiting numerous boutiques in Santa Clara, all at the recommendation of Derek's PA. When the visits yielded no bounty, Sophia debated more boutiques in Palo Alto verses big department stores in San Francisco. The department stores won. Time wasn't her friend, Sophia needed an evening gown, and she needed it yesterday. So remembering Derek's comments, she tried to shop without looking at prices. It worked until she needed to pay.

Nevertheless, Sophia pushed on, determined to make Derek proud at this important gala. As the young man, with way too many piercings, pulled and pinned her long blonde hair she hoped that the Cameron Marc Valvo silk chiffon gown would fit the bill. It was the third dress she tried on at Saks and about the tenth for the day. Yet, from the moment she saw herself in the full length mirror, Sophia knew it was the one she liked.

First, the bright indigo color made her gray eyes shimmer with a blue hue. The plunging V neckline, together with the gathered bust and bodice accentuated her assets. In a nut shell, her breasts looked bigger and her waist looked smaller. The flowing silk chiffon outer layer reminded her of the gauzy skirts she liked to wear. Based on pure aesthetics, it was the gown she wanted; she continued to avoid the dreaded price tag.

The sales associate was very helpful, obviously working on commission. She emphatically expressed Sophia's need for new shoes for this exquisite dress. A mirrored metallic leather sandal completed the ensemble. The heels were a little over four inches, but Sophia had experience in heels while wining and dining art investors.

She shivered at the memory of paying for her outfit. Her sensible-self screamed -- *it's an outfit, for one night!* However, her rarely touched shopping side, purred *but you look gorgeous in it. And Derek will be pleased with the result.* Sophia quieted the internal debate by reasoning *I just made a ton of money on three paintings. I deserve this.*

It was that voice that sang triumphantly, as she signed the receipt for $1600.00 give or take a few dollars. The hairstyle, facial, and professionally applied make-up added to the total of her day.

The man with the piercings slowly spun her. Peering into the large mirror, Sophia viewed his masterpiece from all angles. Completely outside of her comfort zone, Sophia eyed the woman in the mirror. Courageously, she nodded in approval. The make-up was next. *Yes, Sophia told herself, I can do this, for Derek.*

*****

Amber clapped her hands like a school girl when Harry entered her condominium. "You look so handsome all cleaned up; you should try it more often."

His expression warned his sister to not get too excited about this. "Since you're dating Keaton, you two should be attending this."

"I really don't like these kinds of things. I mean, the charity is worthy and all, but the hobnobbing isn't my thing."

Harry eyed her suspiciously, "And what makes you think it's mine?"

She grunted a stifled laugh, "I know it's not, but it is Claire's. She's good at this kind of thing. She'll be good for SiJo."

Harry walked around nervously, not sure if he should sit or stand. The tuxedo felt like a suit of armor.

"Will you relax? You look very handsome and wait until you see Claire's ..." The ringing of Amber's cellphone interrupted her thought. "Sorry, it's Liz. It might be about your car, I have a SiJo driver coming to get you two in about twenty-five minutes."

Harry could only hear Amber's side of the conversation: "Yes, Liz, is everything all right?" "Really?" "When did you find this out?" "All right, well thank you for letting me know. However, I find it hard to believe this information wasn't available sooner." "No, no, it's all right." "Oh. What about the car?" "Okay then, twenty more minutes." "Bye".

He could tell by the change in his sister's tone something was amiss. "What's that all about?"

Amber sighed, "Remember the confrontation in the kitchen between Claire and Emily?"

"How could I forget?"

"Well, do you think she meant what she said?"

"Who, Emily or Claire?"

"Either, but I'm more concerned about Claire."

Harry thought for a moment and then replied, "Do I think she'd still go to this, if Mr. Rawlings were present? Yes. Why?"

"It seems he isn't sitting at your table, because he's one of the speakers. He'll be sitting at the head table."

Forgetting his tailored tuxedo, Harry sank onto the sofa. Subconsciously he blew his blonde hair from his eyes. However, this evening his normally unruly hair was gelled back. The only movement from his deep exhale was a subtle repositioning of his long lashes.

His tone was one not often heard, Amber recognized her brother's pinned up animosity, "You know damn well Liz knew about this, before now."

"No, I don't. She's a good assistant. I can't fire her because you two have history."

"Then fire her because of shit like this. She's trying to derail this evening. It has nothing to do with SiJo; she's doing it because it's *me* with Claire."

"You don't know that."

"Like hell I don't."

Claire took one last, long look at herself in the mirror. She did a slow spin trying to see the whole package. The dress she'd choose with Emily's help was a Donna Karan emerald green gown. It created an hour glass figure, better in Claire's opinion, than the one hidden underneath. Its sweetheart neckline was perfect to showcase her grandmother's necklace. The cap sleeves and crossover design on both the front and back fit perfectly. Of course she'd had it shortened. Now with the Jimmy Choo, sling-back, peep-toed pumps complete with four and a half inch heels, the hem brushed the top of her toes, making her closer to Harry's six plus foot height. Turning ever so slowly her gaze lingered on the cut-out back. It didn't go as low as her white sundress, but nonetheless, it exposed a large portion of skin. Smiling, Claire knew Harry would like that.

Peering closer at the woman in the mirror she analyzed her hair. Claire decided to do it herself; she enjoyed the primping. It'd been a long time since she'd dressed up this much. Yes, she agreed to do it for Amber. Yet, truth be told, she enjoyed the occasional formal occasion. It was part of her life with Tony she sometimes missed. When he first started taking her out, she thought of it like dress-up -- make-believe. Then over time, it was a fun get-a-way from the confines of the estate. It never seemed to matter what was happening in their private lives, once the door of the limousine opened and they stepped in front of the cameras they were the perfect couple. Those memories didn't feel jaded or feigned; instead, they felt warm and exciting.

After the first time they went to the symphony, Claire never feared the events. She learned quickly how to behave and very much enjoyed the *social* Anthony.

Pushing the memories of her and Tony away, she looked again at her hair. Piled high on the back of her head, there were ringlets falling down her exposed neck. She knew it was a style Tony liked, but hopefully so would Harry. And thankfully, Tony wouldn't be there.

As she touched-up her lipstick, she heard Harry and Amber's voices from down the hall. Frowning, Claire realized they didn't sound happy. She did one last scan, grabbed her purse, her light wrap, and headed for the living room. She wanted to know what was happening.

The sound of her heels upon the polished wood floor caused both Amber and Harry's heads to turn in her direction. Immediately, their quarrel ceased and smiles radiated from each face. Amber found her voice first, "Claire, you look beautiful! Thank you so much for doing this; Simon would be so proud."

Simon's name brought a wave of sadness. Claire had been in her room thinking about *Tony*, about to go to this function with *Harry*, and now Amber mentioned *Simon*. Despite the melancholy sentiment, Claire feigned her brightest smile. Perhaps all formal attire came complete with a lovely mask. "Thank you, that's very sweet."

Before Amber could reply, Harry made his way to Claire's side and smiled lovingly down into her painted face. "I wish I were better at words; all I can think is *Wow!*"

Claire felt her cheeks blush. "That says a lot."

"Maybe this thing won't be so bad; after all, I'm gonna have the most beautiful woman on my arm." Harry said as he lifted his elbow. Claire obediently slid her petite hand into the crook of his arm.

"You look pretty amazing in that tuxedo, too." Claire purred, enjoying the adoration radiating from Harry's intensely blue eyes.

Amber beamed, "Seriously, thank you, both of you."

Claire's expression became more serious as she glanced between both Harry and Amber, "What were all the loud voices about?"

Harry straightened his stance; his shoulders filled the confines of his jacket. "Amber just received some news."

Defensively, Claire straightened her posture, too. "What's wrong? What kind of news?"

Amber spoke quickly. As if saying the words in rapid succession would lessen their sting, "Liz just called. While it's true Mr. Rawlings won't be at your table, she just learned he will be there. He's one of the speakers."

Claire's mind once again went into reverse. She remembered many events, sitting at the head table, and listening to her husband speak. "So he'll be at the head table," she said matter-of-factly.

Amber and Harry both released their breaths.

Claire looked at each face, trying to read their expressions. "Did you think I'd be upset? Did you think I'd say *forget it*?"

Amber moved forward and clutched Claire's hands. "I'd understand if you did. I mean it's one thing to plan for this, it's another to have it thrown on you at the last minute."

Claire shrugged, "When it comes to Tony, I've learned the best way to be prepared, is to expect everything and nothing. Do I wish he weren't there? Sure. But I've sat at those head tables. You honestly can't see many faces in the crowd. At least I never did." She reached again for Harry's arm and looked up to his eyes, filled with concern. "Are you still fine with this?"

He shrugged, "Why not? I'm the one with you on my arm."

Claire's face launched into its biggest grin, "Yes, *you* are."

Her subconscious brewed below the surface. Could she really do this? Could she be next to Harry with Tony in the same room? She said you don't see faces, but in the pit of her stomach she knew, at any moment during the evening, she would turn and see, even feel his dark penetrating stare.

Seeing the relieved expressions of her friends, Claire's resolve strengthened. Apparently her mask was still very much intact.

If you prick us do we not bleed? If you tickle us do
we not laugh? If you poison us do we not die?
And if you wrong us shall we not revenge?
-- William Shakespeare

Chapter 32

-Autumn 1985-

"It's good to see you smile." His deep throaty voice lifted her spirits, as much as his fully masculine body filled her. Marie grinned at the face inches away, finding herself lost in the sparkling intensity of his dark mahogany irises.

Watching the beautiful woman beneath him, Nathaniel enjoyed her soft blissful expression as their bodies moved in rhythm. He could lose himself in the gray eyes that muted beneath her long lashes. Her soft moans of pleasure were like music to his ears, as he escorted her through their own private world.

Her eyes parted as he felt her body relax under his weight. He wanted the warmth and closeness to go on forever. Her lips brushed his cheek as she spoke, "It feels good to smile. For the longest time I just couldn't."

Nathaniel didn't want Marie to go there. She'd spent too much time in darkness and despair. When she finally awoke from her fall, the realization that she'd missed Sharron's passing was exacerbated by the knowledge their baby did not survive.

He provided around the clock medical treatment. Her body healed, but her mind refused to mend. She slept most of the time. When she ate, it was only enough to pacify his pleas. On the rare occasion he could engage her in conversation, the hollow look in her eyes and continuous tears, broke his heart. It was almost too much. They'd just buried the love of his life, and suddenly he saw the same vacancy in the eyes of his one source of vitality.

Nathaniel spent his days at work. It was the only place he had control. He could read reports, purchase companies, sell them off like a fire sale, and rake in millions. His CFO, Jared Clawson, kept deals in motion, even when Nathaniel's mind was sidetracked by thoughts of the women, Sharron and Marie, who he wanted to please but continually failed.

There were deals, stocks and securities... Samuel didn't understand. He didn't understand how each victory, each dollar, justified Nathaniel's existence. Sometimes Nathaniel wondered why he was put on this earth, if everything he touched and loved – died, and then he'd see profits as Clawson and Mathews reported another conquest. It filled him with the same resolve he felt as he provided Sharron with the life her father thought she'd never obtain. The satisfaction was superficial compared to the love he'd seen in her eyes or Marie's, but it was enough to sustain him, to propel him to the next deal.

From where Nathaniel sat, Samuel had a different perspective. He didn't know the desolate emptiness that comes with poverty and dejection. He'd always enjoyed his mother's coddling and his wife's health; how could he know what it felt like to have someone disapprove of you, as Sharron's father had him? At least Nathaniel ended the ridiculous notion of sending Marie away.

Oh, the look on his son's face when he learned Marie was pregnant. Samuel's overpowering animosity was respectfully quelled by the sadness of another loss. While Samuel may not have shared the sympathy, Amanda did. On the day Sharron went to heaven, accompanied by Nathaniel and Marie's unborn son, Amanda appreciated the great loss and wisely guided her husband through appropriate conduct.

Thank god, Anton was home. After witnessing the scene on the stairs, his condolences were the only ones Nathaniel would accept. After all, Anton was the one to save *her*. Nathaniel didn't know what he'd have done if he'd lost Marie too.

It took months. Eventually, Nathaniel resorted to psychiatric therapy. Marie didn't realize she was being treated; she never would have permitted it. Her stubbornness, despite her despair, made Nathaniel smile. He hired a therapist to be her *nurse*. She encouraged, no pushed, Marie to perform daily activities: rise, shower, eat, walk, etc. During those activities, the *nurse* engaged Marie in conversation. In time, with encouragement, Marie reentered the world of the living.

She hadn't just endured the loss of their child and Sharron; Marie finally spoke about her first child, a daughter, who she was forbidden to hold or touch. She only saw the baby girl for a few seconds.

When she learned she was pregnant at eighteen, she understandably detested the child. It was after all the result of non-consensual incest. Marie's uncle came to live with her family in an effort to recover from a drug problem. He was a dreamer of sorts, seeing life through music and art. He claimed that drugs intensified his creativity.

When his advances first began, Marie told her mother. Of course her uncle denied the allegations. After questioning her brother, Marie's mother warned Marie to stop lying. A few months later, when Marie became pregnant, her uncle accused *her* of coming on to *him*. Helplessly incapacitated with cocaine, how could he resist?

Marie's parents didn't entertain her stories to the contrary or debate her options. She was shipped away for the end of her senior year. The following summer, her baby was placed in a *good* home, with a competent caring mother.

Marie never returned home and hasn't spoken to any of her family in years. She needed a complete escape. After a few years of odd jobs, she contacted the attorney who handled the adoption. He knew of a possible position. Marie answered a request for *a personal assistant*.

Nathaniel heard her story before. However, when Marie shared it with her nurse, it helped her move through her continued grief. Nathaniel reveled in Marie's daily progress as she shed layers of dark veils. He couldn't be sure, but he hoped, the therapy combined with his support helped his new love learn to live again.

He was unable to help Sharron; he couldn't bring her back. Therefore, in order to resurrect Marie, no holds were barred. Of course, Nathaniel Rawls had a tendency to show support in unusual ways. He wanted Marie to know there was nothing he wouldn't do to aid her recovery. At the same time, he had investigators working to find her daughter. The source of her past anguish was easily located.

Marie's father owned a small business in upstate New York, a car dealership. Nathaniel wondered if an unwed daughter were truly such a great disgrace in 1981 or if it were the allegations of incest that her family feared. As he devised the demise of the family owned business, Nathaniel brought Marie's father's greatest fear to reality. The day Nathaniel showed Marie the paper work, in fact giving her rights to the now defunct car dealership, he wasn't sure how she would react.

Marie couldn't believe Nathaniel's gift. Strolling the paved stones through the estate's gardens, she listened to his deep rich voice and inhaled the spicy scent of autumn. The summer flowers were sleeping, replaced with orange and yellow mums. The various shades of green in the distance were transforming to vibrant shades of red and brown. It seemed as though the nearby hillsides were ablaze with flames, leaving waste in their wake.

Although the world was settling in for the slumber of winter, Marie felt herself coming back to life, enjoying a springtime rejuvenation in the middle of autumn. The journey was draining, yet with each accomplishment she regained strength. Knowing it was the isolating depression that drained her energy, she worked daily to distance herself from the darkness, filling herself with increased vitality.

Marie never thought of herself as vengeful. But every evening as she was forced to eat at the same table as Samuel Rawls, her skin crawled and thoughts of revenge surfaced from recesses unknown. It was the one injustice she willed herself to endure, for Nathaniel. He wanted his *family* together.

In time, she came to realize the unease she felt during the strained performances of cohesiveness made Samuel more uncomfortable. Especially each time she addressed him or his wife by their first name. At times Marie would do it repeatedly, just to watch the muscles in Samuel's neck tighten. His unease soothed her. It seemed as though she did have a bitter revengeful side she'd never explored. Surprisingly, each opportunity to inflict discomfort on Samuel or Amanda fueled her rejuvenation, as much as Nathaniel's love and support.

Now, as she held the ownership papers to a closed, bankrupted car dealership, Marie stood dumbfounded. "I don't know what to say. Why did you do this?"

His eyes intensified, the blackness overtook the already dark brown, "Because they hurt you. I want them to share in your pain." He pulled her closer. "I would make them take all of it, if I could."

There'd been a time she would have argued his reasoning. No longer. She'd experienced pain and loss. She'd been hurt. This feeling of revenge filled places within her soul she'd assumed destined for emptiness. Her smile unknowingly appeared sinister. It was a new sensation; Marie couldn't control the unfamiliar feeling or its outward manifestation. She could, however, thank the man who obviously welded unknown resources to present this unexpected treasure.

Marie gripped the papers and flung her arms around Nathaniel's neck. She stretched out her toes and lifted her face higher. As he always did, he leaned down to accommodate. "Thank you! No one has ever done anything like this for *me*." She kissed his lips, as her body pressed against his.

Gently he pushed her away, he wanted to see her face as he delivered his final gift. "That took care of your parents. Are you not curious about your uncle?" The mention of the man brought a shadow of sadness across her gray eyes. "Marie, I don't intend to upset you. I thought you should know -- he had a relapse with cocaine."

"Is he... dead?"

Nathaniel smirked. His expression was like none she'd ever seen. If it had been directed at her, instead of a reflection of others, she might be afraid. But his expressions couldn't scare her. She trusted him with her whole life. "I considered that," he said, "but decided death was too easy. He is serving a sentence for robbery and attempted murder. The police report suggests he performed those acts in an attempt to score more money for drugs."

Marie considered the implications and searched Nathaniel's eyes for clues.

He added with a smirk, "Unfortunately, he drew the short straw of penitentiaries. His facility is under federal investigation for a highly unusual number of inmate murders. I believe his imprisonment will be difficult. It's doubtful he'll reach the end of his sentence."

She absorbed his words. The last she'd heard of her uncle, he was clean. "But I thought I heard..."

"Your parent's recent financial woes must have contributed to his downward slide."

She once again molded into his warm embrace. The autumn breeze held a hint of the impending winter. The coolness brought clarity to everything. She'd just received the gift of revenge -- of vengeance – as redemption for the wrongs done unto her. Nathaniel had done all he could to restore her world to its proper place. "Thank you, Nathaniel, I love you."

He inhaled the sweet scent of her flowing auburn hair. "I love you, too. I'm still looking for your daughter, but so far I'm hitting dead ends."

Marie placed her head against his sturdy chest. Her words were strong and filled with conviction, "I would like you to stop looking."

He didn't pull her away. Instead he held her tight; sensing the strength in her voice wouldn't be reflected on her face. "Are you sure? Money can open closed files. It just takes time."

She looked up at him, her strong-willed stance now moistened with tears. "I am sure."

He didn't ask for further explanation. If she wanted to offer, he'd listen. Although he wanted Marie to see her daughter, Nathaniel Rawls decided *this* wasn't his call. He would continue the investigation, but he wouldn't supply her with the information until she was ready.

Marie wanted to ask about one last perpetrator. She wanted to ask what punishment Samuel would receive, but she didn't. Perhaps that was her battle to fight. Each dinner, each time she asked him to pass the salt, or stepped on the grand staircase, she shot a shell into his camp. As long as she had Nathaniel's protection, her defenses were impenetrable.

Nathaniel returned to his home office, as Marie retired to his suite. She hadn't stayed upstairs since recovering from her accident. He expected it to feel wrong, having her in the suite he'd shared with Sharron, but it didn't. Sharron hadn't been there for years. During her absence, his grand master bedroom suite became nothing more than a showroom for opulence, an empty space occupied by the best of everything, yet void of anything.

Now, when he entered the suite and found signs of cohabitation, he felt it was once again a *home*, a *refuge*. Sometimes he'd find Marie resting on the sofa in front of the large fireplace. With warmer weather she might be enjoying a rest on the adjacent terrace. The scent of vanilla and flowers lofted from his attached bathroom as lotions, gels, and perfumes filled his countertops and Sharron's dressing table. His closet glowed with colors, dresses, and filmy blouses, where for so long he'd only seen suits in shades of gray and black. He smiled with each welcomed intrusion.

Nathaniel eventually planned to make their comfortable arrangement something more permanent and legal. He knew Samuel would protest, but wasn't that always the case? Nathaniel hoped he could count on Anton's support. His grandson provided it on numerous occasions since the *accident* on the stairs. What he truly didn't know and what terrified Nathaniel was Marie's response to his request. It was no secret she wanted children. He wasn't exactly a spring chicken. Yes, everything worked. Her recent pregnancy proved his swimmers still swam, but would she want to intentionally plan a family with a man three times her age?

He wanted to prove she was more than a caring woman, nursing a sad old man back to life. She deserved to know how special she was to him. He wanted to wine and dine her and bestow the proper title of Mrs. Rawls upon her. However, as close as they'd become, they rarely went out into public. Sharron hadn't been gone that long, yet. They had time.

Nathaniel had a trip scheduled to Europe, more specifically Geneva, soon. He planned to ask Marie to accompany him. Maybe, he'd even share his Switzerland investments with her. He hadn't shared those with anyone. There was something about starting with nothing, that made a man want a reserve, a card in the hole, so to speak.

Focusing back on his desk, Nathaniel read Clawson's latest report. There were two struggling companies in Ohio that looked ripe for the picking. There were also multiple possibilities in Illinois, but that was a trickier battle ground. Sometimes greasing hands cost more than actual purchases.

As he shuffled the reports, a manila folder caught his attention. It was the report Samuel presented to him while Marie struggled to survive the *accident*. Nathaniel thought his son's timing couldn't have been worse. If he would have learned anything from Samuel's investigation, it was unlikely he'd have kicked her out of his home while she was recovering from internal injuries. Nathaniel shook his head. He continued to hope for Samuel's business prowess. Hope may dawn eternal, but it wasn't worth a dime in the face of tenacity. Perhaps there was hope for Anton, or children yet to come.

Nathaniel stuffed Samuel's report in his side private file drawer, under *C* for *Catherine Marie*. After all, with any hope her last name would soon change – to Rawls.

The best laid schemes o' mice an' men.
--Robert Burns

Chapter 33

The traffic slowed as the SiJo limousine moved in short bursts. Claire recognized the sensation, after an almost hour long ride she was finally nearing her destination. Even though it had been a long time since she'd rode in the back of a limousine, her opinion hadn't changed. She liked driving better. It gave her more of a sense of location and direction.

Through the tinted windows she saw multitudes of people gathered behind velvet ropes. Looking around the vast cabin of the car, she wished desperately for Harry. How had their evening changed so dramatically, so fast? Claire tried to convince herself it was all coincidence, but a voice in the back of her head warned otherwise.

Just before the SiJo car arrived to take them to the gala, Amber and Harry's phones rang. The urgent message to both of them was the same: the computer systems at SiJo Gaming had been hacked. It wasn't just their current operations, but also prospective projects and technology. One of their designers recently created a unique application which theoretically threatened cellphone gaming forever, the next Angry Birds. That new creation was in jeopardy. To make it worse, clients' billing information had been assessed -- a potentially huge public relations problem for SiJo. If they couldn't keep billing information secure, no one would ever buy their games.

Fortunately, the breach was discovered virtually minutes after it occurred. Unfortunately, it doesn't take long in *computer terms* to steal millions of gigs of information. Everyone was needed back at SiJo immediately to work on the problem; every creator, forensic specialist, computer specialist, everyone.

As the car inched forward, Claire thought dreamily about Harry in his tuxedo with his hair gelled into place. Despite his unease in such an outfit, he looked wonderful, sexy, and handsome. Mostly he looked different -- a very good different.

It was painful to watch his expression. Claire could tell immediately he was torn. He wanted to go to SiJo: his skill set was needed. It's his sister's company, and he'd do anything to protect it. That being said, Claire knew he also wanted to be with her.

After Amber hung up she looked at both of them and said, "I can't believe this! Harry, if you want to make an appearance at the gala and then come to SiJo, I understand. Lee's at SiJo, but we need you sooner rather than later."

It would have been easier for Claire to assure Amber and Harry of her ability to attend the gala alone if they hadn't just learned of Tony's attendance. Truly, Claire didn't mind going alone; although, she hated the idea of being unescorted and seeing some gorgeous model on Tony's arm. The idea rekindled ideas about him attending this gala in 2010, while she was held captive in his house.

Thoughts start out as single idea: *attend the gala alone*, and soon stream together: *Tony with gorgeous companion*, and become a river flowing uncontrollably: *he went out with other women while I was there; what did he do with those women?* Claire knew what he did with her, many late nights when he'd return home. If she hadn't had the medical examination in prison, these thoughts surely would have propelled her straight to the doctor checking for every possible disease known to man.

Before the figurative damn broke and her thoughts became too difficult to contain, Claire secured her formal mask and spoke earnestly to her friends, "I'll be fine. You two do whatever needs to be done. SiJo has enough problems right now without wasting two dinners at this gala."

Amber responded, "The tickets are part of the donation. If you don't want to go alone, I understand."

Claire kissed Harry's cheek and spoke sincerely, "You two go do what you do. I'll do the one thing I'm good at doing. I'll hob-knob for SiJo. I will do my best to make you two and Simon proud. Now go!"

Harry's angst quickly turned to relief. He kissed Claire. Not on the cheek, as she'd done, but a kiss full of emotion. His lips took hers as his arms embraced her. She sensed thankfulness at her understanding and concern for her evening alone. Thankfully, Amber turned away and pretended not to notice. His voice was strong, "You're amazing. IF you need me, call and I'll get there as soon as possible."

"I'm a big girl. I'll see you here later tonight."

Amber looked at her phone. Her words staccato, "Claire, the car is here."

Harry volunteered, "I'll walk her to the car and meet you in the basement garage."

Now, alone in the limousine, through the windows, Claire watched the people in the car before hers. They were waving to the people behind the velvet ropes. Claire remembered Harry's penetrating blue eyes as he helped her into the SiJo car. His voice was slow and steady, "I know you're a big girl, but if you have any problems with Mr. Rawlings, call me immediately. I hate not being with you. You should know every man there will want to be your escort. You are undoubtedly the most beautiful, brave, and intelligent woman I know."

His words warmed her soul. She smiled bashfully as he closed the door to the SiJo car.

That same car now stopped. While Claire waited for the driver, or an attendant, to open her door, she secured her mask. As the door opened, the voices from behind the rope came into range.

"Ms. Nichols, why are you representing SiJo Gaming?"

"Ms. Nichols, how does it feel to be out of prison?"

She followed Tony's instructions, from so long ago at the Symphony, *"Do not act surprised or shocked. Just flash a beautiful smile and radiate confidence."* Claire smiled, nodded politely to the crowd, and gracefully made her way into the Saint Regis Hotel.

Once through the front door, a woman with an ear piece and an electronic tablet approached. Claire noticed multiple people fitting that description, all directing attendants through a set of double doors.

"Hello, welcome to The Saint Regis. May I have your name and the name of the company you're representing?"

"Claire Nichols, SiJo Gaming."

"Yes, Ms. Nichols, I see your name. There is also a Mr. Harrison Baldwin registered. Is he with you this evening?"

"No, he was unfortunately detained. I will be representing SiJo Gaming alone."

"I see. If you could please follow the others through the double doors ahead and to your left, you will receive further instructions. Thank you for joining us this evening."

Claire answered affirmatively and followed the others through the double doors. Once inside, she found herself in a large room. Men in black tuxedos and women in beautiful gowns stood in groupings, while waiters and waitresses mingled about with trays. Some of the trays contained flutes of champagne while others held hors d'oeuvres. Claire's stomach twisted as whiffs of caviar, smoked salmon, and pâtés lofted through the air. She'd meant to eat something before she left the condo. However, the glitches at SiJo changed her plans.

Before Claire could give food much thought, a young man explained, "In about twenty minutes you'll need to step to those doors. At that time you'll be announced as you enter the gala. Do you have any questions?"

Claire said she did not. Once again she was standing alone in a sea of people. Gathering her inner socialness, Claire scanned the room. As she looked from couple to couple, a nice older man and woman approached, "Hello, Ms. Nichols?"

"Yes."

"My name is Jonas Cunningham. This is my wife, Hilary."

Claire extended her hand. Mr. Cunningham continued, "We're from Shedis-tics. I believe we'll be sharing a table."

Claire filled with immediate relief. It was so nice to talk to someone whom she would be seeing throughout the night. "Yes, I believe we are. It is nice to meet you."

The three spoke for a few minutes when another woman with an earpiece politely interrupted. "Excuse me, Ms. Nichols?"

Claire responded, "Yes, I'm Ms. Nichols."

"If you would please follow me, your presence is requested in another room."

Claire nodded to the Cunninghams and followed the woman leading her away from the doors she'd been told to exit. When they were on the fringe of the reception room, Claire asked, "Excuse me, everyone else is going another direction. What did you mean, my presence is requested?"

The young woman answered, "If you'll follow me, I'm sure you'll understand."

The voice Claire heard earlier, the one warning her about the coincidence of SiJo's recent problems, began speaking with an alarming tone.

*****

After almost thirty minutes in the *waiting room*, Sophia wasn't sure what else to call it, she and Derek were escorted to the main ballroom. The large double doors opened to a great beautiful vista. The outside was suddenly in, highlighted by a flowing fountain under a glass atrium ceiling. It reminded Sophia of fountains in Italy, complete with glittering sculptures, a continual shower, and an enormous pool.

Everywhere she looked Sophia saw finely dressed people in tuxedos and gowns moving gracefully from place to place. The hum of polite chatter and soft music filtered through the air as their names were announced: Mr. and Mrs. Derek Burke of Shedis-tics Incorporated. Holding tight to her husband's elbow, they made their way to the floor. Immediately, a gentleman approached and introduced himself and his wife.

"Derek, this is my wife Hilary."

Derek shook her hand and introduced Sophia. "I'm pleased to meet you, Hilary. This is my wife Sophia. Sophia, this is my boss Roger Cunningham and his wife Hilary."

As the men began to discuss the economy and expectations for the future, Hilary Cunningham pulled Sophia under her wing. Her motherly voice offered more advice than Sophia wanted, "My dear, you look beautiful. I'm so glad to meet you. Roger speaks very highly of Derek. They're all so happy he agreed to come to Shedis-tics. How do you like Santa Clara? How do you like San Francisco? How about the beach, do you like the beach? Have you two had a chance to drive into the mountains? They are simply beautiful this time of year..."

Although she was trying with all her might, Sophia couldn't keep up with Hilary's questions. It was as if the woman never paused to breathe. How was Sophia expected to answer?

Finally Mrs. Cunningham moved them away from their husbands. "Let me introduce you to some of the other wives. Listening to the men talk shop all night can get a little tiresome."

Sophia looked to Derek who appeared completely engrossed in Mr. Cunningham's words. Unwittingly, Sophia allowed herself to be directed around the room. Hilary knew many of the people. After introductions and polite chats they would move away and Hilary would whisper sordid tidbits of information about their private lives. Sophia wondered how she possibly knew so much information.

Making their way back toward their husbands, Hilary whispered, "I'm surprised Mr. Rawlings isn't here yet. I don't think I've ever made it to a function before him. He has a real thing for punctuality, or so Roger says."

"Do you know him?" Sophia asked, suddenly interested in some of Mrs. Cunningham's gossip.

"Not really. We've been introduced a few times. He doesn't usually make it to our area. I think Shedis-tics is pretty small on his food chain. That's why Roger is so excited he'll be here tonight."

"Is he married?" Sophia asked.

Hilary's expression was both surprised and amused. "Oh come on, surely you know his story."

Embarrassed by her lack of knowledge Sophia apologized, "I'm sorry, I really don't follow things like that. Why, should I?"

At that moment a waitress passed by with a tray filled with glasses of champagne. Hilary reached for two glasses, handed one to Sophia and said, "Well, let me fill you in!"

*****

With increased concern and anxiety, Claire followed the woman away from the crowds to an elevator. When the doors opened and the woman entered, Claire decided she'd followed long enough.

"I'm sorry, but I don't want to get into this elevator without knowing where I'm going."

It was at that moment she heard determined footsteps approaching from the direction they'd just traveled. Claire turned toward the source and saw a face from her past. The man approached at a steady pace dressed in a very nice suit.

Claire's mind wheeled with memories. This man had never shown her anything but kindness, except perhaps at their last meeting. Had he purposely left the key cabinet to the cars at Tony's estate open? Was he part of Tony's plan? Did his actions lead to her eventual incarceration? Although these questions and many more formed in her head, her lips pressed together in a straight line. This wasn't the time or place to speak her distress. The only outward signs were the sparks blazing from her eyes toward Tony's driver.

"Ms. Claire, Mr. Rawlings is upstairs and would like to see you."

"Eric." She managed through clenched jaws.

"Yes, now, if you'll please enter the elevator I'll gladly escort you to him." He looked at the woman from the gala, "Thank you, I'll take Ms. Nichols from here."

The woman didn't bother to look back toward Claire for confirmation. She nodded and walked away toward the gala.

While hushed, Claire's voice sounded strong and resilient, "Eric, please tell Mr. Rawlings I no longer make command performances. If he wants to see me, he can come to me."

Seizing her elbow, Eric directed her toward the still open elevator. His voice was low, yet determined, "Ms. Claire, there are many people about. Perhaps this time you could make an exception?"

Surprised by his assertiveness and stunned by his touch, her feet moved obediently into the elevator. When the doors closed, she pulled her elbow free from his grasp and felt the floor move upward.

This wasn't an elevator used by guests, but an industrial lift, presumably used by the staff of the St. Regis. The stainless steel walls marred with fingerprints and floor covered by a large black mat resembled the service elevator at Claire's condominium.

As the doors opened, Eric gallantly turned and asked, "Ms. Nichols, may I assist you?"

She wondered if that meant: *Do you want me to forcibly remove you from this elevator*?

Her stoic expression remained while her words were clipped, "Thank you, I believe I'm capable of walking on my own." She wasn't happy with this man. Yet, she knew Eric was only doing what everyone did around Anthony Rawlings, following orders. Exiting the elevator, they stepped into a brightly lit, empty hallway. The sound of her heels upon the concrete floor echoed through the passage. "I'll follow you, as you seem to know where we're going."

Eric nodded, "Yes, ma'am, this way please."

What choice did she have? The elevator was now closed. The sensor near the doors indicated a key was required to regain entry. The hallway had few options for escape. The few doors they passed held name plates indicating the contents beyond: heating/AC, cleaning supplies, and personal supplies. The destination at the end of the passage was not labeled. Eric opened the door and held it for Claire to pass. She did, each step becoming more difficult to endure. More than anything, she wanted to call Harry, but he was busy with problems at SiJo. She squared her shoulders and entered an elegant posh foyer. Claire knew who she'd find at the end of this journey. Before her were two options, an elevator and a set of double doors. This elevator was adorned with golden mirrored doors.

Eric placed a card below an electronic reader near the double doors, and she heard tumblers shift. Anthony Rawlings' driver and right hand man opened one of the grand doors. Claire obediently entered the threshold of the luxurious penthouse atop the San Francisco St. Regis Hotel. Although every fiber within her body told her to run for the gold elevator, Claire's Jimmy Choo four and a half inch heels moved forward. She heard the click of each step as she followed Eric through the foyer, complete with a winding staircase, toward a beautiful sitting area. Beyond the elaborately furnished room, with multiple sofas, tables and entries to other rooms were windows covering the wall from the polished floor to the ceiling, at least fifteen feet above.

Claire saw the back of *his* head, hair gelled perfectly in place and his customary Armani tuxedo slacks and perfectly pressed white silk shirt. She couldn't remember how many he owned. She knew it was many. Tony's large form appeared dwarfed against the height of the glass pane. Beyond him the sky filled with color, creating a magnificent vista as an amazing sunset glistened in the western sky, with the Golden Gate Bridge in the foreground.

The anger growing within her chest stilled as she heard his voice. Uncharacteristic anger emanated. He was yelling at some poor soul on the phone he held tightly in his right hand. With his left hand he twisted a cord. It was the tie holding back the drapes at the edge of the amazing view.

"She's not to be there. He is to remain." "No, that isn't acceptable." "This has been the plan forever. If you aren't capable, I will find someone who is." He turned, hearing Eric and Claire enter. His eyes smoldered. Despite the dark blackness of his irises, fire flashed from a deep untouchable abyss. Claire searched his expression for a sign of assurance, finding none; she shivered knowing the depths of this man's temper.

The words of protest she'd been silently practicing since entering the elevator, faded into Tony's cloud of rage. With all her soul, Claire prayed she wasn't the one meant to disappear or the reason for his fury.

"Twenty minutes. I'll be waiting." He disconnected his phone and slid it into the pocket of his Armani slacks. "Thank you, Eric. Ms. Claire will remain with me. Please take care of our other issue. I'm late for the benefit and that's very upsetting to me."

"Yes, Mr. Rawlings. Twenty minutes?"

"Not a second more."

Eric nodded as he backed toward the door, "Yes, Sir." Before Claire could blink Eric disappeared down the hall, and she heard the grand double doors close.

Claire gripped her purse and nervously ran her fingers over the silk of the wrap, now lying over her arm. Eric was a source of uneasiness, yet his departure was more unnerving. She stood anxiously before her ex-husband. Straightening her neck, she tried for a formidable yet respectful voice. "Tony, please explain to..."

He didn't allow her to finish her sentence. Instantly, his chest touched hers, and her chin rose with the direction of his forceful grasp.

267

His warm breath hit her face as his harsh words flowed, "I have no intention of being at a social gathering or anywhere else with you and another man. You're a fool to consider such a thing."

The bile bubbling from her stomach caused her knees to tremble, yet her voice remained resilient. "I agreed to attend this gala, weeks ago. I didn't learn of your attendance until this evening."

His grip increased as he held her emerald eyes toward his pits of darkness, "Then your informant is as incompetent as the firewall at SiJo."

Though her stance remained still, her eyes ignited, "What did you do?"

"Nothing. As long as your friends don't have an overwhelming sense of conscious requiring them to inform the public of their near breach, no harm will come."

Claire remained motionless. Her well trained protocol wouldn't allow her to pull away from his hold. Nevertheless, her eyes screamed at his manipulation. "Why?"

As his hand released her face, Claire flexed her neck and shoulders. Taking a step back, Claire assessed the man before her. He was still very agitated. However, she needed to know, "Why did you do this?"

"I told you Claire. I know your weakness. It's your concern for others. God only knows why, but for some reason Amber McCoy has been kind to you. Her company will not be harmed," He paused and walked to the window. The sky of orange and red was now darkening. The land beyond the bridge was speckled with lights as the bridge glowed with artificial illumination. Turning on his heels Tony's gaze devoured her, as his commanding voice filled the tall room, "IF you follow my rules."

Claire's heart sunk. Her knees wobbled, and her stomach twisted. This was her nightmare, her greatest fear. She'd convinced herself she was able to maintain the upper hand. Her inner voice tried to warn her, but Claire hadn't listened. Now it was too late. Suddenly his expression changed.

"Are you not feeling well? You're pale." Was there concern in the voice that only seconds ago was harsh and authoritative?

"I need to sit down."

Tony wrapped his arm around Claire's waist and directed her toward a soft leather love seat. Her knees buckled and a sudden wave of perspiration covered her skin as she settled against the cool plush hide. Claire lowered her head to her knees and tried to inhale. She saw Tony's shiny loafers move away and return. Then his voice reassuringly offered assistance, "Here's some water, drink."

Claire shook her head against the green material of her Donna Karen gown. The feeling of queasiness wouldn't fade. She feared if she drank the water she'd be ill.

"Dinner will be starting downstairs in about an hour. Have you eaten recently?"

Feeling the chill that comes after the rush of heat, Claire looked up into the softening eyes. "No, I haven't." Her voice quivered, revealing the trembling within her body. She wasn't sure if the cause of her trembling was the recent onset of nausea or Tony. "I don't want to go down there with you." She sat straighter, trying desperately for strength. "I'm here for SiJo, for Amber and Simon."

Tony's gaze lingered. He could see her still to pale complexion. Nonetheless, his voice hardened as his posture straightened. "Then you will do as I say."

Her resolve was spent. She once again lowered her head to her lap and asked, "What do you want me to do?"

Entrepreneurs are simply those who understand
that there is little difference between obstacle and opportunity
and are able to turn both to their advantage.
- Niccolo Machiavelli

Chapter 34

Sophia listened as Hilary Cunningham described Anthony Rawlings' marriage to Claire Nichols. Hilary's excitement built as she spoke about both of them being present at this function. Sophia didn't need to feign interest; this was better than a TV show. She couldn't believe this kind of intrigue existed in real life. She anxiously awaited Claire Nichols' presence at their table. According to Mrs. Cunningham, Ms. Nichols was a surprisingly attractive and friendly woman.

Occupied with sipping her champagne, tuning out the crowd, and listening to Hilary's words, Sophia almost missed the vibrating sensation coming from her handbag. Excusing herself from the conversation, Sophia looked at her phone and read the screen: Mr. George 3 missed calls. Walking tentatively from the ballroom into the quiet hall, she returned his call. He answered on the first ring.

"Mrs. Burke, I've been trying to reach you."

"I'm rather busy this evening, Mr. George. What can I do for you?"

"The mystery buyer, he wants to meet with both of us... *tonight*."

Sophia collapsed against the wall, allowing her shoulders the relief of a sturdy anchor. "Tonight? I'm with my husband at a very important event. I can't leave."

Mr. George continued undeterred, "He's at the Saint Regis Hotel in San Francisco and wants both of us there in fifteen minutes. Maybe I can pacify him until you arrive."

Sophia looked toward a group of waiters with wheeled carts and stacks of covered plates. "Mr. George, I'm at the Saint Regis. Where are we supposed to meet?"

"Consigner's desk, before 8 PM."

She looked at her delicate watch, 7:46 PM, and asked, "Will you be here in time?"

"Yes, I'm in a cab as we speak. I've been trying to reach you for over a half an hour."

"I'll be there." Sophia disconnected her call and gathered her nerve. She needed to explain to Derek; she'd only be gone from the festivities for a very short time. Seriously, what luck the buyer wanted to meet at *this* hotel?

*****

Though the large hand which held hers radiated warmth, the unyielding grip was not intended to be misconstrued as comfort. It was undeniably a warning. Tony made it clear; Claire would again follow his rules. Magnanimous as ever, he kindly reminded her of the most important ones: do as I say, public failure is not an option, and be the perfect companion.

Tonight's duties required obeying all three. In order to assure SiJo Gaming's complete recovery from its current troubles, Claire must attend the National Center for Learning Disabilities Gala as Anthony Rawlings' companion. The silk wrap covering her shoulders failed to keep the trembling at bay. Claire stared at their perfect reflections upon the mirrored door of the private golden Penthouse elevator. With each floor of their descent, her mind reeled with this new reality.

Perhaps, someday she'd learn to expect the unexpected, and his actions wouldn't shock her. Yet, as was their history, whenever Anthony Rawlings was in Claire's life, so was the potential for abrupt change. Remembering the past hour, she bowed to the reality of her new paradigm.

In their figurative game of chess, Anthony Rawlings had Claire in *check*. Every move she made, he countered. When she wanted their dinner to be public, he made it private. When she wanted to surprise him at a public event, he chose to make it the stage for their refound allegiance.

*****

After Claire regained her composure in the St. Regis Penthouse, Tony ordered crackers and cheese to the suite. While Claire ate and sipped a soda, Tony asked for her purse. Although, she didn't want to relinquish it, the recent change of events and his familiar domineering demeanor left her momentarily unable to resist. In a matter of minutes her world had returned to his control.

Taking her elegant black clutch, Tony removed her iPhone, turned it off and placed it in the breast pocket of his silk shirt. Then he methodically unzipped and searched each compartment of the bag.

Finally Claire asked, "What are you looking for?"

"Your *work* phone."

"It isn't here. I left it in my condo." That statement was true in all aspects, except that it wasn't a *work* phone, but Claire's only communication with Courtney.

"As you may remember, while at a function such as this, your attention should be on me and your duties at hand. I believe tonight you're representing SiJo Gaming." Despite the recent snack, hearing Tony say Simon's company made Claire's stomach twist. His tone and expression hardened, "As well as representing *it* to the masses downstairs, your behavior will go a long way in solving their current situation, or..." he paused, "making it public."

Claire nodded, then remembering his propensity for verbal responses she replied, "I understand."

"I am glad you do. You'll get your phone back when this evening is done. I believe you'll have enough on your plate, you don't need another distraction."

Next he handed her a printed page. Compartmentalized memories of previous news articles flooded her consciousness. *Never* had a similar situation been favorable. There was the Meredith Bank's article and the information regarding Simon's death. Tonight's information wasn't as dramatic, but the aftershocks could be. Claire's hands trembled as she took the page from his hand.

"What is this?" she asked.

"It's a news release. My press secretary released it moments before you arrived to the penthouse." Smiling he added, "I just saw a text from Shelly; it's already *viral*."

Her stomach twisted, hearing the same word Meredith used regarding him. Move, countermove, the game continued. Claire focused on the page before her.

Associated Press May 24, 2013

Mr. Anthony Rawlings, CEO of Rawlings Industries, asks the public for patience at this difficult time. He believes two years ago he and the world were deceived. Despite circumstances and appearances, he is now convinced his ex-wife, Claire Nichols (Rawlings), is innocent regarding her unfortunate accusation of attempted murder.

This realization came to Mr. Rawlings through a series of personal and private encounters with Ms. Nichols. Listening to instinct and following his heart, a combination of resources which have successfully helped to create his global empire, Mr. Rawlings is now certain of Ms. Nichols innocence.

In an effort to correct the wrongful prosecution by the state of Iowa, Mr. Rawlings attempted to reverse the ruling of the judge, to no avail. In a moment of inspiration, Mr. Rawlings personally contacted Governor Bosley and requested Ms. Nichols' pardon.

With the assistance of Jane Allyson, Esquire and the signature of the late Governor Richard Bosley, the innocent Claire Nichols was pardoned and released from prison March 9, 2013.

Mr. Rawlings regrets initially denying connection to her pardon. He also refuses to answer who he believes was responsible for the poisoning which resulted in his near death and lead to the false accusations. He will only respond, "It is a personal issue."

It has been reported that multiple longtime employees of Mr. Rawlings have been released of their duties.

At the current time, Mr. Rawlings is concentrating on renewing his relationship with Ms. Nichols. He confirms that theirs is a complicated and passionate bond and asks for privacy at this important time of healing.

As she processed the words, Claire's stomach reeled with thoughts of Harry. Did Tony say this news was already viral? Had Harry seen it? Or was he too preoccupied trying to defuse the problems Tony set into motion at SiJo? With all her heart, Claire wanted to call Harry and explain. That wasn't an option. Obviously, that's why Tony took her phone before he handed her the press release.

"Why are you doing this?" Tears threatened to overflow her painted eyes. She couldn't even pretend to be strong as she placed the page on a nearby table.

"I've tried to tell you my feelings for you. I've even apologized to you for past behaviors and attempted to explain." Claire heard his attempted restraint as his tone once again hardened, "And yet, you blatantly flaunt another man at a shared function."

Perhaps it was the food, but strength was returning, if only enough to respond. "I was not *flaunting*. We, you and I, are divorced. This," she picked up the news release, "is false. You didn't secure my pardon. You had nothing to do with it."

"And who's going to refute my claim? Governor Bosley, no, he's dead. Jane Allyson, I think not."

"Why Tony? What have you done to Jane?"

Grinning triumphantly, Tony stood and looked down at Claire, "Again, so much credit. I should be honored."

Claire stood to meet his stance, her words slowed, "Tell me what you've done."

"While I may be able to assume some responsibility, it is quite the opposite of what you suspect. Miss Allyson is currently enjoying the honor of an invitation to one of the most prestigious law firms in Des Moines." Checking his phone, Tony read a text message. His shoulders relaxed and he continued, "As informative as this conversation is, we can continue it later. It's almost eight, as you know this gala started at seven. You may remember -- I do not like to be late."

For the first time since she entered the penthouse, Tony evaluated the woman before him. "My, Claire, you do look lovely. I admit I doubted your financial ability to dress as would warrant my companion for the evening. There's a complete ensemble in the master suite for you, but I like your choice." Scanning her from head to toe, he stepped toward her and lifted the pearl of her grandmother's necklace. His eyes shone in triumph as he said, "Yes, after you touch up your make-up, I believe we'll be ready to attend our reunion gala." Gently dropping the cream colored pearl, he softly brushed the back of his hand against her cheek. His voice dripped with bogus compassion, "Don't look so strained, my dear, this is a happy occasion. You wanted our dinner public. *Your wish is my command.* Besides, you came here to represent SiJo Gaming. I promise this will bring that small company more publicity and positive public relations than would have originally happened." Taking her small hands in his, he squeezed and said, "This is a win, win."

Claire squared her shoulders. Her eyes found the fight she'd momentarily loss. Although the emerald green flashed and her voice seemed stronger, she submissively asked, "Where can I get ready?"

As he directed her upstairs, she noticed his demeanor calming. He had her over the proverbial barrel. If she chose to argue or disobey, SiJo would suffer. He'd given her no alternative. That, plus the content of a text message he'd just received, seemed to mellow him. Claire wondered why *he* could divide his attention between telephones, text messages, and those around him, and she couldn't. Feeling the prickling sensation of the hairs on the back of her neck, she chose not to voice that question.

The ostentatiously large bath of the master bedroom suite contained rows of buttons capable of illuminating the room from every angle. The glass, chrome, mirrors, and tile sparkled as she depressed each switch. Claire beheld her reflection. In many ways she resembled the woman back at Amber's condominium. Yet, the aching behind her temples, paler complexion, and strain behind her eyes reminded her of a woman she used to be, Mrs. Anthony Rawlings.

Some powder, blush, and lipstick helped the complexion. A few acetaminophens from her purse would eventually aid her head. Claire believed only the conclusion of this nightmare would relieve the stress. Nevertheless, when she emerged from the bath and found Tony waiting, in his custom Armani jacket and tie, she secured her mask and appeared the perfect companion. Old habits die hard.

*****

Minutes earlier, Sophia walked briskly through the crowded lobby of the Saint Regis Hotel. She glanced again at her watch, 7:56. Across the sea of people she saw Mr. George with a tall man in a nice suit. She watched as Mr. George acknowledged her to the other man. Both of their postures relaxed. She wondered if they'd been concerned she wouldn't come.

"I'm sorry I'm late. The walk from the grand ballroom was farther than I realized."

Mr. George smiled nervously, "Sophia, let me introduce Eric Hensley. Mr. Hensley, this is our very talented artist, Mrs. Sophia Burke."

Eric extended his hand, "Mrs. Burke, so nice to finally meet you. I apologize for disrupting your evening. I certainly hope this meeting hasn't caused you too much inconvenience."

Sophia smiled, "Well, as you see, I'm dressed for the gala down the hall. However, after your generous allocation of my paintings, I felt unable to deny this request."

"Mrs. Burke, I apologize. I'm not the one who purchased your art, although I have seen it and think very highly of it. I'm here representing someone else. He would like to meet with the two of you privately."

"Privately, Mr. Hensley?" Sophia asked, "I was told this wouldn't take long. My husband is waiting for me; dinner is soon."

"I understand, Mrs. Burke. I will let my employer know that you aren't able..."

The shocked expression on Mr. George's face said more than the words from Mr. Hensley. Sophia interrupted, "No, I apologize. Of course, I'd like to meet with your employer. I do hope we will meet here."

Eric continued, "Yes, upstairs in one of the Presidential suites."

Sophia nodded at both gentlemen, "All right, let's go."

With that, the three of them walked toward a bay of elevators. Once inside Eric slid a plastic card in the reader and pushed the button for the twenty-seventh floor. The presidential suites were located on the floor below the penthouse. As the compartment ascended, Eric removed his telephone. "I must text my employer. He'll be very happy to know you're on your way to the suite."

*****

Anthony and Claire did not pass GO... they did not pass through the waiting room, as she'd done earlier. When the golden elevator opened, a well-dressed gentleman met and greeted them, "Mr. Rawlings, we are so happy to have you with us tonight."

Tony shook the man's hand, "Yes, Mr. Wilkins, I apologize for our tardiness. My companion was not feeling well, but all is better now." Tony inclined his head toward Claire, "Perhaps you remember my companion, Claire," he paused momentarily, "Nichols."

Claire extended her hand, "Mr. Wilkins, it is so nice to see you again."

Though visibly shocked, Mr. Wilkins accepted Claire's hand and smiled weakly, "Ms. Nichols, yes. It is a surprise to see the two of you," he regrouped. "It is always a pleasure." Turning back to Tony, "Now, Mr.

Rawlings, and, Ms. Nichols, if you'll follow me we will make your introductions.

Tony replied, "Although I'm here to speak, I am also representing Shedis-tics and Ms. Nichols is representing SiJo Gaming."

Mr. Wilkins nodded affirmatively and promised proper introductions. Tony once again seized Claire's hand and slowed their pace, allowing Mr. Wilkins to lead the way to the ballroom. He whispered, "Well, if that's any indication, reactions alone should keep this night entertaining."

She smiled and replied, "*Entertaining* is not the word I'd use."

Her quickness delighted him. Though his soft voice divulged his amusement, his grip, and words revealed his warning, "Be careful, Ms. Nichols; don't let your recently discovered independence get you into trouble."

Utilizing her previous southern charm, she replied, "Why, Mr. Rawlings, I believe I am already in more trouble than I can handle."

They both quieted as the doors opened and an MC announced, "Ladies and Gentleman, we are proud to introduce, Mr. Anthony Rawlings and his companion Ms. Claire Nichols." A hush followed by applause echoed through the large ballroom. Except for a few waiters and waitresses, the room of people stilled and looked their direction. The MC continued, "We are honored to have Mr. Rawlings, of Rawlings Industries, with us this evening as one of tonight's prestigious speakers and as a representative of Shedis-tics. Ms. Nichols is also present as a representative of SiJo Gaming." There was more applause and Tony placed his hand in the small of Claire's back. They stepped into the sea of people. Immediately, they were surrounded by people wanting to meet and speak to tonight's honored guests.

A thing long expected takes the form of the unexpected
when at last it comes.
-- Mark Twain

Chapter 35

Intermittently sipping ice water, Claire sat at the head table, two seats to the left of the podium and listened intently to Tony's speech. As the evening progressed, each scene she performed became easier, almost comfortable. After all, it was the role she'd created; she was the original costar in their perfect couple show. The only constraint to her seamless performance was the daunting concern lingering in the back of her mind. Each time her thoughts turned to Harry or Amber, Claire immediately compartmentalized them away. She couldn't continue this charade if she allowed herself to worry about what was happening at SiJo or imagined the hurt in Harry's soft blue eyes when he learned about her evening.

Tony's speech concentrated on the National Center for Learning Disabilities and its many accomplishments. Claire noted how Tony rarely referred to the electronic tablet before him. Yet, he cited statistics and philosophies perfectly. She had to wonder how someone who just came from a confrontation like the one they'd just had upstairs, could perform so flawlessly.

It wasn't just his speech, but everything about him; the way he conversed with others, his attentive looks, and even his light chatty dinner conversation. His social presence always had, and still did, fascinate Claire. No wonder he was so successful; this Anthony Rawlings was truly captivating. With time, she forgot the circumstance of her situation and fell into her own role as his companion.

That was what he wanted, and shouldn't Claire Nichols know, Anthony Rawlings always got what he wanted. Listening as he concluded his speech, she found herself applauding appropriately and smiling approvingly at the handsome professional man before her.

When he turned from the podium and their eyes met, there was a moment when she was once again -- Mrs. Anthony Rawlings. His velvety brown eyes filled with appreciation, directed at her. It was a look only shared with someone who knows you, truly understands the real person. How many people did Tony have like that in his life?

In the few months since her pardon, Claire had rekindled relationships with friends and family, as well as forged new ones. Who did Tony have?

As he took his seat, he reached for Claire's hand, and gently lifted it from its resting place on her lap. This time, his grasp wasn't a warning. Instead he lowered his head, keeping his eyes fixed on hers and brushed her knuckles with a soft sweep of his lips. The warm light touch made her smile. It was then she remembered the room of onlookers. Her cheeks reddened and she whispered, "Very nice speech, Mr. Rawlings."

His smile lit up the room, "Thank you, Mrs. -- Ms. Nichols, you are mighty remarkable yourself."

Someone else was speaking from the podium. Their voices were a faint whisper against the sound from the nearby speaker; Claire raised her eyebrows and asked, "Mighty?" It was a strangely common word to hear from Tony.

He gently squeezed her soft hand, "Mighty." They both smiled and turned to listen to the next orator, a woman from the Center for Learning Disabilities thanking the audience for their support.

Their most interesting exchange occurred before the meal was served. Truthfully, they weren't able to make much progress moving about the room. Person after person and couple after couple made their way to them. When Claire saw Mr. and Mrs. Cunningham from Shedistics waiting for their attention, she decided to warn Tony she'd spoken with them earlier. Her social instinct served her well in the past; she knew it was best to listen. Therefore, before the Cunninghams made their way to Tony and her, Claire excused the two of them from the public conversation and whispered in his ear, "The Cunninghams from Shedistics are making their way to us. You should know I spoke with them a few minutes in the waiting room prior to being asked to your penthouse." Claire practiced her statement. The *asked* could have been *summoned*, or perhaps *dragged*. She decided *asked* sounded best. Her temples throbbed at the pressure of once again weighing each word. She watched displeasure cloud his eyes and braced for his response.

"You were supposed to be brought up immediately, before you had time to talk with anyone."

"Well, that is someone else's concern. I was out of the loop on your plan. I just thought you'd want to know." Maybe she was caving to his plan, but her verbose response was pointedly more abrupt than it would have been years before.

Tony assessed Claire's expression for a moment and responded, "Thank you, I appreciate knowing. Did you discuss..." he hesitated.

She knew he wanted to ask about Harry. "I said I was alone because of an issue at SiJo. However, who I was supposed to be with was never mentioned."

Tony nodded and he replied loud enough for others to hear, "Most certainly, I'll gladly get you something to drink."

Before he could move, a waiter appeared with a tray of crystal fluted glasses, the contents bubbled from the stem to the rim. Tony took two flutes and handed one to Claire with a nod. She returned his nod. Claire understood the conversation was done; he was happy with her honesty. Each such behavior helped her figurative chess king live one more day.

When the couple from Shedis-tics finally arrived, Tony gallantly proceeded, "Mr. and Mrs. Cunningham, it is always a pleasure."

Roger Cunningham replied, "Mr. Rawlings."

Tony continued, "Ms. Nichols tells me you have met?"

Claire wasn't sure, but the Cunninghams appeared embarrassed or apprehensive about their earlier meeting. She joined the conversation, extending her hand, "Yes," she smiled pleasantly at both of them, "I was so lost in that large room. I appreciated your friendly greeting."

The Cunninghams visibly relaxed with her comment. Mrs. Cunningham spoke, "Ms. Nichols, it was a pleasure to meet you. I'm sure this collaboration between Shedis-tics and SiJo will be beneficial."

Claire continued, her mask intact, "I'm sure you're aware, it goes way back. Mr. Rawlings gave Simon his first opportunity in Silicon Valley with his dream job at Shedis-tics. Simon Johnson never forgot where he started and enjoyed the allegiance between the two companies."

Mr. Cunningham replied, "It's easy to forget the origins of our companies. Thank you for reminding us. I'm sure Mr. Johnson would be happy that the allegiance has remained." Claire radiated confidence. Her never wavering smile successfully hid the contained emotions she successfully compartmentalized away. Mr. Cunningham indicated the man to his left. "Mr. Rawlings, Ms. Nichols, this is our promising new associate Derek Burke."

Everyone shook hands. Claire evaluated Derek Burke: tall, polished, and polite. He approached Tony with an honest reverence yet with enough self-confidence to indicate he deserved the praise bestowed upon him. There were so many people who blabbered incoherently in Tony's presence. Claire assessed Tony must also be impressed by Derek's poise because they conversed longer than Tony usually did with one person. Unfortunately, his attention toward this new associate left Claire, once again, at the disposal of Mr. and Mrs. Cunningham. Their friendly greeting earlier in the waiting room turned to gushing compliments about Claire's attire and the gala. *More incoherent babbling*, Claire thought.

Eventually, the next set of attendees made their way to Claire and Tony. When dinner was announced, Claire was relieved beyond words. She'd played her role well -- very well. Even Tony complimented her regarding the Shedis-tics couple. Nevertheless, her body ached from standing in high heels and the stress. The act of sitting was a welcome relief.

At one point, before the speeches, Claire excused herself to visit the ladies room. She expected a warning glance or gesture. Surprisingly, she received neither. All the way to the restroom she considered borrowing someone's cellphone and calling Harry. The problem was -- she didn't know his number. She called it multiple times a day. But, the number was programmed into her phone. After racking her memory, she gave up and made her way back to her new assigned seat.

On her way to Tony, she passed the round table where she should have been sitting. Claire noticed three empty seats. It was the only table within the large room with so many vacancies. The Cunninghams, Derek Burke and another couple were politely chatting. Claire moved quickly, to avoid another conversation with Hilary Cunningham.

*****

Sophia believed she'd suffocate if she spent another minute in the beautiful sitting room of the Saint Regis' Presidential Suite waiting for the mystery buyer. Walking through French doors onto a balcony she observed the lights of the Golden Gate Bridge. Although almost the end of May, the evening air was brisk against her exposed skin. Mindlessly she wrapped her arms around her chest and dissected the view, as only an artist can do. The towers glowed more orange than *gold,* she thought as she as she viewed the illumination from Route One.

She stood motionless at the rail and inhaled the salty air. It wasn't the same as Provincetown. There was something about Provincetown Harbor which was unique from San Francisco Bay. Nevertheless, closing her eyes and listening to the distant rush of waves, the similarities made her homesick. She glanced at her watch, almost nine thirty.

She and Mr. George had been in this suite both alone and with Mr. Hensley for an hour and a half. Though she'd communicated with Derek regularly, she knew he was upset. He should be, she reasoned. This was ridiculous and rude.

Sophia even felt sorry for Mr. Hensley. The poor man was doing his job. It truly wasn't his fault his employer was delayed. The first excuse was about traffic on 280. When eight thirty came and went, Mr. Hensley kindly ordered them dinner. At eight forty five they fired up Mr. Hensley's lap top and virtually viewed Sophia's art. At nine fifteen Mr. Hensley received a text message and excused himself from the suite.

Now Sophia and Mr. George continued to wait. The night air helped relieve Sophia's distress. Although she hadn't been looking forward to Derek's big gala, she knew how much it meant to him. He'd been anxiously anticipating spending this time with his boss and Mr. Cunningham's wife. He was also very excited to meet the CEO of Shedistic's parent company. He'd told Sophia his name and Hilary Cunningham had gone on about a woman named Nichols, but currently the CEO's name escaped Sophia. More than anything she wanted to be back in that crowded, pretentious ballroom.

"Mrs. Burke, I apologize for this inconvenience." Mr. George was now on the balcony too.

"I don't blame you. It's just that my husband is so close, and I should be with him."

"Mrs. Burke, if this weren't important, I wouldn't have asked you to be here."

"Do we even know the name of this mysterious buyer?"

Mr. George rubbed his temple. "No, Mr. Hensley is the one I've been dealing with."

They both turned, upon hearing the door to the suite open. Mr. Hensley entered. When it was clear he was alone, they both exhaled and moved to join him within the suite. His voice was more assured. "I cannot adequately express my sincere apologies regarding this horrid meeting. Circumstances beyond anyone's control have delayed my employer. He would, however, like to offer an olive branch."

Sophia and Mr. George didn't reply. It had been a long evening.

Mr. Hensley continued, "If you two could please have a seat. My employer would like to fund an exhibition of your work, Mrs. Burke. He was thinking of an exhibition which would run in multiple cities, in succession."

Mr. George and Sophia sat. Her tired mind spun with this new offer. First, this mysterious man paid 2.3 million dollars for three of her paintings and now, he wanted to fund a moving exhibit. She momentarily forgot about Derek and the gala. Her thoughts now centered upon Mr. Hensley and the papers before him.

Eric went on, "Mr. George, commission of all sales at all locations would be directed through you. Mrs. Burke, if we could take a few minutes to discuss possible locations?"

Sophia nodded. She wasn't sure her voice could sound composed.

*****

When the final speaker concluded, the MC from earlier came to the podium and announced, "Ladies and gentleman, the orchestra will be in place soon. If everyone could please make their way back out to the atrium, dancing will commence in less than a half an hour."

Claire looked down at her watch. It was only nine-forty, but she was exhausted. If this were Harry she'd let him know. But it wasn't. She was back to weighing each word. "Are we staying for dancing?"

Tony leaned closer, his eyebrows raised, "Do you want to dance?"

"No, I really don't. I'm tired and I'd like to go home. If I could have my phone I'll call for the SiJo car."

Tony leaned back against his chair. His lack of response caused Claire's skin to crawl. The contrary emotions his actions elicited made her feel as though she were with two different men. One minute he was courteous and social, the next he was his old domineering, controlling self. She tried to remain obedient. With each passing minute her insolence increased. Finally, she leaned toward him, smile glistening. From afar they appeared to be having a friendly chat. Claire's voice betrayed her current emotions; she could only restrain them visually, audibly was too much. Her voice cracked as she questioned, "Have I done everything you asked?"

His external facade remained intact, "Yes, but I want more."

Her heart sank, "Please, I'm tired."

"Then perhaps you should go to bed."

She saw the twinkle in his eye. Her mask momentarily shattered, she leaned closer, as panic filled each syllable, "I am *not* agreeing to sleep with you."

His perfect smile remained unwavering; however, his eyes registered darker than she'd seen since the penthouse, "Sleeping, my dear, is not what I had in mind."

She closed her eyes and waited for the distress to pass. When it merely subsided, she turned to her ex-husband, "I will go upstairs with you. I will complete this scenario. I will *not* have sex with you."

"Why do you fight it?"

People mingled close. There were waitresses and waiters clearing tables. Other couples milled near. Claire inhaled and exhaled. The urge to cry was almost beyond her control. "May we please go upstairs? This conversation is upsetting me. If you want to maintain this charade, we'd better leave while I can maintain a smile."

Tony stood and chivalrously offered Claire his hand. She exhaled and took it, allowing her fingers to be swallowed by his girth. "Ms. Nichols, shall we bid our ado's to the appropriate people?"

"Yes, Mr. Rawlings. I am but so ready to close the curtain on this performance."

Tony leaned toward her ear, "The press release is viral. This, my love, was only the first act."

An older couple from the National Center for Learning Disabilities approached. With her stomach in knots, Claire bravely continued her duties. When they finally reached the golden elevator, Tony removed his phone from his jacket and sent a text. Claire remained silent until the doors opened to the Penthouse entry. "May I have my phone?"

Tony looked at his watch, 10:17 PM. "My dear, the night is still young."

*****

Sophia looked at the list of cities: San Francisco, Seattle, Phoenix, Dallas, Chicago, Louisville, Atlanta, Miami, Charlotte, New York, Boston and Bangor. The tour consisted of two weeks in each city. Exhibition halls rented, advertised, and paid. Lodging and food stipends, as well as travel expenses. Mr. George would receive his customary fifteen percent. The mysterious buyer would receive five percent. The rest of all sales would go to Sophia. With two weeks in each city and the occasional time off, the tour would last approximately thirty weeks.

"I have some overseas commitments," Sophia said as Mr. Hensley discussed the exhibitions.

"I'm sure that can be worked out."

"I really need to discuss this with my husband."

"Of course," Eric replied as he glanced at his phone. "Let me give you this written information." Looking to Mr. George, "You have my number. Please call when Mrs. Burke has made her decision."

Mr. George responded, "Yes, we'll talk."

Eric Hensley turned to Sophia, "Mrs. Burke, again, I apologize for the inconvenience. I hope my employer's olive branch will help to make amends for the missed gala. I'm sure you would like to join your husband. I look forward to talking to you again soon."

Sophia stood with the realization she'd been released. "Thank you, Mr. Hensley. Mr. George and I will be back to you soon. Please tell your employer I do appreciate his offer."

Eric walked Sophia to the door of the suite, "I will. Do you need an escort back to the ballroom?"

"No, thank you. I'll be fine."

Eric Hensley nodded as Sophia walked from the suite. As she waited for the elevator Sophia sent a text to Derek. *I'M FINALLY RELEASED. DO YOU STILL WANT ME?*

Her phone vibrated within seconds, *DINNER IS DONE. DANCING IS ABOUT TO START. I'D LOOK FUNNY DANCING ALONE. I ALWAYS WANT YOU!*

Sophia smiled as the mirrored cubical descended to the main level. When the doors opened, she hurried toward the ballroom.

*The single biggest problem with communication
is the illusion that it has taken place.*
-- George Bernard Shaw.

Chapter 36

Perhaps it was her look of desperation or the tears that lingered on her perfectly painted lids. The reason was not yet revealed. Nonetheless, once the golden elevator closed and Tony and Claire were alone in the entry of the Saint Regis Penthouse, he opened his Armani jacket and handed Claire her phone. She contemplated taking it to an isolated area and calling Harry. Instead, she bravely stood before Tony, waited for it to turn on, ignored the icons indicating missed calls and messages, and scrolled for the number of the SiJo driver.

Although Tony stood resolute before her, Claire refused to turn away. Maybe it was a replay of a scene from their past. Maybe it was a move, counter move. Nevertheless, she waited while the phone rang. When the driver answered, she heard, "Ms. Nichols, this is Marcus, are you ready to be picked up?"

Looking Tony in the eyes, she replied, "Hello, Marcus, yes, this is Claire Nichols..."

She didn't complete her sentence. Tony unexpectedly took the iPhone from her hand and spoke, "Hello, Marcus. Ms. Nichols will not need your assistance this evening." Claire could no longer hear Marcus's response, only Tony's: "This is Anthony Rawlings." "That is correct." "Yes, you are relieved of your assignment." "Thank you, good night." He turned off the phone and placed it back in his pocket. His dark chocolate eyes glowed in the dim light of the penthouse.

Claire wanted to fight, she wanted her iPhone back, and she wanted to be back in Palo Alto with Harry and Amber. However, after Tony disconnected the call, she dejectedly walked to the sofa and collapsed. The tight reign she'd had on her emotions all night severed. How could it not? The tension was too much. With tears cascading down her cheeks, Claire closed her eyes and waited. She'd been here before. Not this hotel or this scenario, but one with enough similarity she knew the drill. Her only option was conceding -- until her side regained strength.

Momentarily, Claire remembered Courtney, Brent, Jane, Amber, Harry, John and Emily. She wasn't a lone chess piece -- isolated, without support. The realization fortified her. Claire didn't stand and declare victory. Nonetheless, she silently accepted their support and sat taller. Drying her tears she stared compellingly into the depths of her ex-husband's dark abyss. If those people could stand for her, she'd sit straighter for them. Inhaling deeply and exhaling, Claire asked, "What do I need to do, to leave?"

Tony sat next to his ex-wife. His gaze mellowed. "Eric will take you home whenever you want. You may leave at any time."

She didn't hesitate, "Then I want to leave now."

Tony nodded, and removed his phone from his jacket. It was at that moment she remembered *why* she was there, why she'd done as he asked, "Tony?" Her voice quivered with concern, "Is SiJo secure? Did they get their problem fixed?"

He placed his phone back in his pocket and replied, "Do you want to know what I have been thinking about all night?"

Claire struggled to stay on track, "What you've been thinking about? All right."

"Many things, the first -- how amazing you've been. I've endured many companions since our divorce. I have not enjoyed any of those evenings as much as I have tonight, being with you."

Claire stared; she wondered what part of that statement was supposed to warrant her response, his many companions or her exemplary performance.

Tony continued, "Shelly was not happy with my desired press release, but I decided it was the only answer. Now the world knows of our reconciliation. It is official."

"You say that, as if it's beyond debate."

He peered unquestionably into her emerald eyes, "Beyond challenge. It is public." The *failure is not an option* went without saying.

"SiJo?"

"The breach has been resolved. It *has been* since about eight o'clock this evening."

Claire exhaled, "Thank you."

Tony accepted her gratitude and answered, "Actually, I will have Eric take you to your condominium. It's probably better if you don't know what else I've been pondering."

Claire sat straighter, "Thank you, again. I'm ready to leave." She watched as he nodded. The familiar attraction sucked her into his gravitational pull, and without thinking she took his hand in hers. Propelled by curiosity as well as concern, Claire asked, "What else have you been thinking?"

"Those black lacy panties."

Claire released his hand and stood abruptly. "What did you say?"

"I've been thinking about your black lacy underwear; there was a small bow." His smile turned sensual, "I've been wondering what color you're wearing tonight."

Her voice came out an octave higher, "How do you know about black lace panties?"

Tony stood, his hands grasped her shoulders. Their chests touched and his breath quickened, "Why can't you believe I still love you?"

"Really? After an entire night of blackmailing me into being your companion, threatening my friend's company with disaster, and now learning that you ... that you," her body trembled, tears once again flowed, her voice broke and became a whisper, "raped me."

His tone was more of a plea, "No, Claire. Don't even suggest that." He lifted her chin and their eyes met. "You agreed to everything. You more than consented; you wanted it as much as I did." He released her chin and her face fell against his chest.

She remembered the day he came to the condominium. She'd been up half the night dreaming about *him*, about *them*. She remembered telling him good-bye, *and* she remembered wanting him. She'd convinced herself it didn't happen. After all, who in their right mind would consent? Maybe that was it, when it came to Tony, when had Claire been in her right mind?

Her knees weakened as his arms engulfed her. The sound of his heart echoed in her ear, and the familiar aroma of his cologne filled her subconscious. Claire melted into his embrace; she had no strength left from which to draw. He was right. She wanted him that day. Truthfully, even at this moment she enjoyed the familiar touch. There was something about the continual challenge that kept her senses electrified. The range of emotions he elicited and the depth of understanding they shared, created a bond. She'd fought it all night. Closing her eyes she conceded the current battle. There was no fight left within her.

Tony kissed the top of her head and scooped her up into his arms.

Her voice was soft, but determined, "No. Tony, not tonight."

"I'm putting you on the sofa. You're about to fall."

She nodded against the silk of his shirt. The softness against her cheek and the steady drum of his heart calmed the aching in her temples. Together they sat on a large white sofa facing the tall windows. With Tony's long legs stretched out onto a matching ottoman and his arm still tenderly around her shoulders, Claire removed her high heels and curled her legs onto the plush cushions. Molding to his side she accepted the comfort of his embrace. For the longest time they stayed like that, silent, watching the vista before them.

The towers of the Golden Gate Bridge glowed from the street level illumination. That same light reflected picturesquely onto the water below. The night was clear and the sky appeared a deep blue black. There were no visible stars, yet the moon shone low over the darkened land on the other side of the suspension bridge.

Claire felt his chest rise and fall with the inhale and exhale of a deep breath. His rich voice resonated through the silence, "Are you ready for me to call Eric?"

When he spoke the vibration tickled her cheek. She didn't lift her head. "What I really want are answers."

"What kind of answers."

"Truthful." It was what he'd asked of her in the past. Some of their deepest heart-to-heart discussions occurred in a similar pose, intimate times when they couldn't see one another's expressions. When Tony didn't respond, Claire pushed on, "You say you still love me. You're a very intelligent man. Surely you understand actions speak louder than words."

"You said, no."

"I don't mean sex. I mean actions, like tricking me tonight and setting me up for your attempted murder." His chest rose and fell again. She felt his warm breath blowing across her hair. "Tell me why."

"I told you. It was a loop hole."

Claire shook her head, "I don't understand your puzzles."

"You, too, are very intelligent. I don't believe you've spent the past year and a half without suspicions."

"I truly didn't understand, until I received that box of information."

"And what did you conclude from that?"

She contemplated her answer, as her fingers mindlessly played with the small buttons down the center of his silk shirt. Finally she spoke, "Well, it's hard to answer. You see at first I thought *you'd* sent it. So, I thought you were adding insult to injury, you know, rubbing salt in my wounds."

His embrace tightened, "And you thought I'd do that?"

"What else could I think? You set me up and left me." Her emotion ladened voice trailed into silence. Closing her eyes, she remembered him at the jail in Iowa and saw visions of her prison cell. Her body trembled as she fought to contain the sobs within her chest.

"There are few people in this world whom I've cared about." Tony's voice had a faraway quality. "Few people whose opinion of me I value." He lifted her chin and looked into her moist glistening emerald eyes. "I know you have reason to doubt me. Hell, *reasons*. But, Claire, you are one of those people." She closed her eyes, and he continued speaking, "I need you to understand. I made promises, and I keep my word."

She didn't know where the words came from. It wasn't something she'd been consciously thinking, yet they came anyway, "You made *me* a promise, on December eighteenth..."

He interrupted, each word coming slower than the one before, "Two thousand and ten, in our estate, to love you forever. I keep my word."

His lips found hers and passion glued them together. It wasn't fevered, like a wildfire roaring through the California Mountains. It was deep and painful; the kind of bond that yanks at your heart, until your only desire is to remove the pumping organ with your bare hands.

Abruptly, Claire stood. The room spun from her quick movement. Tony reached up and steadied her. She heard the honest concern in his voice.

"Are you all right? What happened?"

Claire picked up her shoes and smoothed her dress. "I'm fine. I want to go now."

He didn't argue, though his gaze never left hers. He reached inside his pocket and removed his phone. She waited while he spoke to Eric.

"Eric will have the car ready in the private garage in a few minutes." Her expression must have asked her unspoken question about the location. In the past, cars were always outside. Tony replied, "If we enter the car in the garage, we can avoid paparazzi."

"Oh, good idea. I need to use the restroom, and I'll be ready to leave." Claire turned to walk away and then turned back. "We? Tony I don't need you to ride with me." She paused, "I'd prefer you didn't."

"Then I will escort you to the car. If that is acceptable?"

Claire nodded and walked away; her dress swept the cool floor, while her shoes dangled from her fingertips.

Though considerably less tense than the earlier decent, the ride down the golden elevator was awkwardly quiet. Their reflections in the gold mirrored doors were much less polished than before. Claire's eyes displayed signs of her multiple emotional breaks. Her lids were no longer painted to perfection and her mascara was gone. While freshening up in the restroom she cleaned the dark circles from under her eyes. If they'd planned on exiting through the lobby, she would have needed to redo a great deal of her make-up.

Tony's jacket was gone and his tie hung loosely through his unbuttoned collar. His shirt contained clues to the location of her missing mascara. Multiple dark smudges stained the now wrinkled white silk.

When the elevator opened to the private parking area, Eric immediately opened the door to the back seat. Claire nodded to Tony's driver and sat down. She heard Tony's voice, "Ms. Claire would prefer to ride back to Palo Alto alone. Please call me when she is safely to her door."

"Yes, Mr. Rawlings."

Claire heard Tony say, "I can get this." She then saw Eric move around the front of the car to the driver's seat. Next, Tony's face appeared in the opening of the door. She looked into his dark tired eyes. In his outstretched hand was her cellphone. She took it and placed it upon her lap.

"Thank you, Tony. Good-bye."

"Don't forget the news release." His sturdy voice once again held his authoritative CEO tone, the one that gave orders and expected unquestioning obedience. She'd heard that tone for years, directed both at her and at others. Instinctively, the tone heightened her defenses, caused her neck to straighten, and eyes to blaze. She never liked that tone.

"How could I?"

"We will need to discuss it further."

"I'm discussed out." Later Claire would reflect on their candor in Eric's presence. Sometime ago Tony's intimate staff became part of the woodwork. Claire didn't mean to say they weren't people, but, on most occasions she'd forget they were even present.

"I can tell you're tired. Go get some sleep. We can continue our discussion tomorrow before I leave for Iowa."

Claire closed her eyes. The last thing she wanted was Tony in Palo Alto with Harry. "I have plans tomorrow. Call me after you're back to Iowa."

"This would be better discussed in person."

She exhaled, "Let me meet you somewhere."

His eyes returned her blaze. "Ten o'clock. Text me the location. Palo Alto is fine."

Claire nodded. She didn't want to meet, but the concession was better than having him at Amber's condominium. "Tomorrow." she replied.

"Tomorrow, Claire." He closed the door.

Eric eased the Mercedes C-Class out of the underground garage and around the front of the Saint Regis Hotel. Along the sidewalk, under the bright lights of the canopy, were multitudes of people. Some had cameras while others only wanted to see the attendees of the gala, as they made their way to the line of waiting cars. Claire reclined against the soft leather seat, thankful for Tony's discretion, and the tinted windows. No one seemed to notice the dark grey sedan as it made its way to US 101.

Once on the highway Claire turned on her iPhone. The time appeared, 12:13 A.M., where had the night gone? The screen filled with messages: 16 missed calls, 3 voice mails, and 11 text messages. She debated. Should she listen and read, or should she just call?

Sweeping the screen with her finger she sought her call log and tapped Harry's name. Her heart beat rapidly as the sound of ringing filled her ears. Glancing forward she saw Eric's eyes in the rearview mirror. She knew anything she said would be repeated to Tony as soon as she exited the car.

Harry's voice sounded strained, "Claire."

She took a deep breath, "I'm finally on my way home. I should be there in about an hour."

Silence... finally he asked, "Can you talk right now?"

Her heart broke hearing the emotion in his voice. "Not really."

"Is *he* with you?"

She imagined his clenched jaws and strained blue eyes. "No, I'm being driven by his driver."

"And he can hear you?" There seemed to be relief in the knowledge Claire wasn't currently with Tony.

"Yes."

"I'll tell Amber you're on your way. Will you please come here first?"

Although she was exhausted beyond belief and didn't want any more confrontations, Claire knew she owed this to Harry. "Yes, as soon as I can."

"Can we work this out?"

She thought about the news release. Had he seen it? Were there pictures of her and Tony on the internet? What did he think happened? A tear fell from her eye as she replied, "I hope so."

"I'll be waiting."

She nodded into the phone as the connection ended. He didn't say good-bye. She couldn't remember a time in the past when he hadn't said good-bye. Claire leaned her head against the seat and watched the lights of the highway. She thought about checking the messages and missed calls. Instead she watched the lights.

Power resides only where men believe it resides.
— George R.R. Martin, *A Clash of Kings*

Chapter 37

Sophia gripped tightly to Derek's elbow as they walked past the crowd of onlookers. The bright lights of the hotel's canopy illuminated the night. A gentleman wearing a black uniform opened the door of the Shedis-tics' limousine. Gracefully Sophia lowered herself into the spacious compartment and settled into the plush leather seat. Once Derek was beside her, the door closed and the car eased forward. It was the same car which brought them to the gala. Sophia whispered in Derek's ear, "I like some of the perks with your new job!"

Momentarily closing her eyes, Sophia enjoyed the silence of the limousine. Compared to the gala, the tranquility was heaven. With the multitudes of people talking, the music, people dancing, and the paparazzi outside the hotel, for the past three hours noise had been constant. Suddenly she remembered the presidential suite. Sophia struggled with her mixed emotions. She was angry she'd missed part of the gala, sad at disappointing her husband, and excited about the mystery buyer's newest offer.

Derek's familiar touch warmed her hand and brought her thoughts back to the man beside her. She leaned against his sturdy shoulder. Her cheek brushed the sleeve of his new tuxedo while her fingers played with the satin lapels.

"Are you tired?" Derek asked.

"I am, but I enjoyed the dancing very much."

"Me too." He kissed the top of her head.

Sophia exhaled; she'd already apologized a hundred times for missing the meal and speeches. Nevertheless, she felt the need to do it again, "Derek, I'm so sorry I missed part of the gala."

"You don't need to keep apologizing. I understand. It's your job."

Sophia nodded. She rarely thought of herself as employed. Yet, Derek was right; art was her *job*. She reasoned he understood job responsibilities and equating her temporary absence in that way made it easier for him to justify.

Derek continued, "I just wish you could have met Mr. Rawlings. Roger said he doesn't visit often."

"How was his speech?"

"Excellent. What surprised me was how much he knew about *my* projects. The ones I'm currently working on. He asked specific questions. I had this strange feeling I was being quizzed."

Sophia grinned, "Well if you were, my guess is you responded appropriately and received an A."

"I don't know. I hope you're right."

"Hilary sure likes to gossip." Sophia said, stifling a yawn.

"Yes, I noticed. She was in seventh heaven with Mr. Rawlings' ex-wife."

"I think she was disappointed the ex-Mrs. Rawlings didn't sit at our table. However, I think that poor woman is lucky. Hilary would've eaten her alive with her relentless questions."

Derek replied, "Well, I only said hello to Ms. Nichols, but she seemed nice enough."

Sophia sighed, leaning into her husband's arm. "I missed so much. According to Hilary, the whole thing will be all over the gossip pages, probably before we're home. I'm usually not into that kind of thing, but I may make an exception."

Derek lifted his arm and placed it around her shoulders. Sophia again lowered her head to soft material of his tuxedo. His words rang clear and true, "I think people deserve privacy, no matter who they are..."

Nodding in agreement, his voice faded away as she closed her eyes. Her mind filled with thoughts of the moving art exhibit. She hadn't had the chance to mention it to Derek. The gentle vibration of the car soothed her. Sophia decided she didn't have the energy to discuss it now. It could wait until morning.

The next thing Sophia knew, Derek was gently shaking her. His soft voice slowly infiltrated her dreams, "Hey, sleepy head, we're home." Her eyes fluttered; she saw her husband's sweet smile.

The Shedis-tics' driver opened the door and cool night air filled the limousine's cabin. Derek thanked the kind man, and they made their way up the walk to their condominium.

At such an early hour the street was quiet and a velvety dark sky concealed the stars above. Derek leaned down to his wife's ear. With her hair pinned back he had easy access. In a deep sexual voice he whispered, "Have I told you how beautiful you look tonight?"

Her gray eyes sparkled as she looked up to his loving expression. "Yes, but I like hearing it."

Stepping into the foyer of their new home, Derek turned from the closed door and traced his finger from Sophia's ear to the apex of her plunging neckline. The light touch sent chills throughout her body. Suddenly sleep didn't seem important. She was very glad she'd napped. With his hands caressing the gathered waist of her evening gown, his lips lingered near her ear and her breath quickened.

"I was wondering," his words contacted her skin in hot bursts of air, "if perhaps -- you need – help -- getting out -- of this -- amazing dress?"

Sophia nodded as the silk chiffon gown molded against his black tuxedo. Despite the layers of material she could feel his intention against her hip. "I do," she whispered.

Once within the confines of their new bedroom, the day's disappointments and satisfactions melted away. Derek no longer remembered the frustration of sitting alone as everyone else sat in pairs. Sophia forgot the stress of waiting for a mystery buyer who never arrived. Derek's excitement at speaking to Mr. Rawlings faded. Sophia's exhilaration at the new amazing offer waned. Their joy came in each other, the ecstasy of pleasing and being pleased.

When they finally settled into the soft satin sheets and gave into sleep, calm contentment relaxed them. They both glowed with the serenity associated with compete trust in the person by your side.

*****

Text message sent: May 25: 01:17 AM – To: Anthony Rawlings
MS NICHOLS JUST EXITED GRAY MERCEDES. SHE SAFELY ENTERED HER BUILDING.

Claire didn't need to knock on Harry's door. When she turned the corner in the hall, she saw him leaning against the jam in his open doorway. She sighed in relief at the sight of him; his casual appearance made her cheeks rise. She saw his customary faded jeans and black t-shirt had replaced the tailored tuxedo from earlier. His blonde hair now lay in waves, unrestrained by the earlier gel.

Prior to entering the building Claire gave Harry the opportunity to avoid this meeting. She sent him a text message. After all, it was almost one thirty in the morning. It said: *MINUTES AWAY. DO YOU STILL WANT ME TO COME BY?*

His short reply appeared almost immediately, *YES.*

It wasn't possible to read emotion or attitude in a text message. Nevertheless, as Claire neared and her eyes met Harry's, his unhappiness loomed omnipresent, surrounding them in a cloud of despondency. His hardened expression cooled her progress, almost stopping Claire in her tracks. Instead of summer skies, Claire saw ice in his light blue eyes. She searched for miniscule signs of acceptance. Instead she found frost. His lips pressed together in tight straight line.

As her glistening high heels propelled toward him, the scent of whisky filled her lungs.

"Well, if it isn't the belle of the ball?" he asked cynically.

He gestured for Claire to enter. Initially she planned on kissing him *hello.* Even with his bare feet and her shoes, he stood several inches taller. In order to contact his lips or cheek she'd need to stand on her tip-toes, or he'd need to bend. The furrowing of his brow, as she neared, weakened her resolve. Claire looked pleadingly into his cold eyes, as she passed, entering his foyer.

Throughout the entire car ride, Claire divided her time between reliving the evening's confrontations with Tony and imagining her reunion with Harry. It was at least thirty minutes into the trip before she realized she and Eric were driving in complete silence. It wasn't as if they'd ever chatted, but in the past their relationship was cordial. Nevertheless, when Claire recalled his *persuasive* behavior from earlier, she felt no desire for familiarity. Besides, her mind was too full of thoughts and memories; the outside world seemed temporarily irrelevant. It was when those thoughts incited tears that Claire asked Eric to turn on some music. Truly it was an attempt to conceal her crying from Tony's informant.

Interestingly, Claire noted Eric never asked her where she lived. Perhaps more thought provokingly, she never questioned his knowledge. Music was their only topic of conversation. Eric's only words during their entire drive were those in his reply, "Yes, ma'am, do you have a preference?"

She shook her head to the eyes in the rearview mirror and turned again to the side window. The interior of the Mercedes filled with the sounds of Doc Severinsen and Louis Armstrong. Claire doubted the moisture on her cheeks and occasional ragged breath escaped Eric's observation. Nevertheless, she took comfort in the fact the jazz music muffled her involuntary sounds.

In Claire's likely scenarios for their reunion, she imagined Harry sad, hurt, or more optimistically *relieved* that she'd made it back. She imagined his supportive embrace as she explained the events of the night. Not once during her hour long journey did she foresee anger. Why would she? In the three months she's known Harry, she'd never witnessed him upset.

Stepping into his entry, Claire saw and felt the aura of his fury. After dealing with Tony's anger, she was now face-to-face with an obviously irate Harrison Baldwin. Her imagined scenarios paled in comparison. This was worse than she'd predicted.

He displayed the source of his discontentment on the table near the sofa. Laid out for her viewing pleasure were pages of information, multiple internet stories complete with photos featuring her.

Shit, she thought, *this stupid gala only happened five hours ago. How did all of this get out already?*

Claire walked silently to the table and scanned the headlines:

Rawlings' Reunited, Anthony Rawlings Asks for Privacy,

Innocent? Anthony Rawlings' New Claim.

There were more but she just couldn't stomach to read each one. Each article contained pictures. There was one photo of them during the introductions, Tony's arm behind Claire's back. They were both smiling. Another picture was during the meal. He appeared to be smiling at something she was saying, *a friendly conversation*. There was another picture of them standing together talking to another couple. The other couple was not identified. Claire read the caption:

EVERYONE IS TALKING! The big news at this year's National Center for Learning Disabilities Fundraising Gala, in San Francisco, is not the millions of dollars raised for a worthy charity. It is the reunification of Anthony Rawlings and Claire Nichols. Their unexpected inseparability during the festivities begs the question: is this merger only personal or will it include Shedis-tics and SiJo Gaming?

She put down the page and another photo caught her eye. It was one of Tony kissing her hand. The look on her own face made Claire uneasy. The woman in the picture was staring into Tony's eyes with a blushed radiance. Claire remembered; it was right after his speech.

"Yeah, that one caught my attention, too." Harry's emotionally ladened voice returned Claire to present. "I've never seen that look in your eyes. You're acting skills are amazing!"

Tentatively she looked up to Harry. His blue eyes cried out with unspoken angst. She laid the papers back on the table and struggled with her own emotions. Claire needed to feel understood. Instead she felt challenged and fought the urge to launch her defenses. When she spoke, her voice came out flat. "Do you want to hear what happened? Or have you already made your own conclusions?"

He stared in silence. Finally, shrugging his shoulders, he walked to the kitchen, and returned with a partial bottle of Blue Label and an empty tumbler. Pouring himself two fingers of whiskey, he sat down in his recliner, gestured to the sofa and replied, "By all means, make yourself comfortable and fill me in. I can't wait to hear how this *isn't how it looks.*" She sat; he took a drink of the amber liquor and added, "It never is, is it?"

"I've never seen you drink, like this."

"I've had a shitty day. Would you like a glass? Or has your day been all parties and private drivers?"

She saw herself in the mirror at Tony's penthouse. How could he not see that she'd been crying? Claire could feel her swollen eyelids. Did he think she looked like someone who'd had a great day?

"No, thank you." She answered dryly. "Harry..." Claire began. Then she stopped. Her head pounded with her internal debate. Was she mad, sad, defensive or wounded? Abruptly she stood and walked toward the door. "I can't do this." The tears resumed. Claire honestly wondered how she had any tears left. "I can't do more confrontations."

Suddenly, Harry was out of the chair and standing before her. She looked up at his expression. Behind the anger she saw hurt.

She had been wrong; hurt was worse than anger. The smell of whiskey burned her nostrils as his breath blew warmly toward her face. Her stomach clenched, but undeterred she strived to maintain the eye contact.

She attempted to explain, "You deserve to hear everything. I didn't do anything without thinking of you and of Amber. I did it for you! But I can't talk to you about it when you're like this."

She reached for the door handle as his words cut into her heart, "Did you sleep with him?"

Claire wanted to be angry and then she remembered her dream -- that wasn't a dream. She settled for offended, "I can't believe you just asked me that. No. We didn't sleep together tonight."

He seized her shoulders and stared down into her red swollen eyes. "Why?"

"Because, he blackmailed me! With you. And with Amber and SiJo. *He* was responsible for the problems you had tonight at SiJo."

Harry interjected, "No, he wasn't. We found the problem, it was internal. I tried to call you; hell, I was on my way to San Francisco when Amber called me. She saw the news release, and after witnessing our *moment* in her living room, she thought I should know."

Claire's stomach twisted. She wanted desperately to make Harry understand, "But, he did know about it! He threatened to make your problems worse if I didn't concede. And he had that press release issued before I even spoke to him."

Harry released her shoulders and stared incredulously, "I can't fathom how you can continually believe he has that much power. Our computer engineers are top notch. Your ex-husband," Harry struggled with his words, walked to his glass, took another drink, and continued, "or should I say *the man you're working to reconcile with* can't just snap his fingers and bring down our firewall."

"Firewall! That was the word he used. He said it was incompetent. And I didn't answer your calls because he took my phone."

Harry rolled his eyes, "Our firewall is secure. Our people had everything cleared and secure by eight o'clock. I could have been there with you by nine." He took another drink and chuckled, "Now, that sure as hell would've been fun!"

"You had it cleared by *eight*?" she repeated dejectedly.

"Yes, why?"

Claire closed her eyes. She remembered Tony's words. He told her the problem was resolved by eight. It was clear, Harry wouldn't believe her. She made her way to his sofa, and collapsed. The night would never end. "I know I sound ridiculous, but don't you see? Now I'm trapped. He took my plans for public revelation and used them against me."

"How are you trapped?"

The words flowed with welcomed release as she tried to explain. She told him about being summoned to the penthouse, the revelation of their supposed reconciliation, the gala, and their confrontations back in the penthouse. Admittedly, her recollection contained a few omissions. Specifically, she excluded the kiss and the disclosure about her dream. She explained to Harry that the news release was a public disclosure. According to public knowledge, she and Tony were *now working on their relationship. Public failure wasn't an option.*

His shocked expression renewed her stream of tears. After waiting for him to comment, she finally whispered, "You and I aren't official. We haven't even told Amber about us."

"So you're ending this," he waved his arm around, "us... because of a news release?"

"No! I don't want *us* to end. For the time being, we'll just keep it the way it is, under wraps." She tried to smile, "You know, like they say: friends with benefits."

Harry contemplated her words. "So *I'm* friends with benefits and you're going to be out publically with *him*?"

"I have to talk to him about it. I'm supposed to meet with him tomorrow before he leaves for Iowa. But that's my current concession, public only-- no private."

"Well, obviously when it comes to Mr. Rawlings your negotiating skills are stellar! After your little meeting tomorrow you'll probably move back to Iowa. Hell, you won't even need to pack your things. I'm sure he'll gladly buy everything new." Harry's sarcasm saturated words stung. The pain endured from a physical slap would pass faster than the hurt she felt growing in her chest.

Claire stood and turned toward the door. Her dry tone resumed, "I'm going home." She paused, still facing the door and asked, "Unless Amber no longer wants me?"

"She didn't say that. It's your home. No one is kicking you out."

Claire exhaled in relief. After a few steps she turned back, "What about us?"

His blue eyes paled as his broad shoulders sagged, "What *us*? We aren't official. You see, I didn't realize I needed to inform the Associated Press. Maybe, you could devise a handbook?"

She squared her shoulders and stared at him through swollen lids, "*You* are letting him win." After a prolonged silence she lowered her eyes and turned toward the door.

As she stepped into the hall, she heard him say, "No, *you* forfeited.. "

Walking toward Amber's condominium, Claire grasped the magnitude of Tony's current victory. In one critical move he completed a double attack. He exposed a weakness at SiJo Gaming. Even if Harry didn't believe her, Claire knew Tony was responsible for their problems. If she hadn't done as Tony asked, those problems would have become worse. It also proved he could do it again.

Next, in a bold and critical move, he publically exposed their bogus relationship. While risking negative public opinion, he took control of the situation. He effectively removed any power Claire previously believed she possessed. And as a bonus for forcing her moves, Tony damaged her relationship with Harry.

As she opened the door to her dark, quiet condominium, Claire wondered about Amber. How would she behave toward Claire tomorrow? Was Tony systematically removing her external support, in essence whittling away her chess pieces?

Lying in her cool bed, Claire's tired mind tried to regroup. Did she still have any power? Could she fight him? The questions and answers processed slower and slower as she tried to debate her options. Sleep overtook her. There was no doubt. To paraphrase a book her mother used to read to her as a child, it *had been a terrible, horrible, very bad, and very long day.* She couldn't even rise triumphant over sleep.

You cannot make the same mistake twice.
Because the second time you make it, it is not a mistake,
it is a choice.
-- Unknown

Chapter 38

The incessant ringing of her alarm jolted Claire from her sound blissful sleep. Her mind reeled with *why* she'd set an alarm. Rarely did she need to wake at a definite time. Besides, she didn't get to bed until almost three the night before. As she sat up to turn off the noise, her stomach twisted, and she fell against the pillows. Closing her eyes she willed the rapid onset of nausea to pass.

The alarm continued to assault the silence of her normally peaceful room; nevertheless, Claire feared moving to stop the ringing. Perspiration beaded her entire body. Suddenly her light silk nightgown moistened and plastered against her clammy skin. Slowly she tried to remove the covers from her sweat drenched legs. Her focus increased with each movement. Claire prayed if she earnestly concentrated, she could keep the contents of her stomach in-check.

Exhaling repeatedly, she stared at the bright ceiling. Mindlessly she realized she'd forgotten to close the blinds the night before. Through the wrenching intestinal pain, her eyes squinted against the added assault of the unrestrained morning sunlight flooding her room.

Suddenly, Claire remembered the reason for an alarm. She was supposed to meet Tony at ten. Could her impending meeting be the origin of her current illness? Perhaps, even her body didn't want to see him again.

The knock at her door caused Claire to jump. The jolt intensified the nausea, propelling more beads of perspiration to adorn her skin. "Come in." She managed as her face contorted in pain, and she concentrated once again on breathing.

Claire didn't turn her head to see her roommate enter. Nevertheless, she heard the door open and Amber's footsteps approaching the alarm.

"What the heck? It's Saturday morning. Why do you have a damn alarm...?" As Amber turned from the now silenced clock, she beheld her roommate's ashened, perspiration drenched complexion, and her tone mellowed, "Claire, what's the matter?"

Claire didn't speak, but gently shook her head from side to side. The movement was too much. Gathering strength Claire reached for her blankets, threw them back, jumped from the bed, and ran to her bathroom.

It had been a long time since Claire Nichols had been physically sick. The last time she remembered vomiting was when she learned of Simon's death, which seemed ironic, now that she was living in Amber's home. The heaves came in waves.

Amber stood supportingly holding Claire's long auburn hair away from her face, as Claire rested her heavy head on trembling arms and waited for the next upsurge. When it came, Amber remained quiet while Claire's body racked with convulsions. Even after the contents of Claire's stomach were gone, the heaving continued.

In time, the lull between occurrences lengthened. Finally, her body stilled, leaving only a weakened and shivering Claire.

Amber helped her roommate sit on the closed lavatory lid, wetted a washcloth with cool water, handed it to Claire, and directed her to wipe her face. Next, Amber helped Claire to the sink where she repeatedly rinsed her mouth with water. After Amber helped Claire back to bed, Claire closed her eyes and prayed that whatever this was, it was over.

"It could be food poisoning." Amber offered, after Claire's color returned and her breathing normalized. "Maybe you ate something at the gala last night. I wonder if anyone else is having problems. "

Claire nodded her head. Her strength was returning, little by little. "You're probably right. With as bad as last night was, food poisoning would be a highlight." She grasped the hand of the woman now sitting on the side of her bed. "Amber, we need to talk about last night."

Amber visibly bristled and regrouped. "We do," her tone was comforting not harsh, as it had been when she entered the room about the alarm, "but, not right now. Can I get you something? Maybe some toast? It could help settle your stomach."

"What time is it?" Claire asked, panic threatening to disrupt her current non-vomiting state.

"It's a quarter 'til eight. Why did you have that alarm set anyway?" Amber asked as she replaced the cloth on Claire's forehead with a fresh cool compress.

"I have to meet someone at ten."

"Well, I think you're rescheduling."

Closing her eyes she assessed her current state and said, "I can't." She was truly feeling better. Hopefully the offending food was gone. She wondered, *could Tony possibly be sick too?* A weak smile floated across her face. She responded, "I'll take that toast, if you don't mind."

Amber stood, "Sure thing. Do you need anything else?"

"A glass of water?"

Amber squeezed Claire's hand and replied, "Coming right up."

Once she was gone, Claire reached for her phone. When she completed the task requiring movement successfully, Claire reassured herself she was definitely feeling better. If the toast stayed down, she was good to go.

Claire needed to text Tony a meeting location. She wondered *where she wanted to meet him.* Her first thought was *nowhere.* But, that was unacceptable. She remembered a cute cafe in Redwood Shores. It wasn't far, and it wasn't Palo Alto. She Googled the cafe and forwarded the information to Tony, with a text:

I MIGHT BE LATE. HAD AN ISSUE THIS MORNING. THINGS ARE IMPROVING.

Claire knew he wouldn't be happy about her possible tardiness. Nonetheless, remembering the overwhelming sickness, she decided Tony's darkening gaze ranked below projectile vomiting and keeping Amber's toast down on her current list of concerns.

Covering her now cold body with blankets, Claire felt her stomach growl. How could she possibly be hungry after what she'd just experienced?

AT 9:51 AM Claire eased her Honda Accord into the parking lot of the *Patio Cafe* in Redwood Shores. She wasn't late. Her reflection in the rearview mirror frowned back through the glass. Even the blush and lipstick didn't disguise her pallor. On the bright side, she'd kept Amber's toast down, plus a banana. And despite the paleness, she really did feel better.

During her drive to Redwood Shores, Claire fought the urge to turn around and miss this mandatory meeting. Once again, it was fear which propelled her. This time it wasn't the fear of physical punishment. It was the fear of Tony showing up at Amber's. He was right; Claire's concern for others was her weakness. While she dreaded seeing him, she wrestled with fleeting positive thoughts regarding her ex-husband.

She reasoned it was because of their charade last night. During the evening, as much as she hated to admit it, Claire actually relaxed and enjoyed Tony's company. Guiltily, she thought of the picture Harry printed: the one of Tony kissing her hand after his speech. The look on her face exposed her momentary ease and affability. No wonder Harry was upset.

Upset or not, Harry's words still hurt. They may have been brought on by a combination of jealously and liquor, but that didn't make them any less painful. How could Harry honestly feel Claire's affections could change so dramatically in six hours?

The thoughts of Harry turned to thoughts of Emily, John, and Courtney. Her magnitude of missed calls and messages on her iPhone were mostly from Harry, Amber, and Emily. There was also one from Meredith. Claire decided that should wait until after she spoke with Tony. Her *work* phone held missed calls and text messages from Courtney. Since she and Harry spoke last night and Amber wanted to wait, Claire spent a good part of her morning talking to Emily, John, and Courtney.

Apparently, Tony's press release hit the airways last night at approximately 7:30 PT. Emily and John saw it around 10:30 in Indiana. Courtney said Brent read it on his news feed about 9:30 in Iowa. Needless to say, they were all relieved to hear from her this morning. That being said, once the relief passed indignation reigned.

Courtney remained the most supportive. She understood Tony's persuasive nature and promised continued support. Claire appreciated Courtney's constant concern despite her stress regarding her son's upcoming wedding. Understandably, she and Brent weren't happy about Tony's claims of ensuring Claire's pardon. Claire assured Courtney she didn't believe him, and she'd never tell him, or anyone else, who her actual saviors were. Even Jane Allyson didn't know.

Claire repeated her honest account of the entire evening with everyone. There were a few omissions. Courtney was the only one to hear about the kiss. And no one learned about her dream – that wasn't. She wasn't ready to admit that reality to herself.

After everything she'd been through, Claire believed honesty, no matter how difficult to face, was her greatest ally. Remembering the isolation of Iowa and being Mrs. Anthony Rawlings, she vowed, despite the forced charade, she would not allow Tony to distance her closest supporters. Publically, she would do whatever was necessary to keep her loved ones safe, as well as their businesses. Privately, she promised never again to deceive the people around her.

Despite, or possibly because of, Claire's truthfulness, Emily was livid. A few times during their tense conversation Claire considered hanging-up on her sister. After all, Claire wasn't feeling top-notch after the whole food poisoning thing and having her sister's condescending and accusatory voice ringing loudly through her phone didn't aid her recovery.

Walking along the sidewalk toward the cafe, Claire lifted her face to the breeze. Wisps of loose hair blew around her face as she inhaled. The fresh air coming off a small inlet from San Francisco Bay was cool. Her blue jeans and blouse were perfect for the late spring air. Yes, if she were in Indiana or Iowa this late in May it would be much warmer. Nonetheless, she was slowly acclimating to west coast weather.

Parked three cars down, Claire saw a gray sedan with a man inside reading a paper. She hadn't spoken to Phil since San Diego. Now seeing him she decided with Tony near, this wasn't a good time to chat.

Phillip Roach was another of Tony's intrusions. Somehow over the past three months, she'd come to accept him. Was she being *too compliant*, as Emily said? Claire didn't believe so. She truthfully felt she was resisting Tony's control much better than she ever had. Not staying with him last night and not allowing him to visit the condominium this morning were two examples of her noncompliance. Claire contemplated her strength, or lack of, as she stepped into the busy restaurant.

The large glass doors led directly to a counter. The Saturday morning crowd filled the bustling cafe, with people waiting to order food.

The hum of voices filled her ears as the various aromas filled her lungs. She tried desperately to ignore the returning nausea as she made her way to a tall two person table near the window. A ceiling fan above the table provided a continual cool breeze, calming her queasiness. Moments later, she glanced toward the doors and saw Tony walking casually toward her.

Involuntarily she smiled. He looked so laidback and informal, in jeans and a button down shirt. She noticed how his crisp shirt was pressed and untucked. His hair was perfect, and his face freshly shaven. Her eyes went back to the jeans. Claire always liked Tony's long legs in blue jeans. When his dark eyes met hers, her breathing stopped. She immediately judged his expression. His cheeks rose and a small smile came to his lips. Claire exhaled with a sigh of relief. She didn't want more confrontations. If this charade were to proceed, she wanted to learn the specifics and go on with her life.

Unexpectedly, he bent down and kissed her cheek before taking the seat across from her. Claire's eyebrows rose suspiciously as she eyed the man across the table. He responded with a mischievous grin and crooned, "Good morning, Claire. It is nice to see you aren't late."

His pleasant greeting eased her tightly strung nerves, she chuckled, "Yes, you see there was this man I used to know. He was a real stickler for punctuality."

"Really? It seems as though he must have been a good influence. His persistence appears to have paid off." Tony's brown eyes glittered, reflecting the sunlight through the windows.

"I'm not sure about his influence, and *insistence* would better describe it. But since you mention it, persistence is something he's definitely mastered."

"Hmm, sounds like my kind of man. I'd like to meet him."

Claire shook her head good-naturedly, "No, I don't think you'd like him."

Tony's eyes opened wider, "You don't?"

"No, he has real control issues. You two would probably clash."

"Because... you think *I* have control issues?" This time Tony's eyebrows rose.

Claire leaned forward, as if telling a secret. Her eyes sparkled with the lightheartedness of their conversation. "I hate to be the one to break it to you... but yes, you do."

Tony's laughter filled her ears. Finally he asked, "Don't you want something to eat?"

"No, not really, I ate earlier."

"I'll get us some coffee then."

Although she usually loved coffee, the idea didn't sound good on her recently emptied stomach. "Could you get me an iced tea instead?"

Tony eyed her skeptically, "Sure, unsweetened, correct?"

Claire nodded.

When Tony returned with their drinks they began to discuss this public reconciliation. Although the cafe bustled with patrons, their voices remained low and private. "Claire, I'm pleasantly surprised by your accepting attitude this morning."

She sipped her tea, "Don't mistake it for pleasure. I don't like being bullied into this situation. However, I see signs of compromise. It gives me hope."

"Compromise?"

"In your own way, you're trying to be accommodating. If you weren't you would've tried to stop me from leaving last night, or you would've insisted on riding with me. I see that."

Tony nodded, considering her words. Then he asked, "Hope, what do you hope for?"

"That this won't last long. That we can remain friends and be honest with the world."

As she spoke, clouds darkened his gaze. "I see," he took a drink of his coffee. "I hope... you change your mind."

"See what I mean. That's progress. I honestly don't intend to change my mind. However, I will admit, when you aren't being a controlling ass who's threatening my friends or my friends' company," she smiled coyly, "you can be charming."

"Thank you, my dear." He snorted, obviously shocked by her candor, and replied, "When you are being bold and cheeky, the spark in your gorgeous green eyes makes my initial irritation fade. At that point, I see you for what you truly are."

"Oh really, what am I?"

"Sexy as hell," he leaned closer. His words slowing to a sultry tenor, "And when you are being reticent and genteel, I find you irresistible."

She felt her insides quicken and her cheeks blush, just like in the picture. "Well, then I guess I can behave in any manner without fear of consequences."

"As long as you are doing it with me, my affection will prevail."

Claire shivered at the possible implications of his words. Playfulness left her tone, "Tony, I don't intend to be with you all the time. I'm not moving back to Iowa."

"I'm a busy man, Claire; I can't be flying to California every other day."

"Then we won't be seeing each other every other day. By the way, when do you need to be back?"

Dryly he said, "I have my own plane. I don't have a schedule to maintain."

"I'm aware of your plane. I thought you might have meetings or a date or something."

The clouds returned, "I won't be having any *dates* with anyone except you. That was the point of the news release." His voice lowered as his tone hardened, "And neither will you."

She sat straighter, "This is what we need to discuss. Define *date*."

His hesitant expression glared -- his gaze loomed shades darker than moments before. "A date is the going out in public of a man and a woman." He scanned the cafe. "I suppose it could be a man and a man or a woman and a woman; we are in California."

"Well, that happens in Iowa also. But my point is two people can go out in public and be friends, not dating."

"I would prefer you didn't." Before she could choose the words to her reply, he rephrased, "It would not be publically acceptable, so the answer is *no.*"

Trying to keep her voice low, "I'm telling you, not asking your permission."

"This is not debatable."

"Then what is?" She leaned across the table as indignation infiltrated her words, "Why are we even here, discussing anything at all? If it is all predetermined, just lay out the ground rules." She tried to keep her voice low and restrain her emotions. "That's the way you operate. Things don't change!" Moisture stung her eyes as tears threatened her facade of strength. She stared and waited for the explosion. Claire knew it wouldn't be overt. Their location was too public, perhaps a whispered clandestine threat.

Although his eyes remained dark, the tips of Tony's lips moved upward. He reached out and held the hands that lay on the table in front of him. "Yes, sexy as hell."

Claire removed her hands, sat back against the chair, and pressed her lips together.

His tone lightened with a change of subject, "You know, I don't think the cooler weather is good for you. You look pale. You need sun."

"Thanks, I quite like the west coast."

Tony watched, waiting for more outbursts. Finally he said, "I concede. Some things are debatable. I would make you move to Iowa if I could. Don't get me wrong. It isn't that I am incapable. It is that I want you there of your own free will. So that move is debatable."

"Not debatable -- I'm not going."

"Now you see. We each have issues where we don't want to budge. Let's discuss public events."

Claire settled back and listened. Tony talked about the different public events and business trips he had scheduled in the near future. He offered transportation, private accommodations, and money to purchase appropriate attire. He also discussed acceptable behaviors while separated. In many ways it reminded Claire of sitting in his office, listening to the ground rules of living in his house. The memories made her feel uneasy. Slowly she felt her pulse increase and the temperature of the room increase. The breeze from the fan remained but was no longer refreshing.

It was then she noticed the food behind her. The man must have had an entire side of pork. His plate overflowed with bacon. The aroma filled the space around their table.

Although Tony was still talking and Claire had been attentively nodding, she abruptly stood. "Tony, I can't do this. I need to leave."

His shock quickly morphed to irritation, "What?"

"No, not this – *us*. This – *here*. I need to go outside." With that she grabbed her purse and walked briskly toward the door -- away from the mound of pork. Each step eased her discomfort. Nonetheless, it wasn't until she stepped into the sunshine and felt the wind once again on her face that she could truly inhale.

Only steps behind her, Tony reached for her arm and spun her toward him. His expression changed immediately. The rage disappeared into a mixture of displeasure and concern. "What the hell was that?"

"I don't know. I think I must have gotten food poisoning last night. How have you been feeling?"

"I feel fine. Is that what this just was, you not feeling well?"

"Yes, it was that bacon. It smelled horrid!"

Tony laughed. "I thought you liked bacon. Catherine used to have it for you all the time."

Feeling better, Claire smiled, "I did. I do, I think. But I was ill this morning. That's why I thought I might be late."

Concern won the race on Tony's rollercoaster of emotions. "You were ill? I could have come to you."

Her eyes narrowed, "No. I don't want you at Amber's. It just isn't right."

"I've taken you to my *friends*. If that is truly your definition of Amber and her brother, what is the problem?"

There were so many things wrong. First *his friends* reminded Claire of Brent and Courtney, people whom, just this morning, she'd spent over a half hour talking with on the phone. Next, she thought of Tony with Simon's fiancée. And lastly, Harry. At this moment she wasn't sure how to define him. But having Harry and Tony together wouldn't be good, no matter his definition.

"Are we done?" Claire asked.

"There are a few more things to discuss. How do you feel?"

"Better, the fresh air helps."

"I saw a park not far away. Would you like to walk?"

Claire nodded. Truthfully she wanted to go home, but walking was better than staying in that cafe. Tony gently grasped her hand. Conceding the loss of her appendage, their fingers intertwined. The casual contact radiated familiar warmth through her body. They began walking toward Bridge Parkway. Across the small inlet they entered a haven of nature. Trees surrounded a large grassy plane with picnic tables and benches overlooking a lagoon. Scattered about were signs indicating a summer concert season. Everything pointed to warmer weather and blue skies for the future.

While they talked about their agreement, they also chatted -- not about anything in particular, just things. Surprisingly, it felt good and easy. As long as the conversation avoided Harry, Amber, and her incarceration, Claire found herself speaking without weighing each word. They laughed at children on the playground equipment and watched a man set-up a camp to fish in the lagoon.

Claire tried to remember the last time she'd spent such a normal day with her ex-husband. It had been a long time. When Tony looked at his watch and saw that it was after two, he asked Claire if she were up to eating lunch.

"I think I can handle it, as long as there's no bacon," she said with a smile.

They walked back to Tony's car and drove to a small diner with outside seating. When the waiter brought the menus, Claire perfunctorily left hers lying on the table. She couldn't contain her surprise when Tony glanced her way and said, "Since you haven't been feeling well, you'd better look and see what sounds appetizing." It was the first time she'd *ever* ordered her own meal while with him. Maybe things do change?

By the time he took her back to her car, they'd made some compromises and found some common ground. In two weeks she would join him in Chicago for meetings and dinners with investors.

Standing next to Claire's car, Tony asked, "May I kiss you good-bye?"

"Is it a requirement of the news release and mandatory to keep my friends safe?"

"No," he leaned nearer, "it is because I would really like to kiss you."

She found herself on the precipice of a very slippery slope. Her figurative footing was difficult to maintain. While her mind debated, her body leaned into his chest, and her face tipped upward. His strong arms encased her, his hands found their way to the nape of her neck, and his fingers entangled her hair. They may have been in a parking lot, or perhaps the moon. At that moment, neither one knew. The rest of the world disappeared.

Driving toward Palo Alto, she couldn't remember who finally pulled away from the embrace. Whoever it was, the other conceded. She did remember the sensual allure emanating from his eyes. Even in the car, the image reddened her cheeks.

Oh shit! What have I done? Claire asked herself as she contemplated her next assignment.

Perseverance is not a long race;
it is many short races one after another.
- Walter Elliott

Chapter 39

Text message sent: May 25: 4:41PM – To: Anthony Rawlings
MS NICHOLS RETURNED SAFTLY TO HER PARKING GARAGE. MS MCCOY NOT HOME. NO SIGN OF ANYONE ELSE
Phil waited for a response. Either he would spend the evening monitoring Claire Nichols, watching the front door and parking garage, or he'd be done for the night. After the late night, last night, watching Harrison Baldwin drive the 101 toward San Francisco and turn around and go back to Palo Alto, he hoped this night was done. After so much time on Mr. Rawlings' payroll, could Phillip Roach be getting soft?

*****

After her afternoon with Tony, Claire returned to a quiet condominium. She wandered from room to room looking for Amber; instead she found a note on the kitchen counter:

I'm running errands – will be back soon.
I'm having dinner with Keaton. Maybe we can talk
tomorrow? Hope you're feeling better. There is a
message on the house voice mail for you – Amber

It gave Claire hope. Optimistically they would all work this out. She still didn't know what to think about Harry. While out with Tony, Claire checked her phone a couple of times -- not one call or text message from Harry. Of course, he knew where she was and who she was with.

Thinking about Amber on a date with Keaton made Claire happy. Amber may argue the term *date*, but Claire recently listened to the *Rawlings Dictionary*. According to that very reliable source, a date was the term used to define the act of two people going out into public together. She shook her head and rolled her eyes. It was so ridiculous. Somehow she would need to modify his definition.

Claire picked up the telephone receiver in the kitchen. With cellphones, they rarely used this telephone. Yet, Amber maintained SiJo needed a way to reach her, if something happened to her cellphone. Pushing the appropriate buttons Claire waited for the message. *Who would call me on this number?* Claire wondered.

The voice came through the receiver: "You have one saved message - - saved message."

"Claire Nichols. Do I have the right number? I remembered something else. Call me back: 442-555-7732."

Claire listened to the message a second time. The man's voice sounded vaguely familiar, but she wasn't sure who or why? It was probably a reporter. Heaven knows she'd been making the news lately. Whoever it was would call back, if whatever he remembered was truly that important.

It was only a little after five, but with her stomach full of what *she ordered* (Claire smiled while adding that last part to her thought), she was tired. These past had two days worn her out and down. The idea of a warm bath and an early night sounded heavenly. Honestly, she thought about calling, texting, or going over to Harry's, but she didn't have the strength for another confrontation.

Walking toward her room, Claire thought about her afternoon with Tony. She was incredibly thankful it didn't include overt arguing. Her emotions have been working overtime and despite their blackmailing topic of conversation, the calm afternoon was surprisingly therapeutic.

As she opened the door and tapped the switch illuminating her bedroom, Claire stared in shock. The sweet aroma permeated her senses. On her dresser, desk, and bedside stand were large bouquets of long stemmed red roses. Tears fill her eyes as she made her way to a card propped against one of the glittering vases with *Claire* penned on the outside of the small envelope.

Gingerly opening the flap, Claire removed the small rectangle piece of card stock. Relief filled her consciousness and her tired muscles relaxed as she read the words:

If you're reading this, you didn't move away... and I'm a jerk.
Now you know why I don't drink—much.
It makes me an ass! I hope we can talk again – soon...
I promise to be more open. Can you forgive me? Harry

She immediately reached for her iPhone and sent the text: THANK YOU FOR THE BEAUTIFUL FLOWERS! EXCESSIVE, BUT I LOVE THEM. YES, I CAN FORGIVE... IF YOU CAN?   WE CAN TALK TOMORROW? I'M TIRED AND GOING TO BED AFTER A BATH. TOMORROW?

Claire inhaled the jasmine from the dissolved bath salts, as her shoulders submerged under the warm water. Laying her head against the incline of the tub she closed her eyes and let her mind wander. There was too much to process, too many things to think about. From the distance of her room, she heard the sound indicating a received text message. The warmth enveloped her as the salts moisturized her skin. Claire slipped away to the serenity of sleep.

She recognized the room. With each breath the familiar stagnant air filled her lungs. As her eyes adjusted to the pale light, she saw the dimples on the painted cinderblock walls. Claire wrapped the thin blanket tighter, trying to fend off the chill permeating deep into her soul. It wasn't from the controlled temperature of the small cell, but from the solitude. When she stared up she saw all four corners of the small room without turning her head. Only the grid of an air vent disturbed the monotony of the dirty white ceiling. Each wall looked the same -- same color, same height and same length. Pulling her from the intolerable seclusion, the buzzer sounded. Tentatively she moved toward the door with the small window. People could only be seen through the small glass opening if they stood directly on the other side. Her heart beat quickened. Could it be a package or a visitor... someone to talk to? Lifting herself to her tip toes she peered through the pane...Her vision filled with his eyes, only his dark penetrating eyes....

Claire woke with a start. Her heart beat rapidly as her quick movement caused tepid water to splash about the tub onto the tile floor. She must have fallen asleep. Her eyes scanned the luxurious tile, plush towels, and dimmed sconces framing the mirror. The view blurred as tears filled her eyes. Did the tears come from her dream or her relief? She momentarily submerged her face under the now cool water. Lifting her face above the water the aroma of jasmine lingered, reinforcing her current location. She inhaled deeply as her muscles relaxed. She wasn't in prison; she wasn't alone. It was only a nightmare.

The fog dissipated both from the Palo Alto sky and from the sleeping recesses of her mind. Sunshine facilitated the process, as Claire's eyes adjusted to the morning light. She remembered the food poisoning of the day before and evaluated her current condition. The only possible ailment she could identify was hunger. Rolling tentatively toward the clock her eyes widened at the number before her: 9:53.

When Claire checked her phones she found the response from Harry. *I'M GLAD YOU'RE HOME. GET SOME REST. WE'LL TALK TOMORROW.* It made her both happy and sad. She wanted them to work it out. But she dreaded telling him about her public arrangement with Tony.

On her other phone she had a text from Courtney. It was received at 9:17 and said: *FYI -- TONY IS HERE. HE WANTS TO TALK TO US*

ABOUT YOU! I SLIPPED AWAY TO TELL YOU. I WILL TEXT WHEN HE'S GONE. Claire closed her eyes and shook her head, poor Courtney and Brent. Caleb's wedding is in less than a week away and they have Tony on their doorstep. Narcissistic as ever, Claire was sure Tony believed his issues were more important than anything else in their lives. Curiosity grew as Claire contemplated the conversation occurring 2,000 miles away.

Amber entered the kitchen as Claire finished the final stages of preparing her breakfast feast. She had two fried eggs, two pieces of toast, a banana, and a cup of yogurt. Amber's voice sounded light as she asked, "Did you forget how to make coffee?"

Claire grinned. It wasn't that long ago she didn't know how to work the strange little machine. "No, I'm in more of an orange juice mood."

"Harry told me about your talk the other night."

"Well, it wasn't much of a talk."

"Do you really think Anthony is responsible for our problems?"

Claire nodded, her mouth full of banana. Once she'd swallowed she replied, "I do. I honestly don't think it can be proven, unless there is someone working for him, and you can torture a confession out of them."

Having Claire's ravenous hunger appeased and Amber's attitude composed created the perfect environment for them to calmly discuss the gala and recent events. Claire told Amber about her agreement with Tony. How she needed to appear publically with him, and how she was worried about telling Harry. Amber agreed; Harry wouldn't be pleased.

Although upsetting, the thought didn't deter Claire's appetite. Amber laughed as Claire used her toast to sweep the remnants of egg from her plate.

"I only ate lunch yesterday. I'm trying to catch up." Claire responded with a shrug.

Before they finished, the front door opened and they heard Harry's footsteps approaching the kitchen.

"That's my cue to sneak back to my room. You two need some privacy," Amber whispered.

By the time Harry entered the kitchen his sister was gone. Claire looked up from her empty plate and sheepishly said, "Hi, thanks for the flowers."

*****

Sophia watched Derek as he read the newspaper and sipped his coffee. Things were perfect after the gala... she wasn't ready to mention the possible tour. Then yesterday, the time never seemed right. Could it be because she didn't want to do it? It was a fantastic offer... why wouldn't she want to tour the country, all expenses paid. As Sophia watched her husband, she knew the answer... because she wanted to be with him!

The ringing of her cell phone brought Sophia back to reality. The screen said: *Mom*. Sophia frowned. Derek looked up from the paper, "Who is it? Why do you look worried?"

"My Mom, I just talked to her yesterday." With that Sophia swiped the screen. "Hi Mom, what's up?"

When Sophia disconnected the line she turned to Derek's furrowed brow and concerned expression. He'd heard Sophia's end of the conversation, and now he wanted to know more.

"Is it your dad again?"

Sophia nodded, "Yes. Mom's really worried. She said yesterday he went to the store, someplace he'd been a million times. He didn't come home for three hours. She kept trying to reach him on his cell. Finally when he came home, he didn't have the groceries and couldn't remember why he'd been out or where he'd been."

"She needs to get him some help."

"He's stubborn," Sophia said with a sigh. "I'm worried. I think part of it is financial. Dad doesn't want to spend any money on himself."

"Then help them. They sure helped you."

"He won't accept it. But Mom might. Maybe I should go for a visit?"

Derek kissed Sophia's forehead. "I need to leave for that ten day China trip next week. Maybe you could go then."

She took a drink of coffee. "I've also been thinking about the studio in Provincetown. You know, since I have the money from those paintings, I was thinking about hiring someone to keep that studio open, while we're out here. I hate for it to sit closed during peak tourist season."

Derek agreed. The money changed so many things, giving Sophia the ability to do things she'd always wanted.

"I've been meaning to tell you about an offer I received the other night," Sophia said.

Derek looked up again from the newspaper. "What kind of offer?"

"Well, that mysterious buyer, the one who never showed up..."

Derek listened patiently as Sophia described the tour, the cities, the exposure, and the time apart. He wanted to tell her no. However, he didn't want to stop her dream. "That sounds amazing. What do you think about it?"

"I think it is amazing and I'm going to tell Mr. George *no*."

Derek's relief was visible. "Why?"

Sophia put her arms around her husband's neck. Their eyes met soft brown to light gray. She kissed his tender lips. "Do you think I should do it?"

"I want you to do whatever is best for you."

"I want to be with you. And it's not just me, it's *us*. I'm thrilled I've sold these paintings. I love the idea of having studios on each coast. But my mom needs help, and I want to be with you. There are too many things going on for me to travel around the country for two years."

He pulled her close. "Good, I don't want to ever stop your dreams."

"You and me, *we* are my dreams. The rest is just frosting on the cake."

Derek snickered, "You like frosting."

"I do. But too much makes me sick."

"Then by all means, Mrs. Burke, we don't want you feeling ill."

*****

Harry listened again as Claire explained the gala. This time he didn't judge. He didn't interrupt or doubt Claire's theories. They talked about her agreement. Finally Harry asked, "How long is this supposed to go on?"

"I don't know for sure. He gave me dates reaching into July."

His lips started to move, and then he pressed them together.

"The first one is in two weeks, in Chicago. I'll have my own accommodations."

"Really Claire, what's the point?"

"Appearances -- it is all about appearances and manipulation."

"Do you think it will ever end?"

"I don't know. Maybe if we learn something about his past. I need something to hold over him. I'm going to keep talking with Meredith. She's been in contact with some publisher. They no longer want to do a series of articles, but a book."

"Why are you still meeting if this book will never get published?"

"I still have the agreement. If anything happens to me or someone I care about, the book will be published."

"So you're both threatening each other?"

Claire nodded and shrugged, "Yes, it's a great basis for a relationship, don't you think?"

Harry placed his hand over Claire's. "No, it seems pretty messed up to me. I just want a simple honest relationship."

Claire sighed, "That would be wonderful."

He bent down, their noses nearly touched. "I'll accept friends with benefits, for now. Not forever." His lips brushed hers.

Claire's body relaxed and her arms found their way around his neck. "I'll find a way out of this, I will."

Amber joined them as they talked about SiJo. "I felt the tension ease; do you mind if I join you two?"

"Well, I don't know. It is your place." Claire said with a grin. She felt triumphant. Tony tried to take this comraderie away from her. He failed. It was a small victory, the saving of a pawn. But each victorious battle, no matter how small, helped win the war.

"Oh, did you listen to that message?" Amber asked Claire.

"Yes, twice. I have no idea who it is -- probably a reporter or something."

"What are you talking about?" Harry asked.

Claire told him about the message on the house phone. He asked if it'd been erased. When Claire told him no; he listened to the voice mail.

Claire noticed his expression cloud as he replayed the message and wrote down the number.

"Let me do some checking. I don't like people calling this number. It's unlisted."

After Harry left, Amber mentioned Claire's flowers. "You were quite the popular lady yesterday."

"It was very nice of your brother."

"He brought one of the vases. The other two came in separate deliveries. Neither had a card, but I did find one thing strange; the delivery guy said one of the bouquets was for Claire Rawls."

Claire felt the blood drain from her face, "Why didn't you say anything about that before?"

Amber stared at Claire, "I figured it was some code between you and your ex. I didn't want to upset Harry, more."

"I don't think it is – a code. He doesn't like that I even know about his past. He isn't going to flaunt it in a delivery. I'll ask. Honestly I'd feel better if they were from him. Otherwise, it creeps me out."

Her iPhone had two missed calls from Tony, and her work phone had a text message from Courtney, received an hour earlier: *HE JUST LEFT. SAID HE WANTS YOU TO BE HIS PLUS 1 AT THE WEDDING! CALL ME!!!*.

If we had no winter, the spring would not be so pleasant;
if we did not sometimes taste adversity, prosperity
would not be so welcome.
- Anne Bradstreet

Chapter 40

-Late 1988-

Nathaniel held Marie's hands and looked at his beautiful young wife. Her resolve was stronger than that of a woman two or three times her age. At twenty-six she'd experienced more heartbreak and disappointment than most endure in a lifetime.

"I'm doing fine. Nathaniel, please don't worry about me. You are going to be out of this place in only nine more months. Please use your energy taking care of yourself."

"You shouldn't be tied to an old man in a prison cell. You should be enjoying everything life has to offer."

Marie's smile took his breath away. Her gray eyes lit up the dull visitor's room. Concentrating on her, he could forget their surroundings. Her vitality sustained him. Nathaniel didn't know if he could make it without her weekly visits. Mentally he'd replay them word for word in his head for days. The way her hair glistened under the florescent lights, the scent of her perfume, and the feel of her skin ran a continual loop through his memory. Then on about Wednesday, two days before her return, his memories would give way to anticipation. Sometimes he tried to guess what color she'd wear or how she'd fix her hair. He liked her dark blonde hair loose and long, hanging down her slender back. But then again, he liked it up exposing her neck and collar bone.

In so many ways Marie reminded him of Sharron when they were young. Sharron's energy and wit continually enthralled him. Nathaniel knew he was the luckiest man alive to experience two such wonderful women. He wished Marie knew Sharron when she was healthier. He believed they would have been friends. His late wife had a knack for calming him when the world triggered fury. At this moment Marie was doing the same thing. Her steel eyes danced with life while her steady voice reassured.

"You, sir, are not getting rid of me that easily." She gently removed one of her hands from his hold and placed it on top of his. "I love you, and I plan on spending much more time with you. If the next nine months are in this room at an hour a week, then so be it. But after that Mr. Rawls, I get you all to myself."

"But Marie, you deserve..."

She interrupted, "I think you've made me realize I deserve to be loved. And you are the man to do it."

Nathaniel grinned in spite of himself. Marie's radiating beauty left him speechless. It wasn't just the external attributes of Catherine Marie Rawls, but her spirit and kindness. The only time he saw that spirit change was with the mention of his son. Nevertheless, the subject needed to be breached. She was his only source of information. Anton visited occasionally. However, now in graduate school and working, Anton's time was limited.

The idea of Anton supporting himself through graduate school infuriated Nathaniel. This entire mess was ridiculous. The damn FBI should have better things to do, real criminals to find, instead of attacking a man for living the American dream. Truthfully, Nathaniel still had money, a good amount of money. However, accessing it and bringing it back to the United States was too risky.

Since the court seized his home, company, and other assets, he was thankful he'd provided Marie with a comfortable investment portfolio. If they'd been married when he was convicted, she would've lost that too. But, because they weren't, it remained hers.

When he got out of this hell hole, Nathaniel intended to give Marie a real wedding, maybe somewhere on a beach. The justice of the peace, in this visitor's room with Anton as witness, was legal and memorable. However, it wasn't the kind of memory Nathaniel wanted Marie to have of her wedding. If she'd said yes the first twenty-five times he asked, their wedding would have been nicer. Then again, she wouldn't have the financial resolve. It wasn't like she had a fortune, but she could live comfortably.

Neither Samuel nor Amanda visited Nathaniel, ever. After Anton informed Nathaniel of Samuel's testimony, Nathaniel honestly didn't care if he ever laid eyes on his son again. What upset Nathaniel was his son and daughter-in-law's constant intrusion into Marie's life. Since Samuel was part owner and a top executive at Rawls Corporation, his assets too were seized. Despite Samuel's cooperation, he and Amanda were left with nothing. Somehow in Samuel's mind, he felt he deserved what Marie now claimed as hers.

Nathaniel wondered what Samuel would do if he knew about the Switzerland investments. That information was only shared by Nathaniel, his wife, and his grandson. The monies needed to be routinely moved.

The relocation of his investments kept curious individuals from discovering the actual administrator. He didn't physically move the money, but at least twice a year he took a trip to Geneva and reallocated the funds. Throughout the years his nest egg grew. With his inability to travel, Anton was now his proxy.

Nathaniel encouraged Anton's communication with his parents. Family had always been important. Just because he couldn't stand the sight of his son, it didn't mean Anton should lose everyone. When Nathaniel spoke to his grandson, he could tell Anton's respect for his father had lessened. And despite his current location, Nathaniel felt Anton's growing respect for him. Nathaniel believed his investments were in safe hands with his grandson. Anton would never tell his father and disappoint his grandfather.

Nathaniel dreamt night and day of leaving the minimum security prison. That being said, Nathaniel Rawls wasn't a dreamer. He fought in WWII, clawed his way up the textile business, and worked day and night to provide excessively for his family. He understood the possibility he may not walk out of this facility.

There were threats. There were people who wanted what was rumored to be Nathaniel's. Others believed by hurting Nathaniel Rawls, they'd learn the truth about his supposed hidden millions.

Therefore, not only did he trust Anton with the knowledge regarding his monies, Nathaniel also trusted Anton with watching over Marie and her daughter. Anton's resources were limited. Yet, if something happened to Nathaniel, his resources would grow exponentially. The money in Switzerland would be jointly owned by both Marie and Anton.

When Anton brought Nathaniel the information on Sherman Nichols, AKA Cole Mathews, and Jonathon Burke, Nathaniel knew he could trust his grandson with the name and location of Marie's child. She was safe and living with a loving set of parents. Nathaniel hoped one day Marie would want to know more. From what he'd learned, Marie should be proud of the young girl. Though only eight, she appeared the perfect mixture of obedience and precociousness. Looking at her biological mother, why wouldn't she be? They even had the same eyes.

"Have you had any recent problems with Samuel or Amanda?"

Marie lowered her lids momentarily and exhaled. Although, obviously not her favorite subject, Marie answered, "I haven't heard from them this week. I did speak to Anton about Samuel's appeal to have our marriage voided."

"That is ridiculous. He can't do that. Our union is legal."

"Samuel has appealed to the State of New York to find our marriage void, based on your mental capacity."

Their hands disconnected. Nathaniel abruptly stood. His metal chair groaned with the sudden movement screeching across the linoleum floor. "My mental capacity!" His face reddened with exasperation. "My mental capacity -- he's saying I'm crazy?"

Marie's lips tightened. She didn't like seeing Nathaniel this upset. He had other concerns. Nevertheless, she relished his like-mindedness

317

regarding Samuel. She'd endured too many *congenial* family gatherings. When Nathaniel got out of this prison, they'd be able to live without the daily intrusion of her *son-in-law*. "He claims your business actions confirm previous mental instability. And the stress from the trial and now your incarceration have worked together to diminish your ability to make sound decisions."

"Then get a god-damned doctor in here. I'll do their tests – I'll prove to the fucking world I'm sane."

Marie stood. Resolutely she walked toward her husband. His eyes burned with intense darkness; yet, she showed no fear. "He hasn't been granted the right to sue -- yet. Hopefully it will never get that far, and the courts won't allow him to challenge our marriage at all."

Her words pacified him. His eyes softened and the creases between his eyebrows mellowed. She reached again for his hands. What she wanted more than anything was to feel his arms around her and to be swallowed by his strong embrace. The prison had rules regarding contact. If they didn't abide by the rules, Nathaniel's visiting privileges would be denied.

Marie longed to have the man before her resume his control of the world. That power combined with his private tenderness attracted her. The man she loved was unquestionably an enigma. Under no condition was he *insane*.

Nathaniel stroked Marie's cheek. "Mrs. Rawls, I will not let that happen. You are a mighty and remarkable woman. No one will take your name away."

"Mighty?"

"Yes, mighty –defined as having superior power. Your strength in the face of adversity continually amazes me. I'm awed by your constitution." He kissed the top of her hand. "You are *mighty* remarkable, Mrs. Rawls."

Hope is definitely not the same thing as optimism.
It is not the conviction that something will turn out well,
but the certainty that something makes sense,
regardless of how it turns out.
- Vaclav Havel

Chapter 41

Courtney eagerly relayed the conversation. She couldn't wait to tell Claire everything Tony said. His excuse for visiting was to personally discuss the press release. Courtney promised she and Brent did their best to appear astonished and shocked by his change in attitude.

Brent reminded Tony about his threatened civil suit. Courtney even cried remembering her visit to the jail and inability to help. She said Tony claimed his outlook changed after seeing and speaking with Claire in person. He claimed his earlier anger was a form of self-preservation. He didn't want to admit having feelings for the woman he'd been led to believe attempted to kill him. He told his friends he wasn't sure where this reconnection was headed, but he hoped for full reunification.

Then according to Courtney, he *apologized* for his previous behavior and announced he wanted to bring Claire to Caleb's wedding. Courtney said she almost lost it. She'd wanted to get Claire to the wedding for so long. Now with the possibility before her, she told Tony it wasn't up to him, it was up to Julia and Caleb. Courtney didn't want her son's wedding to be a media circus, like the gala.

Graciously, Tony offered assistance with security and promised discreet behavior. They called Caleb and Julia. Courtney said Julia always liked Claire and was respectfully supportive of Tony's choice of guest.

Claire listened in total disbelief. The wedding was in less than a week. She wasn't supposed to see Tony again for two weeks. Nonetheless, she truly wanted to attend the wedding. As they spoke Claire thought about the trip she took with Courtney to Texas. For some reason she remembered her period was right before that trip. At the time she was relieved it occurred before frolicking in the sun and surf.

At that second, while Courtney rambled on enthusiastically about the wedding... Claire realized she hadn't had her menstrual cycle since.

When Courtney paused, Claire asked, "How long ago did we go to Texas?"

"I'm not sure. Things have been so busy. I just know I can't wait to see you again." Perhaps hearing Claire's recent change in tone, Courtney added, "But, you do what you feel is right. If you don't want to be here with him, don't do it. We can get together again after the wedding."

Claire's mind tried to process -- they went to Texas in the middle of April. And now it's almost June. She and Harry first got together in San Diego. When was that? How effective are condoms? How soon does morning sickness start? Those questions and more bombarded her mind as she tried to maintain her conversation, "I want to see you too." Claire managed weakly, "It'll be hard to act like we haven't been in contact."

"Well, don't worry about that. Just decide what you're going to do."

Before Claire could answer her iPhone rang. It was the third call from Tony. "I need to go; he's calling again. I can't avoid his calls all day."

"Love you, Honey. Tell me what you decide, or maybe Tony should. That way I'll react honestly."

"Got to go, bye." Claire disconnected her *work* phone and answered the iPhone.

Tony's call added to Claire's already fried emotions. Besides working things out with Harry and Amber, she'd just learned Tony was going to ask her to the Simmons' wedding in five days, and she'd realized at the very least, her period was three weeks late. Needless to say, she didn't need to feign anxiety; it was real. "Tony, this is the third time you've called this morning. We aren't making any public appearances for two weeks. *Please* give me some space."

"Hello, Claire, so nice to hear your pleasant tone."

"I've got a lot going on. What do you want?"

"Let me say, I would call less frequently *if* you would answer your phone." She didn't respond. He continued, "I made plans for us, for this coming weekend."

Despite the upheaval in her life, she attempted to conceal the smile from her voice, not wanting the emerging expression to reveal her eagerness to attend the wedding. The mixture of emotions caused her voice to crack; hopefully it came across as irritation, "I agreed to go to Chicago, in two weeks. I'm not going anywhere with you next weekend."

"I believe I might be able to persuade you otherwise."

"Is that a threat? What are you going to do this time, arrange a walk-out of SiJo's employees?"

"No, Claire. No threats – I believe you'll *want* to attend this function."

Exasperation evident, she replied, "Why? What function would I possibly want to attend with you?"

"Caleb and Julia's wedding."

Claire gasped. It was unbelievable. Even after Courtney's call, Claire never truly believed she'd have this opportunity. "But, but... all of your friends think I tried to kill you."

"The news release says differently."

"That doesn't mean they've changed their opinion of me. They probably don't want me there." As they continued to speak, Tony convinced Claire her presence was welcomed. She agreed to fly commercial to Iowa City, arriving Thursday afternoon. He wanted the chance for her to meet with his friends before the wedding, which was Saturday.

Claire's agreement contained a few stipulations: She wanted a pre-purchased return ticket for Sunday. Tony agreed.

The next confrontation came when discussing accommodations. Tony wanted her to stay at the estate. Claire's initial response was *no*. Reinforcing her stance, she exclaimed, "This idea is undebatable."

Then Claire thought about Catherine. "The news release said you let some longtime members of your staff go. I know you still have Eric. Is Catherine still at the estate?"

"She is. And she's hoping you will stay here."

Claire exhaled, "My room will need a lock."

"That isn't a problem."

His answer made her bristle. "It needs to be a lock that operates from the *inside*." She clarified, "Also I *will* keep my phone at all times and have access to your Wi-Fi."

He chuckled, "You drive a hard bargain. I told you before you should go into business. You are a master negotiator."

Claire remembered Harry's words: *When it comes to Mr. Rawlings, your negotiating skills are stellar! My guess is that you'll leave your little meeting and move back to Iowa.* She wasn't moving. This was just a visit.

As soon as she hung up with Tony, Claire went to the store and bought a home pregnancy kit. Sitting at her dressing table and waiting for the results, the memories of her phone calls filtrated her thoughts. She wanted to go to Caleb's wedding. However, the results of this test could make everything different.

Claire stared at the white plastic stick and waited for the timer to sound on her iPhone. Did she really need this little piece of plastic to tell her what she already knew? She was experiencing all the symptoms: nausea - more intense in the morning, hunger – all the time and tiredness – even after napping, and thirst – unquenchable at times. Looking at the two small openings within the stick, Claire saw lines begin to form. The directions said: *results in three minutes.* It had been less than one, and the vertical blue line in the control window appeared before her eyes, indicating the test was working.

Her head pounded with questions. What symbol would appear in the other window? Would she see a lone horizontal stripe meaning *not pregnant,* or a horizontal and a vertical stripe indicating *pregnant.*

Essentially the directions said a *plus* sign would form in the case of pregnancy. *Plus* was often synonymous for positive; thinking about that possibility, *positive* was not the word Claire believed she'd use to describe her current mental state.

She closed her eyes and debated her distress. Was it from the nausea twisting her stomach or the fear of the unknown quickening her heart rate? The buzz of the timer triggered her iPhone to vibrate across the dressing table. Claire's eyes opened. Before her on the table was her answer -- the indicator window revealed a blue *plus*.

The bottom fell out of Claire's world. She eased herself from the stool and sank to the bathroom floor. The ceramic tile cooled her legs, while the solid wall supported her head. Mentally she assessed the timeline: mid-early -- April period, two weeks later – dream, three weeks later – San Diego and now – here she was, seven weeks since her last menstruation. How had she not thought of this before?

Reaching for her phone, she scrolled her contacts for Amber's doctor, one of the most sought after gynecologists in the Silicon Valley. After San Diego, Claire called and made an appointment, hoping to get a prescription for birth control pills. The usual waiting period for new patients was up to six months. Amber's referral shortened the wait considerably. Claire's appointment was in another three weeks. However, now things were different, waiting wasn't an option. Then she realized the day, Sunday, she would have to wait another day to call.

Tears moistened her cheeks as she placed her head on her knees and gave in to the overwhelming emotion. Before she could make any decisions, or talk to *anyone*, Claire needed answers. First and foremost, how pregnant was she -- seven weeks or four weeks?

Finally, she made her way back into her bedroom and into the overpowering aroma of roses; thankfully the flowery aroma was pleasurable -- the three bouquets saturated every molecule of the room. She'd meant to ask Tony if he'd sent the other two bouquets. However, with the talk of the wedding and thoughts of the pregnancy, she forgot.

Claire went to her laptop and Googled answers. How effective are condoms? The search engine spun -- answers appeared: *if used correctly*, condoms are 98% effective. With *common* usage the failure rate grows to between 14 and 15%.

What do they mean *if used correctly*? How many ways are there to use a condom?

Monday morning Claire called the doctor's office and was relieved to learn of a Wednesday afternoon opening. If it weren't for her *dream*, Claire would consider asking Harry to join her. However, despite their reconciliation Sunday morning, there was a change in their relationship. It was her news of the wedding that pushed his limits. Although it wasn't declared, instinctively, Claire knew it. The stolen glances and casual touches were gone.

Everything probably happened too fast. Yet, thinking about the possibility they'd used the condoms *commonly* and not *correctly*, Claire was thankful they were still comfortable and friendly with one another. Harry appreciated Claire's bond with Courtney and her desire to attend the ceremony. He couldn't comprehend the necessity of being in Iowa Thursday through Sunday, and most importantly, why she agreed to stay at Mr. Rawlings' estate. Claire told him and Amber the truth. She was staying at the estate for one reason -- to see Catherine.

In many ways, the woman had become Claire's mother. She was the steady force during a very difficult time in Claire's life. Catherine's support and encouragement sustained her. Looking back, there were times Claire wondered if she would've survived without Catherine's care. Amber and Harry still had their mother; they couldn't understand.

When Wednesday arrived, Claire tried with all of her might to retain the wealth of information. In the beginning, the doctor's staff asked a lot of questions, and even though she'd done a home pregnancy test, they instructed her to urinate in a cup, to confirm the pregnancy.

The eerie stillness of the examination room pulled at Claire's already stretched nerves. She longed for a hand to hold or a voice for comfort. Instead, she waited alone on her roller coaster of emotion for the doctor to confirm the blue plus. Since that moment, three days ago -- every minute, every second, she thought about the pregnancy. While shopping for a dress for Caleb's wedding, she stood motionless for minutes upon minutes looking at her flat stomach in the dressing room mirror and wondered: *How long until it begins to grow?*

The last two nights, during the night, she woke to use the bathroom. Last night she heard her own voice saying, "Hey Little One, I know you don't mean anything by this, but just remember I like my sleep. Maybe we can work on some compromises." (Always the master negotiator.) It wasn't until the words were out of her mouth that she contemplated her discussion. Was she actually talking to the cause of her nausea and increased urination?

As she sat alone in the silence of the examination room, Claire realized she wanted their test to confirm the one she took at Amber's condo. She wouldn't have believed it three days ago, but if they came in the room and told her that she wasn't pregnant, Claire would be devastated.

That realization strengthened her. She wanted this baby. Thinking about the paternity, she recognized it didn't matter. It did. But it wouldn't affect her feelings for this child. He or she was hers. The rest would work itself out, or it wouldn't. Keeping this baby safe and healthy was now her number one concern.

Dr. Sizemore entered the small room with her laptop in her hand. "Ms. Nichols, congratulations! You are definitely pregnant."

Claire's smile radiated to her emerald eyes. It wasn't planned. Potentially she was in the middle of a dangerous mine field. Her entire world could explode with one single misstep. None of it mattered. Her world and the treacherous terrain she navigated were suddenly and forever inconsequential. In her figurative game of chess, attacking her opponent was no longer as important as reinforcing and protecting her pieces, especially her one new piece. Claire would forever have someone else to consider.

After some discussion, Dr. Sizemore directed an ultrasound wand and spoke reassuringly, "The external ultrasound works well later in pregnancy. This early we need to use what is called trans-vaginal."

Claire forgot the uncomfortable sensation as she watched the screen before her go in and out of focus. When the doctor finally stilled the picture, all Claire could see was white static, with a dark oval and something white, shaped like a peanut. Dr. Sizemore explained, "This is your baby."

A grid appeared, superimposed on the *peanut* as Dr. Sizemore took measurements.

"Is everything all right?" Claire asked.

"Yes, everything looks perfect. Do you see this small movement?" A white arrow appeared on the screen and pointed to a dark pulsating spot within the peanut. The sound of swishing filled the small room.

Claire nodded.

"That's your baby's heart beating." The sound reminded Claire of the calming swoosh of waves on the shore of her lake in Iowa. Dr. Sizemore continued, "The heartbeat isn't detectable until six weeks Estimated Gestational Age. According to my measurements, Ms. Nichols, you are seven weeks pregnant, give or take a day."

Claire laid her head on the soft pillow of the exam table. Upon the ceiling there was a picture of three adorable babies, all smiling down at Claire. Her eyes filled with tears as she closed out the world and considered her feelings. If the baby were Harry's it'd be so much easier. Or would it? Is *easy* what Claire desired? Tony claimed to still love her. Harry never said he loved her. But then again, could she trust Tony after all he'd done? She needed answers. She needed to know more about the man she'd once married, the man whose baby she now carried.

The doctor pushed a button and printed copies of the ultrasound screen. Instinctively Claire knew who she wanted to see these pictures. With a new determination, Claire realized she couldn't wait to be in Iowa and talk with the woman who'd supported her and could hopefully answer her questions. Claire couldn't wait to talk with Catherine.

*There is sacredness in tears. They are not the mark of weakness
but of power. They are messengers of overwhelming grief
and of unspeakable love.*
-- Washington Irving

Chapter 42

The BMW stopped momentarily at the front entrance as the large iron gates opened. It had been seventeen months since Claire had been on Tony's property. The last time she watched these gates open was that fateful day in January of 2012, the day she drove away. Her heart rate quickened as the car navigated the winding drive. Being early June, the lush vegetation allowed only the occasional ray of sunshine to break through the canopy of leaves, creating a strobe effect as they neared their destination. When the trees cleared and the vista opened, the house before her took Claire's breath away. She remembered its grandeur. However, with time, memories fade. The stately reality flourished in its full glory. Had this mansion really been her *home*? The combination of brick, river stone, and limestone stood a paragon of Tony's affluence. Or perhaps, Claire wondered, was it a monument to Nathaniel Rawls, Tony's grandfather? After all, it did resemble the picture of Tony's childhood home.

Claire struggled to contain her increasing anxiety while Eric pulled the car onto the brickyard in front of the steps. He had met her at the airport and chauffeured her to the mansion. Although she was still unhappy with Eric's physical persuasion last week in San Francisco, his presence was comforting. After all, he too was a steady presence in her past. Nonetheless, his words as he opened the rear door increased her growing fretfulness. Bowing slightly he said, "Welcome home, ma'am."

Her expression revealed her surprise. "Eric, I am visiting."

"Yes, Ms. Claire. I will make sure your bags are in your room as soon as possible."

"Thank you."

Veiled in the shadow of the house, her heels stalled upon the brickyard. Turning a circle, she took in the countryside. The bright blue sky and various shades of green created a palate of color contrasting the landscape of Palo Alto. She inhaled the warm clear air as she stalled, facing the towering front doors and insurmountable steps. Did she really want to willingly enter this house? Moments passed as she stood frozen in time. Though she willed her body to move forward, her feet remained steadfast. Rising emotions paralyzed her. She stood motionless when suddenly the massive door opened and her heart melted. Standing within the frame of the threshold was the woman Claire longed to see.

Catherine's smile prompted tears to trickle from Claire's green eyes. Claire wanted to go up the steps, but her feet refused to move. Lowering her head, she closed her eyes and surrendered to the sobs within her chest. Her shoulders shook with intense anguish.

Unexpectedly, a comforting embrace surrounded Claire. Her head settled onto Catherine's shoulder, as Catherine's arms encircled her petite frame. Stroking Claire's hair, Catherine murmured, "Ms. Claire, it is all right. I'm here."

At first Claire could only nod into Catherine's blouse. Finally Claire reached into her purse, retrieved a tissue, and wiped her eyes and nose. "I'm sorry, Catherine. I've just missed you so much."

The two women embraced. "Oh, Ms. Claire, I have missed you, too. Please come in the house and let us get you settled."

Claire willingly followed. How many times had Claire confidently followed this woman despite lurking apprehension?

Claire paused as she stepped onto the marble entryway floor. The grand staircase wound upward toward the railed second floor. Her eyes continued to move skyward taking in the elaborate chandelier and the shimmering ceiling beyond. Inhaling deeply she peered around the foyer. Even though it had been almost a year and a half she knew every inch of this massive mansion. She took in the archway leading to the sitting room and the sunporch beyond. She saw the hall leading to Tony's office and the French doors to the formal dining room.

Her body trembled as she mentally moved from room to room. Catherine reached for her hand, "Ms. Claire, may I get you something? Perhaps you'd like to rest after your trip?"

Finding her voice, Claire asked, "Is Mr. Rawlings here? Eric said he was still at work."

"He still is, Miss. Eric is on his way to Iowa City to bring him home as soon as he is able." She patted Claire's hand. "He wanted to meet you at the airport; however, there were pressing matters. He should be here in another hour or so."

Claire nodded. With increased concern she asked, "Where am I staying? What room?"

"Mr. Rawlings instructed to have *all* rooms ready. It is your choice."

"My choice?"

"Yes. He said to tell you, *all* of the suites have locks that operate from the inside."

Claire smiled, "Is my old suite available?"

"Oh yes, it is. And it is ready for you. It's even been redecorated. Would you like to see?"

The nausea hit fast. Claire felt her face flush. "I think I need to sit down first. May we go to the porch?"

Catherine noticed the pallor overtaking Claire's complexion and walked her through the sitting room. Together they stepped down into the open sunporch. Instantaneously, a breeze blew Claire's hair and settled her nerves. Beyond the windows and screens she saw Tony's lush backyard bursting with color. Besides the intense green of the lawn, reds, pinks, whites, and yellows shimmered from the flower beds, pots, and gardens in the distance. Instinctively, Claire turned toward the pool. The blueness of the water rivaled the clear Iowa sky as the fountains sprayed high into the air. The lounge chairs and umbrella tables sat ready for occupancy. At one time, it had been Claire's private resort. She closed her eyes and settled onto the rattan loveseat.

"May I get you something, perhaps a drink or something to eat?" Catherine asked with obvious concern.

Claire looked at her watch. Although it said after two in the afternoon, Claire knew it was after four in Iowa. She had an airline lunch in flight, but it wasn't much. "I know we are supposed to dine later, but I could really use something now, something light."

Catherine smiled tenderly, "Of course. Would you like me to bring it to you here or in your suite?"

Tears threatened Claire's resolve. She couldn't think of it as *her* suite. She wasn't even sure she could sleep there. But then again, could she sleep anywhere else? "I would like to stay here right now and enjoy this beautiful afternoon."

Catherine quickly left to find Claire a snack.

When Catherine returned, she had a tray with a bowl of chicken salad, a sleeve of crackers, some grapes, and a tall glass of iced tea. Claire sighed and asked Catherine to join her as she ate. Catherine did. The food was perfect. It warmed Claire's soul to be near this woman. Somehow, no matter the circumstance, Catherine always knew what was best.

While Claire ate, they chatted about nothing -- very superficial. Once Claire's food was gone and color returned to her cheeks, Claire breached the subject looming omnipresent. "Catherine, do you believe I tried to hurt Tony?"

Catherine took Claire's hand and watched their entwined fingers for a longtime. The sounds of nature from the other side of the screens filled their ears until Catherine looked to Claire and said, "Ms. Claire, I have known Mr. Rawlings for a longtime. I was very concerned for his well-being." She squeezed Claire's soft hand. "I know there were times when you were not happy. I know there were times when being with him was difficult. I also know you are the best thing to ever happen to him, and in his own way he loves you more than he has ever loved anyone." She paused, "No. I never believed you could hurt him, not like that."

Claire allowed the tears to flow, not from sadness but from relief. "Thank you Catherine. I wouldn't do that."

"No, Miss, I know you wouldn't. However, you have in you, the ability to hurt him deeper than any poison could. Your absence has been very difficult for him. If you chose to abandon him again, I do not know what will happen."

Indignantly, Claire replied, "I did not abandon him. He left me at that jail in Iowa City."

Catherine's gray eyes pleaded with Claire in a way words would never articulate, "Ms. Claire, I wish I could help you understand the man beneath the facade. One doesn't become who he is without cause. Your presence and absence has affected him beyond the same from anyone else."

Claire stared and her hands trembled. Finally she managed to voice her new realization, "You sent it to me, didn't you?"

"Ms. Claire, we should get you to your suite. Mr. Rawlings will be here soon and the two of you have dinner plans with the Millers, Bronsons, and Simmons'. I also believe Mr. Summer and Ms. Combs will be there."

At this moment Claire didn't care about her impending dinner plans. "Please tell me. Did you send the box of information to me in prison?"

Catherine stood. "Eric took your bags to your suite. Do you need me to escort you upstairs?"

Claire closed her eyes and lowered her face. Her emotions were too intense to contain. "I so hoped..." Her voice trailed away as she swallowed her words.

Catherine knelt before Claire. Her hand rested upon Claire's knee; she spoke in a whisper, "Ms. Claire, I am pleased you are here. There are many things for us to discuss, but we must proceed with care. May I suggest you ready yourself for your evening and tomorrow while Mr. Rawlings is working we can walk, perhaps beyond the gardens?"

The cameras and recordings came to Claire's mind. Her eyes opened wide. With the excitement of seeing Catherine, she'd forgotten about them. Claire wiped her eyes on her napkin, "Yes, I'd like that. I think I need to freshen up. Do you know how long it will be until Mr. Rawlings arrives?"

"Eric sent a text message. They are about to leave Iowa City. He should be here in thirty minutes. Do you need an escort?"

Claire stood and deeply inhaled the fresh air. "No, I'll be fine." She embraced Catherine, "Thank you. I really have missed you. You're the closest person I've had to a mother since my mother passed away."

Catherine's expression surprised Claire. It was a mixture of love and shock.

Claire quickly added, "I'm sorry. I didn't mean to upset you."

With her expression mellowing, Catherine said, "No, Claire it didn't. I never thought anyone would ever think of me that way."

Internally smiling at being addressed by only her first name, Claire hugged the woman before her. "I do. I don't think I would have survived without you. I feel so much better just being with you."

Catherine's gray eyes filled with moisture as she turned her gaze out into the yard. Never in Claire's memory could she remember seeing

328

Catherine cry, even after Claire's *accident*. Catherine was always strong and steady. The crack in this woman's armor made Claire uneasy; she lifted her purse and walked toward the grand staircase. Her suite was at the top of the steps in the southeast wing. She knew the way well.

*****

Tony gripped the telephone as he looked once again at the clock on the dashboard of the BMW: 5:22 PM. The voice on the other end of his conversation was understandably uneasy. Tony had listened to the murmuring as long as his nerves would allow. Finally Tony interrupted, "So she turned down the tour. Did she tell you why?"

"She said there are too many things happening right now. She doesn't want to be gone from her husband for that long."

"Then tell her, she can choose a shorter tour. I thought thirty months was excessive. You were the one who advised bigger and grander. Make is twelve, sixteen cities in twelve months. I want an answer tomorrow."

"Mr. Rawlings, she's gone. She went to visit her father in New Jersey."

"She left town and you didn't inform me?"

"She just left today."

"Mr. George, you are on the verge of losing the best investment you've ever secured. I want her signed to a contract, yesterday."

"Sir, do you want me to follow her to New Jersey?" He said *New Jersey* like it was purgatory.

"Is her husband with her?"

"I don't know, sir. She didn't mention him regarding her trip."

"Get me a verbal answer by tomorrow." Tony disconnected the call. He quickly dialed another number.

"Hello, Mr. Rawlings."

"Danielle, I was just informed Sophia Burke is visiting New Jersey. Is Derek with her?"

"No, sir, Derek left yesterday for a ten day factory visit in Beijing."

"And where are you?"

"Santa Clara"

"Why are you not with him in China? You are supposed to be his *personal assistant*. I am sure we could find someone who is better for your job."

"Sir, Derek is a nice man. He's not interested in cheating on his wife."

Tony's sneer lingered, as his eyes remained cool, "People get lonely in other countries. You will leave immediately. Keep me apprised of your success."

"Yes, sir."

Tony disconnected his call and placed his phone on the seat to his right. Looking up to the rearview mirror, Tony asked, "Eric, tell me again about Ms. Claire. How is she?"

"She was strong until she reached your home."

"What happened?"

"She broke down, crying on the brickyard ..." Eric explained everything up until Catherine took Claire gingerly in to the house.

Tony listened. Not in seventeen months had he felt the anticipation of reaching his home as he did today. He couldn't believe she was really back. Drumming his fingers silently on the leather seat, he watched the road pass before him. If he were driving, he would have this car doing one hundred and ten.

*****

Her shoes clicked along the marble second floor landing until the carpet of the southeast corridor enveloped her heels and muted her steps. Each door she passed along the corridor made Claire wonder if she'd chosen the right room. The door to *her* suite stood ajar. She tentatively stood at the threshold. It had been a long time since she'd spent thirteen days trapped within the confines of this suite. Yet, despite the happy memories associated with this room, that incarceration was what tumbled out her hidden compartment.

By entering, was she exposing her queen, or worse her king? Everyone knows if her king were captured, the game would be done.

Bravely she reached into her purse and looked at her iPhone. Yes, she had a signal. Her queen had protection. Most of her support was miles away. However, a bishop or a rook could move across the entire board in an undeterred motion.

The suite was as luxurious as she remembered. Some of the colors and textures had changed, but the opulence remained. The wood work was still white, and now the walls were copper. Claire walked to the tall open balcony doors as a gentle breeze blew the now burgundy and gold draperies. The new valances were classic brocade contrasting elegantly with the copper colored walls. Taking the curtains between her fingers, Claire assessed the fabric, lighter than the ones before. She watched as the satin moved freely in the gentle wind.

Mindlessly, she stepped onto the concrete balcony and stared out into the vista. She'd viewed this scene in every season. Today greens filled the landscape, so many trees and so many shades.

"Welcome back, Ms. Claire."

Claire spun toward the sound of Cindy's voice. She took in the young lady's genuine smile. "Cindy, it's good to see you."

"And you too, ma'am. I took the liberty of placing your luggage in the dressing room and hung your dresses, so they wouldn't wrinkle."

"Thank you. How have you been?"

"Very good, ma'am, and how... It is so nice to have you back with us."

Claire knew Cindy was about to ask how she'd been, but stopped. They all knew she'd been in prison, not exactly a great conversation starter. "Cindy, lately I've been very good. And I'm just here for a visit, to attend a wedding. But it's good to see you. Thank you again for putting my things away."

330

"Can I get you anything else, ma'am?"

"Not right now. I believe I'm going to rest and then get ready for dinner."

Cindy nodded as she left the suite, closing the door behind her. Claire gazed about the room. The sofa and chair were now a silvery taupe plush material. It looked very soft. The fireplace held wonderful memories of warmth and serenity. Her heart quickened as she saw the now closed door.

Claire steadily walked to the lever handle and pulled. The door easily opened to the empty hallway. She saw the button upon the lever, on the suite side of the door. Above the lever was a new addition. Claire smiled at the dead bolt. No key could enter if she secured the new lock.

Walking into the dressing room Claire saw new clothes hanging from the racks. There weren't as many as there had been when she arrived the first time. Nevertheless, there were dresses, blouses, slacks, skirts, jeans, and tops. And the shoe rack contained multiple pairs in various styles. Of course they were all very expensive. Instead of complaining, she wondered again if things really change. With curiosity, Claire began opening drawers. The second drawer she opened contained bras in many colors and textures. The third drawer contained panties, various colors and styles. These clothes should have upset her. Instead, the new lingerie filled her with promise.

On the small dining table was a crystal vase filled with an array of wild flowers. Next to the vase she found the note:

I am very pleased you chose this room.
As you may have noticed, your lock is only operational
from within. Below is the username and password
to the Wi-Fi. I am a man of my word.

Were there similar notes in other rooms? What if she would have requested the first room on the left in the southeast corridor? Claire didn't allow her thoughts to linger. Was she predictable or was he overly prepared?

Claire sat at the table. The flight, her reunion with Catherine, seeing Tony's estate, and being back in this suite, left her drained but surprisingly content. Using the information on Tony's note, she connected her iPad and iPhone to the internet. She then sent a text message to her various chess pieces: *I ARRIVED SAFELY. I HAVE MY PHONE AND A LOCK ON THE INSIDE OF MY DOOR. ALL IS WELL. I WILL TEXT AGAIN LATER.*

Courage isn't having the strength to go on -
it is going on when you don't have strength.
— Napoleon Bonaparte

Chapter 43

Somewhere, Claire heard knocking, was it real, or was it in her dream? She tried to analyze, but she couldn't; she couldn't distance herself from the warmth and pleasure cocooning her body. She floated on the softest sheets, upon a bed of perfect firmness. Somewhere between sleep and awake, the knocking stopped, replaced by her name.

"Claire -- Claire, you need to wake. We're supposed to be to Tim and Sue's in an hour." Tony spoke from the moment he entered the suite. He didn't want to give her the wrong impression, although *that* impression was paramount in his mind. She looked so peaceful, sleeping on *this* bed, in *this* suite. With all his might, Tony wanted to reconnect the electronic lock and keep Claire there forever.

He couldn't succumb to his thoughts. If Claire were ever to be his, she needed to *want* to be here. If he were to stop her stupid articles from appearing, he needed to tread lightly. The fact she was here was, in itself, a miracle. Approaching the bed, her serene expression transfixed him. Hoping not to startle her, he spoke louder, "Claire? Claire?" Partially out of necessity; but, more out of desire, Tony touched her exposed skin, "Claire?"

She began to stir. His fingers caressed the light blue satin bra straps, visible above the blankets on her exposed shoulders. The allure of moving the covers and discovering the remainder of her attire was almost irresistible. Tony wondered if she could possibly be wearing matching light blue panties.

Her blissful nap slipped away. Slowly she opened her eyes to his voice. Suddenly, they opened wide. Claire abruptly sat, pulling the blankets around her body. "Tony!" Claire pulled the covers higher, "what are you doing in here? You promised."

332

He chuckled at her modesty, "I promised a lock. The door wasn't locked. I knocked, multiple times. You must have been very tired."

Her panic diminished at his casual tone, "I think I was. I have that jittery just awakened feeling." She laid her head back onto the pillow, and her long chestnut hair fell in waves around her face. The late afternoon sunlight shimmered off of her emerald eyes. "What time is it?"

"Six thirty and we need to be to Tim and Sue's in an hour." Tony remained motionless, grinning at Claire.

"Well, if you're going to stand there, go find me a robe so I can get ready."

He didn't speak but walked slowly into the dressing room. Claire's eyebrows rose and lips pursed into a straight line, when he emerged holding a black silk transparent negligee cover. The smirk on his face revealed his attempt at humor. Her only response was a slow shake of her head. With a feigned pout he reentered the dressing room and returned again with a long pink cashmere robe.

"That's better. Now if you don't mind?"

Tony gallantly turned away as Claire covered herself with the robe. "Don't you think this is a bit ridiculous?" He asked. "We were married."

"No, I don't," she answered. After securing the robe Claire said, "You may turn around now." When he did, she couldn't help notice the twinkle in his soft suede eyes.

"I thought we could talk about tonight."

She looked up to his still amused expression. "Not now. I need to get ready. We can talk in the car. If you leave me alone, I'll be ready in thirty minutes."

Mockingly, he bowed, blew her a kiss, and left the room. Instinctively, she listened to the door close. Upon hearing the normal sounds associated with the mechanisms of a latching door knob, Claire walked into the attached bathroom. It was exactly the same: white tile, chrome fixtures, and glass shower. The only change was the color of the towels, now copper, matching the walls in the bedroom.

Thirty minutes hour later, Claire descended the grand staircase to see Tony casually leaning against one of the grand doors, with his hands in the pockets of his navy slacks. She noticed his white "v" neck shirt and unbuttoned sports coat. Her choice of slacks and blouse would blend perfectly.

Claire tried to ignore his non-wavering gaze as she made her way to the foyer. Once her heeled sandals touched the marble floor he straightened and said, "You look amazing -- as usual. Is that an outfit you brought or one from the closet?"

"One I brought. The closet seems silly. I'm leaving in three days."

"You refused to take a credit card to shop. So I hired someone to shop for you. You may decide to wear some of those clothes to our public functions."

Claire shook her head as she stopped before him. "Tony, I'm not falling into that same trap. I don't want the media accusing me of *reconciling* with you for your money."

"Tonight there won't be media, just friends."

Claire exhaled, and her shoulders slumped.

"What's the matter?" He asked.

"Are you sure they want me there? I would rather face the media than *your friends* considering what they think I did." That was another of Claire's prepared speeches. She'd thought about saying *after what you made it look like I did* or *after what you did*, but she believed she'd found the best wording.

Tony grasped her hand. "I promise. I've spoken to everyone, most in person. Mary Ann and Eli I spoke to on the phone."

"And they ..."

"And they *understand*. I was distraught, but we are reconciling."

Claire closed her eyes. Why was she forced to face these people as the villain? Wasn't she the victim, the heroine? Exhaling, she allowed Tony to lead her through the grand doors, down the steps, to the bricks below. Waiting for them on the circular drive was a Lexus LFA. The silver car reminded Claire of the Batmobile. Tony opened the passenger door and she eased herself into the low seat. The red and black interior included a very impressive dashboard. As Tony settled himself into the driver's seat, his broad smile and shimmering eyes held her gaze. Without a doubt, Tony loved his cars. She got the distinct impression this vehicle could go very fast.

"This is a very nice car. Would you mind not going too fast?"

"It can do zero to sixty in three point six seconds."

"I believe you. Do you remember my reaction to the bacon the other day?"

Tony frowned, "Yes, are you still not well?"

"I'm not back to myself."

He scowled, "Maybe you should see a doctor."

Claire looked through the windshield as Tony put the Batmobile in drive and eased down the driveway. "I have an appointment in a few weeks." That was true. She did. It was her four week obstetrical visit. According to Dr. Sizemore, she would be seen every four weeks until week twenty eight. Then the appointments would be every two weeks, eventually every week. Of course, she didn't say any of that to Tony. Instead she prayed her stomach would not revolt against the low riding Batmobile.

As they passed the impressive double gates, thoughts of that fateful day and her drive away from this place, infiltrated her mind. She stared at the blue skies, as the road before them wound and twisted though fields and forests. Claire closed her eyes and laid her head against the headrest. They would be there soon. *Please let me keep Catherine's snack down.* She silently prayed.

Tony turned down the radio. As the volume decreased so did his smile. It was barely visible when he said, "We need to discuss tonight and your behavior."

Claire opened her eyes and peered to her left. She wasn't alone she told herself. (Maybe her greatest ally came in a pawn or bishop, but nonetheless, she had allies!). "Tony, I wouldn't be here, of my own free will, if I didn't completely comprehend my behavior. Don't patronize me. I've done this dance before."

Tony's eyes darkened, "Are you saying when you were with my friends in the past, it was a performance?"

"No." Claire sat taller; the car glided onward and Tony continued to make marked looks to his right. "I'm saying, there were times I wasn't happy with you, but no one knew."

"You aren't happy with me?"

Grasping the large hand holding the steering wheel, she explained, "Tony, we are doing what you want, it's a performance." She considered their child. "I can't say I don't want it to be real. But for now, it isn't. Let's not add unnecessary layers to this charade."

He considered her words, and finally asked, "So there is a part of you, I will settle for a small part, which wants what we are about to do, to be real?"

She exhaled, "Yes, Tony, a small part of me," and *of you* -- she thought, "wants *us* to be real."

The scenes passed, and a comfortable banter ensued, until they neared Tim and Sue's home. Tony slowed the car and his tone, "Perhaps we should review rules?"

Claire closed her eyes and replied, "Maybe I could save us some time and summarize? Do as you say. No public failure and do not divulge private information."

Tony exhaled, "Are you summarizing or mocking?"

"For the sake of argument, I'll call it summarizing. As I said earlier, I've done this before. Perhaps you've forgotten, but I'm perfectly capable of doing as you wish."

"No, Claire, I have not forgotten your abilities. I just need confirmation that we're on the same page as we enter the Bronson's."

Her patience waning, "Tell me the number, and I'll turn right to it."

The car was now stopped along the side of the country road. Tony grasped Claire's chin and turned her glaring green eyes toward him. "I believe I'm tiring of the sexy, bold, and cheeky."

Her strong tone didn't vacillate, "Then stop this charade."

He maintained his hold, peering intently into the fire of her emerald eyes. Finally he asked with obvious restraint, "May I please, have reticent and genteel while in the presence of others?"

Her lashes fluttered, fire ebbed, and her southern belle emerged, "Why Mr. Rawlings, your wish is my command."

The darkness before her grew. She found herself lost in the abyss of his stare. Time stilled as her chin remained captive between his thumb and finger. Their distance decreased and his lips neared hers. "Kiss me." It was his wish, his command. Powerless, her eyes closed, lips parted and their mouths united. His hand released her chin and reached for her shoulders. The restraint of the seatbelts held their bodies in place, yet their hands and lips searched for one another.

When they parted, Tony replied breathlessly, "If we weren't expected at the Bronson's any minute, I'd like to put more effort into exploring the *wish and command* possibilities."

Claire leaned her head against the seat and laughed. The tension within the sleek sports car had been mounting. With the kiss, the pressure released, like a valve on their boiler. The sudden relief allowed Claire a moment of honesty, "I'm nervous to see all of them again."

Once again he reached for her chin. This time he gently pulled her eyes toward his. What was once black, now faded into soft brown velvet. "There may be questions, personal questions. This isn't the press. They're people who know me, know us. They're going to want to know what happened."

Claire nodded, accepting Tony's advice. He continued to create a believable scenario -- a story which they'd each know and could refer, with consistency. The blending of their stories was essential to making the world believe their reunion. Dutifully she listened to every word, knowing her performance affected the lives of many.

This dinner was another of his forced moves. Claire needed to evaluate the chess board and strategize her next appropriate move. She couldn't afford to lose any more pieces. As she considered their baby -- too much was at stake.

The cars parked in the driveway indicated they were the last to arrive. Claire tried not to imagine the conversation occurring within. Of course, she'd probably learn the truth from Courtney later. For fear of being discovered, Claire left her *work* phone in California. Talking intimately with her dearest friend would wait until Claire was back in Palo Alto.

Claire compliantly stayed within the grip of the sleek bucket seat, struggling to quell her growing anxiety, until Tony parked the LFA and chivalrously came around to open her door. Upon seeing her expression, Tony whispered, "I'm not leading you into the den of lions."

"No, you've already done that."

His polished expression wavered, "This time, I won't leave you. I'll stay by your side. You won't be alone."

His valiant tone strengthened her. Nodding, Claire grasped his extended hand. Being alone was always her greatest fear. As their fingers intertwined she realized she wanted his support and presence. Walking toward the house, Tony leaned down, "I'd hoped seeing everyone here first would be easier than seeing them for the first time in a crowd."

"It probably will be; nevertheless, I think I'm going to be ill."

He stopped their forward movement and assessed the woman before him. "Your color looks good. You look amazing. I promise," he squeezed her hand, "I'm right here." His grin broadened, "A man of my word."

She reached up and kissed his cheek. "Thank you."

Before they could push the door bell, Tim opened the wooden barrier. With Sue by his side, he politely offered, "Welcome to our home. Tony, Claire," he nodded with a smile.

"Please come in," Sue added. She motioned toward the large sitting room full of familiar faces. Feeling the cool insincerity, Claire secured her mask and clung tighter to Tony.

Silence prevailed as Tom, Bev, Brent, Courtney, Mary Ann, and Eli turned and watched Tony and Claire enter with Tim and Sue. Courtney was the first to move. Without speaking she sat her wine glass on the large square table before the sofa. Ignoring Tony, Courtney approached Claire, her blue eyes glistening with tears. It wasn't as dramatic as their reunion in Texas, but Courtney's embrace squeezed the air from Claire's lungs. Helpless, Tony released Claire's hand as the two women clung to one another weeping. Courtney whispered in Claire's ear. *Could others hear?* They didn't know.

"I'm so sorry; I'm so sorry."

Claire nodded, swallowing her sobs. This wasn't an act. It was the reunion of two friends. The ice was broken, another release. Eventually the rest of the room began to talk. Sue, Bev, and Mary Ann led the women to the kitchen. Dabbing their eyes, all the women gave Claire the support she'd feared Tony's friends would withhold. Everyone claimed to have doubted Claire's guilt. They all apologized for not being more supportive. Claire knew the man in the other room was the reason for their disobliging behavior. Nonetheless, she bashfully accepted their belated validation.

When they returned to the living room, Claire devotedly sat beside her ex-husband. His expression displayed genuine pleasure with the ladies' response. When he reached for Claire's hand and gently brushed her knuckles with his thumb, their faces bowed toward one another and their noses touched. The light contact provoked an approving smile from her lips.

Their Oscar worthy performance was outstanding, possibly under serious consideration for nomination. Throughout the entire evening Tony was Claire's anchor. By the time dinner was complete, even Claire believed the words coming from her mouth.

With Tony engrossed in conversation in the living room, Claire made her way to the kitchen. She'd spent the evening nursing a glass of wine, for appearances; however, water seemed to be the only liquid capable of quenching her ever present thirst. Leaving the others behind, Claire wondered, *was thirst another symptom of pregnancy?* She stood at the sink, filling her goblet when Brent approached and nonchalantly whispered, "Did you get my message?"

Claire looked nervously toward the other room, "No, I left *that* phone in California."

He continued, "I saw some paperwork on a recent Rawlings hire. The man's name caught my attention." Claire looked questionably at him. Brent whispered. "Burke."

Her mind twirled; there were so many things going through it. She tried to make a connection. "I'm sorry, should I know that name?"

Brent glanced to the other room to see everyone still talking. "Jonathon Burke worked with your grandfather..."

Claire's eyes opened wide, "Yes, the securities officer."

Brent nodded and whispered, "I understand why you're doing what you're doing. But, please remember who you're dealing with *and* be careful."

Ignoring his warning, Claire asked, "Is there a connection between the Rawlings employee and Jonathon?"

"I haven't had the chance to follow through, but I will."

"Oh, there you are..." Courtney came loudly into the kitchen with Tony close behind. Claire finished putting ice in her water glass, grinned, and walked toward Tony.

"What are you two in here talking about?" Tony asked. Claire heard his question, but at the same time her mind tried to process the new information. Are other people suffering because of Nathaniel and Tony's vendetta?

"Monterey," Brent said. Claire pushed her new concern away and turned toward Brent with a grin. Brent continued, "Yes, Courtney and I've been there a few times and really enjoyed it. I wondered, with Claire living in Palo Alto, if she'd been."

Claire interjected as she smiled toward Tony, "I was telling him the only time I'd been there -- was with you."

Tony placed his arm around her back. "We did go there, didn't we?"

Courtney said, "I hate to leave this get-together, but we have a lot to do before the rehearsal and dessert celebration." She addressed Tony and Claire, "You two will be there, won't you?"

Unsure of their plans, Claire looked to Tony. He replied, "Of course, we will. That's why we met tonight. I hoped Claire's reintroductions would be easier if she could meet first with friends. Hopefully this will allow her additional support with increased people." His arm gently squeezed his ex-wife to his side. She smiled appropriately to *his* friends.

"Well, you have ours. Oh, Claire," Courtney asked, "Could I have your cellphone number? I'd love to talk more after the wedding."

A flashback of a similar situation years earlier entered Claire's thoughts. Before she could answer, Tony responded. "Courtney, I'll give her your number tonight. She can call or text, and then you will have each other's number."

The women nodded. "We'll do that." Claire said with a smile. *Maybe things do change,* she pondered.

"Now if you'll excuse us, we need to say our good-byes," Brent offered as they turned to leave.

Tony stopped them. "Wait, we should probably go, too. Claire's had a pretty emotionally packed day. Besides, I believe the four of us need to speak privately. Perhaps, out by the cars?"

338

Claire's insides suddenly twisted. She refused to look toward the Simmons; what could he want to discuss privately? Did he know about their clandestine relationship and support?

"All right," Courtney managed, "But we do have a lot to do." Her tone sounded as if she were agitated by the delay; however, Claire knew the same concerned inflections would be present if she spoke. So she didn't.

Tony thanked Tim and Sue for hosting the dinner and the four of them said goodbye to the others. However, before they could leave Sue and asked, "Could you please wait just a minute?" Without waiting for an answer she hurried away toward the stairs.

Courtney seized Claire's hand. "I think she's going to get Sean. He's upstairs with the nanny."

A lump developed in Claire's throat, recognizing Sue's ultimate gesture of acceptance. Through pleading eyes she looked to Tony, silently conveying her desire to stay and see Tim and Sue's son. He shrugged. Claire turned back to Courtney, "Can you stay for a few more minutes. I know you have a lot to do, and Tony wants to talk..."

"Oh, I always have time for babies. Wait until you see him." Turning to Brent she asked expectantly, "How long do you think it will be until Caleb and Julia make us grandparents?"

"I'm not old enough to be a grandparent."

Courtney laughed, "You are, and so am I. But *I* don't look like it!"

"No, you don't." They all lightheartedly agreed.

Moments later, Sue appeared with a pajama clad, very blonde, little boy in her arms. He alternated nestling into his mother's shoulder and peering at the people around him while all the while, his little arms wrapped tightly around Sue's neck.

"Claire, I wanted you to meet Sean. I'm sorry. This is past his bedtime and the poor little guy is getting tired."

Claire's heart melted, "Hello, Little Guy, it is nice to meet you." She looked at his small frame, calculated Sean's age and asked, "He is what, about fifteen months?"

"Almost," Sue smiled. "He's so much fun, getting into everything and learning new words every day."

Tim approached the group; Sean held out his arms. Tim lovingly swung his son into his embrace and added, "Believe me; it makes you think about every word, when little ears are listening."

The attention made Sean awaken. He smiled mischievously at the Simmons, Tony, and Claire, while intermittently hiding his face in Tim's shoulder.

"Thank you." Tears teetered on Claire's lids as she reached out tussling Sean's soft curly hair. "I think you might have some difficulty getting him back to sleep."

Everyone scoffed jokingly and said goodbye.

Tony and Claire followed the Simmons' out to the cars. Stepping away from the brightly lit home, Claire noticed the black velvet sky sprinkled with millions of stars, exactly as she'd remembered. Pulling her attentions away from the beautiful sky, Claire braced herself as Tony began to speak addressing all three of them.

"I'm doing my best to be honest with Claire. And I expect the same from her." Swallowing, she attempted an innocent expression as he looked down at her and continued, "That's why I thought we should get this out in the open."

There are two mistakes one can make along the road to truth...
not going all the way, and not starting.
- Buddha

Chapter 44

"Tony, I think the Simmons' need to..."
Tony interrupted Claire's attempt to avoid this discussion. "This won't take long." He turned to Brent. "I've trusted Brent with many things through the years." Claire saw Brent's stance stiffen. Were they all about to be reprimanded? Tony went on, "That's why I wanted him to be the one to tell you about his progress regarding your brother-in-law."

Brent visibly exhaled. Apparently, Claire hadn't been the only one holding her breath. "Yes," Brent said, looking at Claire as relief shone from his tired eyes. "Well, it seems some new information has come to the attention of the New York State Bar Association. This hasn't been released to anyone, not even John. If my informant is correct, this new information will cause his case to come up for review soon. We are hoping the review will result in the reinstatement of his law license."

Claire sprung skyward and clasped her hands with the news. "Oh, thank you." The tears teetering in the house now spilled onto her cheeks. "Thank you, Brent. Thank you, Tony. I won't say a word. When will you know if it will be up for review?"

Brent answered, "It'll take a few months. I should be kept apprised of updates."

Tony offered his hand to Brent, "Thank you," he shook Brent's hand. "I apologize for delaying your departure, but I wanted Claire to hear it from you."

Courtney's relief made her giddy, "That's all right. However, now we need to go. I'm so glad this was good news." Reaching out for Claire's hand, "Now you need some rest. Tony's right, you've had too many things thrown at you. Look how emotional you are."

Claire nodded and managed, "We'll see you tomorrow night. And, I'll call." The words spoken out loud felt liberating.

Tony grasped Claire's hand, and they walked back to the silver Batmobile. As he opened her door, he bent down and whispered, "A man of my word."

She smiled all the way to her emerald eyes and kissed his cheek. "Thank you, I really mean that."

The country roads wound like a ribbon before them. Claire closed her eyes and tried to comprehend the evening. There were so many things to think about. Yet, the only vision which managed to find its way to her consciousness was Sean, the way his pudgy little arms encircled Sue's neck, his giggle as Tim propelled him in the air, and his security at landing on Tim's strong stable shoulder. Would their child ever have that? Would Claire's baby have a father willing to embrace him unconditionally?

Tony's squeeze of Claire's knee brought her back to the present. She focused on his words, part of a statement already in progress. "... it takes longer than you would expect. But, Brent thinks it can be resolved before the end of the year."

Claire turned, "That's a long time away. How long did it take to set him up?"

Tony turned. His expression suddenly darkened. "I'd rather not talk about that."

With her preoccupation of Sean, she'd forgotten to weigh her words. "Why? I know you did it. You told Brent and Courtney you wanted to be honest. So be honest."

Tony's neck stiffened and he peered forward through the windshield. Finally he spoke, "From the time he turned down my job offer."

Claire sat straighter and looked out the side window. She tried to keep her mind on the passing scenes. Subtle interruptions in the nocturnal darkness were visible with the occasional house or opening in the trees. The light from the quarter moon illuminated each field or a yard they passed. Although, the familiar terrain gave Claire comfort, she wrestled with Tony's confession.

"You asked. Now, you won't comment?" Tony asked.

"I don't know what to say. Do you want my bold and cheeky response or the reticent and genteel one?"

Claire saw his knuckles blanch upon the steering wheel. She waited. Instinctively she knew she'd baited him enough. He'd been honest. She should give him credit for that.

"This is why I haven't answered all of your questions. You may think you're ready for answers, but you're not. Bits and pieces may help you understand. But, the blatant truth is too much."

Claire watched the passing scenes without comment. It wasn't that words didn't form in her head; they did. She chose to keep them to herself. In the past her silence may have been the result of fear regarding Tony's reaction. Exhaustion was her current motivator. Without a doubt, Claire was tired of confrontation.

342

When Tony pulled the silver Batmobile onto the brick circular drive in front of his house, Claire turned to him. Sincerely and serenely, she placed her hand on top of his and spoke softly with confidence, "Thank you." He turned -- showering her with the intensity of his dark glare. Every fiber of his expression displayed his unspoken resentment regarding at her recent silence. Undeterred she continued, "Thank you for supporting me tonight with your friends. I was very nervous. It turned out much better than I could have possibly hoped. And thank you for helping John. I know you don't like him, and you created his problems, but helping him now – it means a lot to me." She leaned in and lightly kissed his lips.

The touch ignited feelings deep within her. The change in Tony's breathing revealed a similar response. She searched his eyes in the dark stillness of the car.

"Claire, I am trying to give you space. But I'm on the edge."

She leaned back and undid her seatbelt. "I know you're trying. And I appreciate it." She opened her door and started toward the house. She heard his door slam as he made his way to her, grasping her arm; he stopped her progress. They stood in the night upon the brick drive. His chest pressed against her hypersensitive breasts.

"I am very glad you are here."

Claire smiled and looked up at the mansion before her. "I'm surprised at how much I like being here. I was afraid the bad memories would overpower the good."

Tension escaped his lips in an audible sigh as a grin emerged, "Does that mean... the good overpower the bad?"

Claire shrugged. "I don't know. I wish I could say *yes*. You said you want honesty, and honestly, I don't know. They're both there. It's just that the familiarity of *here* is heartwarming."

He kissed the top of her head and with lightened eyes offered, "I need to go into the office tomorrow morning. I hope to be done and home by noon. The dessert celebration isn't until eight. Would you like to go for a walk tomorrow?"

"A walk?"

His encouraging smile peeked her curiosity. "Yes, Claire, to your lake?"

She smiled and nodded. "I would. Very much, I would like that."

He kissed the hand he'd secured. "Please allow me to escort you to your suite. I will give you Courtney's number and you may use the lock you requested. Actually," his eyes narrowed, "I suggest you do."

Claire pressed against his chest. "You know, we never did this."

"This what?"

"We never *dated*. I guess twice, in Atlanta." Her smile didn't falter at the reference. "I like it."

He gently squeezed her hand, and they ascended the front steps. "We better get you behind a locked door, so I don't do anything to ruin this *date*." He emphasized the word.

Claire smiled slyly, "Actually, according to a definition I recently heard, we need to be in public for this to be a date."

Tony's only response was another small squeeze of her hand. However, as they entered the well-lit foyer, her emerald eyes sparkled at his upturned lips.

Once behind her secured door, Claire hit *call* on the contact Tony had just added to her phone. After three rings she heard Courtney's voice. "Hi Courtney, I was just checking the number Tony gave me..." They didn't talk long. Courtney asked if Claire was okay. Claire assured her she was alone, behind a locked door, and fine. When she hung up, she sent a text message to Emily, Amber, and Harry. It said the same thing: *I VISITED WITH TONY'S CLOSE FRIENDS. ALL WENT WELL. NOW SAFELY ALONE AND GOING TO SLEEP. WILL TEXT TOMORROW.*

On the table, Claire found a note:

> *Mr. Rawlings turned off the cameras in your suite.*
> *Please call the number below when you wake. Your breakfast*
> *will be brought to you. Sleep well - good night, Catherine*

Claire thought about the changes she'd seen in Tony. Was her opinion swayed because of their child? Did she see positives where she should be seeing warnings? Claire recalled Brent's advice: *Remember who you're dealing with.*

Wasn't that a two edged sword? She had many memories of Tony, and a lot were good. Of course, there was a flip side. Perhaps, she should think about them. However, she didn't want her baby overwrought with negativity.

Inhaling the cool night air, the country noises and moon lit vista enveloped Claire as she stepped onto the balcony. Despite the change in decor, the familiarity of the suite, balcony, and nocturnal murmurings comforted her. She felt her body relax and exhaustion prevail. Moments later she snuggled into the soft sheets as sounds of crickets and cicadas through the open French doors serenaded her to sleep.

The next morning Claire woke after ten. She blamed the time difference. Nonetheless, she lay motionless for moments, assessing her physical state. When she'd determined she was not going to be ill, she made her way to the bathroom. Next, she called the number from Catherine's note. Claire didn't leave her breakfast to chance. When Cindy answered, Claire was very specific, "Hello, Cindy, I'm finally awake. Could someone please bring me...?"

Cindy brought dry scrambled eggs, toast, and fruit and served it on the balcony. Claire ate her breakfast and drank tea and orange juice while a soft breeze blew her unbound hair around her face. Taking in the beautiful, green, peaceful scene, it was difficult not to enjoy her surroundings. Everything was perfect.

When Claire finally descended the grand stairs, it was almost twelve. She'd wanted to speak with Catherine. And although Tony was due home any minute, Catherine was waiting for her near the sun porch.

"Do you think we have time for a walk?" Claire asked.

"Yes, not too long. However, I believe it would be good for you to *walk*."

The two women strode in step out of the sun porch and down into the backyard. Even though the midday sun heated the June day, a warm breeze kept the air moving and comfortable. Together they made their way to the gardens. Flowers of all colors adorned the paths. Following the flagstone stepping stones they made their way to a stone bench at the edge of Tony's yard.

"This is visible, not audible." Catherine said. Claire nodded. "Ms. Claire..."

"Just Claire, please?" Claire asked with a smile.

Catherine smiled, "Claire, thank you for what you said yesterday. You will never know how much it means to me. Mr. Rawlings asked me about a box of information sent to you in prison. Why do you believe it was sent?"

Claire's insides fluttered. She didn't know if it was their baby finally waking or anxiety produced by the possibility of answers to her many questions. "I think it depends on who sent it. At first I thought it was sent by Tony. If that were the case, I thought it was done maliciously – bragging about the things he's done." She paused. When Catherine didn't respond, Claire continued. "Now I'm not sure. And I don't understand all of the contents."

"What don't you understand?"

"How long have you known Tony?"

"A long time," Catherine's expression revealed someone reminiscing. "I met him the day he graduated high school."

Claire gasped, she had no idea they went back that far. "So you knew him when he was Anton?" Catherine nodded. Claire asked, "Did you know his family: his parents and his grandparents?"

"Yes, I did."

There were so many questions going through Claire's mind. She didn't know which ones to vocalize. "He never talks about his family. Well, he's mentioned his grandfather a few times. Please tell me about them."

Catherine focused on Claire, "Someday, perhaps. Today is about Anton. He needs you more than he is willing to admit, even now. I hope you can see the strides he has accomplished and the concessions he's made."

Claire fought the emotions within her. She steadied her shoulders, "I do. I also have memories. Not just the ones of here. You mentioned sometimes being with him was difficult. You and I both know that's an understatement." Claire inhaled deeply and continued, "I also have memories of prison. Tell me why he did that to me."

345

"Mr. Rawlings is a man of his word. The problem was, he made two different promises and he felt honored to keep them both. He hoped that by fulfilling one, in a different than expected way, he may have the chance to rectify the other." Catherine squeezed Claire's hand. "That's up to you. Please give him the chance."

"Why are you so loyal to him?"

"He is like my family. I have seen what life has done to him and how he has triumphed on so many levels. He has been loyal to me, also."

"But, if I'm to interpret the box correctly, he's done some terrible things."

"Ms. – I mean, Claire, we have all done some terrible things. That doesn't mean we aren't capable of good. You've shown me that, too."

As Claire was about to respond, they both heard the approaching footsteps. Coming from the house, Tony advanced carrying a large satchel. His concerned expression mellowed when his dark eyes met Claire's. Abruptly, Catherine stood.

"Catherine." His one word greeting could easily be interpreted as a reprimand.

"Tony," Claire reached for him. "What do you have?"

Slowly, his piercing gaze left Catherine and turned toward Claire. She watched the light overtake the dark and a smile emerge. "I see you're wearing the hiking boots."

"Well, yes, you promised a walk," Claire responded.

"I have our lunch. Shall we picnic at your lake?"

Catherine said, "I will leave you two to your afternoon." Her eyes pleaded at Claire before she nodded and turned away.

"I hope I remember the way." Claire said as they began walking toward the trees.

"Did I interrupt something?" he asked.

"Girl talk. I've missed Catherine terribly." With a tightening in her stomach brought on by concern for the woman she held dear, Claire hoped Tony's lack of response meant this conversation was done.

She did remember the way. With each step the directions came back to her. When the trees opened to her meadow, Claire sighed with relief. Everything was just as she'd remembered. The shadowed fringes contained remnants of morning glories the color of the Iowa sky. Daisies and mustard plants added yellow and golden highlights to the otherwise green clearing. Although Tony and Claire talked during their hike, they also enjoyed the quiet serenity of nature.

The buzz of the occasional insect and the rustle of the leaves above, brought on by the gentle wind, filled their ears. As they neared the lake, Claire noticed the fresh aroma of the water penetrating her lungs with each breath.

The new boots she'd found in the well-stocked closet stood upon the pebbles of the lake's edge while the waves lapped the shore. Out over the water, the sun shone in sparkling prisms like colored flashes above the rippled lake. Tony squeezed her hand and whispered, "It's as beautiful as I remember."

"Have you been here -- recently?"

"No, I'd be lost without you." Claire wondered if he meant he'd be lost in the woods or if the statement held deeper meaning.

They laid the blanket upon the shore and unpacked the lunch. She made no attempt to hide her ravenous hunger. Claire blamed her appetite on the exercise.

Later in the afternoon as the warmth continued to build, Claire took off her shoes and socks and ventured into the water. The soft underwater terrain squished beneath her toes. The warm sun on her skin and the cool water on her feet created the perfect balance.

"We could swim?" Tony offered.

"I didn't bring a bathing suit."

"Me either," he managed with a sultry grin. Claire laughed and declined his offer. Instead, they lounged on the blanket in their shorts. As the sun's rays intensified, Tony removed his shirt. Claire found the view from the blanket very enjoyable.

No man chooses evil because it is evil;
he only mistakes it for happiness, the good he seeks.
-- Mary Wollstonecraft Shelley

Chapter 45

-September 1989-

A nton eased his rental car in the parking space at the Royal Hotel on Century Boulevard. Thankfully the low watt overhead lights did little to brighten the shabby cracked asphalt lot. Even if he tried, he couldn't ignore the beat-up old automobiles filling many of the available spaces. With the demise of his family's fortune, Anton had fallen. He was extremely thankful he hadn't fallen this far. And under normal circumstances he'd never step into the likes of this flea infested hotel.

It was a place where whores and junkies rented rooms by the hour. For some it was a living, for others – their death. It was the last place in Santa Monica anyone would expect a Rawls to stay. For that reason and that reason alone, it is where Anton safely stowed his step-grandmother.

Technically, Marie wasn't his step-grandmother any longer. Nathaniel suffered a massive heart attack four months ago. His death came two months before the completion of his sentence. The news sent shock waves through Anton's family like a 7.0 earthquake.

Prior to Nathaniel's passing, Samuel Rawls sought legal declaration voiding his father's marriage to Catherine Marie London. While few states allowed third party challenges to marriage, New York had a unique rule allowing the ability to annul a marriage and defeat the property consequences of said marriage. Both Nathaniel and Marie fought Samuel's efforts. Despite Nathaniel's incarceration, his power managed to keep Samuel's allegations out of court.

Although Samuel never visited his father in the minimum security prison, the moment he learned of Nathaniel's passing, his attorney successfully filed the necessary paperwork. Because Samuel had begun the annulment prior to his father's death, the legal action survived.

In order to *void* a marriage, one of the following situations must be proven: fraud, duress, mental incompetence (either permanent or temporary), undue influence, sham, jest, and underage (voidable in a majority of jurisdictions). Samuel's suit claimed mental incompetence and undue influence.

It wasn't property from the marriage Samuel sought. Most of the family assets were gone, seized by the federal government. Rawls Corporation was sold. It no longer existed as a whole but parted out to many different procurers. The contents of the large home in upstate New Jersey were auctioned to the highest bidders, and the estate now belonged to a prominent sports star. The resulting proceeds sat in trusts, waiting to be funneled to those wronged investors. Of course, the attorneys would take their share first. What was left would eventually make its way to the people taking part in the claims and various class action suits.

Thankfully, Samuel wasn't aware of Nathaniel's overseas money. Samuel's main objective was Marie's name. His case was only to strip *Rawls* from her title. Vindictive, yes, but Samuel Rawls learned from the best. In one bold move, he punished Marie for replacing his mother and Nathaniel for wronging their family.

Anton tried to act as mediator. His father was not receptive. It didn't matter to Samuel that Marie loved his father, that she had sat through every minute of his trial, and that she visited Nathaniel every week for twenty-two months.

Nathaniel had always been gruff and commanding, but there were times a softer side emerged. In Anton's memory those instances usually involved his grandmother or Marie. Anton remembered one of his last visits with his grandfather. They were in the dingy pale green visitor's room, and Nathaniel was giving Anton business advice.

"Boy, when I'm out of here we're going to start new."

"Yes, Sir, I told you about the project I'm working on with a friend."

Nathaniel answered, "Yes, something about computers and getting information fast."

"Yes, it's called a search engine. We have some great ideas..."

"I don't know about that. I do know you need money to make money. I know you can begin this start-up computer search thing and when it hits – move on. Buy, invest, sell, and just remember, it's the bottom line. Your father always worried about people." Nathaniel stood and paced behind the table. A habit he had when he was thinking, especially when the subject agitated him. It reminded Anton of watching a caged lion. "Where are those damn people now?"   Nathaniel asked. Not waiting for a response, he continued, "They're gone! They don't give a damn about me, Marie, you, or even your damn parents. Do you think any of them give a shit if you have the money to grow this idea of yours?"

"No, Sir, but that doesn't matter. I will make this work."

"Damn right, but it is money that will help you. I've spoken with Marie about this. Regarding the money we've discussed, you can use as much as you need to get your project working. When I'm out of here, I'll help with the growing, investing, and selling. Be smart, boy. If you have too much, the damn feds will be on you before you know it."

"Thank you, sir. But I can't take Marie's money."

"I know your father thinks very little of her. But that woman is one *mighty* remarkable woman. She doesn't care about the money. Just don't let your father get to her. I'm an old man. It helps me to know she has you on the outside to take care of her, if things get too rough."

"I will do that, sir."

*****

As Anton walked in the shadows toward room 12 A, he thought about how rough things had become. He never expected this family feud to end this way, but he wasn't completely surprised.

When he came to Santa Monica to visit his parents, Anton wanted to discuss the recent ruling successfully voiding Marie's marriage. He wasn't relishing the idea of listening to his parents' victory speech.

Anton wanted to stop the law suit; he tried. By tolerating the ruling to pass, he felt he'd disappointed his grandfather. He'd hoped this visit could bring about a compromise. Samuel had made his point. Now that Marie was planning on appealing the decision, perhaps Samuel could allow her to proceed.

Anton never had the chance to talk to his father or his mother. When he entered their bungalow three days ago, he found them dead. Immediately, Anton knew Marie had made it there first.

Her rendition of events was not too farfetched, if you knew the history. According to Marie, she went to their home to *talk*. It was Samuel who exploded first. He ordered her off his property. When she refused and asked to explain, Amanda entered the conversation. Supporting her husband, she told Marie to leave. It was Marie's second time to attempt this discussion. More than anything, she wanted to make them understand.

Marie was determined to talk until they listened. Amanda was the one to surprise Marie with a gun. Marie's memories were fuzzy after that. There was a struggle. She didn't intend to kill them, but once Samuel was shot, Marie knew if either lived, she'd be arrested. She couldn't endure what Nathaniel had in prison; she just couldn't. The combination of pent-up rage, years of degradation, fear and self-preservation all fueled Marie's ability to stage the final scene. She knew the exuberance of the gun shots nullified the murder/suicide theory. Yet, Marie hoped the scene she staged would aid in that notion.

Next, Marie turned up their television and cleaned away evidence of their scuffle. Her finger prints were wiped away. By all accounts she was still in New York. She'd driven the three thousand miles in her own old Honda, using cash along the way. There were no records of her traveling to California. No one knew she was there, except Anton.

Opening the door of 12 A, Anton entered the small stale hotel room. The stench of old tobacco and bodily fluids filled Anton's senses. It was enough to quench any desire he'd previously had of food. Nonetheless, he brought food from a local drive through. Placing the bag and cups on the small table, he said, "I brought this for you."

"Anton, I want to get out of this dump. When will it be safe for me to leave?"

He paced the only space large enough to take more than three steps, near the end of the bed. He considered sitting; however, the filth and stains on the furniture quickly changed his mind. "A few more days. I've been talking to the police and making all the necessary arrangements. So far the neighbor, Chester, is cooperating. He made one statement that first night to some cop. After that, he conveniently forgot about my *father's sister's* visit."

"It's going to cost money to keep him quiet, isn't it?"

"Yes, but I've negotiated. It won't all be up front, more of a yearly settlement."

"Did he agree?" Marie asked.

"I'm a very good negotiator. He understands -- sudden wealth brings questions. This will be mutually beneficial. Over time his payments will increase and it assures us of his future cooperation."

Marie stood before Anton. He looked at the woman his grandfather loved. She looked so much older than three years his senior. Her tired gray eyes cried out in anguish over the events of the past few months. She'd lost her husband, her name, and now her money. Anton knew he could turn her in to the police and go on with his life. Marie knew that too.

"I will repay you for this." She said, with her eyes lowered trying not to notice the grime on the worn carpet. Marie continued, "I know you are doing this for Nathaniel, not for me. But, I thank you."

He lifted her chin; she was his grandfather's wife. She needed to act as such. "You are right. And you are a Rawls; don't ever look down like that. I am the one who failed him by not stopping my father's law suit. I will not fail him again."

"I came to your family as hired help. I am not above doing that again. I can work for you."

Anton stared. His mind filled with memories of his family. He remembered the dinners in the grand dining room -- his grandfather, grandmother, father, mother, Marie, and him. How had it come down to just the two of them? "I'm not sure how this arrangement will work. I don't exactly have need for household staff at this point."

"You will." In the midst of total chaos, Marie's tone rang with confidence. "You are Nathaniel's grandson. You will succeed. I have no doubt."

Anton remembered Nathaniel's evaluation: *She is mighty remarkable.* He replied, "I will not abandon you. In a few more days we should be able to move you. Once we get you back to New York, we will create a timeline, an iron clad alibi for your whereabouts during my parent's death. The future will work itself out."

"It will, Anton. I have confidence in you." She reached for his shoulders, there was no sexual attraction. They were family. Marie felt as if she were looking into Nathaniel's eyes each time she stared into Anton's deep dark irises. The touch was merely a point of contact. They were together in this mess and bound forever by Nathaniel. "You know, your grandfather had plans for after his release. I've had a lot of time to think about those during these past few days."

"He told me." Her determination impressed Anton.

"I can help. I *want* to help. Truly I didn't intend to kill your parents, but I'm not sorry they're gone. I could lie and tell you I am. But, I won't." Anton nodded. "There are others who assisted in putting Nathaniel in prison, your father was but one."

"I have names. However, this will take time and money."

Marie smiled, "I have time. You make us more money."

The truth is rarely pure and never simple.
- Oscar Wilde

Chapter 46

Sophia exhaled and spoke determinedly, "Mr. George, I'll consider the most recent offer, but I'm afraid I cannot give you an answer today or tomorrow." She didn't wait for his response. "I will call you when I make my decision. Good-bye."

Silvia looked questionably at her daughter. "You are too busy to be babysitting your old parents."

"I'm hardly babysitting. You and Pop are helping me get this studio ready to open."

"I think getting away from home for a while has been good for your father, a change of scenery and all."

Sophia smiled. The thought came to her as she was flying to Princeton. She wanted to spend time with her parents and get the studio open. At first her parents balked at the idea. It wasn't until she told them how much work she needed to do that they willingly consented. Sophia knew if they felt needed, they'd be willing to go.

It was a good change of scenery for Sophia too. With Derek overseas, she didn't want to be stuck in California. Besides, Mr. George was beginning to annoy her with his persistence. Although smaller than the studio in Palo Alto, her studio in Provincetown was home.

She and Derek had worked so quickly to secure some of her art for shipping, they'd left this studio in disarray. Sophia still had many paintings and chalk and charcoal drawings stored here. Now, she and her parents needed to work to choose the best ones to display. Once the choices were made, the pieces needed to be framed, or stretched and framed, depending upon the medium.

Sophia's parents never claimed personal artistic skills. Nevertheless, when it came to displaying art, they were professionals. Silvia laughed saying they'd been doing it since Sophia was barely two years old – displaying her creations on the refrigerator door. Carlo's memory may have difficulties, but when it came to constructing an appropriate frame for his daughter's masterpieces, he was still on the top of his game.

Derek wouldn't be back to Santa Clara for another week. It was the perfect time for Sophia to enjoy her family, her cottage by the shore, prepare her studio, and hire someone to manage it while she's away. The income from her recent sales truly gave her more freedom than ever before.

*****

Tony and Claire returned to the house before five thirty. Claire hoped for a nap, before readying for the dessert celebration at Brent and Courtney's house. Catherine promised dinner on the patio at seven, saying they shouldn't go to a dessert and wine celebration on empty stomachs. Thinking of her condition, Claire agreed.

Back in her suite, Claire checked her phone. Of course, she had multiple text messages from her sister. The main request was for a call. Claire didn't want to call. She would willingly text, but she didn't want to hear Emily's voice or lectures. However, Claire worried, if she only sent a text, Emily would suspect Tony's manipulation.

Dreading the conversation, Claire hit *call.* Emily answered on the first ring. "Claire, are you all right?" Claire assured her sister she was fine. She still had her ticket to return to California on Sunday and those plans haven't changed. Claire promised to be careful and politely hung-up before Emily's words became too annoying.

After sending text messages to Amber and Harry, Claire climbed into the beautiful four poster bed, settled into the soft sheets, and slipped away. The memories of her lake and their afternoon floated through her subconscious. Being alone, she didn't try to subdue the smile that continually crept onto her face.

Her dream didn't make sense... when she drifted to sleep she was in the copper colored suite, yet as she looked around the walls were once again a rich beige and heavy golden draperies covered the windows. Claire reached for her cellphone but it was missing. Easing herself from the warm covers she searched for her iPad. It was no longer on the table. She saw the television, but instinctively knew the channels were limited. Her breathing quickened as she paced the confines of the luxurious room. No matter how hard she concentrated, she couldn't fill her lungs with adequate oxygen. The beautiful walls were closing in around her. She needed air, fresh air. Quickly she moved to the heavy golden drapes and exposed the tall French doors of her balcony. When the lever refused to budge, her heart rate quickened. Why wouldn't the doors open? The condensation on the small panes indicated cold on the other side. She peered through the small windows and registered the scene outside. The green leaves and vibrant colors were gone. In their place she saw skeletons of bare trees and visions of black and white. Inches of snow sat undisturbed on the rail of the balcony.

Claire's knees became weak. If it were winter, where was her baby? Claire's hand moved to her midsection finding her flat stomach. She wasn't visibly pregnant, so their child must be born. Claire scanned the suite for a crib, nothing. She ran to the hallway door. The lever wouldn't move. No! She was locked in! Where was her baby? Tears of panic rushed from her eyes as she beat upon the door. Panic filled her voice as she screamed at the top of her lungs. This was no longer *her* nightmare; it was her child's too.

"Ms. Claire, Ms. Claire, you are having a dream." Catherine's words quieted the screams which summoned Catherine to Claire's suite. She'd heard Claire's panicked screams from down the hall.

Claire opened her eyes to Catherine's concerned gaze. "Oh, Catherine – I was dreaming. It wasn't real, was it?"

"Yes, you were dreaming. Thankfully, your door wasn't locked. I am here for you. Everything is all right. Whatever it was, it was just a dream."

Claire allowed Catherine to embrace her before lying back upon the soft pillow. Trembling slightly she scanned the suite. The copper walls were back. Her stomach twisted as tears escaped her eyes. "Catherine, did you ever want to be a mother?"

The older woman straightened her back, "Why are you asking?"

Claire struggled to sit up. Her heartbeat beginning to calm, "I got the feeling yesterday when I told you that I've thought of you in that way, that it made you uncomfortable. I'm sorry."

Catherine's expression mellowed, "Don't be sorry. I took it as a compliment."

Claire smiled, "Good, that's how it was intended."

"Yes -- is the answer to your question. However, I've come to realize some people are not meant to be parents. There are better people to raise children."

"Why do you say that?"

"Some people have made too many poor choices to subject a child to their views."

Claire asked earnestly, "So you think a person's past would influence their ability to parent?"

"Of course, how could it not? Some people do not deserve to influence a child. Take Mr. Rawlings for example. He is the way he is in part due to the environment in which he was raised."

"What were his parents like?"

"You need to ask him that question. I believe he could have done much better."

Claire pondered Catherine's words and asked, "What about his grandparents?"

Catherine's expression softened. "In that category, Mr. Rawlings did do much better." Catherine pulled herself from her memories. "Ms." –

she smiled, "Claire, dinner will be ready soon. Are you better – from your dream? You need to get ready for the Simmons' celebration."

Truthfully, Claire could scarcely concentrate on Catherine's words. She had too many thoughts going through her mind. *Tony's parents were not good examples. Would that make him a bad father? If Catherine believed a person's past could make them undeserving of children, what about Tony's past sins?* Claire thought about the transgressions she knew to be true: *his stalking obsession of her, removing Simon from her life early on, (although that turned out well for Simon's career) and then Simon's death. Somehow Claire still believed Tony was involved. Also her kidnapping, his treatment of her when she first arrived, his controlling domineering side, how he set her up for attempted murder, and the demise of John's career; did it matter that he was now attempting redemption? What about the reason she was with him now? What about his recent blackmailing?*

"Thank you, Catherine, for giving me some answers."

Catherine nodded.

Claire continued her voice distant as her mind wrestled with these new thoughts, "I will get ready and be down for dinner."

This evening was more formal than the last, but not as formal as the wedding. As she readied for the festivities, Claire's nausea returned. Sitting on the edge of the large whirlpool tub wrapped in the pink cashmere robe, she fought the onset, as perspiration drenched her recently painted face. She heard the knock on the door of the suite, but she couldn't form the words to bid entrance. Claire knew she should be ready and downstairs, but her body wouldn't let her move.

His voice came from the other side of the bathroom door. Slowly she heard the turning of the knob. Whatever his expression and tone had been before, distress now prevailed. Tony fell to his knees before a shivering ashened Claire, "What is the matter with you? Are you sick? I will get you the best doctors..."

She heard his voice but their long ago lunch was no longer content to remain within her stomach. The problem was they'd eaten hours before. Claire ran to the lavatory enclosed within a small attached room and submitted mostly to dry heaves as her petite body convulsed. This wasn't how she had wanted to tell him, *if* she was to tell him at all.

When her body finally calmed, Claire stood, attempted poise, and reentered the main part of the bathroom. She walked to the sink, rinsed her mouth, and turned toward Tony. She hadn't noticed before how handsomely he was dressed, quite the contrast to her current condition. Her hair was still done, but her cosmetics needed repair. And although quite expensive, her robe was hardly celebration attire. Looking to his worried face, she finally found her voice, "Tony, I'm not sick."

He gently reached for her shoulders. "What do you mean? You're obviously ill. I'll call Brent. They'll understand."

"No, I want to go. I will be better soon. It doesn't usually hit this hard in the afternoon. I think I'm just stressed."

"What doesn't hit..?" For an extremely intelligent man, he was slow at fitting the pieces of this puzzle together. His eyes widened and he released her shoulders. Suddenly his concerned tone morphed, now more slow and harsh, "*What* doesn't hit?"

"The nausea." Claire wasn't feeling the positive aura one would hope in such a conversation.

"Brought on by what?"

Hell, her make-up needed touch up anyway. She felt the tears pool and blinked, allowing them to descend her cheeks. "I'm seven weeks pregnant, almost eight." Claire could see the wheels turning in his head. "Yes, Tony, *we* are going to have a baby."

His expression momentarily appeared blank. There was no manipulation, no hidden agenda, only shock. Did Claire ever remember seeing Tony speechless? If she did, she couldn't recall. Finally she saw his emotions swirl through his ever darkening eyes. He asked, "How did this happen?"

She looked at him incredulously, "That is a great question, since I have no recall of letting you back into my condominium, but nonetheless, the timing works perfectly."

He slowly turned circles, pacing as he could within the confines of the bathroom, "What are we going to do about ..." he motioned toward her midsection, "...this?"

Indignantly, she stood straighter. "I don't know what *we* are going to do. *I'm* going to have a baby, with or without you."

"But you're twenty-nine years old; I'm forty-eight!"

"Yes, and when we married our age difference was the same."

"We never discussed children."

"It's a little late for discussion." Claire felt her strength returning with the fury now surging through her veins. Damn him for not responding the way she wanted him to! "Now if you'll excuse me, I will be downstairs in ten minutes for dinner, and we can continue your charade."

Tony shook his head and stepped toward his ex-wife. "I'm sorry. You surprised me. Let me think about this for a while."

"Fine, Tony, *think* all you want. Your thoughts and decisions don't matter. I'm having this baby."

"Of course you are. I never suggested otherwise. I will be downstairs on the patio." He kissed her cheek and left. She collapsed again on the edge of the tub. *Well that went well!* She thought sarcastically. Then she remembered the little life inside of her and audibly comforted, "It will be all right. No matter what -- *we* will be fine. Don't worry about your father -- I'm not." *Was it good to lie to your child, even if you were doing it for their own good?*

When Claire stepped onto the patio, Tony attentively stood and pulled out her chair. Her hair was perfect; make-up repaired, and dress lovely. Her growing breasts filled the bodice more than they would have before. Even her color was back to normal with a glow of sun on her cheeks from their day on the lake shore.

Sincerely he asked, "How are you feeling?"

Genteel and reticent, she responded, "I am feeling better, thank you for asking." And then Claire did what Tony had done to her over and over. She conversed about anything and everything except the pregnancy. On his few attempts to discuss it, she changed the subject. Her change of subject wasn't as direct as saying, "The subject is closed" but subtly she'd mention something else. For instance her dress -- it was one from the closet. She told Tony how much she liked it and thanked him for having it bought.

The dessert celebration proceeded with equal poise. Claire stayed dutifully by his side and said and did everything to continue their charade. After all, this gathering contained people they didn't know. It was Claire's experience that information can be leaked at any moment by any source. To everyone, they appeared the happy couple trying for reconciliation.

When the waiter offered glasses of champagne, Claire smirked as Tony asked for non-alcoholic. Even he drank the disgustingly sweet bubbly grape juice. It didn't make up for his initial reaction, but it did incite a genuine smile on Claire's lips.

On their way back to the estate, Tony detoured to a secluded back road. The June night was warmer than the one before, and the stars were bright. Although she didn't know where they were going, Claire didn't ask. She remained reserved, answering questions, and continuing courteous conversation. Finally after a bumpy dirt road, Tony stopped the Mercedes. His headlights faded into the darkness illuminating a meadow. "Do you know where we are?"

Claire looked from side to side. Beyond the meadow were trees, but they were no more distinctive than any other trees. "I don't."

He got out of the car and walked to her door. After opening it, he extended his hand and asked, "Will you please walk with me a moment?"

Claire looked down at her shoes. They too were from his closet of clothes, Casadsi platform pumps with a very thin four inch heel. She wasn't sure of their cost, but from experience she was certain they weren't intended for hiking. "I don't think my shoes are meant for..."

"I don't give a damn about the shoes." His polite invitation gave way to the emotions he'd been suppressing all evening.

Claire shrugged and accepted his outstretched hand. Her facade once again in place she replied, "Of course, Mr. Rawlings, I'd be delighted."

They took a few steps when Claire stumbled, falling into Tony's strong embrace. She straightened and secured herself. "Have you figured out where we are?" He asked.

"I really don't know."

"This is where I brought you the day I apologized for your accident." Claire's back straightened and her chin rose indignantly. He added, "I meant every word that day."

"Tony, I don't want to talk about..."

"I have done some things in my life I'm not proud of. I never in all of my life considered having a child."

Claire turned to look at his face. The faint glow of the moon saved them from total blackness and shadowed his features. He continued, "I can run businesses, I can make deals, and I can multi-task better than most." His volume increased, "Nothing frightens me. I can take on an entire board of directors and know that tomorrow they will all be jobless. I have eliminated adversaries and obstacles." He turned toward his ex-wife, "This is totally new territory."

Her facade melted, "I know, it scares me too."

"Do I?"

His question surprised her. Claire considered her answer and spoke, "I'm afraid of what you're capable of doing. You made a point of showing me your control over my friends' futures." She reached for his hand. "But of you – personally -- not anymore. There was a time. But I've changed and you've changed. No, I'm not."

"I don't want you and this baby living in California."

"I know. But Tony, I can't go back to the past."

"To here?"

"No, I love *here*. I won't go back to your supreme control over my every move. I can't. And I can't allow that kind of life for our child."

"*Our* child." He repeated as he gently touched her midsection.

Claire nodded, "I went to the doctor on Wednesday. She did an ultrasound. I saw the image of our baby and his heart beating. The sound of his heart reminded me of my lake, here. From that moment on, everything felt right."

"You keep saying *him*?"

She mused, "I have no idea of gender. *Him* sounds better than *it*, don't you think?"

Tony thought about her words. Finally he said, "You know you're very good at pretending. I knew it before, but tonight you were perfect at every turn. I felt your anger, yet you appeared perfect. How do I really know how you feel?"

"How do I know how *you* feel? Or that you won't do something to me like you did before, with the attempted murder thing."

Tony lowered his lips to the top of her head, "I guess we need to trust one another."

"Can we do that?" Claire asked.

"I don't know." He answered, as he took her hand and helped her back to the car.

On the ride home Tony asked questions and Claire answered. No one else knows about the pregnancy. She wanted to see him and decide what she'd do. However, from the moment she saw the ultrasound, Claire knew, *not having* this baby was not an option. She told him about the sickness, what she'd thought was food poisoning and the bacon. He asked when she knew. It was Sunday, less than a week ago. She did a home pregnancy test. Wednesday she saw the doctor and Thursday she flew here.

At the bottom of the stairs, Claire said good night to Tony.

Before releasing her hand, Tony said, "I would like to join you, just to talk."

"Not tonight. I've got a lot to think about."

He didn't argue.

When she reached her suite, she closed the door and collapsed on the soft sofa. The vibration in her purse caught her attention, three missed calls from Harry. If it were one, she could wait until morning, but three needed attention. There were no voice mails, but she did have a text message, simply saying: *CALL AS SOON AS YOU CAN.*

Harry answered on the first ring. "Claire?"

"Yes, what's the matter?"

"Amber's condo was broken into tonight."

Claire's heart stopped, "Is she all right?"

"Yes, she was out with Keaton."

"How did it happen? I thought security had been tightened?"

"It has. Now it's been stepped up another notch."

"Did they catch the person?"

"No, whoever it was got away. Security noticed the breach. Do you think Mr. Rawlings is responsible for this, too?"

Claire sat straighter, indignantly she replied, "No." Her mind whirled; he wouldn't do that, would he? "Besides, he's here." She hastily added, "In Iowa, not here in this room."

"Well, the thing is – whoever it was tore *your* room apart. Drawers dumped, closet torn apart. We won't know until you come home and do inventory, but so far we've determined the only thing missing is your laptop. Or do you have it?"

As the blood left her face, she felt violated, "No, I have my tablet, but my laptop should be on the desk." Her once strong voice quivered, "They only disturbed my room?"

"Yes."

*Love comes when manipulation stops; when you think more
about the other person than about his or her reactions to you.
When you dare to reveal yourself fully.
When you dare to be vulnerable.*
- Dr. Joyce Brothers

Chapter 47

Reality began to focus as Claire's blissful dreams gave way to the intermittent beeping of her iPhone. She tried to push the sound of her unanswered text messages away and stay in her warm safe cocoon. Undaunted, the beeping continued. Blindly, Claire reached next to her on the large ornately carved four poster bed, for her iPhone. It was where she'd left it, after falling asleep talking to Amber until very late, Iowa time. Claire concentrated on the time: 7:35.

She assessed her body. How did she feel about waking this early? After a few moments she determined neither her body nor her baby were protesting. Claire focused, reading the text messages. The first from Amber: *IM GLAD WE TALKED. SEE YOU SUNDAY.* The next from Tony: *IF YOU ARE FEELING UP TO BREAKFAST, MEET ME ON THE PATIO AT 8.* Claire wondered if that was an invitation or a mandate. Either way, her presence was requested in less than a half an hour.

Making her way to the bathroom and washing her face, Claire decided, *If Tony wants to see me this early, this is what he gets.* She wrapped herself in the pink robe and made her way to the patio. The morning summer sun rose in the southeast, beginning its ascent considerably earlier than Claire. Therefore, by the time she arrived to the patio, it was making its way over the trees and illuminating the brick terrace with its morning brilliance. As soon as Tony saw Claire through the French doors, he moved his coffee cup away and stood.

"Good morning, I wasn't sure you would wake for my text."

"Good morning," she smiled, "I did." She sat, at the seat complete with a place setting, obviously for her. Immediately, Cindy was beside her.

"Ms. Claire, would you like some coffee or some tea?"

"Tea, thank you, Cindy."

Cindy scurried away toward the kitchen, leaving Tony and Claire alone in the warming fresh country air.

"How are you feeling this morning?" he asked with concern evident in his tone.

"I'm feeling well, which is surprising, thinking how early this is in California."

Tony smirked, "I think you're getting used to being in Iowa. It probably isn't a great idea to keep changing time zones; maybe you should stay here."

Claire smiled half-heartedly. "I don't think that would resolve any of my current issues."

"Oh, but you're mistaken. It would be ever so helpful." Tony reached for the bowl of fresh fruit. "Would you like some fruit?"

After Claire spooned some fresh melon and grapes into her bowl, she asked, "Why did you summon me here so early?"

He reached for her hand, "Claire, why do you think everything has double meaning?"

She swallowed the juicy fruit and replied, "Because, I know you."

Tony laughed, "Better than most."

"What's your plan?"

"I wanted to discuss the day. I plan to work from home this morning and was hoping we could spend time together before the wedding."

"I told Sue I might be available to meet her and Sean this morning in Iowa City. I think I'd like that."

Tony sat back and contemplated. Finally he said, "Eric can drive you."

She tried her best to keep her defenses at bay, "I was thinking -- perhaps you have a car that isn't worth half a million, that you'd let me borrow for a quick drive into town?"

Claire watched Tony's mental and physical wheels turn. She knew she'd sent his controlling impulses into overdrive. The muscles in his neck intermittently protruded as his jaw clenched and unclenched. She drank some orange juice and enjoyed the show.

Finally he asked with a smirk, "Are you enjoying yourself?"

Claire grinned, "Immensely, thanks for asking."

Clouds darkened his expression, "The last time you drove away..."

"This time I am talking to you about it," she interrupted. "I want to meet Sue for coffee. I will return, and you and I will go to the wedding - together."

"I thought coffee made you ill?"

Claire smirked, "Coffee is an aphorism for getting together. I can guarantee I will not be having coffee."

"Getting together? About what?"

Claire sat straighter. "This is what I don't want."

"Concern Claire -- that is what I have. After all, someone broke into your condominium last night. Don't you think you should be concerned?"

Cindy brought eggs and toast to Claire and sat them in front of her. After Claire thanked her, she left. Her attention returned to Tony. "How do you know about that?"

"So you aren't surprised?"

"No. I spoke to others about it last night. And I suppose I'm not surprised you know."

"Others?"

"Yes, Tony – friends, Harry called. I spoke to him and to Amber. They are both well, *thank you for asking.*"

"Why are you not more upset?"

"I was initially, but now I think you're responsible."

His spine straightened. "Claire, why would *I* have someone break into *your* condo?"

"I don't know. Whoever it was took my laptop. The only secret information on there is about you." Claire continued to eat.

Tony sat his cup of coffee on the table, "Me?"

"Yes, I've been trying to reconstruct the information from the box I received. I've spent a lot of time looking up information about your grandfather and father. It's on my laptop." Claire watched as his jaws once again clenched and unclenched.

"I have nothing to do with this break in," Tony said. "I do, however, think you should consider staying here. It is significantly safer."

"Well, Tony, I'm being honest with you. That laptop contains information regarding Nathaniel and Samuel Rawls. If you weren't the person responsible for its disappearance, perhaps you'd like to learn who has it."

"I will do my best. This is getting out of hand."

"Well, back to my original question, do you have a car I can take into town for coffee with Sue? I need to call her."

Tony leaned forward, "Claire, are you asking? I'm having difficulty with your wording."

"Are we in the presence of others?" She looked to her right and saw the empty pool deck. She looked to her left and saw the southeast wing of the mansion; she knew the woods and gardens were behind her. "No, I'm not asking permission to go into town, only permission to use one of your cars. I would hate to be accused of stealing."

With her get-together complete, Claire maneuvered the BMW toward Tony's estate and contemplated the long winding drive. She tried unsuccessfully to diminish the beauty of it. She'd driven off his estate twice; this was her first solo drive back onto it. Looking at the dashboard clock, it was nearly eleven. The wedding wasn't until five thirty.

Coffee with Sue was nice. Sue obviously felt guilty for not supporting Claire in her troubles. In many ways Claire felt bad lying to Sue now about her and Tony's reconciliation. Or was she? Claire's emotions were so jumbled -- sometimes she didn't know what was real and what was pretend. To Claire, the best part of their meeting was seeing Sean again. While the ladies chatted, he busied himself with toys. Claire smiled, remembering how Sue picked the bright colored rattles off the floor at least fifty times.

Claire pulled the car to the front door, not worrying about taking it around to the garage. Eric would do that. As she walked up the steps toward the house Claire realized how easy it was to slip into that place where others did things for her. Was this part of Tony's plan? Did he want her to remember the perks of being here?

She opened the door to the massive sparkling entry. While she decided if she wanted to go upstairs to her suite or down the hall to Tony's office, Catherine came hurriedly down the hall to greet her. "Claire, you are back!"

"Yes, I just went to town," Claire looked questionably at Catherine, "Did you think I wouldn't come back?"

"I was only concerned when Mr. Rawlings told me you'd taken one of the cars."

"Where is he?" Claire asked.

"He is in his office. Would you like me to let him know you are back?"

Claire remembered his rules: she was only allowed in his office by invitation or summons. Claire decided this was another opportunity to push the envelope. "No, thank you. I will." She saw Catherine's surprised expression as Claire turned toward the corridor and walked to office. Should she knock?

As she contemplated, she heard his voice from behind the large doors, "... that was two days ago. I wanted an answer yesterday. Your incompetence is..." His speech stalled, hearing the simultaneous knock and opening of his door. Claire watched his expression morph through a series of emotions. Wasn't there a time when she couldn't read his thoughts? Seeing him go from anger -- at the person on the telephone -- to shock at the unrequested intrusion and finally to amusement by Claire's forwardness, she wondered how anyone couldn't read his every thought. With a mischievous smile, he continued speaking. Although his heart was no longer in his tirade, he attempted to conceal that from the poor soul on the other end of the line. "It seems as though another pressing matter has come to my attention. We will postpone this conversation. Mr. George, I expect to hear from you Monday morning. Do not disappoint me." He disconnected the line. His eyes remained fixed on Claire's from the moment she opened the door.

She smiled as he walked around the large mahogany desk toward her. His movements were graceful yet powerful, like a lion stalking its prey. The light behind his intense dark chocolate eyes made her tingle with anticipation. She'd seen that sultry look before. *Why was she smiling?* She'd come to his office to let him know she was back, and suddenly the temperature of the regal room was rising exponentially.

She thought about his words on the phone. She'd heard that closing statement a hundred times. "That should be your tag line."

"Oh, but you are so right." He was now only inches away, looking down into her confident expression. His cologne penetrated her nostrils and filled her lungs. "I do not like being disappointed."

"I remember that about you." She hesitated. If she just leaned forward, they would be touching. She stood straight, fighting the urge for contact. "Your car has been returned in one piece, scarcely a scratch."

The tips of his lips twitched and his eyebrow cocked, "A scratch?"

Claire's grin broadened, "Wasn't that your concern, that I might scratch it?"

He took the initiative and leaned forward. Their subtle touch increased the beating of her heart. Almost instantaneously, her tender breasts responded to the sensation of his massive chest. "I don't recall being concerned with a scratch," he said. "The whole damn car can be replaced. I believe my concern was with your safe return." Because, Claire hadn't resisted their contact, Tony chose to make another move, wrapping his arms around the small of her back. With their proximity, her face tipped upward.

Her mind told her to back away. However, she could barely hear the instructions over the intense pulsation of blood in her ears. Her words slowed with breathy expectation, "I have returned."

With one hand still behind her, Tony gently brought her chin skyward. His touch combined with a new husky tone caused Claire's emerald eyes to flutter. She felt the vibration of his speech against her chest, "You, my dear, are continually teaching me new things?"

"What, pray-tell, have I taught you?"

His lips tenderly brushed hers. "I believe I mentioned before, I liked the black panties. The other night, the light blue satin bra straps monopolized my thoughts. Every time I looked at you, I wondered if it was part of a matching set." Claire nodded, their noses touching with the movement of her head. "And just now, I realized how much more satisfying it is to have you bring yourself home, freely – willingly, than to know you have been driven, perhaps reluctantly."

"It seems - s...." Claire giggled, "You can teach an old dog new tricks." The breath of his laugh bathed her face in warmth. She went on, "and as I recall, you've taught me quite a few things too." Her mind screamed to stop. Did she really want to go here? Yet, her mouth seemed to be attached to another part of her anatomy. That part knew exactly where it wanted to go.

"I had been thinking about the pool, but I'm up for review, if you are willing?"

She smiled at the reference. He was definitely up for review. She could feel him up against her hip. This wasn't her plan either. But for some reason it felt right. Maybe she needed to know. Lifting her hands to his dark hair, Claire allowed her fingers to weave their way through his thick black mane as her green eyes opened wide, searching his softening brown irises.

He pulled her closer, pressing himself against her. She lowered her lids and willingly consented. Parting their lips, their tongues engaged.

The passion ignited Claire in ways she'd forgotten. In ways she'd safely compartmentalized away. Even with Harry.

None of it made sense. Claire wanted Tony to pay for his sins. She wanted to bring him down. And, and ... and she wanted what they had, but more... better. She wanted what seemed to be staring her in the face.

Tony -- his magnetism, his control, his dominance -- was erotic. Claire also wanted freedoms and liberties. She wanted a non-monitored telephone, the ability to come and go, and freedoms -- and him.

Didn't their child deserve to know his or her father? Could Tony ever be a man to swing his small child into his arms with a laugh? Claire told herself, she was consenting for their child, but currently *her* needs wholly dominated her thoughts.

As Claire's arms encircled his neck, her breasts tingled against his solid muscular chest. Everything she did or said was brought on by deep suppressed carnal desire. She'd spent too much time during the past three years thinking. Today she wanted to respond and react... she wanted her screaming consciousness to take a much needed break. Claire wanted Tony.

When he bent down with his nose touching hers and asked, "Are you sure?"

Claire didn't hesitate. "Yes. I'm sure."

Tony didn't ask again. Instead he bent slightly and scooped Claire into his arms. They did not stay in the regal office; instead, Tony carried her away from the grand staircase, down the corridor to his room, laying Claire on the large regal bed.

Today she wore pink underwear, matching the color of her top. Once again his skilled fingers played with the bow directly below her bellybutton. After removing the lace bra, he caressed her growing breasts. Their tenderness intensified his manipulation, rousing stimulation and bringing Claire unknown ecstasy. His prowess within the defined skill set was unequaled. Multiple times Claire gripped Tony's shoulders or the satin sheets trying desperately to remain earth bound as her body surged toward heaven.

When they were both satisfied, she laid within the crook of his arm enjoying the feel of her head on his shoulder and his intoxicating scent. Claire thought about what she'd done. Unashamedly, she didn't regret her decisions. His steady breathing was an aphrodisiac, electrifying her already taut body. Was this insatiable need, too, a result of the pregnancy? The more he gave, the more she wanted.

The draperies of his large windows were open. The midday sunshine illuminated his suite. Seeing past the glass, the crystal blue sky reminded her of the pool. "Do you think we could have lunch at the pool and enjoy some of this day outside?"

He turned to her with a grin matching his sultry stare, "I would like to stay here forever, but I like the idea of getting you more sun."

Her lips found his neck and began to roam, between suckles she said, "At this second, I wouldn't argue, with staying here." The low growl elicited by her actions was enough to split her body wide open. "But, I'm hungry, and that sky, looks beautiful."

He rolled her onto her back as her long brown hair fanned the pillow behind her glowing face. "Not as beautiful as you look this moment."

Claire felt her cheeks blush. Her eyes went to the grand ceiling above as she felt his lips nuzzle her collar bone and move south. "Mr. Rawlings, I believe we were discussing lunch?"

His smile filled her as much as his actions. Claire didn't want to enjoy it or him. But she did. When she sat to get out of his bed, her vision turned toward his grand fireplace. There were so many good memories associated with that hearth and the warmth radiating from it. What caught her attention causing the air to leave her lungs was *above* the fireplace.

"Tony," she stammered, "how long have you had that there?"

His expression changed. Had he forgotten her wedding portrait was hanging above his fireplace? "Ever since you left."

Perhaps it is impossible to wear an identity
without becoming what you pretend to be.
– Orson Scott Card

Chapter 48

Pictures of Tony and Claire flooded the internet. Someone at Brent and Courtney's house made good use of their cellphone. There were even pictures of Claire with Sue in Iowa City. Claire wondered, *isn't there any real news happening in the world?*

As she viewed each picture, Claire questioned her expressions. How long could she continue to argue her facade? Was she truly that accomplished at lying, or had Tony's bold move and forced togetherness induced his desired outcome? Could Claire possibly be enjoying herself with him?

As she completed the final touches of her wedding attire, Claire thought about their afternoon. From his office, to his suite, and the pool deck with the warm sultry water...his expressions and touches kept her body on high alert. Even while napping under the shade of a large umbrella, Claire remembered the feel of his large strong hands caressing her skin with sunscreen. It wasn't the first time her body rebelled against her better judgment. Claire reasoned, *tomorrow I will fight. Today I want to enjoy.*

Radiant was the word in Tony's mind as he watched Claire descend the grand staircase. With the blush of afternoon sun on her cheeks, her hair and makeup done to perfection, and the light green Herve Leger dress she'd found in the closet, Claire looked radiant.

As the Gucci, strappy, five inch heeled sandals clicked across the marble floor, the adoration she saw in his eyes made her cheeks redden.

"I think it's true what they say," Tony purred.

She raised an eyebrow, "What do they say?"

"You are glowing – absolutely radiant!"

"Thank you, Mr. Rawlings." She took in his toned muscular body, covered exquisitely with his customary Armani silk suit. "You are rather handsome yourself."

They made their way to Tony's waiting Mercedes and drove to Davenport. On the way Claire asked about Eric. Other than picking her up from the airport, she hadn't seen him her entire stay.

"Well, if you recall, I offered his services this morning for your trip into town."

Claire blushed at the memory of her return. "Perhaps I should have taken you up on that offer?"

His hand caressed her knee, "I believe I'm very happy with your choices; bold and cheeky is proving to be another pleasurable lesson."

"Why, Anthony," her faux southern belle accent purposefully elongated the *yyy*, "who would have guessed, you could be open to new things?"

Thankfully, she was sitting and seat belted into the soft leather seat, because Tony's expression made her knees weak. And the sound of his deep sensual voice caused her insides to melt, "I am always open to new things, especially so -- if they involve you."

Once again she felt the blood rush to her cheeks as they rose in a genuine smile, causing her emerald eyes to glisten. Claire turned and watched the passing scenes beyond the passenger side window. Was she flirting? Was he?

Entering the cathedral, Claire and Tony blended into the groom's guests. Claire couldn't believe she was actually attending Caleb Simmons' wedding. It had been a dream of hers since learning the date in a letter from Courtney while in prison. Glancing down at her hand resting comfortably in Tony's, she thought about how long ago prison seemed. Never in a million years could she have predicted her current location, watching Courtney and Brent escorted down the aisle. Courtney looked beautiful in a mother-of-the-groom sunburst gown. Claire had heard all about it when Courtney first purchased it. Again, neither woman ever foresaw Claire seeing it in person.

As the ceremony progressed, Caleb appeared handsome and confident. Julia's smile lit the entire cathedral. Her gown's train flowed behind her as her father escorted her to the front of the church. Claire couldn't help think about her own wedding. As the memories came, so did the tears. She dabbed her eyes while Tony gently squeezed her hand. Without thinking she leaned against his strong shoulder and accepted his unspoken support.

They sat with Tony's friends during the reception. Claire was thankful Tony insisted on getting together prior to the wedding festivities. It made the reception much more comfortable. After the meal and cake, the music began. While the new Mr. and Mrs. Simmons danced, Tony and Claire watched from their seats. Again he held her hand. She wondered if he was thinking about their first dance as husband and wife. She remembered feeling like a princess in his arms. After the couple danced with Julia's parents, Claire watched Caleb dance with Courtney and Julia with Brent. Claire couldn't imagine being anywhere else. Next the dance floor opened to the guests. When the music slowed Claire accepted Tony's invitation and joined him under the soft lights.

Perhaps it was their afternoon activities, but Claire's body molded unconsciously to his. He directed their every step gracefully guiding her across the floor.

"I know I fought you about all of this," she whispered, "but I'm so happy to be here right now."

His embrace of her slender waist tightened, "I couldn't be happier myself." He leaned away to see her face, "And I hope you realize, *this* isn't a charade."

Claire pressed her lips together in a straight line. With all of her might she wanted to argue, but she couldn't lie. Shaking her head from side to side, she admitted, "Right now, I know that."

Tony pulled her close as the rest of the guests disappeared. Claire closed her eyes, felt the warmth of his embrace, and allowed her body to go wherever he led.

*****

It wasn't difficult to access her laptop. A few different tries and her password was easily discovered. The information within was more than he could ever have imagined. Just recently he'd formed his own ideas about Anthony Rawlings being Anton Rawls, but now he had it in black and white. She had so much information about the Rawls family. Years ago he'd tried to do similar research, but everything came up a dead end. Why wouldn't it? By 1990, the Rawls family ceased to exist.

According to Ms. Nichols fine research, Sharron died first of natural causes. There was very little information about her, especially during the last three years of her life. She didn't even appear in any family photos. Nathaniel passed away in May of 1989, while incarcerated in a minimum security prison in New York. Next, yes, he liked this part: Samuel and Amanda died in a *murder / suicide* in Santa Monica, California. Why did Ms. Nichols have a question mark next to the murder / suicide? Obviously she questioned the accuracy of the assessment.

He often wondered how Anton got the police investigators to go along with that conclusion. Perhaps, he made the same bargain with them that he had with him. Ms. Nichols even had copies of police, ballistic, and autopsy reports. The scanned copy of the 911 call caught his attention. Apparently, Anton hadn't been as thorough as he thought. This must have been how she and Harrison Baldwin found him. His name appeared on the report.

Smirking, Patrick Chester thought it funny; he'd actually thought Ms. Nichols was Anton's daughter. Seeing her recently all over the internet, she wasn't Anton's (aka Anthony Rawlings) daughter; she was his ex-wife. According to the gossip people, they were working on reconciling. Patrick wondered if Mr. Anthony Rawlings had any idea of the wealth of information his ex-wife had accumulated against him.

Patrick considered the possibility of blackmailing Claire Nichols, too. But she wasn't exactly living in the lap of luxury. Oh, her condominium was nice, in a very high priced part of town. She even kept affluent company. Amber McCoy, CEO of SiJo Gaming, was valued at quite a bit. Her brother, Harrison Baldwin, wasn't hurting for cash either. Nevertheless, in comparison to Anthony Rawlings, they were paupers.

Why had Patrick accepted such measly annual supplements, when Anthony Rawlings could so easily afford more? Of course, it was because up until Ms. Nichols made an appearance at his home, he never suspected Anton Rawls of being the great Anthony Rawlings. The way Patrick saw it; he was due twenty plus years of back payments.

The missing information on Ms. Nichols laptop was about Samuel Rawls' sister. Patrick didn't even know her name; he never did. He just remembered Amanda Rawls referring to the woman as Samuel's sister. Funny, as he scanned Ms. Nichol's research, it didn't even look like Samuel had a sister. That didn't matter. For all the time, Anton – Anthony -- had paid to keep the information about that woman hidden, she must be someone important. Patrick wondered if Mr. Rawlings would pay a bonus for keeping this information away from Claire Nichols. Seriously, what man wants his wife or ex-wife to learn he's been paying to keep a secret about another woman?

Another picture just hit the internet. Wasn't today's technology wonderful? The photo was taken only minutes ago, via someone's cellphone -- amazing quality for a phone. The picture was of Anthony Rawlings and Claire Nichols dancing. They seemed very dressed up. The caption mentioned a wedding reception. Patrick Chester smiled. The sinister grin was truly too large for his face. He knew without a doubt, the real money was right there, in Mr. Rawlings' arms. The mega-billionaire would gladly pay big, no huge, for the safe return of that woman. And to think he'd had her right on his property. If he'd only known what a gold mine she was the day she and Mr. Baldwin visited. That didn't matter. Patrick knew now.

Searching the laptop he found her travel itinerary. Ms. Nichols' flight was due back to San Francisco at 17:40:00, tomorrow. She had a first class ticket. *That figures*, Patrick thought. *Well, her accommodations won't be as luxurious once I get a hold of her.*

*****

To: Anthony Rawlings
From: Phillip Roach
Date: June 8, 2013
Re: Ms. Nichols

I have confirmed with security at Ms. Nichol's condominium, her unit was indeed breached. It was not until the perpetrator was leaving her unit that security devises indicated a violation. That means it is safe to assume, since her room was the only one manhandled, she was indeed the target. Until Ms. Nichols can confirm, the only item taken was her laptop.

According to the records of my indicators, the front door to her condo was opened Friday, June 7, at 8:15, the violation was noted when the door once again opened at 8:27 pm. Security cameras do not show a clear picture of the person in question. It appears to be a man who is bald or balding. I will increase my surveillance and report any suspicious activity.

Please confirm the time and place of her arrival. I know her reservations have been changed. I look forward to the new times and places. Thank you.

*****

The guests began to thin, when Tony suggested they head back to the estate. Claire hated leaving Courtney, Brent, and her other friends. She didn't know when she would see them again. Of course, since she and Tony were in the midst of *reconciliation*, she couldn't voice her concerns. Instead, she smiled politely and warmly offered her farewells.

Once they were alone in the seclusion of Tony's car, Claire settled against the soft seat and thought fondly about her day. Her mind went from the breakfast on the patio, to driving Tony's car, coffee with Sean and Sue, her return to the estate and their mutual physical admiration, poolside, the wedding, and finally the reception. Each scene filled her with hope, with promise of what could be.

These thoughts kept her from talking and overpowered her consciousness. She was mindlessly lost when Tony asked, "Have you spoken to anyone from Palo Alto lately?"

Her insides clenched with apprehension. She didn't like discussing Harry and Amber with Tony. "I haven't even looked at my phone since we left for the wedding. Why? Has something else happened?"

"Not to my knowledge. However, my source tells me the intruder to your unit was not interrupted. His only intention was to access *your* room and take your laptop."

Her world of happiness and hope evaporated, "Why would anyone want *my* laptop?"

"What was on it?"

Claire considered the contents of her hard drive. "I don't know, my bank accounts, my travel itinerary, information about your past, and a rough draft from Meredith about her bo... articles."

Tony's knuckles blanched as he gripped the stirring wheel. "I thought this stupid Meredith Banks thing was over?"

"It is. With the money you gave me, to give her – she'll keep it quiet, unless, as you and I decided, something happens to me or someone I care about."

After taking a deep breath Tony asked, "What do you have regarding my past?"

Claire sat straighter, "Seriously, I've spent so much time on this, it's hard to condense it into an elevator pitch."

With the eerie green of the dashboard, his black eyes transcended the darkness. "Give it a try. I'm sure you can do it."

Claire inhaled, "Fine. I confirmed Nathaniel and Sharron Rawls had a son named Samuel. He married a woman named Amanda; they had a son name Anton, born February 12, 1965, the same day as you. That plus a picture in Newsweek showing your grandfather's home confirmed to me that you are indeed Anton."

"Well, you know that's true. Why are you continuing this research?"

"I really don't want to discuss this... please?"

"Despite your suspicions, I had nothing to do with the break-in. I need to know what the perpetrator now knows."

"My computer is password protected. No one besides me can access it."

Tony's ambivalent expression spoke volumes regarding her *secure* laptop.

Finally she said, "Obviously you disagree. If someone is able to access my information, there are documents and reports from your parents' death."

For a moment, Claire feared their future. Tony seemed unable to peer forward although the Mercedes cruised that direction at unknown speeds. His eyes bore into her soul. "What possible business of yours is my parents' death?"

Claire straightened defiantly, "I suppose before it was morbid curiosity. I wanted to know if you were truly capable of hurting your own parents. Now – however --" she hesitated and sat straighter, defiantly, "now it is very much my business. I need to know about *my* child's family history."

The tenseness in Tony's strong shoulders eased. "I suppose that's correct." In a moonlit glow, the countryside continued to pass outside the windows. Tony confessed, "I did not harm my parents."

Claire reached for him, covering his hand with the warmth of hers, "I know that now. I've known for a while it wasn't you; it was a woman in a blue Honda." Claire felt the atmosphere within the car tighten. She went on, "Whoever that woman is -- you have been protecting her for years."

"Protecting her?"

"Yes, whoever she is, you've kept her secret secure."

It felt as if Tony were wrestling with himself, wanting to ask more questions, yet not wanting to divulge more information. After a moment he asked, "So all of this is on your laptop?"

Claire nodded, "Yes."

They drove in silence until Tony said, "I want you to seriously reconsider your return flight. The estate is much safer and more secure than a condominium which has already been broken into."

Claire squeezed his knee. "I've had a wonderful time. Please don't ruin it. Let's please take all of this one day at a time? I'd like to think about tonight now and tomorrow later."

His grip loosened upon the innocent wheel as he contemplated her words.

When they reached Tony's estate, he left the Mercedes sitting in front of the steps, gallantly opened Claire's door, and kissed her hand. Earlier, in the dashboard light she'd watched the man she'd once loved fight his emotions. The intensity in his black eyes and grip upon the soft leather steering wheel no longer frightened her. Hadn't Catherine asked her to see how hard he is trying? Claire did. And now, that same gorgeous man had her hand at his lips with an equal but different intensity in his gaze. The aura surrounding them wasn't about laptops or airplane tickets but about pure and simple desire. She could over analyze; however, the way his lips electrified her skin and melted her insides, nullified any arguments she could form.

They walked hand in hand into the house. At the base of the grand staircase, Tony hesitantly whispered, "I suppose this is good-night?"

She stretched her toes allowing her lips to linger on his. When she pulled away, she suckled his neck, just above his perfectly starched collar. Tony's grasp of her small waist tightened as a low groan escaped his clenched teeth. "That's up to you." Claire purred, "I don't plan on using that lock."

With their fingers entwined, they made their way toward her suite. At the door, Tony stopped to kiss the woman before him. "There is more for us to discuss...."

Claire's finger touched his lips. She watched as the pressed straight line below her touch slowly formed a sensual grin. With her face tilted upward she whispered, "Tonight is about us... non-charade, non-performance. If you want something different, go downstairs."

The copper walls and satin drapes were different, but the suite was the same. It held so many memories. Their history was made within these walls. Yet, as they came together it didn't feel like the past. It felt new, rejuvenated, consensual, and real.

Their bodies united like they'd never been apart, but their roles were different.

Prison and being away hardened Claire. No longer could she trust without question or believe without confirmation. That didn't mean she couldn't trust or believe – it meant she needed the ability to question without fear and confirm on her own terms. As she surrendered to his erotic caresses, Claire pushed the questions away. Right now their carnal needs demanded attention. She craved what only he could give.

With all his entrepreneurial success, Tony's private life had been anything but. He never wanted love. Why would he? He wasn't even sure it existed, until her -- the woman now willingly beneath him. Her beautiful eyes saw into his soul. And her petite body dominated his mind. Somehow despite all of his mistakes and manipulation, Tony was once again where he longed to be. He wanted to control her and limit her access to his past and his heart. However, he knew it was too late. She'd managed to open places he didn't know existed. And now they had a child coming. He felt his power slipping through his fingers. Nevertheless, as her eyes opened and Tony watched the shimmering emerald irises glow and her lips form a smile, he no longer cared.

Hope is the dream of a waking man.
- Aristotle

Chapter 49

Claire didn't knock, and she didn't enter reverently. The sudden rush of his office door made Tony turn toward the commotion. His emails could wait. Her displeasure radiated throughout the room before she uttered a word.

"Tony, what the hell have you done?"

"What are you talking about?"

"After I got dressed, I checked my emails. One is a confirmation of my airline reservation *cancellation.*" She stood defiantly before him, "I did not cancel my reservation. I called the airline. They informed me my seat was sold. They have no open seats for my original flight or any others until tomorrow. I told you -- I was going back to California today; you promised me!"

He smirked, taking her tirade too well and fueling Claire's anger. "I promised you," he said with a smooth calm voice, "a return ticket. I am a man of my word; you have a ticket."

"A voided ticket --semantics! I want to be on that flight!"

"Claire, listen to reason." He gestured toward the chairs, "Have a seat."

She looked at the straight backed chairs near his desk. How many times had she sat in those seats while he rattled off rules or perimeters for her behavior?

"No." As the word left her lips, she watched the muscles in his neck tighten and his eyebrow rise.

"Very well, stand if you prefer. How are you feeling today?"

Claire glared. "You're not changing the subject. I'm going home."

"I hoped you would consider yourself home."

Claire exhaled, paced the length of the desk and back, and collapsed into one of the chairs she'd just refused. "Tony, why do you have to push and push?" Exasperation came through her tone, "I truly have had a wonderful weekend, and I've surprisingly enjoyed being on your estate. But I have a life. I have plans. Amber is leaving for a conference, and I want to see her before she leaves. John and Emily will be in Palo Alto Monday. They're spending four days looking for housing. I need to be there."

"Amber is leaving? You will be alone?"

She misinterpreted his question, "I will not be with anyone in public, if that's what you're asking."

His voice hardened, "That goes without saying. I'm asking -- will you be alone?" His volume rose, "Christ, Claire! Your condominium was broken into. It isn't safe!"

"You are trying to scare me into staying. I'm not falling for it. My building has top notch security, Harry is utilizing more SiJo resources, and then there are always your people watching me. I lead a damn parade!"

"Your laptop was stolen."

"Stuff happens – it isn't cause to stop living."

He tried to reason, "We have plans beginning Friday in Chicago. *In your condition*, you shouldn't be flying all over the country." She pressed her lips tightly together. The words forming in her head were not appropriate and would not add positively to their conversation. He exhaled and added, "In a commercial plane. Do you know how many people get ill after breathing that recycled air?"

"You're really stretching here. Tell me, how I'm getting back to California *today?*"

He sighed, "I want to take you back upstairs and lock that door," his eyes glared as he added with excessive emphasis, "from the *outside*."

Claire stood and walked toward him. Her closed lips formed a soft smile as she peered deep into his dark eyes. There was a time the expression before her would have frightened her, that was no longer the case. Framing his freshly shaven face between her petite hands, she bent toward him. Their noses touched, and she brushed her lips to his. "Tony, I believe you. I know that's what you want. I drove to town yesterday, and I came back." She kissed him again. "I will go to California today, and I will be back to Chicago on Friday. Remember what we said the other night?" She didn't wait for his answer, "We said we needed to trust each other."

He closed his eyes and nodded; his face still in her hands.

She continued in her soft and steady voice, "I trust you not to lock my suite from the outside. You need to trust me to return."

He reached out and encircled her waist, caressing the small of her back, above her slacks and beneath her blouse. She allowed herself to be pulled onto his lap. In response, she embraced his neck and listened to his gentler tone. "You don't need to believe me. I know I need to earn that right. But I *did not* have anything to do with the break-in. It wasn't a plan to scare you into staying here. I'm concerned," he kissed her lips and moved his hands to her stomach. "And not just for you."

Claire lowered her face to his broad shoulder as tears formed, "Thank you. From the moment I saw the little blue plus, I've been concerned, too. You have to know, I will do anything necessary to keep me and our baby safe. I just need to be in California, especially this week. I have a lot going on."

"What if I told you, you shouldn't have a lot going on? You deserve to rest and allow others to do for you. If Catherine knew about the baby, you'd never lift another finger."

Claire suddenly remembered the two computerized pictures she had in the pocket of her slacks. "I have something to show you."

He raised his brow, "Oh?"

She ignored his reference and removed the ultrasound picture from the pocket of her slacks. Tony's eyes widened with wonder. "Is this what I think it is?"

Claire nodded, barely able to contain her emotion. "Yes, it's our little one's first picture."

"I want her to have your eyes." He declared.

Claire smiled. "I know you are used to getting your way, but sex and eye color are non-negotiable."

"I don't know ... sex sounds great and I love your eyes." His twinkled, "Would you like to negotiate?"

Claire shook her head, feeling the blush on her cheeks. "How am I getting..." she almost said *home*, but rephrased, "back to California."

"The same way you're getting to Chicago -- in a private plane. It's a safer mode of transportation, with no public record of your itinerary."

She exhaled with relief and thanked him. Tony explained the time of departure was negotiable, but asked that she stay in Iowa until after they share an early dinner. Claire chose not to argue. She was leaving; time was inconsequential.

Claire went back to her suite, finished packing, and called Amber and Harry, telling them her change in plans. Unfortunately, she would miss Amber. Her roommate promised to return on Thursday, before Claire needed to leave again. Another problem created by her new itinerary was her car. It was parked at San Francisco International Airport. She would now be flying into the private commuter airport in Palo Alto.

"I can take a SiJo car into San Francisco and bring your car back," Harry offered as they spoke on the phone.

"Thank you, but I'll just take a taxi home and get my car tomorrow when I pick John and Emily up from the airport."

"No, Claire, I'll be glad to get you. Just text me with the time of your departure."

She inhaled. Claire knew she and Harry needed to talk. Nevertheless, she didn't want to face him, yet. "I don't want to put you out."

He hesitated; Claire heard his heavy sigh. Finally he asked, "Will you text?"

"Yes, thank you." After customary and polite good-byes, they both disconnected. Her recently settled stomach tied in knots, in anticipation of their discussion.

Claire walked onto her balcony and leaned against the concrete and stone ledge. She had a few hours before their afternoon dinner and the air was warming nicely. Her clothes were packed, but she knew there were bathing suits in the dressing room. Watching the gentle rustling of the leaves in the vast sea of green, she lifted her face to the sun and felt the warm breeze against her skin. While she debated a swim, she heard a knock on the door.

Claire called into her suite, "Come in."

Catherine entered. "You are leaving?"

Catherine's sad grey eyes tugged at Claire's heart. She reached for the kind woman's hands. "Yes, and I'll be back. Thank you, for all you've done to make my visit special."

Claire saw a spark of hope as Catherine asked, "You'll be back?"

"I will... I believe you. He is trying."

Catherine smiled a satisfied smile, until they both turned toward the opening of Claire's door. Tony performed a perfunctory knock as he pushed the door further open. "Oh, am I interrupting?"

Claire walked to Tony and took his hand. "No," her emerald eyes gleamed toward him, "but since you're here...?"

He looked at her, questioning, "Yes?"

"I think I'd like to share something with Catherine, but not without you."

His features softened as a glow overtook his face.

"Catherine, I suggest you sit." Tony suggested.

She did. And although her expression revealed alarm or suspense, she didn't speak.

Claire reached into her pocket, removed their baby's picture, and handed it to Catherine. The woman took the ultrasound picture and stared. Finally her eyes widened and for the second time, Claire saw tears form on her lids. "You are pregnant?" She asked Claire, who nodded in response. Then turning to Tony and seeing his proud expression, Catherine continued, "The two of you?" She sprang from the sofa and embraced Claire. "Oh my, a Rawls - Nichols baby. I can't believe it."

Claire allowed herself to be swallowed by Catherine's embrace. Looking to Tony she was instantly surprised by his expression. The smile that was present only seconds ago was gone. *Why is he glaring?* Claire wondered. *She's happy – what's his problem?*

Claire and Tony decided to spend a few hours at the pool while they waited for dinner. With the rising humidity, the tepid water felt wonderfully refreshing. When Claire wasn't submerged, she sat with her feet dangling in the cool blue liquid and enjoyed the view of Tony swimming the length of the pool and back. His strong arms fanned outward as he pushed against the water. The muscles in his back, shoulders, and arms defined with each stroke.

In the light of the sun, Claire noticed a few renegade gray hairs in Tony's black mane. She thought it made him look distinguished.

However, with his recent *age* comment, she chose not to mention them. When he surfaced at her feet, she giggled as he pretended to pull her into the water. Just when she thought she was safe, he stood and scooped her into his arms. All of her squealing was to no avail.

After a few playful moments of feigned fighting, she relaxed, and floated in his arms. The sun bathed her exposed skin as he supported her shoulders and legs. His words were a statement, intended as a question, "I want to show you something."

"I'm curious." She asked with a seductive smile. "Is it something I've seen before?"

He returned her sparkling gaze, "Yes, but not what you're thinking."

It was her turn to raise an eyebrow. He led her up the steps and out of the pool. The afternoon heat made for a smooth transition from water to air. The breeze only dried their skin as they walked to one of the umbrella tables. Sitting knee to knee, Tony reached into the pocket of his bathing suit. Claire gasped as her eyes adjusted to the umbrella's shadow. In Tony's outstretched palm, sparkling in the reflection of the June brilliance was Claire's engagement ring, the one she sold.

Only her eyes moved as she looked from his hand to his face. *Was he mad? What was he going to say? How did he get it?* So many thoughts assaulted her mind. His true intent was not even on her radar.

Despite her concerns, his expression seemed soft-- almost fearful.

"Tony, how did you...?"

"I bought them back."

Her stomach twisted, "I'm sorry. I needed money....'

He interrupted, "If I gave them back, will you promise not to sell them?"

"Why would you give them back?" she asked in all sincerity.

"Do I need to get on one knee? I suppose I didn't do that the first time."

She stood suddenly and backed away, almost tripping over the heavy iron chair. If she'd made him speechless with her pregnancy announcement, he'd certainly returned the favor with his proposal. Finally, as her eyes remained large, she said, "No, I'm not ready for anything like that."

His eyes dropped. "No, never – or no, not yet."

She saw his pain and instinctively moved forward. Kneeling before him, she said, "Tony, slow down. I told you, I like the dating thing... we never did that. Please don't push too hard. In the last week we've survived a major game changer. I think we need to proceed with caution." *Everyone knows the game of chess requires planning and strategizing. Making moves too quickly often proves lethal for the offending piece.*

He reached for her left hand and slipped the diamond ring onto her fourth finger. Prisms of color and light radiated from the large center stone as the smaller diamonds sparkled around its perimeter and from the embedded band. Of course it fit. It was hers. With a mischievous smile, Tony said, "I just wanted to make sure it still fit."

Removing the platinum engagement ring, she handed it back to him. "I appreciate the offer. Don't make me give you a definite answer. If I do, you won't be happy. Let's be content with what we have, for now."

Reluctantly he accepted the ring. Holding her hand he bent his head and kissed her fingers, one by one. The warm sensation began where his lips contacted her skin and immediately radiated throughout her body. As he suckled each finger he confessed, "I have made some bad decisions... and done some things I regret in my life... but without a doubt... what I regret the most... is divorcing you." His penetrating gaze held her emerald eyes captive. "If you tell me there is hope, that one day you'll be Mrs. Rawlings again, I will wait."

She didn't reply. She was busy enjoying the sensation of his lips. It started with her fingers, moved to her hand, arm, shoulder, and by the time he reached the nape of her neck, Claire was moaning and lost to the world around her.

"May I get you out of this wet suit, *Ms. Nichols*?" He emphasized her name.

She answered heatedly, "Yes... and Mr. Rawlings... there is always hope."

Text message, from Claire's iPhone to Harry's number: *THE PLANE IS ABOUT TO TAKE OFF FROM IOWA CITY. IT'S A LITTLE AFTER 4. SHOULD BE IN PALO ALTO AROUND 6:15 OR 6:30 PT.* She hit send. Then thinking about it more she wrote a second message: *THANK YOU FOR PICKING ME UP.*

She settled into the plush white leather of the reclining chair and fastened her seatbelt. Closing her eyes she tried to think about Harry; however, her thoughts continually returned to Tony.

The copilot, a woman Claire didn't know, spoke. The competent voice returned Claire from her daydreams. "Ms. Nichols, we are about to take-off. If you'd like to make any calls or send any messages, please complete them in the next few minutes. Once we are at cruising altitude I will be happy to get you anything you need."

"Thank you," Claire read her name badge, "Grace, I think I'm going to try to sleep."

"Yes, Ma'am," the woman disappeared behind the door to the cockpit.

Claire removed her phone one more time. With an uncontained smile she wrote: *THANK YOU FOR A LOVELY WEEKEND. I'M SO THANKFUL I WAS ABLE TO ATTEND THE WEDDING.* Send.

She saw the icon for an incoming message: *I WILL BE THERE.* Claire frowned. It was from Harry. His normal pleasantries were gone. She knew without a doubt, tonight's conversation wouldn't be pleasant. A beep and another message: *I HOPE THAT WAS NOT THE ONLY PART OF THE WEEKEND YOU ENJOYED?* Her grin returned; the plane was starting to move. She replied: *I BELIEVE THERE WERE OTHER PARTS TOO. BUT SINCE YOUR PLANE IS MOVING, I NEED TO TURN OFF*

MY PHONE -- CAN'T ELABORATE. She hit send and turned her phone to Airplane Mode.

With the seat reclined and a soft light blanket, Claire drifted off to sleep. It had been a long eventful four days. Just before sleep she realized Tony was right about something else: this was a nicer way to fly.

Simultaneously another text message conversation occurred. Interestingly, this one too was volleying between Iowa City and Palo Alto:

IC (Iowa City): *WHAT NEW INFORMATION DO YOU HAVE RE: BREAK IN?*

PA (Palo Alto): *BUILDING SECURITY TO SEND ME ENLARGED IMAGE OF PERP - WILL FORWARD AS SOON AS I RECEIVE. NOT CLEAR ENOUGH TO BE USED WITH RECOGNITION SOFT WARE.*

IC: *SEND VIA E-MAIL, EASIER TO ENLARGE ON MY END.*

IC: *MS NICHOLS WILL ARRIVE PALO ALTO AFTER 6 PT. KEEP HER IN YOUR VIEW UNTIL SAFELY RETURNED TO HER CONDO. ARE YOUR SENSORS IN PLACE?*

PA: *YES SIR. MS MCCOY JUST EXITED UNIT.*

IC: *SHE IS GOING OUT OF TOWN.*

PA: *HER FLIGHT PLAN IS FOR LOS ANGLES WITH RETURN FLIGHT THURSDAY.* (Phil wanted to show Mr. Rawlings he knew what was happening.)

IC: *KEEP ME CONSTANTLY APPRISED*

PA: *YES SIR.*

*****

Patrick waited by the exit to her terminal. He didn't know if she had checked luggage or not, but he could follow from a distance. It took some patience, but he had the panel van parked right next to her Honda Accord. The element of surprise was always the best. It wasn't like he'd ever kidnapped someone before, but he'd watched enough episodes of crime shows to know the necessary tools and form a well thought out plan.

He double checked the monitor. Yes, this was her flight; nevertheless, as passenger after passenger passed, she was AWOL. Didn't first class usually deplane first?

After the stream of people waned, Patrick walked confidently to the American Airlines counter. "Excuse me," he said politely. "I'm waiting for a friend. She was supposed to be on Flight 1103 from Iowa. Can you tell me if she made her flight?"

Once Patrick gave the attendant Claire's information, the man checked his computer. "I'm sorry, sir. We don't have anyone by that name scheduled on this flight. Perhaps she changed her reservations."

"Can you check?"

"No, sorry." The attendant looked disgusted, "Privacy issues, you know? I can't look in her account. I *can* see if she's on another flight scheduled to arrive later today."

Patrick's heart raced; damn this was going to be perfect. Maybe there was still a chance. "Yes, please."

After prolonged scanning, the attendant confessed, "I'm sorry, sir. I don't see a Claire Nichols on any of our flights. United has two coming in this evening from Iowa City. Perhaps she switched carriers."

"Thank you." Patrick huffed as he walked away. *Now what?*

*****

Derek's face filled the screen of Sophia's laptop. It amazed Sophia how even half a world apart, his voice sounded like they were in the same room. "I called corporate. She's on her way back to California and being reassigned."

Sophia couldn't believe her ears. "So what are you going to do about an assistant?"

"They'll assign me a temporary and when I get back, I guess I get to start interviewing potential candidates."

"I'm really sorry I was right about Danni's intentions." She smiled into the camera, "However, I'm very glad you stopped her in her tracks."

"Yea, Baby, I need to get some work done here. I just wanted to be honest with you."

Sophia's smile transcended the oceans. "Thank you. When will you be home?"

"I'm scheduled to fly back Friday. I hope this doesn't postpone things."

"Me either. I love you."

"I love you, too," Derek said as he disconnected their Skype call.

For a few moments Sophia stared at the blank screen. She couldn't believe Danni flew all the way to China to seduce her husband. Of course, that wasn't the reason she listed on her travel request. It had something to do with negotiation assistance.

"Sophie, did I hear that husband of yours in here?" Carlos asked as he walked into Sophia's kitchen.

"No, Pop. Remember, he's in China. I was just talking to him on the computer."

"China? He's in China? Why would he be there? He should be here with you. He could help me make some more frames. I think we can get a few more sketches stretched today."

"That sounds great. I want to be back to California by Friday."

"You and that man of yours need to move back here. New Jersey is where you belong."

"Yes, Pop."

She decided not to remind him that *here* was Provincetown not Princeton. It wouldn't matter in another ten minutes anyway. She and her mom told him a hundred times about Derek's trip to China.

Sophia smiled as she thought about her father's agenda for stretching sketches. Why could he remember some things and not others?

If she hadn't spent the past week with him, she wouldn't have believed how far he had deteriorated. Sophia wanted to talk to her mom about hired help. She worried her mom was doing too much. Sometimes you just need help.

*Anger is not the opposite of love, for the opposite of love is
indifference. To be angry is to care tremendously.*
                              - Doris Moreland Jones

Chapter 50

-January 2011-

Tony woke with a start; his wife, for just over a month, rolled
from his shoulder to her side. In the silence he heard Claire's
soft rhythmic breathing. She was sleeping peacefully -- a far
cry from earlier. Closing his eyes he remembered their night, their words,
and her tears. When they went to bed everything was fine. Then out of
nowhere she said told him she was bored and wanted to join him on
business trips. Normally he'd like that, but lately nothing was normal; he
had too many fires to count.   Fires Claire never would or could
understand.

Truthfully, he'd been holding so much in lately, so many issues:
Rawlings Industries, Sophia Rossi – no Burke, and John Vandersol.

Lifting his head to his elbow, he watched her. Tony couldn't fathom
how someone so seemingly compliant could so easily incite his emotions.
He could keep his cool in the middle of chaos; yet, a few simple words
from her and his reactions were uncontrollable. *No*, Tony thought, *not
uncontrollable.* He'd gone there once -- he wouldn't go there again.

Then why did she need to remind him? Her insolent question...
when he told her she had invitations, but he had chosen not to share
them, explaining he wanted her safe from more *accidents*... she had the
audacity to ask ... from whom? Tony's body trembled with pent-up anger
– *from whom?* He knew what she was implying. Of course, she said,
from *whom* were the invitations... but Tony knew what she meant – from
whom would an accidents occur. It wasn't like he didn't think about that
every damn day! He'd never regretted his actions more, but you can't
turn back time.

There was something about Claire, something about her veiled assertiveness, something which provoked Tony like no one else. She could bring out the best in him. No question, as he watched her petite body curl into a ball and snuggle into the soft pillow, he wanted to please her. Not just please, love – indulge – spoil and pamper her, beyond her greatest dreams. However, she could also elicit the worst in him. Tonight was no exception.

Damn, if he didn't want to wake her and tell her he was sorry – explain she was experiencing his frustration with so many other things. He thought about her words, *Thank you, I'd really like to see Courtney and Sue*. She had the uncanny ability to say the right thing. Nevertheless, he questioned her sincerity... could she be playing him? Had he fallen victim to her persuasion? Is that why he offered Phoenix?

Tony slid out of bed, stood silently, and watched as Claire remained sleeping. He wouldn't be as cautious upstairs, but he wanted to leave the room. Ironically, it was her desire to *leave* which escalated tonight's emotion. Nonetheless, if she were awake, he couldn't leave her in *his* suite – alone. Her rhythmic breathing continued. Tony eased himself into a pair of nylon shorts and a t-shirt and quietly entered the corridor.

His bare feet padded the marble hall into the foyer, past the grand stairs, and toward his office. The path was dark, yet he knew every step. Quietly, he eased himself into the confines of his grand office, pushed the switch, and illuminated the room.

Bored! She said she was bored. Tony tried to push Claire from his thoughts. He hit the mouse and watched his desktop come to life. Searching his private inbox, he found the email he'd been anticipating:

To: Anthony Rawlings
From: Cameron Andrews
Date: January 26, 2011
Re: Ms. Burke

Although Ms. Burke is now living in Boston in her husband's apartment, I've just confirmed they made an offer on a small cottage in Provincetown, Mass. I'll notify you immediately if their offer is accepted.

Derek Burkes' employment record is straight forward. I've attached his dossier. I will continue to monitor. Please inform me if you would like my activities to change in any way. CA

Tony fired of a response:

To: Cameron Andrews
From: Anthony Rawlings
Date: January 27, 2011
Re: Ms. Rossi-Burke
Let me know the value of the cottage and their offer.

He hit send.

Tony rubbed his temples and silently berated himself. He'd looked away for a couple of weeks. A couple of weeks to marry and honeymoon and everything changed -- Sophia married! She wasn't even seeing anyone when he went to her art show in New England, the beginning of December, just two weeks before his own wedding.

Closing his eyes, he remembered seeing her across the room. She was stunning, wearing a long red gown with sparkling, dangling earrings which hung to her shoulders. It wasn't a style he'd like on Claire, but they looked beautiful on Sophia. Her people skills were constantly improving; her gray eyes looked confident and steadfast.

Then a month later, she not only married; she married Derek Burke.

Derek Burke wasn't a *large* blip on Tony's radar screen, but Tony knew of him. When Sherman Nichols, aka Cole Mathews, worked to bring Nathaniel Rawls and all of Rawls Corporation down, he was assisted by Jonathon Burke, a securities officer. Their testimony, along with Anton's father's, hammered the final nails in Nathaniel's coffin, literally, as far as Tony was concerned.

Nathaniel's quest was to return the favor -- to bring down these men and their families. Sherman had one son, Jordon, who had two daughters, Emily and Claire. Jonathon had one daughter, Allison. Though married, she had no children. Well, at first they thought she had a daughter, Cindy. It later turned out Cindy wasn't her biological child, but rather the child of her husband's sister. All very complicated -- the first miscue on their road to fulfilling Nathaniel's quest; after Allison and her husband tragically perished in a hiking accident, Cindy was left alone. Marie reached out, posing as one of Allison's old friends. Since that time, Cindy has worked on the estate. All of her needs were met: college tuition, (she was currently taking online courses) clothes, and housing. She has also accumulated a nice nest egg. Never would Cindy suspect her saviors were anything but.

The direct line of Jonathon Burke was gone.

Nevertheless, the reason Derek Burke was on Tony's radar was in reality Cindy was his cousin; Derek's grandfather was Jonathon's brother. In the past month, Tony had spent a great deal of time learning more about Derek Burke. A few of Tony's recent trips weren't *business* at all. He couldn't very well take Claire to watch the new Mr. and Mrs. Burke in person.

Tony's observation: Derek was nothing like Sophia -- their relationship wouldn't last.

Past suitors were tested, induced with great temptations. All failed. Sophia may have interpreted it as personal failure; however, Tony believed he was only accelerating the future, in essence, saving her from greater heartache. He needed to decide how to do the same with Derek; test him, before it was too late. This would take time.

After all, just because, Tony allowed his defenses to wane, he couldn't allow Sophia's rash decision to change his ultimate plans. Her art career was finally receiving warranted attention. She truly had talent. He even owned many of her pieces. They were displayed in New York, Phoenix, and Dallas... if he remembered correctly. It didn't seem right to have her work displayed at the estate. Damn, if he hadn't been so preoccupied with Claire...

Leaning back in his luxurious leather chair, Tony's mind slipped back to his wife. He didn't regret marrying her; it surprised him how much he usually enjoyed being with her. In the past, beautiful women had their purpose, like anything else: a nice car, a priceless antique... It took Tony awhile to realize Claire was different, not someone to use when he wanted and forget until the desire returned. No, she wasn't like one of his many expensive cars. And she wasn't just a beautiful ornament to have on his arm at functions, although she played that role to perfection.

Tony's realization hit months ago when he realized it didn't matter if she were dressed in designer gowns with perfect hair and perfect makeup or newly awake with no makeup and tussled hair. He no longer saw the difference. For a man who valued outward appearance as much as Anthony Rawlings, that insight was shocking.

When he first brought her to the estate, he never intended to enjoy her, much less love her. Truthfully, it was initially determined she and her sister would have *accidents*, much sooner -- years sooner, like their parents. However, as he began following Claire and her life, there was an undeniable attraction. Then at her parent's funeral for no particular reason, Tony fought the urge to comfort her. At that moment, he knew he wanted her for himself. Truthfully, Emily's survival has been a byproduct.

As a man who makes money -- lots of money, buying and selling -- rarely does Anthony Rawlings become emotionally vested in projects or people. Initially, he saw Claire the same way; however, after his acquisition, as weeks and months passed, despite her situation, she worked her way into his being -- into every fiber. Her strength to meet him with eyes on fire while her words and body appeased, fascinated Tony. Never had anyone done that.

Smiling, he recalled their amazing honeymoon. The isolation of the island paradise kept he and Claire within the confines of a private bubble. Yet, as always, life intervenes. Back to Iowa meant disruptions. Being a multibillion dollar company, there were always issues with Rawlings Industry. The stock price was up, but there were always fires in need of dousing. A recent acquisition in Missouri was currently raging.

On top of Rawlings Industries and Sophia, Tony had to deal with John Vandersol. The man absolutely infuriated Tony. Never had he met a more arrogant, self-righteous prick. Tony did his research. He knew John was accomplished. Every account Tony uncovered was flattering -- some to the point of nausea. It was hard to believe anyone could be as perfect as everyone's account of John Vandersol.

During their first meeting, Tony was determined to play nice, for Claire. It was after all, his olive branch to his fiancée. Thanksgiving went well. The ladies didn't seem to recognize the subtle feather ruffling and posturing which occurred on multiple occasions.

He tried to endure John because of Emily, Claire's sister. Tony knew Claire wanted to see her family. He also knew Claire obeyed his rules while alone with her sister. After all, he listened intently to the recordings of each private conversation; from their after dinner catch-up in New York, to their giggling girls' sleep over prior to the wedding. Never once did Claire allude to her and Tony's less than conventional beginning. He was extremely proud of his wife's obedience.

Allowing his mind to change directions, perhaps Claire had earned the right to spend some time away from the estate. He would reconsider that possibility.

Rubbing his temples, Tony contemplated John Vandersol's future as he remembered the man's past. Their first open disagreement occurred the night following Thanksgiving, regarding the prenuptial agreement. Tony was both amused and shocked by John's impudence. The man actually thought he could persuade Claire to defy Tony's authority. Smiling to himself, Tony knew he'd trained Claire too well. Public defiance from his wife wasn't a concern. Nonetheless, John's audacity agitated Tony beyond words.

And then there was the wedding rehearsal -- where John *didn't* give Claire away. It was at that moment, as Tony stared into Claire's anxious eyes, when Tony determined *John Vandersol will pay.* This insolent man not only upset him, but his words caused Tony's future wife distress. Her connection with John was his only saving grace. By causing *her* discomfort, at *her* own wedding rehearsal, John secured his own demise.

Tony's first plan was brilliant: offer John a job. It *appeared* as though Tony was taking the high road, recognizing John's superior legal abilities, offering him an exorbitant amount of money and pleasing Claire. It was win – win. Rawlings Industries could always use another competent attorney, but he'd be under Tony's thumb.

Nonetheless, in the ultimate act of defiance, John Vandersol refused Tony's offer. It was an act which has infuriated Tony ever since he learned of it two weeks ago. He hadn't told Claire until a few hours ago.

Tony was certain Claire understood the implications (her ability to see her sister now or in the future was in serious jeopardy) without Tony spelling them out. That was good because the thought of his wife's family caused his blood to boil, and it was truly better for Claire, if he didn't experience that feeling while in her presence.

Tony poured himself a drink, perhaps it would help him sleep. Pacing the confines of his regal office he contemplated his wife further. He thought about Catherine's words. She claimed Claire's strength in the face of Tony's adversity was proof of Claire's true competence. Truly, Catherine's encouragement regarding their relationship helped propel it beyond the original plan. Catherine claimed she saw Nathaniel's positive qualities in Tony when he was with Claire. Comparing him to Nathaniel was no small compliment. Catherine's approval of Claire continued to mean a great deal to Tony.

That was why Tony wanted Claire at the estate, safe, with Catherine to watch over her. With Rawlings Industries, Sophia, and John Vandersol, Tony didn't need to be concerned about Claire, too. Her role as Mrs. Rawlings had just begun. And admittedly, in most situations, she'd done well. However, there were a few occasions she'd forgotten the significance of her new title. He didn't want to spend his days worrying how her actions reflected upon him.

Claire said she wasn't a spouse or a partner. That wasn't true. He wanted her as both... however; Anthony Rawlings never shared control. His percentage always held more weight... therefore; it didn't matter if she was bored: if he wanted her at the estate -- that was where she would be.

All changes, even the most longed for, have their melancholy;
for what we leave behind us is a part of ourselves;
we must die to one life before we can enter another.
– Anatole France

Chapter 51

"**M**s. Nichols, we're almost to Palo Alto." Grace's voice penetrated Claire's dream, resounding through the hum of engines. "Ms. Nichols, please return your seat to its upright position."

Claire opened her eyes, seeing the luxurious interior of Tony's private plane and the nice copilot standing before her. Recognizing she'd slept the entire flight, Claire slowly obeyed. She nodded at Grace as she pushed the appropriate buttons and returned her lounge to its chair position. It was true; no commercial seat, even in first class, could provide the comfort and serenity Claire had just enjoyed for over four hours.

As wakefulness came, so did hunger. Earlier in the afternoon she enjoyed one of her favorite meals: grilled salmon, asparagus, salad, and red potatoes. And since Tony claimed not to have requested the delicious menu, they both suspected Catherine. Nevertheless, as Claire adjusted her watch to Pacific Time, she realized dinner was over five hours ago. Contemplating her future, she wondered if the twisting in her stomach was hunger or the thought of her impending discussion with Harry and her future travel plans next Friday morning.

Claire wanted to talk with Harry, be honest, and explain her thoughts. The problem with her plan -- Claire didn't know her own thoughts. Harry deserved honesty; she wasn't completely sure what that entailed. She truly never meant to lead him on – she liked him. Perhaps no one would believe her, but up until recently, she never expected to even consider allowing Tony back into her life. Even now she didn't know if their charade was an act or if real feelings were emerging.

From the moment Tony left her in the jail in Iowa, she thought *they* were ancient history. If she didn't, would she have spent hours upon hours sitting with Meredith Banks recounting some of the most horrific times of her life? Would she have spent day after day researching Tony's family history? No -- no, she wouldn't.

And when he blackmailed her at the gala, she had no intentions to truly reconcile. It was all a sham. But ... Claire had to admit, there were moments... flashes of feelings. She tried to ignore them. Unfortunately, the press didn't. Harry was right about some of the pictures; Claire wasn't that good of an actress. The look in her eyes couldn't be feigned. Nonetheless, that didn't mean she wanted reconciliation. Well, not until... the little blue plus and pulsating black dot appeared.

If Claire allowed herself to somehow look past Tony's faults and peer into the man who claimed never ending love, she could see his good. She could see what Catherine wanted her to see; he was trying.

As the plane descended, Claire struggled with her wedding portrait. Tony left her alone at the jail and stared at her every night above his fireplace. It didn't make sense. And when she noticed it, he seemed surprised, obviously accustomed to its presence. She attempted to understand what he and Catherine tried to explain. Tony said he did what he did to save *her* -- from *him*. Catherine explained Tony made two promises; he tried to keep one in a way as to also keep the other. Was that the *loop-hole* he mentioned? In San Francisco, after the gala, Tony reminded Claire of his promise to love her forever, made in front of family and friends. Claire needed to know the specifics of his *other* promise and confirm to whom it was made. Was it his grandfather, as she'd suspected, or the woman in the blue Honda?

Claire closed her eyes and contemplated Brent's recent information: Burke, the same name as the securities officer. Could Tony possibly be doing the same thing to someone else – like he did to her? Claire knew one thing for sure; no one else was in her suite.

Didn't she owe it to herself and to their child to give this reconciliation a try? How could she possibly explain all of that to Harry? He knew the truth about Tony's past behaviors. The night of the gala Harry was upset and said hurtful things. Nevertheless, Claire doubted he could ever treat someone the way he treated her in the beginning. How could she make anyone understand she would willingly choose Tony over Harry?

As the plane came to a stop on the tarmac, Claire stood. Her stomach knotted in anticipation of their conversation. Suddenly, she remembered the second part of her week -- John and Emily's arrival tomorrow. If her impending conversation with Harry would be difficult, talking to her family would be impossible. Feeling light headed, Claire sat down against the plush seat and closed her eyes.

"Ms. Nichols, are you well? You're very pale."

Claire peered toward Grace's concerned expression, "I think I just stood too fast."

"Yes, ma'am. We'll have your luggage out to you in a few minutes."

"Thank you," Claire said as the door began to open. Remaining seated she inhaled the fresh air and returned her iPhone to normal. There were three text messages. The first one was from Tony, sent just as she left Iowa: *OH, BUT HOW I WOULD LOVE FOR YOU TO ELABORATE!* The color quickly returned to her cheeks.

The second was received only a few minutes ago. *I'M HERE,* from Harry.

The third came immediately after Harry's. *YOU SHOULD BE LANDING, PLEASE LET ME KNOW YOU HAVE ARRIVED SAFELY,* from Tony.

With the fresh air filling the cabin, Claire quickly replied to the third text: *JUST LANDED. THANK YOU AGAIN FOR EVERYTHING. I SLEPT THE ENTIRE FLIGHT... VERY COMFORTABLE WITHOUT ALL THAT RECYCLED AIR!* Smiling she hit *send.*

The comfortable California breeze refreshed Claire as she stood at the door atop the steps. Looking around she saw Harry standing casually near one of the hangers. Immediately, she recognized his blonde hair moving slightly in the breeze. Her eyes moved from there to his well-fitted black t-shirt tucked casually into the slim waist of his faded jeans. Claire remembered telling Courtney about Harry, describing him as the anti-Tony. That was so true and yet not. Both were incredibly accomplished, strong men. Tonight's conversation would be much easier if Claire could in some way blame Harry. However, she knew none of this was Harry's fault.

She smiled his direction and he nodded, stepping toward her as she descended the stairs.

*****

Sitting behind his large mahogany desk, Tony tried in vain to read the documents on his computer. The words entered his mind and disappeared before he could digest their meaning. He watched the clock in the corner of his monitor. Finally the iPhone to his right sounded and vibrated upon the smooth glossy surface. Hastily he swiped the screen. 1 Text Message: *JUST LANDED. THANK YOU AGAIN FOR EVERYTHING. I SLEPT THE ENTIRE FLIGHT... VERY COMFORTABLE WITHOUT ALL THAT RECYCLED AIR!* He smiled at her cheekiness. Maybe the recycled air was a stretch, but he would undoubtedly prefer her in Iowa to California. Nevertheless, they made progress this weekend. They both knew it. His phone sounded and vibrated again. 1 Text Message: *MS. NICHOLS PLANE JUST LANDED. MR. BALDWIN WAITING AND LUGGAGE BEING PUT INTO HIS CAR. I WILL FOLLOW.*

Tony's neck muscles tightened. Does picking her up at the airport constitute a date? Tony tried to tell himself it didn't. Besides, would he rather have her in a taxi with some stranger? They spent four days together, made love on three different occasions, and have a baby coming. While reasoning words went through his thoughts, the clenched jaws and tightened shoulders revealed the jealousy cursing through his veins.

Tony replied to Phillip Roach: *KEEP HER IN SIGHT. LET ME KNOW IF THERE ARE ANY STOPS ON THE WAY TO THE CONDO. WHERE IS THAT PICTURE?* He hit *send.*

Text message number two, to Claire: *OUR AGREEMENT FORBIDS PUBLIC EXPOSURE WITH ANYONE ELSE! I THOUGHT I'D MADE THAT CLEAR! WE HAVE AN UNDERSTANDING!* (Exclamation marks were so often overused in text messages.) Tony hesitated. He repeatedly hit the backspace key.

He typed once again: *IM GLAD THE AIR WAS TO YOUR LIKING. REMEMBER OUR AGREEMENT. CALL WHEN YOU'RE SETTLED.* The restraint was difficult, but he knew he wasn't going to win her back without effort. The damn press would have a field day if they saw her with Mr. Baldwin, but Tony reminded himself to do what he'd told her to do -- trust. Exhaling he tried. It was especially difficult if you'd never done it before.

The sound and vibration announced another arriving text message: *THE PICTURE WAS SENT TO YOUR EMAIL. LET ME KNOW IF YOU DON'T HAVE IT.*

Shit, Tony had been trying to read the acquisition documents and forgot to check his email. He switched screens. There was the email from Phillip Roach with attachment. He opened the attachment. The photo quality was poor, obviously enlarged too many times, creating a very grainy image. Tony pushed the plush carpet with his feet, as his leather chair moved away from the screen hoping for a clearer picture. He saw a man with little to no hair. Was he older and balding or younger with his head shaved? Looking closer Tony guessed the man was older. Normally, Tony was excellent with names and faces. He saw a hint of familiarity, but Tony couldn't remember why. Perhaps it had been a long time since he'd seen him, or maybe he'd been on television or in the news. Regardless, the twinge of recognition made Tony uncomfortable. Why would someone he recognized be stealing Claire's laptop?

Two more text messages came through his iPhone. The first one, from Claire: *I DO. I WILL LATER.* Tony exhaled. It took every fiber of self-restraint to not get on another plane and go get her. Second message, from Phillip Roach: *DID YOU GET THE EMAIL? I CAN RESEND.*

*****

On a Sunday night the light traffic around Palo Alto flowed well. Nevertheless, within Harry's Mustang their polite conversation was strained through the dense unspoken tension. Harry asked, "How was the wedding?"

Claire told him about Caleb, Julia, Courtney, and Brent and how nice it was to talk openly. She rambled about one thing and another, avoiding their impending discussion.

As the tension began to wane, Harry asked, "Would you like to get something to eat?"

Claire thought about it. She was hungry. Yet, Tony's reminder about their *agreement* came to mind. Even more deterring was the thought of her and Harry's future talk. "I think I'd like to order something to the condo," she said, as they neared the four story building. "It will be more private, and we need to talk."

Harry eyed her suspiciously, "Talk?"

Claire exhaled. "Oh, come on. You have more questions than you're politely asking. I think we need to be honest about what's going on."

"I thought we were."

Claire exhaled. "Please, I need to tell you a few things."

"Maybe I don't want to hear them." Harry waved at the security guard as he pulled the Mustang into the underground parking garage. "Hey, there's a van in your spot." Harry noticed as they wove around to his assigned parking spot. "I don't remember seeing that before. I could call..." He hesitated, "or maybe you should call security and have it moved."

Claire didn't care about the stupid van. She wouldn't have her car back from the airport until tomorrow. "If it's here in the morning I will. It's probably someone's guest who doesn't know about the assigned spots." She looked at his light blue eyes, "Please, can we order some delivery and talk?"

"Yeah, fine." He got out of the car and began removing her bags from his trunk. "My place or yours?"

Claire pulled the smaller bag, while Harry pulled the larger. Stepping into the elevator she replied, "How about yours?" She reasoned it would be easier for her to leave if things got too uncomfortable. "I'll take my bags in and freshen up. Then I'll be over."

"Don't forget, your room's a mess."

She had forgotten. There were too many things competing for space in her head. "Oh yeah, I'll do a quick inventory and let you know if I think anything else is missing."

Harry walked Claire to her door and let go of her large suitcase. "Are you sure you're okay seeing your room by yourself?"

Claire shrugged. "Yeah, I'm fine. Why don't you call for some food?" She thought a moment as she unlocked her door, "Just no sushi, all right?"

Harry's blue eyes squinted, allowing his amazingly long lashes to linger near his cheeks, and his head tilted to the side. "But you like sushi," seeing her wrinkled nose he asked, "How about Chinese?"

She nodded. "Chinese sounds great. Extra rice," she added with a smile.

*****

Parked across the street from 7165 Forest Avenue in his nondescript grey Camry, Phillip watched the lights turn on in the large windows on the fourth floor. He typed the text message while engaging his laptop. *MS NICHOLS ARRIVED TO CONDO. NO STOPS ON WAY.* He checked his laptop. The sensors would indicate if only her apartment opened or if both hers and Mr. Baldwin's opened. The sensors were new, but with the recent break-in and an unlimited budget, no piece of technology was beyond his scope.

There must be something wrong with his sensors. Yes, Claire's door just opened and now Mr. Baldwin's door opened. However, the data indicated Claire's door also opened twenty minutes ago. Phillip's heart raced as he looked up toward the windows. He pulled out his phone; Mr. Rawlings answered on the first ring. Common pleasantries disappeared, "I just read my sensors. She's in her unit *and* it was opened twenty minutes ago." Phil's voice came with deep breaths as he raced across the street.

Ignoring Mr. Rawlings' bellowing voice, Phil hastily entered Claire's building and approached the security desk, "Has anyone been to unit 4 A recently?" The security guard looked at Phil questionably. Phil repeated himself louder, "The unit that was broken into last week? Has anyone been up there?" Phil could still hear Mr. Rawlings yelling through the phone.

"Yes, there was a delivery. The man had the appropriate documents."

Phil revealed the picture he'd sent Mr. Rawlings, "Is this the man?"

The security guard looked at the picture, "I don't know. He had documents. Yeah, maybe... he was bald."

"Call 911 and get me up there right away!" Phil's voice rose above Mr. Rawlings'.

*****

Tony could hear everything and do nothing. How long would it take to get up four flights? He disconnected from Phillip Roach and scrolled his contacts, finding Harrison Baldwin. He hit *call*.

*****

Claire pulled her luggage into the foyer. She'd forgotten about her room being a mess. Maybe Tony didn't have anything to do with it. If that were the case, she was glad she'd been out of town when it happened. Suddenly, she wished Amber were home.

Turning on lights, she headed toward the kitchen. Even though Harry was calling for dinner, she thought a little snack might help her nerves before she faced her wrecked room and their conversation. She watched as the overhead lights flooded the living room and darkened the outside world beyond the large windows.

Which occurred first, the sound of his footsteps or sensing his presence? Claire's heart raced as she spun around. She recognized the man immediately -- Patrick Chester, the neighbor from Santa Monica. In an attempt to hide her panic, she feigned indignation, "What are you doing in my house?"

He walked toward her, his beady eyes narrowing while his smile widened.

She repeated her question, "What are you doing in my house? Get out!"

He continued forward. She backed toward the windows and assessed an escape. If she ran through the kitchen, could she get back to the door and out before him?

"You made me think you're Anton's daughter." Patrick laughed. The menacing sound made the hairs on the back of Claire's neck prickle. "You're not his daughter unless that's what they call whores who seduce Sugar Daddy's!" His volume rose with each word.

The distance between them lessened as her back pressed against the cool glass. "I never told you I was..."

Without warning his hand forcefully contacted her left cheek causing her to stumble sideways. She caught herself against the glass before falling to the floor. He grabbed her hair and pulled her back to her feet. Tears filled her eyes as her scalp screamed in pain.

"Shut up!" He shouted. His foul breath making her stomach lurch.

She thought about her baby, "Please, you can have whatever you want. Just don't hurt me."

"I said shut up!" He slapped her again, releasing her hair and allowing her to fall. Her head bounced off the sill and onto the wood floor. Claire pulled her knees into her chest, as she tried to shield herself and her baby. Patrick's foot connected her ribs pushing the air from her lungs.

As she struggled for air she heard his voice, "You're coming with me. I'm going to get everything I deserve...." His fist now entwined her hair, pulling her body upward. She scrambled, trying to move -- to stop the pain. He dragged her body across the floor. The room grew steadily darker, while in the distance she heard Harry's voice -- yelling. Pain intensified -- in her head --- her chest --- a loud noise -- everything faded away.

I hope you aren't too ugly. What a collection of scars you have.
Be grateful. Our scars have the ability to give us the reality
that our past is real.
- Red Dragon

Chapter 52

Consciousness came slowly; she felt the throbbing in her head and the intense pain in her side. As the feelings intensified so did her nausea. Claire couldn't remember where she was... it felt wrong. Wanting to see her surroundings, she tried to open her eyes. Why did she hurt so much? Why wouldn't her eyes open? Panic intensified her nausea. Instinctively she knew getting sick would increase her pain; she tried to breathe and distance herself from the agony. Beyond the darkness she heard sounds. Her mind scrambled, beeps -- she heard beeps... what were the beeps?

As the fog cleared, the beeps steadily became louder and their origin registered. She was hearing monitors. She also felt a strange sensation in her arm. Claire tried to touch it, but her hand wouldn't move. Why wasn't her body responding to her thoughts?

Voices... she strained to hear the voices. Was it Tony? Oh, she wanted Tony. What about their baby? No, it wasn't Tony's voice – it was Harry's. Her body didn't move; yet, she felt tears escape from her closed eyes.

That feeling in her arm -- she remembered it. She'd felt it before, but when? The pain in her head made it impossible to concentrate.

"How long will she be unconscious?" Harry's concerned tone disengaged Claire from her thoughts, filling her with conflicting feelings.

"That's up to her. She's fighting her injuries the only way the body knows. Her energy is needed to repair the trauma; she'll wake when she can. In the meantime, we'll keep her monitored."

"You said she was pregnant."

Claire's heart ached. Did Harry say *was*?

"Mr. Baldwin, Ms. Nichols *is* pregnant. The baby is strong and healthy. Ms. Nichols is fighting for two right now."

Claire wasn't sure what else they said. The only thing that mattered was that her baby was healthy. She drifted back to the place where her body didn't hurt.

The beeping continued even in her dreams. She rolled slightly and the tightness in her arm intensified. Claire suddenly remembered when she'd had that feeling ... it was after her *accident*!

She concentrated on lifting her lids... slowly they obeyed. The florescent beams lit the room as they flowed from under the cabinets. The tubes in the crook of her elbow came into view. She was right; it was the same sensation she had after her accident. As her eyes continued to focus, she saw his golden hair resting near the foot of her bed. Although sleeping in a chair, Harry had his head resting on the bed with his hand over her leg. She remembered him picking her up at the airport; they were going to talk. She went into her condominium, and then... there was fog. Claire closed her eyes... Patrick Chester. She couldn't remember anything else.

Claire tried to talk, "Harry?"

He didn't move.

"Harry?"

The blonde head bobbled as Harry raised his head, and his light blue, tired eyes peered toward Claire's face. "Oh, Claire, you're awake."

He climbed toward her as he grasped her hand. "I need to let everyone else know."

"Everyone else?" Her voice sounded raspy.

"Amber, Emily, John, and Keaton are out there somewhere."

Her heart sank. Where was Tony? Maybe he didn't know she was hurt. Of course he knew! Where was he?

"Harry, what happened?" The words were difficult to form with her mouth too dry.

He gripped her hand and brushed her knuckles with his lips, "Claire, I'm so sorry."

She was reeling from everything, "Why are you apologizing? Can I please have some water?"

He reached for the Styrofoam cup sitting nearby. Sipping the water from the offered straw, she relished the coolness as it moisturized her throat. Experience told her not to drink too much. She tried her question again, "What happened?"

"Let's talk about that after we tell everyone you're awake." Claire nodded. There was no need for urgency, somewhere in her memory she'd heard her baby was all right.

Harry hit the nurse button. When the woman in light green scrubs came into the room, she took Claire's vitals and promised more information after the doctor's examination. Claire wanted to ask about the baby; however, Harry's presence made her hesitate.

When Dr. Sizemore entered the room, she asked Harry to leave. He kissed Claire's forehead and walked into the hall. She heard Amber,

Emily, and John's hushed voices as they questioned Harry beyond the closing door.

"Dr. Sizemore, I don't know what happened, but please tell me, is my baby all right?"

"Yes, Ms. Nichols. I've already shared with Mr. Baldwin that your baby's vitals are strong."

"Mr. Baldwin?" Claire asked, puzzled.

"Yes, he said that the two of you..." the doctor's face blanched. "I know that I shouldn't have, but I guess I assumed. Ms. Nichols, I'm sorry."

Claire couldn't stop the tears. *Oh my god! Harry knows I'm pregnant and thinks it's his!* Her thoughts came with such velocity her head spun.

"My head hurts – Doctor."

"Ms. Nichols, you hit your head very hard. You don't show signs of a concussion; however, the MRI indicated you've had one before."

Claire nodded. That's what Dr. Leonard said after her *accident.* "Yes, I did. That was a while ago. Does that matter now?"

"Well, yes. Any damage to your brain after a previous injury is significant. You also have bruised ribs. You are quite lucky they aren't broken. Again, I saw evidence of past broken ribs. Ms. Nichols, were you in an automobile accident, in the past?"

Claire inhaled; the action caused her side to hurt. "I had an accident in 2010. Will any of that affect my baby?"

"No, we have pain medicine that won't hurt your baby. I want you to get some rest. If you do, we can probably release you tomorrow or Thursday."

Claire's mind reeled, "Thursday? What day is it?"

"It's Tuesday. You've been unconscious for about thirty hours."

Thirty hours, why wasn't Tony here? As happy as Claire was about her baby being healthy, Tony's absence caused equal sadness. "Please send Mr. Baldwin back in."

"I will, but you have an entire waiting room of people. Would you like me to let them all come see you?"

"Harry told me they were here." She failed to sound happy.

Dr. Sizemore squeezed Claire's hand, "You have a great support system. I apologize for sharing your secret, but everyone is thrilled."

Although the aching in her heart made it difficult, Claire tried to smile. "Thank you, Doctor, just Mr. Baldwin, please."

Dr. Sizemore left Claire's room. Moments later, Harry peered his light blue eyes around the tall, imitation wood door. "May I come back in?" he asked bashfully.

Claire nodded through her tears. "Harry, I remember your voice when Chester was hurting me; please tell me what happened."

Harry sat on the edge of Claire's bed, took her hand, and inhaled and exhaled. Chronologically he recounted the events of Sunday night. "I left you at your door. Oh Claire, I'm so sorry I didn't go in with you."

She touched his arm. "I remember you weren't too happy with me. It's okay."

"I went to my place and began looking for the number for Chinese take-out. My phone started ringing. It was a blocked number. The first time, I'm sorry to say, I ignored it. The second set of rings I gave in...."

"Yes?"

"It was your ex-husband. I wasn't in a friendly mood. He was talking so fast I had a hard time following. Basically, he knew someone was in your condo and wanted me to get to you as soon as possible. Honestly, I thought it was some kind of set up. I mean, I'm right there, he's across the country, how could he know what's happening in your condo?" Harry paused, "I must agree," he said with a grin, "Anthony Rawlings can be very persuasive. I expected to find you doing inventory in your room. I used my key and entered." He shook his head.

"Thank you, Harry. I think you saved my life. Mr. Chester said something about taking me...or me going with him."

"It was his van we saw in your space. Do you remember that?"

Claire nodded. The action made the room lose focus. She closed her eyes, laid her head back, and tried to keep the world still.

"He had a note ready and supplies in the van. Claire, he planned on kidnapping you and ransoming you, to Mr. Rawlings. He wanted more money."

Claire felt the world slip away... she was supposed to be kidnapped???

"Claire?" Harry's questioning voice kept her earthbound. "Why didn't you tell me?"

She looked to the soft blue eyes staring down at her.

Harry continued, "I'm so sorry. You tried to tell me we needed to talk -- I was an ass. I keep saying the same thing, but I want you to know that I'm really sorry!"

"What happened to Patrick Chester?"

"When I started to open the door I heard the commotion in the living room. You were on the ground and he was..." Claire saw the anguish in Harry's expression; she turned her hand and squeezed his. He continued, "He was pulling you by your hair." Harry took another breath, in and out. "I screamed at him and at the same time, building security and Phil, you know, the guy you call your bodyguard? They came rushing in. Chester freaked. He started to reach for something. I think we all assumed it was a gun. The security guard shot first."

Claire listened in horror. "Is he dead?"

Harry nodded. "By that time you were unconscious. This is entirely my fault. I never should have taken you to his house. I never suspected he would see you as a..."

Harry's voice trailed away as voices in the hall became loud and angry. Claire heard John's rising above the fray, "*You are not* welcome here. I can't believe you would have the nerve to show your face after all you've done."

"I want to see her."

Claire's heart leapt -- Tony. "Oh, it's Tony!" She couldn't hide the happiness from her voice or expression while simultaneously seeing the pain in Harry's. "Didn't you say his call is what got you to me in time?" Harry nodded. "Then don't you think he should be able to see I'm all right?"

"I don't think *in your condition* you need to be upset by him."

Claire closed her eyes as tears slid down her cheeks, "Please, Harry, before he and John exchange blows."

Begrudgingly, Harry rose from the side of her bed and walked toward the voices. When he opened the door, the harsh words came even clearer to Claire. She heard Harry above the others, "John, stop. Claire wants to see Mr. Rawlings."

Emily's voice prevailed, "I haven't even seen her yet. She's my sister."

"*Claire* wants to see *him* now."

"Thank you, Mr. Baldwin."

Although Claire heard restraint in Tony's words, the deep baritone voice filled her with relief. Tears trickled from her eyes as she turned toward the door frame and saw her two men. She remained silent as Tony offer his hand to Harry and the two men shook. It was then she noticed Tony's wrinkled shirt and slacks, his unkempt hair and evidence of a three day beard. Harry looked as equally unkempt; it was just not as unusual to see him in that condition. They both walked into the room. Though she tried, she couldn't read Tony's expression. She watched as he took in her appearance and slowly approached her bed. She wasn't sure how she looked, but suspected by his darkening eyes and protruding neck muscles, it wasn't good.

The silence turned deafening as Tony's presence overtook the small hospital room. Claire turned to see Harry watching Tony suspiciously. She suddenly feared he would try to stop Tony's progress. Breaking the tension Claire spoke to Harry, "Please give us a moment alone." She saw his indecision. "Harry, I promise I'll be fine." Her words broke Tony's trance.

"Mr. Baldwin, I will only stay as long as Claire allows."

Claire exhaled at Tony's manners. She knew he was speaking as the social Anthony, not from his soul. Nevertheless, his charisma prevailed and Harry approached Claire. When he bent to kiss her, she pleaded with her eyes. Instead of continuing his descent, he squeezed her hand. The sad realization in his eyes broke her heart. He said, "I'm right on the other side of that door."

"Thank you," she feigned a smile, "for everything."

After a prolonged stare at Claire and again at Tony, Harry exited the room. As he did, Claire heard the protests of her family. She didn't care.

She looked up to the man looming above her, gloom emanating from every pore. His expression should terrify her; it was probably the reason Harry didn't want to leave, but she wasn't afraid. Tears of relief flowed as she reached for him and said, "I'm so glad you're here."

He took her hand, "The last time I saw you like this…"

"I'm all right."

"If that son-of-a-bitch weren't dead, I'd kill him myself."

By the sound of Tony's voice, Claire didn't doubt the accuracy. "Tony, *we* are both okay."

His eyes opened wide and his shoulders relaxed, "I haven't been able to get any specific information. I just assumed…"

"The doctor was just here. She said our baby is fine."

Moisture filled his eyes as he pulled away and paced near the end of her bed. Finally he spoke, "Claire, just like your accident, this is my fault, too." She shook her head but he continued. "I don't know how Chester found you or knew of our connection. I don't even know how he knew me. I knew him when I was Anton." He moved closer and started to reach for her chin, but stopped. "And now look what he's done."

Claire squeezed his large hand and lifted it to her face, "Thank you for coming. I feel so much better having you here."

As her face inclined to his touch, Tony's forehead fell to her chest and he sighed with relief. "I knew my presence wouldn't be welcome. I've been waiting on another floor for word of your waking."

That's why he wasn't here -- Claire thought as her lips turned upward and said, "Yes, I heard your welcoming committee."

He looked into her eyes and his voice hardened, "When you're well enough to travel, you're coming home where you'll be safe and where Catherine can take care of you."

She narrowed her eyes, "That didn't sound like a question."

His eyes narrowed in response, "It shouldn't. I would hate to mislead you; it wasn't."

Claire exhaled, "Chester is dead, no more danger."

He leaned toward her, "Are you seriously going to argue about this, covered in bruises and carrying my baby?"

He was close; she raised her chin and kissed his pursed lips. "Not right now," she smiled. "Let me get some rest and get a little stronger and then I will." She watched his eyes soften as a smile caused his cheeks to rise.

"Good," he kissed her again. "I look forward to it." He squeezed her hand. "We don't know if Patrick Chester was working alone. Until we find out and find your laptop, this isn't negotiable."

Claire debated protesting. While Tony's expression warned otherwise, that wasn't what stopped her. She wasn't sure she wanted to argue. What if there was someone else? "I need some sleep for this headache to go away, and then I'll respond with the appropriate cheekiness for you."

His eyes continued to lighten, "Even looking like you do, I think you're sexy as hell." He gently kissed her forehead, "Do you think now is a good time to tell your entourage our news?"

Claire looked down. "No, they know." Tony's eyebrows went up. "The doctor told Harry before I woke. He told everyone else."

Dark clouds returned to his gaze, "Why would the doctor tell *him*?"

"She assumed he was the father."

His words slowed as his posture straightened, "And does *he* assume that as well?"

Claire thought she might be ill. She was single. She and Tony weren't married, engaged, or anything else. At least they weren't when she and Harry...So why did she feel so guilty. Shyly she replied, "Yes."

If she'd slapped him, he couldn't have stood faster. For a split second Claire feared he was heading for the door. She worried more for Harry than for herself. However, Tony stopped his progress and paced around the small hospital room, keeping his eyes fixed on his shoes moving rapidly upon the glossy linoleum. Claire didn't speak; Tony needed to work this out himself. Instead, she laid her head upon the pillow and closed her eyes.

His voice brought her back, "You're sure *I'm* the father?"

Claire opened her eyes, her voice steady, "Yes, you were at the condominium two weeks before Harry and me... Well, at the ultrasound the doctor said the heartbeat isn't detectable until six weeks. If he were the father, I would have barely been five weeks along. At that time, I was seven." She reached for his hand. After a moment of hesitation he stepped to her. She continued, "Tony, I didn't know we were together until you confirmed it at the gala. I remember it, but I'd convinced myself it was a dream."

He sighed and sat again on her bedside. "You were very tired, but you were talking. You mentioned something about a dream. I may be guilty of taking advantage of a tired woman, but nothing else."

"How did you get back in the condo? I remember closing and locking the door."

"You closed it, but you didn't lock it. Or, it didn't lock. I came back to say something, and I heard something fall. It sounded like it broke. I listened but didn't hear anything else. So, I decided to check on you. The door opened." He confessed, "I didn't knock. You were on the couch. I carried you to your bedroom. I can say *with honorable intentions*, but that wouldn't be entirely true. Claire, I asked you multiple times. You never said no."

She sighed, "I remember wanting you. I'd spent half the night dreaming about you, until I gave up and stayed awake. That's why I was so tired."

His smile lit her world. "You dreamt about me?"

"Yes, it was after our dinner. I hadn't seen you since ... the jail in Iowa."

He softly kissed her lips, and his eyes sparkled, "You dreamt about me?"

She smirked, "Yes, you egotistical narcissist. I did."

"I've dreamt about you, too. I think it may have something to do with seeing your beautiful face above my fireplace every night before I fall asleep."

The door opened, and they turned to see the nurse return. "I'm sorry, sir, Ms. Nichols needs her rest. I'm closing her door to visitors for a while."

Tony stood with Claire's hand still in his. "What about...?" he asked.

"I'll tell them. I was about to tell Harry when you showed up."

Tony turned to the nurse, "How long is *a while*?"

She looked to Claire. Suddenly, Claire realized the nurse was probably sent to save her. Claire replied, "*I* want Mr. Rawlings here whenever possible."

The nurse spoke to Tony, "Let her sleep through the night."

Tony nodded, "I can do that." He bent down and kissed Claire, "I'll be back in the morning."

"Good. I think you look like you could use some sleep too." Although her head hurt, her emerald eyes glistened through her bruised face.

As she turned to watch him leave, she saw four sets of eyes watching their goodbye and focusing on Tony as he politely passed their human wall. The door closed.

"Nurse, I'm sorry I don't know your name."

"Terri."

"Terri?" Claire asked softly. "Could you please tell my other visitors I need rest? I really don't have the energy to talk with *any* of them."

Terri nodded, "I can do that. This medicine should help your pain and help you sleep."

"It won't hurt the baby?"

"No, it's completely safe."

Claire watched as Terri injected something into her IV. She closed her eyes and allowed the medicine to take effect as Terri walked to the hall and addressed Claire's entourage.

Blissfully, sleep took her away.

A woman must not depend on the protection of man,
but must be taught to protect herself.
- Susan B. Anthony

Chapter 53

Claire woke to a piercing pain in her head and a throbbing ache in her side. She tried to keep herself still and evaluate the nausea building within. She remembered eating with Tony on Sunday afternoon; had she eaten since? There couldn't be anything in her empty stomach to revolt, yet it was. She hit the nurse *call* button and peered out the window, attempting to divert her attentions. Her window looked over the roofs of the sprawling hospital and beyond to Stanford's Medical Campus. Past the campus in the distance, she saw the mountains. The lightening sky and lingering fog told her morning had finally arrived. It was Wednesday and her family and friends had been waiting all night, for multiple nights.

She needed to talk to them. She knew Harry deserved a private discussion; hopefully, the others would agree to a group session. Claire didn't relish the idea of repeating her story over and over. She turned to the sound of the opening door.

"Hello, Ms. Nichols, I'm Abbey your day nurse."

"Please, call me Claire."

"Claire, what can I do for you?"

Claire asked about getting up and out of the bed. After Abbey checked the chart, she assisted Claire to the bathroom. On the way, Claire worried about her reflection. She hadn't seen herself yet. She knew from Tony's reaction she looked as bruised as she felt. Steeling herself for the worse, she bravely faced the woman in the mirror.

Walking to and from the bathroom required help. By the time they were done, her tubes were disconnected, she was sponged clean, her teeth brushed, and thankfully, her bladder emptied. Claire would have loved to wash her hair and add makeup to cover the various shades of bruises on her checks and temples, and the deep purple under her left eye. Nevertheless, she felt better.

This was in many ways easier than her *accident*. Although she tried not to make comparisons, they were staring her in the face: injury to head and ribs. Ironically the injuries ensued by a crazy greedy monster were less than those obtained by the man who claimed to love her. Claire continued to remind herself, Harry stopped Patrick. What would have happened if he hadn't -- if Tony hadn't called Harry -- if Phil and security hadn't come? With her accident, no one stopped Tony. He stopped himself -- eventually. The most monumental difference was internally. Following her *accident*, Claire lost all desire to continue forward. She remembered a black hole of apathy. She didn't feel that way now. Despite her battered appearance, Claire's desire to live was stronger than it had ever been. She saw hope for better tomorrows with every new day.

As Abbey helped Claire back to bed, she handed Claire a folded note. "This is for you. I was supposed to deliver it once you woke."

Claire took the paper and opened it:

> *I hope you and our baby are feeling better.*
> *Perhaps you'll feel up to arguing your destination*
> *following your release.*
> *(I am definitely ready)* Claire couldn't help but smile.
> *I want to see you.*
> *However, I realize you need to speak to the others and*
> *I don't want you to overdo. I'm staying nearby.*
> *Call me at the number below when you're ready*
> *for my visit. I'll be there in minutes.*

Fighting tears, she closed the note. At one time, Tony would never have given her the time and space she needed to deal with her family and friends. Although she wanted to feel his reassuring embrace, at this moment, his absence meant more and filled her heart with reassurance.

"Is there anything else I can get you?" Abbey asked.

"I would love some food. Can I eat?"

"Yes, I'll get you an order card. You have many people who've been patiently waiting. Are you ready for visitors?"

"If Mr. Baldwin is here, would you please ask him to come in?"

Claire's pulse increased and her stomach twisted. As Harry entered, she saw his clean shirt and freshly shaven face. "You went home?"

He held her hand; the spark she'd seen in his eyes yesterday was gone, the resulting dullness infiltrated his voice, "According to the nurse you didn't want visitors. She said you were going to sleep. I knew you and the baby were healthy, so I went home."

"Good, I'm glad you got a good night's sleep."

"I went home. I didn't say I got a good night's sleep."

Claire raised her eyebrows.

"Tell me, Claire, what you wanted to tell me Sunday night. It wasn't that *we* are having a baby, was it?"

She squeezed his hand. "No. It wasn't."

His face lowered to his chest. "I knew that last night, as soon as I saw *his* face and your expression when he arrived."

"Thank you for saving him from John."

"I don't think your ex needs saving from anyone. Although you have to admit John has legitimate reasons for his feelings."

Claire knew Harry was right, and she didn't want to rehash any of that. "Still, thanks."

"He saved you. I don't want to even think about the injuries you endured because I didn't answer his first call."

"Harry, there are plenty of medals to go around; one is definitely yours!"

"Tell me – when?" His voice now distant, "Was it the night of the gala?"

"No!" She fought the urge to be defensive. "I told you, nothing happened that night." She took a deep breath and continued, "It was the day he came to the condominium. I don't want to discuss it, but the ultrasound confirmed the baby is two weeks older than it could be if you were the father."

Harry nodded. Finally, he asked, "He already knew, didn't he?"

"Yes, I told him this past weekend. I wasn't sure I would, but I did."

"What else happened this past weekend?"

Claire looked down. "Harry, I can't tell you how much your friendship has meant to me; you've been so supportive. I understand if you want to hate me." She looked up into his sad expression. His blue eyes looked distant. Her heart ached knowing she was the cause, "But, I hope you won't."

He stood and walked toward the door, "Are you ready to tell everyone? They want to see you."

To Harry's credit, he didn't let on to the others that there were issues, or that he wasn't the father of Claire's baby. Immediately, Emily embraced her sister and began crying. Next it was Amber's turn. Besides telling Claire how happy they were she was all right, they both told her how delighted they were about the baby. Both couldn't wait to be aunts. After enduring everyone's good wishes, Claire braced herself for comments about Tony's visit.

She decided it was better to allow everyone their say. The comments started slow and continued with increased velocity. Finally, Harry stopped the barrage, "Are any of you interested to hear Claire's point of view?"

Although she was grateful for his support, in a way, it made her feel worse. "I let him in. I wanted him here, because things have changed." How could Claire make her chess pieces understand? "I'm not denying any of his past sins. However, some of what we've assumed were his I've learned weren't. But, nonetheless, I'm very much aware of all he's done. With that said, the baby I'm carrying isn't Harry's." She waited while realization came to those around her. Amber went to Harry's side and put her arm around him.

"I've known since last night," Harry told his sister, "but I thought Claire should be the one to tell everyone. I'm disappointed, but listen; she's still having a baby, that's a miracle."

"Anthony's baby?!" Emily exclaimed. "How could you?!"

"Yes," Claire replied defensively, "*your* niece or nephew."

John didn't speak. His eyes sent daggers toward anyone willing to look his way. Finally, he walked from the room. When the door shut, Claire exhaled.

Emily used the moment to attack, "I don't know why you're relieved John left. I'll have you know, your attack, injuries, and probably your pregnancy would be all over the internet and television if it weren't for John. He immediately set about with a *do not disclose order* against the hospital. Your newly found friend – lover – ex-captor -- I don't even know what to call *him*, took away John's life and law license, but your brother-in-law still managed to be here for you."

"Please, tell him thank you. What does the press know?" Suddenly she thought of Meredith. Claire didn't want her book under production.

Harry sounded as though he were describing an unknown news story. "The police and ambulance were called to your condominium. You went to the hospital in an ambulance. An intruder was taken from your condominium after suffering deadly gunshot wounds."

"Could someone bring me my phone? I need to call someone."

"It's at the condo." Amber replied. "You're probably coming home today, can it wait?"

Claire didn't know. She didn't want Meredith publishing anything prematurely.

Their conversation was interrupted by the delivery of Claire's breakfast. She opened each plate with reserved anticipation: eggs, orange juice, toast, and tea. As she inspected the food, Abbey reentered.

"Ladies and gentleman, I understand how happy you are to have Claire and baby Nichols doing well. But, she needs her rest. I'm restricting her to two visitors at a time."

Harry spoke first, "I need to get to work. Claire, I wish you well, and I'm trying. We both need some time."

Her eyes filled with tears. "Thank you."

Amber came forward and hugged Claire. "I'm disappointed and confused. But more than anything, I'm happy you and your baby are safe." Her smile sparkled, "I guess it wasn't food poisoning, was it?"

Claire shook her head and smiled. "No, it wasn't."

"I don't know your plans, but you can stay with me as long as you want."

Claire remembered her impending argument with Tony. "I really don't know what I'm going to do, but thanks for the offer."

Once Amber left the room and Emily and Claire were alone, Emily spoke first, "What do you mean you don't know what you're going to do? Are you seriously considering moving back to that prison?"

Claire closed her eyes. "I don't know. Tony wants me to move back to Iowa. I was resisting, but, after Patrick Chester, I just don't know. At least on his estate, I'm safe and so is my baby."

"Safe? Is that what their calling imprisonment these days?"

Claire regretted telling Emily the truth of her and Tony's past. She thought of Tony's recent words: *You may think you're ready for answers, but you're not. Bits and pieces may help you understand. But, the blatant truth is too much.* Claire tried to explain, "I can't make you understand, but when I was there last week, things were different."

"Right -- and once you decide to stay, I'm sure it will stay that way."

"I'm going to call him. He'll be here soon. The nurse said I can have two visitors. Emily, the choice is yours. When he arrives you can stay or go, but he's coming. I want him here."

The next time the door opened, an orderly entered carrying two large bouquets of flowers. The first one had a card which simply read: Tony. The second bouquet was from Courtney and Brent, with wishes for fast healing. Claire wondered if Tony told them about the baby.

Emily stayed until Tony arrived. When he did, she kissed Claire on her cheek and said, "We have more places to see today. I'll check on you later." She turned, made eye contact with Tony, and left.

He immediately went to Claire's bedside, "Well, I seem to have that effect on all of your family."

Claire's eyebrows rose, "All? Did you see John again?"

"Briefly, he's in the lounge down the hall."

Wrinkling her nose in anticipation, "Did you two speak?"

"No." Tony grinned, "I'm pretty sure if you ever decide to accept the ring I offered, he *won't* give you away – *again.*"

Claire sat taller, "I'm not anyone's to give away. And I don't care any longer what others think."

"Does that mean..." His brown eyes twinkled as he lifted her hand. When she smiled in response, she winced at the pain near her swollen eye. Tony's voice hardened, "I wish that ass hole were still alive, so I could kill him."

She rested her head against the pillows and closed her eyes to the pain. "It means ... we're dating."

Looking around the small room, Tony whispered jokingly, "This hardly seems public."

Claire's eyes sprang open. "I need to contact Meredith. I don't want her to misconstrue this and think it means she can publish her book, but my phone is at the condo."

Tony removed his iPhone from his pocket. "I have her number."

Claire eyed him suspiciously, "How do you have her number? And now that I'm thinking about it, how did you have Harry's?"

He looked down, "Before I answer, you must admit the information was useful."

"Yes, I admit that. How?"

He handed her his phone with *Meredith Banks* on the screen. "You just need to hit call."

"I know how to use a phone, thank you." She waited. She remembered how Tony didn't like asking the same question more than once. She knew the feeling and continued to stare.

"The night of the gala I copied your contacts."

Claire shook her head and hit *call*. While she spoke to Meredith another orderly entered her room with another bouquet of flowers. Tony accepted the arrangement and sat it on the large window ledge. He reached for the card and began to carry it to Claire. Suddenly, he stopped. Claire watched as he opened the envelope and the color drained from his face. She wondered if it were from Harry.

"Thank you, Meredith, our agreement is still intact." "Yes, I'm fine." "This had nothing to do with Tony." "I need to go." "Thank you, good-bye." She disconnected the call. "Tony what is it?"

He hesitated. "I'll be back in a minute." He started to leave her room with the card.

"No, you don't." Her voice rose. "Show me that card."

When he turned toward her, his expression was scarier than she'd seen in years. "Claire, you and our baby do not need to be concerned. I'll find out who is responsible for this, and by the way, we are talking to your doctor about a referral for Iowa City. You are moving home as soon as you're released."

She didn't want to argue. It wasn't just his expression, the darkness of his eyes, or the determined tone. She saw fear masked under his sudden fury. "Tony," she spoke softly. "Please let me see the card. I'm not arguing. I need to know what *I* need to do to protect our baby."

Slowly he walked toward her. His furrowed brow and intense glare revealed his conflicting emotions.

Claire pleaded, "I know you want to protect me, but you have to let *me* protect me."

He handed her the card and she read the envelope: *Claire Nichols Rawls.* The air left her lungs. She opened the envelope and read the note:

*I hear **you** are well. Now there's*
another body to add to the count.

"What does that mean?" She asked, as the fear she felt Sunday night returned.

"I don't know. I know it means you're coming home with me."

Claire nodded.

Trouble is part of your life. If you don't share it,
you don't give the person who loves you
a chance to love you enough.
- Dinah Shore

Chapter 54

L ate Wednesday afternoon Dr. Sizemore released Claire from the hospital and gave her a referral to Iowa City. Tony wanted to drive her directly to the airport; however, Claire convinced him to take her back to her condominium and pack some of her things. She didn't know if her trip to Iowa was for a week, a month, or forever.

Entering her bedroom, the sight of her things strewn across the room and drawers emptied all over the floor... paralyzed her movement. Her knees weakened as Tony's strong embrace steadied her. Together they worked to right the mess.

When they finally had her room almost in order, building security called. There was a package waiting downstairs for Claire. They wanted to confirm her presence before bringing it to her unit. Leaving Tony in her room, she went to the door and greeted the security guard with the potted plant. It wasn't the same man who saved her. But everyone within 365 Forest Avenue knew what had transpired.

"Ms. Nichols, we're all so glad you're safe."

"Thank you, I am."

"Here's your delivery. Obviously, lots of people are worried about you." The young man handed her the plastic wrapped arrangement and scanned the envelope. "This is you, right?"

Claire read the card: *Claire Nichols Rawls.*

Feeling suddenly faint, she called for Tony. He immediately appeared by her side, took the card, saw the name, and rudely ordered, "Take this away".

Claire didn't have the presence of mind or words to mend Tony's negativity. Instead, she merely nodded. The guard apologized and left with the plant.

Tony opened the envelope – nothing... not even a card within. "I'll find out who's doing this, I promise."

The conviction in his voice reassured Claire. Tony meant every word. She stood straighter, nodded, held back tears, and walked past him toward her room. Before she could pass, Tony seized her arm and stopped her movement. Claire looked up at him indignantly and watched his eyes darken as his voice echoed against the long hallway and wooden floors, "You are not staying here another night."

Her bruise-covered face and pained expression were more than Tony could take. It wasn't a debatable statement.

Claire nodded, "I know. I want to pack."

He released her arm, "While you do, I'll make some calls. May I go into the living room?"

"Yes, Amber knows we're here. She's giving us space."

"She doesn't want to see me." His statement wasn't judgmental -- just a statement. Either way, he was right; Amber was purposely avoiding the condominium. She wasn't the only one opposed to Claire's decisions. Emily repeatedly chided her. John avoided her at all costs, and Claire hadn't spoken to Harry since the hospital room.

With the recent turn of events, Tony's estate seemed much safer than California, if only temporarily. Claire packed while Tony made calls. His efforts were rewarded as he learned: the flowers and plant came from two separate florists. One was ordered over the telephone, the other over the internet. The caller ordering the flowers claimed to be *Mrs. Rawls* and used a purchased credit card, the kind available at any retailer across the country. The internet order appeared to be made by Claire herself; all the information entered into the order form was hers. It was also purchased with the same type of credit card, but from a different retailer. Tony also had people working to track the origin of the credit cards and someone checking the fingerprint of the computer placing the internet order.

Claire didn't understand it all, but if it led Tony to the person sending the threatening gifts, she was all for it.

Although Tony repeatedly told Claire she didn't need any of her clothes or anything that wasn't of emotional value, she packed as much as her luggage would hold. Her belongings were the things she'd accumulated on her own; everything from her lingerie to the flip-flops she wore on the beach with Courtney meant something. Securing her jewelry in a small velvet bag she fingered her new diamond stud earrings. Admittedly, they weren't as large as the ones she sold. But, nevertheless, they were hers, bought by her. She didn't want to part with them.

Claire struggled with her research. Even though her laptop was still missing, she had hard copies of everything. Did she want to take all of that to Tony's? Claire decided she should. She didn't know anymore who to believe or who to trust. What if someone used her information to hurt Tony? It was safer with her.

By the time Claire finished packing, it was late and she was tired.

412

Tony conceded, "We can spend the night in Palo Alto at my hotel. Tomorrow we'll come back for your things and leave for Iowa." Claire agreed. There was no need for debate. Every time she walked into the living room, in her mind, she saw Patrick Chester.

As she settled into the passenger seat of his rental car, exhaustion hit. By the time they arrived at the Marriott where he'd rented the Presidential Suite, Claire was sound asleep. Tony's words woke her gently as he opened the door and kissed her cheek, "I'd gladly carry you to my suite, but I'm afraid we'd attract more attention than either of us wants."

Despite the stress of the day and of the past few days, his sensitive smile and tender tone made her anxious expression morph into a smile. "I'm pretty sure I can walk." She stood sorely and melted against his chest. "I could do this alone, but I'm so thankful I don't have to." She brushed her lips against his. "Thank you."

When they reached the suite, Claire looked around at the modern furnishings and beautiful view. The living room had lovely glass doors leading to a balcony, an archway leading to a dining room, and a doorway she assumed lead to a bedroom.

Tony offered, "Perhaps we should order some food?"

"I just want a shower and some sleep," Claire said as she walked toward the bedroom.

The warm water assaulted her bruised skin and at the same time felt wonderfully refreshing. She towel dried and combed her hair and brushed her teeth (if they could share a bed and a baby, why not a toothbrush?). She turned off the lights and settled into the large king sized bed wearing one of Tony's t-shirts. She'd seen her reflection in the bathroom mirror and didn't want Tony to see the large bruises on her ribs. Although sleep loomed, she yearned to feel his embrace. The last few days left her anxious and Tony's presence reassured her. Closing her eyes, she realized how safe she felt near him. Thinking about the stories she'd recently recounted to Meredith, Claire knew that hadn't always been the case, but now she longed for his presence.

As she was about to drift away, she heard a knock at the door. Claire assumed Tony must have ordered dinner. She rolled over, wincing from her sore ribs, cradled a pillow, and drifted away.

Sometime later, Claire woke with a start. She'd been dreaming, no, not dreaming – it was a nightmare: darkness, Chester, gun shots... She reached for Tony, but his side of the bed was cool.

His t-shirt fell to her thighs as she quietly walked toward the living room. Her bare feet silently made their way down the hall. In the near darkness she saw the back of Tony's head, bobbing in silence. The sofa where he sat was made up like a bed, complete with sheets, blankets, and pillows.

Claire walked around the sofa and met his gaze, "Tony? Are you all right?"

She saw the amber liquid in his glass, his vacant expression, and smelled the bourbon in the air. After his dark eyes looked her up and down, he finally replied, "No."

"What's this?" She motioned toward the sofa. "Why aren't you in bed with me?"

"I don't trust myself."

Claire tilted her head sideways, "I trust you..."

His stare looked through her, "I went in there and kissed you. You were sound asleep." Claire smiled, he continued, "I watched you, saw your expression and your bruises." Claire flinched; she didn't like her appearance. He grasped her dangling hand. "Stop that."

"What?"

"You're beautiful!"

She pulled her hand away, "I've seen me. Beautiful isn't a word I'd use."

Tony leaned back and rubbed his face. With a new focus, he demanded, "Take off my t-shirt."

Claire stood taller. Her chin rose indignantly. "Excuse me?"

He stood. His body towered over her as his voice hardened, "Take off my shirt."

"Tony, I didn't bring any night clothes... I didn't think you'd ..."

"I don't give a damn about the shirt. I want to see you."

Claire stammered. It'd been a while since she'd experienced this domineering personality. "See me?"

"I can see your face and your legs... I want to see what that bastard did to you."

She reached for his hand and kept her voice steady, "I'm fine, but I want you to come to bed...with me."

His stoic expression remained, "I planned to call for dinner. Instead, I found the bar. It's been a rather stressful few days." Claire inched closer. His sudden grasp on her shoulders stopped her progress. "I should never have let you return to California." Shaking his head, he released her, and stepped backward. In a tone she remembered, he commanded, "I believe I've said this more than once... take off the damn t-shirt."

Her innate training prevailed; disobeying wasn't an option. She reached for the hem. Trembling, she lifted the cotton above her head and exposed her battered body, covered only by a pair of flesh-colored lace panties.

His hardened expression continued in silence... until her trembling registered. Suddenly, he fell to his knees and gently clutched her hips. His lips gently brushed her stomach and tenderly caressed her battered midsection. The domineering voice disappeared; his actions spoke of love and possession. Holding his head for support, her fingers wove through his hair. Claire whispered, "Please, Tony, please, can we go to bed?"

His lips continued to caress her bruised body. Each kiss electrified her skin, melting her insides until her legs turned to jelly. When her knees buckled, she knelt before him and their eyes met.

"You're mine." His words weren't debatable. He wasn't asking.

"Tony, bed... please?"

414

"I'm trying so hard. You have no idea the restraint I'm enlisting...yet, all I can think about are *his* hands on you."

"Tony, I'm fine. I'm all right. I'm with you."

"But, you weren't. You were with him."

"He just wanted your money..."

Tony clutched her frame. His dark eyes burned with desire and despair. "I'm not talking about Chester."

Claire froze. Her heart pounded in her chest. Somewhere deep, she knew the scene in the hospital went too well. She framed Tony's face and watched as he searched her emerald eyes. With all her might, she tried to keep them subdued. "*I* wasn't with *you*," she whispered. "*We* weren't together."

His loud visceral response was unreadable.

"But now..." her lips touched his, "now, I want to be... *please,* Tony."

One of the hands which held her waist now roughly seized her loose damp hair, pulling her head back, and exposing her slender neck. His lips met the soft skin with equal force. A shocked moan escaped her lips. Tony's unbridled passion ignited her, creating a sudden rush of heat overpowering any impulses of pain crying out from her tender scalp. His rough stubble scratched her collar bone, and his voice resonated throughout the suite like a low growl, "Are you sure?"

The fervent lust tightened her insides. Momentarily, speech was lost. Finally, she whimpered, "I am."

He continued his unrelenting assault, holding her tighter, wildly claiming everything before him. His fire consumed everything in its path, a passion which held no bounds. Claire never felt so desired; her whole body ached for his touch. When he paused she saw the flames in his dark eyes. The inferno wasn't frightening; it fueled her desire. His low growl became more demanding, "You are mine."

She kissed his stubbly neck, hearing, as well as feeling, a rumble from the back of his throat. Once again he pulled her hair, tipped her head, and bathed her in the aroma of whiskey. His glaring abyss penetrated as he demanded, "Say it!"

Her emerald eyes begged for understanding, uncertain of what he wanted.

"Say you are mine and nobody else's."

Despite his command and her powerful yearning, Claire's eyes shone. Her voice resonated above his growl, "Yes, Tony, *you* are mine and nobody else's."

She watched. A spark penetrated his dark gaze – a flash of light where only moments before darkness prevailed. Through the crack in his facade of domination, he responded. It began as a whisper and rose in volume. "Yes...mighty fine and sexy as hell," claiming her lips he added, "and mine!"

Suddenly, he stood, seized her wrist and pulled her up toward the bedroom. Before she could comment, the world shifted and she was upon the king sized bed. His hungry mouth on hers made protesting impossible. Truly, it wasn't her plan.

Once her breathing became labored, he moved to the end of the bed. Beginning at her ankles he worked his way toward her injuries. Each touch released energy, freed aggression, and exposed affection. If she winced, he caressed. If she moaned, he encouraged. With each kiss, each touch, Tony reminded Claire of her desires. The outside world was lost... gone beyond comprehension. He elicited thoughts and desires she'd compartmentalized away. His lips found places she'd abandoned. His teeth nipped at nubs which yearned for attention. His long talented fingers and skillful tongue probed and tantalized. Within no time, Claire found herself begging for mercy and at the same time pleading for more.

It was different than the day in the condo or from her visit to Iowa. It was different than ever before. This was deep, raw, and primal -- unbridled carnal passion. While it started with possession, its culmination was unification and reconciliation. Tony began this ecstasy, but Claire met him move for move. Truthfully, she didn't like the reports of him with other women, either. The handsome, possessive, domineering, loving man before her was *hers*. And although she wasn't ready to commit, she wanted everything he offered.

When they finally submitted to sleep, no desire was left unfulfilled.

The next morning at Amber's condo, they were met by a crew of men to carry her belongings from the fourth floor to a waiting van and from the van to his airplane. While the men moved her things, Claire's mail arrived.

If she hadn't already been frightened into moving to Iowa, the package she received would have pushed her over the edge. It was a large, light, thick, soft, manila envelope addressed in handwriting Claire didn't recognize, with no return address. She didn't want to seem paranoid; after all, it was addressed to: *Claire Nichols*. Nevertheless, when she opened the envelope and a small yellow layette fell to the floor with a note which simply read: *Congratulations*. Claire feared she'd faint. Tony assessed the package.

They both knew it was a threat, not only aimed at Claire, but at their baby. Yet, the benign nature gave them nothing they could take to the police.

Tony grabbed Claire's purse and phone and immediately walked her from the condominium to his rental car. "We're going to the airport. Whatever you want that doesn't make this move can be sent later. I don't want you here another minute."

Claire broke down in the passenger's seat, no longer able to contain her tears. She didn't know what the future held, only that she needed to get away from California.

Once they were safely in the air and flying east, Claire's anxiety began to lessen. Lying on the long white leather sofa with her head on Tony's lap, she closed her eyes. The hum of the engines pacified as he smoothed her long hair away from her wounded face. His words surprised her.

"Claire, this whole mess is my fault. I'm so sorry."

She sat up. He looked older, less confident, perhaps even frightened. "What do you mean it's your fault?"

"That man, Patrick Chester. He attacked you because of me."

"That's not your fault. It's because of your money. That's not your fault." She touched his cheek. "I know you were overbearingly controlling before, but I get it. I think about our baby. If I could, I'd never let him or her leave the estate. There are too many crazy people out there."

"I'll hire you security. For the time being I don't want you going anywhere without them."

Claire nodded. "I don't like it, but I'll do it. But..." she looked him in the eye. "I will come and go as I please, or I'm leaving."

His back straightened and he reached for her chin. "Remember what you just said about our child?"

"I'm not a child. I will not risk my life or our child's." She exhaled. "I can see why informing you of my activities is important, but I'm not asking permission."

He closed his eyes and exhaled, "You will have someone with you."

She noticed it wasn't a question. "Yes, Tony. I will take whomever you hire as a body guard with me. But does this person have to be with me on the estate?"

He released her chin. "I don't know. This is all new to me." He gently squeezed her hand, "We can feel it out together."

Claire nodded and laid her head back on his lap.

"Can I tell you a story?"

She looked up at his face. He wasn't looking down at her, but staring away to another time and another place. Claire nodded, "Yes."

"There was this man -- young man, actually. He didn't have the greatest role models growing up. The positive traits he saw in people and what he learned to respect were power, unbridled control over those around him, veracity, and ambition, the belief that nothing was beyond his reach – nothing, meaning the acquiring of a company, money, or even people. And reliability -- once a promise was made, no matter what, it was kept."

Claire listened as Tony spoke about this young man who emulated his grandfather. In his own way, he'd made his grandfather into the person everyone would want to be. Few people truly knew the grandfather. Of those that did, most disliked him. However, they respected him and his abilities. That was until some decisions he made and people he trusted turned on him. The young man's father helped in the family demise. The only support this young man believed he had was from his grandfather and his grandfather's new wife.

Claire followed along until this point. Nathaniel had a new wife? She remembered reading where Sharron Rawls died years before his arrest. Why hadn't she seen anything about another wife? She wanted to ask, but never before had Tony shared. She remained silent, hoping he'd reveal more.

Tony went on explaining: emotions were high, threats and promises were made. The new wife and this young man's parents did not get along. One night there was an incident. Tony looked down into Claire's eyes; he rephrased *an accident*. It wasn't intentional, but things got out of control. The young man wasn't there. He arrived too late to help his parents. Since they were beyond help, he chose to help the woman his grandfather loved. The only person who could refute the premise of murder/ suicide was a neighbor. That neighbor, like everyone else, had a price. For over twenty years the young man worked to shield the woman he promised his grandfather he would protect.

Tony's eyes once again met Claire's. "When I changed my name, I hoped to distance myself from the Rawls sins. I'm not sure how or why Patrick Chester made the connection from Anton Rawls to Anthony Rawlings, but I'm so sorry he did."

Claire sat up, "It's my fault."

His eyes refocused, "What? How?"

"We found his name on a police report. Your parents' injuries weren't consistent with murder/suicide. Patrick Chester lived in a very nice neighborhood with very nice cars. His lifestyle didn't match his profession or income. He had an annual installment that continued to grow. We suspected the annual payments were payoffs for silence. In the original report he mentioned a woman in a blue Honda. The woman was never mentioned again. A month or more ago, I went to his house."

Tony's regret changed to hostility before her eyes, "You did what?"

Claire couldn't justify her behavior. She melted against the soft cushions, "I know-- it was stupid."

His hands were on her shoulders, "Why would you even think..."

She allowed the tears to fall, "It wasn't *your* fault. It was mine. I'm the one who put our baby at risk." His arms surrounded her. With her face pressed against his chest, she asked, "The woman, she wasn't your aunt was she?" Claire felt Tony shaking his head. "She was your *grandmother?*"

He shrugged, "I guess. I've never really thought of her that way. My parents successfully petitioned her and Nathaniel's marriage to be voided. She wasn't legally able to maintain the name Rawls."

"You've been paying for her freedom for all these years. Do you ever see her?"

"I do. But she doesn't want to be identified."

Claire nodded. She didn't blame the lady. There was no statute of limitations on murder in California; the less people that knew, the better. "Thank you for telling me the truth."

He pushed her away and looked into her eyes, "No more detective work." This again wasn't a question. Claire nodded and settled against his chest. Inhaling his cologne and listening to the beat of his heart, Claire

418

closed her eyes. She didn't want to ponder the new information. She wanted it all to go away.

Claire awoke as the plane touched down in Iowa.

Your memory is a monster; you forget - it doesn't. It simply files things away. It keeps things for you, or hides things from you -- and summons them to your recall with a will of its own.
You think you have a memory; but it has you!
– John Irving

Chapter 55

O ver the next few days and weeks Claire settled into an old, yet unfamiliar, pattern on Tony's estate. Things were different and the same. She had her iPhone and iPad. Tony even bought her a new laptop; her old one was still missing. Apparently, the police found Patrick Chester's van and hotel room. Unfortunately, the laptop was in neither place. His house in Santa Monica was also thoroughly searched. Nothing was there either. His wife and daughter were shocked. They had no idea why a loving husband and father would decide to kidnap someone. Repeatedly, they told the police and press, "This wasn't like him at all. We don't understand what drove him to such behavior."

The missing laptop led everyone to assume there might be an undetected accomplice. For that reason, Claire was more than content to stay behind the large iron gates. She rarely left the estate. When she did, it was usually to attend functions with Tony. The first few dates on their prearranged schedule were missed due to her appearance. Claire didn't want the press taking pictures of her with the remnants of Patrick Chester's handiwork around her eye or on her cheeks. During those first few weeks she called friends and family. Courtney and Sue made multiple visits. She even told them about the baby.

One afternoon Claire led Courtney out to the gardens. They settled onto the same bench that Catherine had told Claire was visibly accessible to the cameras but not audibly. Claire explained her change of heart to her dear friend. Courtney told Claire about Brent's research. Derek Burke was related to Jonathon Burke, but not directly. And Brent couldn't find anything remotely negative regarding him or his wife. The news fortified

Claire. With all of her heart she wanted to believe Tony's vendetta was done.

The two women embraced. Courtney promised to always be there for Claire, if Claire promised to be honest. With tears in her eyes, Claire said, "I refuse to be anything else, and Tony knows that."

Courtney smiled and hugged her again. "If this is really what you want, I'm happy for you. I want you to be happy."

"I'm not sure about forever, but right now, Tony is what I want."

Courtney smiled, "You know I love babies?"

"Good, I think ours is in need of an aunt. Emily isn't very happy with me."

Tony hired a bodyguard, Clay, an ex-secret service agent. As long as Claire stayed on the estate, he stayed behind the scenes. However, if she and Tony left the grounds, he rode shotgun with Eric. If Claire left by herself, he drove. If Tony chose to drive somewhere with Claire, Clay followed closely behind. He was much more intrusive than Phil had ever been. She almost asked for Phil; at least he'd be familiar. Sometimes Claire wondered what happened to him.

Claire never moved back to the second floor suite. The first night she arrived at the estate, she stayed in Tony's room. After that, all of her new and old things were moved there. The technology which once barred her from his suite was no longer an issue. Besides, once their baby was born, neither one wanted to maintain separate rooms. The underutilized room beside Tony's suite was in the midst of renovation. It would be a lovely nursery, accessible from their suite and the corridor.

By early August, Claire's baby bump was visible, especially when wearing a bathing suit. Although it made her self-conscious, Tony complimented her changing anatomy. Her midsection wasn't the only part of her growing. Her new doctor in Iowa City maintained everything was progressing well. Somehow they'd managed to keep the pregnancy from the press. This was amazing since the media seemed to know almost everything else including Claire's change of address. Thankfully, nothing was ever printed about the threatening packages she'd received. The name *Rawls* never appeared in print or on the internet.

Living within their secure bubble, Claire began to relax and enjoy her life again. She would spend days sunbathing at the pool or hiking to her lake and listening to the waves lap the shore. When she closed her eyes, the sound of the water upon the pebbles continued to remind her of the sound of their baby's heartbeat at that first ultrasound. As their little one grew, the heart rate increased. It was too early to learn the baby's sex, but the doctor said the faster the heart rate the better the chance of a girl. When he said that, Tony squeezed Claire's hand and whispered, "I bet she has your eyes, too."

Claire smiled and shook her head. It never ceased to amaze her how Tony managed to get his way.

Memories of Patrick Chester's attack kept Claire content within the safety of Tony's estate. Catherine's presence helped Claire fight the feeling of isolation. Catherine's ongoing support was therapeutic as their relationship moved beyond anything it had ever been. Nonetheless, when Claire asked, Catherine wouldn't reveal any more about Tony's past. Claire believed Catherine wanted her and Tony back together. She'd achieved her goal.

On a warm and breezy day in late August, Claire's bubble burst. She might never have realized it, if she hadn't decided to come in early from the pool. From the sunporch she heard loud voices coming from Tony's office. Claire quietly walked down the marble corridor to investigate. She heard Tony, but she couldn't tell who he was talking to -- *yelling at* would be a more accurate description.

Nearing the closed grand doors, Claire recognized the significant change in their relationship. Never in the past would she have willingly walked toward his voice holding the threatening brash tones she currently heard. Most significantly she no longer feared opening the doors and learning the reason for his tirade.

Not wanting to interrupt, she gently opened the door and slid inside the office. Immediately she realized she was standing in a bathing suit, flip flops, and a cover-up while Tony wore a suit. Obviously, he'd come straight from the office. His eyes flickered toward her. She saw the darkness she'd heard in his voice. The office was full. Facing Tony, she recognized the backs of Eric, Catherine, and Clay. When she entered, Clay was speaking. She heard the end of his statement, "...no, sir. We've intercepted the others. This is the first one to make it onto the estate."

Claire panned the room. Sitting on Tony's desk was an open package. She wanted to know what was in the package and, most importantly, if it were addressed to her. Tony's eyes were now solely on her and soon everyone turned her direction.

"You are all very loud. Is this about me?" Claire asked.

"Claire, please don't worry about this. I'm taking care of it." Tony's voice strained in an attempt to modulate his tone from the one he'd been using on everyone else.

She stepped toward him. His eyes went to Catherine, "Catherine, if you could please help Ms. Claire, she may need some assistance."

Claire stopped. Yes, there were others in the room, but if this were about her and her baby, she had the right to know. "Clay, what *others* have you intercepted?"

"Ma'am, nothing that concerns you."

"I don't believe you."

Catherine approached Claire with her arm out, "Claire, let's get you something to drink. It is very hot outside." Claire heard Catherine's voice from the hall; she'd been loud too. Something was happening.

"I am not leaving."

"Claire." The finality in Tony's tone, the way he said her name, the one syllable, could easily be translated: *Not now Claire. I'm handling this. Leave now.*

Claire shot Catherine a *do not touch me* look and walked to the other side of the desk. She didn't intend to make a scene in front of everyone, but she wasn't leaving without answers. Standing beside Tony she said, "Catherine, Eric, and Clay, could you please excuse us for a minute. Mr. Rawlings and I need to speak privately. I would assume he's not done with you, so please stay close. This won't take long."

Everyone in the room turned to Tony. The tension was palpable. Finally, Tony clenched his teeth and proclaimed, "Do not go far. I'm *not* done. Clay make some calls. After Ms. Claire and I have finished, I want answers."

Everyone hurried from Tony's office as Claire turned toward her ex-husband. She'd seen the intensity of his eyes before. However, she knew the blackness was meant for someone else. She wanted to know who. "What's happening?"

"How did you hear? You were at the pool."

"How could I not hear? Everyone in a three mile radius could hear you. Tell me, what's so important to bring you home early from work? The sooner I know, the sooner you can continue your *meeting.*"

"Damn it, Claire. I don't want you worrying." He paced to the window and back. "Besides, who in their right mind would come in here while I'm teetering on the edge of sanity? Did you see how fast they all left?"

Claire smiled as she placed her hands on lapels of his dark suit. "No one. Just ask my family, I'm definitely not in my right mind. And if I'm correct, the only thing that can get you this worked up is something about me." She turned and picked up the package. It was addressed to *Claire Nichols Rawls* with the estate's street address. "So, I don't get to open my own mail anymore?"

"Seriously, some asshole found you here, knows our address, and you want to complain about opening mail?"

She turned and faced him. With her spine straight and chin up she kept her voice calm, "No, it scares the hell out of me, but anyone can learn this address; it's public record. The stupid press has told anyone who wants to listen that I'm living here." She lifted the box, "What was in it? And how many packages or letters have come that I don't know about?"

"It was a silver baby rattle, engraved."

"Where is it?"

"Clay bagged it. He's having it processed for finger prints. Hopefully the asshole touched it."

"Engraved...what did it say?"

He seized her shoulders and pulled her close. "Claire, let me handle this. Show me you have faith in me."

Her face tilted upward, "I wouldn't be here if I didn't." She kissed him. "What did it say?"

"Baby Nichols-Rawls."

"That isn't so bad, considering the way it was addressed. Why didn't you want me to know that?"

He directed her to his large leather chair. She obediently bent her knees, and he said, "That wasn't all. Under the name it read: R.I.P."

She couldn't hide the shock or fear suddenly flowing through her. Protectively her hand covered her midsection as her body began to tremble. "Oh my god, Tony..."

He knelt before her, his voice now soft, "I told you once before, too much information isn't good for you. Will you please learn to trust me and enjoy the bliss I'm trying so hard to provide?"

"But... that has to be considered a threat. Can't you take it to the police?"

"We are. But what will they do that we aren't already doing?"

When his arms encircled her, she lost her fight with tears and took comfort in his lingering embrace. When a semblance of calm prevailed, she said, "I'm going to lie down. Will you please come to our room when you're done with the others? Or are you going back to work?"

"No, I'm staying here. I'll be there as soon as we're done."

Later he explained the new cards and packages began arriving to the estate mid-July. The first was a congratulations card about a baby. Sometimes they were flowers, sometimes presents. The notes were always addressed to *Claire Nichols Rawls* and the sources of origin would range from the west to east coast. Even the font changed on the cards. The benign contents made it difficult to involve the authorities, but the recent change in text now had the police's attention.

During the first week of September, Tony needed to take a ten day trip to Europe. He asked Claire to join him again and again. Her growing anxiety caused by the spontaneous deliveries made Claire question every decision. She didn't know if it was safer to stay within the gates without Tony or to be with him overseas. She chose the familiarity of the estate.

The first attempt to unlawfully enter the estate occurred three days after Tony left. Though initially concealed from Claire, when she finally learned the details, she learned Clay thwarted the failed attempt. No perpetrator was caught, but, thankfully, a possible threat was adverted, and a previously unknown kink in their security was identified.

The next incident occurred as Clay drove Claire back to the estate one warm afternoon. Keeping her gaze toward the tinted window, the changing leaves of the vast countryside went unnoticed as Claire's mind reviewed her busy day. They'd traveled early to Iowa City where Clay escorted her to her doctor's appointment. She thought wistfully about the doctor's words. If she and Tony chose, with the assistance of an ultrasound at her next appointment, they could learn the gender of their baby. Claire smiled wondering if they wanted to know. Yes, they occasionally joked about their green-eyed daughter, but did she want to know? One thing was for sure, if the answer was *yes*, she didn't want to attend that appointment without him.

As often happened, especially with the increased flutterings she felt, Claire realized her hand was protectively shielding her growing baby. She thought about the maternity clothes she'd purchased before meeting Courtney for a delicious lunch. The press would be all over that, but hiding her pregnancy was becoming impossible. Without even considering a desire to drive, Claire's eyes closed to her favorite pregnancy side-effect: her afternoon nap.

Feeling the change in acceleration, Claire was jarred awake. By the time she focused, she saw the car to their left. Like the car in which she rode, the windows were too dark to see through. Clay held fast as the other car bumped and pushed against the side panels of Tony's prized Mercedes. If the roads had been wet or snowy, the outcome may have been different. Thankfully, the roads were clear. By the time Clay pulled over, the other car disappeared over a hill and Claire's breathing was shallow and her heart rate accelerated. The other car didn't have a license plate.

"Are you all right, ma'am?" Clay asked as he removed the cellphone from his pocket.

"Yes, please get me home."

He spoke softly into his phone as he eased the car back onto the road. When she entered the mansion she went quietly to their suite and collapsed on the large bed. *Would this ever end? Would her baby ever be safe?* She'd tried to call Tony. Her mind spun with what-ifs as his phone went straight to voicemail. *What time was it in Europe?* She couldn't think.

Claire was almost asleep when the knock came on the suite door. With puffy eyes and an aching head, she managed, "Come in."

Catherine entered, "I just heard what happened. Are you all right? Should we call your doctor?"

"I'm fine," though the anguish in her voice revealed otherwise.

Catherine approached the bed. "Can I help?"

"I don't think anyone can help. I've tried to reach Tony, but I keep getting his voicemail." Claire shook her head. "It feels the same -- although I know it's different."

"I don't understand."

Claire sat up. "I know I have my phone and access to friends and internet, but I feel trapped."

Catherine held her hand, "You aren't. You see the difference from before, don't you?"

Claire nodded, "I do. This time, it isn't Tony -- it's this person. Who would want to hurt me or our child? I don't understand. I'm afraid it will never end." When Catherine failed to offer Claire the reassurance she sought, Claire's tears resumed. She buried her face in the soft plush pillows. Catherine gently rubbed her back until Claire's tears subsided and sleep overtook her.

Later that evening Catherine personally delivered Claire's meal to her suite. When Claire saw Catherine's return, she couldn't hide her

425

surprise, "Catherine, I hadn't planned on eating in here tonight. Outside would be nice." The cooler late summer evenings combined with the red and golden leaves made the back patio very enjoyable. Although she was nestled on the leather sofa with her reader, the tepid breeze from the open French doors beckoned Claire outside.

Without acknowledging Claire's words, Catherine pushed the cart to the side of the small dining table and silently began placing dishes upon the surface. When she'd finished there were two place settings. She turned solemnly toward Claire and said, "I think it's time we talk. As you probably know, there are no cameras in here. This is the best place."

Immediately noticing the change in Catherine's demeanor, Claire nodded. Curiosity overpowered her thoughts. Claire needed to know what Catherine wanted to say. Their discussion took them late into the night.

How long had she sought the truth about Tony's promise to Nathaniel? Now with all her might she wished for ignorance.

Tony's hesitance and Catherine's reluctance at disclosing the full truth was easily understood. As the evening progressed, Claire wondered how Catherine knew so much. Of course, she'd been within the walls of the Rawlings and Rawls' homes for a very long time, and there wasn't much which occurred within those walls that Catherine didn't know.

With all of Claire's heart she wanted to call Tony and verify the story she'd just heard. But as Catherine explained, if she called Tony and opted for the escape Catherine offered, she risked too much. The New York Bar Association recently agreed to revisit John's case. John still wasn't speaking to Claire, but Emily was, a little. And then there were Amber and Harry. After what happened to Simon years ago, a part of Claire feared for Harry ever since she confessed their brief relationship. Tony had stayed true to his word. Her friends and family were safe; however, if he thought she left him of her own accord, he would no longer be bound by his promise.

Catherine was right. It had to look like this unknown perpetrator took her. It was the only way to keep everyone she loved safe.

Although, her heart told her to stop and trust the man she knew she loved, her mind replayed the words Catherine shared, "Anton promised to keep Nathaniel's vow -- *Everyone associated with Nathaniel's downfall will pay ... their children, their children's children, and children's children's children...*"

How could she stay? Even if she'd already paid her due, Claire couldn't allow her child to pay.

The temperature of her and Tony's suite dropped as Catherine presented her final and most persuasive argument. Catherine stood from the table, disappeared into the closet, and returned with Claire's missing laptop. When Claire saw it she thought she'd be ill. "I thought my laptop was missing?" Claire asked as dread filled her chest.

"I believe the final word was," Catherine set the laptop on the table in front of Claire, "the *police* weren't able to locate your laptop."

Semantics, Claire thought. "When was it found?"

426

"From what I understand, it was before you regained consciousness after Patrick Chester's attack."

"I don't understand..." Claire looked into Catherine's gray eyes hoping for an answer capable of quelling the dread growing within her. "That missing laptop is why I moved back here."

Catherine closed her eyes and nodded, "Anton knew if you felt threatened you'd be more likely to move."

Claire tried desperately to comprehend Catherine's words while her new world crashed around her. "What about the packages?"

"Those are real." Claire heard the emotion in Catherine's voice, "At least I think they are."

By the time Catherine left the suite, the tepid air had become cold. Walking to the French doors, Claire stepped onto the private patio and looked up at the velvety sky ladened with millions of stars. Struggling with her decision, the cool autumn air cleared Claire's mind and her thoughts moved to her future. In and out, inhale and exhale. Her future was her baby's future. Claire knew she needed to make her child's safety her first priority. Feeling the calming effects of Iowa's tranquility she contemplated her decision. Tony wasn't due back to Iowa for four more days. If she followed through on Catherine's plan, by the time he returned she'd be long gone and no one would suspect him.

The stars blurred as she thought about the dark chocolate eyes she'd never see again. Her heart ached. Nevertheless, her child's safety was paramount in her mind. Suddenly, Claire prayed, not for the green-eyed daughter Tony sought, but for a dark-eyed son...

*****

Sophia felt she was getting better and better at timing her personal events around Derek's travel. While he was on his second trip to the orient, she executed a very successful art exhibit at her Provincetown studio. Although she often exhibited at the Palo Alto studio, since Mr. George was called away and the new curator was in place, she wasn't as comfortable there. It was all right while she was in Santa Clara. But more than anything, she relished her time on the East coast.

Her recently found success and artificially high sales prices out West increased her notoriety throughout the East coast art community. This translated into more guests and investors interested in her three day gallery exhibit.

As she settled into their cottage on the cape, Sophia poured herself a glass of wine and waited for the familiar ringing of her laptop. Derek's Skype call was due any minute. Although the time difference made communication difficult, they'd worked out a manageable schedule. Derek's new assistant was both efficient and experienced with business travel. His suggestions aided in making their separation easier. Sophia never heard what happened to Danni. The last thing Derek said was that she was transferred to another office under the Rawlings Industries

427

umbrella. Personally, Sophia could care less. She was just glad the woman wasn't around her husband anymore.

The ringing of her laptop brought Sophia's focus to the screen. After a moment or two of circles turning, she saw her husband's soft brown eyes shining from the other side of the world. "Hey, Beautiful, how did day three of your exhibit go?"

"It went very well."

"Do you ever wish you'd taken that offer for the traveling exhibit?"

"Are you kidding?" Sophia lifted her glass of wine and toasted her husband's image. "This is too much work. I'd rather spend my time painting and enjoying time with you."

Derek's smile filled the monitor. "I like that, too!"

"Hey, I sold three pieces to Jackson Wilson."

"Are you sure he isn't your secret mystery buyer?"

"No, I'm not sure. But that would be silly. I've never seen the mystery guy and Jackson is at every showing I have east of the Mississippi."

"Three pieces -- impressive. Did you get the same price as the ones last spring in Palo Alto?"

"No, but thanks to those, my price has definitely gone up."

"Babe, I think I'm going to tell Shedis-tics to forget future travel, I'm going to be a kept man."

Sophia giggled. "I'm not sure I'd go that far, but I could come up with a few things to keep you busy."

"Have I ever told you how much I love to hear your laugh, even when your smile has that nice red wine glow?"

Sophia quickly ran her tongue over her teeth. "You're awful. Maybe the wine is adding to my humor -- plus exhaustion; it's been three long days!"

"Yeah, I'm sorry I couldn't be there with you."

"Me too. But I like staying busy while you're gone."

When they finally disconnected their call, Sophia climbed into bed and allowed her thoughts to center on the man on the other side of the world. Her silly red wine smile stayed until dreams took her to another place.

*We gain strength, and courage, and confidence by each experience
in which we really stop to look fear in the face...
we must do that which we think we cannot.*
- Eleanor Roosevelt

Chapter 56

Predawn murkiness weighed heavily on Claire's tired eyelids. Blinking back the threatening gloom, she gazed into the rearview mirror. Behind her the eastern sky filled with reds and oranges from the rising sun. She feigned optimism and promised herself: *it is a new day.*

The text message on the disposable phone, one resembling her old *work* phone, instructed her to pull over on I 80, at mile marker 145. With each mile she drove toward Des Moines, the mile markers decreased while her anxiety proportionately increased.

The phone in her hand and the folder of information on the passenger's seat were the extent of preparation she'd received for her escape. Everything happened so fast Claire hadn't even had a chance to look through the material. After she reentered the house from the patio, her new phone and the folder of information were waiting on the small dining table within the suite. Part of her wondered how Catherine had been able to supply her with so much support so fast. After all, Claire's decision to leave the estate was only minutes old. While light overtook the sky and she neared her designated mile marker, multiple questions swirled through Claire's mind. She tried desperately to push away the uneasiness.

She cranked the radio and air conditioning, plummeting the car's internal temperature while simultaneously increasing the interior volume. Curiosity was powerful but not as powerful as sleepiness. She needed her eyes to remain open.

In the distance, waiting at her designated mile marker, Claire saw a dark gray SUV. Suddenly, her need for rest evaporated. The SUV grew as she approached. Of all the questions swirling through her mind, the one that came pressing to the forefront -- the one that screamed in her head and echoed throughout her consciousness was... *How can I put my life and my child's life in the hands of this unknown person?*

As if on cue, the darkness gave way and rays of sunshine infiltrated the windshield. Prisms of color and points of radiance flickered throughout the interior of the freezing cold BMW as beams hit the large diamond on Claire's trembling left hand. She'd only recently agreed to wear the ring, and now she was leaving her fiancé. It was more than Claire could fathom.

If she turned around and talked to Tony, could she explain Catherine's stories, and would Tony understand her fright? Could things be all right?

Berating her indecisiveness and battling a combination of sleepiness and fright, Claire felt as if wavering would prevail. It wasn't until she slowed, passed the SUV, and saw the sole occupant of the gray utility vehicle that she was able to see freedom from the unknown terror and promised vendetta which threatened her and her child's life. Claire recognized the white hair immediately. She swiftly pulled the BMW over to the shoulder of the highway, feeling the vibration of the uneven surface. Slowly, she backed along the gravel until the trunk of her sedan rested only a few feet from Phillip Roach's bumper.

Catherine had connected her with the perfect person to help her escape. This realization reinforced Claire's steely determination. Stiffening her spine, she placed the car in park, grabbed the folder of information, the disposable cellphone, turned off the BMW, laid the key on the driver's seat, locked and shut the car's door.

A line of semi-trucks passed, blowing Claire's hair and exposing her determined expression. She made her way toward Phil's SUV. Over the rush of traffic she heard the click of the unlocking doors. Claire opened the passenger door and climbed into the seat beside her old bodyguard.

She was the first to speak, "I thought you worked for Tony."

"I did. How do you think Ms. London found my name?"

Claire raised her eyebrows.

"He hasn't needed me since you moved to Iowa."

"How do I know you won't tell him where I am?"

"Because, I work for money. According to Ms. London, once I get you to Geneva, you will pay me more to keep quiet. Secrets are my specialty."

"And you can do this?" Claire asked as she felt the SUV ease back onto I 80.

"Oh, Ms. Nichols, my talents were wasted as your babysitter. I'm very capable."

Claire looked at the man to her left. "Don't you think you should call me Claire?"

He smiled, "Actually, no. You have new documents. Claire Nichols is gone."

He handed her a stack of passports. Each folder contained the international document and a corresponding state issued driver's license, each from different states. The documents and licenses held digitally enhanced pictures. They were all her, but not; in some she was blonde, some red headed, and others her hair was darker than normal – almost black. Upon further scrutinization she read her eye color also varied. "I understand how my hair can change, but how can my eye's change?"

Phil pointed to the back seat. Claire picked up a small cosmetic case. Inside were multiple pairs of colored contact lenses. He took the next exit and turned around, heading the SUV east toward the rising sun. Claire reached into her purse for her sunglasses.

"We'll need to get rid of your purse and the clothes you're wearing." He noticed the large stone on her left hand. "And that -- isn't that the same ring you sold?"

She fought the tears that suddenly filled her eyes and nodded.

"Can *you* do this?" Phil asked.

She swallowed. "I don't have a choice. Where are we going? Are you taking me back to Iowa City?" There was a hint of optimism in her voice.

"Cincinnati. You're flying from Cincinnati to Florence later this afternoon." He turned toward her. And although her gaze was out the side window, Phil could see her trembling shoulders. "We have to stop on the way so you can change your clothes and your hair." He waited until the silence grew uncomfortable, "Unless you want to go back to Iowa City?"

Claire felt the movement of her baby inside of her. Her voice quivered, "No. This is something I need to do." She reclined the seat and refused to turn toward Phil. "I think I'd like to rest while we drive to this hotel." She knew he'd watched her for months. She remembered the note he sent the night Tony came to her hotel in San Diego. She couldn't let him see the tears which refused to stay behind the Cartier sunglasses. He'd know immediately -- Iowa City was her destination of choice.

*****

There were so many things Sophia needed to do at her studio. An exhibit throws everything off kilter. Cassie, the assistant she hired to keep the Cape studio open while she was in California, was supposed to meet her at nine. Waking and sleeping at appropriate hours had never been Sophia's gift. She was better of late, but the exhibit wore her out. When she rolled over and saw the bright Cape Cod sun streaming through her windows, she jumped from bed knowing she'd overslept.

It was a quarter after nine before she made her way out the door. Luckily, it wasn't a long walk to the studio. Derek kept talking about her buying a bigger studio, but honestly, she was happy with the one her parents helped her start. As she closed her front door and breathed in the wonderful salt air, her purse began to vibrate. Immediately, she assumed it was Cassie wondering if she would make their meeting. Glancing at the screen of her phone, Sophia saw an unknown number with the Princeton, New Jersey, prefix. She hit: *Answer*.

"Mrs. Sophia Burke?"

"Yes, this is she." The bright sunshine faded.

"Ms. Burke, I'm sorry to be making this call, but a blue Camry was discovered this morning. We don't know the cause of the accident, but we believe both of your parents were discovered within the car. It may have been due to wet leaves. We had a hard rain here last night. Or with the year of your parent's car, it could be an acceleration issue. Their car hit a tree. The coroner believes they both died instantly. We need you to travel to New Jersey to identify the bodies."

Sophia collapsed onto the steps of her cottage as the tears grew and sobs formed in her chest. Her mind tried to process. She managed to speak, "Okay, I can do that."

"Visible identification will be difficult. We were hoping for familiar DNA."

"I'm sorry. That won't work. I'm adopted."

"Are there any other siblings?"

"No, I'm an only child."

"Perhaps you will be able to identify their belongings."

"I will be there as soon as I can." Her mind tried to process, "Can you tell me who was driving?"

"It was your father, Mrs. Burke. May I ask why you're asking?"

"Curiosity, Officer, perhaps shock."

"I understand. Please ask for me, Officer McPherson, when you arrive."

"I will. Thank you." Sophia disconnected the call and called Derek's international phone.

Although she knew it would be best to claim *an acceleration problem* or possibly *wet leaves* as the officer suggested, Sophia knew that wasn't the cause. Officer McPherson said Pop was driving. Why hadn't her mom listened? Sophia pleaded with her to take away Pop's keys. It wasn't his fault. Not really, yet Sophia knew in her heart, it was. What would she do without them?

*****

The mid-morning sun moved higher as Tony's private plane touched down in Iowa. After the call from Clay he cut his European trip short and immediately headed home. If someone tried to push Claire off the road, he needed to be there. Tony tried Claire's phone again. No answer. He hadn't been able to reach her since the near accident, even her voicemail wouldn't activate.

Getting into the car, he tried Catherine's phone. When the line connected, Tony couldn't comprehend Catherine's words, "What do you mean she left yesterday and hasn't come back? How could she leave without Clay?"

"She said she was tired of the constant surveillance and needed a break."

"When? Why haven't you called me or the police?"

432

Catherine tried to justify her reasoning, "Yesterday evening... I assumed she'd be back. It wasn't until this morning we realized she never returned. You were in the air; I couldn't reach you. I haven't called the police; what was I supposed to say? A twenty-nine year old woman drove away on her own and now I can't reach her? Once Clay learned she'd disappeared, he followed the GPS. Your car was just located outside Des Moines... Anton, I'm so sorry. I truly thought she would return after she got her break. You know how the hormones are making her emotional. I'm very worried."

Eric couldn't drive the car fast enough for Tony. "Eric! Hit the damn gas! I need to be home!" His mind scrambled as he spoke to Catherine through the phone, "Des Moines? Jane Allyson is there. I'll contact her."

"Claire left her phone and iPad here. I can tell you, she's missed many calls from people, especially her sister."

"Shit. Someone will need to contact Emily." The jet lag was nothing compared to the chaos in his mind. "What if Chester's accomplice has her? We need to get the police involved. Have I received any ransom requests?"

"No, nothing here."

"So, a car tries to run Clay off the road and later that same day Claire decides to leave. Doesn't anyone else think this is suspicious?" His question was rhetorical; he'd disconnected their call.

A few minutes later, the front door of the estate burst open. Tony entered barking orders into his phone and around the room. He wanted everyone in his office *yesterday*. He wanted the security detail, Tom and Brent, the local police chief, and he even contacted the FBI. His call to Jane Allyson went to her secretary. Ms. Allyson was in court and won't be available for another few hours; however, the secretary knew nothing about Ms. Nichols.

Tony even called Emily and Harry. Surprisingly, the call with Harry went better than the one with Emily. He ended up hanging up on her. Harry promised to call with any news and assured Tony they'd not seen or heard from Claire but would contact him if they did.

Tony contacted his office; there'd been no ransom requests or other messages. Patricia would check the satellite offices and get back to him immediately.

Although she'd only been missing a short time, with Tony's influence, APB's went out to all airports and every flight's manifest and passenger list was scrutinized for *Claire Nichols*. Her name didn't appear as anyone who'd flown in the past 48 hours or who had reservations.

While Tony assembled the greater part of his posse, Chief Newburg of the Iowa City Police Department, excused himself to take a call. When he returned he reluctantly approached Tony, "Mr. Rawlings, I need to speak to you privately."

Tony looked around the room. His legal consultants were present as well as Catherine and his security detail. "Does this have to do with Ms. Nichols?"

"Yes, sir, it does."

"Then I don't see any reason you can't speak in front of these people. We all want to find her."

"I think this would be better alone."

Tony's heart sank. He looked around. "Everyone but Catherine and Brent step out of my office for a minute."

Chief Newburg waited until the grand doors closed, leaving the four of them alone. "Mr. Rawlings, a Mr. and Mrs. John Vandersol have contacted the Palo Alto, California, Police Department. Their department has formally contacted our department. You are being accused of culpability in the disappearance of Ms. Claire Nichols. If she is not found, they want you charged with her disappearance and possible death, as well as the same for her child."

Tony collapsed into his leather chair. "Chief, that is the most ridiculous thing I've ever heard. *I* called you here."

"If they'd contacted our office personally, I could agree with you and talk them down. Unfortunately, since they've involved another agency, we have to follow through. Mr. Rawlings, may we search your house?"

"Yes. Of course, do anything you need to do to find her. But don't waste too much time here. Find where she went. Find out if she's with some maniac. You know she was attacked in California? We have brought threatening mailings to you. She could be with some crazy person right now." His dark eyes fumed as he fought the desire to argue his innocence.

"I understand, Mr. Rawlings. We will get to the bottom of this."

Chief Newburg called for additional officers and began taking statements from Anthony Rawlings and his household employees. The process lasted deep into the night. Most of the staff were blissfully ignorant. Chief Newburg wondered how so many people could reside under the same roof and have no idea what was happening with one another.

By the time they finished, Tony figured Claire had possibly been in the hands of some zealot for an additional five hours. It took all of Brent's persuasive power to keep Tony from calling Emily and John and telling them exactly what he thought of their charges. After all, Claire's baby was his baby. He'd never cause her or it harm. He reasoned: *All right, maybe I did. Now, I wouldn't.*

During the questioning, another team of investigators descended upon the house. They went from room to room and searched everything. One investigator, searching their private suite found Claire's box of research. He deemed the information worthy to be designated as evidence and took it back to the station for processing. They also asked about the estates security system. Was there video footage? Could they access saved files?

The press was already hot on the hunt. Someone leaked to the media that the ICPD was investigating Anthony Rawlings and his estate in conjunction with the reported disappearance of his ex-wife and current live-in relationship, Claire (Rawlings) Nichols.

As soon as everyone left, Tony returned numerous calls from his publicist who was working feverishly to restrain the outgoing information. Shelly was doing her best, but stalling or limiting was all she could promise. It was coming too fast and too furious; curtailing it was impossible.

Any emotion, if it is sincere, is involuntary.
- Mark Twain

Chapter 57

-*Moments before Tony's plane touched down in Iowa-*

At a roadside motel, somewhere in Illinois, Claire dried her newly temporarily-died red hair while Phillip explained the first part of her escape. "You'll stay in Florence for a few days before you make your way across Italy toward Switzerland." His voice came through the thin bathroom door as she changed into the clothes he'd brought. "The secret of staying hidden is moving, but not too erratically."

She slid the squeaky pocket door, creating an opening large enough for her to exit the ugly pink and black tiled bathroom. The smell of stale smoke overtook her senses as her eyes scanned the shabby motel room. Thread bare carpet highlighted the traffic areas. Despite the surroundings, Claire's voice sounded stronger than before, "Eventually I want to settle. I have a child to raise."

From the corner of her eye, in the cloudy mirror above the low dresser, she saw her unfamiliar reflection. She noticed the looseness of the new clothes. They hid her pregnancy much better than her previous outfit.

"You will, after you acquire the money from the account in Geneva."

Claire nodded. Catherine's documents had specific instructions for accessing Nathaniel Rawls' hidden fortune. It seemed appropriate. If *his* decree could send her into hiding -- *his* money could finance her future. Claire even justified it as her baby's grandfather's support. It was amazing how the mind can twist things, making them legitimate, especially under duress.

Phil went on, "You'll have a week to travel from Florence to Geneva. I'll meet you there next Thursday. Your hotel reservation is set in Geneva.

I need to know where to meet you. It's too dangerous for you to have contact with anyone in the United States, even me. While leaving the U.S. you're *Lauren Michaels*. In Geneva, minus the time you're in the bank, you're *Isabelle Alexander*. Hopefully, once I'm there, we'll discuss your eventual destination."

"Hopefully?" Claire asked.

"Your transaction must be complete. Temporary identities are one thing; securing a permanent identity with a new residence is expensive."

Claire nodded. She wondered how much money the Switzerland account held.

Phil left Claire at a cafe in Burlington, a suburb of Cincinnati. From there she called a taxi which took her to the Cincinnati International Airport. She had to admit, he was smart. The curbs at the airport had video surveillance. With this plan, if she were to be identified, he wasn't connected.

Claire realized she was flying international with nothing more than a carry-on; Phil supplied her with the basics. She would need to purchase everything else new in Italy. His plan provided her with enough starter cash to sustain her until she completed her financial transaction in Geneva.

The first security check was unnerving. Claire summoned every mask she'd ever worn. Once she passed to the other side of the check point and nodded to the last TSA agent, she sighed with relief. From that point on, *Ms. Lauren Michaels* confidently met each agent and scan head-on.

Lauren was thirty thousand feet in the air, crossing the Atlantic Ocean, by the time the police finished searching Anthony Rawlings' estate. The striking green-eyed woman with deep amber hair rode economy-class, wedged between a mother with a sleeping child and a man in a cheap suit. The man to her left was not only a barrier to the aisle, but after he consumed too many seven dollar beers, his attempts at flirting made her debate the pros and cons of committing assault and battery.

It took all her self-restraint to not pull the large diamond from her purse and wiggle it under his nose. In her daydream she curtly said, "Leave me alone, jerk; I'm engaged." But sadly she realized that was no longer true.

The diamond was the only instruction from Phil, Claire didn't follow. She could leave her Prada purse, her overpriced clothes, and her Cartier sunglasses... just not the ring. Claire closed her eyes and remembered the afternoon she'd finally accepted it...

It was a Saturday; Tony was working from home. She'd spent most of the morning out in the gardens. Before, when they were married, Claire longed to work in the gardens, planting and tending his beautiful plants. Back then she worried it wasn't appropriate. Now she didn't care and didn't ask. One day she started talking with James, the gardener. He helped her find the tools. Tony never complained. On the contrary, he

437

delighted in her hobbies, often asking questions about her plants and supporting her desire to get her hands dirty and tend the small living things.

On that particular Saturday, after digging, dividing, replanting, and weeding, Claire decided to cool off in the pool. Tony must have seen her swimming. She'd only been in the cool water for a few minutes when he joined her. While they talked and swam in liquid bliss, he reached for her hand. Seeing the dirt still under her nails he mentioned, "I think you need a manicure after all this manual labor."

Claire giggled and pulled her hand away. "I wasn't planning on having anyone look that closely. Besides, I haven't had a chance to shower yet."

"Now that sounds intriguing!" His eyes twinkled as his lips formed a mischievous grin. "In the meantime, I know a way to deflect people's attention from your nails."

She was holding his shoulders and the moment for no particular reason felt right. Later, Claire decided it was the ordinary calmness she liked; nothing special, just realness that comes with every day. Her answer surprised him, "Well, that shower I'm about to take..." Her emerald eyes returned his sparkle. "Perhaps if you can figure a way to bring the ring in there, I'd slip it on. I mean..." She cooed into his ear, "I wouldn't want it to go down the drain."

Grasping her growing waist, he gently pushed her away and stared deeply into her eyes. Claire remembered feeling the familiar tug as his gaze lingered. "Are you finally saying yes, you will be Mrs. Rawlings again?"

She nodded and kissed his neck. Her insides tightened at the sound of his responding growl. When her lips finally released his neck, she replied, "I'm willing to go from *dating* to *engaged* – can we not rush the married part?"

His dazzling smile melted her completely. Claire wanted the shower, the ring, and whatever would come next. However, his gaze turned serious as did his tone, "There is one condition."

After trying so long for her to accept his proposal, the addition of a stipulation surprised Claire. "Yes?" she asked tentatively.

"I don't want to have to track it down again. Do not sell it, give it away, or leave it any place but on your beautiful finger." It was one of those non-debatable statements.

Nodding with a seductive smile, Claire whispered, "I promise." She sealed the deal with a lingering kiss.

She couldn't leave the ring behind.

-Three days later-

Tony stared at the monitors in his office. The large screen was sub-divided into many smaller screens. At the top was a live feed from outside his office door. He didn't want intruders. Below were multiple smaller screens changing constantly with various locations on the estate. The bulk of the screen held two videos. He controlled the speed and sound of each one. On the left he saw Claire in his garages, rushing to the key cabinet and removing the key to a Mercedes Benz. In the lower right corner the date read: 01/17/12. On the right was the video of Claire walking casually to the key cabinet which no longer held a lock. He watched as she removed the keys to a BMW and calmly walked toward the car. The date in the lower right corner read: 09/04/13. Repeatedly, he paused the action and scrutinized the scenes. With all his might he tried to read Claire's facial expressions.

In twenty twelve, he saw fear as Claire looked nervously all about her. On the video recorded only days earlier, Tony wondered what he saw. No, he knew her look; it was a mask of steely determination. What he didn't know was the emotion hidden underneath.

The police also saw the twenty thirteen video. They believed it proved she left of her own free will. But if that were true, wouldn't she have taken more belongings? Wouldn't she have taken more money? She had access. She had credit cards and an ATM card... yet they were all found in an Illinois hotel.

At nearly two in the morning, Tony was all alone. The various screens displaying the estate were devoid of people. Everyone was fast asleep. Even the crickets outside his open windows knew to leave him in silence. Yet, with no one to hear, he spoke the question he'd been wrestling with for days, "Why, Claire? Why?" In one gulp he downed the amber liquid from the crystal tumbler. Though the rich Glen Garioch Whiskey went down smoothly, it didn't ease the ache in his head or the pain in his chest.

His facade of the last few days successfully drained his strength. Tony knew he needed sleep, but how could he sleep in *their* bed? He couldn't even stand to enter their room or see the unfinished nursery. It was the *not knowing* that hurt the most. If he knew she was safe. If he knew she did this of her own free will... but he didn't know. Last time -- in 2012 -- he knew. And the pain he'd put her through back then added to his current torment.

In the past few days he'd spent untold amounts of money, had private and public agencies search every inch of Iowa, the surrounding states, country – damn -- the world. There were plenty of tips... a large reward will bring those. Yet, none paid off. How could Claire evaporate into thin air?

The BMW was thoroughly searched by Iowa's top CSI. Only her finger prints, Clay's, Eric's, and his were discovered... but no unknown clues.

During the last three days he'd hardly left the confines of his home office. Entering the attached bath, he saw his almost unrecognizable reflection in the mirror. His facial hair had never been so long. Rubbing his hands through the now soft stubble, he stared into his own eyes. For the first time in his life he'd dared to believe in happily-ever-after. He learned at a young age it was unattainable. Therefore, he'd never even tried... until Claire. And somehow, for a few short months, it was at his fingertips. The wealth, homes, and appearance of stability and sanity... all meant nothing when he saw the pictures of Claire with Harry. Tony couldn't be at that damn gala and know she was there with *him*. Hell, Tony didn't even know about their baby. He just knew, for the first time in his life, Anthony Rawlings would risk public scrutiny to have what he wanted most. What mattered to him above anything else... the problem was making *her* realize it.

Tony turned off the screens of his computer and lay on the soft leather sofa. His mind went back to two thousand ten and eleven. On this very couch... on this luxurious carpet... he smiled... on his desk... there was hardly a place they hadn't been together. Damn, they'd been great. Despite the happy memories, the twisting in his heart tightened. The things he'd done to her -- the regret was almost paralyzing.

Then somehow in this totally screwed up world -- when all was said and done -- she'd taken him back.

The pounding in his head brought moisture to his eyes. His words were barely audible. That was all right; they weren't intended for anyone except the woman who wasn't there. "I'm so sorry... for everything... why? ... why did you leave me?" As the tears coated his cheeks he told himself, *Anthony Rawlings doesn't cry. He doesn't apologize, and he doesn't cry...*

*****

Once settled in Florence, *Isabelle* utilized an Internet Cafe to surf the web and learn the latest news happening back in Iowa. The face of Claire Nichols appeared in multiple thumbnails. She scrolled over the pictures which looked nothing like the blue-eyed woman with short dark hair staring at the monitor.

Different titles appeared: Missing – Day Three, Reward Offered, Ex–Husband "Person of Interest", and Vanished – Memoirs left behind.

Claire read each article scrutinizing every detail. The first article spoke analytically about Claire's disappearance. It described the incident where her car was attacked by another car, how that evening she went for a drive and never returned. The article highlighted photos of her and Tony at recent events. It even showed a recent photo of them out to eat. Claire tried to see the restaurant. She was pretty sure it was in Chicago and on her left hand she could see her engagement ring.

The next article said: Anthony Rawlings believes his ex-wife was coerced off his estate and kidnapped. He states the incident in California as evidence of a probable attack. To this end he is currently offering a reward of $100,000 for information leading to the safe return of his ex-wife. The Iowa City Police Department hired additional personnel to help with the onslaught of calls and emails. Mr. Rawlings offered to reimburse ICPD for the extra expense.

The "Person of Interest" story claimed John and Emily Vandersol, Claire Nichols only family, made allegations suggesting Anthony Rawlings look no farther than the mirror. They allege the wealthy tycoon is responsible for the disappearance of Claire Nichols, claiming he's done it before (see story related to memoirs). The office of Mr. Marcus Evergreen, Johnson County Prosecutor, Iowa City, Iowa, stated formal charges against Mr. Rawlings are under consideration.

Mr. Rawlings' attorneys are working overtime. While defending his innocence they are also battling Parrott Press. The publishing company is seeking to publish Ms. Nichols memoirs immediately. A written agreement between the author, Ms. Nichols, and Mr. Rawlings states said manuscript may only be published in the event of possible harm to Ms. Nichols. Parrott Press believes her disappearance fits this description. Advanced orders of: *My Life as It Didn't Appear - Unofficial biography of Claire Rawlings Nichols* have exceeded one million.

Isabelle read in disbelief. If Tony were in Europe when she left, how could anyone suspect him? She never meant to implicate him. That's why Catherine recommended Claire leave immediately, so she would disappear while he was out of town. And, what about Meredith's book? Catherine said Tony's lawyers would stop it. What if they didn't? Claire hated herself for going through with those interviews. Lastly, John and Emily's actions infuriated Claire. If only she could call them... but she knew it wasn't an option.

For the last two days *Isabelle* reviewed Catherine's specific instructions regarding the hidden fortune. She also practiced her Italian and used it whenever possible. According to Catherine, Nathaniel's money was hidden at an institution in Geneva, Switzerland. She said Tony had accessed the money for different things throughout the years. Nevertheless, Catherine believed it had accrued nicely since Nathaniel's death. According to the documents, there was a safety deposit box within the institution which could only be accessed by two people: Anton or Marie Rawls. Catherine provided Claire with Marie's information. And Phil supplied her with identification under the same alias. Sometime during their fateful late night talk, Claire asked Catherine, "Were you still with the Rawls when Nathaniel remarried."

"I was."

So many questions came to Claire's mind: Nathaniel's second wife was the woman Tony protected, the woman Patrick Chester thought was Samuel's sister. She was the woman who killed Samuel and Amanda. But that was a long time ago, and Tony said the woman was still alive. Claire asked, "Was she younger than Nathaniel?"

"Yes," Catherine answered and then asked, "You are younger than Anton. Do you think that's wrong?"

"No, I'm just trying to figure things out." Claire wanted to ask more. However, she needed to concentrate first and foremost on her escape.

Besides, Claire had the feeling her questions made Catherine uncomfortable.

As Catherine described the financial institution in Geneva, Claire remembered the place. Near the end of her European journey, so long ago with Tony, she'd met him at the same institution before they went for lunch. Claire remembered being early and waiting patiently for him to emerge from behind the gated area. This time she'd be the one behind the gates.

Catherine provided Claire with the number of the safety deposit box, as well as a copy of the required key. Both were necessary to access the safety deposit box. The moment Claire saw the key Catherine placed in a small envelope, she recognized it. It was the odd shaped key Tony used to roll from finger to finger when agitated. Years ago, Claire hated that key. Its presence meant her day had just taken a turn for the worse. Now, its replica would unlock her and her baby's future.

Things are not always what they seem;
the first appearance deceives many. The intelligence of a few,
perceives what has been carefully hidden.
- Roman poet Phaedrus

Chapter 58

-One week after Claire's disappearance-

Derek held his wife's hand admiring her strength. Bravely, she faced mourner after mourner, as each offered their condolences. No one mentioned Carlo's recent mental state. It wasn't as if everyone didn't know. The unsaid tragedy was that he'd taken Silvia with him. They all pitied Sophia, losing both parents at once.

When Derek arrived in New Jersey from Taiwan, Sophia had already faced too many things alone. She'd visited the morgue. Fortunately, the coroner hadn't allowed her to view her parents' remains. After striking the tree their Camry burst into flames. She did identify some of their possessions. Her parent's wedding rings, though charred, survived the inferno. Sophia recognized them immediately.

Although she grieved their loss, Sophia reasoned it was better for them to be together. She couldn't imagine consoling her mother if her father died alone. Derek embraced his wife as she rationalized the tragedy. It was late one night while holding her trembling body, she uttered the words he never expected to hear. Though muffled by tears, her resolve was steadfast, "I've lost my only parents... I never want to go through this again."

He understood what she was saying. She didn't want to find her birth parents. He whispered, "Anyone can give birth... a parent is the person who loves you every day without condition."

Sophia nodded into his chest. "Mine were the best. Please don't let me forget that... if I ever change my mind... please remind me."

He hugged her tight and promised.

*****

Other than the meal she'd shared with Tony at the French restaurant in Palo Alto, Claire hadn't had the opportunity to practice her newly acquired languages. Nonetheless, as she traveled through Italy and Switzerland, her Italian came back with a little more than a hint of an American accent. That didn't seem to matter. She spoke well enough to gain access to the locked vault in Geneva.

Appearing with short-dark hair and gray eyes to match the ID with the name *C. Marie Rawls*, *Marie* entered the vault with a bank official. Her hands trembled as they approached the safety deposit box once opened by Nathaniel. According to the ledgers, it was regularly accessed by Anton Rawls, usually twice a year. Claire signed the same ledger: *Marie Rawls* and presented her identification. The officer never flinched. He asked, "*Seniora Rawls, la sua chiave?*" (Ms. Rawls, do you have the key?)

"*Si, signore, grazie.*" (Yes, sir, thank you) She prayed the financial executive couldn't hear the pounding of her heart or sense her wet palms. She placed the small replicated key in his outstretched palm. *Marie* smiled when he gently closed his fingers around her petite hand. The man was less concerned with her identity and more interested in her proximity. She responded boldly, "*Signore, ti ringrazio per il vostro aiuto.*" (Sir, I appreciate your assistance here)

"*Forse più tardi?*" (Maybe later?)

"*Prima la mia missione.*" (First, my mission)

He released her hand with a friendly, "*Si, naturalmente.*" (Yes, naturally)

With his invitation momentarily dismissed, the officer inserted a key from his large ring. Next, he took *Marie*'s key. When he fumbled momentarily, her breathing stopped and her heart forgot to beat. Then, all at once the metal key breached the archaic lock. The tumblers turned; he slid the long box from its home. Remembering to exhale, *Marie* worked diligently to maintain her stoic expression as she followed him to a private room.

Once alone, Claire opened the lid and gasped. She'd come this far, she'd given up her life, listened to Catherine's advice... all for a virtually empty box. However, virtually was not entirely. Slowly Claire removed the documents. In the next forty-five minutes she read all the information.

Nathaniel planned everything to a *T*. His original intention was for Marie or Anton to tend to his fortune. He left specific instructions about maintaining an overseas cache. The money was to be constantly rotated, moved, and secured. All pertinent information regarding the accounts was to stay locked in this box. Only the person in possession of these documents could access the monies. Being as he didn't know for sure which heir would maintain his secret, everything was accessible with a numeric code. No names were associated with the financial accounts. This layer of security also aided in concealing the true ownership. Tracing the money to a Rawls, or anyone in the United States, was virtually impossible. The Switzerland financial system specialized in maintaining hidden fortunes. Only in the case of broken laws would they share information with the United States government.

In nineteen seventy something, when Nathaniel created his hidden treasure, it probably seemed very *James Bond*. Claire wondered if Tony changed the rules or had gotten more high tech? She would need to find-out. She'd gone too far to turn back.

Currently there were seven different accounts. The last time monies were transferred was six months ago. It really was time for a transfer. She wondered why he hadn't done it while recently overseas.

Claire wished for Phil's assistance; he'd be joining her in another day. However, this was something she needed to do on her own. Feigning confidence, *Marie Rawls* took the documentation to the front of the institution and requested a representative.

Over the next ninety minutes *Marie* watched and scrutinized computer screens. Her months of required attendance in Tony's office paid off. She frowned at unsuccessful investments and discussed better reserves for better returns. If ever a time to wear a mask, this was it. As the afternoon progressed, she systematically moved and invested over 200 million dollars. The monies were once again dispersed throughout the world market with a portion liquid and accessible. The only difference was that now *she* was the only one holding a means to their access.

By the time she feigned reinserting the documentation into the box, a presumed action based upon prior transactions, she was ready to faint. Tony's personal reserve was now hers. It wasn't stolen out of spite. Her desire for vengeance was gone. Claire willingly admitted her feelings of hate were only a close cousin to the love she now felt. And she knew Tony loved her. But thankfully, Catherine helped her see the truth. No matter how much he loved her and their child, his need to fulfill his promise to Nathaniel would always prevail.

Claire couldn't live with that. Besides, didn't their child deserve to live like a Rawls? With a heavy heart, Claire justified she didn't steal his money -- only reappropriated it -- to his child.

With the papers in her purse, *Marie Rawls* disappeared and *Isabelle Alexander* stepped onto the bustling Geneva sidewalk a mega millionaire. Faces didn't register. While in the heart of Geneva's financial district, *Isabelle* didn't notice the magnificent blue waters ahead or the grand snow covered Alps around. As she walked from the bank to her hotel, not even the phenomenal shopping within the sleek cosmopolitan buildings beckoned her.

While the slender heels of her Luciano Padovan sling-back platform pumps clicked along the sidewalk toward Lake Geneva, Claire's self-absorbed thoughts filled every fiber of her being. How many times had she told Tony his money didn't matter? How many times had she shunned the idea of wealth? Nevertheless, she'd just done the unthinkable. If it weren't for the uncomfortable gray contacts, she'd surrender to the tears threatening to flow. She fought the impulse.

Isabelle Alexander needed to be strong, just as *Marie Rawls* had been moments earlier.

The documents inside her purse were the key to over $200,000,000. More than anything, she longed to throw them in the nearest gutter. The only thing stopping the growing compulsion was the child moving inside of her. Never in Claire's entire life had she hated herself as much as she did at this moment. Thankfully, her love for her baby overpowered her self-loathing.

Claire's common sense demanded she go directly to her hotel and secure the documents inside a locked safe. Nevertheless, she was tired of listening to her mind. She needed to know what was happening in the USA, in Iowa, and at Tony's estate. She had so many questions. And over the past week she'd formed many more: First and foremost... who was the real Marie Rawls? Tony admitted to seeing her since she killed his parents. Catherine admitted to being with the Rawls family when Nathaniel married Marie. This woman existed. Why hadn't she turned up in any of their research?

The vibrant sky and tall limestone buildings disappeared beyond the sea of sidewalk tables and happy tourists. *Isabelle* politely intermingled and scanned the landscape. Slipping into an internet cafe, she ordered a tall tea. No question, her Italian was improving with each passing day. She settled into an available swivel chair next to a computer, logged onto the Wi-Fi, and transcended the ocean in search of information.

Information began to materialize:

Parrott Press Wins Battle Against Rawlings Industries – Representative Promises Claire Nichols' Rawlings Memoirs Published By October First.

Claire's heart sank... was there any way to stop this mess? Next story:

Palo Alto Police Question Iowa City Police Regarding Lack of Cooperation with Anthony Rawlings. As of yet, no charges had been filed or restrictions placed on Mr. Rawlings' travel. Mr. and Mrs. Vandersol have requested his passport be seized. Marcus Evergreen, Iowa City Prosecutor, was quoted as saying, "Mr. Rawlings is an upstanding law abiding citizen. Until we are convinced otherwise, he is free to live his life. He has a home and multibillion dollar business empire. We have no reason to assume he is a flight risk."

Claire exited the current stories and began searching New Jersey records -- nothing on Marie Rawls. She remembered Nathaniel was incarcerated in 1987. Claire wasn't sure when he married Marie.

However, if he married her while in prison, that would have been in New York. Claire entered *Marie Rawls* into the data base of *Marriage Licenses - New York State*. She narrowed the search to 1986 – 1989.

Claire held her breath as the small sentence surfaced:

February 25, 1988, Nathaniel Rawls and Catherine Marie London– license of marriage.

Claire stared at the screen... *Catherine Marie London.*

She wasn't sure how long she stared; a minute, an hour, a day, maybe ten? Claire's world once again swayed from its axis. *Catherine is Marie! Marie is Catherine!* What does that mean?

She closed her eyes and reviewed. The nausea from her early pregnancy returned. The stress at the bank was nothing compared to the mayhem in her mind. It meant *Catherine* killed Samuel and Amanda Rawls. It meant Tony paid Patrick Chester yearly for *Catherine's* freedom. It meant *Catherine* loved Nathaniel. According to Tony, Nathaniel loved her, too.

Despite the damn gray contacts, Claire's tears of fear, rage, and sadness swelled behind the pigmented disks. She didn't want to believe the thoughts and theories flooding her mind. She loved Catherine. The woman sustained her during the time of Tony's domination. Claire reassured herself: *Catherine is protecting me again.*

However, she had to wonder, was this truly protection?

Catherine knew Claire's greatest fear -- her biggest terror. She knew it was isolation. Catherine provided money – lots of money. However, suddenly Claire questioned -- how was this kinder than thirteen days sequestered in her suite? She and her baby would have every need met. Yet, when all was said and done, Claire's need for love and companionship would remain unsatisfied for the rest of her life.

She laid ten Swiss Francs on the counter and stepped out into the bustling cosmopolitan city. Her hotel was only blocks away.

Claire, no *Isabelle,* entered the Hotel d'Angleterre in a mental fog. Her mind whirled with new and old information. The concierge's greeting caught her off guard. "*Buon pomeriggio, Seniora Alexander. Senior Alexander è qui, ti aspetta.*" (Good afternoon Mrs. Alexander, Mr. Alexander is waiting for you.)

Mr. Alexander? She thought. "*Grazie, dove?*" (Thank you, where?)

"*Egli è nella vostra suite, seniora.*" (In your suite, ma'am)

Claire nodded and tried to smile. Panic from years before bubbled from the depths of her soul. The past few months with Tony held no hint of domination, yet she knew it existed. And now, if he were upstairs in her suite, what did that mean? Did he think she'd left him for his money? Did Catherine tell him? Was this all just a set-up, a test? Had she just failed? Claire decided company would be beneficial, "*Mi sembra di aver smarrito la mia chiave, potreste aiutarmi?*" (I seem to have misplaced my key, could you help me?)

"*Si, seniora.*" The concierge accompanied *Seniora Alexander* to the third floor suite. As they rode the elevator in silence, Claire's mind spun with questions. When the doors opened, anticipation prevailed. She prayed, *Please let Tony be here, and let us work this out.*

She foresaw anger. But she'd seen it before. Claire squared her shoulders and stiffened her neck. Once his impending tirade was complete, she'd explain. She wanted to face the man she'd just left.

The concierge inserted the key and penetrated the lock on the polished wooden door.

Before he pulled the opulent lever, the door opened. Instead of brown darkness she saw intense hazel. Flecks of gold shimmered within her *husband's* gray-green eyes while his white hair lay casually over his forehead. Claire sighed as Phil beckoned her into the suite.

"Il mio amore!" (My love) He pulled her hand toward him; her body followed. Instantly his lips were on hers. She fought her urge to fight, knowing the concierge was watching their show.

Claire lifted her hands to Phil's shoulders and pushed, "Lei mi sorprende." (You surprise me)

In English, "Didn't they tell you I was here? I didn't mean to surprise you."

The concierge stood faithfully near, in the open door. Phil immediately reached into his pocket, removed some Swiss Francs, and thanked him for his help. When the door closed Claire freed herself and retaliated, "They said *Mr. Alexander* was here, my husband. I didn't know who to expect."

"You seem disappointed?" Phil questioned. "I had to be your husband, to be allowed entry."

Grasping her arm, he directed her to the main room. The doors of the balcony were open to the lake below. For moments they stood silently and watched the docks as yachts came and went. The hum of people below filled the silence as the sun made its way toward the Alps elongating the shadows below.

Claire's mind tried unsuccessfully to prioritize her myriad of thoughts. After a time Phil's arm surrounded her shoulders. She turned toward him; her words harsh, "The concierge is gone - the show is over."

He removed his arm, "Did you complete your transaction?"

"I didn't expect you until tomorrow."

"I had to get to you. I'm scheduled to return to the United States early tomorrow morning. I have an appointment with the ICPD. They want to discuss the disappearance of a woman I was hired to trail." His eyes twinkled, "You know, there is a $100,000 reward!"

"So you're here to turn me in?"

His hazel eyes closed, jaws clenched, and head shook. "No, Claire, I'm here to make sure you completed your little endeavor at the financial institution today and to set up a meeting to move you to your permanent residence. Where will that be?"

448

Claire's neck straightened. She walked onto the balcony and peered over the wrought iron rail. Phil followed closely behind. His words were a mere whisper against the sounds of the blossoming nightlife below. "You know, the last time I followed you on to a balcony, you played me for a fool. Is that your intent tonight?"

Claire turned toward him. "You know it isn't. Things have changed."

"Some things."

"In San Antonio I was protecting someone."

"In San Antonio you out smarted me. I can't tell you how much that impressed me." He stepped closer. "Until that trip," his breath bathed her cheeks, "I had preconceived ideas about you."

Claire stood her ground and looked up into his eyes, "Preconceived?"

His gaze searched her contact covered eyes, "I researched you, you know?" She didn't answer. "From the beginning of my assignment with Mr. Rawlings, I read all about *Claire Rawlings Nichols* and made assessments based on that research. I predetermined you to be this woman who tried to kill her multibillion dollar husband -- a gold-digger. I assumed he hired me to keep an eye on you, to let him know if you were getting close. I assumed he was afraid you might try it again. Then I saw you for the first time; you were walking down that street in Palo Alto. The wind was blowing your hair." He reached out, removed the dark wig, and loosened strands of her once again chestnut hair from the confines of the hair pins. She shook her head allowing the trusses to fall free. "I knew Mr. Rawlings wanted you, not because he was afraid. He wanted *you*. His insistence at knowing your every move proved he wasn't willing to give you up. Then, you tricked me in San Antonio."

He stepped away. Slowly Phil settled at the wrought iron table, leaving Claire against the rail as the glow of the setting sun framed her beautiful face. She smiled at his reference as he went on, "I learned that week, you were so much more than a beautiful woman. You're smart, strong, sneaky, and conniving."

"If I recall, you called me a bitch."

A grin filled his face. "I assure you, it was meant as a compliment. I find those qualities very endearing." He leaned forward, "I immediately became enthralled. From that moment, I've fought an intense desire to have you for myself."

Claire lowered her eyes. Although she didn't want to encourage him; she needed his help, "Thank you," she said demurely.

"For what?"

"For all you've done."

His head tilted sideways, questioning her.

She went on, "Thank you -- for your kind note in San Diego, for saving my life in Palo Alto, and for wasting your talents babysitting me for months on end."

"Clair... *Isabelle*," he corrected, "I wish I could've been there sooner, in Palo Alto."

Her smile turned bashful; she walked back into the suite. Phil rose and followed her within. "You, Harry, Tony, and the security guy all saved me." She turned her intense gaze on him, "Right now, I'm nervous. Phil, I have so many questions – things aren't adding up." His gaze stopped her. She needed to collect her thoughts. Exhaling she said, "I'm going to go get these damn contacts out. Help yourself to the bar."

Phil smiled, "Good, I like your eyes much better green." He turned and walked toward the highboy containing bottles of fine liquors. Phil poured himself two fingers of Cognac as Claire disappeared into the bedroom.

When she returned, wearing a casual pair of yoga pants, a t-shirt, and no contacts, she saw Phil's intense glower. As their eyes met he said, "I've watched both of you." He finished the Cognac and added more to his glass. "I realize this whole thing is to hurt your ex-husband," he shrugged his shoulders, "which could work out well for me. But... I have to say, I've watched a lot of people. Love and hate are both strong emotions. You've sacrificed everyone you hold dear to hurt Anthony Rawlings. You could've gone on living in California. The governor of Iowa wiped your record clean. Yet, your anger, your crusade was continually met by him. You told me it was a game to him. I think it was a game to both of you, a real life chess game. Every move you made he countered. In order to get his king, you sacrificed your queen, a bold move. One I believe will work. But at what cost?"

Claire stood dumbfounded. She didn't understand Phil's words. "What are you saying? You think I'm here to hurt Tony?"

Phil swallowed the remaining contents of his tumbler, "That's what Ms. London said. She said you wanted away from him. You were afraid to leave him, of what he'd do... so this was the plan." Claire tried to follow. "Pretty creative; you exploited Mr. Rawlings' obsession with you, his Achilles heel, to penetrate his invincibility."

Claire didn't speak, she couldn't. Her mind swirled as the cyclone of thoughts became a category five hurricane. Phil took her silence as an invitation to continue his notion. "I read your theories of retaliation, for sins of past generations. I'm not saying they aren't true. Nonetheless, don't you find it odd? The only person who continues to survive is you."

Claire stuttered, "You... you read my theories? Where?"

"On your laptop -- of course."

Claire involuntarily took two steps backward. Her legs hit the sofa and she crumbled into the soft cushions. "You found my laptop?"

"Yes, the night you were attacked. It was in Patrick Chester's hotel room."

Her eyes flashed, "And you gave it to Tony?"

He shrugged as he poured another two fingers, "I tried. He was preoccupied -- with you. Actually, he was in the air when I found it. I reached Ms. London instead. She's the one who told me your plan, very ingenious." He tipped his glass in Claire's direction.

Claire realized the liquor was helping his honesty. "What *exactly* did she say?"

"She told me to bring it to Iowa; I did. You were still in the hospital."

"So Tony never got the laptop?"

"She told me she'd give it to him. He contacted me after you woke. He told me you were going to Iowa, and my job was done. He wasn't happy with me. I think he blamed me for Patrick Chester getting to you. Honestly, I don't think we ever discussed the laptop." Phil cocked his head to one side, "Your ex can be difficult."

She lowered her head near her knees; the fullness of her midsection restricted her motion. She straightened. "Yes, a very ingenious plan; however, I can't take credit." Claire leaned toward Phil, "You told me before, you work for money. Who's paying you – now?"

"You -- Ms. London gave me the starter money, but you're paying me for everything else. Did your transaction work?"

"Are you still reporting to her?"

"No, not since I told her you were out of the U.S. She didn't want to know more – *plausible deniability*."

Claire pointed to the house phone. "Would you call for some dinner? I have many questions and would prefer to not spend this evening in public." She softened her tone, "If that is all right with my *husband*?"

Phil smiled, "That's fine. I enjoy the privacy."

Claire smiled a tired smile. She was suddenly exhausted, mentally and physically drained.

After their dinner arrived, Phil and Claire settled onto the wrought iron table on the balcony. She needed more answers before she could decide her future or that of her child's. Their discussion continued as the shadows turned to twilight and darkness prevailed. Though sitting in the center of nature's beauty, Geneva's abundant artificial radiance impeded the stars. Manufactured glitter extended everywhere, even onto Lake Geneva as the reflection added illumination to the night.

Phil informed Claire, "Due to your family's insistence, Mr. Rawlings is currently being pursued by the police and media as a *person of interest* in your disappearance."

Claire frowned, "That wasn't supposed to happen. If anyone should be considered *a person of interest*, it should be the person who sent me the scary things and tried to run Clay off the road."

Phil looked at Claire quizzically, "Well, that would make it difficult for me to help you, then. Wouldn't it?"

Her hand suddenly trembled as she sat her water glass upon the table and stared. "What are you saying?"

Phil saw Claire's sudden fear and casually covered her hand, "I never intended to hurt you."

Her eyes widened as she retrieved her hand, "I don't understand?"

"Claire, Ms. London said you were involved. It all led to this escape. I would never have sent those awful packages or pushed your car if I didn't think you were behind it."

"Did Ms. London explain *my plan* when you delivered the laptop?"

"Well, afterwards. I received text messages telling me to travel around and mail different things. She was very specific about what to do." Claire's complexion paled as she listened to Catherine's complex scheme -

- one that reduced both her and Tony to pawns in the ongoing game of chess.

"So, you had no intentions of hurting me or my baby?"

Wrinkles surrounded Phil's hazel eyes. "I work for money. However, I believe I've already revealed my true feelings on this subject," his eyebrows rose, "in San Diego?"

Claire held her breath.

He once again covered her hand, "I'd never hurt you."

She exhaled. Patrick Chester didn't have an accomplice. The sudden relief was intoxicating. Her expression mellowed. Instantaneously, the relief evaporated. There was another culprit -- one Claire would have willingly allowed total access to her child. The thought nauseated her. Could Catherine have made Nathaniel the same promise Tony made to him?

If she did, now that she no longer needed Tony to keep Patrick Chester silent, wasn't Tony too *a child,* of *a child*? After all, Samuel helped convict Nathaniel...Catherine killed Samuel...Tony is Samuel's son. Everything was coming together...

Claire leaned closer -- their faces only inches apart. "Phil, thank you."

"For what?"

"For what you're about to do. I promise – I'll make it worth your while."

His hazel eyes questioned, "The next step is getting you settled."

Claire turned her hand palm up and closed her fingers around his. She inhaled and exhaled as a devious smile overtook her face. "Senior Alexander, let's enjoy the beautiful view and discuss the *next step.*"

Her plan shocked, surprised, and disappointed Phil. She truly was much smarter than he'd initially given her credit. Now with the fortune she'd successfully acquired, the combination was impressive. And although his role was different than what he'd hoped, he was more than willing to accommodate.

Phil said, "I don't think you should stay here too long. Where do you want to go?"

With her tired eyes lingering on the vista before her, she thoughtfully replied, "Back to Italy, I've been thinking about Venice. I've never been."

"Then let's decide on a hotel. I'll meet you there in a week. By that time, I should have more information and some permanent destinations for you. Tell me your requirements again."

Claire shifted and met his expectant gaze. "You're worried about my plan, aren't you?"

"Yes. I'll feel better when you're settled and safe."

"Thank you. It's nice to know someone's worried about me." She said as she sipped her iced water.

"There're many people back in the states worried about you."

Claire sat tall, her expression strong. She couldn't allow herself to think about those people, not yet. Now that she knew the truth... *she* was the one putting them through hell, not Tony, not Catherine. Nevertheless, it was Catherine's impending hell that forced her moves. Placing her hand on her mid-section, she knew winning this game was truly the difference between life and death.

If she was a child of a child, and Tony was a child of a child... their baby was doubly doomed.

Her voice held no hint of emotion. "I like tropical, secluded, and remote. I truly don't care about amenities. Just give me warmth, water, and sunshine." She gazed over Lake Geneva and turned back to Phil, "And medical care needs to be accessible."

Claire looked at her watch, 12:02 AM. She glanced to Phil, "I'm going to do it."

He nodded. "It's a little after five there, Wednesday evening... he may not be in his office."

"I have to try." Claire rose and went into the suite. Her disposable international phone was on the table. She reached for it and called information in Iowa City. "I need the office number for the Prosecutor for Iowa City, please." Moments later, "I would like to speak to Marcus Evergreen." "I'm sure he'll talk with me." "Tell him *it's an out of work weather girl.*" Claire waited a moment and then smiled at Phil. Her heartbeat quickened.

For the first time she could see the entire game board, a few more moves and her opponent would be in *check*. Her call was being forwarded...

The voice came through the receiver, "Hello? This is Marcus Evergreen."

"Mr. Evergreen, I was wondering if perhaps this time you'd be willing to listen to the truth?"

All truths are easy to understand once they are discovered.
The trick is to discover them.
- Gallolao

Chapter 59

-Claire Nichols, missing for over two weeks-

Tony settled into his plush leather chair. Perhaps because of the chaos happening around him or his desire to be away from people, his home office was the only place he could truly concentrate. He made daily appearances at his Iowa City office, but all traveling had been postponed, indefinitely. So far, none of the thousands of tips produced any clues into Claire's disappearance. Tony rubbed his temples; it was as if she evaporated into thin air... like every hope or dream he'd ever had for his future.

He didn't want to believe she chose to leave him. Yet, on another level, he did. If she left of her own free will, she was safe. Their baby was safe. If, as he suspected, she'd been lured away and was at the hands of some maniac, her future and that of their baby's were unknown.

With each passing day doubts infiltrated his mind. If she left of her own free will, had any of the past four months been real? She'd accepted his ring. He told her every day how much he loved her. Had it all been a charade? Did she have her own agenda of revenge for his past sins? Tony didn't want to think so... he just didn't know.

Tony scanned his emails. Nothing caught his attention. He didn't care anymore. Thankfully he had Tim, Tom, and Brent. For all practical purposes, Tim was running Rawlings Industries. Brent and Tom were busy with company matters as well as Tony's personal matters. The Vandersols were taking every opportunity to declare Tony's guilt to the world. Hell, at this point he'd turn himself in, if it would bring Claire home.

The large office doors opened. Catherine entered. "I came to check on you."

"I'm fine." His furrowed brow and the dark circles under his deep wrinkled eyes said otherwise.

"Anton, I'm sorry I didn't try to stop her."

Tony shook his head, "I'm not having this discussion with you."

"But the Vandersols? If they have their way, you will be taken in on questioning, soon."

"They're vindictive idiots. The prosecutor will see through them."

"Yes – but if her memoirs are published, *it appears*..."

Tony's eyes pierced, "What did you say?"

Catherine straightened her neck. "I said, if Claire's memoirs are published, the world will know about your predisposition toward violence."

His eyes darkened with each word, "*Catherine*, you know I had nothing to do with her disappearance."

She sat as her tone mellowed, "I do. But I understand the Vandersol's concern."

Tony's attention turned toward his emails. One caught his attention. He clicked and read. According to his informant, Sophia had returned to Provincetown following her parents' funeral. Under normal circumstances, he would have attended their funeral. These, however, were anything but normal. He looked back to Catherine.

"You judge me? You haven't given a damn about your daughter in thirty plus years."

Catherine sat straighter. "I'll have that discussion with you in another thirty years, when you haven't had contact with your child. Then we can discuss similarities."

His hand hit his desk. The pen set and wireless mouse helplessly jumped. "I've told you your daughter lost her adoptive parents. Yet, you don't give a damn!"

She leaned toward him, questioning, "Did you?"

"Of course not!" His eyebrows rose. "Did you?"

"You know, I don't even know her name."

This was only their second open conversation on the subject of Catherine's daughter.

"I doubt there is anything in this house you don't know. Her information is in my private files."

Catherine exhaled, "How did it happen? How did her parents die?"

"I'm not sure." Tony shrugged. "Her adoptive father was beginning to show signs of dementia. He was driving."

Catherine's eyes closed. *Dementia*... her thoughts immediately went to Sharron Rawls. "How bad?" Her voice was but a whisper.

Tony sat straighter, "He wasn't like grandmother, not yet."

"Then she's better off. At least she didn't need to witness..."

Tony closed his eyes, "Catherine, she could use a parent."

Her gray eyes stared; the silence grew. Finally she replied, "*Mr. Rawlings*, I am sure you will do whatever *you* feel is best. I have made my feelings clear." She stood and started toward the door. Suddenly she turned back toward the desk, "Mr. Evergreen called -- again. He wants to speak with you in person."

Tony turned from Catherine back to the computer screen. The NASDEQ indicator for Rawlings Industries displayed the stock's continued downward spiral. It didn't matter that he wasn't responsible for Claire's disappearance. The effects of the Vandersol's claims were also being felt on the Dow Jones. He checked his watch. At least the weekend would stall the continued drop. There were only a few more minutes until the end of Friday's trading session. The fun would resume again on Monday.

He picked up the telephone. "Hello, this is Anthony Rawlings. I'd like to speak to Marcus Evergreen." "I see." "Please inform him I have business taking me out of town for a few days. I should be back by Monday." "Thank you."

Next, he used his iPhone and called Eric. "Get the plane ready. I'm leaving for Provincetown in a few hours."

*****

Sophia shivered as she walked into her art studio. After record setting heat over the summer, she couldn't believe the coolness of the autumn. She considered turning on the furnace to remove the cool dampness from the air and from her art.

Looking out the front windows, she stared past the sidewalk full of Saturday tourists at the low clouds. She came to her studio to get out of the cottage. With Derek on his way back to Taiwan to attend a few unavoidable meetings, she needed a reprieve from life's recent dealings. Next week they'd be back together in California.

Sophia sighed as she set her purse in the back room. There were so many things to do regarding her parents' estate. Never had she imagined they'd incurred so much debt helping with her dreams. Thankfully, due to her recent sales, she could settle their accounts. She wondered why they never said anything. No wonder they wouldn't consider hiring someone to help with Pop. Sophia's heart ached with *what-ifs*. Their love for her took everything, even their lives. Over the last few days, Derek repeatedly tried to convince Sophia they wouldn't have wanted it any other way; she hoped and prayed he was right.

The bell pulled Sophia from her sad spiral. Damn, she meant to lock the front door. It wasn't that she was afraid. This was a great town. She just wanted some quiet time alone.

As she stepped into the studio, the man at the counter looked familiar. Maybe he'd been at a gallery event, or she'd seen him on TV. She couldn't be sure, but his eyes were so dark and mesmerizing. "I'm sorry; I'm not open today. I just forgot to lock the door," Sophia said as she approached Tony.

"That is all right. I can come back," Tony said with an agreeable smile. "It is just that I travel a lot and happened to be in town. A friend of mine told me about your gallery. He was here a week or so ago and bought three pieces. I'm very interested in nature, and he said you have a wonderful selection."

Sophia exhaled and smiled. Of course, talk of her art could lift the dark cloud that held her hostage. "Are you a friend of Jackson Wilson?" Tony's smile widened as he nodded. She continued, "He's one of my biggest fans."

"I don't get this way often. Are you sure you couldn't give me a speed tour? By the way, my name is Anthony, Anthony Rawlings."

Sophia stuck out her hand. "Where are my manners? I'm so sorry. My name is Sophia, Sophia Burke. I would be happy to give you a tour." She couldn't help looking at those eyes.

"With one condition," Anthony said, his eyes shining, "you let me buy you dinner and a drink after the tour."

Sophia gently took the man's elbow and led him around the studio. After a few minutes of enjoying his charm, she decided, why not? After the last two weeks, what harm could one dinner and a drink do... after all; a new investor could help with her parents' debt.

Sophia's mind moved slowly with recent events; however, when the word *investor* came to her, she recognized the name of the man beside her. "Rawlings?" She stepped back. "Are you the Anthony Rawlings, as in Rawlings Industries and Shedis-tics?"

He grinned, "The one and only."

She tried to hide her shock. "I'm not sure if you know this... I mean you have thousands of employees, but my husband works for you at Shedis-tics."

Tony turned toward the painting. "This is lovely. What was your inspiration?"

Sophia tried to concentrate, the mountains were from memory. "The inspiration was a mountain range in Geneva, Switzerland. It's a beautiful place. Have you ever been?"

He nodded. Sophia saw sadness behind those memorizing eyes. "Mr. Rawlings is everything all right?" She'd been so wrapped up in her own personal tragedy she hadn't been following the news.

His eyes refocused on her. "I'd like to purchase this."

She never remembered making an easier sale. "You don't have to do that, just because we identified our connection."

"Oh, Mrs. Burke, there is more. Could we possibly discuss it all over dinner?"

Sophia looked at her watch. "It's ten in the morning."

He smiled, "Then lunch? Could I meet you at the Bistro at the top of Bradford Street, say one o'clock?"

"They don't serve meals until after 5:30."

Tony exhaled, "Well, I'm not on my usual game. I'm staying at the Inn at Crown Pointe, so once again... dinner... say six?"

"Do you want to know the price of the painting?"

"You can tell me during dinner. I'll write you a check." He smiled, "If you think I'm good for it?"

Despite the absurdity of this encounter, Derek had said good things about Anthony Rawlings. "I accept. I'll see you at six."

Tony bowed gallantly. "Mrs. Burke, it is a pleasure to finally speak with you in person. I look forward to our talk."

She watched as he walked into the cool autumn morning. *Mmm, tonight's conversation with Derek will be interesting*, she thought as the bell on the door jingled signifying Mr. Rawlings' exit. Sophia quickly walked toward the handle and secured the lock. She'd had enough odd visits for one day.

Tony paced the confines of his executive suite thinking about Sophia. He wondered what she would be like if she'd been raised a Rawls, instead of a Rossi. In actuality, she was a London; however, that was irrelevant.

Nathaniel Rawls wanted to bring Sophia into the family as soon as he found her. At first Tony wasn't sure; although, he never dared voice his opinion to his grandfather. Yet over time, as Nathaniel's intention remained steadfast, Anton agreed. With Sophia's talent, an affluent education and influence could have propelled her beyond her current meager status.

Although Sophia's adoption was completely legal, the true reason Nathaniel's desire never materialized was Marie/Catherine. Even in 2013, she didn't want to know or even have knowledge of her daughter. Catherine didn't know Sophia's name, her occupation, anything...

Catherine knew Tony knew. Tony even suspected Catherine knew he'd been watching over her. Until the death of Sophia's adoptive parents, they'd never discussed it. Tony wasn't sure how to approach the subject, especially now with Sophia married into a line connected to Jonathon Burke. Yet, he reasoned, Catherine was supportive of him and Claire; perhaps she could also be supportive of Sophia's choice.

Heaven knows, Tony didn't approve of Derek Burke initially. However, over time the man passed every test Tony posed. Tony wanted to be sure Derek was the right person. After three years of enticements, Derek and Sophia were still together.

Tony thought pensively about Claire. If only he could say the same about them.

The knock at the door startled him. His original thought to ignore it evaporated as the rapping grew louder. "Mr. Rawlings, open the door." He stared toward the wooden barrier. "Mr. Rawlings, this is the FBI. If you don't open the door, we have a member of the Inn's staff present to open it."

His dark eyes stared as he pulled the door toward him, "FBI... is this about Claire?"

A man in a dark suit presented a badge, "Yes, sir."

"Have you found her?"

"Mr. Rawlings, we need to take you in for questioning."

The weak can never forgive.
Forgiveness is the attribute of the strong.
— Mahatma Gandhi

Epilogue

Claire rolled on the large bed, relishing the soft sheets against her skin. Smiling, she reached for the man whose warmth filled her days and nights. Instead, her touch met cool satin. Lingering in her cocoon, she enjoyed the ceiling fan's gentle breeze as it moved the humid air around the grand bedroom. When she closed her eyes the scent of his cologne permeated her senses. Beyond her haven, she heard the sounds of morning: birds singing their morning wake-up songs and the ever present surf.

Forcing herself from the heavenly bubble, she reached for her robe, and walked toward the veranda. A veil of tropical vegetation filtered the sun's sultry penetration. Stepping around the fragrant flowers and large lush leaves, she took in the marvelous view. Even after over two months, it still took her breath away. Leaning against the folding wall, one that, due to her instance, remained mostly open allowing the indoors to be outdoors; she relished the blue. Truly, *blue* couldn't describe the panorama: endless blue sky with wisps of white filled the space above the horizon. Below the horizon, Crayola would be at a lost to describe the shades. On most mornings turquoise dominated. Sometimes if the sun was just right, the waves sparkled florescent. Farther out, away from the shore and her paradise, the waters darkened. The blue became indigo, purple or gray, often reminding her of the fog covered mountains near Palo Alto.

Wearing a white bikini and white lace cover she made her way to the front lanai. As her bare feet padded across the smooth bamboo floor, Madeline's friendly rich voice brought her to present. "Madame el, may I bring you tea?"

Claire smiled, "Yes, Madeline, thank you. But please, no food... I'm not hungry." The baby's increased growth reduced her stomach to a mere fraction of its old size. She filled so easily these days.

Madeline and Francis were brought to this island paradise thirty-five years ago by their wealthy employer. He died, but they stayed. Since that time they've worked and maintained this heavenly home, on the other side of the world from their native Haiti, for multiple owners. When Claire purchased the paradise retreat, the couple came as part of the package. They were invaluable, especially during the first few weeks while she was alone.

She couldn't imagine being there without them.

They did everything and anything to make Claire feel welcome and safe. Madeline's dark, radiant skin and cheerful smile brightened every room. She absolutely glistened when Francis was near. Being married for over forty years and unable to have children themselves, they have tirelessly cared for family after family. As a matter of fact, when they first learned the estate, the island, the retreat, was purchased by a single female, they tried unsuccessfully to hide their disappointment. However, as soon as Madeline saw Claire's midsection, she praised God for giving them another child to tend.

Within days, customary staff – lady of the house, protocol was forgotten. Claire spent hours with Madeline in the state of the art kitchen, learning to cook foods she'd never previously tried. She also spent time with Francis, caring for the tropical gardens and fruit trees. The three would sit down together and eat. To Madeline's insistence, each meal began with a prayer. It was a ritual Claire hadn't practiced since she was young. After so much change and discord in her life, she's found it comforting.

Of course, as is always true, things change. Claire was no longer alone. It took some time for her husband to make his way to their paradise. Too many disappearances at once would add to the speculations of critics. Since his arrival, Madeline and Francis stepped back -- some. Claire refused to allow them to be lost to archaic protocol. They may be her employees, but they were also her friends. With Claire's insistence, all four of them sit together for midday meal. Although breakfast remained a relaxed time for Claire, it was usually a rush for Francis and Madeline; they had things to do. Claire's husband's schedule varied, sometimes he joined her for coffee and breakfast, and sometimes he went out and about. He liked exploring the area, reading the internet news, or taking the boat to the local village center. Evening meals were reserved for the two of them. After all, they were officially newlyweds and as such, needed time alone.

"No, Madame el, you must eat. I'll bring you muffins and fresh fruit."

Claire shook her head. Arguing would be pointless.

At the early hour, the lush vegetation entwined above the lanai shaded the lounge chairs near the pool. Claire settled into the cushioned seat, elevated her feet, turned on her iPad, and waited for the daily news to load. She may be thousands and thousands of miles away, but technology made the world a smaller place. Events across the globe would soon be as visible, as if she were on the same continent.

It wasn't the first story to appear on her homepage, but her own picture immediately caught Claire's attention. She clicked and read the title:

"Family Files Charges against Iowa City Police Department, Prosecutor, and Anthony Rawlings."

Shaking her head, Claire read: Associated Press.

John and Emily Vandersol have filed formal charges against the Iowa City Police Department, Marcus Evergreen, I.C. Prosecutor, and Anthony Rawlings(in absentia).

Mr. and Mrs. Vandersol have requested a hearing based on evidence discovered at the home of Anthony Rawlings. The request states the evidence, currently undisclosed, is sufficient to establish probable cause against Anthony Rawlings. The Vandersols also charge Mr. Rawlings with extortion. "Anyone else would be sitting in jail. It's only because of his wealth and influence that ICPD and Mr. Evergreen have not filed charges. Their delay is corruption." (Another of the many charges listed). The Vandersols claim the prosecutor and police department worked together to protect Anthony Rawlings. In doing so, the ICPD jeopardized the investigation of Ms. Claire Nichols' disappearance. Mrs. Vandersol also charged Mr. Rawlings (in absentia) with the disappearance and possible death of her unborn niece or nephew.

Claire's hand rubbed her very large midsection. Now in her thirty-fifth week, she smiled knowing no harm had come to her unborn child. She honestly didn't believe that would be the case if she'd remained at Catherine's disposal. She continued reading:

Ms. Nichols was last seen September 4, 2013. Mr. Anthony Rawlings disappeared after his private plane made an emergency landing in the Appalachian Mountains, September 21, 2013. The FBI will not confirm or deny the survival of Mr. Rawlings following this incident. The FBI refused additional comments claiming an ongoing investigation. Currently, no charges have been filed.

Rawlings Industries is currently operating with a temporary CEO and the same Board of Directors. It has been speculated that the pending charges will force the SEC to investigate Rawlings Industries. Since September the share price has dropped from $142.37 to $86.84 at last call.

Despite her reading material, when Claire realized she'd eaten all of Madeline's food, a smile appeared on her face.

Madeline's voice came above the sound of surf. "Madame el, may I get you more tea or perhaps some water?"

"Madeline, I would love some water. It's getting hotter by the minute."

"Then perhaps you should be in the water?" The rich, husky voice came from behind. She couldn't see the handsome source. Yet, instantaneously her neck tensed and goose bumps appeared on her arms and legs. It amazed Claire how something as benign as a voice could continue to incite such a visceral response.

Madeline saw Claire's reaction and laughed. Francis and Madeline wanted Claire to be happy. It didn't take them long to realize this man was exactly what their employer needed. Madeline's laugh made Claire giggle.

Claire loved Madeline's laugh, so deep and rich, just like her voice, "Madame el, I will bring you some water, and Monsieur?"

"I would like some coffee please, Madeline?" He bowed toward the woman.

She laughed at his gesture, "Why, of course. I will bring it out soon." With that, she disappeared, leaving the lady and gentleman of the house alone.

Her husband reached for Claire's shoulder and gently massaged. While the sound of his voice instigated chills, the touch of his hand sent her body into mayhem. It hadn't changed; she hoped it never would.

*****

Catherine sat at Tony's grand desk. It wasn't like he'd be sitting there anytime soon. Thanks to his kind provisions in his absence, Catherine Marie London was listed as executor of Anthony Rawlings' estate and anything related to it. The title came with a nice trust fund. That money plus the large sum she'd accumulated over the years left her more than financially solvent.

It took almost twenty-five years, but Marie had finally fulfilled Nathaniel's desire. She was finally the lady of the manor. Maybe her name wasn't Rawls, but that didn't matter. Nathaniel told her many times how he wanted her to live, and it wasn't as Anton's housekeeper. Catherine Marie leaned back against the plush leather and scanned the grand office. There was no doubt; the room was much more regal from this perspective.

Catherine opened the drawer on the lower right, to inspect Anton's private files. She fingered the tabs... in this paperless world it surprised her he'd kept these printed documents. Thankfully, the ICPD hadn't felt the need to confiscate them as evidence.

She eyed the scribed names. There were so many. How could she figure out which one was her daughter? Catherine saw her own name.

Maybe there was a clue in there. When she opened the file, she feared her heart would stop pumping. The writing wasn't Anton's. Catherine knew his writing well enough to duplicate it easily. This writing was Nathaniel's.

Scribbled in the margin of a contract was the name *Sophia Rossi*. Catherine went through the drawer again. The only Sophia was *Sophia Burke*. Suddenly she no longer remembered her husband's love, she remembered his vendetta. Burke? *Burke?* There was no way *her* daughter could be connected to Jonathon Burke.

Catherine removed the *Sophia Burke* file and opened the folder. Above the typed name Sophia Rossi, was the scribbled name *Sophia Rossi Burke...* Catherine searched the pages. There was a plethora of outdated information. Nonetheless, written above the text on the second page was a telephone number. Catherine couldn't resist. She used the blocked house phone.

Derek answered his wife's cellphone. The past few weeks were too much. She wasn't up for solicitors or blocked numbers. "Hello?"

Catherine hesitated, questioning the correctness of the number. She expected a woman's voice. "I'm sorry, I'm looking for the beautiful baby girl I was forced to give away thirty-three years ago."

Derek listened. Sophia had said she didn't want to know her birth parents. Nevertheless, this may be their only chance to learn the truth. "I'm sorry; my wife is indisposed right now. She's had a difficult few weeks."

"Yes, that's the reason I'm calling. I never wanted to interfere with her and her adoptive parents. But now...." Catherine wasn't sure how to finish that sentence. Now she was lonely and wanted to at least meet her daughter? Now she thought her daughter might be more open to learning about her birth mother? Now she had nothing better to do...

Thankfully she didn't need to finish the sentence. Derek interjected. "Tell me the date you gave birth."

Catherine sat taller. Who was this man demanding information? She sure as hell wasn't intimidated. She'd loved Nathaniel Rawls and outlasted Anton Rawls... this man was nothing in comparison. However, she answered, "July 19, 1980."

Catherine heard muffled voices. Then a woman's voice, "Please, don't call again. My parents are dead. I don't know you."

Marie sat straighter. Of course she deserved this response. Nonetheless, part of reasoned maybe she could fill a void left by the death of her daughter's adoptive parents. If nothing else, she could look out for the young woman from afar, as Anton and Nathaniel had done. "I'm sorry, I won't call you again."

Resolutely, the young woman swallowed her emotions. "Wait, if you could give me your number, I'll think about it. Then when I'm ready I can call you."

Catherine breathed a sigh of relief... this was more than she'd expected. "Yes, of course."

Derek's voice came back through the receiver, "You may give me the number. When my wife is ready, *if* she is ready, she will call you. Please do not call her phone again."

Catherine heard her daughter's sobs in the background and gave the number of a disposable phone to her son-in-law. After he repeated the number, he disconnected the line.

Catherine grinned. She'd found her daughter. Her daughter was married – to a man named *Burke*. She needed more information. That was all right, as before, she had the time. And without a doubt, Catherine was up for a new challenge.

CONVICTED

Book # 3 of Bestselling Consequences Series

You must stick to your conviction,
but be ready to abandon your assumptions.
-Denis Waitley

Coming: Late 2013!

TRUTH

Stay Connected...

Your opinion counts! Please share your thoughts about The Bestselling Consequences Series: *Consequences, Truth & Convicted:*

*Amazon, *Consequences by Romig*, Customer Reviews
Truth by Romig, Customer Reviews

*Barnes & Noble, *Consequences by Romig*, Customer Reviews and *Truth by Romig*, Customer Reviews

*Goodreads.com/Aleatha Romig

Consequences Review:
http://www.goodreads.com/book/show/12368985-consequences

Truth Review:
http://www.goodreads.com/book/show/16070018-truth

Contact Aleatha:
aleatharomig@gmail.com

Learn the latest information regarding Consequences, Truth, Convicted, and other writing endeavors:

"Like"- http://Facebook.com/Aleatha Romig
"Follow" - @aleatharomig on Twitter!
"Follow"- Goodreads.com/Aleatha Romig
"Visit" Aleatha's Blog: http://aleatharomig.blogspot.com

TRUTH

Made in the USA
Lexington, KY
12 August 2013